The Best-selling
Windhaven Saga!

Book One
WINDHAVEN PLANTATION

This glorious family saga begins as young Lucien Bouchard leaves his ancestral home in France to pioneer a bold new destiny in America.

Book Two
STORM OVER WINDHAVEN

The Bouchard family fights for home and honor against the shattering forces of greed, bigotry, and violence.

Book Three
LEGACY OF WINDHAVEN

The Civil War destroys the beautiful Windhaven chateau, but the blood of old Lucien runs deep and a brave heritage survives amidst the ruins and ashes. The men and women of Windhaven must move on to a new beginning in Texas, where cattle replaces cotton as their way of life and renegade Comanches and Mexican bandits assault their attempts to establish a home in the plains. Only love, fierce pride, and stubborn strength enable the Bouchards to withstand the brutality and bitter tragedy they continually face. This magnificent legacy is the key to their future, for they will endure. They have inherited the proud passions of a man who knew that the conquest of adversity was the price of fortune.

The Windhaven Saga:

WINDHAVEN PLANTATION

STORM OVER WINDHAVEN

LEGACY OF WINDHAVEN

RETURN TO WINDHAVEN

WINDHAVEN'S PERIL

TRIALS OF WINDHAVEN

DEFENDERS OF WINDHAVEN

Legacy of Windhaven

Marie de Jourlet

PINNACLE BOOKS   LOS ANGELES

LEGACY OF WINDHAVEN

Copyright © 1978 by Book Creations Inc. (Canaan, New York 12029).

An original Pinnacle Books edition, published for the first time anywhere.

Produced by Lyle Kenyon Engel.

ISBN: 0-523-41267-3

First printing, March 1978
Second printing, November 1979
Third printing, June 1980
Fourth printing, November 1980

Cover illustration by Bruce Minney

Printed in the United States of America

PINNACLE BOOKS, INC.
2029 Century Park East
Los Angeles, California 90067

Dedicated to Lyle Kenyon Engel, whose kindness, integrity and benevolent wisdom have given both impetus and inspiration to this book.

ACKNOWLEDGMENTS

Any author of an historical novel must be able to provide not only the flesh of the story, but also to make certain that the bones are accurately placed and sturdily composed, if the reader is to have credibility in the story told. Accordingly, I must express my indebtedness to those who graciously furnished vital documentation, the "bones" of this new Windhaven story. My sincere thanks are due to: Joseph Milton Nance, Professor of History, College of Liberal Arts, Texas A & M University, College Station, Texas; Mrs. Evelyn M. King, Assistant Director for Special Collections, Sterling C. Evans Library, Texas A & M University Libraries, College Station, Texas; Dr. John Talmadge, Jr., Houston, Texas; my good friend Donald B. Hamilton of Santa Fe, New Mexico, a great novelist and one who has himself written many superb books about post-Civil War Texas; Thomas L. Miller, Bryan, Texas; Stanley McElderry, Director of the Regensteiner Library of the University of Chicago; and Rich Padnos, good friend, gourmet and history buff who himself did much research into the period which this book covers.

The author wishes to express her grateful thanks to Dave Richmond, head of the gun department of Abercrombie & Fitch, Chicago, for detailing the actual guns and ammunition used during the period of this novel and for offering many valuable suggestions.

Finally, I acknowledge my heartfelt debt to Mrs. Doris Samuels, typist-transcriber, who as a schoolteacher, brings an editing skill to her flawless mechanical tasks.

CHAPTER ONE

It had been a long, sullen night, this fateful Thursday, April 13, 1865. Along the swiftly moving Alabama River, swollen with the first heavy spring rains, there were the sounds of lapping water and the calls of the nightbirds and the rustling of trees in the forests which lined the winding banks. Luke Bouchard and his wife Lucy, their son Lucien Edmond and his lovely young wife Maxine, as well as Sybella and griefstricken Maybelle, kept their mournful vigil on the grounds of what had once been the old Williamson plantation. They were watching the clouds of dense smoke rising above the trees and even the bluff upriver . . . the smoke of the fire which was consuming the red-brick chateau with its two proud towers, the Windhaven which had been Lucien Bouchard's dream come at last to reality and now to destruction in these final hours of the terrible Civil War.

It was Luke who had rallied them, even allaying Sybella's fears for her courageous husband Matthew Forsden, who had remained behind at Windhaven to defend it and to confront the vengeance-driven Union troops under Captain Arnold Huxter. Sybella had tried to dissuade

Matthew from putting his life in unnecessary danger, and he had gently reproved her by saying, "My dearest Sybella, don't you remember when we first met, that you hired me as your overseer? Well, it's still my duty to oversee Windhaven, and to see if I can't talk those soldiers out of destroying that beautiful place where we had such great happiness all these long years. I'm not afraid, and I'll have no weapons. Soldiers won't hurt an old man like me."

Luke, with his grandfather's vision, had promised that they would build a new Windhaven on a new frontier; that they would go to Texas, that vast country where there were still few settlers and where they could begin again, now that the war was over. Even Sybella, having seen the flames leaping from the chateau, found her own spirit restored by her stepson's undaunted vow. And it was she who consoled Maybelle, by saying gently, "Come, Maybelle, we'll have a new beginning, you'll see. Life isn't over just because property and possessions are gone. We've our health, our love for one another, our devotion as a family. That's what's made Windhaven endure, that's what dear Lucien has taught us. He and his Dimarte are there on the bluff, and they see the fire, but I'm sure their spirits are with us now, urging us to think of the new life ahead. Come, dear, there's nothing more we can do until the morning. A good night's sleep, and we'll all be ready to face what lies ahead for us."

There had been strange portents throughout the land during this silent night. On the plains of the Indian Territory, which would one day be known as Oklahoma, a middle-aged Creek brave named Emataba, son of Turintaka who had been *Mico* over the displaced villagers of Econchate, stood outside his wigwam and stared at the night sky, then gasped with wonder at the sudden blaze of a falling star which hurtled from the heavens. "Protect us from this evil omen, oh Ibofanaga," he murmured to himself. "Do not abandon us to this strange land to which you have brought us so far from our ancestral home. Our people are without spirit or hope."

Along the coastline of Baja California, there was an

2

ominous rumbling, giant boulders from the cliffs toppled into the ocean, and then again all was still. A sudden wind sent waves crashing against the southernmost tip of Florida, and then again there was only silence and the sea itself was still. And slowly the dawn began to brush away the shadows of this long night to herald the day of Good Friday.

The tall, gaunt man, his black suit flapping about his ungainly frame, had opened the polished rosewood door of his bedroom at seven this Good Friday morning and bidden the night guard in the hall a gracious "Good morning." The circles under his tired eyes were pouched, the skin of his face was almost saffron, and his scraggly black beard thinned and died as it approached the hairline. His thick lips, more brown than red, were drawn back in a semi-smile, for already there were men waiting to see him, asking for favors, having slept all night long in the White House hall. Behind the new dome of the Capitol, the sun was fighting an energetic battle with sullen gray clouds.

Already the streets of Washington were full of people, for the business day would begin a half hour hence, and the flagstone and wooden walks clattered with the tread of heavy boots, while teams of horses pulled heavy brewery wagons and loads of produce to the taverns and markets. Ducks and chickens waddled solemnly along Pennsylvania Avenue, edging around the horses, while pigs wallowed and grunted in the puddles from the rain the night before.

Around noon of this day, the tall, gaunt man told his Cabinet a haunting story. He was sure that something momentous was about to happen, for he had had a dream that always came just before some great event. He had experienced it before the firing on Fort Sumter, before the battles of Bull Run, before Antietam and Stone's River, before Gettysburg and Vicksburg.

It was inevitable that several of the Cabinet ministers asked what the dream was, and it was Gideon Welles, the Secretary of the Navy, who wrote it down: "Mr. Lincoln said that he seemed to be in a singular, indescribable vessel . . . and that he was moving with great rapidity toward the dark and indefinite shore."

It was only a little more than a month since March 4, 1865, the rainy day of Abraham Lincoln's second inauguration as President of the United States. His address had taken a little more than five minutes, and it had ended with the words: "With malice towards none; with charity for all; with firmness in the right, as God gives us to see the right, let us strive on to finish the work we are in; to bind up the nation's wounds, to care for him who shall have borne the battle, and for his widow, and his orphan—to do all which may achieve and cherish a just, and a lasting peace, upon ourselves, and with all nations." That speech had received only perfunctory attention from the press which labeled it far too conciliatory toward the enemy South. The real news of that inauguration had not been published, but whispered: Andrew Johnson, Lincoln's Vice-President, had arrived red-faced, nervous and visibly intoxicated on the arm of the outgoing Vice-President, Hannibal Hamlin, who introduced him. And in a few short minutes the new Vice-President had disgraced himself in a speech that abounded in phrases like "humble as I am, plebeian as I may be deemed." There was disgust on all the faces in the crowd, a disgust that Andrew Johnson was to feel the rest of his days. And yet, on this very day, Abraham Lincoln was to express a desire to see "Andy" to discuss matters which he felt would be of lasting importance to the nation he had fought so arduously to preserve.

As the dawn's first light brightened the somber sky, Djamba, the tall, powerful Mandingo who knew himself to be bound to the Bouchard family by far more than the original shackles of servitude—for these had been removed by Luke long years before—rose from his improvised bed on a blanket near the Williamson plantation, and turned to stare upriver. Only a few desultory whorls of smoke lifted from the red-brick chateau toward the still dreary sky. By now, he was sure, the fire had all but burned itself out. Soon it would be safe to go there and to search for what possessions, keepsakes, heirlooms, might still be left untouched.

Although he was now fifty-three, his bearing was still

erect, and only a few streaks of gray in his hair attested to his age. He flexed his fingers as he continued to stare toward the chateau, and his thin nostrils sniffed the air, his eyes narrowing as if seeking to detect the presence of an enemy. Then he scowled and shook his head.

"Father, do you think the soldiers have gone by now?" it was Lucas, his twenty-four-year-old son, nearly as tall as Djamba, his skin a lighter brown because his mother Celia had been a mulatto.

Djamba whirled, then his features relaxed, and he nodded soberly. "Surely by now, Lucas. And there wasn't any need for burning Windhaven nohow. Mistah Luke and his grandfather, they never harmed a soul, and all they did was raise food and cotton. Now maybe that's a crime because they're from the South, and the North has won the war. Still and all, there wasn't any need to burn that beautiful house. I hope there'll still be some of the fine things Miz Sybella prizes so much—but you know what I'm feared of most, Lucas."

Lucas nodded, looking at the ground. "You'll be thinking of Mr. Forsden, won't you, Father? He's not back yet. He said he was going to watch over the place and try to get the soldiers to leave it be."

"Yes. And they didn't leave it be, the smoke shows us that, doesn't it? And I feel he's been hurt or worse. When I woke this morning, I heard the hooting of an owl, and this early in the day, it's bad luck. Just like it was back in the country where I was born, Lucas. There's death in the air, and not just here. I had a strange dream last night."

"A dream, Father?"

"Yes, Lucas. I dreamed I was hunting the lion again and I had my spear, and the lion stood on the ridge of a hill staring down at me, his black mane ruffling in the wind, and his tail lashing as he worked himself into anger so he'd attack me. And then I turned to the east and I saw a tall man in a black suit with a beard, and the saddest face I ever saw, watching me. And just then, a hyena sprang out of the bushes behind him and clawed him and pulled him down, and then I woke up." Djamba shuddered, shook his head again, then muttered, "I wish I had a *juju* to take away the curse of that bad dream. But

5

that's enough of that kind of talk. Lucas, boy, whyn't you go round to the kitchen and see if you can have your mammy and Prissy get us a mess of vittles for the folks? They'll be up and stirring soon enough, and they'll be wanting to go back to Windhaven to see how bad it is."

Lucas hesitated a moment, then hesitantly asked, "Do you think any of the workers will still be over there, Father?"

"Maybe some of them," Djamba gloomily responded. "They were scared when they heard the soldiers were coming, and they lit out early yesterday, just the way they did over here. 'Course, there's some that's loyal, like that Kru field hand Harry, who Mistah Luke made a foreman years back, and of course his wife Betty. Over at Windhaven, I'm sure that Jimmy, who tended the stables all these years, he won't have run away, he'll have tried to save what horses he can. But we'll have to wait and see till later in the day, Lucas, just how many come back. Now you hustle and get those vittles started, boy!"

"I'm going right now, Father."

In the kitchen, gray-haired Celia and her daughter Prissy had already begun preparations for the morning meal, and when Lucas entered, he found the Hausa, George, who had been stableboy on the old Williamson plantation and was now foreman and nearly fifty years of age, talking earnestly to his mother and sister. "Land's sake, Miz Celia m'am," he was saying, "we still got plenty of hard-workin' folk 'round here who didn't run away and wouldn't nohow. Dat wouldn't be fair to Mistah Luke, not aftah all he done foah us all these years long before Massa Lincoln done freed us. Ah'll help de folks in dere cabins wid brekfust effen you'll help me out wid a l'il bacon 'n some cornpone—dat's effen you kin spare any."

"You wait here, George, I'll find you some supplies right enough. Morning, Lucas boy," Celia looked up and briskly nodded at her smiling, tall young son. "Don't just stand there grinning like you're still asleep, boy, make yourself useful. Help your sister tote me in some more wood for the fire. Pretty soon Miz Sybella and Miz Lucy 'n Maybelle and Maxine, they'll be up wanting their breakfast. Mistah Luke's already been in bright and early,

6

just had himself a cup of coffee and said he'd wait till his son and Miz Maxine woke up 'fore he'd ride over to Windhaven."

"Yes, Mama. The reason I was took back, Daddy just sent me in to ask you to start fixing breakfast, that's a fact," Lucas chuckled good-naturedly. "I'll get the axe and cut some more wood. Prissy, you stay here and mind Mama, you hear?"

"Get along with you, Lucas," Celia smiled fondly and waved a ladle at him, at which Lucas pretended to back out in terror with a hand upraised to fend off the feigned blow.

Prissy, now thirty, was exceptionally attractive and still unmarried. A quadroon and the illegitimate child of the now dead Mark Bouchard and Celia, her skin was akin to the tone of yellow ivory, with a round, heart-shaped face, large, soulful brown eyes, full ripe mouth and delicately flaring nostrils. Her black hair was primly combed from her forehead and braided into a thick oval knot at the back of her neck, while her red calico dress hinted at a buxom figure. She stooped to the oven, drew out a freshly baked rack of cornpone, and began to lift the piping hot square cakes with a clean hand towel and drop them into a basket on the table. "You can take these back for a starter, George."

"Mighty kind, Missy, mighty kind of you and your mama. Lawd Gawd, wut we gwine do now, Windhaven done burned down and all them damn Union soljers round de place? I been talkin' all night long to these shif'less, no-count *nigras* tellin' 'em de leas' dey kin do is stay wheah dey bin treated so good, not run off like a passel of wild hosses jist 'cause dere's soljers. I tol' dem dey ain't gwine shoot us no-count nigras, but jist the same, lots of 'em done run off durin' the night. I feels mighty bad 'bout dat, Miz Prissy m'am, I sho nuff does." He lifted the basket, hesitated and shook his head, then gave Prissy a stealthy, adoring look. It was no secret to the comely quadroon that the former Williamson stableboy was mighty sweet on her, though he had never dared express himself in other than longing looks and a tendency to be nervously talkative whenever he found himself in her presence.

"You're a good man, George, and I know Mr. Luke is going to appreciate what you've tried to do. But you mustn't force them. Those who want to stay will do it, and those who want to go are free anyway by what Mr. Lincoln said, you know. If they think they can start a new life somewheres else, you've got to give them their chance. Now you come back and I'll fill up that basket again. There's plenty here, and I'll cut you some bacon, but Mama won't have time to fry it for you, she's too busy preparing for everybody else—you understand, don't you, George?"

"Yassum, thankee, that's real nice. Ah'll be back directly, sho will enjoy dat bacon and so will Harry 'n his Betty. Dey says to tell you dey's stayin', no matter what, Miz Prissy." He touched his hand to his forehead and hurried out of the kitchen, while Prissy smiled and then went back to stand beside her mother.

"That George, I do declare, he gets more moonstruck over you every day, Prissy girl," Celia teased her daughter. "You know, child, I never said a word to you all these years about jumping the broom with anybody, but I'm just wondering now if you oughtn't to be setting your mind to picking some good steady man to look after you. Your pa and me, we won't be around forever, you know. I heard Mistah Luke say last night he was figuring on going to Texas and start all over again, now the war is over and Windhaven's burned. It's a mighty big country, from all I've heard tell, Prissy. It'd be mighty lonely there if you didn't have some nice fellow you could set up house with. You just think about it. Maybe George, hm?"

"Oh, Mama!" Prissy giggled and flushed as she lowered her eyes and pretended to be busy drawing out a new pan of cornpone cakes from the oven. "He's too old for me. Besides, he's so shy, he'd never get up the courage to ask me to jump the broom. He's not even kissed me once all these years."

"Well, I don't say he's the one, but you just mind what I told you. Now why don't you cut that bacon for him, and then you can help me fix breakfast for the men and

8

womenfolks. Like as not they'll all be up by now, honey."

"I will, Mama." Prissy straightened, glanced nervously around, then faltered, "Mama?"

"What is it, child?"

"Yesterday, Mama, when I heard the Yankee soldiers were coming, I went to the dining room and I got all that fine silver, you know, the one with the monogram on it that stands for Windhaven."

"Yes, Prissy, I know what you mean. Land's sakes, I'm certainly glad you thought about that! What did you do with the silver?"

"I put it in a burlap bag, Mama, and I buried it just inside the stable, near that first stall where old Midnight used to be."

"That was smart, honey. Now when the folks are at breakfast, you'll tell Mistah Luke. I know he'll thank you for what you did, honey. His old grandpappy was mighty proud of that fine silver, and I know I always polished it extra-special hard at least twice a week, even if we never did have company, just so it'd keep looking beautiful and shiny."

Luke Bouchard hardly looked his forty-nine years, still tall, wiry, and with only a hint of gray in his thick blond hair. But his pleasant face was grave as he stood by his horse. He spoke to Sybella: "Mother, it may not be safe to go back there. Djamba and Lucas and I will see if we can get into the building, if it isn't too badly damaged or still on fire, and try to save what we can."

"Luke, you know why I want to go with you. It's Matthew. He hasn't come back yet, and I'm afraid for him. Please, Luke. I wouldn't feel right if I stayed behind and let you tell me what I'm so terribly afraid to know—please, son!"

Luke's eyes moistened, for he had always deeply loved and admired his courageous stepmother. And to have her call him "son" as she had just done, remembering how her two real sons had died, Mark and then Paul whom she had borne so late in life, greatly moved him. Partly turning away to hide his emotion, he gruffly called to the

Hausa, "George, you'd best saddle a mare for Mrs. Forsden."

"Directly, Mistah Luke, suh," the Hausa nodded and hurried toward the stable.

"May I go, too, Father?" Lucien Edmond asked as he stood beside his beautiful wife Maxine, an arm around her waist. Carla and Hugo, their little girl and boy, were dawdling over breakfast in the kitchen, and Celia was telling them an exciting story about a sly raccoon who outwitted a pack of hunting dogs, in order to distract them from the somber events of this day. She, too, had the premonition that Matthew Forsden was no longer alive.

"No, Lucien Edmond, it's best you stay here, just in case any Union soldiers should come by on a last foray. I doubt that they will. Just the same, it's well to be on the alert. You remember that teakwood case in old Mr. Williamson's secretary, with the two derringers in it? Make sure they're loaded. I'm not so much afraid of Union soldiers as I am of deserters and looters who will be taking advantage of the situation to line their own pockets as well as to rape and kill."

Lucien Edmond's dark-brown eyes lowered as he accepted his father's order. "Of course, Father. I'll look after everyone."

"You may as well get used to standing guard, son," Luke humorously added, "because I've a feeling that when we go to Texas and find a place to settle, there'll be plenty of standing guard to be done, from all I've heard tell of the Indians and bandits in that country. No matter—Prissy, I can't tell you how grateful all of us are for your forethought about the silver. You're sure you can ride a horse, though, because we could dig up the silver if you'd just tell us exactly where you hid it."

Prissy shook her head. "I hid it real good, Mistah Bouchard. 'Sides, maybe I can help find some more of Miz Sybella's things that we forgot when we were all in such a powerful hurry to leave the house yesterday."

"Very well then, Prissy. George, help her on the mare—that's it. I'll help you, Mother," this last to Sybella who smiled as he grasped her waist and helped her into the lady's saddle which George had secured to a piebald mare. "Well then, we'll take the path along the river, it's the easiest, and we can see if there's any activity around Windhaven as we near it."

"I'm sure the soldiers are all gone by now, Mistah Luke," Djamba said. "Just before you came out after breakfast, Walter, the footman over at Windhaven, came back through the woods. He'd been hiding there all night long, and he says there's no one around the place, no soldiers, nobody."

"That's good news indeed. Well, let's be off then."

Sybella turned back to smile at Prissy, "I declare, Prissy, you've more resourcefulness than any of us had given you credit for. First saving the silver and the jewelry the way you did, and now I see you really do know how to ride a horse. That's something I didn't know at all, in all these years!"

"Daddy showed me, lots of time in the evening when the chores were done. I love horses so, it was easy!" Prissy self-consciously flushed and tightened her hold on the reins.

The smell of smoke clung to the humid air, but the fire had burned itself out by the time the five riders reached the edge of the fields which flanked the towering red bluff. With a cry, Sybella Forsden dismounted and ran toward the chateau. There, lying sprawled face down in front of the still smouldering portico, Matthew Forsden lay, having defended the chateau to his very last breath.

She sank down on her knees, cupping his cold cheeks in her trembling hands, to lift his face toward her own. The widened eyes, the startled curve of the mouth bespoke not so much the agony of death but his amazement that he would be shot down unarmed for the sole crime of having begged the Union captain to spare this house where he had known such happiness.

"Oh, Matthew, my dearest husband, what a price you've had to pay for being so honorable—and so loving. Now you are with our Paul!" she murmured in a low, quivering voice meant only for the dead man's ears. Luke, Djamba and Lucas had dismounted. They stood holding the reins of their horses, as did Prissy hers, holding back

11

from this agonizing farewell, their own eyes filled with tears to know Sybella's suffering and desolation.

"You knew I didn't want you to stay here, my darling," Sybella murmured as the tears coursed unchecked down her wrinkled cheeks. "I would have rather had you beside me than all the houses in the world, you know that, my husband." She bent down and reverently kissed his forehead, then his lips and eyes. "What heroes they must have been, how proud they must have thought themselves to shoot down a harmless old man who faced them without a weapon! And now I'm alone, Matthew, and you and Paul must watch over me just as Grandfather Lucien is watching over all of us. May God grant your soul eternal peace and bless you for the years of happiness you gave me, my dearest one."

As she knelt there, she grasped his lifeless body by the shoulders and with all her strength, rolled him onto his back. "It's not right for you to lie with your face in the dust, my darling," she murmured. Then she looked up at the others who had come with her. "Can we bury him at the foot of the bluff so that he'll watch over Windhaven forever, Luke?" her voice broke as she strove to compose herself.

"Of course, Mother. Djamba and I will do it at once. Prissy, look after Mrs. Forsden, that's a good girl," Luke gently said.

The powerful Mandingo watched Sybella, and there were tears in his eyes. The dreadful premonition he had had when Matthew Forsden had so staunchly declared that he would protect the chateau from the marauders had come true. Once again, Djamba suffered inwardly with her, as he had done when Henry Bouchard had died of a sudden heart attack. More than that, even after all these years, he knew that what he had always felt for Sybella was the truest, deepest love a man could have for any woman—a love that had been doomed before it could even begin because of the very nature of things . . . because, although he had once been a king, his skin was black and hers was white.

There was a spade lying abandoned at the edge of the fields, along with the other planting tools the workers had

12

flung aside in their hour of flight with the knowledge that General Wilson's troops were heading from Montgomery toward Windhaven. Lucas retrieved it, as his father and Luke Bouchard gently lifted Matthew Forsden's body and carried it toward the towering bluff. And when it was done, Djamba and his son knelt while Luke uttered a prayer in which gratitude and sorrow were mingled and in which he bade farewell to his valiant old stepfather.

By the time they returned, Sybella had dried her tears and was staring at the gutted red-brick chateau, Prissy beside her with an arm around her waist to support her. "The fire seems to be out," she said dully as the three men came toward her. "Perhaps the wing where Grandfather Lucien lived was spared—perhaps you can find some mementos in his room. I want to take them to wherever we're going. I want him to know somehow that when we begin again, those things dear to him will be with us so that his memory will live on. I've kept the watch I gave Matthew some Christmases ago, the one I had inscribed 'from your loving, grateful wife, and may time be gentle with you always.' I took it out of his pocket before—" she could not finish, bowing her head as her shoulders shook with muffled weeping.

"I'll stay with you, Miz Sybella," Prissy consolingly murmured, blinking her eyes to clear them of the tears.

"Oh no, dear Prissy. I'll be all right now. Matthew's at peace, and if there's a hereafter, he and Paul and Grandfather Lucien and Dimarte and their tiny baby are reunited, and I know they're praying for our happiness wherever it's to be. I want to stand here and look at Windhaven and remember it as it was. That strong red brick wasn't burned, only the inside. It's a little blackened, but it's still strong. It shows how long we've been together and how many adversities we've overcome in all that time, just as in some way God will give us courage to overcome our present trouble." She straightened, took a deep breath and forced a smile to her trembling lips.

"If you're sure," Prissy hesitated. "I'll just go dig up that silver, then, Miz Sybella, m'am. Oh yes, I'd better see if there's any horses left. Daddy told me I should look.

13

Now you rest easy there, it won't take me but a little minute, Miz Sybella."

The door to the entrance of Windhaven swung crookedly on its hinges; the troopers had savagely flung it to one side as they had hurried in to put the torch to this den of slavers, as Captain Arnold Huxter had termed it. Luke caught his breath at the sight of the charred, collapsed stairway which had once so proudly risen beyond the foyer up to the second floor. The old grandfather's clock in the corner to the left of the door had been smashed into kindling wood by the butt of a trooper's rifle. "Chances are the landing's been burned away too, Djamba," he forced his voice to be casual, though the sight of these blackened ruins filled him with a silent fury. "We could go up by either of the stairways in the two towers, of course, but I doubt that we'd be able to get to any of the rooms. We'd best start looking on both sides of the ground level. See if you and Lucas can salvage any of the pieces of furniture—but don't take needless risks. The smoke isn't too bad, thank heaven for that. I'll go to Grandfather's room."

"Yes, Mistah Luke. Come on, Lucas boy, let's have a look-see in the library and the dining room. Mind the way you step there, see those pieces of timber, with dots of fire at the ends? It's terrible they had to burn this beautiful place, just terrible."

As Djamba and Lucas carefully moved down the charred remnants of what had once been a carpeted corridor along the right wing, Luke cautiously advanced in the opposite direction to the room Lucien Bouchard had lived in almost from the very day the chateau had been officially completed. What had saddened him most was the sight of that blackened portico which he himself had helped to put into place as his joyous contribution to his grandfather's dream-come-true, that replica of old Lucien's birthplace in Yves-sur-lac in Normandy in what had been another world, another lifetime.

To his pleased surprise, old Lucien's room had been left almost untouched; the depredations of the fire had done most of the damage to the stairway and the landings along the second floor, and partly to the right wing. But

14

here, old Lucien's bed was still intact and his famous escritoire was undamaged except for smoke stains.

Thoughtfully Luke stood before this writing desk, which summoned up the gilded era of Watteau and the elegance of the French court. He put his hand to the top drawer and drew it out slowly. There was a dirk which clattered along the thin wooden surface, and he picked it up wonderingly. Then he remembered: once, long ago, old Lucien had told him how, when he had come to New Orleans the first time, he had saved a pretty young lady from assault by river ruffians and disarmed one of them of this very dirk. And he had used that dirk to save the life of a Creek girl, Shehonoy, the wife of the warrior he had been forced to kill in his journey from Mobile to Econchate. Her life had been spared, although she had been banished from the village; and she had been the friend of his beloved Dimarte.

He pocketed the dirk, closed the drawer, and then tentatively tried to lift the writing desk. It was not too heavy, and with care he could manage it. Slowly he retraced his footsteps and set the escritoire down just beyond the stone steps that led to the entrance of Windhaven.

Djamba and Lucas had made a cursory inspection of the library and dining room, and found that several pieces of furniture could be saved. The smoke here, however, was even more intense than on the other side, and so they hurried out. Luke waved to them and called, "How is it in there?"

"Another few hours, Mistah Luke, and we can go back when the smoke dies down. There's plenty we can save. But what's that now?" From beyond the chateau, all three of them suddenly heard what sounded like a muffled cry, brusquely silenced.

"The stable—Prissy!" Djamba exclaimed, his eyes suddenly bright with anxiety.

Prissy had pushed open the stable door and turned to retrieve the shovel which she had propped against the wall just inside, when she uttered a startled gasp and put her hand to her mouth, recoiling from what she saw. Sprawled on the straw-covered floor, lying almost at her feet, was the body of the lanky Kru, Jimmy. His kinky gray hair was soaked with blood from the ugly wound of a saber which had cut his skull open like a melon. "Ohh, my Gawd, my Gawd!" Prissy gasped, chokingly, paralyzed with a sick nausea. Beyond her, she heard one of the horses nicker, and then suddenly two dark forms emerged from the stalls and were on her before she could cry out. One of them clapped a dirty hand over her mouth and grabbed one of her wrists with the other, while his companion gripped her by the waist and both hustled her to the very back of the stable and flung her down to a pallet of hay. "You make one sound, gal, just one sound, we'll serve you like we done that nosey nigger," the man with his hand over her mouth hissed.

Prissy's eyes rolled to the whites, sweat drenched her plump, ripe body, and she lay motionless, hardly daring to breathe. "Come on, Jeb, see what me'n Buford got ourselves here," he exultantly crowed.

A third man, clad in Confederate gray like his two companions, straightened from his crouching pose in one of the empty stalls and hurried to join them. "Wal now, ain't she a sight for us pore boys!" he sniggered, reaching out a grimy hand to squeeze one of Prissy's full ripe heaving breasts. She moaned and writhed, shrinking under his harsh caress, and he snarled, "Just one peep, bitch, you're a gonner, don't fergit it! We's Second Alabama Cavalry—leastways, we wuz till last month when we saw who was gonna win. Hell, Case 'n Buford 'n me, we come from Marion County, and we pore whites didn't hold with these goddamn seceshers nohow! We didn't have cash to buy ourselves off, so they done went and conscripted us, but hell, it's over now and we're gonna have ourselves some fun to make up fer takin' orders from these fancy-dandy officers. Hell," he turned away to spit contemptuously, "all the goddamn Confederates's got is officers, seems like. Now then, gal, whatcha doin' here anyhow? Take your hand off a mite, Case boy, let the bitch speak up—but mind you, gal, jist one yell, you're done. Now then, whatcha lookin' fer in this stable, that's what I want to know."

"I—I hid something for the people that own this place—I came back to get it for them—" Prissy gasped,

16

her voice faint and trembling. She winced as the bony fingers of the man called Case prodded at her breasts, while his companion who crouched on the other side of her and gripped her shoulder with one hand began to glide the other over her thighs.

"Somethin's mighty valuable, seems like, or you wouldn't be riskin' your purty neck to come git it," the man who squatted just beyond her head and whose torn gray shirt bore a corporal's chevrons, leered. Then he reached out and slapped her brutally across the mouth, "Don't yell, gal, don't yell, don't you dare! Now, what's this you hid and where'd you hide it?"

"Aw, fer Chrissake, Jeb," Buford whined, a man in his late twenties, with heavy jowls and stubbly yellow beard, "Let's poke her first 'n then we can make her tell where the stuff is. I'm fair bursting, and this bitch's nice and juicy, cain't you tell jist by the feel of her tits?"

"Oh please, oh no, please Gawd, don't do that to me, please—I'll—I'll get you money—you can have the horses—" Prissy began to babble hysterically, though she forced herself to lower the tone of her voice in her mortal terror.

"Now ain't she a smart one, Jeb," Case, in his early thirties, with yellowing teeth and a knife scar along the left jawbone, jeered. "We're takin' those horses anyhow, so that's no bargain. But I'll tell you one thing, you start yellin' or makin' a fuss, we'll switch you till you tell us where the stuff is hid, and then we'll kill you. So you'd best just make up your mind to accommodate us good old Alabammy boys right off, and tell us nice and proper where you hid it and we'll let you go when we've had our fun and got the swag. What is it anyway, jewels or gold? Better be hard money, sister, or you'll get what that uppity nigger got when he come round about dawn to see if there was hosses left here. Hell, we wuz in the woods when them Union troopers stopped by to fire the place, and then they went off and they didn't trouble the stables at all. Mighty thoughtful of 'em. Guess somehow they knew there was Union sympathizers watchin' on 'em!" he guffawed, then bent his head down till he was staring into Prissy's agonized face. "Hell, this ain't no white bitch, it's

17

a high-yaller. Most likely she's been a sucker outa the white master's git. That's lighter than a mustee, that's for sure. Come on, strip her down. No need to treat her like a lady."

With this, the corporal called Jeb by his companions, tall and rangy, with a wizened, pockmarked face, nodded to Case and Buford who grasped Prissy's wrists and shoved them up toward him. Clutching them tightly in his right hand and clapping his left palm over her mouth, he repeated, "Peel her down raw."

Mad with shame and terror, Prissy writhed and kicked, but Case seized both her ankles in his bony hands while Buford, his face florid and twisted in lust, ripped off her calico dress and then the cotton chemise.

"Man, lookit that, willya!" he exulted, running his hand over the inside of Prissy's flexing, desperately clenching thighs. "Now who's gonna go first, that's what I wanna know!"

"I wuz the one killed that nigger, seems like I got the right. Didn't I tell you boys to wait till those troopers done their work and that there'd be swag aplenty fur us all?" Jeb spoke up. "You come hold her hands, Buford, I'll bust her good. Then you and then Case can have your turns. She's built to take on a platoon of Alabammy boys and not even work up a sweat, hee hee hee!"

"Aw right then, but fur Gawd's sake, don't take all day at her, I'm fair nigh burstin' here!" Buford complained as he crawled over to replace the corporal's chevrons and clutched Prissy's slim wrists in one hand while the other covered her mouth. In that instant when they were changing hold of her, however, Prissy twisted her face to one side and uttered a wild scream before it was silenced by Buford's fleshy palm which mashed her lips down against her teeth and drew blood.

"Goddamn nigger bitch, we oughta gutcha right now for that," Jeb snarled as he unbuttoned his trousers and got between Prissy's writhing thighs. "Hold her ankles good, Case, till I get planted in her, then she can kick like an ornery mule if she's a mind ta!" With this, he forced himself down against her struggling naked body.

Arching and twisting as best she could, Prissy averted

her ravisher's intended penetration for a moment, and he swore violently: "Hold her tight, you sons of bitches, till I get in her!"

At that moment, Djamba flung open the stable door, armed with a pitchfork he had found just outside, and Luke, dirk in hand, advanced beside him while Lucas, who had seized a short heavy piece of fire wood, warily moved behind them and to the side.

"Prissy—what's happened, girl?" Djamba called.

"Kill 'em, boys, kill 'em all!" Jeb savagely shouted as he flung himself off the helpless, naked, quadroon's body and crawled, his breeches rucked down about his knees, toward the bloodied saber he had left near the straw pallet on which Prissy was stretched.

With an oath, Buford released Prissy's wrists and rummaged for the pistol he had laid behind him. Djamba drew back his arm and flung the pitchfork as he might have done the spear against the black-maned lion long years ago. As the deserter straightened, leveling the pistol, the tines of the pitchfork caught him in the throat and flung him back against the wall. The pistol dropped to the ground as he weakly clawed at the impaling metal, then slumped down to a seated pose, lifeless.

"I'll gut you bastids fur that!" Jeb raged as he lifted the bloody saber and rushed at Luke. But the tall slim grandson of Lucien Bouchard stepped back, right finger and thumb gripping the sharp point of the pirate dirk, then flung it forward with all his strength. Jeb stopped in midrush, stared stupidly down at his left chest into which the dirk had fatally penetrated, uttered a gurgling cry, dropped the saber and pitched forward on his face.

Case, the scar-faced deserter, was shrieking blasphemies as he ran to the dead Buford and tried to tug the pitchfork out of the dead man's throat so as to use it as a weapon. Before he could, Lucas had bounded forward and struck with all his strength. The heavy piece of fire wood smashed Case's skull and sent him sprawling across Buford's lap without a sound.

Prissy had stumbled away, crouching in one of the stalls, weeping hysterically in the aftermath. Djamba, his chest heaving, his strong fingers flexing, exhaling his rage, turned to the empty stall nearest him and picked up a horse blanket, moved to where his stepdaughter crouched and gently tendered it, saying, "Wrap this round you, girl, cry it out now, it's all over."

Luke stood over the fallen Jeb, grimaced as he bent down to pull the dirk out of the ruffian's heart and to wipe it on the tattered gray breeches. He stared at it, then pocketed it, and said, as if to himself, "Will such senseless horror ever end? Why must men forsake their God-given intelligence and act like beasts?"

"Shall we bury them, Daddy?" Lucas asked.

"In my country, jackals like these would be left for the buzzards and the hyenas to devour. But yes, my son, we'll bury them here so if they've any friends of their sort, they won't be found. Mistah Luke, I'm grateful for what you did for my girl Prissy; mighty grateful. Thank the Lord we got here in time before they hurt her. Come on now, Lucas boy, let's put them under the ground and then Prissy can show us where she hid Mistah Luke's silver."

Back at the Williamson house, young Lucien Edmond, his curly hair damp from a sudden shower which had broken just after the three men and Prissy had set out for Windhaven, was opening the shiny teakwood case in which old Edward Williamson had kept a matched pair of derringers. Curiously, he took out one of the little hand guns and laid it in his palm, then shook his head. "To think that such a toy as this could take a man's life," he mused, and then replaced it and closed the case.

At 10:15 on this very night, John Wilkes Booth would pull the trigger of "such a toy" and plunge a nation into mourning.

CHAPTER TWO

Luke Bouchard and Djamba and Lucas had ridden back to the Williamson plantation with Sybella and Prissy. Both women needed rest after their bitter ordeals at Windhaven. Sybella had already wept her tears for Matthew Forsden, and was silent and dry-eyed by the time she dismounted from her mare and walked slowly into the Williamson house. Celia had seen the five riders from the kitchen and hurried out, greatly concerned over her daughter and her mistress. When she saw Sybella go into the house without a word to anyone, she reverently crossed herself as she turned to Djamba and murmured, "The Yankees done killed Mistah Matthew, didn't they, Djamba?"

"Yes, Celia. And it was all so useless and so cruel. Prissy's fine, we had a little trouble in the stable but she's fine now, aren't you, girl?"

Prissy, still trembling in reaction to her encounter with the three Confederate deserters in the stable, nodded, leaning against him and closing her eyes as he put his arm around her waist. Luke watched them, and then nodded understandingly to Djamba and went inside the house to comfort his stepmother as best he could.

"My poor girl, my sweet Prissy, what happened back there?" Celia urgently demanded as she took Prissy's hands in hers and kissed her daughter.

"Now don't you fret, Celia, it's all over now," Djamba said. "There were some deserters hiding there in the stable, but thank the Lord, Mistah Luke and Lucas and I took care of them before they could cause any serious trouble. It's all right now, honey. Celia, take Prissy into the kitchen and give her a good strong cup of coffee and stay with her. Directly we've had a spell of rest, Lucas and I are going back to Windhaven and try to take out more of the things that the fire hasn't ruined. We've already saved a few of old Mistah Lucien's things."

"I'm so glad, Djamba. Come along, Prissy honey, cry all you want, it's good for you. Thank the good Gawd, you're all right now. Come along, child."

Luke Bouchard stood in the hallway of the Williamson house, frowning as he brushed his palm over the sleeves and chest of his fawn-colored waistcoat, begrimed with smoke and dust. Thinking of his grandfather, he wondered if what had just happened in the stable was a kind of evil omen for the future. Or was it, again, the end of one era and the beginning of another, predicated upon the perilous times that were in store for a land which had known such dreadful internecine warfare? *Once again I've had to kill,* he thought to himself, *against all my beliefs and convictions, yet somehow I didn't stop to think or to reason about it. I thought only of saving Djamba's daughter. Beyond what we learned, there may be a greater law that dictates to all of us what we must do, even against the written word of the Scriptures at times. Is it an instinct of the heart which guides us all in these lawless times? I pray unto God that He judge me by the motive which impelled my hand.*

Luke paused near the guest bedroom which Sybella had occupied since the hasty flight from Windhaven. Against his will, hearing voices, he stood listening.

"Forgive me, Mother," it was Maybelle Bouchard who spoke softly and earnestly. "Last night, when I saw the

22

flames rise over Windhaven, I thought only of myself and how my settled way of life was being violently disrupted. What a self-centered, thoughtless fool I've been, Mother. Can you find it in your heart to forgive me?"

And then Sybella's voice, firm without wavering, though soft-toned: "But there's nothing to forgive, my dear. You've had greater heartaches than I. You've had all these years when my son Mark deserted you, leaving you to bring up Laurette, never knowing what would happen to him, with all that bitterness between you because he never wanted the integrity and responsibility of a true marriage. But I've been lucky. I've been loved by two men. Yes, I've lost them both, and I've lost my other son, Paul, who fell at Shiloh, but the love I had for them and which they returned in such full measure can sustain me now. So you see, dear, it's been much harder for you. You're still attractive, still full of life. Perhaps going to Texas will be a chance for us to begin all over again. And if this tragedy has a meaning, it's that it's brought us all the closer together, and we can share the very best that's in all of us with one another."

"Oh, Mother, I shan't be afraid any more, I shan't, not ever again, thanks to you!" Luke heard Maybelle exclaim as she burst into tears. And as he moved silently by the partly opened door, he saw the two women embrace, comforting each other, and he in turn was comforted.

Luke, Djamba and Lucas had gone back to Windhaven that fateful Friday afternoon and worked until twilight to bring out what the fire had not consumed: a few chairs and tables, Arabella's old writing desk, old Lucien's comfortable four-poster bed, and most of the kitchen cooking ware, as well as the monogrammed family silver which Prissy had buried in the stable. They had hitched horses to two wagons left in the Williamson stable and brought back this salvage. Once again the silence of the night had fallen, but there were no sounds of crackling flames, no volleys of gunfire, only the lapping of the river against its winding banks and the calls of the nightbirds to herald the end of this momentous day.

Everyone in the Williamson house slept longer than

23

usual, exhausted by the emotions and anxieties of the day before, so that it was nearly noontime on Saturday when they finished breakfast and Djamba entered the Williamson dining room to bend down beside Luke and murmur, "Some of them have come back, Mistah Luke, they're out there by the cabins, asking to see you. Some of them from Windhaven, too. I told them you'd be out directly you'd finished your meal."

"Thank you, Djamba. Did any of them say anything about Yankee troops in the vicinity?"

"Not a word, Mistah Luke. Old George, he rode out on a horse early this morning to scout, as you might say, and there's no sign of any soldiers miles around. And the fire has burned itself out at Windhaven."

"We've taken all we can, it would be dangerous to try to get to the second floor, Djamba. I'm grateful to you and Lucas for all the help you gave me yesterday."

"No, Mistah Luke, it's I who are grateful to you, for Prissy's sake. She's fine now. She went down on her knees last night and asked the good Lord to bless you and your family."

Luke closed his eyes and nodded, emotion once again welling up in him, then laid down his napkin and rose from the table. "If you'll all excuse me for a few moments, I want to talk to the hands who've come back. Maybe some of them would be willing to go along with us and help us build a new Windhaven," he smiled at Lucien Edmond as he spoke, and his son nodded and reached for Maxine's hand.

It was an unseasonably warm day for April, and the sun blazed down on the rows of cabins beyond the Williamson house. Some twenty men and women and their little children stood waiting patiently as Luke strode out to greet them, flanked by Djamba and Lucas. As he came toward them, he saw that George was weeping silently, tears coursing down his black cheeks.

"Oh, Mistah Luke, dey done shot and killed Massa Lincoln!" George hoarsely exclaimed. "Jist now, a young niggah on a hoss rode up from Montgomery, and he said de news came over the telegraph early dis mohnin', it true, Mistah Luke!"

A chorus of soft groans from the other blacks punctuated George's anguished declaration. Djamba turned to his son and murmured, "Then that was what I saw in my dream night before last, Lucas. That great good man pulled down by a hyena, and there I was with my spear and I could do nothing to save him. God help this sorrowful land, now that he's gone from us!"

"George, did that man say who shot the President?" Luke anxiously demanded.

The graying Hausa shook his head and brushed the back of his hand across his eyes to clear them of the tears: "Nossuh, Mistah Luke, jist say somebody he shot Massa Lincoln, dat's all! He done freed us all, and now he daid—what we po' niggahs gwine do now?"

"That is terrible news, George, the worst kind of news now that this war is over. The North will cry for vengeance more than ever, especially if the assassin is a Southerner. But you know that you were freed long ago, long before President Lincoln issued his Emancipation Proclamation. My grandfather and I determined that there should be no such thing as slavery. You know also, all of you," he raised his voice now to address the gathered crowd of blacks, "that, just as my grandfather did, I arranged to pay all of you wages and to place them in your names in my account at Mobile."

"Yassuh, we knows dat, Mistah Luke," Harry spoke up, and his wife Betty smiled agreement, "only you allus saw we got whatevah clothes 'n baccy 'n things we needed, so we nevah needed no wages. Wut we all wants to know right now is dis, if you kin tell us dat, Mistah Luke—is you gwine stay heah on this land, now they burned that big red house upriver?"

Luke bowed his head for a moment, choosing his words with care. "No, Harry, and I'll tell you why. The North has won the war, and many of its leaders will want to punish the people of the South for having broken away from the Union. I think the North will send soldiers and agents down here to tell us what we must do, perhaps even to break up the big plantations. You will most likely be given the opportunity to buy the land and to work it for yourselves."

25

"None of us is gwine have money enough fer dat, Mistah Luke, no mattah how much wages you gwine pay us," Harry called back, dolefully shaking his head amid a chorus of "dat's right—he say de troof, Harry do!" from his companions.

"But, Mistah Luke," George interposed, "we knows we's free, why cain't we wuhk heah and keep de land foah you? Won't dem Yankees let us niggahs do dat if we sez we wants to?"

Luke shook his head. "I may be wrong, George, but I'm pretty sure that those in power in the North will make sure that any landowner who gave comfort to the people of the South will lose his land. Even though I always paid the taxes, even though all I did during this dreadful war was to furnish food to the soldiers and to my neighbors, they'll still call me a Confedrate rebel, a secessionist, a slaveholder. And if they try to sell you the land, they'll set such a high price in hard money that you'll never be able to meet it, yes, as Harry just said, even if you had in your hands right now all the wages that all of you have earned in working for me these last years."

"Den you ain't gwine stay heah, even on de ol' Williamson place nohow, is you, Mistah Luke?" George pursued.

"It's true that I'd thought of trying, George. But I've decided to go with my family to Texas, because it's a huge country with plenty of opportunity for everyone, and very little touched by this war. It'll be a chance to build a new life where we never again shall have to talk about slaves and masters; where, I pray to God, no man will look at another and scorn him because his skin is black or because his politics are different. That's the real meaning of freedom, George."

"Would you take us there with you, Mistah Luke?" Harry spoke up. He moved forward toward Luke Bouchard, his eyes bright with enthusiasm.

"I'd be proud to have you come with me, Harry, and I'd pay you good wages as a free man. Mind you, it'll be a hard life for all of us, but you'd be your own master, and I promise to try to be a good employer to you and to all of you who want to follow us. What we called Wind-

26

haven is gone now, but there'll be a new Windhaven in Texas one day, and all of you can help us build it and be proud of it as we shall be."

"I'll go, Mistah Luke, me 'n Betty, we wants to go wherever you does," Harry grinned and, hesitating a moment, came forward to hold out his hand, then stepped back as if startled by his own boldness.

But Luke smilingly shook his head and grasped Harry's hand and shook it. "God bless you, Harry, and you too, Betty. But now, I want all of you to think about it very hard, before you say you want to come along. There'll be dangers and hardships. I've heard there are Indians there, and it's close to Mexico, and there are bandits who ride across the border to rob and to kill."

"Seems lak to me, den, Mistah Luke," Harry chuckled, glancing back and winking at the others, "dat you gwine need all de help you kin git so nobody gwine bother you, ain't dat right?"

"Yes, you're right, Harry," Luke smilingly nodded. "Yet there's something I want all of you to think about before you make your final decision. I'm very grateful for your loyalty. But you see, we're not going to grow cotton as we did so much here on the Williamson place and over there at Windhaven. Of course, there are people who do grow cotton in some parts of Texas, but my son Lucien Edmond and I have agreed that we should think about cattle as the real way to make the money we'll all need to have a good life. Some of you here, I know, have worked with the cows and the bulls I've brought from Mobile. But most of you have been in the fields with corn and cotton and some fruits, and working with cattle may be very strenuous and difficult for you. That's why I want you to think this over. Besides, it'll be a little time before we can leave here. We'll have to go to Mobile first, then New Orleans, and then take a steamer on to Texas. So there's plenty of time to decide carefully what you really want to do."

"We knows already, we wants to go wid you, Mistah Luke!" Harry exclaimed, then turned to face the others: "Don't you all say the same, jist lak me?" And again

27

there was a chorus of "Yassuh—dat's right—we wants to go wid Mistah Luke anywheah he take us!"

Luke could not suppress the tears that came to his eyes to observe such an unhesitating demonstration of trust. He turned for a moment to stare toward the bluff in which his grandfather lay and said softly to himself, "It was your words, your wishes and your dreams they cheered, not mine, grandfather. And I feel that your spirit will be with us in the new land."

He turned back, serenely purposeful, and spoke to Djamba who stood beside him: "There's much I can't tell them yet because I don't know it all myself, Djamba. Talk to all of them, tell them what you know of your work with the cattle. Those who are older, like Harry and George, may not be strong enough for such work, but they can help us build a place to live, perhaps a stable. All of them have skills which will be useful."

"Yes, Mistah Luke, I'll talk with them and tell them what you said. And I think, if you want to know the truth, there'll be some more coming back out of the woods now that the soldiers have all gone, and they'll be wanting to go along with you too. They want to earn their freedom just as I do, Mistah Luke. You see, I was a slave first, after I was a king, and I've learned that freedom isn't just a word. You can't rightly say you have it till you've worked hard at earning it for yourself."

CHAPTER THREE

Arabella Hunter stared into the dusty, cracked mirror in her bedroom at the Montgomery Hotel and smiled wanly at her reflection. She was remembering the cheval glass in the bedroom which she had shared with her younger sister Fleurette, trying on her new pink dress, and how Fleurette had been so engrossed with the sight of the bird at the window that she hadn't even looked around. To think that that had been thirty years ago—how swiftly the years had gone by!

Yet they had dealt kindly with her, she had to admit as she glanced quickly round to send a covert glance at her tall, gray-haired husband who was seated at the opposite end of the large room. True, the slim figure of her teens had given way to more buxom contours, thanks to motherhood, yet her husband still found her desirable. In an age when it was common practice for a slaveholder to choose a black concubine at whim, James Hunter had not once availed himself of the privilege, nor, for that matter, shown interest in any other woman except herself. That alone was enough to flatter Arabella and enable her to meet the maturing of the years with a joyous grace. Her skin was still smooth and creamy as it had been in her youth, though she was now all of forty-one. Her black hair was styled with little curls at the top of the forehead and a thick chignon falling below her nape, since that was the way he liked it. And as she made a saucy *moué* in the mirror, her soft mouth still evinced her willful and mercurial nature.

With a sudden warm surge of memory, she smiled to recall how Sybella had chided her for flirting with that Creole dandy—what was his name?—yes, Edouard Villiers, and once told her that love was not meant to be a mirror in which one could see one's beauties and virtues reflected, since that was only vanity.

And she remembered, too, how, just a little more than a year after their marriage, wanting to test her flirtatious powers, she had danced with a dashing young bachelor at a party in Selma, let him bring her a cup of punch and had rewarded him with one of her dazzling smiles and the trailing of her soft fingers across his wrist. That night, alone in their conjugal bedroom, James Hunter had said not a word to her. But just as she had been about to clamber into bed, in her long nightgown, he had grasped her round the waist, pulled her across his lap as he seated himself on the edge of the bed, and proceeded to administer a sound spanking with her own silver-backed hairbrush, a wedding present from Sybella. And that night, she was certain of it, their daughter Melinda had been conceived.

She rose now and turned to him to watch him as he finished the letter he was writing to his cousin in Texas. "James dear," she murmured softly, "before we go to Galveston, could we maybe stop over at Windhaven so I can visit Mother and my stepfather?"

"I don't see why not, Bella," he rose and turned to her with a quick smile. "Just written to Cousin Jeremy in Galveston. I told him that with any luck, we ought to be there in about two weeks. I've heard that General Wilson's men burned at least four steamboats on the Alabama, so that will hold up transportation down to Mobile for some little time, even though the war is over now. But since there's a dock there, and it's a regular steamboat stop, there's no reason why we couldn't spend a few days with your family, and I'm sure they'd like to see Melinda and Andrew."

"Oh, thank you, James," Arabella exclaimed as she came forward to hug him. His arms tightened round her and they kissed warmly and fondly, like two lovers who had long since divined each other's ardors and desires. Arabella uttered a contented little sigh as she nestled her head against his chest and closed her eyes: "That's it, James, hold me, I need your strength now. We'll be starting all over again, won't we?"

"It's not as bad as that, Bella dear. Jeremy Danton has offered me a good job, and I've learned enough about cotton running my father's plantation, as you know. Besides, there's my law practice, and Cousin Jeremy thinks I can be very helpful in looking after the legal side of his ginning and exporting business."

"You make it sound so easy, James. But I'm not afraid, as long as I'll be with you."

"We've come through the worst of it, Bella, you and I. You remember when we first met at Mrs. Gurley's, and I admired your watercolors? I told myself then you were a clever but flighty young lady who had a reserve of resourcefulness that the right man could bring out in you— and I was right."

"Do you know what I was thinking just then while I was looking into the mirror, James?" she shyly whispered, her face coloring hotly at the recollection. "That time I flirted with poor young Wilson Larkins, and how you gave me such an awful spanking that night. I thought for certain I was going to ask Mama to get me a divorce from you—but I'm ever so glad I didn't."

"I am too, you saucy minx," he whispered as he kissed her again. "No, we've got our health and we still love each other, we've got our two fine children, and there's this strongbox with enough stake in it to see us through the future in Texas. And now, let's collect our offspring and go downstairs for breakfast and learn today's news."

"You go down first, dear, while I get the children ready." Then, with a flash of her adolescent piquancy, she pressed close against him, her fingers gripping his shoulders as she whispered, "I'll tell you one thing, Mr. Hunter, the news I really want is when you and I can share a bedroom to ourselves again. Not that Melinda isn't the most adorable little lady, and I'm sure it's a treat for Andrew to lie beside his daddy, but the sooner we get to Galveston where we can have a room all to ourselves, the happier I'll be."

James Hunter chuckled indulgently and gave Arabella a pat on the hip as he gently disengaged himself. "I must say, Bella," his eyes were twinkling though his tone was feignedly grave, "there are some husbands who would find such a wish most uncircumspect in a dutiful wife after nearly fifteen years."

Arabella colored hotly, then gave him a saucy wink as she murmured, "I declare, Mr. Hunter, are you blaming me because you're such a satisfying lover that I haven't the slightest interest in any other man?"

James Hunter smiled at her and then walked with a hardly perceptible limp toward the door and opened it. Turning, he said softly, "Well, my dear, if we spend a few days at Windhaven, I'm certain there's room enough there to spare us a place just for ourselves. I'll be back shortly."

The lobby of the little hotel was crowded with excited, jostling storekeepers, citizens and guests, beleaguering the elderly clerk for the latest news that had come over the wires on this Monday, April 17, 1865. "Please, gentlemen," Caleb Hoskins tried to make his reedy voice audible above the hubbub, "the boy just came in from the telegraph office, and if you'll be quiet, I'll read you what I have, that's the best I can do!"

James Hunter, halting on the stairway, called out, "Read the dispatch, Mr. Hoskins!" The elderly clerk glanced up and grinned, "Morning, Major Hunter sir. That's just what I'm trying to do if these folks will let me." Then, galvanized by the urging of his important guest—for Major James Hunter had been twice decorated for gallantry under fire—he held up his hand and bawled, "Now you men shut up so Major Hunter can hear the latest."

One of the merchants nearest the counter scowled and

called out, "Major, is it? I don't see any gray uniform there, Hoskins, what are you giving us?"

"Now, now, Mr. Bedwell, that's no way to talk!" The clerk indignantly retorted. "I'll have you know that Major Hunter there was decorated by General Joe Johnston hisself. They mustered him out 'cause of his wounds, that's why he's not got a uniform on. And the war's over, you all know that. Now hush yourselves a mite and lemme read this."

"All right, go ahead, then, Hoskins!" the merchant muttered, with an apologetic glance up the stairs at the sober-faced, gray-haired man who stood there.

"Well, here it is, then. This is from Washington. Assassin of the President identified as actor John Wilkes Booth. Assassination attempt made on the life of Secretary of State William H. Seward. The assassin of the President still at large at time of this dispatch. There it is now."

"My God," James Hunter ejaculated, "Edwin Booth's younger brother!"

He came slowly down the stairs and shouldered his way toward a tall lanky middle-aged man wearing a top hat and long blue frockcoat and holding a silver-headed cane. "Mr. Asbury, sir, good morning to you. You remember, we met in Selma last spring."

Garner Asbury turned, took off his top hat and inclined his head with a cordial smile. "Upon my word, so we did, sir. Here's my hand on it. And I'm happy to see that you're apparently well, in spite of the war."

"Thank you, sir! Now tell me, Mr. Asbury, since you're clerk of Montgomery, can you give me local news which we don't find in that dispatch? Have General Wilson's troops left the area?"

"That they have, sir. Governor Watts left for Union Springs with the hope of establishing our capital at Eufaula, and our farsighted mayor ordered the burning of nearly a hundred thousand bales of cotton so that it wouldn't fall into the hands of the Yankees."

"There was no destruction, then, as in my own city of Selma?" James Hunter anxiously pursued.

"No, most of the troops were marched through the city without any incident, though of course there were a few

33

isolated cases of robbery by stragglers. They destroyed the railroad depot and the mills and foundry—military objectives."

"Of course."

Garner Asbury chuckled humorlessly. "Do you know, sir, that the editor of our *Advertiser* attributed the minimum of looting to the absence of liquor, but then, you see, we saw to it that all barrels containing whiskey were emptied before the Yankees got here. And I can tell you something else—some of General Wilson's forces met our gallant boys at Girard yesterday—I had the news from a courier early this morning. I'm very much afraid it's the last gallant, useless effort of our Confederacy."

"You've been most helpful, Mr. Asbury. I wonder, do you know the Windhaven plantation, near Pintilalla Creek?"

"I do indeed, sir. That, I'm sorry to say, was one of the places those Yankee troopers burned. Seems the captain leading a large group of them hated what he called damned Southern aristocrat slave owners."

"Oh my God! My—my wife was a Bouchard, and lived there before I met her. We were hoping to go downriver and have a reunion with the family."

"I'd say that anyone there would have gone farther on downriver and taken what refuge they could, Major Hunter."

James Hunter frowned and bit his lips. "I'm indebted to you, sir. I think—yes, I think I know where they might have gone. I bid you a very good day, Mr. Asbury."

"And many more to you and your charming wife, Major. I'm sorry about the Bouchard's place, and please give my condolences to your wife. If you don't mind my asking: what do you think you'll do now?"

"I'm thinking of joining my cousin in Texas, at Galveston."

"You'll find many good Southerners there already. And I shouldn't be surprised if many more are on their way, wanting to get as far away as possible from the infernal Yankees. Well, I must get back to my desk. I have to register complaints from citizens with grievances—not that it will do them any good to complain these days."

Hurrying back up the stairs, James Hunter knocked at the door of his wife's room and was admitted by Arabella, who had just finished inspecting Melinda's and Andrew's outdoor attire. Melinda, black-haired like her mother and with the same sensuously ripe mouth, large hazel eyes and upturned nose, immediately sought her father's attention by performing a pretty pirouette in her modish white linen dress. Andrew, his curly dark-brown hair a thick shock in urgent need of scissors, squinted at her. He wore a Russian-style embroidered tunic, a lingerie under-blouse, tight striped ticking trousers, and a cloth cap with leather visor. He turned now to Arabella, his round face tightening with annoyance and showing the hint of his father's firm chin, as he complained in a loud whisper, "Aw, Mama, make her stop showing off all the time!"

James Hunter chuckled, came forward and lifted his son up in the air, then set him down and clapped him on the shoulder: "You're too young yet to realize, Andy boy, that that's a woman's perogative. Give or take another five or six years, I've no doubt you'll change your opinion of the fair sex, just as I did when I first met your mother."

"How you do go on, Mr. Hunter," Arabella coquettishly bridled, her quick smile showing that she was far from being displeased at this husbandly jibe. "What's the news, dear? Can we go to Windhaven?"

James Hunter scowled, put his hand on Melinda's head and playfully rumpled her curls as he answered slowly, "I'm afraid there's bad news about that, Bella. The city clerk just informed me that some of General Wilson's troopers visited the house, and they set fire to it. None of the family was hurt, though—at least there's no report of it."

She looked pale. "Oh God, how dreadful! Could they all be safe? How could we find out?"

"Now, now, Bella, don't upset yourself. I'm quite sure they all must have gone downriver to the Williamson place, and so far as I can tell, Windhaven was just about the only property that the troopers damaged. They've evacuated the area, and now that we've had the news of Appomattox, there can be no doubt that the war's over at

35

last. I'm told that Joe Johnston and Sherman are meeting today in North Carolina to wrap up the rest of the surrender of Confederate armies."

"Oh, I must find out about Mother—do you think we could go to the Williamson place today, James?"

"I'm going to see if I can rent a carriage and some horses, Bella. It's a fair drive from here, and if I'm lucky, we ought to get there a little after sundown. Melinda, Andrew, you both look just fine. Now you stay here and keep your mother company and behave yourselves until I get back."

CHAPTER FOUR

"I'm still hungry, Mama," Melinda pouted as she climbed into the buggy and took her place at Arabella's right, while Andrew promptly moved himself up as close as he could get on the other side and gave his sister a defiant look.

"I shouldn't wonder, darling," Arabella sighed as she watched her husband climb into the front and grip the reins. "I do hope these poor starved-looking horses will have strength enough to get us to the Williamson place, James, dear."

"I was lucky to get even these, Bella. Had to pay the livery man a hundred dollars in gold, and even then he was grumbling it wasn't enough. I told him I'd have one of the blacks over at the Williamson place drive the buggy and horses back when we arrived. Have you got the box safely hidden under your feet, my dear?"

"Of course, James. And my long cape will help cover it, too. My gracious, it's going to be a very warm day. I wish I didn't have to wear this cape."

"Even though the soldiers have gone, Bella, there's still a danger from deserters and looters following them and seeing what booty they can pick up from the places the Yankees have burned. It's a tragedy we can't have some form of martial law now and shoot riffraff like that out of hand. Well now, Melly, Andy, all comfortable now and ready? I warn you, it's going to be a long journey, but I promise you there'll be plenty to eat when we get to your grandmother's."

The dingy little restaurant next to the hotel where they had eaten a belated breakfast had had little to offer. With coffee going at seventy dollars a pound, all the portly widow who ran the place could offer was a hot, brownish liquid made out of okra seeds which had been matured and thoroughly browned. The homemade bread, baked out of moldy corn meal, had been liberally dosed with the ashes of red corncobs to make it rise since bicarbonate of soda had not been available almost since the outbreak of the Civil War. Happily for the children's sake, the widow had graciously opened one of the last of her jars of home-made raspberry preserves as a spread. Melinda and Andrew had wrinkled their noses at the taste of the skim milk, till their father sternly told them that they were lucky to get even that. And James Hunter, by dint of handing the dolefully complaining widow a five-dollar gold piece, had induced her to fry one of the scrawny chickens in her back yard, and had contented himself with a meager wing while Arabella and the children shared the remainder of the none too meaty dish.

He had donned his gray military cape, and Arabella shuddered as she saw the sinister, dark butts of pistols protruding from the tops of the pockets. "A necessary precaution, I assure you, Bella," he told her when she had started at the sight of them. "Don't forget, that box you've got back there contains all we've got left in the world. I don't propose to have some lazy deserter take it away from us. And you know yourself how hard it was to come by when all we had for our crops was payment in Confederate greenbacks. I can tell you now, my dear, I sold a few heirlooms to come by hard money, and I don't regret it. And now, let's get a good start. We'll take the road along the river, it'll lead us past Windhaven and on to the Williamson place."

Once out of town, the road along the winding Alabama River led past thickets of elderberry and blackberry bushes, and then a long stretch of piny woods. The sun was oppressively hot, and the air was sticky with the first hint of an early summer.

James Hunter warily watched the woods and the thick clusters of bushes to his left. The horses were docile and kept a fair pace, so that he could hold the reins with his right hand and keep his left hand at the butt of the pistol. Both weapons had been primed and cocked, in case of ambush.

About three in the afternoon, he stopped to water the horses and to allow Melinda and Andrew time to stretch their legs and to go into the bushes, while Arabella primly chose a place of privacy some distance away. He stood guard, but there was no sign of any movement on either side of the river. A stillness pervaded the humid air, and even the river ran quietly.

He sighed softly and shook his head. It was hard to think of leaving this beautiful country where he had been born, come to manhood, courted his beautiful, spirited wife and seen his children enjoy their formative years. Yet his mother had died on the very day Fort Sumter was fired on, and he had buried his father twelve years ago, and now their comfortable old house back in Selma was razed to the ground. And worst of all, he could foresee the coming trials imposed on the South by the vengeful victors of this war whose cause he had once believed was invincible. Galveston would mean a new beginning, a chance to forget the heartbreak and the disillusion of the past.

"We're all ready to travel again, James," Arabella blithely announced as she got into the buggy and held out her hand to Andrew first this time, who seated himself and made a spiteful face at his sister. "Oh now, Andrew, that was unworthy of a gentleman! Don't you know I love you both equally much? Come up, Melinda, and it won't be long before Grandma Sybella will have a nice cool glass of lemonade for you both."

James Hunter chuckled, grasped the reins and clucked at the two lean black horses, who obediently started off along the winding road. "We're making better time than I'd hoped for, Bella," he called back. "I'm sure we'll be there by sundown."

"If only this sun weren't so dreadfully hot, James, dear," Arabella sighed as she hugged her children close to her. "Isn't there a road through those trees there?"

"Yes, but if you don't mind, I'd just as soon stay along the river bank. It'll be safer, if you gather my meaning."

"Oh—yes—yes, of course, James. Do you—do you think there's really any danger?"

"I can only pray there won't be, my dear. And I can tell you that from my experiences on the battlefield, there were always those miserable vultures who tried to rob the dead and the wounded. I had to shoot a few myself, and so did my men. Let's talk of more cheerful things, though, Bella. When I was renting these horses and the buggy from the livery man, he was saying something about hearing that the steamboats would be going down the river again in a couple of weeks. I'd told Cousin Jeremy in my letter that he might expect us around June at the very latest, and of course that I was beholden to him for his kind offer of employment. In his last letter, he wrote that there'll be no trouble finding a nice little house for us."

"It will be nice to have our own house again, James. Even if it isn't as big and comfortable as the one back in Selma. And I do hope there'll be a good school for Melinda and Andrew."

"Oh gosh, Mama, will we have to go to school right away?" Melinda turned to ask, her face anxious.

"Not the very first day, silly," Arabella bent to kiss her on the tip of her daintily turned-up nose. "But you remember, you're the one that wants to be a grown-up lady, and grown-up ladies have to have plenty of schooling before they're ready to take their place in the social world."

"Oh, all right then," Melinda petulantly acquiesced and snuggled closer to her mother, comforted by the latter's arms around her waist while Andrew, not to be outdone, leaned forward to kiss Arabella on the side of her chin and whisper, "I just love you so, Mama!"

By four o'clock, they came within view of a towering

red-brick chateau which stood just beyond the borders of the wide creek. Arabella uttered a cry of anguish: "Oh, James, just look at Windhaven! Why did the Yankees have to burn it? Grandfather Lucien and my half-brother Luke weren't slavers, and they never did anything against the North! What useless, hateful vandalism!"

"It's the senseless hatred that breaks out in every war, Bella—but hold on, don't look back, I'm going to gallop the horses, and I only pray they're up to it!" James Hunter suddenly muttered as he lowered his left hand to the pocket of his cape and grasped a pistol. Then, lifting the reins in his right hand, he brought them down like a whip, calling out, "Go, go on!" and the two lean black horses lunged forward just as, from behind them near the side of the red-brick chateau, two men broke into a lope toward the buggy. One of them was squat and short, with a long curly red beard; the other tall and lean, with a broken nose and a dark-bluish bruise left by a rifle butt on his left cheekbone; both were dressed in tattered gray uniforms.

"Hold up there, Mister!" the bearded deserter bawled. But James Hunter ignored the summons and, letting go of the pistol for a moment, seized the buggy whip and lashed at the horses to quicken their gait.

There was the sound of a pistol shot as the tall deserter leveled an old fowling piece at the buggy, and James Hunter heard the ball whistle past his head. Dropping the whip and turning, he retrieved the pistol in his left-hand cape pocket, aimed it and fired. A hoarse shout of anger rose as the lanky man clapped a hand to his shoulder and tried to reload the pistol, but dropped it. A few moments more, and the buggy sped beyond the chateau and on past the bluff where old Lucien and his Dimarte lay at rest.

"Oh James, he shot at you—oh my God, are you hurt, darling?" Arabella feverishly cried.

"No, no, though it was a bit too close for comfort. They won't catch up with us, don't worry, darling. I didn't see any horses, and for certain there wouldn't be any left in the stable by now—Luke would have seen to it. I'm going to drive these poor horses just as fast as I can. We've only a few miles left and we'll be safe."

41

At the edge of the chateau, the lanky deserter violently swore as he shoved the old pistol into the pocket of his tattered gray trousers, and snarled at his bearded companion, "Missed the damned secesh bigwig, and it's all your fault, Nate. If you'd thought to bring along that old geezer's rifle he clubbed me with back in Selma last week, 'steada jist killing him and taking off with the swag, I coulda picked that bastard off right between his eyes. Now get busy and tie me a rag or somepin 'roun' my shoulder—he creased me, damn his nigger-hoardin' soul!"

"Never mind, Lem," the squat man reassured him as he ripped off a piece from his own dirty, tattered cambric shirt and made an improvised bandage. "Hold still, if you want this to stay on right—they're sure to be more folks along this road before long, I'm thinking. Just prime your piece and we'll watch here. Then we'll git ourselves some hosses and a little cash and maybe, if there's some cute female sashayin' along, have ourselves a lotta real shaggin' fun!"

"We better git somepin, Nate," the lanky deserter growled, wincing as he inspected the dirty bandage. "Wal, bleeding' seems to have stopped some, so I guess I'll be all right. That old man didn't have much back in Selma, neither. Mostly worthless greenbacks and only about a couple dollars hard money and that watch you took out of his vest after you gutted him. But why the hell didn't you take along your knife after you done the job? Now all we got 'tween us is this ol' pistol, and it ain't good but for one shot at a time."

"Shet your ornery mouth, Lem," the squat deserter angrily rebuked him. "You know damn well patrols was coming down that street 'n if we'd been seen with a knife or a rifle, we coulda got ourselves hung or shot. Jist stay peaceful and outa sight till the next buggy comes along—like I told you, there's bound to be more folks hightailin' it out of Montgomery, seein' if they can git a steamboat down to Mobile."

Now twenty-eight, Laurette had never been lovelier than she was in this the fourth month of her pregnancy. All through this last year of the war, she had lived with her thirty-year-old husband Charles Douglas in the rambling white frame house which his sister Ruthann owned at the southern end of Montgomery, where she earned her livelihood as a teacher in a nearby school. Ruthann Douglas, ten years older than her quiet-spoken brown-haired brother, had taken to Laurette from the very first, and both of them had spent many happy hours together sharing the books of Ruthann's excellent library. And nothing could have delighted the shy, reticent spinster more than to learn that she was to become an aunt by next fall. Her own fiancé had been killed in the war with Mexico, and she had loved him so deeply that she found it impossible to think of marrying any other man. She plunged herself into teaching, found fulfillment in stimulating the acquisitive minds of her pupils.

Ruthann Douglas detested war and had predicted, even before its outset, that the South would be crushed by the superior forces of the North and by the thriving industries which the Confederacy could not equal. She had been secretly overjoyed when her brother had been wounded badly enough to be discharged as unfit for military duty in the spring of 1862. He had gone back to the store in Tuscaloosa, where he had been born, but at the end of 1864 the shortage of supplies had rendered such a venture impractical, and he had agreed to stay with his sister and manage the little produce farm which she had begun as a hobby, and later ran as a necessity, on half an acre of land which she owned behind the frame house.

On this Monday morning, the postman had brought her a piece of news which had distressed her, and she had debated with herself whether to tell Laurette. Mr. Carruthers had insisted on detailing the depredations which those "damned Yankees" had committed right here in Montgomery and downriver as they rode southward on their way to Georgia for a reunion of all the massed Union forces. "Why, Miss Douglas ma'am," he had said, "those scalawags in blue fired up at least four of our good steamboats, like the *River Queen* and the *Tensaw*. And that's not all, not by a long shot, Miss Douglas ma'am! No ma'am, they had to go downriver and burn some of the purtiest houses we ever had round these parts—like that

43

big red castle down near Lowndesboro. It's a criminal shame, that's what it is. Now I hear tell, now the war's over, we can ask for damages from the federal government—but if you ask me, we can ask till doomsday and we won't get a penny from those good-for-nothing Yankees!"

She had patiently waited throughout his lengthy narrative, then gently thanked him for the news, and gone into the living room where Charles Douglas was reading the *Advertiser*. He was six feet one inch tall, with a pleasant, angular face, and Roman nose, twinkling blue eyes with an irrepressible, though quiet, sense of humor which in part he shared with his sister. His hair was long, with extensive sideburns, but he had always balked at wearing a beard on the grounds that too often it was an excuse to hide a weak chin, which his was assuredly not. As she entered, he looked up from the newspaper: "Something wrong, Sis?"

"Oh, just that gabby old Mr. Carruthers and his mournful tales about what the Yankee troops did. You know that you can discount a good deal of what he says. I declare, that man is a prophet of doom."

"Come on now, Sis, I can tell by that frown on your forehead that some of the news must have been serious. What is it?"

"Charlie, I don't think you should tell Laurette. Mr. Carruthers said that the troops went downriver and burned Windhaven. But it's so strong and sturdy, made of that good red brick from the river clay. How could it burn?"

"The inside could burn, Ruthann, you know that. But it does worry me, especially wondering what happened to her folks. I know that some of the Bouchard family were living at the old Williamson house, and undoubtedly, that's where all of them must have gone when there was news of the Yankee troops coming their way."

"I pray the Lord so, for Laurette's dear sake. You know, Charlie, you couldn't have picked a sweeter girl in all this world—or rather, if I'd been left the choice to make for you, I couldn't have found anyone nicer and more thoughtful than Laurette."

44

"I'm glad you feel that way, Ruthann. I'm a lucky man, and I know it. I have Laurette, and I managed to get out of the war with only a limp as damage. But you can't eat good luck. I've been thinking about what I'm going to do to earn a living. And I've come to the conclusion that it might be a good idea to get out of the South altogether. What would you think about moving with me to Chicago?"

"Chicago?" the thin tall spinster gasped, adjusting her spectacles and regarding her brother with amazement. "Why in the world would you ever go there? Why, it's the heart of Yankee country."

"Sis, you're smarter than that, because you're a teacher and a good one. I'm sure there are plenty of Yankees who don't hate the South, just as there must be plenty of Southerners who don't hate the North. This war was about two different kinds of economy, and from what I've seen thus far, I'm inclined to think that the people who beat us have considerable more ingenuity and a lot more opportunity going for them than we ever will with our concentration on cotton and slaves. Now that slavery's over, these big plantation owners are going to be hurting for labor. I'd even go so far as to bet that big plantations will be broken down into what you might call subsistence or tenant farming."

"Yes, I think you're right, Charlie. But still, what's there for you in Chicago?"

"It's becoming one of the biggest cities in the whole United States, that's what, Ruthann. Why, they've got department stores there with sections of goods for all types of customers, from little babies on up to old men and women. Now you know, I liked running that store in Tuscaloosa. I'd like even better learning all I could about how a big store is run for profit, how you get more customers, make them come back again and again because they like your way of doing business. I like selling to people as much as you like teaching children, Ruthann."

"Yes, I think you'd do well wherever you'd go, Charlie, and Laurette would be a great help to you in business. But do you know anybody in Chicago?"

"Well, Sis, just before the war, a fellow by the name of Levi Tallon came down with his wife on a vacation, and he stopped in the store and we chatted a while. He said he had a small fashion goods store on Wabash Avenue in Chicago, and that if I was interested some day, I might look him up. I wrote him a letter just after I got out of the army and went back to the store, and about four months later I got a letter back saying that he had a bigger place and that his offer still held. He guessed the war would last another year or two, and he wasn't too far off at that. So I've just about decided, Ruthann, to give Laurette a sort of little vacation, go on down to New Orleans, let her have a week or two there shopping and enjoying those fancy restaurants and the theater, and then taking the steamboat up the Mississippi to Cairo, and then the steam cars on into Chicago."

"But wouldn't you rather wait till she's had her baby?"

"In one way yes, Sis, but you've seen yourself how Laurette has been fretting recently. She's a little depressed, and I think deep down inside she knows that life here isn't going to be the same as it was before the war. The only thing, she'd be away from her mother and grandmother and her Aunt Arabella, but I think we could all still keep in touch. What I do want to know, Sis, is would you consider coming along with us?"

Ruthann Douglas shook her head. "No, Charlie, much as I'd love to, I won't. There'll be need for schools again now the war is over. As you said, children have been my life, even though I never had any of my own. Maybe that's why I love them all the more dearly. Besides, what would an old-maid schoolteacher do, tagging along with you and your sweet young wife and the baby you're going to have, 'way up there in cold Chicago? No, I'm going to stay right here and, you mark my words, that school of mine will be reopening come fall. Charlie, do you have enough money to start all over again up there? I've a little I can give you—"

"Oh no, Sis, that's out! I've managed to save about fifteen hundred in gold, and I've got it in a money belt, and

46

that'll get us to Chicago and stake us a while till I can see about this job Levi Tallon might have for us. But what you've just told me about Windhaven has sort of speeded up my decision to make the move. I think Laurette would feel much easier in her mind if we drove down there and on to the Williamson place to make sure that her folks are all right. We could stay there a bit, or else go down to Mobile where I've got a friend who's got a big house and wouldn't mind having guests for a week or so till we could organize ourselves and get on to New Orleans."

His sister stared at him, then smiled and nodded. "You always did have more gumption than I did, Charlie. All right, I'll go make breakfast—Laurette's had a nice long sleep and it's good for her. You go wake her up and tell her. Thanks goodness I've still got old Henry locked up safe in my barn and that buggy of mine I use to drive to school is still in good condition. You'd have a difficult time buying or renting horses these days, I'm certain of that."

"But if I take your horse and buggy, Sis, what will you do next fall?"

"Maybe one of the freedmen over at the Williamson place would be nice enough to drive them back here, if you paid him for his trouble, Charlie. We're all going to have to get used to paying for labor now and not looking upon it as our birthright because we're whites and they're blacks."

"You're certainly right about that. I'll go wake Laurette."

The sorrel stallion nickered as Charles Douglas held out a piece of sugar in his palm, scratched the spirited animal's ears with his forefinger. Laurette, her face taut with anxiety, and her eyes misty with tears of concern, had said her goodbys to Ruthann Douglas and promised to write every day. She wore a light green cotton frock with puffed sleeves, and had donned a light spring cape of nankeen and a soft yellow bonnet to protect herself from the glaring sun. In her reticule, she carried a few keepsakes and mementos and the few pieces of jewelry which her husband had already given her, wearing a plain gold wedding band but leaving the engagement ring hidden in the reticule.

"I know it's been a shock for you, Laury darling," Charles said as he hobbled over to the front seat of the buggy, then gently helped her. "But this way, you'll have a chance to visit your folks and get used to the idea of this move of ours."

"I don't mind at all, darling, really I don't. I'd go anywhere with you in the first place, and I certainly agree that there'll be more future for you as a merchant in a city like Chicago than here, or in Tuscaloosa," Laurette firmly declared as she leaned forward to kiss him before clambering into the buggy.

"Good girl! We'll have a second honeymoon in New Orleans first, and maybe I can telegraph Mr. Tallon to expect me and get a reply back so it won't be a wild-goose chase." He got into the buggy, favoring his right leg. Carefully, he propped his long ivory-knobbed cane between his legs, took the reins in both hands, glanced around to make sure that Laurette was comfortable, and started down the road out of town and along the river.

The sorrel stallion was in fine mettle, making good time. And so it was that about half an hour after James and Arabella Hunter had passed along the road winding past the chateau toward the Williamson plantation, Charles Douglas drew on the reins as they neared the red-brick chateau. Laurette put her hand to her mouth and tears came to her eyes to see the desolation of what had once been the imposing, sturdy beauty of that castle-like house in which old Lucien Bouchard's dream of Windhaven had been so magnificently realized.

"Oh Charles, I can't bear to see it this way." Laurette stared longingly at the two towers, as if by sheer will power she could restore the smoke-blackened edifice to its former majesty. "How many years it took Great-grandfather to build this out of the wilderness where there were only Indians and a few venturesome white settlers! What a tragedy it seems to abandon it now."

"Perhaps one day the state will make it an historic landmark, Laury darling," Charles Douglas said encouragingly. "Well, shall we go on? I don't like those clouds over to the north, and I'd like to get to the Williamson place before a storm breaks."

"I'm quite all right now. And I feel sure they're all safe. Yes, by all means, let's go on, dear."

Just then, from around the edge of the chateau, Lem and Nate moved toward the buggy, and the former leveled his fowling piece at Charles Douglas as he called, "Not so fast, my find bucko! Suppose you jist git down from that buggy and state your business!"

"I don't see that it's any concern of yours, sir," Charles Douglas coolly replied as he made the reins fast, then turned to contemplate the two approaching deserters, his hand gripping the ivory knob of the cane.

"A fancy swell, no less. Now there's a cane I'd mighty admire having, brother," the squat deserter sniggered. "S'pose you jist git down from there, you and your little lady."

"Now here's a fancy piece, Nate boy," Lem leered as he reached out a grimy hand toward Laurette. "I'll help you down jist like a gennelman would, honey. Don't be 'fraid now, me 'n Nate'll treat you real nice. No tricks, Mister, I'd just as soon blow your brains out as look at you!" This as Charles slowly and painfully clambered down from the front seat of the buggy, still holding his cane.

But as Lem turned slightly to confront Laurette's husband, the young woman suddenly grasped his right wrist with both hands and forced the old weapon upwards. "Now, Charlie!" she cried out.

Charles Douglas yanked out the top of the cane and bared a long sharp sword. With a single lunge, he thrust Lem through the heart and then, tugging out the blade, turned on Nate. The stocky rogue, shocked by the sudden reversal of events, stood gaping, as if transfixed. Setting his lips. Charles Douglas thrust the sharp, bloodied point of the sword into his heart, then wrenched it out, leaning back, trembling violently in emotional reaction.

Laurette turned her back on the two sprawled dead deserters, hiding her face in her hands, and burst into hysterical sobs.

Dropping the sword, Charles took her in his arms and comforted her. Slowly he helped her into the buggy. "Don't look," he hoarsely admonished. "Try not to think about it, honey. My God, I was in the war a year and I fired my rifle at lots of blue uniforms, and I don't think I ever hit a one, and now I've had to kill two men. But I had to, Laurette."

"I know, Charlie. I love you so, Charlie Douglas. You'd have given up your life for me, and you know you would have. Hurry, before I break down like a silly girl and cry. "I'm fine, the baby's fine, just hurry!"

Two hours later, in the dining room of the old Williamson house, Laurette and Charles Douglas, seated across from James Hunter and Arabella, with Melinda and Andrew flanking them, enjoyed what by comparison with the flare in Montgomery was a bounteous meal, eagerly prepared by Celia and Prissy.

"Of course you'll stay with us, James, Charles," Luke Bouchard spoke up from the head of the table. "I've made some inquiries, and it's going to be at least ten days to two weeks before there's a steamboat doing business downriver to Mobile. James, you and Arabella and the children can go with us on the steamboat to Galveston, and most likely we will be on that same packet. I've got to talk to John Brunton at the counting house in New Orleans and find out his ideas about the best place in Texas for us to settle for our cattle-raising venture. I'm not sure it's near Galveston, but I'll find out directly I'm down there. Meanwhile, the Bouchard clan will have a festive reunion before we go our separate ways, and, God willing, there'll be many more reunions in the years to come."

Then he turned to his right and handed Lucien Edmond a little jewel box. "I found this ruby ring in Grandfather Lucien's escritoire," he said. "It's the ring his mother gave him when he left Normandy, the ring he put on the finger of his Dimarte, and then Amelia, and finally Priscilla. It's a priceless heirloom, my son. Give it to your Maxine, and may it bring her long life and joy in your togetherness. Grandfather never wanted to part with it, not

50

even to exchange for the land he always yearned to own and to settle on. I think now that we're leaving Windhaven to find our own new Windhaven, he would approve of what I've done."

CHAPTER FIVE

During the next weeks, the members of the Bouchard family enjoyed the simple domestic pleasures of a complete family reunion, for only Fleurette was missing from their devoted circle. She and Ben Wilson, the Quaker medical corporal in the Union Army, had been married in Richmond in January, after Ben had been released after his convalescence from a shoulder hit by a sniper's bullet while he had been trying to bandage the wounds of a dying Confederate officer. Because he had borne no arms against the South and had been seen performing that act of humanity on the battlefield by a colonel heading Confederate forces, Ben Wilson had not been sent to Libby prison, but allowed to remain in Richmond on his word of honor that he would not try to escape or leave until the war was over. Sybella had had a letter from Fleurette in mid-February, with the joyous news of the marriage and her husband's plans to return to Pittsburgh and become a doctor. During his enforced stay in Richmond, he had already endeared himself to his captors by going daily to the very hospital to which he had been brought and where Fleurette had nursed him, acting as a medical orderly and doing what he could to alleviate the suffering of the wounded and the dying.

Meanwhile, Luke Bouchard had asked Djamba to talk with the blacks who had begged for the chance to accompany the Bouchard clan to their new home, for the practical side of the venture had to be considered, quite apart from sentiment and loyalty. It would be essential to have large supplies of food and clothing, in the event that even so many as a dozen blacks and their families accompanied the descendants of Lucien Bouchard. And with New Orleans under the domination of federal forces commanded by General Benjamin F. Butler, the acquisition of such supplies might be impossible.

But foremost in Luke's mind was the knowledge that wherever they might choose to settle in Texas, life would be arduous and full of hardships, perhaps even more than his beloved grandfather had encountered in what had once been the paradise of Econchate. The raising of cattle and the driving of them to market was not a job for men in their fifties, and many of the blacks who had begged for the chance to accompany him to Texas were of that age group or near it.

By the end of the second week, Djamba and Luke conferred on this weighty problem and the powerful and seemingly ageless Mandingo declared, "I've talked to all of them, Mistah Luke, and I've told them about the dangers and the hardships and some of them have changed their minds and said they'd take their chances now that they're free. There's some talk that the government will have a freedman's bureau all through the South to find these blacks homes and work, and I guess it's maybe because they're mainly scared of something new they don't know anything about and would rather stay where they are and hope for the best."

"I wouldn't fault any man for that, Djamba. Who are the ones that you think can be of the most help to us and can work side by side with us and endure all the hardships which I know await us?"

"Well, there's George, of course, and you know yourself that's because he's stuck on Prissy," Djamba chuckled. "But he's still spry and he can do plenty of

54

things around the house and help build one too. Then there's William, the Angola, from over at Windhaven, and of course Harry and his wife Betty, and Carl, the Ashanti foreman. Then there's three good sturdy blacks in their thirties, and they know something about riding a horse and they've worked with me and Lucas on the cattle you've had here, Mistah Luke. There's Dave, the Kru, Frank, the Fulani, and Ned, the Hausa. Dave and Frank never did jump over the broom with any gal, and Ned's wife ran off in January with some big buck downriver, so those three for sure are eager to try their hand at cattle-raising."

"That's eight, then, and the four of your family, an even dozen, Djamba." Luke frowned, deep in thought. "But didn't Harry and Betty have two sons?"

"Yes, Mistah Luke. But you remember, the oldest boy, Eddie, he died from a snakebite just before last Christmas, and the other boy, Benny, he up and ran away last week and told his folks he was going to try to make his way alone up North and see if he couldn't find himself a good job now that he was free."

"I wish him well, Djamba. Yes, now I can understand all the more why Harry and Betty want to come along with us. All right, then. There'll be my wife Lucy, my son Lucien Edmond and his wife Maxine and their two children Carla and Hugo, and of course Mrs. Forsden and Miss Maybelle. And my daughter Mara, of course." He chuckled wryly. "In fact, perhaps as much as myself, Mara is impatient to be off and to begin the new life. Heaven knows she's had heartbreak enough around here. I only hope we'll have good neighbors wherever we pick to settle down in Texas, so that she'll find the right husband. But it's not going to be too easy, she's always had very independent ideas about everything, especially marriage. Well, now, Djamba, the *Advertiser* today printed President Johnson's removal of the restrictions of domestic trade in all Confederate territory east of the Mississippi, within Union military lines. That means that any day now the steamboats will be going up and down the Alabama, so we'd best get all our belongings packed and ready to be out there on the wharf when the first one comes our way bound for Mobile."

And it was on May 2, 1865, the day on which President Andrew Johnson proclaimed the offer of a reward of $100,000 for the arrest of Jefferson Davis, who had been charged with complicity in the assassination of the martyred Lincoln, that the *Alabama Sun*, its paddle-wheels churning the placid Alabama River, anchored at the wharf of the Williamson plantation to take aboard the Windhaven clan and their twelve loyal blacks who would follow Luke, and his son Lucien Edmond, to whatever destiny awaited them in Texas.

The elderly captain of the steamboat grumbled when he saw the gathering on the wharf and the two wagons which contained those effects which the Bouchards had been able to salvage. But Luke pressed several gold pieces into his hand, and he promptly barked orders to the black stevedores to hurry the wagons into the hold and then beckoned to the purser to find accommodations for "these fine, worthy folks."

Lucy stood beside her husband at the rail as the *Alabama Sun* slowly pulled away from the wharf, her eyes clouded with tears. Nearby, Maybelle, her face drawn and desolate, stood beside Sybella as they watched the ruins of Windhaven and the beloved old Williamson house recede into the distance. "What counts most, my dearest Lucy," Luke turned to his wife, "is that we're all together now. There's strength in this, against the worst dangers and hardships that even the most fearful of us can foresee. Grandfather Lucien never wanted to be an aristocrat—he hated the idea of being a parasite—yet all the same, he *was* an aristocrat, a patrician of honesty and goodness and decency. Those virtues, if we can maintain them, will sustain us."

"I feel so sorry for Sybella and Maybelle," Lucy replied, "beginning all over at such an age and after the heartbreaking losses they've endured. Especially Sybella, losing her wonderful husband in such a senseless, cruel way."

"We'll look after them, you and I, Lucy dear," Luke promised. "They've come together more than ever now

56

just because of their grief, and Maybelle will be able to draw upon my wonderful stepmother's endless courage. Indeed, Lucy, Sybella may well be the strongest Bouchard of them all before we're done!"

Part of the Union flotilla lay anchored in the great bay of Mobile, including several of the iron-armored fighting ships which had wrought such deadly havoc on the Confederate navy. At the dock, a fussy Union captain impatiently waited for the passengers to disembark, demanding identification. When Luke produced his papers, he pleasantly asked, "For whom are you looking, Captain?"

"For that damned rebel assassin of yours, old Jeff Davis, that's who, Mister!" the officer snapped. "He's still at large, but we'll smoke him out before much longer, don't you fret. Have you business, sir, in Mobile?"

"Why, yes, Captain. First I have to make a call on the counting house where I did business, and then we're bound for New Orleans. After that, perhaps Texas."

"You'll have to take an oath of loyalty to the Union. We Northerners are going to make sure that none of you rebels starts trouble all over again, no matter where you go!"

"I've always been loyal to the Union. I wasn't a slaveholder and I didn't bear arms against your side, Captain. I think Mr. Vance Alderson at the counting house can vouch for the Bouchards."

"I'll see about that. All right, you can go ashore, you and your party. What about those niggers? They're not yours any longer."

"Long ago, I drew up the manumission papers of every black working on my land," Luke Bouchard patiently explained. "These workers of mine especially asked for the opportunity to come with us and to help us build our new home wherever it will be."

"Well," the captain shrugged, "no business of mine. So long as you know they're freedmen now and pay 'em wages, that'll keep your nose clean. All right, next!"

"Lucien Edmond," Luke called to his son, "would you inquire about accommodations at the hotel here? Ask Captain Morrell to have our wagons put ashore and see if you can get the stevedores to cover them with a tarpaulin.

We'll board for New Orleans most likely tomorrow, as soon as I can find out what the steamer schedule is. I'm going in to the counting house over there and see just how we stand. Come along, Lucy, Mr. Alderson asked to meet you the last time I was down here with a load of cotton, and I'm looking forward to the opportunity of showing off my beautiful wife."

"I declare, Luke Bouchard," Lucy smilingly teased, "you've just reversed the usual process of a suitor. You're more dashing now than when you married me—and I like it very much that way, Mr. Luke Bouchard sir. Let's go, by all means."

What had once been the old log trading house of Swanson & McGillivray, and then Swanson & Strothers, was now an imposing brick building, having been several times enlarged to store not only foodstuffs but also munitions during the just-ended war. Vance Alderson, a stocky, bearded man in his early fifties, resplendent in gray frock coat and starched shirt with lace cuffs, a diamond stickpin in his cravat, came forward to greet Luke Bouchard and to bow and kiss the hand which Lucy smilingly tendered him. "What a pleasure at last to meet you, Mrs. Bouchard! I'd guessed that you were beautiful, from all your husband had to say about you, but I assure you he didn't do you justice."

"Such flattery sounds as if we'd never had a war, Mr. Alderson. And I assure you I don't deserve it."

"In my judgment you do and far more. But now, sir, how may I serve you? As you know, Mobile fell on April twelfth. In spite of that and the blockade during the war, our bank is in somewhat better condition than yours in New Orleans, I'm afraid."

"What do you mean by that, Mr. Alderson?" Luke anxiously demanded.

Vance Alderson shook his head. "Of course you know that General Butler, whom they call the Beast of New Orleans, is lording it all over that great city. One of the first things he did was to take over all the banks and oust their officers, for the very greedy purpose of being able to print his own scrip and to flood the city with it."

"Then John Brunton isn't in charge there any more?"

"No, Mr. Bouchard, he's not. It's a good thing you stopped here to inquire, for I know that you've got important holdings in that bank. I want to give you an account of what you have here, though it's none too salubrious, I can assure you. All our paper money is worthless."

"That much I could have guessed. But as I recall, the last time I had an accounting from you, we still had about three or four thousand dollars in gold," Luke pursued.

"That's true enough, and even though all the accounts have been confiscated by Federal authority, I can easily get you that much money released once you sign the loyalty oath. But now back to Brunton. He's a friend of mine, too, Mr. Bouchard. Not only did they force him out of the bank, but they seized his beautiful house upriver. I hesitate to tell you where you can find him now, seeing that your wife is present."

"I'm not prudish, Mr. Alderson. You won't offend me. From what Luke has told me about your dealings with the Bouchard family, I know you to be a man of the highest principle and integrity, so you couldn't offend me by telling the truth," Lucy encouraged him.

"Well then," Vance Alderson reddened and nervously adjusted his frock coat, "fortunately he was able to put aside some hard money for himself by converting some of his assets when he saw what was going to happen. And damned—excuse me, Mrs. Bouchard—if he didn't go ahead and buy a fancy house, if you take my meaning."

"Of course. And that's where I'll find him in New Orleans?" Luke smilingly inquired.

"That's it precisely, Mr. Bouchard. At a place on Honorée Street known as *The Union House*. That's what you might call changing with the times. His clients are mainly well-to-do carpetbaggers—you've probably heard the term—and well-to-do Union officers. The fortunes of war, you see."

"The only problem is that I've got about fifty thousand dollars in gold which Grandfather left me in the Bank of Liverpool," Luke mused aloud.

"No need to worry about that, Mr. Bouchard," Vance Alderson eagerly assured him. "Brunton can wire New

York to his factors there, and they'll cable on and get your money. It'll probably take at least five weeks, maybe six. There's no difficulty about that."

"That's good news indeed, and I'm very grateful to you, Mr. Alderson."

"Now, sir, have you and your folks a place to stay here in Mobile till you can take the steamer to New Orleans? That might be another day or two, seeing as how there are no regular schedules yet. It would be my pleasure and my honor to offer hospitality to you during your stay here in Mobile."

"That's most generous. I'd asked my son Lucien Edmond to see about hotel accommodations—"

"He'll find nothing, Mr. Bouchard," Vance Alderson emphatically shook his head. "Right now, looks like everybody in Alabama is trying to get out of the state before those Yankees come down here and treat us the way Butler's been treating the citizens of New Orleans. We've been lucky so far, but everybody who wants to get away is passing through here. He won't find anything. They're even sleeping in the hallways the last few nights. No, sir, you'd best accept my offer. I'll have my boy hitch up the horses and drive you and your wife over to the house. It's at the end of town."

"Again, all my thanks, and tomorrow, when we're rested, I'll be back and we can close out the account for good."

"In a way, I'm glad to hear you say that, Mr. Bouchard," Vance Alderson sighed and shook his head. "The name of Bouchard, beginning with your wonderful grandfather, is the most distinguished among all the clients we've served all these years. And yet, for most of the people who've lived here all their lives, the years ahead are going to be dreadful. Look at yourself, with at least from fifteen to eighteen thousand dollars of what was good solid money in Southern banks wiped out like a puff of smoke. Think of all the soldiers coming back to find that their pay is worthless, many of their homes destroyed by Union troops, no future on the land—because, sure as you're born, Mr. Bouchard, men like that Thaddeus Stevens of Pennsylvania will insist that all of us be treated like slaves in bondage because we were traitors to the Union. No sir, I'll be glad to see your name expunged on our records and know that it'll appear somewhere far from here where the only way they'll judge a man is by what he does and the hard work he puts into his life."

"Amen to that," Luke Bouchard said softly as he gripped the banker's hand.

[A]

CHAPTER SIX

It was three days before Luke Bouchard could arrange for passage to New Orleans for all those who had accompanied him downriver from the gutted chateau of Windhaven and the abandoned Williamson house, including the twelve blacks whose official status—a vital point in view of the imminent regulations to be imposed by the North regarding former slaves and their owners—was that of free and consenting hired workers. Thanks to the hospitality of Vance Alderson, the Bouchard family was reasonably comfortable in the large house, while Djamba and the other blacks solved the problem of sleeping quarters by pitching tents in the spacious yard of the Alderson house.

On the afternoon of their last day in Mobile, Luke Bouchard and Lucien Edmond visited the trading house to close out the long-standing Bouchard account. "Here, Mr. Bouchard, is your three thousand dollars in gold," Vance Alderson declared as he counted out the shining coins. His young clerk stood attentively by, holding a small chamois bag in which the coins could be neatly packed into paper-wrapped rolls.

"There are still about a dozen of my workers who decided to remain on the land and take their chances with whatever disposition the Northern authorities will make," Luke Bouchard eyed his son. "You remember, I hope, that when the first Bouchard to deal with this house opened his account here, he indicated on the ledger that such and such wages were to be paid to each black according to length of service and occupation. Well, I should like to send two thousand of this money back to those loyal workers. I wonder if it could be arranged."

"Of course, Mr. Bouchard," Vance Alderson smilingly agreed. "As it happens, Lawrence, my young clerk here, is going up to Montgomery on other business matters of this house, and he'd be glad to deliver the money to whomever you designate."

"Good. I'm only sorry that the balance in scrip and paper money no longer exists. I should certainly have liked to divide it with those hard-working and devoted men and women who stood beside us and did so much to bring about the prosperity of Windhaven."

"You and your grandfather are indeed a rare breed, Mr. Bouchard," Vance Alderson gravely replied as he separated the coins and indicated that the clerk was to wrap a third of them and put them in the bag to be given Luke Bouchard. "My predecessor often told me how conscientiously your grandfather saw to it that the Creeks received a full half of all the profits of his ventures in cotton and other goods. Although I've been a slaveholder myself, I've always admired what Lucien Bouchard and you yourself, sir, were able to do in the very heart of slave-owning country. I daresay you and your grandfather must have had to come to grips at times with some of your more outspoken neighbors on the issue."

"Not really, Mr. Alderson," Luke Bouchard gently smiled, "neither Grandfather nor I ever forced our views on any other man. He was my inspiration, and since I believed in what he did, I concern myself with those around me and those dependent on me. I'm neither a rabble-rouser nor a soap-box orator.

"Now, Mr. Alderson, my family and I are deeply indebted to you for your hospitality, and as a last favor I might ask of you to point out any difficulties we might face in New Orleans while we're waiting for the transfer of the funds in the Bank of Liverpool."

"You say you're planning on settling in Texas, then, Mr. Bouchard?"

"Yes, because from what I've heard about it, it's ideal for raising cattle. During the last few years and just prior to the war, my son and I experimented with a few pedigreed bulls and some cows, as well hogs and sows. With the country expanding I feel I'd be contributing not only to the well-being of all of my family by helping to produce a part of it, but also the well-being of countless others. And that's a rewarding venture."

"Well now, Mr. Bouchard, I've no doubt that John Brunton can tell you much more about Texas than I can. As I recall, he has a second or third cousin, who moved out there back in the Fifties. But I can give you some advice about New Orleans. You'll probably have no trouble finding lodging in the best hotels. And although they have what they call slave quarters for your blacks, they'd never take as many as you've brought along with you. At the far end of the city, there are poorer sections inhabited by decent people who never owned slaves and are sympathetic to providing for them. Matter of fact, I happen to know a freed black by the name of John Dewton. I'll give you his address as well, and I'm sure that old John would see that your people were made comfortable."

"That's extremely kind of you, Mr. Alderson, my heartfelt thanks."

"You'll most likely have to sign a loyalty oath there, and I'd take pains not to call too much attention to myself in front of Butler's ambitious officers. That man's a disgrace!"

"I think I read an editorial in the *Advertiser* to that effect, though it didn't give all the details," Luke humorously chuckled.

"Well, sir, Benjamin Butler started as a Massachusetts politician. Matter of fact, he was a Democrat and went to the 1860 Charleston convention bound and determined to elect none other than Jefferson Davis as President of the United States. He's done a complete about-face, because

65

he was once a pro-slavery Southern sympathizer. Once he became a Northern commander, he dared to proclaim the view that fugitive slaves be considered contraband of war. He marched into Baltimore and acted like a Caesar, and was quickly relieved from that post."

"A contentious man, I'd say."

"Much more than that, sir. He is a martinet. They made him the Federal commander of New Orleans back in May of 1862. He had the gall to issue that General Order No. 28, declaring that any woman who, by word or deed, insulted the Union flag, uniform or army, made herself liable to be treated as a woman of the town, plying her vocation. Why, sir, when one gently bred woman rejoiced aloud to see the funeral possession of a dead Union officer pass by her house, she was arrested, almost stripped naked, then given uncomfortable lodgings on desolate Ship Island under heavy male guard. Scandalous, sir, scandalous!"

"Not the behavior of a gentleman, I'll agree," Luke Bouchard answered.

"But that's past and done with now. What matters is that Butler's a shrewd profiteer. As I told you, that's one reason he took over all the banks and ousted poor old Mr. Brunton, so that he could have unlimited access to issuing his own useless paper money and then lining his own pockets with gold. His first act when he entered New Orleans was to hang a man who had torn down and mangled a flag hoisted by Farragut's men, but that patriotic citizen—rebel if you wish to call him such—did this before the Union formally took possession of New Orleans, and so legally that man had committed no crime and did not deserve hanging. But today, you'll find a good deal of contraband trading going on in cotton, sugar, salt, yes, even weapons. And Ben Butler's brother Andrew—whom they call Colonel but who isn't in the army at all—is making deals and raking in profits that some of my friends in New Orleans tell me amount to about two million dollars by now."

Luke Bouchard shook his head. "That sounds very much as if trafficking with the so-called enemy was going on even before the war was over."

"Exactly, sir. Now I mentioned weapons, and if you're going to a huge, lawless and practically uninhabited country like Texas, you'd best provide yourself with a good supply of them. There are bandits and Indians there who aren't overly friendly to whites. But John Brunton can tell you where you can get weapons without great risk to yourself. As a Confederate and former landowner, once you've taken that loyalty oath, it wouldn't do to have Butler's boys suspect that you're buying up arms and munitions—they might accuse you of trying to continue the war and hang you for treason."

"Once again, Mr. Alderson, I'm deeply grateful to you for your very valuable advice. I promise you I shall take pains not to be hanged. I have planned no treason, only the defense of my family against lawlessness." Luke Bouchard rose, and he and Lucien Edmond shook Vance Alderson's hand. "Again, my sincerest thanks, and I'll write you from New Orleans after our plans are finalized."

"Godspeed and good fortune to you and your family, Mr. Bouchard."

"So this is your first visit to the Queen City since the war began, is it, Mr. Bouchard?" grizzled Edmund Devries, captain of the *Carondolet*, standing on the quarterdeck of the steamboat, turned to his neatly dressed passenger and regarded him with a knowing deference. "You'll find she's changed a good deal. If I were given to metaphors, sir, I'd say she's a beautiful woman who's become begrimed and put on her shabbiest dress as if she's ashamed of what's been happening to her, and that's a fact, Mr. Bouchard."

The paddlewheels were chugging the placid waters as the crowded steamboat slowly and majestically headed into the port of New Orleans. The sun shone brightly down upon the close growths of sedge, grass and rushes which lined the distant banks on either side, and cypress flanked the shores in continuous panels of deep green, shot with the mystic gray of Spanish moss. On the slopes could be seen bright patches of yellow jasmine, wild azalea, silverbell, dogwood and redbud, and on the stagnant water

67

washing the banks were the floating leaves of water hya-
cinth. Overhead, plovers and black skimmers turned in
their desultory flight and headed back to shore.

As soon as Luke and Lucy had boarded the *Carondolet*
along with the other members of the Bouchard family,
Captain Devries had invited them to his private cabin and
had had his steward break out a fine old bottle of sherry,
while at the same time summoning his purser to see to it
that comfortable accommodations were provided for all.
Having heard that Luke had brought along a dozen freed
blacks, he had scowled and shook his head: "They'll have
to stay down in the hold, Mr. Bouchard, no offense to you
and your charming wife, believe me. And you'll find that
once we dock at New Orleans, you'll not be able to get a
carriage for them. They'll have to go shank's mare to
whatever quarters they can find. There's something they
call Jim Crow already put into operation by those blue-
uniformed bullies who are running the city now."

"But, Captain Devries," Luke Bouchard had countered,
"I was of the opinion that this war was fought over slavery and that with President Lincoln's proclamation,
there'd be no distinctions made any longer."

"You're an idealist and a dreamer, sir, believe me," the
grizzled captain had chuckled. "Just because those
Yankees didn't like the notion of us Southerners enjoying
the benefits of free black labor while they're paying good
wages up in their territories, doesn't mean by a long shot
that they're going to welcome the *nigra* with open arms
and declare that he's free and equal with them."

"In Mobile, Mr. Alderson told me that I could arrange
for their accommodation at John Dewton's house."

"And so you can, Mr. Bouchard. Only I'm afraid
they'll have to walk to the very west end of New Orleans,
and it's a stiff hike. Believe me, sir, I'm telling you the
truth. Oh, you'll find *nigra* stevedores and soldiers loading
shipments of cotton and salt and the like, and they're
from the North, but you won't find them rubbing elbows
with their white companions in uniform at any saloon,
and they'd best not try for fraternization like that either.
Now as to you and your charming wife and your companions and family, Mr. Bouchard, I can recommend the

68

Verandah Hotel. The desk clerk is a drinking companion of mine, sir, and if you run into any trouble there, just tell him—he's Josiah Clarke—that Ed Devries says there'll be no more drinks stood for unless he takes care of my good passengers."

"That's most kind of you, Captain Devries."

The conversation with Devries saddened Luke Bouchard, and he was thinking of it as the steamboat neared its dock. He and his grandfather had never believed in slaves, had set them free so far as the legal limitations of the state had permitted. Yet now that they were declared nationally free as the result of the outcome of this bloody war between brothers of a growing young nation, they were enslaved by an unwritten decree of racial discrimination. He had already spoken with Djamba and apologized for the discomfort and inconvenience that would face these loyal dozen blacks. But the Mandingo had smiled, shaken his head and replied softly, "We are bound to follow you, and it doesn't matter if it's on foot or on horseback, Mistah Luke. Besides, none of us has ever seen New Orleans, and walking that long spell is sure to give us a good look-see at it."

At the stern, crowding against the rail and exclaiming volubly over the sights of the wharf and the levee beyond, Melinda and Andrew Hunter, standing beside little Carla and Hugo Bouchard, expressed their delight and curiosity at the sight of bales of cotton being hauled aboard by sweating, half-naked stevedores, urged on by blue-uniformed soldiers; by vendors of all types of goods loudly hawking their wares; by bustling, important-looking men in stovepipe hats and long black frockcoats, carrying *sacs de nuit*, (the forerunner of the fateful carpetbag that would soon be the symbol of Northern pillaging of the conquered South). But even here on the wharf and the levee, Luke Bouchard could realize at once, there was some of the gaiety, the color, the fascinating complexity of mingling peoples from many states—and most of all, there were almost no women to be seen, except here and there for a painted, powdered streetwalker seeking to ply her trade by mingling with the soldiers and nudging and whispering to them.

He could already see the tragic changes brought about by war, a war that now, in retrospect, seemed senseless, and yet whose aftermath was to affect the lives of even those not yet born. It was, he knew, a challenge even more perilous than that which had confronted his beloved grandfather. And he knew also that he must face it courageously, adapting himself to the strange new rules of a life that would be full of adventure, lawlessness and selfish struggle for survival.

CHAPTER SEVEN

"You'll find carriages down there near the levee to take your people to the hotel, Mr. Bouchard," Captain Edmund Devries pointed to the back of the open wharf at which the *Carondolet* had just docked. "Mind you now, be sure to tell that old scoundrel, Josiah, I said he was to give you the best rooms in the house."

"I'm indebted to you again, Captain Devries. One more thing—could you tell me where I might keep my wagons safely till I'm ready to board a packet for Texas? It might be some weeks before I'm ready to set out."

The steamboat master scowled and tugged at his straggly beard, deep in thought. "You'll just have to take your chances, sir. Like as not you might find a few handymen down there swarming around the dock offering to do odd jobs or to take you to the best cathouse in town, and you'll just have to be a good judge of character to see who'll be trustworthy enough to look after your wagons. New Orleans hasn't changed a bit since before the war, not so far as lack of sheds and covering for cargoes is concerned. When I think of all the cotton and tobacco that rotted along here, and the money lost, I could have been long since retired on what's been wasted. But you'd best pick people of your own kind, Mr. Bouchard, not any of those thieving Yankees. They're all swarming in like vultures to pick up whatever they can."

"Well then, we'll take our chances, and again, all my thanks. Come along, Lucien Edmond. I'm beginning to see it was a wise idea not to have taken too many possessions along, especially clothing. I'll go down first and help the ladies off the gangplank."

It was early afternoon of a sultry day, and the sun pitilessly beat down on the crowded wharf. The voices of the soldiers, vendors, stevedores, rose like the sudden chattering of monkeys in a zoo, and the accents of those voices turned the crowded wharf into a veritable Tower of Babel. Luke turned to Djamba, who had come up from the hold to receive instructions: "I'm told it's a good five or six miles due west along muddy streets to the end of the city, Djamba. You and the rest will have to make it as best you can, I'm afraid. When you're settled at John Dewton's, send one of the younger men back to inquire for me at the Verandah Hotel. I'll know better then what our plans are."

"I'll do that, Mistah Luke. Never you mind, we'll manage. I've walked through mud before in my own country when the rains came, and the fields back at Windhaven were muddy enough before planting time."

Luke Bouchard smiled and nodded, put his hand on Djamba's shoulder and gripped it firmly. "It'll be different once we get to Texas, that I promise all of you. And good luck to you. Here are a few gold pieces, they'll buy you food and lodging at that freedman's house."

Then, with a friendly wave to the captain, Luke Bouchard started down the gangplank and waited there for his stepmother Sybella to be the first to disembark, helping her down to stand on the level wooden planking. Maybelle and Lucy were next, then Lucien Edmond, protectively helping his wife Maxine and their two small children down the gangplank. Then came James Hunter, cautiously favoring his limp, with Arabella steadying him, and Melinda and Andrew, agog at the thriving, noisy scene before them, trailing behind their parents. Charles

72

Douglas, steadying himself with his sword-cane in his right hand as Laurette moved beside him, an arm around his waist to help him, followed. Last was Mara Bouchard, who went down slowly, staring back out at the gulf into which the *Carondolet* had sailed to bring them all to this harbor which lay between them and their unknown new adventure. Her eyes were somber and sorrowful, her face unsmiling, as she took a deep breath and then descended. Behind her lay the ghost of the past, the man to whom she had been affianced now dead and she herself at twenty-eight, though still spirited and handsome, feeling herself a spinster loved only by her mother and father.

"I think two carriages will take all of you to the hotel," Luke declared. "Lucien Edmond, be sure to talk to Josiah Clarke, just as Captain Devries suggested. I'll be along directly, I want to see if I can find some men to store our wagons for us till we're ready to go on to Texas."

"I'll take care of things, Father. Come along, Mara dear, it's best not to linger," he called to his sister who looked around her, seeing the blue-uniformed soldiers everywhere, reminding her of Bobby Jordan's death and of the burning of Windhaven. With a sigh, she turned to her brother and held out her hand, tears glistening on her long curly lashes. "I hope we can leave here soon, Lucien Edmond," she murmured. "I don't ever want to see soldiers' uniforms again, not ever. I hope we can go someplace where people aren't thinking of killing and burning and destroying, but working together and having children and planning a good rich life."

"Never you mind, Mara, Father'll see to it. And sure as you're born, there's going to be someone waiting for you in Texas, and you'll be glad you've left Alabama to find him," her brother assured her. "Now let's get all the others collected while I go see if I can get to those two carriages over there by that big storage shed." He put two fingers to his lips and emitted a loud whistle, waving the other arm to attract the waiting drivers.

Luke, kissing Lucy and assuring her that he would join her and the others at the hotel just as soon as he could conclude the business of safeguarding all the Bouchard heirlooms contained in the two wagons which stevedores

73

were now unloading from the hold, walked to the back of the dock, his eyes scrutinizing the faces of the jostling vendors and onlookers. His attention was drawn to two smiling young men who leaned against the rough wooden wall of an abandoned shed. A corpulent, pockmarked Union sergeant passing by them hawked and spat at their feet, but they only shrugged. One of them, who had lost his right arm, called out good-naturedly, "You won the war, Yank, guess that gives you the right to crow a spell. But if I hadn't lost this arm at Chickamauga, I might just take a notion you wasn't being real polite just then."

"Go on, you damned Reb cripple, you probably blew off your arm falling over your own musket in retreat," the Union sergeant contemptuously riposted, then pushed his way past the two to grab the elbow of a painted jade, to whisper into her ear, then lead her away from the wharf.

Luke Bouchard made his way toward the two men, both dressed in frayed buckskin jackets and tattered trousers and heavy hob-nailed shoes, and sympathetically said, "I couldn't help overhearing what that sergeant said to you. It was despicable and cowardly. I take it that you both served the Southern cause?"

"Mighty friendly of you, stranger, to take an interest in us pore mountain boys," the one-armed man grinned broadly. "I'm Andy Haskins, down from Tennessee, and this here's Joe Duvray, he's a Georgia cracker. When I had my arm blown off by a shell at Chickamauga, it was Joe that saved my life and dragged me to shelter and put on a tourniquet to stop the bleeding till they could get me to a field hospital. Only, mister, you don't have to feel sorry for me. If I ever got that sergeant off somewheres alone where I could teach him manners, he'd find out that even left-handed I could whale the hell out of him or, if it came to a duel, blow his stupid brains out or flip a Bowie knife through his nasty heart."

"How is it that you're down here in New Orleans?" Luke inquired. "By the way, my name is Luke Bouchard, from near Montgomery. My family and I are on our way to Texas to try to start all over again."

"I envy you, Mr. Bouchard," Andy Haskins replied, dolefully shaking his head. "Me 'n Joe were trying to get

74

us up a stake so we can pull out of this town. Can't be soon enough so suit us both, either. We were figgerin' maybe we'd try our luck at Californy, maybe there's still some gold left we could prospect for. But Texas, now that's a great big country and I don't think they've got too many Yankees out there yet."

"I've got two wagons being hauled ashore right now, Andy," Luke Bouchard declared. "I was wondering if I could hire someone to look after them till I can settle my affairs and leave on the steamer. Might be quite a time, because I've got to wait for some money sent me from England, but I'd be glad to pay you well for your services. And maybe both of you might even want to think about coming along with us to Texas. I'm going to raise cattle there."

"Joe, this sounds like our lucky day," the tall, rangy one-armed light brown-haired man chuckled happily as he turned to his stocky tow-headed and younger companion. "You see, Mr. Bouchard, Joe here grew up with horses on his uncle's farm, and me, I was riding after coons and bear and foxes by the time I wasn't any bigger than a tadpole—leastways, that's what my own daddy said. And if you're raising cattle, you'll need riders to round them up and corral them, won't you?"

"Why, indeed I will," Luke Bouchard smiled back as he held out his hand, which both men in turn heartily shook. From his moneybelt Luke took out two gold coins and handed one to each young Southerner. "Tell you what, here's a double eagle for each of you. I'll be staying at the Verandah Hotel with my family. Where can I find you, and where do you think you can store these wagons safely till I'm ready to move them again?"

"We've been here a month, Mr. Bouchard, and not all those Yankees are as unfriendly as that whore-loving sergeant you just saw," Andy Haskins wryly answered. "A couple of blocks from the wharf here, there's an old livery stable and the owner's been letting us sleep there in exchange for looking after the few spavined critters he's got left. I reckon if I shared a little of this gold with him, he wouldn't care what else I stored in his stable. It's over on Duval Street, Mr. Bouchard. Fact is, Joe 'n me'll go get a couple of his horses, hitch them up to your wagons, take them right over there and they'll be safe as you can git them in this town right now."

"I'm much obliged to you gentlemen. As soon as I've settled my family, I'll look for you here or at the stable, then?"

"You'll be sure to find us, Mr. Bouchard. Joe 'n me, we thank you kindly, most kindly, sir. You see, when we got back home from the war, we found our homes burned down to ashes, and our folks all dead. Joe had just his old uncle and granny, and I just had my ailin' paw, but they was dead just the same, and that was all the kinfolk we had. So working for you, Mr. Bouchard, that'll sure perk our spirits up more than a mite. We're beholden to you." Andy Haskins held out his hand and Luke Bouchard shook it, then nodded to both men and turned to find a carriage that would take him to the hotel.

Built in 1837, the Verandah Hotel was renowned throughout the nation for its splendid dining room with its high ceiling comprising three superb elliptic domes from which glittering chandeliers hung. At the lady's private entrance on St. Charles Street, a superb statue of Venus stood in tribute to the fair sex. As the black driver halted his horse close to the brick-paved sidewalk, he looked back at Luke Bouchard and grumbled, "Mebbe you bettah hab me wait foah you, suh, you ain't likely to git no lodgin' dere, dey's full up from whut ah heahs."

"I'll take my chances, driver. Here's your fee and thank you," Luke smiled as he lifted down his valise and made certain that the chamois bag with its well-wrapped golden coins was safely in his breeches pocket.

The lobby seemed proportionately as crowded and noisy as the wharf, with ladies in flounced, long-skirted dresses, puffed sleeves and beribboned bonnets animatedly conversing with top-hatted, long-frockcoated gentlemen, while Union officers, merchants and factors stood here and there in small groups conversing in whispers and glancing around to make certain that their conversation was not being overheard.

Luke politely made his way to the desk, presided over by a tall man in his sixties, with gleaming bald cranium but thick white sidewhiskers and Van Dyke beard. "I was looking for Mr. Josiah Clarke," he said pleasantly.

"I'm he, sir. Ah," his pale-blue eyes twinkled behind the thick spectacles, "you must be Mr. Luke Bouchard. No fear, sir, I've already had the boys take your family's luggage up to their rooms. The minute your son—a fine young man—told me about old Captain Edmund, I knew he was sending me quality guests. You know, he saved my life about twenty years ago from a gang of river pirates trying to board his steamboat just off Barataria."

He chuckled reminiscently and scratched his bald head. "But I must say, Mr. Bouchard, as you can see, we've had to take the overflow of the Exchange, so the best I could do was a small room for the Douglases," he glanced down at the register, "a larger one for the Hunters and their two children, one for you and your wife, another for your son and his wife and their two small children, and then a deplorably small room at the back of the hotel for Mrs. Forsden and Miss Maybelle and Miss Mara. If I'd had longer notice, I might have done better. Perhaps in a few days, when some of these officers you see here in the lobby have been transferred to Natchez and Vicksburg, there'll be an opportunity for me to transfer you to more commodious quarters."

The last hard spring rain had been in mid-April, so fortunately the New Orleans streets were not quite such muddy quagmires. Nonetheless, the going was hard and slow as Djamba led the way, holding Celia's hand, while Lucas behind him held onto his sister Prissy's hand and joked with her to brighten her mood. Since the near-tragic episode in the Windhaven stable, the attractive quadroon had had many a night shattered by nightmarish dreams, seeing again the leering faces of her would be ravishers, remembering their violent deaths. Only the steadfastly loyal determination to follow her beloved mistress Sybella Forsden had strengthened her for this arduous journey. And now, in this weary trudging just below the raised paved sidewalks, hearing the obscene catcalls of male passersby directed at her, the jeering insults leveled at her black companions, Prissy tasted the bitter dregs of what

77

she had been spared at Windhaven: the demeaning knowledge of being an inferior, despised and mocked simply because her skin was not white.

"Oh, Lucas," she murmured to her brother, as the group paused to let a carriage cross at the intersection of Royal and Ernestine Streets, "why should all these folks treat us so mean? They don't even know who we are, that we're not slaves—and even if we still were, we'd have been freed by Mistah Lincoln's word, wouldn't we?"

"Yes, honey, 'deed we would have been. But you see, Prissy gal, you can't change the way people feel about other people just by saying words, even making them laws. 'Pears like it's going to take lots of time before everybody forgets the color of our skin, and we're just going to have to work hard, keep out of trouble and prove to them we've got as much right to get along on this earth as they have," Lucas gravely responded.

As they neared the middle of the city, they passed the elegant Creole houses with their iron-work balconies, porte-cochères and walled-in patios. Djamba looked up across the street to a large balcony and gestured with his thumb as he remarked to his son, "Lucas, see those pointed ends? They'd make us fine spears, strong enough to kill lions with if we were hunting back where I was born. Maybe, when Mistah Luke starts looking for weapons to take to Texas, I'll see if I can't get me some of those spear-ends, whittle me a piece of sapling, split it down the middle, then tar it and rope it so it'll stay fast."

"I've heard the Indians uses lances and spears, Daddy," Lucas agreed with a nod, "they kill buffalo by running or riding up close and spearing 'em. Old Jed from Mistah Williamson's plantation told me he had buffalo meat once, mighty tasty it was too. Maybe we'll find some of that where we're going."

"Could be, son. Well now, Harry, Betty, want to stop a little and rest? It's been hard going, I know," Djamba asked, turning to the gray-haired Kru and his buxom wife.

"Now you looky here, Djamba," Harry bridled, "I'se no older'n you are, 'n effen you kin keep up, my Betty 'n me we kin do jist as good any time. 'Sides, sooner we git to this feller Dewton's house, sooner we can rest and hab us a mess ob vittles."

"We all feels de same way," Frank, the wiry, good-natured twenty-seven-year-old Fulani, chimed in, "time we wastes talkin' 'bout how we feels, we be there."

"All right, all right. I'd as soon get there quickly too. Look out for that carriage crossing ahead of us. Glad to hear you're all feeling so fit 'n eager," Djamba grinned as he waved his arm to signal for the group to continue their plodding trek.

Half an hour later, they began to enter the poorer section of the city, where the houses were more isolated from one another and of dingy once-white wooden frame and even log construction. As they paused to catch their breath and shoulder their burlap sacks of such belongings as they had taken from the plantation cabins, Djamba turned to his left to observe the cause for the sudden outbreak of angry voices on the opposite sidewalk, just outside a glass-windowed little restaurant-saloon.

"Hell, you lousy redbone, git off the sidewalk! Don't you know only white men belong on it? I've a good mind to drown you in the mud—the idea, thinking yerself good as a white man! Hey, Harvey, let's teach this damn stinkin' Injun manners!" this from a florid-faced, squat man in his mid-forties wearing a bowler hat, a dirty pea-green jacket and a pair of Union Army fatigue trousers. Beside him, his elbows pulled behind his back and gripped by two angry-looking frock-coated top-hatted Creole dandies in their thirties, was a tall slim young man in his mid-twenties, his black hair braided and dangling nearly to his waist, an eagle feather thrust through the topknot. He wore faded black cotton trousers, a red calico shirt, and a pair of wornout Army-issue boots. On the sidewalk in front of him lay a wooden tray with straps and the spilled and trampled meat pies which the tray had borne.

"I've got a better idea yet," one of the Creoles drawled as he put his right hand into the pocket of his fawn waistcoat and drew out a derringer. "I'll send him to the happy hunting grounds these Injuns are always palavering about."

Djamba turned to Lucas. "We've got to stop them, son.

I don't know what that poor fellow's done, but certainly nothing to deserve killing."

"I'm with you, Daddy. Let's go. Wait up, the rest of you," Lucas called to the group as he and Djamba headed across the street.

"Hold on there, why do you want to shoot that man?" Djamba called just as the Creole leveled the derringer against the back of the captive's neck.

"You talkin to me, *nigra*?" the man with the derringer insolently drawled. "Just you keep out of this, it's not your affair."

"Excuse me, Mister, but I think it is," Djamba showed his teeth in an amiable grin as he clambered onto the raised sidewalk, while Lucas swiftly flanked him at the right, standing next to the other Creole who held the young redbone's elbow in both hands.

"Maybe you'd like a bullet too, *nigra*! It's come to a fine state of affairs when *nigras* and redbones step out on sidewalks reserved for whites," the first Creole gloweringly declared as he shifted the derringer towards Djamba.

But the powerful Mandingo seized the squat man in the bowler hat around the waist and flung him out into the muddy street as, crouching, he ducked under the exploding derringer. A moment later, he had wrested the weapon from the outraged Creole's hand, pocketed it, then clutched the Creole by the throat with his strong hands and began to shake him as a terrier shakes a rat. "Now you're not going to kill anybody, Mister, understand?" he said softly, his eyes boring into the Creole's congested, fear-twisted face.

Meanwhile Lucas, one hand gripping the other Creole's throat, the other twisting his wrist, had forced him to release his hold of the intended victim, and, smiling pleasantly, murmured, "Friend, if you'll take some good advice, you'll go right away from here and mind your own business from now on. Otherwise I can just as easily break your neck as I can your arm, and I'm not choosey which I pick, if you catch my meaning."

"Yes—ah—ughh l–let go—I–I'll go—please," the man gasped, wincing at the pressure of Lucas' fingers against

80

his bruised throat. Released, he ran around the corner like one possessed, without once looking back.

The young redbone turned to Djamba and Lucas, his dark eyes glowing. "You are good friends to Simata. But I would not have you think me a coward. My father was Kiowa, a strong warrior. My mother, black like you, but freed many years ago by her white master. She still alive but very sick. She make these meat pies, I try to sell to buy medicine to make her well again."

"But why were those men so angry? Did you try to sell the pies in there? Food is sold in there, I think. But that should not be enough to make them want to kill you," Djamba wonderingly asked.

The young redbone shook his head. "No, Simata ask only for water to drink, he walk all this morning, try to sell pies, not much luck. Man who owns place in there, he not angry with Simata, only those white eyes."

"Look, Simata," Djamba put his hand into his trousers pocket and drew out one of the coins Luke Bouchard had given him. "Go buy medicine for your mother. We go to the house of John Dewton—you have heard of him?"

"I know of this man, he good man, yes."

"We are to stay there till the man for whom we work is ready to go to Texas."

"That was where my father came from, he rode the plains with his tribe."

"Then perhaps you can be of great help to us, Simata. Come visit us at the house of John Dewton when you can, and we shall talk."

81

CHAPTER EIGHT

The lavish dining room of the Verandah Hotel would
have reminded old Lucien Bouchard of those festive ban-
quets which his doughty father, the Count Etienne de
Bouchard, used to give at the chateau of Yves-sur-lac in
Normandy during the years of his boyhood, before the
French revolution. Indeed, only the presence of high-
ranking Union officers at several of the tables indicated
that this was only a month after the fall of the Confederacy and the beginning of its humiliation in the bitter
dust of defeat. Waiters dressed in black with immaculate
white aprons hurried here and there, and the
mustachioed Creole *maitre d'* who escorted the Bouchard
family to a single extended table at the very back of the
huge salon might have come from one of the greatest
Parisian restaurants.

Quail, terrapin, rich gumbo in true New Orleans style,
succulent Westphalian hams cooked in champagne, monu-
mental roasts of beef, sweetbreads, mutton cutlets, pigeons
in compote, duckling with green peas, boiled turkeys and
oyster sauce, pompano in port wine sauce, even haunches
of venison and bear prepared with applesauce, appeared

on the bill of fare for the most demanding gourmet. For now that the North had emerged victorious, communication lines were again available and supplies could pour into a city once besieged and nearly starving.

Luke Bouchard at his head of the table smiled across at his intrepid stepmother Sybella who presided at the other end, and lifted a glass of sherry to toast her and the others: "To our new home, to our new life, to peace and happiness for all of us," he said. And then he added, admiringly, "And to you, Sybella, the most undaunted spirit among us all, whose courage gives us new hope and strength for the future."

"Thank you, Luke. But you give me too much credit. I've drawn from your courage, and I think that's because yours came from the grandfather who showed the way to us all," Sybella responded.

The family prepared to enjoy their celebration.

"I've seen to the wagons and they're in good hands," Luke declared. "In fact, the two Southern boys I engaged to look after them are hoping to find a new beginning themselves, and since they've been around horses a good part of their young lives, it's quite possible they might want to come along with us to Texas. They could be very useful. After a few days, when we've all had a chance to rest after the trying times we've been through, I'll have them over for dinner and you can meet them."

And so, for a little time, even in alien surroundings, the Bouchards drew pleasure and strength from this festive reunion. Before it was over, Maxine excused herself on behalf of little Carla and Hugo, who, once they had eaten, had begun to show signs of sleepiness and the natural irritability which very young children display after a wearying day. Luke took advantage of this lull in the celebration to rise and smilingly declare, "I too must ask your indulgence to be excused, though I'm sure you will all readily understand the necessity. I must find John Brunton, who represents our holdings in the old Rigalle bank, so I can arrange through him the transfer of the funds Grandfather farsightedly had deposited abroad. Thank God for it; otherwise we'd have very little." Then he turned to Lucy and added, "Please don't wait up for me, Lucy dear. It appears that Mr. Brunton, through fortunes of war, is engaged in a nocturnal business that thrives on late hours. I promise to come in quietly and not waken you."

He shook hands with James Hunter and Charles Douglas, bade the rest a cordial good night and promised to let them have the news at breakfast the next morning. Then, beckoning to the *maitre d'*, he paid the bill, over the protests of Arabella's and Laurette's husbands, and with a genial wave, left. He walked out to the sidewalk and hailed a passing handsom, driven by a black freedman who expertly tugged on the reins to direct his horse toward the raised curb.

"Thank you, driver. Can you take me to The Union House?" Luke looked up inquiringly as he prepared to clamber in.

"Shonuff kin, suh! Ah kin tell you's a mighty fine, discriminatin' gennlemun, yessuh—'n you gotta be mighty rich too, effen you gwine take yoah pleasure dere, suh! Ah heah tell dey jist got two brand-new fancy gals to tend to de gennlemun folks, a mighty purty red-haired gal all de way from Pensacola, 'n den dere's a high-yeller gal wut come from Natchez dat's got all the menfolks askin' foah her, suh!"

Luke chuckled as he leaned back and surveyed the relatively deserted sidewalks on both sides of the street. Here and there a Union soldier walked with a flamboyantly dressed girl on his arm, and across the street a fat gray-haired merchant was gallantly helping a bejeweled *cocotte* into a carriage. But it was evident that most of the residents of the Queen City preferred to remain indoors, so long as General Butler's troops remained in view.

"I wasn't aware it was quite so famous, driver," he called up to the hansom cabman. "As a matter of fact, I'm supposed to meet a Mr. John Brunton there. Do you know him?"

"Sho' do, suh! He de man wut own de Union House."

"Good. He's the one I want to see there."

The bald-headed driver cackled gleefully as he slapped the reins to urge his recalcitrant horse to make a turn to the left. "Now ah would hab rightly said, suh, you wuz gwine to visit wid one ob dem fancy gals. You's a fine-looking' gennlemun, you hab de gals fightin' to see who you gwine pick, dat's wut I tell mahself, suh!"

"Your flattery is most kind," Luke whimsically retorted, "But my business is with Mr. Brunton, not the ladies. As it happens, I'm happily married."

"Hee hee, so's most ob de gennlemun wut goes dere, suh, no offense meant!" Then, his tone sobering, he leaned down to study his handsome passenger and remarked, "De truf is, suh, mebee you bettah off effen you gwine meet up wid Mistah Brunton. Mostly, it's de Yankee officers 'n traders dat come down from de North 'long wid dem, spends dere money at de Union House. An' dey ain't none too friendly to us Southern folk yit, nossuh!"

"I'll bear that in mind, and thank you, driver." The hansom cab pulled up before a two-story home, evidently only recently built and of sturdy red brick, with a lofty attic between two thick gables. As the driver drew on the reins, a doorman in red waistcoat and black trousers, with black silk top hat, bowed low and helped Luke Bouchard out of the hansom cab. He turned to pay the driver and added a sizable *pourboire*, then turned to the doorman and asked, "Would you be kind enough to direct me to Mr. John Brunton. I have business with him."

"Certainly, sir. May I tell him your name?"

"It's Luke Bouchard from Windhaven, if you please. And thank you for your trouble."

"My pleasure, Mr. Bouchard. If you'll just wait in the parlor, I'll see that Mr. Brunton is advised of your visit." The doorman swung open the heavy walnut door of the establishment, and stepped back to allow Luke to enter. He found himself in a wide, short foyer, where, standing facing him attentively and with a fetching smile, was a charming, petite black-haired girl who could have been no more than eighteen, dressed like a French soubrette, with lace cap jauntily perched atop her fluffy black curls, her surprisingly buxom figure emphasized by a puffed red velveteen jacket and billowing, full-length green sateen skirt which very nearly concealed the toes of her high-buttoned fawn-hued cloth shoes. She dropped him an elegant curtsy and murmured in a deliciously husky voice tinged with an unmistakable French accent, "May I take M'sieu's cape and hat?"

"Mais certainement, Mam'selle," Luke Bouchard replied drawing a dimpled smile from the pretty little soubrette as she came forward to take his hat and cape. As she did so, she murmured softly, *"Je m'appelle* Mitzi, if M'sieu wishes to ask for me. But of course, M'sieu is so tall and handsome, he is certain to prefer *les belles joyeuses* in the parlor."

Gallantly, Luke took her hand and brought it to his lips, replying, "If I were here in search of pleasure. *ma belle poupée,* it would assuredly be Mitzi I should ask for."

Her exquisite blush was totally spontaneous and not at all feigned as she glanced wonderingly at her hand and then at him. Meanwhile, the doorman had gone through the parlor and up the winding, velvet-carpeted stairs in search of the proprietor of the establishment. "You see, I am here to see M'sieu Brunton," Luke explained.

"Oh, that is very good! Perhaps M'sieu will not forget Mitzi the next time he visits, when it is not to see *le patron*?" her large, limpid brown eyes glowed with an unmistakable invitation.

"Rest assured that I shall not forget you. And now if you will excuse me, *ma belle,*" Luke gracefully bowed as he might have to a lady of title, and moved into the spacious and lavishly furnished parlor. Here, one could believe that there had never been an agonizing, prolonged war, not in this sybaritic setting of rococo luxury. There were overstuffed sofas with antimacassars, hand-carved cherrywood tables adorned with oil lamps whose shades were fringed with multi-colored beads, others on which ivory statuettes—all depicting the unadorned female form —served as decor. The windows were discreetly covered with red velvet drapes with fringed tassels at tops, bottoms and sides, and on one wall there was a magnificent oil, from the period of Watteau, which showed a satyr chasing naked nymphs through a forest glen.

On the sofa nearest him, a Union captain, short, fat

and thickly bearded, conversed softly, with a tall, stately young woman in her mid-twenties, her brown hair coiffed in a high pompadour, wearing a green silk dress which bared her shoulders and the cleft of her dazzlingly opulent bosom. With her hands demurely folded in her lap, listening attentively to his words, she looked more like a prim belle at a ball than a *fille de joie*. At the other end of the long sofa, a tall, gangling, bushy blond-haired man in a green waistcoat and tan-colored breeches and black boots, conversed animatedly but in a lowered tone of voice with a young woman, not quite twenty, whose fiery-red hair vividly contrasted with the demure high-necked, yellow silk gown which clung to her voluptuous body. Indeed, Luke thought to himself, this must be the celebrated newcomer from Pensacola, and the hansom cab driver's appraisal of her failed to do her full justice.

On the sofa beyond, a cadaverous-looking man in his early fifties, wearing the insignia of a Union colonel of cavalry, reached forward to clink his goblet against one held by a coquettish, young woman in a cerise silk evening gown which bared her shoulders and whose dark-brown hair fell in a luxuriant sheaf to the middle of her back. In one of the overstuffed armchairs across from him and to his left, a scowling, heavy-set cotton buyer from Massachusetts listened morosely, twirling his empty wine goblet between his pudgy hands, while a magnificently sensual mulatto half his age and wearing a low-cut green sateen frock perched on one arm of the chair and whispered into his ear.

In another chair directly opposite from Luke, a red-faced, burly Union captain, his empty champagne goblet lying on the floor near his feet and his trousers wet with what he had spilled from obviously more than one libation, lolled back, each of his arms encircling the waists of two slim girls who looked enough alike to be twins and who were not more than eighteen, one dressed in a circumspect, black silk gown, the other in the provocative *déshabillé* of a red silk wrapper whose open upper folds disclosed the lacy frills of a black silk chemise.

"My dear fellow, what a pleasure to see you again after all these years!" a hearty baritone voice boomed out from the stairway, and Luke Bouchard turned to see John Brunton, tall as himself, with sardonic features, keen, searching dark-blue eyes, a pointed gray beard and neatly groomed sideburns. He was dressed in formal black evening clothes, with a white silk cravat from which a diamond stickpin glittered. Clinging to his arm was a supple, willowy, yellow-haired young woman in her mid-twenties, in a long purple silk evening gown whose train she had neatly gathered up in her left hand to disclose exquisitely chiseled ankles and gold-cloth slippers.

"John Brunton, I hardly recognized you," Luke Bouchard smilingly came forward up the stairs and shook the lean, wiry hand of his former banker.

"That's not surprising after so many years and a war intervening, Luke. Come upstairs to my private office, and Laure, be a dear and bring us a bottle of the best champagne in the house and a plate of *petits gateaux*." Then he added for Luke's benefit, "Laure is, shall we say, the *maitresse de la maison*."

"*Enchanté de faire votre connaissance*, M'selle Laure," Luke courteously inclined his head.

"I like your friend very much, *m'amour*," the lovely blonde told John Brunton in a stage whisper. "I shall be back in a moment. Until then, M'sieur Bouchard."

She went down into the parlor and passed through the exit hallway at the back, while Brunton gestured up the stairway. "It's at the end of the landing, my friend. Yes, it's been years indeed. And you see me now as an opportunist."

"I see you in the midst of luxury and gaiety, it seems," Luke chuckled as he followed his host down the thickly carpeted hallway to a small door at the left which Brunton opened.

"Well, I'll be frank with you, Luke. If I'd been an obvious Confederate sympathizer, you'd never have found me in a place like this. More likely in one of Ben Butler's squalid prisons. The fact is, when my dear old patron Antoine Rigalle began to groom me to take over his bank, I had already observed what financial wisdom your esteemed grandfather had shown in transferring his profits to hard gold coin in a reputable and solid English bank.

Of course, the Confederacy was hoping till the very last day that the British government would take its side and furnish munitions and supplies and even loans, but that never materialized, as you well know. At any rate, well before the war began, I took the precaution of turning some of my own rather fortunate land speculations into specie deposited in the very same bank where your grandfather left his gold. As a consequence, when New Orleans fell to Farragut's siege, and when our forthright conquering general ousted me from my post at the bank, I was able to change occupations the way a chamelon changes its color. It wasn't too difficult, since I had plenty of gold and wasn't on the proscribed list of enemies to the North. And of course I know why you've come to see me. Now tell me, what's happened to Windhaven since I last saw you?"

"It's been burned, John. We managed to save a few heirlooms, but the most grievous tragedy was the wanton murder of poor old Matthew Forsden."

"Sybella's husband? I'm dreadfully sorry to hear that. How did it happen?"

"He insisted on staying behind when the rest of us went over to the Williamson house after we'd heard that General Wilson's troops had burned Selma and were on the way to Montgomery. He intended to try to assure the soldiers that Windhaven was not a nest of slavers, that there were no weapons, but apparently some heedless trooper shot him down. It was a terrible blow for my courageous stepmother, John. As you know, she lost her son Paul at Shiloh."

"So you wrote me, yes. So you've abandoned Windhaven as well as the plantation you took over when you married that lovely Williamson girl? Ah, here's Laure with our refreshments. *Merci, ma Mignonne,* and now if you'll be sweet enough to leave us, I'll make it up to you later this evening."

The young woman had set a tray with an open bottle of champagne, glasses and a plate of little cakes down on the tabouret near the low-backed couch on which John Brunton and Luke Bouchard were sitting.

As she straightened, she glanced flirtatiously at Luke

Bouchard and murmured, "If you persist in neglecting me so, *m'amour*, perhaps I can induce M'sieu Bouchard to console me."

"If that occurs, *ma très belle, ma très chère,*" John Brunton casually drawled but with a twinkle in his eyes, "I promise that you will have considerable difficulty in sitting comfortably for at least a fortnight. Now, *va-t'en, vite, sinon—*" he drew back his right hand, the palm open, and with a delighted little laugh, Laure hurried out of the room and closed the door behind her.

As John Brunton poured out two brimming glasses of the sparkling champagne, Luke Bouchard said, "I should say that you have certainly successfully recouped your losses, judging by that charming companion. I don't recall that you had any such attractive employees at the bank when I used to call on you."

"We had no females there whatsoever, and you know it very well, Luke Bouchard," he raised his glass. "To the future, yours and your family's and mine, and may the next venture of the Bouchards prosper as fortunately as mine seems to have done."

"I'll drink to that willingly, John." Luke sipped from his glass, and set it down on the tray. "You see, it was Vance Alderson in Mobile who told me where to find you."

"He's a good friend, and I'm sorry to see that the fortunes of war left him strapped. Most of his trading was in paper, Southern paper, and you know by now exactly what that's worth—enough to light a few imported Havana cigars. But Mobile is a valuable port, Vance is enterprising, and he'll rise to the top again, I'm sure of it. But now to your affairs, Luke. You'll be wanting to get your hands on that balance in gold in the Bank of Liverpool."

"As soon as possible. From what I've learned about the Union takeover in this city, I'm afraid I'll have to carry it with me till I can deposit most of it in a safe bank in Texas."

"So that's where you're going, is it?"

"Yes, though I'll want your advice about exactly where you think I should settle. It's obvious that the new frontiers west of the Mississippi offer the only chance for a new start for someone like myself who's been identified with the South for so many years. I furnished no help to the Union, but on the other hand, all I did for the South was to provide food, horses and some beef when it became apparent that cotton couldn't be shipped out of the country because of the blockade."

"There were plenty of speculators who managed to sell their cotton to the other side, as you can guess, Luke. One of them's down in the parlor at this very moment, an old sobersides from Boston who married a Virginia girl, kept his connections in the South while professing loyalty to the North, and managed to wangle himself a fortune by playing both ends against the middle."

"That could never have been my way or Grandfather's. What I did do at Windhaven, well before the war, was to try my hand at raising beef, bringing in a pedigreed bull with a dozen cows. My son, Lucien Edmond, and I feel that our future should be devoted to the profitable raising and even breeding of cattle. Doesn't it seem logical to you? The country will need more food than ever now that the war is over, now that people will be pushing out as far as California, settling even in Indian territory."

John Brunton nodded as he poured more champagne into Luke's glass, then his own. "Your reasoning is sound, and Texas is certainly ideal. There's plenty of wild cattle coming up across the Mexican border into southwestern Texas, belonging to anyone who can round them up, brand them and market them. It's the marketing that'll be difficult. There aren't any railroads, though I'm sure that soon there'll be one cutting through the Midwest and on toward California before much longer. It means you'll have to drive those cattle with a good crew of experienced riders, a long, hard drive to Missouri or perhaps Colorado to find your buyers."

"As to riders, I've brought along a dozen faithful blacks, though I'll admit that perhaps only half of them would qualify for the business of raising cattle and driving them to market," Luke mused.

"I've an older cousin, Daniel Nichols, in San Antonio. He went there in the early Fifties, established himself as a merchant, and now he owns a hotel as well. We've written back and forth, and he's told me a lot about the problems Texas faces. Right now, there's still some fighting going on, even though this war is to all intents and purposes officially over. However, by the time you get your money from the Bank of Liverpool, it certainly ought to be finished. And there are a few other things to consider besides, Luke. You say you're taking blacks with you—a good part of Texas has already been settled by diehard Southerners who were brought up with the tradition that a black is a nigger and a nigger is a slave from birth to death. Neighbors like that wouldn't take kindly to your emancipated ideas, I'm afraid. So that would rule out certain parts of Texas for you, unless you want to start with hostility lined up against you before you even begin your venture."

"I shouldn't care for that. And that's exactly why I came to see you, to seek your advice."

"We'll be talking again, Luke, but the first thing I'm going to do tomorrow is get off a telegraph to New York to David Larson, a good banking friend of mine with whom I used to do business at the old Rigalle house. In turn, he'll cable Liverpool and then your draft will be sent on the steamship here to New Orleans. That will take about four or five weeks at best. And when you get it, I'd advise the utmost caution in receiving the consignment, because you wouldn't care to have any busybodies or Union soldiers knowing about the cargo you were taking ashore."

"Hardly," Luke smiled wryly.

"Have some of those cakes, Laure baked them herself. I hope you haven't altered your good opinion of me, finding me in such surroundings."

"The thought hadn't occurred to me, John. You had to survive, and I think you've managed very well."

The former banker frowned and tugged at his beard, then took a sip of his champagne. "Understand, Luke, I haven't given up my career as a banker forever. Shall we say, this was a temporary expedient. One of these days, Ben Butler's regime will be over, and I hope we can get back to normal. Meanwhile, Laure runs the house and chooses the young ladies, and she's most selective, I can assure you. I may tell you also that they retain at least three-quarters of their earnings here, the rest being devoted entirely to the expense of maintaining so lavish an establishment. I don't need the profit, thanks to my earnings on those land deals I was telling you about. But the value of being here and offering an establishment like this to high-ranking and better paid Union officers is that our young ladies learn a good deal behind closed doors, such as how long Ben Butler intends to keep control of the banks, what contraband deals he has going, what new restrictions he intends to levy upon our citizens. All useful information which in due course will enable me to reopen my bank once the time is right. So much for my affairs. But, since you're here as my guest, Luke, it would be my pleasure to offer you the companionship of any girl in the house except, of course, Laure."

Luke Bouchard flushed and set down his champagne glass with a clatter, looking sheepish as he did so. "From what I saw down in the parlor, John, any one of your charming young ladies would delight the most demanding and fastidious man alive. But I must decline with thanks. It's just that I've never yet broken my marriage vow."

"I thought you'd say that, Luke. I admire and respect you for it. Well then, we'll be seeing a good deal of each other the next few weeks. Where are you staying, by the way?"

"At the Verandah Hotel. My half-sister Arabella and her husband James Hunter and their two children are with us, and they'll be going on to Galveston, where Hunter is to have a job in the cotton business with his cousin. I wrote you that Laurette had married a young Tuscaloosa merchant, Charles Douglas. They're here too, and they plan to go on to Chicago where he'll work in a department store. The only one not here is my other half-sister Fleurette who married a Union medical corpsman. She's gone back with him to his home in Pittsburgh where he's going to be a doctor."

"The Bouchard clan will leave its roots throughout this country before its final history is written, I'm certain," John Brunton smiled as he reached toward the nearly empty champagne bottle.

94

"No more for me, thank you, John. I'd better be getting back to the hotel. But it's good to see you again, and I'm happy for your good fortune."

"Yes," John Brunton got to his feet, uttering a long sigh, "I guess you and I are to be congratulated for the way we've survived this war. Others weren't quite so lucky. By the way, do you remember that gambler, Pierre Lourat?"

"Yes," Luke soberly replied. "More than that, I remember my half-brother Mark's association with him and how Mark died. Killed as a smuggler and a profiteer."

"Pierre Lourat died this last January. Someone waylaid him in an alley and stabbed him in the back. It's said that a woman did it." John Brunton shrugged, took out a silver cigar case, offered it to Luke, who smilingly shook his head, then selected one, bit off the end and lit it from a glowing red wax taper set in a silver candlestick on the secretary. "The strange thing is, two days later some boatmen fished the body of a woman out of the river near the levee. Someone had seen her jump into the river late the night before, and reported it to the patrol sergeant in charge of the the levee district. She was identified as Louisa Voisin. It seems she ran a *maison de luxe* for this Lourat fellow. Luke, you look pale as a ghost, as if someone had just walked over your grave. Did you happen to know the woman, by any chance?"

"Yes, John, I knew her," Luke Bouchard slowly replied. "She was the daughter of the woman with whom my grandfather was in love, the woman who decided to marry his older brother Jean so that she could become a countess, and I think it was mainly because of that unrequited love for her that Lucien Bouchard came to Econchate to found his Windhaven."

CHAPTER NINE

It was nearly sundown when Djamba, Lucas, Prissy and Celia and the eight other Windhaven blacks reached the desolate western edge of the Queen City, beyond which they could see only a few frame houses and stretches of swampy marshland. John Dewton's house—for it must be his, according to the description Djamba had been given—towered like a tired bastion at the edge of the bleak wilderness. It was an old two-story house, the roof tarred several times over and still showing signs of deterioration, wooden shutters nailed from the inside against the lopsided windows, and a veranda whose timbers showed signs of rot. Yet at the back there was a neat fence of barrel staves deeply hammered into the ground and extending for at least a hundred feet beyond the back of the house. One could see chickens scratching for handfuls of grain, and, at the far back, sectioned off by a rectangle of neatly laid red bricks, a sow and four young sucklings nuzzling her swollen teats. Close by was a smaller brick enclosure for the old boar.

"Mighty lonely place for any man to live in, Djamba,"

Harry squinted at the house, turned to the Mandingo with a doubtful frown.

"Well, Harry, maybe that's because this far away he knows he won't get into any trouble with white men who don't like his color. Now let's see if I can rouse him. No sign of life around, but—"

As Djamba spoke, the door of the house opened and a powerfully built black stepped onto the sill, cradling a musket in his muscular arms. "Wut you nigras doin' heah?" he irritably demanded.

"No harm at all, Mr. Dewton," Djamba smilingly advanced, holding up both hands to signify his peaceful intentions. "We heard about you from Mr. Alderson in Mobile and Captain Devries, that you might have room for us. We've got money to pay for lodging and maybe some food if you can spare it."

The elderly black, who was as tall as Djamba, his hair white and thick as merino wool, his forehead broad and high-arching, with a thick, flattened nose which suggested pugilistic encounters in his youth, clad in heavy blue levis and a frayed red cambric shirt, chuckled and stood the musket's heavy wooden butt on the sill beside him as he nodded. "Well now, you's more'n welcome den, ef dose two fine gennlemun sen' you heah." Turning his head to look back into the room, he bawled, "Hezzy, go put some vittles on de fiah! We's got visitors fuh suppah, gal." Then, genially, "You folks come right on in. The porch is fine ef you come on straight up, doan go messin' roun' de sides. Ah been meanin' to fix it, been too busy to git 'round to it. Mebbe some of you strong young nigras kin help out wid chores, pay fur yer keep."

"We'd be glad to, Mr. Dewton," Lucas amiably spoke up.

Djamba took Celia's hand and helped her up the steps to the veranda and straight on through the door, Lucas and Prissy following, and then Harry and his Betty, and after them, the others. To their surprise, the spacious living room of the old house was in almost unbelievable contrast with the dilapidated exterior: a comfortable old couch, some old but sturdy straight-backed chairs, even a walnut writing desk over at one side. And the stairway leading to the second floor had thick, serviceable red carpeting.

"Let de women sit deyselves on the couch deah," John Dewton commanded, "de oldah men take de chairs, and de rest of you young bucks, you kin stand like me. Heah's Hezzy, she mah third wife and mighty spry when she doan get to feelin' lazy." He turned to wave a large, thick-fingered hand at a young light-colored black woman not yet thirty, with a red bandanna bound over the top of her head and wearing a neat gingham dress. She eyed him respectfully, then giggled softly and immediately covered her sensual mouth with her palm as she saw his eyes narrow and glint with annoyance.

"Mind yo' manners, gal. You see, her real name's Hepzibah, only I call her Hezzy 'cause it soun' lak hussy, which is wut she acts lak—specially when she see a young buck around she favors. Doan lemme catch you makin' eyes at any ob dese yeah nigras, gal, less'n you wants me to take my stick to youah fat tail."

"Ah won't nohow, Mistah John," the attractive black woman giggled again, shook her head vigorously to confirm her promise. "Jist came in to see how many of you I'se got to fix foah. Dey's twelve all tol', ain't dat right?"

"She's smart, she kin count," John Dewton chuckled good-naturedly. "Off you go now, woman, dese yeah folks look mighty tired. Git!" And as she passed, he whirled and swung his hamlike hand to resound on her plump bottom, making her squeal and hurry out of the room, not without an admiring backward glance at her obviously masterful, though far older, husband.

"Now den, who you folks, wheah you gwine? Reckon you musta come from Alabammy-way, ef ol' Mistah Vance done gib you mah name."

"We did, Mr. Dewton. We came from up around Lowndesboro. My name's Djamba, and this is my son Lucas, my wife Celia, and my daughter, Prissy. The rest of you, speak up your names to Mr. Dewton so he knows them," Djamba turned to his followers.

"I see, I see," the powerful white-haired black nodded, eying Djamba with obvious respect. "Well, y'all free niggers now, wheah you gwine, you ain't told me that yet."

"We were set free long before Mr. Lincoln read the Proclamation, Mr. Dewton," Djamba explained. "When the Yankees burned Mr. Luke Bouchard's plantation, he and his family said they'd make a new start and go to Texas, raise themselves some cattle and such. We asked if we could come along and work for him at wakes."

"Wal now, not such a consarned bad idea at that. Texas is wide open. 'Round here things ain't so good. You already found out, all you fine plantation bucks that got your papuhs and wuz jist hungerin' to see wut freedom wuz really like, dat heah in N'Orleans dey ain't quite ready to sit down wid you at the de table and pass you de po'k chops and de bread, ain't dat right?"

"Yes, we walked in the street to get here, Mr. Dewton," Djamba smiled. "Would you have room to put us all up for a few weeks till Mr. Bouchard can get his money from the bank in England, get himself supplies and maybe have some wagons built and buy himself some guns?"

"What you want guns foah, boy?" John Dewton suspiciously demanded, lifting his musket up to his chest again and warily eying the powerful Mandingo.

"Well, not to start the war over again, that's for certain, Mr. Dewton. But Mr. Bouchard says there'll probably be unfriendly Indians there and maybe bandits, and there isn't any law out there, so a man has to have a gun handy to defend his property and his life."

"Dat make sense, I reckon. Well, we'll talk about it all after supper. Den mebbe you bucks might like to come along wid me 'n see a bear fight a hound dog." He suddenly scowled and shook his head. "Leastways, you might want to help me stop a damn-fool friend ob mine from gittin' his dog clawed to bits all 'cause he's a gamblin' fool and thinks it kin beat the bear."

"A bear and a dog? That's not an even match, Mr. Dewton," Lucas politely spoke up.

"I didn't say it wuz," the white-haired black snapped back with an angry glare. "Wut dey do is have deyselves some sport in an ol' barn down a ways here near the swamps. They got an ol' bear and dey puts a muzzle on him and dey let the dog go at him in the ring. Once in a while, if a dog's mighty quick and knows where to bite the varmit, he kin win and make his massa a nice piece ob money. Mos' time, it's de bear wins. I told my friend Zeke he was a goddamn fool to take de young dog he found jist last month and put it up against dat ol' bear. Some feller kicked the hounddog out and Zeke found it and took it home and 'fixed it up. Now he's gonna git it torn to bits tonight less'n I stop him. And dey's gwine to be a ruckus if I does dat all by myself, even wid disyeah musket."

"I'll go along, how about you, Daddy?" Lucas turned to his father and the tall Mandingo nodded.

"Good! Now den, I heah Hezzy callin' from de kitchen—come sit yerselves 'n eat up hearty. One thing I will say about that no-good, lazy, light-color *nigra* gal, she sho kin cook when she's a mind to!"

Over a bountiful supper of chicken gumbo, chitterlings and juicy succulent blackberry pie, John Dewton entertained his guests with anecdotes from his past. Slyly insisting that he was still in his prime and hardly a day past fifty and glaring at his young wife when she dared gigglingly whisper, "Dat man, he closer to Methusalah den fifty, 'n dat's a fac'!" he explained how a Portuguese slave trader had captured him and a dozen others from his village near the Belgian Congo and brought him to this very city when he had been a stripling of twelve. He'd been sold to a Creole master, run away after a year, been whipped and sold to a Louisiana sugarcane planter where he'd toiled for a decade. When the planter had decided to go back to France, John Dewton had passed into the hands of a kindly old veterinarian, who had taught him a good deal about animal husbandry, finally freed him a dozen years ago and paid his wages to go on working for him. With this money, John Dewton had bought the ramshackle house and acquired a hog and a sow and chickens, now made his living doing odd jobs, nursing sick pets and renting out space in the house to freed blacks like Djamba and his followers.

"It's a consarned shame ah nebbah had no sons to stay roun' 'n help me wid de house 'n de hosses 'n pigs 'n cows 'n dogs ah's had to look after," he lamented. "Mah other two wives, all dey could gimme wuz gal suckahs. But mebbe Hezzy heah'll change things." Then, abruptly, he stood up and glowered at Djamba and Lucas: "Wal, s'pose we git to dat bear fight. Gwine start purty soon, 'n ah hopes ah kin talk some sense into dat no-count buckra Zeke."

"Will there be white men there betting on that kind of fight, Mr. Dewton?" Djamba thoughtfully asked. "We don't want to stir up trouble. Fact is, Mr. Bouchard hopes that when he gets to Texas, he won't have to be up against neighbors that don't hold with blacks and whites mixing."

"Hee hee, now ah'd say dat disyeah massa you's wukkin' for, he lookin' for de Garden ob Eden, dat wut he aftah!" Then, his face sobering, the white-haired black softly added, "But ah sho does wish all ob you luck findin' a place like dat. Sho, dey's gonna be white men bettin', only wut ah wants is to peel Zeke loose fum dat barn 'foah he gits notions to bet all de cash he got and lose it. You see, Zeke, he near 'bout my age, he's an Angola, and dey gits fool notions you gotta talk 'em outa all de time. Nawsuh, we ain't gwine raise no fuss wid any white man, gibs you mah word on dat!"

Turning to his wife, he growled, "Hezzy, you git on wid youah chores, woman. When you's done, you see to it dat ornery ol' hog Moses, he hab his feed and stay in de pen ah built him last week so's he wouldn't moles' his sow 'n dem l'il piglets. Mind you do dat now. If when ah gits back ah finds you been shinin' up to dese hyeah bucks gwine stay wid us, ah'll take a strap to youah backside, 'n you knows I kin do it good even at mah age!"

"You sho nuff kin, Mistah Dewton," Hepzibah giggled, then scurried out toward the kitchen as he clenched his fist and shook it at her.

Djamba, Lucas, the tall sturdy Kru, Dave, and the stocky young Hausa, Ned, accompanied John Dewton toward an old red barn about half a mile northwest of the latter's house. Against the dark, moonless sky, the eerie flames of two torches served as a beacon to those who sought the excitement of this primitive entertainment. En route, the white-haired black explained, "Disyeah Kaintuck mountain man wut own de bear, he jist as mean 'n ornery as dat animal he got. Made hisself a bundle by now. Y'see, a man's got to put up twenny dollars in hahd cash just to entah, 'n den he natcherly keep on bettin' wid all de folks dat favors another hound. He kin git flat busted in de time it take dat bear to claw his dog daid. 'N Zeke jist de kind of crazy *nigra* won't be satisfied till he put up all de cash he got left. He a shiftless, no-good *nigra*, Zeke is, but he save mah hide in a fight wid a man who drawed a knife on me when we wuz fightin' wid ouah fists, 'n ah ain't likely to forgit wut he done. Le's go in now. Cos' you twenny cents to git into de barn, though— you brung money wid you?"

"I have some, Mr. Dewton," Djamba put his hand into his breeches' pocket and drew out a handful of small coins which Luke Bouchard had given him along with the gold pieces.

"Das good, das real good." Passing between the flaming torches, John Dewton at the head shouldering his musket, they reached the partly open door of the old red barn. Inside, by the light of several kerosene lamps, they could see crude benches at the rear on which about twenty men sat, some rivermen with jugs of whiskey in their laps, a few Creole dandies dressed in the height of fashion, even a few blue-uniformed soldiers though of no higher rank than sergeant.

Standing at the entrance to the barn, a wizened little man with weasel-like features, wearing a bowler hat and a dusty black frockcoat far too large for him, stuck out a grimy hand for the entrance fee, which Djamba promptly paid. Recognizing John Dewton, he cackled, "Better not shoot old Hank's bear, he'd gut you for fair!"

"Jist brought it along 'n case dat bear gits loose and starts chasin' de folks watchin' de show," the white-haired black chuckled. "Dere's Zeke now, see him? He right outside dat ring, talkin' to his hound dog."

A makeshift arena had been formed by a huge circle of fence staves. At the back of it and nearest to the barn door, was an upright old iron cannon which had been set deep into the ground. A heavy chain had been wound several times round it and reinforced with knotted ropes to make it hold fast to the bear's collar, the last link of the chain being soldered to a metal ring in the collar. It was a squat black bear, old and surly, blindfolded and muzzled, and beside it stood a tall gray-haired, sour-faced man in fringed buckskin breeches and jacket, muttering softly to his fearsome pet.

Crouching outside the far end of the ring were four men, holding their dogs in check, exhorting them for the coming fight. John Dewton ambled over toward a stocky, gray-haired pockmarked black who was stroking the angular head of a half-starved dog that looked mangy, lean gray, with mournful amber eyes and long lean muzzle.

"So you think dat mangy hound kin whup that bear, does you, Zeke?" John Dewton chuckled as he planted the musket butt on the ground and stared down at his friend.

"Ah sho does, John boy. Ah's gwine bet a hunnerd dollahs he kin. See, ah got a good draw now, ah goes third. Ah figgers by den, dose first two houn's, dey gwine wear out dat o' bear, so's mine kin finish him off."

"Dat poah ol' sick-lookin' dog, he don't look like he kin even tree a coon, much less tackle dat bear."

"We'll see. Now, dey gittin' ready! Who yo' friends dere, John?" Zeke peered at the quartet who stood beside his friend.

"From Alabammy. Dey's boun' foah Texas. We talk about dat when you's done. By rights, you oughta be done right now, effen you had any sense."

The mountain man had now removed the bear's blindfold, made a gesture for silence toward the noisy onlookers at the benches far beyond, and then bawled in a reedy voice, "Now then, gennlemun, you know the rules. Each houn's got five minutes, 'n I'll say when my bear's had enough. After all, he makes my livin' for me, I ain't figgerin' to have you kill him daid nohow." Out of the pocket of his buckskin jacket, he took out an old silver watch on a fob and chain, held it up for all to see. "When I call 'Time!' fust houn' gits let in."

Djamba and Lucas exchanged meaningful glances and
104

Lucas shook his head. "Hunting's one thing," Djamba whispered to his son, "baiting's another, and I don't hold with it. That dog Zeke's got doesn't look as if he's the baiting kind either. Maybe we can talk him out of it. "

The Kentuckian put the watch back into his pocket and called, "Time!" and a hubbub of voices rose from the benches as the first man, a fat German saloon keeper, pulled aside one of the staves of the picket fence and exclaimed, "*Gehe*, Hermann!" His dog, a vicious-looking mongrel with long tail and heavy jaws, bounded forward as the bear, with an answering snarl, reared on its hind legs and pawed at the air. The mongrel made several forward lunges, barking, to which the bear responded with fierce growls, and then suddenly the dog rushed forward and tried to bite the bear's leg. Instantly the enraged animal slashed down its right paw and an agonized howl went up as the mongrel retreated, its belly viciously ripped and blood pouring out onto the grayish earth.

"*Gott verdammte Hund,*" the German saloon keeper swore. Cautiously moving forward, he lifted a heavy cudgel and struck the yelping, dying mongrel on the head, silencing it, then dragged the bloody carcass out beyond the picket fence and replaced the stave. Next he turned back toward the benches and sullenly bent to one of the spectators, taking out a purse and counting out coins to pay his lost bet.

The second dog fared no better, though it lasted three minutes, circling and lunging. As it moved in for one attack, the bear snarled and seized it by the throat, lifting it in the air and strangling it.

"My God, we've got to stop this," Djamba muttered.

"Next one, time!" the Kentuckian called out. "Yes, you fellers didn't pick your dogs too good tonight. Better luck tomorrow, mebbe. Wal now, what's holding you up there, nigger?"

Zeke had risen, pulled away the stave to make an opening for his dog to enter, but the animal only whined and crouched low, its amber eyes fixed on the bear which had dropped to all fours now, shaking its head as if to warn all future challengers of a similar fate.

"Damn you, Jasper," Zeke whiningly complained, "Git

on in dere, ah's got mah money ridin' on yo' wurthless hide!"

But the dog merely flattened its belly on the ground.

Catcalls came from the impatient specators on the benches: "Forfeit the bastard! Why'd you let a nigger in here anyhow? Throw him in with the bear, that's what!"

Zeke, in desperation, brutally kicked the dog in the ribs. The animal yowled as it rolled over, then began to drag itself away looking fearfully back at its master.

Djamba stepped forward and seized Zeke by the shoulders, "That'll be enough of that. I'll buy that dog from you, mister."

"Who the hell you talkin' to, nigger?"

"To you, Zeke. If you kick that dog again, I'll break your neck, I mean it. Here, I'll give you the twenty dollars you paid to enter it against that bear. You'd better take it, those people out there are getting nasty!"

"Goddamn it, gimme the money. Ain't got no use for a yeller, shif'less houn' like dat anyway!" Zeke whined.

Djamba bent down, stroking the dog's head, crooning to it, while he looked at the animal's side. Carefully, he touched the place where Zeke had kicked it. "You're lucky you didn't break any ribs. I'll take it now. Lucas, let's get out of here."

Gently cradling the dog in his arms, Djamba strode out of the barn and into the night.

CHAPTER TEN

Exactly a week after their first meal of celebration in the Verandah Hotel, the Bouchards gathered there again, this time to bid farewell and good fortune to Laurette and her husband Charles Douglas, who were leaving for Chicago the next morning on the steamboat *River Princess*.

James and Arabella would be leaving soon, too, for Galveston, but their plans had been temporarily side-tracked. The seaport was still under Union siege and there appeared to be no immediate end to hostilities. But Arabella had cheerfully welcomed this delay as an opportunity to spend more time with her mother. "You see, James dear," she had pointed out, "you know that your job's safe once you get there, and it can't be very long before the port is open again. Besides, it's like a second honeymoon for us!"

Three days earlier, the news had come that Jefferson Davis had been captured at Irwinsville, Georgia, and at once imprisoned in the Fortress Monroe. And on the very day of this second reunion dinner at the Verandah, a Confederate force under General Slaughter had bested Union soldiers under Colonel Barrett at Palo Pinto,

Texas, in what was destined to be the final military engagement of this stubbornly fought war.

After Charles and Laurette had departed, with many good wishes from the entire family, Luke Bouchard excused himself and took a hansom cab to The Union House to learn whether his former banker had managed to arrange for the shipment of the English gold. The doorman recognized him and informed him that John Brunton was in his office. Lovely Laure, who had been standing on the edge of the parlor chatting with several uniformed officers, at once came forward to greet him, her eyes merry with recognition and amusement.

"Well, Mr. Bouchard, perhaps this time you've come to ask my help in selecting a companion for the night?" she teased as she took his hat and cape.

"I'm sorry to disappoint you, Mam'selle Laure, but once again I've come to see the head of the house," Luke smilingly retorted.

"But, my dear Mr. Bouchard," she countered, her eyes sweeping him up and down as if to detail every facet of his still athletic body, "didn't John tell you that I manage this house? Therefore I should say I'm the head of it. And besides, I'll let you in on a little domestic secret—he and I plan to be married in a few weeks. I don't think he told you my last name—though of course when a woman marries, it's always changed. But then, since I've never been one of the girls here, so to speak, I've been very proud of my last name, whereas there's never any need for theirs. It's Prindeville. My father was a Creole and a member of the city council until—" here she lowered her voice, glancing quickly back into the parlor to make certain that the officers could not overhear her, "until that detestable Massachusetts politician masquerading as a general took over New Orleans. It was too much for Papa; he killed himself when his bank was taken over and his house confiscated. It was John who brought me here and gave me something to do to keep my mind off my grief. And as you'll see one of these days, Mr. Bouchard, I'll still have a chance at avenging Papa. Now I'll go tell John you're waiting to see him."

With this, she slowly ascended the stairs, looking backward over her shoulders at him with a coy little smile. She wore an exquisite red velveteen frock, which bared her shoulders and upper back, though contrastingly it covered her magnificent bosom. Gathering her skirt up in one hand, she allowed Luke Bouchard to admire the chiseled grace of ankles sheathed in white silk stockings.

He flushed hotly under her amused, covert scrutiny and turned to look into the parlor. More than he cared to admit, Laure's physical presence troubled him. Not once in all the years since he had married gentle, faithful Lucy, had he thought of another woman, nor had there been any need. Yet now, in this chaotic interlude between the ending of one phase of his productive life and the beginning of another that was still unknown, he felt himself impressionably aware of events, of people, of sensory things in a way that he had never known before. Perhaps, he told himself, that terrible violence in the Windhaven stable which had recalled how the slave trader James Buffery had died at his hand, had wrought this singular change in him. And now, the delicate fragrance of Laure Prindeville's perfume, her coquettish glances and voluptuous costume made him drive his nails into his palms as if to exorcise some unbidden demon that might undo him. He struggled to revive his sober resolves for guiding his family to a new life in the vast land which lay beyond them.

"Come on upstairs, Luke, Laure should have had the sense to bring you right up to me," John Brunton called from the top of the staircase. "I've good news for you, and it's something that delights me too, because it shows that I still haven't lost all the valuable contacts I made before the war."

A few minutes later, in his private office, the former banker filled his glass and Luke's with an excellent red wine from the Loire, while Laure prettily excused herself on the pretext that she was needed in the parlor. After she had gone, John Brunton clinked his glass with Luke's and then explained, "I don't know why the idea didn't occur to me when we met last week, Luke. But as soon as you'd left, I realized that of course you wouldn't want to be carrying all that heavy gold around from here to Texas. So I telegraphed David Larson to have the Bank

109

of Liverpool send a draft through the leading Boston bank and then on here to New Orleans."

"Why through Boston, John?"

"Ben Butler happens to depend on the support of the Boston banks, he being a politico from Massachusetts. He'd have to honor such a draft when it comes to any legitimate bank in New Orleans, even if he's got control of it. And the draft will stipulate that you can take such gold as you need here and now, and convert the rest into another draft which will be honored at any bank in Texas."

"Yes, that's good news indeed. Now another thing I must do before I leave New Orleans is to buy guns to protect us against hostile Indians and bandits. Also, yesterday, when I was out walking with Lucy and Lucien Edmond, I came across the shop of a wagonmaker just past the Vieux Carré, Dagronard, I believe."

"Oh yes, old Emile. He's the finest in the city."

"The two young men I met at the wharf when we landed here and who are looking after the wagons I brought from Windhaven, gave me some excellent pointers on having special wagons constructed. I should have some particularly sturdy wagons for supplies, and if we're going to round up cattle and take them on long drives I'll need a chuckwagon for meals on the trail."

"Yes, you'll certainly need those. But as to the weapons, that's going to take a bit of doing. You could probably find plenty of abandoned Confederate guns, the most accurate rifles come from the North. You'll have to find some Union officer who'll look the other way for a sufficient price to let you, a former plantation owner from Alabama, acquire weapons which some might think would be used to continue the war all over again."

"Of course you know that's not my intention in the least."

"Certainly I know that. So what Laure and I are going to do—and perhaps Laure more than I, since she's down there in the parlor all the time chatting with Union officers—is to find some officer who perhaps is getting out of the army and who's got an eye out for a quick and greedy profit. I warn you in advance, Luke, you'll have to expect to pay anywhere from five to twenty times what a good rifle would be worth. And you'll have to be careful of the way you make the deal—not to give your man more than a third down until the arms are delivered. And then to make sure that he hasn't planned some kind of ambush so he can shoot you down and pocket your money."

"I deeply appreciate your concern, and I'll certainly be guided by your advice, John. You've been a good friend to me all these years, and I've never needed one more than now. I promise you this, when one day I make Windhaven Range into a successful venture, I'll see to it that if you're back in the New Orleans bank, my profits will be put into your supervision, with, I surely hope, a handsome profit to yourself."

"Thanks, Luke. I'll say just this, once Butler's men leave New Orleans and I get back into the banking business, I'm going to plunge a little more, not only into land but also building. To be sure, there'll be Northern money invested here in the years that will follow, but if any sensible peacetime arrangement can be worked out by the Federal government, even a New Orleans banker with sound judgment can prosper. Now, have another glass of wine. By this time next week, I'm pretty sure we'll have an answering letter back from the Bank of Liverpool. Here's to you, your family and to our continued association."

"I'll drink to that gladly, but it appears there's another toast I should make—Laure was boasting, or so I rather inferred, that one of these days soon, you'll be giving up your bachelor habits."

"So the minx was as forward as that, before I was ready to let her announce the news? One of these days, I shall really have to chastise her," John Brunton grinned. "But it's true. I know I'm more than twice her age, but that's not important any more. She does feel grateful to me, and at the outset I felt sympathy for her. But now our feelings go beyond all that. Say what you will about there being no fool like an old fool, Luke, but I suspect she'll keep me young and hold me away from my dotage a good deal longer than if I remained a bachelor."

111

"I rather think she will at that, John. So here's to you and Laure, and long happy years to you both!"

After he had left John Brunton, Luke Bouchard got into a carriage and ordered the driver to take him to the house of John Dewton. At first the elderly driver demurred because of the length of the journey and the lateness of the hour, but a few coins overcame his objections. About an hour later, still grumbling over the tedious trip through the muddy streets, he drew the carriage to a halt. "Now you'll take me back in a few minutes, driver, and there'll be more money for you," Luke assured him. "I'll make it worth your while, and since you look tired, why not come in with me and perhaps they'll give you a cup of coffee or, if you prefer, something cool to drink?"

"Dat mighty thoughtful, suh. Ah believes ah will, thankee."

They ascended the old steps and crossed the veranda, and Luke rapped at the door of the house. The light of a kerosene lamp showed through the chinks in the boarded-up shutters which served as windows, for there was no glass, and after a moment, John Dewton's harshly suspicious voice boomed out at them, "Who dat, wut you want disyeah time ob night?"

"It's Luke Bouchard, Mr. Dewton. I'm sorry to have disturbed you, but I wanted to meet you and also talk to Djamba and the others who are staying with you."

"Ah'll open up den, Mr. Bouchard. Been waitin' to meet you, ebbah since Djamba 'n Lucas told me what a fine massa you wuz to dem all dese yeahs," his voice was eager now as he unbolted the door and opened it.

"I brought the driver of the carriage along. Perhaps you could give him something to drink."

"Sho, c'mon in, nigra. Hezzy, go git some of dat berry juice you been keepin' down in de dry well, it nice and cool by now. Bring Mr. Bouchard a nice big glass too, you heah, gal?"

"Come in, come in," he urged as he closed the door behind Luke and the driver. "Disyeah's mighty lak a meetin' house. Why, we got usselves a redbone visitin' too."

112

In the living room, the young redbone Simata was seated beside Lucas and Frank, while Djamba, recognizing Luke Bouchard, hurried forward with a huge grin on his amiable face. "Real glad you could come, Mr. Bouchard. Specially because Simata here has been telling us all about Texas, where his father rode with the Kiowa band many years ago."

"I'm glad to know you, Simata." Luke came forward and held out his hand which the young Indian hesitantly took, as if uncertain how to reply to so unexpected a gesture from a white man.

"We found Simata on our way to Mr. Dewton's house," Djamba explained to Luke. "Some drunken men were treating him badly, and we helped him. He knows a great deal about Texas, and he says he would like to come along with us, because he could be a scout. He knows the friendly and the unfriendly Indians of that country, and a good deal about the land and the cattle that roam it and what grows on it."

"Indeed, I think you could be of great help to us, Simata, and we would pay you well to scout for us. You would be as well treated by my family as you have been by Djamba and Lucas and the others," Luke warmly offered.

"I would like to see again the land I knew as a boy," Simata assented, his eyes narrowing as if seeing what those in the room could not see. "Do you know of my father's people, the Kiowas?"

"No, Simata, only that they were a race of brave warriors and moved across the western plains. My grandfather lived for many years with the Creeks, who were sent into Indian Territory to the north of Texas long before this war."

"This is what your man Djamba has told me," Simata nodded, frowning as he sought to choose his words. "Long, long ago, I think even before your grandfather came to this land, the Kiowas and the Crows were friends and lived far away, near the headwaters of the Missouri. Long after that, the elders say, they made treaty with the Comanches and came southward to the Arkansas. When my father was a boy, he rode with his father on the plains

113

near *Nuevo* Mexico, near the trail that is called Santa Fe. When I was born, he and his people had come into Texas. Ah, I remember the stories he told me of the herds of buffalo, of the wild mustangs, the fierce bulls and cows with long horns that were everywhere. The hunting was good, there were few white-eyes then. Now, it begins as with the Creeks you knew." Simata eloquently shrugged, bowed his head and closed his eyes.

"How was it you came here to live in New Orleans, Simata?" Luke asked after a respectful pause.

"My mother had been slave to a white-eyes who grew cotton near San Antonio," the young halfbreed replied. "When he grew ill and knew his time was upon him, he set her free. She set out by wagon to return to my grandmother, in New Orleans. Along the way, my father captured her and made her his squaw. At first, she did not wish this, but then—she was happy he had made her his. Ten summers ago, when the Great Spirit called him, my mother brought me here. Before the war between the white-eyes began, I worked in a stable for a very rich white-eyes. Later, my mother baked breads and cakes and made the meat pies your man Djamba saw me carry that day he and his son came to do battle for me. Truly, they are my blood brothers."

"And your mother, Simata?" Luke gently asked.

The young halfbreed's face was bleak as he said tonelessly, "Her spirit is once again with my father's. The medicine I brought did not save her from the river fever. I am alone now, and that is why I would go with you to Texas."

"And you shall, Simata, I promise you. My family and I must wait here perhaps another month till the gold my grandfather left for me far across the great ocean is sent here. I mean to have strong wagons made to take us to the land where we shall settle. I hope to herd the long-horned cattle you spoke of. Do you know of land where I might find these cattle, where I should not be robbing the Kiowa and the Comanche of their buffaloes?"

Simata pursed his lips and pondered a moment. "I remember, when I had but twelve summers yet could ride horse and shoot my arrows straight as a full-grown war-

114

rior, that my father and his tribe came to land that was flat and dry, with sand and black earth all around. It was near the Nueces River, and the white-eyes, the Spanish, called it Carrizo Springs, because that is their word for the tall reed that grows all around the land near the river. The hunting was good! We saw turkeys and the wild hog, the *javelina,* the fox, the coyote, the raccoon, and many squirrels—aiyee, we did not want for meat at our campfires that moon!"

"And there were cattle, with the long horns?"

"As many as the buffalo—no, even more as I remember. They belong to those who can catch and kill them."

"We shall catch them, tame them, and sell them to others who will kill them for the good meat that will feed many families, Simata. And you shall help us, and since you are Kiowa, you can help us speak your tongue with those of your people who may hunt and come upon us, so they will know we are not enemies."

Simata grunted laconically, shook his head. "It is not the Kiowa you must fear, but the Comanche. I speak some words of that tongue, for my father taught me. But there are many tribes, and they move swiftly, for they are great horsemen, almost as good as we Kiowas. One chief may be your friend, a dozen others may draw lance or arrow on you because you are white-eyes, and they will not hold council first. That is what you must fear most."

Luke put his hand on Simata's shoulder and said gently, "My grandfather learned to speak the tongue of the Creeks as well as his own, and all Creeks were his brothers. Before we leave for Texas, Simata, you will teach me the Kiowa and what Comanche you know, and with your wisdom, I shall try to be their brother too."

CHAPTER ELEVEN

Two days after his meeting with Simata, Luke Bouchard visited the shop of the wagonmaker, Emile Dagronard, two blocks east of the Vieux Carré, accompanied by Andy Haskins and Joe Duvray. John Brunton had generously loaned him five thousand dollars for wagons and also for guns. "You can pay me back when your own draft comes through," Brunton had said. "In the meantime, as I told you, Laure and the girls are keeping their eyes and ears open for some officer who has access to weapons and who wants to sell them for a good profit. Do remember me to your sweet wife Lucy, and don't forget, before you finally leave our fair city, I want you and all your family to be my guests for a farewell dinner."

Emile Dagronard was a frail-looking man in his mid-sixties, with a white goatee and a thin, reedy voice. But there was nothing frail about the vehemence with which he cursed, in a most fluent and flowery French, at two of his workers who had incorrectly forge a wheel. Luke stood listening till the old man had finished his eloquent tirade against the stupidity of imbeciles who could not have drawn the picture of a tree on the Cro-Magnon caves of their prehistoric ancestors from whom they had undoubtedly descended without any greater intellect having been granted them over those thousands of years, and then said in French, "I haven't heard such beautiful use of the language, M'sieu Dagronard, since my grandfather used to read Voltaire to me."

The old wagonmaker wheeled, his eyebrows knitting at this unexpected interruption, and then grinned and shrugged. *"Que voulez-vous,* M'sieu? When one deals with assistants whose only virtue is that they work hard but have little imagination of their own, one must do the best one can. Now may I serve you?"

"Yes, I am Luke Bouchard, and my family and I and my friends here plan to settle in Texas. I want to commission some wagons from you, and I can pay you a deposit now, or, if your price is not too high, the entire sum as you choose. You may know John Brunton, he was my banker before the war."

"Le diable me prend, mais bien sûr, je connais John Brunton!" the old wagonmaker exploded. "The old rascal has gone into a much more delightful occupation than presiding over a stuffy bank, as I am sure you know."

"Yes," Luke replied, "I had that impression also. However, he has arranged through his contacts in New York to have money, which my grandfather left in an English bank, sent to me here in New Orleans, and so you need have no worry about my ability to pay your price. I want the strongest wagons you can make, and I have brought my good friends Andy Haskins and Joe Duvray and this Kiowa scout Simata with me because they have given me some very good ideas on what I may need in that part of the country."

"I shall do my very best, M'sieu Bouchard. That you are a friend of John Brunton assures your credit with me at once. Money, *eh bien,* it is a necessary evil but always good to have. And now to business. How many of you will there be?"

"Well, I'll be taking a dozen negroes, loyal workers now free, plus these three men, and nine in my family."

"A round two dozen by my quick counting, then, M'sieu Bouchard. Well now, you should have at least four wagons, sturdily covered, with good heavy wheels—I hope, however, you are not thinking of going to Texas by land? That would take you through muddy swamps and even the best wagons I can provide would founder."

"Have no fear of that, M'sieu Dagronard. We'll most likely take the steamboat to Corpus Christi, and then overland on ground that I'm told is dry and flat."

"Then that presents no problem. It's wild country there, M'sieu Bouchard, and I suggest that you allow me to make openings in the covers of your wagons so that you can poke your rifles through. I don't mean to alarm you, but attacks are always possible."

"An excellent suggestion, and Simata here has already anticipated you. In case we are ambushed, such a precaution could easily save our lives."

"Very good. Now, what about furnishings?"

"We have two wagons full which Andy and Joe here have been guarding. They're flat wagons, sturdy enough, but not really suitable for our future purpose."

"Then a fifth wagon, by all means."

"Yes, and also for the future, we need a chuckwagon."

"Of course, of course, I know just exactly what you'll need. Six wagons. Let me see now," the old man scowled and his lips moved as he quickly figured the price. "Two thousand dollars in gold, M'sieu Bouchard, and I guarantee you the best wagons you'll find anywhere. *Pardieu!* I almost wish that I could come with you, for they will be such fine wagons that I should like to ride along with them and see how well they serve you, M'sieu Bouchard!"

Luke smiled and shook hands with the old wagon-maker, then showed him the draft which John Brunton had given him. "Tomorrow," he promised, "I'll come by the shop and give you the two thousand. When do you think I may have them, M'sieu Dagronard?"

"I'll hire a few more workers, *ça va sans dire*, and this is now the middle of May—a month from now they will be ready to be hauled aboard your steamboat, and that is the promise of Emile Dagronard who does not easily give a promise and never breaks one when he does. *Parole d' honneur*, M'sieu."

Andy Haskins and Joe Duvray, as well as Simata, while

119

the two men had been discussing the wagons, had been inspecting a heavy Army supply wagon in another part of the shop. Simata grunted his approbation of the work, "Wagons heavy, need strong horses to pull these."

Overhearing this, Luke turned, a look of dismay on his handsome face. "Devil take me!—Simata does well to remind me of the most obvious thing of all! Yes, of course I'll need horses." Turning back to the old wagonmaker, he demanded, "Most likely four horses to each of the four heavy wagons and two apiece to the chuck wagon and the other wagon which will carry our belongings. Do you know where I can get about twenty good horses, M'sieu Dagronard?"

"I can get them for you myself. But you won't need them until the wagons are ready and you're going to leave New Orleans, and by then I'll have found the horses you require. Visit my shop in a week or ten days, M'sieu Bouchard. I'll tell you how much they'll cost, and you can be sure that I'll get you the best price I can. I've some friends who still have good stables, even though the accursed Yankees—though I shouldn't say it too loudly, since that very wagon there has been commissioned by one of General Butler's own captains—try to steal everything in sight."

"Until next week, then, and it's been a pleasure meeting you. And if you do change your mind and come along to see how well your wagons ride, you'll certainly be welcome," Luke said as he took his leave.

After lunch the next day, Luke Bouchard went to the old Rigalle bank and presented the draft which John Brunton had made out in his name, quietly collected the money in *rouleaux* of gold coins, politely thanked the cashier, and hailed a hansom cab to take him to the shop of Emile Dagronard, where he opened the chamois bag and drew out two of the *rouleaux*. "Here's payment in full, *mon ami*. And next week I'll talk to you about the horses to pull these wagons you're going to make for me."

"For a customer like you, M'sieu Bouchard, I'll gladly move heaven and earth, which I assure you would be easier to move than those two idiots who still have not got that wheel properly aligned on the wagon which you see still standing there before you," the old wagonmaker sardonically declared, shaking his fist at the two crestfallen, stocky Creole laborers who had aroused his displeasure. "I swear to you, Aristide, Jules, if, by the time the sun goes down, that wheel is not in place, you will draw your pay without a reference, and good riddance to you both!" Then he whispered to Luke, "They are really very good workers, M'sieu Bouchard, but at times they need the lash of my old tongue to drive them on."

For the rest of the afternoon and early evening, Luke found himself free, his family being occupied in shopping and other pursuits. He decided, on impulse, to visit The Union House to report to John Brunton what he had been able to achieve thus far, thanks to the generous loan which the former banker had made to him. At the house, the pretty little maid whom he had noticed on the occasion of his first visit warily opened the door to him, and then, recognizing him, giggled and held it open for him to enter. "You are very early, M'sieu. Did you wish to see one of the young ladies, perhaps Barbara or Matilde?"

"No, *ma petite* Mitzi, I came to pay a call on M'sieu Brunton, *s'il vous plaît*."

"Oh, I am so sorry, but M'sieu Brunton has gone out for the afternoon. But I will tell Mam'selle Laure that you are here. Ah, *la voilà maintenant!*" as the young woman came down the stairs.

"Why, M'sieu Bouchard, how delightful to see you again! I have some very good news for you. Come upstairs, and we shall have a glass of wine, and then I shall tell you what it is," she invited.

He flushed hotly under her gaze, as she turned now and slowly climbed the stairs again, glancing back over her shoulder to make certain that he was following. She wore a red silk wrapper which enveloped her voluptuous body like a cocoon, following the play of her rounded, resilient thighs, tightening over the jouncy hillocks of her buttocks, emphasizing the graceful slimness of her waist. She wore silver-cloth slippers, and he could not help seeing the flash of tan silk hose as the wrapper shifted above her slim chiseled ankles.

She led him down the hallway, not to the room which he had visited before, but to another at the right. Opening the door, she glanced back over her shoulder again, and lazily drawled, "I think you will find this much more comfortable than John's dreary old office."

He gave her a quick bow, hesitated a moment, his face warm, and then followed. Laure Prindeville closed the door, and as he moved forward ahead of her, slyly drew the bolt. "What do you think of it, M'sieu Luke?" she huskily murmured, moving close beside him till he was conscious of the delicate scent of jasmine and the fragrance of her golden hair which hung long and shimmering to the middle of her back, a fillet of silver thread tying round its middle, the curls at the end floating freely.

There was a long low backless couch, with soft poufs upon it, a loveseat, and a writing desk with a heavily upholstered chair beside it at the large window whose exquisite lace curtains had been drawn. To the right, almost dominating the room, was a large canopied four-poster bed with green velvet cover and soft white sheets and two huge pillows with lace-embroidered cases. On the wall to his left was an oil painting by some local Creole artist, depicting a naked Venus Calliphyge standing in a conch shell, one soft hand over her sex, the other arm extended as an invitation, a coy smile upon her full sensual lips. Luke glanced at it and felt ill at ease. Laure had moved toward the foot of the bed and stood against one of the upright posts, leaning back, smiling almost mockingly at him as she reached both hands behind her to the rail to steady herself.

"It's a sumptuous room, Mam'selle Laure," he replied.

"If you could only see how you look, M'sieu Bouchard!" she suddenly giggled, crinkling her nose in a most exquisite and provocative moue. "Like a naughty schoolboy who's been kept after class and isn't sure exactly why his teacher is going to rebuke him, but thinks maybe he deserves it just the same."

"Oh, come now, you're exaggerating."

"You think so? But you do feel guilty, because you're alone with me in my room. Oh, but I assure you, no man enters here, not even John. He, too, is very scrupulous

122

about such matters, and it will not be till our wedding night which is only a week away."

"Didn't you say you had some news to give me, Mam'selle Laure?" he tried to change the subject.

"Oh yes, and the glass of wine I promised also. Be a gallant, and serve us both the wine, *chéri*."

He eyed her a moment, then shrugged and turned to a handsome mahogany sideboard near the writing desk on which a cut-glass decanter with goblets stood on a silver tray, poured out a glass of Tokay and brought it to her, then returned to pour himself only half a glass, drew out the chair beside the desk and seated himself, watching her intently. Laure smiled, lifted the glass toward him as if to toast him, then sipped it slowly, her eyes never leaving his face. Presently she said, "John had the reply from the bank this morning, by telegraph from his friend in New York. The draft is on the way, on the steamship *New Caledonia,* and it should arrive by about the middle of next month."

"That's welcome news indeed, Laure. But you didn't have to bring me here to tell me that."

"No, that's true. I brought you here for quite another reason, *mon ami.*"

"And that is?" he put down his glass, rose from his chair and stood watching her, his face quizzically expectant for her answer.

"John told me that you're after someone who'll sell you guns to take with you to Texas, isn't that true?"

"You know it is. And so?"

"Oh please, *mon cher* Luke, don't act like a school teacher now, browbeating a dull-witted pupil," she flashed with a saucy curl of her red lips. "John has told me so much about you and the life you led at that Windhaven of yours, that I felt I knew you even before we met. Oh yes, it's true. When the Union troops entered New Orleans and when John was ousted from his bank, I was an orphan and I had no one to turn to and everything was gone. What I felt for him was gratitude, and I respected him because he's wise and he still has youthful ways, of course. Then, when he started this house and put me in charge of it, he began to talk about the people he'd served at the old Rigalle bank, and about your grandfather and what a wonderful man he was, fighting against the wilderness and surviving all the hardships, living with those Indians. I looked upon you as a kind of hero, *mon cher*. And now that I've met you, you don't really act at all like a hero, but like a rather dull and self-centered person who doggedly clings to an idea and hasn't time for any diversions."

"I'm afraid you've wasted a great deal of time trying to analyze me, Mam'selle Laure, when there's really no need for all that," Luke Bouchard blandly replied. "I'll agree it's most flattering to hear that you should be interested in me at all, but since you're going to marry John, what I am or am not should really be of no concern."

"Oh, but it is, you've no idea how much it is," she drained her glass and set it down quickly, shattering it. Then, felinely, she moved toward him, her slim hands smoothing the belted wrapper, her lips curved in a tantalizing smile till at last she stood facing him. "Even John doesn't yet know that I've finally found the man who'll sell you all the guns you want at a price, *mon cher*. And for that, I think I'm entitled to some greater consideration than mere thanks."

"Who is this man?"

"You see, it's exactly as I said, you're like a bulldog, tenaciously biting into a notion and refusing to let go of it. I'll tell you, then. You'll have to arrange to meet him, but he's a frequent visitor here. His name is Captain George Soltis. He was attached to the Quartermaster's staff when General Butler took over New Orleans, and his term of enlistment expired just a week ago and he's getting out of the service. He was boasting to Elaine—you remember, that red-haired wench you saw in the parlor when you first came here to see John—that he's wangled himself quite a supply of ammunition and arms and that he expects to make a great deal of money so that he can enjoy his retirement from the Army in high style. And, judging from the way he's thrown his money around here, I'd say he's already found some buyers for his merchandise. So I think you'd best let me arrange a meeting before he disposes of everything he has to offer."

"I'm grateful to you for the news, and I'd indeed be grateful if you could arrange such a meeting with this Captain Soltis."

"I may and I may not. That depends on you, *mon cher*." She wound her beautifully rounded arms around his neck and approached her tantalizing moist full mouth toward his. "Show me just how grateful you'll be, and maybe I can arrange a meeting tomorrow night."

Luke could not help blushing as he put his hands to Laure Prindeville's wrists and gently disengaged them, lowering her arms to her sides, then stepping back. "I promise you that I'll make you a very handsome wedding present on the day that you and John are wed," he answered.

Laure Prindeville tilted back her head and laughed softly. "I'm not the sort of woman to be bought with gewgaws, *mon cher*. Otherwise, I'd be no better than the girls in the parlor, and I've never been one of those. On the other hand, since you seem to treat me as if I were a vestal virgin just because you know that I'm going to marry your friend John, I'll tell you that I'm not a virgin at all." Her eyes darkened and her lips tightened as at a distasteful memory. "A Yankee corporal saw to that when he and his bullying soldiers broke into Papa's house and started ransacking it. Oh, he was very polite, this corporal. He promised me that if I'd let him, he'd see to it that the other soldiers didn't touch me. Of course, if I wouldn't, then they'd all take their turns. And Papa wasn't there, because the night before he'd put a bullet through his brain." She drew a long breath, then moved even closer to him, put her hands against his sides and murmured, "So you see, *mon cher,* you won't be taking anything that belongs to John. And I'll let you in on a little secret—he's already sampled one or two of the delightful girls in the parlor. And I expect him to, because he's a man, after all. Now then, *cher* Luke, what are you?"

"Please, Laure, you're acting like a willful child. John Brunton has been my friend for years, and even granting what you've just told me—which I should rather not have heard—it still wouldn't excuse my betraying his trust."

"You are either a saint or a fool, and I don't believe you're either one, not really." She raised a hand to caress his cheek and Luke, again flushing hotly, struck it away and stepped back, his lips tight with anger. "And now you're looking at me as if I were a fallen woman," she giggled softly.

"Not at all. I'm just remembering what John said to you that first time I came here, that if you could induce me to console you for his neglect, you might have considerable difficulty in sitting comfortably for at least a fortnight."

"Oh yes, I remember he did say that, didn't he? But he isn't going to know about this, is he?"

"I don't know what you mean by *this*, Mam'selle, but I ask you in all kindness to end the little game and to be content with my gratitude for your help."

"But I find the game most interesting. I've never met a man before like you, *cher* Luke."

"In that case, perhaps I may serve as John's proxy."

"What do you mean—you're hurting my wrist—stop it—let me go—oh no—please—Luke darling—not like this—"

He had suddenly seized her wrist and dragged her over to the huge couch. Seating himself, he pulled her unceremoniously across his lap, clamped his right leg across her slim ankles, and, his left arm circling her supple waist, began to apply the flat of his right hand vigorously and rapidly to her buttocks. Laure Prindeville squealed and wriggled, thrusting back a hand to try to protect herself, but he swiftly seized it in his left hand, pinned it high on her back, and went on spanking with gusto.

"Ouu—please—*ça me brûle—assez, je t'en prie*—oww—stop—oh I beg of you—you're hurting—oh you brute—I'll tell John—you'll see—I'll tell him you assaulted me—you've hurt me—aiii—oh please, Luke darling, please let me off now—it does hurt—ouuu!!"

He was trembling now, and his face was crimson, not only with embarrassment and anger, but a sudden, inexplicably carnal fury. For as his hand repeatedly rose and fell, flattening the resilient curves of Laure Prindeville's ripely contoured buttocks, he was conscious that she wore nothing under her wrapper and that her squirmings and

126

twistings served to display her body to its most tempting advantage. He stopped at last, ashamed of the vindictively sensual impulse which had made him inflict so ignominious a punishment. And instantly contrite, but as secretly aware of the far from impersonal motives which had led him to this act, he released her.

Laure Prindeville was sobbing softly, tears running down her flushed cheeks as she stumbled to her feet. Then, like a chastised little girl, she began to rub her buttocks vigorously, after having first stealthily loosened the sequined belt that fastened her wrapper. It opened, and Luke stared at the Circe-like beauty of her tumultuously swelling naked round, dark-tipped breasts, at the smooth sleek belly with its shallow dimple, at the thick dark-golden fleece which covered the plump mount of Venus, at the long sculptured, quivering thighs sheathed halfway by the elegant silk hose held in place at mid-thigh by green satin-elastic rosette garters.

"Laure—I didn't mean—forgive me—Laure—" his voice was hoarse, trembling. He rose, extending his hand. Laure Prindeville sank down on her knees, squeezed his hand, kissed it effusively, turned it, then glided her soft warm tongue against his palm, while her other hand reached out toward his turgescent loins.

"No—Laure—we mustn't—I didn't mean this—no— oh *mon Dieu*—Laure—oh God forgive me—yes, you treacherous sweet bitch—you'll have the gratitude you wanted—"

He drew her up by the armpits, their mouths fused together, and with a gasp which was half laughter, half pain, Laure Prindeville drew him down upon the lush couch atop her.

Old Lucien had told him how he had saved the life of Shehanoy in the village of Econchate because she had tried to avenge her warrior husband's death at his hand. But he had not told Luke what had ensued between her attempt to stab him with his own knife and the pronouncement of her death sentence by Tunkamara, the *Mico* of Econchate. Now, more than three score and ten years after Lucien Bouchard had yielded to the most atavistic and primal instinct of man, his grandson cast aside all scruples as Lucien Bouchard himself had once done. There was no cogent world, no future, no thought, only the sensation of giving and taking without quarter on either side, as Laure Prindeville, her hair tumbling over his face, her hands urging him, abetted him with every sinuous, arching response of her lithe nakedness.

The fury of their culmination left them dazed and shuddering upon the couch. When at last they felt sanity returning, when Luke Bouchard tore himself away at last from Laure, it was to stand with his back to her, his face haggard with shame. Even if he had thought of such a thing at that moment, it could not have comforted him that once a Roman philosopher had coined the proverb that every animal is sad after coitus. He could think only now that he had broken his marriage vow, and that he had added to that moral sin the ethical one of betraying an old and steadfast friend.

Only vaguely he heard Laure Prindeville murmur, "Forgive me, my dearest Luke. You should have used a whip on me and then told John to do the same. I didn't know—I couldn't. How very much you must love her, and how blessed she is to be your wife. Forgive me. I truly mean it. I—I'll get word to you at the hotel when Captain Soltis will visit here again."

CHAPTER TWELVE

Luke Bouchard stumbled down the steps of The Union House, and spent the next hour walking the streets of the Vieux Carré in self-recrimination. His chief concern, quite apart from the realization that for the first time in his marriage he had been unfaithful to Lucy, was whether his impulsive act would wreck his friendship with John Brunton. He took some small consolation from the fact that what had happened between himself and Laure would never recur. Nor was it likely that his friend would ever become aware of it, for Laure was, he realized from her last words, a sensitive woman. Still he knew that each time he saw her again, he would not be able to avoid being reminded of the devastating if brief passion which had consumed them both.

Exactly because he was not a selfish profligate who took carnal pleasures where he could, but rather a rational man who consciously patterned himself after his grandfather's quiet integrity, he found himself tortured by misgivings. Somewhere within his conscience, there was a small glib voice saying that the end justified the means, that only a fool would reject so tempting an offer of brief ecstasy, that it had in no way altered either of their lives or those dependent upon him. Yes, all of that was true, except for the fact that if he had controlled himself somehow, he could have limited himself to chastising Laure for having played the wanton with him, yes, and still gleaned the information she had teasingly withheld from him. It was not so much that this act of sexual abandon had been in itself a mortal sin—though he felt that it truly was. Instead, he was most disturbed by the discovery of the violence hidden within his very soul. It was unexpected and unknown to him, and he ached with despair and self-loathing as he paused now and again to peer vacantly into shop windows.

How well he could remember the books he had read in his grandfather's library, how often as a boy he had posed theoretical questions to his grandfather, and how always old Lucien had urged him to think for himself, to reason out the logic behind the cold bare facts of what he had read in the books so that he would not accept them blindly as unshakable gospel. He remembered having read John Bunyan's *A Pilgrim's Progress* and, having been impressed by the portrait of those seven deadly sins which plagued mankind, had once asked old Lucien, "Grandfather, which is the worst sin of all, do you think?" And Lucien had sighed, shaken his head, and then taken his hand and said, "Luke, the philosophers say greed or lust or vanity, but for my part, I deem hypocrisy to be the greatest taint in a man's soul. Be the best that you can be, and know that you have tried to be thus, but do not ape either your betters or your inferiors if by doing so you are false to yourself." And that, of course, had been a paraphrase of Shakespeare's own adage that if a man be true to himself, he could not then be false to any man.

How easy it would be to rationalize, to tell himself that a single lapse of marital fidelity could never shatter a union so dear and so enduring as his with Lucy. The only sobering yet somewhat cheering thought was that by having recognized the dark shadow which lurked within him, as perhaps it does in every man alive, he would be the more on guard to prevent its again taking possession of his being. And thus in this solitary, brooding promenade,

130

Luke Bouchard came upon the simple yet terrifying wisdom of Socrates, who centuries before had said, "Know thyself."

Nor could he help remembering how fearful at times old Lucien had been that the traits of cruelty, violence and lechery which had appeared in Henry, Luke's own father, might have been the heritage of that older brother Jean who had been the very antithesis of Lucien Bouchard himself; how his own half-brother Mark had hated him, Luke, enough to propose a duel to the death. Was there, then, a subtle taint in the Bouchard blood which had impelled Luke, all unknowingly, to the frenetic possession of Laure? And now, on the very threshold of entering into a new life upon an unknown frontier which was certain to abound in danger and hardship, would the struggle for survival draw him into new, unprincipled, amoral acts?

He found himself outside a jeweler's little shop and went in. On the counter, he saw a little silver tray on which lay an assortment of golden lockets. One of them was in the shape of a heart with a thin, hand-wrought chain of the most exquisite workmanship. The dapper, bearded proprietor discreetly watched him as he reached for the locket and lifted it up, turning it this way and that. "Would it be possible, M'sieu, to have initials engraved on the back of this heart?" Luke asked.

"But of a certainty, M'sieu. I could have it done by tomorrow."

"If you will, then. The initials WR, together without periods."

"It shall be done to your utmost satisfaction. That locket is from France, M'sieu, as my father and I were," the little jeweler vouchsafed.

"That is where my grandfather came from, from Yves-sur-lac in Normandy."

The jeweler's face brightened. "My father also came from Normandy, M'sieu, from Harfleur. It is not far from Bolbec."

"I know," Luke Bouchard said slowly, "Bolbec was the nearest town to the provincial village in which my grandfather was born."

The jeweler shook his head. "Truly, it is said that this is a small world, M'sieu. The initials WR then, as you have directed. They stand for your family name, I presume?"

"No," Luke told him. "For our intended new home, Windhaven Range. Let me pay you now for the locket and the work."

On his way back to the hotel, Luke stopped at a flower stall and bought a large bouquet of jasmine and magnolia. He would leave them with the *maitre d'* of the dining room, so they might be placed on the table where he and Lucy and his daughter Mara would dine tonight.

It was the next evening, just before dinner, and Luke Bouchard opened the little case the jeweler had given him, took the ends of the delicate chain and gently fitted them around Lucy's slim neck, deftly locking the tiny clasp.

"Oh, Luke! How exquisite it is, and how like you to be so thoughtful!" Lucy flushed with pleasure as she cupped the little golden heart in her palm and turned it over. "The initials WR—for Windhaven Range, aren't they? What a good omen it will be for us!"

"Pray God that is so, my darling. Are you bored with having to wait so long here before we start our journey? I'm hoping that within four weeks we'll have Grandfather's legacy and can complete all our arrangements."

"The time will be all too short, my dearest husband. There'll be so much to do when we find our new home, it will be all so new and different, that our days here are a kind of second honeymoon for us. And it's so nice to have Arabella and her children with us all this time. She and James are looking forward to going along on the same steamboat. So you see, it will be as if we are all going together to start our new life, and we mustn't ever lose touch with all of our family."

"We shan't, I promise you that. Perhaps one day we'll see Ben and Fleurette and Charles and Laurette and their children as neighbors. It could happen, you know."

"Yes, indeed it could, Luke. But wherever the rest of them go, we'll always be together in our loyalty of love, and that's what makes a family strong and able to endure, no matter what the hardships are."

He lifted the locket to his lips and kissed it, and then took her in his arms and kissed her tenderly. "There's no one I know who has more loyalty and trust and love than you, Lucy. Each new day with you reminds me how lucky I was that you let me show you through Windhaven that January night of our housewarming."

She smiled up at him as she held him tightly and murmured, "I'm the lucky one, Luke. You see, even that very first night, I knew you were the man I've always wanted. Just like the Chevalier Bayard, *sans peur et sans reproche.*"

"No, Lucy, no man's beyond reproach. And there's one fear I'll always have, and that's of losing you and your love. And now, the rest will be waiting, so let's go down to dinner. I want them all to see your new locket and to say silent prayers to the success of our new Windhaven Range."

As dessert and Creole coffee—alas, a far weaker brew because of the Union blockade than New Orleans diners were wont to enjoy—were being served, a waiter approached Luke at the head of the table, and whispered, "This note was just delivered for you, M'sieu."

"Merci bien." Luke whispered back and handed him a silver coin. Then, turning to the others, he said, "Please excuse me, this note may be important."

Opening it, he read the two lines written in a woman's hand:

Captain Soltis will be here at ten this evening.
Come well before he arrives, I'll prime you for him.

Luke folded the note and put it into his waistcoat pocket, then took out his watch. It was nearly a quarter of nine.

"I hope you will all excuse me," he turned to smile at them. "This matter concerns my trying to buy weapons for our own defense when we settle in the wilds of Texas." He rose, turned to Lucy, took her hand and brought it to his lips. "I'll try not to be too late, my dearest, but you'd best not wait up for me."

"Do be careful, Luke. The very word, weapons, scares me; it brings back all the horror and suffering of the war," Lucy murmured, her face clouded with anxiety. "From whom will you buy them? Can you trust him?"

"Never fear, darling, I'll be most cautious. From what I've been told, the man's a greedy profiteer. But I'll see to it that he doesn't take advantage of me." Again he kissed her hand. Then, raising his voice, declared, "Good night to all of you, and I'll see you in the morning. Our plans are going forward, and I'm most optimistic about them."

Again it was the liveried doorman, recognizing him as he got out of the hansom cab, who welcomed him to The Union House and opened the front door for him to enter. Mitzi took his hat and cape, giving him a roguish smile, and said, "Mam'selle Laure is waiting for you in the office of the *patron,* M'sieu. If you wish, I shall be glad to show you the way."

Luke Bouchard could not help smiling back at this charming little *soubrette* whose appeal was so refreshingly playful. He gave her a courtly bow, a hand over his heart, and riposted, "I am sure I could ask for no lovelier guide, but I know the way already. Thank you for your trouble, Mitzi."

He ascended the stairs and went directly to John Brunton's office, knocked at the door, and was admitted by Laure Prindeville. This time, however, she was dressed as befitted her role of madam of the establishment, in a full-length green bombazine dress whose flounced skirt thrust out behind to proclaim her wearing of a cage-shaped, steel-wired petticoat. Her hair had been restyled into an imposing pompadour, giving her an aspect not only of height but also of severity.

He found himself silent before her, and he was disconcerted by the sudden flush in his cheeks as she calmly scrutinized him, but she put him at ease by coming directly to the point: "I'm glad that you did come early, *mon ami.* This officer I told you about, he's giving up his commission next week and going back home to Cincinnati. So this is the best possible time for you to arrange your business with him."

134

"Thank you for helping me, Laure. May I ask if John is on the premises this evening?"

An amused twinkle softened the cool scrutiny of her green eyes, and her lips twitched in the hint of a faint smile as she replied, "Of course you may ask. He went to dine at the house of an old friend and then to play chess. Oh, that reminds me—we're going to be married a week from tomorrow, and John wished me to ask you if you would do us the honor of standing up as his best man."

"Nothing could give me greater pleasure, Laure."

Now her smile was teasing as she softly murmured, "You said that from the heart, I am sure, *mon ami*. Have no fear, I shall make John a very good wife. And you're thinking that once I'm married, you'll be out of danger so far as I'm concerned."

"I didn't mean that—" he stumbled, furious with himself because he was crimson-faced before her teasing mockery.

Instantly she was contrite. "Forgive me again, dear Luke. But I mean it, I truly do. I shan't ever forget what happened, and maybe for the rest of my life I'll wonder what it would have been like to have found a man like you before the war, before all the horrible things that happened to Papa and me. And that's the last I'll say on that subject. Now to business. Do sit down, and this time I'll bring *you* a glass of wine."

He watched her, as she moved with stately decorum to the decanter, poured out a glass for each of them and brought it to him. Then, seating herself at John Brunton's desk and turning the chair so that she could face him, she resumed: "George Soltis is a fat, arrogant and greedy boor. He's a schemer, too, so be on your guard. Pay him only a little of what he may ask for what you want, and don't give him the rest until you've safely secured what you've bought. John has heard some nasty rumors about him."

"I'm grateful for that information, Laure. I bought with me a *roleau* of a thousand dollars in gold."

"Give him only a small part of that as a payment in good faith. But there's one thing more, and it may be embarrassing for you—I'm sure it will be, knowing what I now know about you, my dear friend." She turned her face from him, lifted her wine glass and sipped at it, and now he could see that her own satiny cheeks were vividly colored.

He waited till Laure had set her glass down and coughed delicately. "You see, *mon cher,* he's very coarse in his ways. He's a *voyeur*—do you know what that means?"

"The word means one who watches, Laure. I think I understand."

"Not completely, Luke. He's coming for a rendezvous with Elaine, and he's engaged our *salle des miroirs.*"

"And so?"

She turned to look directly at him, and again her lips were curved in that faintly derisive smile which had so inflamed him that never-to-be-forgotten night. "Sometimes, when the good captain is in his cups, he'll boast about his virility and how irresistible he is to the fair sex. Several times, he's actually demanded that some other client of our establishment accompany him to witness his, shall we say, performance. And it's very possible that he'll ask that of you tonight, especially if he's in a good mood because he thinks he's made a very profitable deal."

"*Mon Dieu!* That's gross! The man is shameless!" Luke exclaimed, his face again reddening.

"Of course he is, *mon cher.* But he's a stubborn idiot, and if you're the least bit standoffish, he's just as likely to fly into a rage and try to have you thrown out of the house. And then, of course, you'd lose your chance to get the weapons you need. I say all this because Elaine has told me that it's happened several times, and even she, for all she enjoys a good romp in bed because she's a lusty wench, is offended by his behavior. Still and all, he tosses his money around like a drunken sailor, and as John's already told you, his main reason for running a house like this and catering to men like George Soltis is to forearm himself against the future when the Reconstruction starts in New Orleans."

"Yes, I understand that. Well then, it seems I must play a role myself tonight. What would you have me do?"

"If he does invite you to follow him into the *salle des*

miroirs, mon cher, I'm afraid you'll have to take one of our young ladies with you."

"Oh come now—that's impossible!" Luke rose, scowling with embarrassment.

"Wait a bit, dear Luke. You said yourself you'd have to play a role. But that doesn't mean you'll have to imitate him. Now you're blushing again like a schoolboy. Yes, I'm very glad that I'm going to be John Brunton's very respectable wife very soon, or else I might find it hard to resist teasing you as much as I do. No, seriously, all you'll need to do is perhaps kiss and cuddle your partner while you both watch our valiant captain demonstrate his prowess with Elaine. And I think I know the very partner for you, our adorable little Mitzi. Do you know, that forward minx asked me the other night if I could arrange a little *entretien* between the two of you, and she insisted that she would be insulted if you offered her a single *sou*. She's extremely fond of you, it appears."

"This begins to sound like some bawdy farce by the Marquis de Sade himself," Luke irritatedly snorted.

"That's exactly it, a farce and nothing more. If there were any other source of getting you your weapons, I'd be the last in the world to suggest you lend yourself to what I know will be distressing for you."

"It seems I have no choice, Laure. All right then."

"Good! Now he'll be here promptly at ten, and I'm going to usher him into the little salon just off the parlor where Elaine will be waiting for him. You'll be there with Mitzi, drinking champagne. I'll tell him that you wanted to meet him, and then the rest is up to you. *Ça va?*"

"*Ça va bien, j'espère,*" Luke Bouchard sighed as he bent his head and brought Laure Prindeville's hand to his lips.

"Oh, oh, *ça sera tres drôle, n'est-ce pas,* M'sieu Luke?" Mitzi giggled as she led Luke Bouchard by the hand into the ornately furnished private salon just off the parlor, closed the door and gestured to him to take his ease in one of the loveseats. This done, with another provocative giggle, she scurried over and plumped herself down in his lap, winding her arms around his neck and murmuring,

"I've wanted to do this from the very first time I saw you, *c'est vrai, crois moi*, M'sieu!"

Nervously, Luke shifted himself in the deep seat, and awkwardly placed his hands against Mitzi's waist to steady her. The petite maid of The Union House had, for this occasion, put on a stunning black satin peignoir, under which she wore a silk chemise and two lace-trimmed petticoats, clockwork black net hose and dainty silver-cloth slippers. With her pert, heartshaped face and enormous eyes she hardly looked her eighteen years. Not quite five feet in height, her body was that of a pocket Venus, and the alluring French perfume which she had liberally applied made Luke Bouchard uneasily loosen his cravat as he was made fully conscious of his dainty burden. "You're very sweet, *ma poupée*," he murmured, staring at the door of the salon and hoping that Captain George Soltis would appear without more delay. Whimsically, he found himself wondering just how his grandfather would have reacted to so scandalous a comedy as he was about to play.

Suddenly the door was opened by Laure herself. Moving ahead of her was a stocky man in his late thirties, with bushy sideburns and a waxed mustache, wearing the uniform of a captain in the Union Quartermaster Corps. Behind him, her face blandly disdainful, was the same young red-haired woman whom Luke had observed in the parlor, on the evening of his reunion with John Brunton. She carried an ivory fan in one hand, which she repeatedly opened and closed, then tapped her mouth to hide a yawn.

"Captain, this is the gentleman I mentioned to you, M'sieu Luke Bouchard." Laure made the introduction as she indicated Luke with a graceful wave of her hand.

"Well now," Captain George Soltis sniggered, "I'd say this friend of yours rates high in the establishment, Mam'selle Laure! I myself, as you well know, have often asked you to pair me with that little vixen of a Mitzi, but you've always said she wasn't one of the regulars."

"And she isn't, Captain. But it seems she's taken a fancy to M'sieu Bouchard. You should know, gallant that

138

you are, that there's no accounting for a woman's caprices of the heart," Laure wittily observed.

Luke was crimson with embarrassment, for Mitzi remained perched on his lap with her arms still clinging around his neck. He whispered to her, and with a giggle, she extricated herself and dropped a curtsy to the smirking officer.

"Mam'selle Laure said that you had some business with me, Mr. Bouchard, sir. Perhaps we'd best have the ladies wait elsewhere while we discuss it. Might I ask first where you're from and whom you represent?"

"I'm from near Montgomery, in Alabama, Captain Soltis, and I represent my famliy and my workers who are going to Texas to raise cattle."

The officer's forehead creased into an unpleasant frown. "One of those damned Rebs, are you?"

"Not entirely, Captain Soltis. My grandfather came from France, lived with the Creeks, was given land which he later bought from the government, produced cotton and food crops, and never owned a slave, no more than did I myself. The blacks who have come with me were freed long before President Lincoln ordered their emancipation, and they are to be paid wages for their labor, decent wages such as any loyal, industrious worker is entitled to."

"Fine-sounding, I'll give you that, Mr. Bouchard." Captain George Soltis seated himself in a loveseat opposite Luke. The three young women, meanwhile, discreetly withdrew, closing the door behind them. "Now then, sir, I'm sure you can show me credentials? And I assume that you're ready to take the loyalty oath that President Johnson is shortly going to demand of every damned Reb."

"I can furnish you with ample credentials, Captain Soltis. John Brunton can vouch for me also. More to the point, my grandfather left me a very large sum in gold in an English bank, a draft for which is now en route to New Orleans, and I've brought some earnest money along with me, knowing that we might discuss our business in private here."

"You come to the point, I'll say that for you, Mr.

Bouchard," the captain chuckled. "So you're going to raise cattle in Texas, are you? You're sure you're not going to help that emperor whom wily old Napoleon III has put on the throne of Mexico and maybe go to join Marshal Bazaine's troops, which happens to be the only reason that Austrian fop still holds his throne?"

"It's true that I'm of French descent, Captain, but my grandfather left France because he foresaw the revolution against the monarchy. I myself believe that Mexico ought to be a republic, and I agree with you in your appraisal of Napoleon III. No, one branch of my family is bound for Galveston as soon as naval hostilities are ended there, to take a post with a cousin who produces cotton. The rest of us will go there, buy land and start a ranch. I'm sure you'll agree that this country will need plenty of beef as the frontiers are pushed farther and farther westward."

"No doubt about it. And you're smart if you don't get mixed up with that Mexican empire business. Benito Juarez is the acknowledged president of that country, and maybe all you Rebs hoped that by putting Maximilian on a throne the Froggies were going to take your side in the fracas we won so handily. I'll tell you something in confidence, though, Mr. Bouchard—Napoleon III won't be able to keep Bazaine and his troops there forever, and the *Juaristas* are getting stronger every day. Once the Froggies pull out, I wouldn't give you one of your Confederate greenbacks for the chance of poor old Maximilian."

"Again I'm inclined to agree with you, Captain Soltis."

The stocky officer grinned and crossed his legs, waggling his booted foot as he contemplated it with exaggerated attention. "You know, Mr. Bouchard, for a Johnny Reb, you're a most agreeable fellow. We might just be able to do some business after all, that's if you've got gold as you say you do. Now a draft is fine, but I take it yours hasn't come yet."

"I've brought along a *rouleau* of gold in the amount of a thousand dollars, Captain Soltis, as a down payment in good faith."

"That sounds still better. Mind you, I'm not saying I could give you all you want, but you won't get anything until it's paid for in full."

140

"I expect to pay you the balance upon your delivery of the arms I require."

"We're getting along just fine, Mr. Bouchard, just fine. Now tell me, what do you think you're going to need to keep you safe in the wilds of Texas?"

"I'd like to get the newest repeating rifles. The single-shot breech-loading rifles are accurate at long range, but they're more suited to sharpshooting in a war. We'll need to get off a great many shots in a hurry if we're besieged by Indians or bandits."

"You're a mighty smart man for a Reb, Mr. Bouchard, I'll give you that. Muzzle-loaders were mighty popular with us boys in blue at the start of the war, but we cut back on them long before it ended. Why, you can get piles of them for about fifty cents now. What you'll need is the new Spencer repeater. It's a breech-loader, all right, and it weighs just ten pounds and it's forty-two inches long. It handles eight shots, seven in the magazine and one in the chamber. You pull the trigger, then you cock the hammer each time and lever off the rest of the shots. It's accurate, too. It's a .52 caliber with rimfire cartridges. One of these days some gunsmith's going to come up with a center-fire metal cartridge and then you'll really see some shooting. Yes, I can get you some of those Spencers and maybe a few Sharpe carbines—they're shorter and more compact at closer range when you're in a hurry."

"And perhaps some of the Colt six-shooters, the .36 caliber as hand arms, Soltis."

"For a peaceful man, Mr. Bouchard, you know a little something about firearms. Well, as long as you tell me you're not going to try to start the war all over again or join up with Maximilian's palace guard, I guess we can do a little business. You'd best take the 1851 Navy Colt, with its Smith and Wesson cartridges. Some of those other pepperpots don't have rifled cartridges, so when you pull the trigger, you might find all the other shots exploding at the same time—messy and dangerous. How many rifles and carbines do you figure you'll need?"

Luke thought rapidly, closing his eyes as he figured in his head: "I'd like to get a dozen Spencers, about five carbines and half a dozen six-shooters. And of course ammunition."

The stocky officer uncrossed his legs, stood up abruptly and scowled, tugging at the tips of his black mustache. "That'll run you into plenty of gold, Mr. Bouchard. If you don't mind spending a little more, I might just be able to get you some real new Spencer repeating carbines—just a few of them, mind you, because they're being made under contract for our side these days by the Burnside Rifle Company. That model's a seven-shot repeater chambered for the .50 caliber .56/50 Spencer rimfire cartridge. And you'll need some of the Blakeslee cartridge boxes, the best there are these days. They're leather-covered, and inside you'll find wooden blocks drilled with tin holes into which you can fit a tin magazine tube with seven cartridges to refill the butt magazines of your Spencers. They've got a kick like a mule to them, both the rifles and the carbines, but they'll do the job for you. Let's see now—" he closed his eyes, doing his own mental figuring, a greedy smile on his sensual lips—"I'll take the thousand in gold right now, and three thousand more when everything's ready. I'll have to arrange to get it to you where not too many other people will see what sort of business we're transacting— you understand me, Mr. Bouchard?"

"Perhaps it could be delivered out near the swamps, near the house of John Dewton. My blacks are staying there for the time being." Luke realized the price was extortionate; but he had already appraised the captain and knew that haggling would be futile.

"I know where it is. Excellent! Well now," the officer came forward and held out his hand, "let's shake on it. I tell you what, Mr. Bouchard. I'm a man that loves company, and I always celebrate a deal with the best champagne in the house and the prettiest, fanciest girl who knows how to give a man a real cuddle, if you get my meaning."

"I think I do, Captain. Permit me the privilege of being your host this evening—your champagne and your entertainment will be on me." Luke Bouchard opened his frockcoat to disclose a money belt, and took from it several bright pieces of gold, which he cupped in his palm and showed to the Union officer whose eyes glinted.

"Capital, Mr. Bouchard. Just one thing more—it's a little habit of mine, and I hope you won't find it amiss. When I poke a girl to celebrate a deal of this kind, I like to have a discriminating partner enjoy his own pleasure in my company. As it happens, I've engaged Brunton's special mirrored room for this evening, and that tasty new redhead you saw me with is, I do declare, the hottest girl in all New Orleans. Now why don't you come along with little Mitzi, and perhaps Laney and I can help stoke your own fires, Mr. Bouchard sir."

Luke was hard-put to suppress his distaste as he blandly responded, "I must confess, Captain, that this would be an entirely new experience for me."

The stocky officer guffawed and clapped him on the back. "Why, then, Johnny Reb, I'll try to outdo myself just for your benefit. I'd say it's fitting and proper that a Union officer help instruct a secessionist in how to go about the business of enjoyable living after a dirty, bloody war."

He swung open the door of the salon, and saw Mitzi and Elaine waiting out in the hallway. "We mustn't keep the ladies waiting, eh, Mr. Bouchard? Come on, Laney, my friend here is going to pay your fee. Mitzi, go fetch a couple of bottles of the best champagne—Mr. Bouchard's standing us all treat tonight. And now, you red-haired slut, show me to this fancy room where we'll do our best to heat up the tired blood of this Southerner!"

The redhead, who was nearly as tall as Luke Bouchard himself, tapped her closed ivory fan against the officer's cheek and huskily murmured, "But I'm sure you know the way by now, George dear. Come along, then." She led him down the carpeted hallway to the room at the very front of the second-floor landing. She took out a silver key, fitted it into the lock of the broad door and opened it. Mitzi, clinging to Luke's arm, giggled and whispered, "This will be a treat for me too, M'sieu Luke, I've only been in here once or twice to serve champagne. Oh, *mon Dieu,* that reminds me, I must go get the bottles the captain ordered. Make yourself comfortable, *chéri,* and I'll be back *tout de suite.*"

Luke Bouchard had dropped the golden coins into Elaine's little sewn-on pocket, and she flashed him a quick, sympathetic smile, her large, hazel eyes swiftly appraising him. Her face was oval, her cheekbones high-set, with a dainty aquiline nose whose thin, sensuous wings subtly flared to denote the characteristically mercurial temperament of a redhead. Her thick, flaming-red curls covered the nape of her slender neck, as well as the top of her high-arching forehead, and atop her head they seemed like the tangled serpents of the legendary Medusa: there was a feral, primal, earthiness to her, blended with a cool poise which even Luke Bouchard, now more than ever resolved to hold himself in check, found to be disconcertingly provocative.

He caught his breath at the startling decor of this room, surely the first of its kind he had ever seen. It had all the baroque splendor of the palace of Versailles, from the thick carpeting as well as Oriental rugs and ornately quilted throw rugs, to the majestic double-sized bed with four tall posters and a Jacob's ladder at one side. The ceiling was entirely of mirrors which concealed sturdy masonry above, and the large bay window which looked out onto the street below had been shuttered and the thick purple draperies were drawn. On each side of those curtains, the walls were likewise covered with mirrors as were those behind and directly opposite the bed. Luke could see his own reflection across the room and, as he glanced upwards, saw his own startled face reflected back at him.

To his left was an enormous backless couch, covered with lace-trimmed poufs; and in front of the mock fireplace was a huge, thickly upholstered loveseat covered in blazing red which vied with Elaine's own tousled curls.

Already the mustachioed captain was divesting himself of his coat, and Elaine attentively knelt to tug off his boots as he leaned back with his hands gripping the top of the doubly thick mattress to support himself, greedily staring down at her, then glancing over at Luke with a bawdy wink. "The privileges of the conqueror, eh, Mr.

Bouchard? Laney here knows how to treat a poor humble captain as if I were that womanizing Marshal Bazaine."

Though tempted to remark that this was a case of the pot's calling the kettle black, Luke wisely held his tongue and permitted himself only a politely assenting murmur as he uncomfortably stood waiting, not exactly sure what would be demanded of him.

Yet before Mitzi could return with the two bottles of champagne in a bucket filled with ice, wheeling a little cart which conveyed the bucket, four crystal goblets of Venetian fabrication, and a silver plate of *petit fours,* he watched incredulously as Elaine, her face expressionless and her manner quietly deferential, stripped the paunchy, hairy officer naked.

"Ah, here's the bubbly at last, it took you long enough, Mitzi girl!" Captain George Soltis chuckled, in evidently rare good humor. "Now then, Mr. Bouchard, since we've agreed on a down payment, and I've a fancy for that money belt of yours, whyn't you make me a present of it? I'll wear it now, if you've no objection. And you, Laney, put my boots back on. A man likes to die with his boots on, even if it's in bed, eh, Mr. Bouchard?"

Numbly, as if he were standing aside and observing himself in a dream, Luke unfastened the money belt and moved mutely toward the huge bed. Already the officer's manhood was in obscene evidence as he chuckled again, took the belt and clasped it round his own thick waist, then thrust out his right foot while the kneeling redhead tugged back on the boot, and then the other.

Mitzi hastened to pour a brimming goblet and bring it to the naked man, who, his left hand stroking Elaine's neck, reached out to take it and, with a lewd wink, demanded, "Mitzi, you see all the money I've got in this belt round me? Can I bribe you to share this bed with me for a spell if our good friend Mr. Bouchard has no objections?"

"*Hélas, non, merci, m'sieu le capitaine,*" Mitzi charmingly shook her head, her piquant face wearing an expression of profound regret. "Madam Laure made it very clear that I belonged to this gentleman for the evening. *Je le regrette infiniment,* but she is in charge and I must do as she tells me. You will forgive me, *mon brave général?*"

"That's the best promotion I've ever had, you tricksy little French bitch, you," Captain George Soltis guffawed, then drained his goblet with a single gulp. Mitzi took it from him and refilled it promptly. Then she filled goblets for herself and Luke, and brought them back to him, whispering, "We shall watch from the loveseat in front of the fireplace, M'sieu Luke, it will please him." And then, with a little glint in her eyes, she whispered for only him to hear, "If M'sieu wishes, nothing would give me greater *plaisir* than to give him *plaisir* in return. *Je parle du coeur, vraiment!*"

Luke found himself blushing as he accepted the goblet from the charming *soubrette* and allowed himself to be led over to the loveseat in front of the mock fireplace. Mitzi sat down beside him and leaned against him, sipping her champagne. She watched with glowing eyes as Captain Soltis sprawled on his back on the bed, his booted heels digging down into the sheets, while Elaine calmly unbuttoned her gown and let it slither down to her ankles. She was naked save for black silk stockings which clambered to midthigh and were held there by purple satin, elastic rosette garters. Taking her ivory fan, she bent to the smirking naked officer and, spreading the ivory wands, began to touch him lightly over his hairy paps and belly, then caressed the insides of his thighs down to the knees and back again, while he moaned and arched in feverish anticiaption.

"Come on now, you feisty roan mare you, see how well you can ride this Union stallion!" he panted. Elaine knelt beside him now, bending her head and brushing her flaming curls against his side, his armpit, his chest and belly, while he clenched his fists in avid torment. Luke tried not to look, but from everywhere in the room and the ceiling came the pale luster of Elaine's naked body, the insolent firm ovals of her jutting buttocks, with the tempting glimpse of the pouting pink maw of her sex between her willowy thighs, the ripe, pear-shaped globes of her breasts swaying pendant as she hovered beside the sprawled officer.

146

"C'est amusant, et très méchant, n'est-ce pas, mon amour?" Mitzi whispered, and Luke felt her soft little hand grope along his lower thigh. He gripped her wrist to halt her caress, fearful of its consequences. He could only stare bemused at the bed beyond him, while from the mirrors the images of Elaine and the captain forced themselves upon his senses.

"Que c'est drôle, comme il fait l'amour, M'sieu Luke! *N'as-tu pas le désir de l'imiter avec moi?"* Mitzi whispered to him, pressing against him. He battled the demon of lust which struggled within him as she wriggled onto his lap, throwing her arms around his neck. "Oooh, *vois-tu ça? Ça m'excite, vraiment, mais pas toi, chéri?"* she hissed as Elaine sank down upon her groaning partner, tensing and flattening herself. He watched as Soltis reached over Elaine's shoulder, wrested away her fan, and began to smack it against her buttocks and upper thighs.

He dared not answer Mitzi's sly question: despite his revulsion at the coarse behavior of this man whom he was forced to court only because of his need for the weapons, Luke Bouchard felt himself almost hypnotized by what ensued before him, unable to take his eyes from Elaine's lascivious gyrations as the feverishly roused officer exhorted her to an even swifter pace by cursing her obscenely and beating even faster her now vividly reddened posterior and thighs with the ivory implement of flagellation. Luke's hands gripped Mitzi's wrists like a vise to prevent her overwhelming his tormented body with more direct attempts to make him accede to her blandishments, as he stared, motionless, beads of sweat dotting his lined forehead.

Now, in their frenzy, the couple on the luxurious bed rolled back and forth, over and over, their cries of passion pounding through his brain. Only when they stopped could he close his eyes and tremble with the knowledge that this time he had forced the demon back into sullen retreat, that this time there would be no such abandon of self and psyche and honor as there had been with Laure.

"You wore me to a frazzle, you sweet red-haired bitch," Captain George Soltis said languidly as he rolled away from the naked young courtesan. "Now get me more champagne, we'll rest a bit, then see if you can do me as nicely the next time." Lifting his head, he chuckled lewdly at Luke Bouchard: "Thanks, Johnny Reb. Now I'd say our little arrangement is properly launched. When you've got the rest of the money, send word to me through Laney here, she'll know where to find me."

"Thank you, Captain. It should be within a few weeks." Luke uneasily but gently pushed Mitzi off his lap as she turned to pout at him. Rising, drawing a deep breath, he added, "I must thank you for an instructive evening, Captain, and apologize for having an engagement which will deprive me of the rest of it. I bid you a happy night."

CHAPTER THIRTEEN

Luke Bouchard, dressed like an elegant Southern gentleman in his best frockcoat, ruffled shirt and flowing cravat, stood behind John Brunton in the Little Church of the Angels on Lemaire Street on the afternoon of May 26, 1865, as the former banker took his marriage vows with beautiful Laure Prindeville before the kindly old priest. Lucy, as well as Lucien Edmond and Mara, Sybella and Maybelle watched from the pews. It was Luke's duty to hand his friend the simple gold band which John Brunton placed on Laure's finger. As he did so, Laure looked at him and her lips wreathed in a sudden dazzling smile; then she turned to bestow it on her husband-to-be as if it had been meant for him and not Luke. And only by that sign did she remind Luke of that secret which they shared and would never divulge.

The wedding supper at Moreau's, held in a private room off the main dining chamber, was sobered by the news that on this very day General Kirby Smith had surrendered to the Union General Canby all the remaining Confederate forces west of the Mississippi, thus putting a formal end to Southern resistance. Now all the fighting was over, save for the diehard resistance of a valiant Confederate force who still held the seaport of Galveston. No news of any surrender had as yet been heard, and so Arabella and James Hunter and their two children would have to wait in New Orleans until the port was opened to peaceful commerce.

After John and Laure Brunton had bidden *au revoir* to their convivial guests and taken a carriage to the honeymoon suite awaiting them at the Exchange Hotel, Lucy turned to Luke and murmured, "Such a lovely, witty young woman. It's obvious that she adores him. I suppose some people would say that the difference in ages is wrong, but John's so full of life and zest. I do hope they'll be happy and have a long life together."

"Yes, Lucy my darling, she's beautiful and, as you said, intelligent too. Not unlike yourself, my dear. Do you know that on the very first evening I met you and we began to talk about books we liked, I knew that you were the wife I wanted for the rest of my life."

She put her hand in his under the table and gave him so happy a look that he knew he could forget his momentary lapse. Now Laure was forever out of his reach, even if he had wished to explore the dark pleasures of conjugal infidelity. John Brunton would be able to make her happy. She would find in him not only a still quite capable lover, but also a father-protector to console her for the tragic suicide of her own father who had been John Brunton's friend. It was, indeed, the happiest possible ending.

And now also it was a time to keep his mind alert and ready for their journey to Texas, for within a few weeks the draft from England would be in his hands, the wagons and the arms and ammuniton ready for delivery. He and his family would be isolated newcomers in a sparsely populated land which was part of the United States, yet still uncharted over hundreds of desolate miles, still as fiercely independent in spirit as it had been when a handful of men at the Alamo had defied the overwhelming might of General Santa Anna.

Moreover, there was a new and most significant factor for him to consider in his migration. Though he despised

Captain Soltis, he paid heed to what he had said about Maximilian in Mexico and his support by French troops. In the New Orleans *Times-Picayune,* a story had appeared just the other day from the headquarters of Ulysses S. Grant, to the effect that he was sending General Sheridan to Texas with orders to assemble a large military force on the Rio Grande with the object of driving the French power out of Mexico. And Luke himself was certain that the French would not risk a war with the United States; the spendthrift Napoleon III would this time think twice before pouring out what remained in his dwindling treasury to risk a conflict whose outcome would surely destroy France as a European power for long years to come. Luke knew he would have to learn all he could about Mexico since what happened below the border of the Rio Grande could very well bring disaster to his future Windhaven Range.

Old John Dewton had carefully examined the mournful gray dog which Djamba had purchased from its angry owner after the animal had refused to challenge the bear. Zeke's brutal kick had, fortunately, only bruised a rib; and within a few days the dog had made friends with everyone in the rickety old house on the edge of the swamps. Mostly, it followed Djamba.

"You done got yerself a friend in dat dere houn' dog, Djamba boy," John Dewton cackled. "He don't pay no heed to no one else. Dat dog might come in real handy where you gwine. Mebbe you could even teach him how to run after de cattle 'n git 'em to go de way you wants 'em to go."

"That's what I've been thinking, John," Djamba nodded. "Of course, I'll have to try him out and see if he's afraid. I think we should give him a name he can come to, to give him back his pride, and then to see what he can do."

"Sounds lak dat make good sense, Djamba. Wut you plannin' on callin' him?"

"Jubal. It is a name I came upon in the Bible that Mr. Luke gave me to read many years ago. It is the name of a good man who took pride in his work before the Lord.

Maybe with such a name and a new chance, Jubal here will show what courage and skill he really has."

"Ah see you been teachin' him already, throwin' sticks n' sich fer him to fetch. And he yo friend foah life, any fool kin see dat, Djamba."

"Sometimes when a man is alone and there are no other men around, an animal will stand by him and take a man's place by its friendship and its loyalty. I have seen this in my own country when I was young, when a boy from our village who was crippled by a leopard found a baby monkey and made a pet of it. There were those of us who looked down on the boy because he could no longer walk straight and would never be a warrior, and the monkey seemed to know this and it made the boy feel how much it needed him, and so the boy was happy and did not mind the cruel things that stupid and thoughtless people of our village would say to him." He smiled, his eyes half-closed, as if projecting himself back to that primitive land where once he had been a young king with his life before him, and his hand again stroked the ears of the hound squatting patiently before him.

"Later that boy became the witch doctor of our village, one of the wisest of men, and those who had once mocked him and hated him because he was a cripple came humbly to him to seek his advice and to make spells that would save them from the evil spirits. And it was the monkey which made him feel that he was not despised and that he could use his brain instead of his arms and legs and so become even more respected than the fiercest warrior among us. Yes, John, it may well be that Jubal here will show us the courage deep within him and be a friend to some of us when we are most in need of one."

Djamba rose and gestured to his son Lucas: "Do you remember, Lucas, how on that afternoon when we walked to John's house, we saw those balconies with their rows of spikes shaped like a fan?"

"I remember, Father, and how you said they could be made into spears."

"That's true. And Simata has said that perhaps we can find an old house in which no one lives now, where we can take some of these spikes and make spears. We can take the spikes to a blacksmith who will shorten the shafts to the right length. Then we will split strong pieces of bamboo placing a spike-pointed piece between each of the two halves of a bamboo shoot, binding them with cord, or better still, wire."

The young redbone had come across the living room of the old house in time to hear the latter part of this conversation. "Simata will help make the spears," he said. "They must have good balance in the hand so that when one throws them, they will carry true to the mark. I have seen such spears made in the land of my father. There was good hunting when my father rode with the Kiowa warriors, there was meat for the fire and to be dried and smoked and kept for the days when game was scarce."

"Do you know of an old house where there is such a balcony from which we might take these spearheads, Simata?" Djamba asked.

"Simata knows. Not far from that place where you and your friends came to help me, there is a very old house and no one lives in there now. People say that ghosts come to walk in it at night, and so no one goes near it. I will show this place to you, and we shall make good strong spears."

On the night of the very day that John Brunton and Laure Prindeville were married, the young half-breed led Djamba and Lucas back along the way which they had taken to John Dewton's house and turned southward at the Rue de Mousselines. Here there were isolated old houses made of heavily walled red brick, two stories, with Spanish style courtyards. "It is the very last house along this street," Simata said. "Blind Tom, who sells pralines as I sold my mother's meat pies, told me once that an old woman lived here for many years, locking herself up inside and cruelly treating her female slaves. When I asked him why this was, Blind Tom told me that many years before that, this woman's husband had been unfaithful to her with a girl of color and run away with her to Natchez. So she punished all the other slaves because of what he and that girl had done."

Around the house was a crumbling brick wall no higher

than the waist of a man, and Simata pointed to a breach in it.

The trio passed through the jagged hole and came upon a giant cypress tree which seemed to guard the side of the old house. Behind it was what remained of a once beautifully tended garden set off in a kind of patio with cracked stone tile making a footpath between beds of rank weeds and dead stalks which had once been flowers. Simata pointed to the side of the house, along whose second floor there ran an exquisite balcony framed in ornate cast iron with patterns of flowers, leaves, acorns, many arrows, vines and even trees. The floor of the balcony was of white sandstone, now crumbling, and here and there had eroded to expose the base of the iron shafts made by some now nameless *forgeron,* perhaps a gifted slave.

"The arrows are sharp, they will make good heads for the spears," Djamba agreed. And then he turned to Simata and added, "In my village, the witch doctor—what you would call the medicine man—said once that if that which is linked with evil is used for good, the evil will be wiped out just as the heavy rain washes away the dirt and cobwebs of decay."

The three of them tried the door of the old house and found it open. Ascending to the second floor, and cautiously stepping out onto the stone balcony, Djamba grasped the center of the cast-iron railing and wrenched at it. Part of it came loose. All three tugged and pulled until it fell crashing to the ground below.

"We can carry this to the blacksmith, who can separate the sections with arrows for our spears," Djamba declared.

"I know such a man not far from here, who works many times late into the night. Perhaps he will still be there if we go to him now," Simata suggested.

An hour later, Djamba nodded with satisfaction as the blacksmith finished his work. "It is good. Here are the heads from which we can make six strong spears, their wands long enough for good balance in throwing once we have enclosed the lower half in a strong bamboo pole."

"They are sharp," Simata agreed, his eyes shining as he

remembered his boyhood days riding beside his father. "They will bring down much game, and if enemies attack, they may save our lives."

"Or, better still, the lives of those most dear to us," Djamba said softly.

CHAPTER FOURTEEN

Three days after General Kirby Smith surrendered, President Andrew Johnson issued a proclamation of amnesty, "to all ordinary persons who were in the late rebellion and who will take the oath of allegiance to the United States, the exceptions being Confederate officers and persons worth over $20,000." On the same day, the reconstruction of North Carolina began through Presidential proclamation, with the appointment of W. W. Holden as provisional governor. The President had already formally recognized the appointment of Francis H. Pierpont as the new governor of Virginia. Thus began the final events of this long, bloody and tragic war.

Exactly one week after the marriage of John Brunton and Laure Prindeville, the Confederate force which had so valiantly defended the last seaport stronghold of Galveston ran up the white flag of surrender, marking the official end of the war. Now all hostilities on every sea and land front had ceased; now would come the inevitable struggles of reconstruction, not peaceful reconstruction such as Lincoln had wished, and as Johnson was trying to bring about, but instead a radical rebuilding shaped by a spiteful few in power, and aimed at punitive reprisal.

As soon as Luke Bouchard read of the Presidential amnesty, he went to see John Brunton. "I know exactly what's on your mind, Luke, the former banker said. "You're thinking about that draft for $50,000 exceeding the limit and marking you as a dangerous rebel, aren't you? Look, Luke, when it comes through, take your son Lucien Edmond and your stepmother down to the New Orleans bank on which it will be drawn. Put it into three drafts, so that not one will exceed the $20,000 limit. Technically, then, no one can bother you."

"I confess that that solution occurred to me, but I was afraid that the technicality of three drafts wouldn't work. But I am relieved that you feel it will. Perhaps the new provisional government here won't be out to confiscate property illegally, as some have feared."

John Brunton smiled. "My feeling is that now Andy Johnson is starting to name provisional governors and re-establish Federal administration in the rest of the Confederacy, our unsavory Beast of New Orleans will soon be pulling out along with all of his greedy crew. Maybe we can get back on an even keel within the next several years. I've been talking to Daniel Coureux, whose father left him one of the largest banks in this city. The old man was smart enough, like your grandfather Lucien, to keep his money in gold in London, and Daniel intends to re-open his bank, perhaps in partnership with me. Both of us have excellent contacts, and he's not quite half my age, so the combination ought to make us prosper. Now I meant to ask you, what sort of deal did you make with that fellow Soltis?"

"I gave him a thousand dollars, and he'll get three thousand more as soon as the draft comes through. Yes, I know, even Laure told me to be on my guard against him, but I could tell that if I tried to haggle or plead lack of funds, he'd either raise his price or else show no interest in doing any business at all with me."

"Well, the price of the commodity depends to a large extent on how badly a man needs it, I'll agree to that. Only be very careful when he finally delivers your weapons and you're ready to hand over the rest of the cash, Luke. I've heard a few more unpleasant rumors about our man who enjoys the mirrored room so much—that must have been a disgusting exhibition for you to have to sit through, by the way."

Luke flushed and lowered his eyes. "I shouldn't care to do it again, that's for certain. Perhaps it taught me something too, something useful even about myself."

"Well, I will say that you broke poor little Mitzi's heart. She was so certain that you'd be so inflamed watching those two go at it that you'd forget all your backwoods morality and make love to her the way she's dreamed you would ever since she first saw you."

"Tell her for me that I'm deeply flattered and honored, and also remind her of the French proverb that for many, the pleasure of anticipation far exceeds the realization."

"That sounds exactly like what old Lucien might have said in your place," John Brunton laughed. Then his face sobered: "What I was getting at about Soltis, Luke, was that he's sold a few consignments of weapons that he doesn't have to account for and in at least one instance I've heard about, he recouped not only his money but also got the weapons back. He's got a couple of bully boys who help him deliver his merchandise, though he doesn't take part in the actual delivery himself so that he can't be involved if anything goes wrong. I'd suggest that when you meet with him or his emissaries, you get your hands on some weapons in advance just in case there's treachery."

"I'd thought of that, and now that you've told me your suspicions, I'll take precautions. Those two young fellows I met down at the levee, Andy Haskins and Joe Duvray, will surely be able to help me in that respect. And Djamba tells me that he's been to a blacksmith and turned some abandoned wrought-iron balcony framework into half-a-dozen beautifully balanced throwing spears."

"That's all very well, Luke, but Soltis' bullies will have the latest rifles and pistols. I wish you'd get some, too. You'd best set up your meeting in a place where your men can hide themselves and be in a position to strike quickly if they have to."

"Yes, you're quite right. Well, thank you again for all

159

you've done. And give your beautiful Laure my very warmest wishes for long happy years to the both of you. If God wills, maybe Lucy and my son and Maxine and I can put you up at the hacienda one day on Windhaven Range."

Following his visit with John Brunton, Luke Bouchard took a carriage to the shop of the crochety old wagon-maker Emile Dagronard, who welcomed him enthusiastically. *"Pardieu,* work like this makes me feel good, M'sieu Bouchard! If I were only ten years younger, I'd close up my shop and come along with you." He sighed heavily, shook his head. *"Eh bien,* what would you? But at least, I shall know that when you are on your journey, you will be driving the finest wagons I have ever made, and so perhaps in that way I shall have had a small part in your venture. Come see for yourself—the work progresses well, it will be finished just as I have promised you, two more weeks at the most."

He led Luke by the arm out into the rear of the shop, where half a dozen workmen were placing hubs, cutting sturdy canvas, fabricating the shafts to which the horses would be hitched *"Voila!* I have made you axles of metal, they will enable you to load more on the wagons. You may wish to carry kegs of water when you go through dry prairie country, for example. And I'll furnish you with some cans of tallow, for you must lubricate the moving parts of metal as they rub against one another."

"Yes," Luke admiringly agreed, "I can see how strong those wheels are. You know your business—indeed, you are an artist at it."

"I will not say you are wrong, M'sieu Bouchard, for it is true I have some small skill and many years at my trade. But see what I have done with the canvas. It can be opened out and supported like a tent with those poles you see the men polishing. That will give you the shade which you will need wherever you go in Texas, M'sieu. Also, I have had the bodies of the wagons made out of the tough, *très dur* yellow wood from the *bois d'arc* tree. They call it—*comment s'appelle ça*—ah, *oui,* Osage orange."

"It does seem very sturdy, M'sieu Dagronard."

"It is the very best that can be used for such work, *croyez-moi*! Now, see what I have done with this chuck-wagon, as you call it." He led Luke Bouchard over to another wagon. At its rear was a huge box with shelves, drawers and partitions, which could hold small packages of food, beans, coffee, meat, sourdough for biscuits, as well as cutlery and tin or iron dishes. Larger supplies of food would be carried in the body of the huge wagon itself. The lid or wall of the chuck box was ingeniously hinged and had a leg which unfolded to support it. The lid or back side then opened downwards to provide a tabletop on which the cook could work.

"Magnificent!" Luke praised the white-haired old wagonmaker.

"Rien du tout, only common sense, M'sieu Bouchard," Emile Dagronard modestly disparaged his imaginative skill. "Now see, on this wagon, they are putting up the canvas. It is what you would call a prairie schooner, *n'est-ce-pas?* Observe, *s'il vous plaît,* the flaps I have had made, with buttons that can be quickly unfastened. Aristide, open one for M'sieu Bouchard—*voyez-vous ça?* It is a round hole, through which one can aim a rifle and sight it in case *les sauvages rouges* attack you on your journey."

"You have thought of everything, it appears. I am more than satisfied," Luke Bouchard smilingly held out his hand to the old wagonmaker, who shook it vigorously, and, as he led Luke to the door of his shop, promised, "When you wish them moved to the steamboat, M'sieu Bouchard, I shall have my men help you. And I shall come along myself to instruct the stevedores, so they do not damage them when they haul them aboard. Ah, if you knew how at night I dream of seeing myself riding along with you!"

CHAPTER FIFTEEN

On the evening of June 20, a waiter made his way to the table where Luke Bouchard was dining with his family. He handed Luke an envelope addressed in John Brunton's handwriting, and waited while Luke opened the letter, then blinked his eyes with surprise as Luke pressed a ten-dollar gold piece into his palm.

"It must really be good news, Luke dear," Lucy smilingly turned to her husband.

"It is indeed, my darling. John Brunton tells me that the draft from the Bank of Liverpool has finally come through the Boston Federal Bank to the Consolidated Bank of New Orleans. Tomorrow morning, we shall have the stake we need for our new venture. And my first act will be to pay John back the five thousand dollars he so kindly loaned me so that I could pay for my wagons and put down an advance on the rifles and ammunition."

"That means you'll be ready to leave for Texas at once, doesn't it, Luke?" Arabella Hunter eagerly asked her older half-brother. Then, reaching for her husband's hand, she added, "Oh, James, we'll go with them at last! I can hardly wait to settle down in our own house and get

163

Melinda and Andrew back under my control. I must confess, dearly as I love them, the wonders of New Orleans have made them so excitable and impatient lately, I'll be happy when we go back to a placid domestic routine."

"You know perfectly well you mean nothing of the sort, you sly minx," James Hunter chuckled. "I think they've been wonderfully behaved considering all the changes and excitement they've been subjected to the past month or so." He glanced affectionately at his pretty thirteen-year-old daughter and at eleven-year-old Andrew, who was trying very hard to eavesdrop on his parents' conversation.

"Oh?" Arabella gave her husband an archly ingenuous look, widening her eyes and making a soft pout of her lips. "And what, pray tell, Mr. Hunter, do you think is my main concern if not settling down in a house at last and having a sensible arrangement for the children?"

"My dearest Bella," James Hunter wryly chuckled, "you appear to forget that I have had the distinct pleasure of living with you for years enough to know that what you're really after is getting me off all to yourself and trying to manage me."

"Oh, la, what a spiteful thing to say before everyone, sir!" she bridled, unable to hide the sudden blush which suffused her cheeks. "But all the same, James, I shall be glad to be far away from all those ill-mannered soldiers. Why, I declare, whenever Melinda and Andrew and I go shopping, they stare at me and make the most scurrilous remarks till I wish I could slap them and teach them how to behave to a lady!"

"I shouldn't advise that, my dear," James Hunter dryly retorted, "and certainly not in view of General Butler's notorious order concerning any outward manifestations of disrespect toward his conquering retinue. But, to change the subject to a far happier one, Luke isn't the only one with news this evening. This afternoon, I had a telegraph from Cousin Jeremy, and he's found a nice little house for us all, with a yard and a garden. And there's a surprise for Melinda and Andrew waiting for them, too."

"Oh, Papa, what is it, do tell us!" Melinda clapped her

hands and anxiously leaned over the table toward her father. Andrew, trying to look very grown-up as if such things as surprises were beneath his dignity, tossed his head and shrugged, but all the same could not suppress the sudden excited look in his eyes.

"Well now, puss, if I told you, there'd be no surprise, would there?" James Hunter winked at his impetuous daughter. "I'm afraid you'll just have to wait till we get there." Then, turning to Luke, he asked, "Have you heard any news about when they expect the packets to leave New Orleans for Texas ports?"

"I was down at the levee yesterday, James," Luke replied. "I met an old Scotsman who used to run a steamboat on the Mississippi, and he thinks that by the end of the week his vessel will be seaworthy enough to make the journey. He told me that he expects clearance any day now, and so I booked passage with him for us all. That's why I'm doubly glad this news came from my good friend John Brunton. Jamie McMurtrie is a typically canny Scot, eager for a good profit, and when I told him about the wagons and the horses I intend to ship, he began by saying that he couldn't spare me all that room. I told him in a day or two I'd have a substantial bonus to give him, and he at once began to feel much less gloomy about the available space on the *William Wallace*."

"What a funny name for a ship, Papa!" Andrew spoke up.

"Not at all, Andy," his father remonstrated. "You just haven't got that far in your studies of history. Sir William Wallace was a great Scottish hero who fought against the English king, Edward I, and gave his life for his people. When we board, you'll be able to talk to this captain. He'll probably tell you many wonderful stories about his native land." Then, turning back to Luke, he added, "We'll be ready to leave whenever you are, Luke."

"I'll go to the bank tomorrow and arrange for the drafts to be converted to what gold I'll need here and the rest changed into drafts on whatever stable Texas bank is recommended. Then I must arrange a meeting with this man who's selling me the weapons."

"Do be careful, darling, it worries me to think you have to get them from an enemy officer."

"You mustn't worry, Lucy, I plan to take every precaution. John has already put me on my guard against the man. But there's absolutely no other source, and we must have those guns and ammunition. Before the war, the Texas Rangers maintained law and order, but they've been disbanded and so every man has to be a kind of law unto himself and be ready to defend himself." Turning to his son, he added, "I'll want you to come to the bank with me tomorrow morning, Lucien Edmond. And you too, Mother," he smiled at Sybella. "The three of us will divide this money so as not to exceed the limit set by President Johnson. Mother, you'll tell them that a part of this draft belongs to you under the terms of Matthew Forsden's will. I foresee no difficulties. The Boston draft has to be honored; even General Butler himself couldn't prevent that. And now, let's all drink a toast to the safe beginning of what I pray will be a prosperous journey and new homecoming for all of us."

"But Luke, dear," Sybella unexpectedly spoke up. "aren't you forgetting that a single woman, even a widow, can't inherit property? If it was true in Alabama, it will certainly be true here."

Luke clapped a hand to his forehead, then shook his head in self-condemnation. "Mother, once again you're the wisest and most level-headed of all of us. I'd forgotten that, I confess, and so did John Brunton—Well then, there's no help for it, it will have to be another man who claims the third portion of that draft. And now that I think of it, so as not to arouse too much suspicion, we'd best make separate trips to the bank and each take a portion which will be under the Presidential limit."

"But that's very easy, Luke dear," again Sybella gently interposed. "Why not let Djamba claim that last portion? After all, he's a free man now and most of all, he's black. From what I've heard around the city, General Butler has purposely formed black regiments in order to force upon the conquered Southerners the knowledge of how the Union intends to turn the tables."

"That's a capital idea, Mother!" He lifted his glass again. "Let me amend my toast, and drink it in honor of Sybella Forsden, whose courage and astuteness will guide us all to our new Windhaven venture!"

The Consolidated Bank of New Orleans had once been the house of Jules Ronsart, then of Antoine Rigalle, and, till the fall of New Orleans to Farragut, of John Brunton. On the glass window which fronted the *Rue de Toulouse,* those illustrious names had been obliterated with thick black paint, and in their stead, a wooden plank had been nailed high above the door on which the new name was daubed in blood-red paint. Inside, the furnishings were still the same, but Luke Bouchard recognized none of the new bank's personnel. All of them had come in the wake of General Benjamin F. Butler's domination of every financial institution in New Orleans; they had been handpicked by him and his brother, and their very first task had been to confiscate many of the outstanding accounts owned by hitherto wealthy Confederates.

Outside the door, two soldiers in Union uniform stood with rifle butts lowered to the sidewalk in the at-ease position, and he flushed as he saw them eye him with a sneer, recognizing in his frockcoat and elegant breeches the costume of a Southern gentleman. One of them, a burly private with a pointed beard and pug nose, derisively offered, "If you're thinking of drawing out your savings, Johnny Reb, better not waste Mr. Pendergast's time. If it's in gold, it belongs to the Union now."

"That's putting the right to it, Amos boy," his companion, a lean, lantern-jawed corporal, guffawed.

Luke Bouchard ignored their taunts, and entered the bank. He went directly to the window where in the old days the teller for drafts and promissory notes had stood. Behind it stood a pimply faced clerk in his early thirties. "Yes, can I do something for you?" he asked with a sly wink aimed at his colleague to his right, who had looked up for a moment from his work of counting out Federal scrip to a Union lieutenant who stood beside Luke Bouchard.

"Yes, if you will, please. I've just had a notice that

there is a draft from the Bank of Liverpool into this bank in the name of Luke Bouchard. If you would verify that with me, please, I should be grateful to you," Luke pleasantly replied.

The teller's thin eyebrows arched with surprise, then he frowned at the unexpected request from a man whom he had already sized up as "one of those damned, fancy Creole dandies who give themselves airs even when they haven't got a pot to piss in." The disconcerted clerk grumbled, "Well, I don't know about that, I'll go see Mr. Pendergast, he'd know about such things."

A few moments later, out of the private office which John Brunton had been the last to occupy in this historic bank before it passed into enemy hands, a fussy little man in his early fifties, in a green waistcoat and somber black trousers, hurried forward, closely followed by the officious clerk. "Good morning to you, sir. I'm Edward Pendergast, director of the bank, you see. Mr. Tentron here tells me you're looking for an English draft, is that right?"

"Yes, that's quite correct, Mr. Pendergast. It's from the Bank of Liverpool in the amount of fifty thousand dollars, made out to Luke Bouchard. I have ample identification to show you." With this, Luke produced an old letter of credit issued by Antoine Rigalle and a statement of the Bouchard account rendered by John Brunton two years before the outbreak of the war.

"Yes, yes, it seems in order. Well now, sir, I presume you've taken the oath of allegiance?"

"Yes, and I have proof of it."

"Very good. But you know also about the limit the President has set?"

"I propose to take out only eighteen thousand dollars, of which I should like six thousand in gold with the balance in a draft that would be valid at a major financial institution in Texas, Mr. Pendergast," Luke Bouchard explained.

Edward Pendergast squinted hard at Luke Bouchard, then scratched his head. "I can arrange that for you, Mr. Bouchard. And the balance of thirty-two thousand dollars?"

"That belongs equally to my son Lucien Edmond, as earnings from his own crops, and to a black freeman, Djamba Forsden, for his labor as foreman of my own plantation at Windhaven."

The bank manager looked hard at this unusual customer. "You're very shrewd, Mr. Bouchard. You have, shall we say, a Yankee ingenuity when it comes to money. Or maybe you've just pretended to give this nigger of yours sixteen thousand dollars to hornswoggle us."

"Oh no, Mr. Pendergast, quite the contrary, I assure you. Mr. Forsden was set free nearly thirty years ago, and that money represents the honest wages he's earned since then."

"Well, now, I must say, sir, if that's the case, I'm surprised you didn't come over to our side with notions like that."

"When my grandfather Lucien Bouchard founded Windhaven near Montgomery not long after the French Revolution, Mr. Pendergast, one of his first acts was to set free the slaves whom the Creeks had given him. He did not hold with slavery, nor do I. As to the politics of this war, my own opinion is that nobody really ever wins a war and the ordinary people caught up in it are almost always the losers. My grandfather's concern, like mine, Mr. Pendergast, was to produce crops that would assure the welfare of his family, his neighbors and everyone who benefited from what he grew on his land, regardless of their geographic or political location."

Once again Edward Pendergast coughed and glanced at the clerk who stood open-mouthed beside him staring at Luke Bouchard, and then, "Very well, Mr. Bouchard. When this nigger of yours comes in for his money, I'd like to see his manumission paper—not that I doubt the word of an enlightened gentleman like you, you understand. But you see, we have to be careful these days. There are still plenty of Southern traitors trying to fleece us and take off for Mexico or the west with funds they're not entitled to." Then, turning to his clerk, he sharply ordered, "Tentron, get Mr. Bouchard the gold and the draft he'll require. See to it at once!"

Later that same afternoon, Lucien Edmond entered the

Consolidated Bank of New Orleans and withdrew $3,000 in gold and a draft for $13,000 which, as Edward Pendergast himself had recommended to Luke Bouchard, would be issued on the Citizens' Bank of San Antonio. And on the following morning, Djamba entered the bank and presented his manumission paper to the fussy little bank manager and took out the balance of old Lucien's legacy in the form of a draft on the same San Antonio bank.

Edward Pendergast himself waited upon the powerful Mandingo, and chuckled and rubbed his hands together in evident pleasure at which he believed to be the supreme humiliation toward a conquered Southern planter. "Sure you don't want to keep that $16,000 here with us, Mr. Forsden?" he gave Djamba his most ingratiating smile. "A big strong black buck like you, if he played his cards right, could make himself a pile of money here in New Orleans now that we've made all your white masters crawl off with their tails between their legs."

"No, thank you, Mr. Pendergast, I've hired out to Mr. Bouchard to manage his ranch in Texas. I'll use the money to buy some land for myself after I've got him started," the Mandingo politely retorted.

Edward Pendergast watched him write his name to acknowledge receipt of the draft which the clerk had just prepared, squinted at the signature, and then, leaning forward over the counter, slyly insinuated, "Now just between you and me, boy, give me the straight truth of it. That name you've got, Forsden, that belongs most likely to the white master you used to have. Say, you're a big one, you are. You know, I wouldn't be surprised at all if some of this money wasn't a secret reward from your former mistress for, shall we say, services rendered. Services, that is, that she wouldn't want to name to her husband."

Djamba's face contorted with a sudden savage rage, and it took all his self-control to quell the murderous impulse that flared within him.

Slowly he forced himself to look at the two men with a deferential, almost apologetic expression as he softly replied, "No sir, it wasn't that way at all. You see, I got

170

myself a good-looking wife and a son and a daughter, and that did me just fine, sir. Now may I have my money?"

He pocketed the draft after neatly folding it, inclined his head toward the bank manager and his clerk, and then walked out onto the sidewalk. He drew several deep breaths, closed his eyes for a moment, and then began to walk back to the Verandah Hotel where Luke Bouchard was waiting.

As Djamba walked, the look on his face was that of a man who had been granted his fondest wish only to have it snatched away again. It had been Sybella's own suggestion that Djamba use her dead husband's name in order to trick the greedy profiteers at the bank. And though Djamba had understood the purpose and the necessity of this ruse, it had been a painful reminder of his own secret yearning for the most valiant and beautiful and desirable woman he had ever known .. . . a yearning that could never be fulfilled, and one that torturingly had been brought agonizingly close by having her name linked with his as if, indeed, they had been man and wife.

CHAPTER SIXTEEN

On the afternoon of the same day on which Djamba had successfully collected the third and final portion of old Lucien Bouchard's legacy to his grandson Luke, the latter sent a messenger to Captain George Soltis at his rooms in the St. Charles Hotel. The profligate Union officer had just formally tendered his resignation from the army to Major Arnold Parkinson, who commanded the quartermaster corps stationed in the Queen City. Parkinson himself, a Bible-reading zealot from Connecticut, had little stomach for the unbridled thievery, as he called it, which had followed the military occupation of New Orleans. In his view, the role of a conquering force was to administer impartial justice. He was hardly popular with General Butler, but his military record was impeccable; he had twice been decorated for valor at both Chickamauga and Shiloh, and, what was still more important, he had powerful friends in the War Office in Washington.

When an orderly had brought him Soltis' resignation, he had chuckled sardonically, "It's about time, or I'd have tried to cashier the scoundrel," and swiftly signed his name with a flourish to signify that the resignation would be accepted and set into force upon the same date as his signature. Also lying on his desk, buried under a sheaf of ordinances and dispatches, was a corporal's report that a hidden storeroom in the American quarter of the city had been broken into and looted of its camouflaged stores of rifles, carbines, pistols and ammunition. It would not occupy Parkinson's attention for a few days yet, since he was presently engaged in taking steps to pacify the citizenry of New Orleans, making sure that they did not take action—possibly justified—against the unruly Union soldiers in the town.

Although Parkinson detested slavery, he was of the private opinion that General Butler had committed a terrible tactical blunder in organizing Negro regiments. Forcing them upon citizens who for several generations had regarded the blacks as inferiors and who could not be expected, simply by the brutal facts of having lost the war, to accept them overnight as equals, much less as superiors. In Parkinson's view, Butler's intention to drive home the galling turnabout of racial relations into the mind of every Southerner was merely sadistic.

When Luke Bouchard's messenger reached Captain George Soltis, he found the latter slouching in an overstuffed armchair, his right hand gripping the neck of a bottle of port and his left hand cuddling a quadroon prostitute whom he had seen the night before plying her trade near a tavern he frequented, and whom he had brought to his rooms so that he might celebrate his resignation from the army.

"Get off my lap, Queenie, you sweet fat bitch," he jovially ordered as the young messenger hesitated on the threshold of the door, blushing violently at the bawdy scene. "What's this you've got for me, boy? Don't be bashful, Queenie'll soon fix that, won't you, honey?"

"I declare," the plump quadroon, who was in her early twenties and wore only a gaudy blue frock, cloth slippers and black silk stockings held up on thighs with red elastic garters, giggled and playfully slapped the stocky officer with the tips of her fingers. "You are the naughtiest man, but seeing as how you're so generous with poor little Queenie, I reckon I wouldn't mind if that young fel-

low poked me—that is, if he wants to. Do you, sonny?"
This last to the furiously embarrassed youth who could
not have been more than eighteen.

He swallowed hard, then shook his head, while Captain
George Soltis burst into braying laughter: "Aw, Queenie,
can't you see you're making the poor little mama's boy
blush like sin? Bet he's never even kissed a girl yet—have
you, bub?"

"N-no, s-sir, that is—I mean—" the youth floundered.

"Well, make up your mind. Let's see what's in this note
you brought." He tore open the envelope and quickly
scanned its contents, then chuckled. "Good news is what
you brought, boy. Mighty good news. Going to make myself a little money tonight. And just to show you I'm a
fair-minded man, I'm going to let you take little Queenie
here over to that couch and learn what poking is. Go on,
honey, take your dress off, show him what a gal's really
made of."

"No please—I mean—I—I'd rather not—thank you,
Captain, but I've got to be getting back to my work at the
hotel—" The youth bit his lips and pretended not to look
as the quadroon seized the hem of her long-skirted frock
and swiftly drew it up over her head and shoulders, then
tossed it into the officer's lap, standing naked except for
her stockings, garters and slippers. "Like what you see,
mama's boy?" she purred, winking at her *pro tem*
paramour.

"Don't be afraid to look, sonny, you won't go blind.
Take a look at those big juicy tits Queenie's got—and I'm
here to tell you from personal experience that that sweet
box of hers will squeeze out every drop of sap you've got
in your pecker. Go ahead, she's paid for through tomorrow night, it's on me, boy!" the captain smirkingly urged.

But the youth had turned and fled, slamming the door
behind him, and Captain George Soltis guffawed heartily
as he slapped his thigh, then shook his head. "Poor little
bastard, couldn't believe I'd be that generous, could he,
Queenie? Now, seeing you show yourself off like that just
made me randy as hell. Get over to that couch and spread
yourself, I'm going to fooferaw you good. Man alive, I

feel like a bull right now after the news that boy just brought."

The young quadroon nonchalantly ambled toward the long low couch, sprawled on it, lifting one knee and running both hands over the dimpled kneecap, then drawing her fingertips along her thigh toward the thick black forest of her *mons*. "You're really feeling good, Georgie man," she crooned. "Come here to Queenie, she'll make you feel lots better. But what's all this good news you just got?"

He thrust the note into the pocket of a red velvet dressing robe which he had obliged a storekeeper to make him a present of two nights before, unbelted the robe and flung it off, standing naked in his boots. "That'd be telling, honey. Poking and business don't mix, so just you keep your mind on the one, and I'll keep mine on the other. But I'll say this, I've got me a sucker right where I want him, and I'll have money enough to keep you being nice to me for as long as I choose. Now let's see how long you can make me last." He moved toward her, chuckling with sadistic pleasure over the news he had just received and his own ingenious plan to turn it to still greater advantage and profit to himself.

"Come in, come in, boys. Pour yourselves a drink, there's lots more where that bottle came from." Captain George Soltis waved his arm with a grandiose sweeping gesture to welcome three surly-looking men into the garishly furnished parlor of his hotel rooms. "Glad you could make it. There's a job I've lined up for you tonight, and the pay'll be double if you bring it off the way you handled old Connaught."

"You mean get the cash, do the stupid bastard in, then bring back the stuff to that old hayloft on Mercier Street where we've been keeping it?" The leader of the trio, a stocky man in his late forties, wearing a tattered blue coat with the chevrons of a Union corporal, moved forward to a side table, lifted a half-empty bottle of corn whiskey and poured himself out a liberal portion into a champagne goblet, then gulped it down and belched loudly. "Cripes, Soltis, seems like to me you ought to offer us boys champagne, not this pig's swill, considerin' how much we made you on the Connaught job."

"Never you mind, Scraggs, and you too, Dudley and Morse," the stocky officer sniggered. "If you pull this one off, I'll buy each of you a bottle of the best French champagne you can find in New Orleans, and that's a promise. And it's going to be an easier job than with Connaught. Some damned Reb is putting up four thousand for the rifles, carbines and revolvers with ammunition I've written down on this piece of paper. Mind you give him full measure and put them in a buggy with a tarpaulin over all of it. You're to meet him at eleven tonight near that rundown old house on the edge of town, you know, the one that crazy John Dewton lives in with that menagerie he's got in his back yard. About a mile from there, due northwest."

"I get the drift," Lemuel Scraggs grunted assent, then turned to his two cronies. Jesse Dudley was a wiry young man in his late twenties, several inches over six feet tall, with a vacuous smile and placid blue eyes hiding the mentality of a psychotic killer. Norton Morse, a stolid, man in his early thirties who had originally been a pig farmer from Ohio and who wore a clean new Union uniform with sergeant's stripes, looked back at Lemuel Scraggs as if seeking assurance, then addressed the captain: "What we gotta know, Cap'n, is what sort of man this Reb of yours is. Now you take that skinny old bastard Connaught, he give Lem and me a real fight before Jesse here got a chance to use his knife in the old geezer's guts. Gave us a devil of a time, he did."

"You won't have any trouble like that, I'm pretty sure, Norton boy," the captain chuckled. "I'm to get three thousand in gold and don't you boys take a penny less, understand? Our customer's name is Luke Bouchard, all the way from Alabama. Gave me a lot of palaver about starting new in Texas and raising cattle. Says he's taken the oath of allegiance and doesn't have any politics one way or the other about the war—as if he thought I'd fall for a yarn like that."

"I get your drift, Cap'n," Lemuel Scraggs chuckled,

"So he's not likely to be a fighting man then, is he, Cap'n?"

"He strikes me as one of those fancy gentlemen slave-owners, mealymouthed and righteous, who'd have a man believe he never owned a slave or used a whip on one. What's more to the point, he's rich. He told me he was waiting for some money, and the note I got this afternoon shows that he's got it. Your job is to collect it, and then take care of him nice and neat, mind you. That ought to be easy, way out there near the swamps with nobody around to see you boys at work. Now I'll come along just to make sure everything goes the way it should, but I'll stay a good distance away from you on horseback."

"We take all the risks and you get all the profits, Cap'n," Lemuel Scraggs complained in a whining voice as he again glanced at the empty whiskey bottle.

"There's two hundred apiece for you boys, and a little bonus right now, if you're hankering after something nicer than corn whiskey," Captain George Soltis grinned.

"Now what could that be, Cap'n?" Lemuel Scraggs's beady brown eyes narrowed intently on the stocky captain's flushed, smirking face.

"I've got a prime piece of quadroon pokemeat in the next room, and she's been giving me a real good time until this noon when I caught her going through my breeches and trying to take a little money that didn't belong to her. I've got her tied up and waiting for punishment. I just thought you boys might like to dish it out. Now mind you, don't mark her up too much, and don't spoil her either, because when this business is over tonight, I'd like to come back and find her a little more humble and ready to service me the way a bitch like her really can. Come along, I'll show you what I mean."

Soltis, still wearing only his dressing robe and boots, flung open the door and stepped to one side as he nodded to the trio. Spreadeagled on the four-poster, canopied bed, naked except for her black stockings and elastic garters, the young quadroon lay, a handkerchief thrust into her mouth and a black bandanna wound over it tightly and knotted at the back of her neck. Her eyes were bulging and glassy with terror, and her breasts rose and fell

178

with the feverish rhythm of apprehension. Already, on the insides of her thighs and the satiny smoothness of her belly, angry striations still blazed, imprinted by the strokes of a narrow black leather belt which lay between her straddled thighs. The thick mossy niches of her distended armpits were damp with fear-sweat, and beads of perspiration glistened along her sides. As she saw the four men approach the bed, she mewled in terror and madly tugged at her tethered wrists and ankles, writhing to free herself.

"Wal now, Cap'n, this is a mite better'n corn whiskey, I'll give you that," Lemuel Scraggs hoarsely muttered as he pulled off his coat and unfastened the fly of his breeches. "But I'll still hold you to that offer of champagne when the job's done tonight, Cap'n."

"I never go back on my word, Lem, you ought to know that by now. Now you boys won't mind if I sit myself down here in this chair out of the way and smoke myself a segar, will you?" Captain George Soltis leeringly insinuated.

"Hell, Cap'n, you do what you like. I'll be first with this purty bitch, and then we'll let Jesse try his luck. You, Norton, takes you a long time to work up a lather over a wench, as I've noticed before, so you can just hold your fire till we're done."

"Aw, Lem boy, what you wanna go and talk mean like that for?" Norton Morse complained, peevishly scratching the back of his shaggy neck, his eyes riveted on the struggling naked girl before him. "I ain't never had a piece as fancy as this to work on, so how'd you know I couldn't make out real fine this time?"

Lemuel Scraggs had disdained the little Jacob's ladder by the side of the bed and, without bothering to take off his boots, seated himself on the edge of the bed and swung himself over beside the terrified quadroon captive. Seizing the discarded belt and doubling it in his right hand, he knelt up, leaning toward her. His bony left hand playfully roamed over her shrinking belly, reached one of her feverishly swelling breasts and lasciviously and lingeringly kneaded it, as he raised the belt and brought it down with a savage thwack diagonally over the other. A strident cry was muffled by the gag as Queenie madly arched against her bonds, then fell back, writhing and shuddering, tears running down her cheeks and her hugely widened eyes beseeching pity.

Already Jesse Dudley had doffed his buckskin jacket and, his expressionless blue eyes unwaveringly fixed on the quadroon's congested face, was fumbling with the fly of his ragged denim breeches, while Norton Morse, his face perspiring, began to tug off his blue uniform coat and to massage his crotch as he licked his lips and stared at the quadroon.

"A mighty techy l'il piece you got yourself here, Cap'n," Scraggs leered as he moved his left hand to the other breast and directed a backhanded slash of the double belt against the shuddering, opulent round globe it had just left. An even more plaintive and long-drawn cry was torn from the naked young sufferer, her eyes rolling toward the ceiling as if praying for divine salvation. Meanwhile the stocky officer had flung himself onto a thickly upholstered chaise longue, his left thumb and forefinger caressing the tips of his mustache, his other hand buried under the folds of the red velvet robe, his eyes glittering like a satyr's.

"Yes sir, a mighty techy piece," Scraggs chuckled thickly as he thrust his left hand down between the girl's straddled thighs and, after keeping her in agonized suspense by stroking the satiny insides, suddenly poked his gnarled long forefinger between the poutingly open lips of her vulva, then applied without warning half a dozen whistling, smacking strokes of the doubled belt over her breasts and belly. "You got her real hot for us, Cap'n, but I'll get her a helluva lot hotter before I'm done with her. Lookit her buck and wiggle her big arse, boys, she wants it real bad, and I've got just what she's lookin' for. Ain't that right, honey?" He punctuated this question with several more sonorous thwacks of the leather against her armpits and chest and sides, giggling inanely as she arched and tried to throw herself from side to side to evade the lashes which raised new bright-red streaks on the satin of her naked skin. His forefinger delved deeply, turned and twisted, and the girl flung her head back, her eyes rolling to the whites, her body stiffening, then visited

180

by convulsive shudders. "Didn't I tell you? She's hot to trot, that's what, Cap'n!"

"For Chrissake, Lem, get on with it before I bust," Norton Morse plaintively whined, unbuttoning his breeches and rubbing himself with feverish alacrity.

"I told you to hold your fire, Norton." Scraggs turned back to bare decaying, yellowing teeth in a taunting grin at his frustrated crony. "You ain't even got it up yet, boy, how'd you expect to service Queenie even if it was your turn right now, huh? Just watch and mebbe you'll get the notion 'fore I'm done poking her!"

With a last vicious cut of the belt over the unfortunate victim's quivering belly, Scraggs stretched himself over the tethered quadroon, slipping his hands under her buttocks and digging his dirty fingernails into the well-fleshed hillocks as he imbedded himself with a ferocious lunge. Again Queenie mewled, closed her eyes, her head turning rapidly from side to side, her eyes tightly closed, but the quick, convulsive flaring and clenching of her nostrils betrayed the torment she was enduring.

Jesse Dudley growled, "Get on with it, Lem. You marked her enough with that belt. When you really want to mark a bitch, a knife's better anyhow."

Lemuel Scraggs glanced back over his shoulder and, although he was the leader of the unsavory trio, he nervously observed the angry tightening of the younger man's thin lips. He cleared his throat and nodded, then turned back to his now pitifully sobbing prey and began to ravish her with brutal, rapid probings, his fleshy lips noisily sucking at one of her nipples as he gouged her buttocks with his fingernails and rampantly violated her. When he had finished, he clambered off the bed, stood staring down a moment, a smirk of satisfaction on his coarse, unshaven face, then waved his hand: "She's all yours, Jesse."

The blond Missourian, who had joined the Union Army hastily to avoid being lynched by an irate group of citizens of a small river town where he had been jailed for having beaten a young prostitute nearly to death, drew out a soiled kerchief from the pocket of his breeches, bent to the whimpering quadroon and sadistically rubbed and chafed her sex till she tried to twist herself away, as he softly remarked, "I'm a little more particular than Norton here. Now let's see if I can't really make this bitch wiggle." Then to the terrified, half-fainting girl, he sibilantly hissed, "You better show me a good time, bitch, or I'll work you over with my clasp knife and you'll be begging for the belt instead—won't she, Lem?"

"That's sure right, honey," Scraggs guffawed as he moved to the side of the bed and peered down into the girl's tear-ravaged face. "You don't want to trifle none with Jesse here, he's as good as an Injun with that knife of his—why, he can peel your whole skin off and make hisself a pair of long johns out of it if he's a mind to."

Queenie twisted her face to one side and closed her eyes again, as the blond gangling Missourian drew a sharp gleaming clasp knife out of its leather sheath strapped round his waist and laid the flat of the blade against her lower belly. Her body shuddered at the feel of the cold metal, and a prolonged whimpering sob escaped her. "You're gonna treat me real good, aren't you, bitch?" Jesse Dudley hissed as he glided the flat of the blade against each of her panting breasts, then down again to her belly. "Nod your head and lemme know how nice you're gonna be for Jesse!"

Queenie frantically nodded, turning her face and opening her eyes to regard her younger tormenter, staring at him with a supplicating gaze as he grinned mirthlessly and lifted the clasp knife to show its viciously sharp-honed point.

"Just don't forget it, then. Let's see how nice you can be if you've a mind to, bitch," he counseled as he laid the knife down at her right side and then stretched himself over her, his long slim fingers pinching and tugging at her breasts. In his chair, the goggling officer leaned forward, the fingers of his left hand dug into the soft, yielding upholstery, his mouth open and slavering at the sight. Norton Morse licked his dry lips, glanced down with agonized frustration at his still flaccid tool, hastening his manipulations as he, too, watched with glazed, dilated eyes.

Jesse Dudley stretched out his warped pleasure with

the whimpering, pinioned naked quadroon, his fingers mauling and pinching her breasts and buttocks and armpits as he prodded her abused sexual orifice with the stiffening point of his virility, making her squirm and start and arch and shudder in her desperate attempt to prove her total submission and avert the torture with which he had threatened her. When he at last entered her, she proffered herself in the most abject, wanton way to demonstrate her obedience, and he purposely held himself in rein until by sheer dint of prolongation he had drawn her oversensitized nerves to the breaking point. Then, rapaciously, violently, he achieved his climax and left her writhing and moaning, on the brink of total surrender but as yet denied it by the frightening revulsion of his sadism.

And it was Norton Morse who, at last granted his long-delayed turn at the unfortunate quadroon, flung himself down on her sweating, shuddering body and, still impotent, managed by his frenetic grindings against her to draw her to an hysterical culmination which left her sprawled, inert and seemingly lifeless on that bed of depraved martyrdom. . . .

The moon was a hazy scimitar in a murky sky, and the air was fetid from the miasma of the marshy swamps. From the top of a stunted pine tree, a screech owl hooted. Its mate answered as mournfully, hidden in a thick grove of cypress trees.

The haze of the swamps blurred and obscured the tiny glimmer of light in John Dewton's rickety old house far to the southeast. Now, for a moment, even that source of light was blotted out by the figure of a uniformed man on horseback, who reined in his black gelding, leaned forward over the horse's neck and waited as he heard an almost echoing sound of horses' hooves nearing him. Then, drawing on the reins, he turned the gelding farther off to the northwest until he came to a giant live oak tree. There he dismounted, and squatted down, his left hand holding the reins, his right unconsciously toying with the sharp tips of his waxed mustache.

The sounds of the other hooves came closer and closer now, until, at about the point of the jagged pine tree, the squatting man could see emerge out of the darkness of the night an old dray horse drawing an open buggy at the head of which one man perched on a box marked "Property of the U.S. Army." Sprawled at their ease beside the long wooden cases containing rifles and the others packed with revolvers and cartridges, Jesse Dudley and Norton Morse exchanged whispered conversation. Lemuel Scraggs stopped the wagon, swung himself down, and chuckled, "Look, alive, boys, I reckon this is the place we're to meet the Reb. Where the hell is he, now?"

"Don't rush things so, Lem," Jesse Dudley whispered, "just make sure he doesn't bring along a passel of friends. The Cap'n wants this nice and sweet and neat."

"Jist git your knife ready, Jesse, you can make it as neat as you please. My job's to get the cash and you, Norton, see if you can pump him any about where his kinfolks are planning to go. The Cap'n thinks they might be just as loaded with cash as this fancy gentleman Reb is hisself," Lemuel Scraggs declared in a stage whisper.

With a groan, Norton Morse slipped down off the wagon, looked nervously around. "A place like this gives me the creeps," he complained. " 'Sides, my back hurts me somethin' fierce."

"It ain't your back, it's your peter," Lemuel Scraggs softly sniggered. "I like to bust a gut laughin' when I saw how hard you wuz workin' on that pore bitch. She got all the fun and you jist laid there like a rooster with its head cut off—hey, what's that? Seems like I heard someone comin' out of those cypress trees—yeah, it's the Reb. Norton, go on over and talk nice 'n gentle to him. I'll come along and when you've pumped him dry, I'll take his cash. You, Jesse, finish him off quick."

"I don't need a two-bit corporal like you to tell me my business," Jesse Dudley snarled as he put his left hand to the handle of his clasp knife, half-drew it out of its sheath, then shoved it back.

Luke Bouchard had stepped out of the grove of cypress trees, a moneybelt fastened round his waist.

"You Luke Bouchard?" Norton Morse wheedlingly demanded as he moved slowly forward.

"That's right. You must be Captain Soltis's men with the merchandise I'm buying."

"That's right, Mr. Bouchard sir. 'Course, there's a little matter of cash on the barrelhead before you get what's in this wagon, Mr. Bouchard sir."

"Now, now, Norton boy," Lemuel Scraggs said, an ingratiating smile making his face uglier than ever, "ain't no cause to be so hasty with Mr. Bouchard here. Anybody can see, jist one look at him, he's a real fancy gennelmun, he is."

"Sure nuff. I didn't mean any harm," the heavyset sergeant furtively glanced at his older crony, then obsequiously addressed Luke Bouchard: "It's only, and you can understand it, Mr. Bouchard, we ain't used to meetin' folks we don't know out in these here swamps. Snakes 'n God knows what else crawlin' around. So what I want to ask you right off, and I hope you won't take no offense, is jist how many of you figgers on goin' off to Texas with all these firearms and ammo? 'Pears like to me you got enough to start a small-scale war."

"I assure you gentlemen that what I'm buying from you is defense against a war, not to be used on the attacking side unless I'm attacked. I've been told that there are plenty of Indians and bandits in the area we're going to, and it just makes good sense to have protection along. I personally am a man of peace."

"Well, sure now, Mr. Bouchard, we all kin see that," Norton Morse glanced back at both his companions, as Jesse Dudley had moved up to the withers of the horse and was stroking them with his right hand, his pale blue eyes detailing every feature of Luke Bouchard's face. " 'Bout how many would you say are going along with you, Mr. Bouchard, sir?"

"About two dozen, including my black workers to whom I'm paying a wage because they're free men and always have been," Luke Bouchard curtly replied. "I like this meeting place and the time and surroundings no better than you gentlemen. I'd prefer to give you the money and make certain that I'm getting what Captain Soltis offered, and then you can be on your way."

"That'll be three thousand, then, Mr. Bouchard," Lemuel Scraggs stepped forward with an oafish grin. "Sure hope you brought every penny of it, too. The Cap'n's mighty particular about settling accounts right the first time."

"I've brought it all in this moneybelt, and I'll turn it over to you. Feel free to count it, you'll find the exact amount agreed upon," Luke Bouchard declared as he unfastened the belt and held it out in both hands toward the leader of the trio.

"What part of Texas do you hanker after, Mr. Bouchard, would you say?" Norton Morse persisted, his voice taking on an uneasy whine as he observed Jesse Dudley's movement slightly forward toward the tall debonair man with the moneybelt.

"Where I can find plenty of cattle to put my brand on and drive to market, that's where," Luke Bouchard answered, his eyes fixed on Jesse Dudley's blandly expressionless face, flickering an instant down to the young Missourian's left hand which rested on the handle of the clasp knife. "I didn't expect we'd discuss my plans, gentlemen. I assumed that Captain Soltis was satisfied with the transaction and that you'd take the money and turn over the contents of that wagon."

"Sure we will. Hand over the belt now," Lemuel Scraggs commanded, his lips curling in an avaricious smile. He moved a step forward, reaching out to take the belt, then hissed out of the side of his mouth, "Get him, Jesse!"

But Luke Bouchard stepped back, swung the end of the belt with its heavy rolls of gold coins sewn in rows along the lining, squarely into Lemuel Scraggs' astonished face, smashing the bridge of his nose. With a frenzied oath of pain and rage, the leader stumbled back, jostling Jesse Dudley who, with a snarl, moved clear of the leader and drew out his clasp knife, transferring it to his right hand and holding it out with the point aiming upwards at Luke Bouchard's belly.

Drawing back the belt again, Luke swung it down to coil around the Missourian's right wrist, and at the same time launched a sudden kick with his booted right foot that caught the gangling blond killer in the kneecap. Jesse

186

Dudley yowled in agony, doubling over and grabbing at his knee, dropping his clasp knife in the process.

"Why, you ornery, dirty-dealing Reb you!" Norton Morse swore as he thrust his hand down into the pocket of his blue breeches in search of the always loaded derringer he carried with him. Then he stood transfixed, his eyes widening with horrified surprise, and then they darkened and the light went out of them forever as a long bamboo rod with an arrow-headed tip made of delicate wrought iron hurtled out of the dense grove and pierced his back. His left hand groped behind him, trying to grip the shaft and drag it out, and then he toppled forward onto his knees and bowed his head to the ground. His feet kicked out convulsively and then he lay still.

Scraggs, his left hand clamped over his broken, bleeding nose, fumbled with his other hand for a six-shooter bulging in the rear pocket of his tattered breeches. Before he could reach it, however, Andy Haskins came loping out of the grove of cypress trees, the murderously sharp tip of a nine-inch Bowie knife clutched between his left thumb and forefinger. Drawing back his arm, he took careful aim and flung the weapon. Lemuel Scraggs uttered a gurgling shriek, twisted halfway round, as the knife buried itself in the back of his scrawny neck. His arms dropped limply to his sides, and he pitched forward onto the moist ground.

By now, the gangling young Missourian, ferociously grinding his teeth against the agonizing pain of his bruised kneecap, had straightened and, his clasp knife retrieved, advanced toward Luke Bouchard. His eyes were narrowed, and his nostrils flared with blood-lust as he hissed, "I'm going to gut you, you Reb bastard, gut you so's you'll die real nice and slow." He made a vicious upward-driving lunge at Luke Bouchard who, having anticipated it, nimbly sprang to one side. From Jesse Dudley's left, Djamba now hurried forward, spear in hand. Gripping the bamboo shaft with both of his powerful hands, he drove the spear point into Jesse Dudley's left side as far as he could plunge it. With a yowling shriek of death-agony, the blond Missourian turned his contorted face toward his assailant, lifted the knife in a last murderous

187

effort, and then his hand opened and the knife dropped as he tried to seize the spear and wrench it out. Blood gushed from his mouth and he sagged down onto his knees, as the Mandingo, with a grimace of disgust, wrenched the spear out of the deep wound and thrust it this time into the Missourian's heart.

Out of the grove of cypress trees, Joe Duvray and Lucas, as well as old John Dewton himself, the last armed with an old but still serviceable musket, emerged to join Andy Haskins, Djamba and Luke Bouchard.

"We'd best bury this carrion in the swamp quickly as we can, Mr. Bouchard," Lucas suggested.

"And don't go leaving the moneybelt here either," Andy Haskins grinned as he picked it up and handed it back to Luke Bouchard, who fastened it around his waist.

"It's plain to see that these weapons were stolen by our good friend Captain Soltis," Luke said with a weary smile. "But I don't think he'll come after us when he finds out he's not getting his money. He'd have a little too much explaining to do, I think."

Beyond them, Soltis, who was looking on in abject terror, quickly mounted his horse and, bending low over its neck to hide himself in the oppressive darkness of the humid night, galloped away to the northwest.

"You can hide the stuff in dat wagon in my cellar, Mr. Bouchard," old John Dewton cackled in rare good humor. "Shore did mah old eyes a spell of good to see how you bested dem murderin' Yankee skunks. Ah wuz afraid ah was gonna have to use mah musket there, but you shore held off those three rascals, purtiest thing ah done seen in a coon's age." He lifted his musket and contemplatively stared at it, then shook his head. "Anyhow, shootin' woulda been too good fer de likes of dem devils." He cackled again and shook his head. "Andy, ah nebbah in mah whole life seen a one-armed man throw a purtier beeline wid a knife dan dat!"

Then, moving to the wagon and squinting at the inscription on the cases, he added, "Ah got some paint ah kin use so's nobody gwine see dat dese guns 'n sech didn't 'zacty belong to de man who tried to sell 'em to you, Mistah Bouchard!"

CHAPTER SEVENTEEN

John Brunton poured a brimming glassful of Madeira from the cut-glass decanter on the sideboard in his private office, walked over to Luke Bouchard and handed it to him, then filled his own and lifted it. "To your new Windhaven venture, and to Windhaven Range, and may both be even more successful than the first Windhaven!"

Luke Bouchard stared at the exquisitely wrought goblet in his hand, turning it slowly so that the flickering lights of the candles in filigree iron stands set into the walls, played their dusky golden reflections all around its facets. "I know that toast of yours is meant to be a happy one, John. Indeed it is in many ways—and yet somehow I've a certain sadness in thinking of the future because it's certain to relegate the past to oblivion."

"You're philosophical tonight, Luke. You're an unusual man, a philosopher and yet a man of action—indeed, remembering what Antoine Rigalle told me about your grandfather Lucien, I'm beginning to think that you're perhaps his reincarnation."

Luke raised his eyes and considered his friend with an almost wondering look. "It's very strange you should use that word, John. I don't know what mood's suddenly got into me, but here tonight, with our sailing planned for tomorrow, I find myself thinking more and more of Grandfather's chateau on the Alabama River. I remember how very proud I was to help set the portico in place to mark the entrance into that house, a house that was the realization of his fondest dream through all those years with the Creeks."

"I quite understand. Old Maurice Arnaut used to boast to Antoine that he had never undertaken so rewarding a commission in all his years as a renowned architect. I think he began to share your grandfather's dream as it took shape. Poor fellow, he died of yellow fever—perhaps that, too, was destiny, for you may recall that by coming to supervise the work on the chateau, he escaped a pestilential epidemic at the time. Ah well, who is to say that destiny doesn't have many strange crossroads to bring us all eventually to the end originally planned for us?" John Brunton smiled sadly, and drank from his goblet, then set it down.

Luke Bouchard stood facing him, still twisting the goblet in his hand and regarding it, a nostalgic look on his handsome face. "Who knows what Grandfather's destiny might have been if I'd been his son and not his grandson, John? Perhaps his Windhaven might have been erected long before it really was, and perhaps he could have devoted that tolerant, searching mind of his toward influencing the selfish planters who could see no further than their acres of cotton and their toiling slaves. Perhaps if he'd been free to go into the legislature and influence those around him, there might even have been no war. If only the South could have understood that the rotation of crops and the development of its own manufactured products could have made it economically free of the North—but our lives are full of ifs, I'm afraid." At last he put the goblet to his lips and drank.

John Brunton walked back to his desk and seated himself. "I've a feeling I know what you're thinking, Luke. It's about that house, isn't it? You're wondering what's going to happen to it now that the war is over and you're going to Texas."

"Yes. From the outside, apart from the blackening of smoke, it still stands in all its pride and dignity. The towers are still there. Did you know that it was in one of those towers that my grandfather used to commune with his first love, the Creek maiden Dimarte? He died there, too. So much has taken place at Windhaven. What will happen now, John?"

"What's going to happen throughout the South, I'm afraid, Luke. The provisional governors will make sure that you can't go back there, even though the war is over. Every black is to have fifty acres and a mule—that's part of the reconstruction program. The large holdings of land will be parceled off; that too is a Northern precaution to make sure that the aristocratic gentlemen planters never get a chance to return to their acres."

"I know, I know. And yet, John, you owned neither land nor slaves. What is there to prevent your buying the chateau and, since they've set a figure of fifty acres, even that small portion of Grandfather's old estate?"

John Brunton frowned, nursed his chin and pondered a moment. "I daresay it could be done, but it would take time and money. And surely, to put that chateau back into good condition after the fire which burned so much of the wood and the furnishings inside, would cost a pretty penny."

"But it could be done, couldn't it?" Luke stared eagerly at his friend.

"Perhaps. But understand this, Luke, even if I were to act for you and buy it, the provisional government now being set up would investigate me thoroughly, and you wouldn't dare go back to it for a good long while. In my considered judgment, the bitterness engendered by this war is going to grow more intense rather than less. It might be as much as five, even ten years before all these hatreds and prejudices die away."

Luke strode forward to the desk, put his palms on the edge and leaned forward, his eyes aglow with eagerness. "At least it's worth thinking about. When I get to Texas, I should have at least half of the gold which Grandfather left. And I plan to replace it by raising cattle and selling them to the best available market. Make discreet in-

191

quiries, John, find out what happened to the chateau, whether anyone's going to live in it. How much it would cost to make it livable again. Write me in care of the bank in San Antonio. I'll keep in touch with you, let you know what progress Lucien Edmond and I are making in this new venture. And if the price is not too high, try to buy it and the fifty acres to go with it. Understand, I don't say I'd go back there—there are too many painful memories now. But perhaps one day Lucien Edmond, as he grows older and his children come of age, may consider that first Windhaven as a home of peace and retirement in his advancing years."

"I'll make inquiries, you can depend on it. And now, will you drink to that promise?"

"With all my heart," Luke Bouchard laughingly agreed and raised the goblet to his lips again.

"Well, now, you've got your wagons and the horses to draw them, and you've bought good supplies of flour, beans, bacon, salt and the other staples you'll need to get yourself settled." The banker resumed in a cheerful tone, "And that Scottish captain of yours is going to weigh anchor two days from now?"

"Yes, it's all settled. His stevedores will load the wagons and the horses tomorrow, and I've paid him his bonus. In spite of all his grumbling, I rather think he's pleased to make such a handsome profit. Thanks to the transaction in weapons about which I've already told you, I could spare a little extra gold to make him more enthusiastic about all the space my passage was going to take up on the *William Wallace*."

"I'll drink to your cleverness in besting a rogue like Soltis, Luke, and most heartily!" John Brunton finished his Madeira and set the goblet down with a clatter on the top of his desk, then rose. "He can hardly dare accuse you to his superiors, because that would mean explaining where he got the weapons he was going to turn over to you. Our newspaper had a story running all the past week about the mysterious plundering of a camouflaged warehouse. It won't be long before what honest officers there still are in New Orleans will put two and two together and come up with the four that spells out Soltis's name. And you say you've heard nothing from him? Neither have I. He hasn't been to The Union House since Laure introduced you to him."

"And how is your beautiful wife, John?" At the mention of her name, Luke flushed and turned sideways, staring at one of the candle-lamps.

"She's made me young again, I can tell you, Luke. By God, a man's as old as he feels, not what his birth certificate says. At least that's the way I look at it right now. She's devoted to me, she's beautiful and young, and I can't let my gray hairs remind me that I'm old enough to be her father and a good deal more. I'll always be grateful to her for that."

"You give her my warmest regards, and accept my good wishes for the happiness of both of you, John. I don't know what I should have done without your help and your friendship."

"I was glad to be of service. But I've a feeling somehow, Luke, that if I hadn't been around to help out, you'd still have managed on your own with that ingenuity and courage you surely inherited from your grandfather. In a world of scoundrels, and we see so many around us, it's always rewarding to find an honest, decent man. I wonder if the war has made too many of us forget what honor means."

Luke Bouchard had closed his eyes, his face taut and anxious, and he was silent for a long moment till finally he turned to face his friend and to hold out his hand. "You're embarrassing me, John, making me sound like one of those legendary Greek heroes. I assure you I'm only a very mortal man with a mortal man's failings."

"I've never noticed any of the latter, Luke. Devil take it, but you're in a dark mood at a time when you should be hardly able to contain yourself for excitement over all that's going to happen to you in the next few weeks!" He chuckled and shook his head. "If I didn't know you better, I'd offer you right now one of my most luxurious salons and a charming *fille de joie* to make those lines in your forehead and that distant look in your eyes vanish for tonight at least."

"But you do know me better than that, John. And so

I'll say goodnight, and I hope that you'll keep your promise to see us off at the dock."

"Depend on it. And I'll keep my promise, too, about finding out what happened to your grandfather's chateau."

Well before sundown of this same day, Luke Bouchard engaged two carriages to drive himself and his son Lucien Edmond, Lucy and Maxine, Sybella and Maybelle, as well as Mara, to John Dewton's house, where Djamba, Simata, Andy Haskins and Joe Duvray awaited them.

Andy Haskins raised his eyebrows and expressed mild surprise: "You brought the ladies, Mr. Bouchard? You mean you're going to have them watch us men have target practice?"

Luke smilingly shook his head. "Quite the contrary, Andy. You're going to teach them how to handle a rifle, a carbine and a revolver."

"Hold on there, Mr. Bouchard," the genial one-armed Tennesseean anxiously protested, "have you got any idea of what a kick those rifles and carbines are gonna have? Why, begging your pardon, Mr. Bouchard, but delicate ladies shouldn't have no truck with firearms, not in my book."

"Ordinarily I'd defer to your superior wisdom, Andy," Luke chuckled, "but I'm going to overrule you this time and for a very good reason. This morning, John Brunton told me that there are several roving bands of bandits who cross the Rio Grande and terrorize the few white settlers just over the border, pretending to be *Juaristas* who want to liberate Mexico from the Austrian tyrant, as they call him. From what I've heard about Maximilian, he's a dreamer and an idealist, and I'm beginning to believe that he let himself be maneuvered by that wily scoundrel, Napoleon III, into accepting the very uneasy throne of Mexico. The United States will never recognize a monarchy so close to home, you can be sure of that. All of which means every one of us who go to Texas ought to be able to know how to load and unload and fire a weapon—such knowledge may save our lives in case we're attacked."

"I see your point, Mr. Bouchard, but I'm afraid the

194

ladies are going to be in for an uncomfortable time, and I was just thinking of them."

"Spoken with true Southern gallantry," Luke laughed gently, "but I've asked them and they've all agreed to take practice with us. And of course, ladies go first, Andy, so you and Joe can start the lesson while we watch."

"Father, have all the supplies been arranged for?" Lucien Edmond turned to him with a questioning look.

"Yes, I finished the last details this afternoon. I've arranged for all supplies to be taken to the *William Wallace* and loaded tomorrow afternoon. We'll sail at noon of the next day. Although I'm told there's ample water in much of the region through which our wagon train will pass, we'll have kegs of fresh water on hand. You know yourself, Lucien Edmond, that horses have an uncanny way of knowing just where they're going to find water long before we humans do. In any case, we shan't go thirsty."

"Simata help you scout ahead for water," the young redbone eagerly assented. "Many underground rivers and springs besides the Nueces. You'll find plenty water. Good hunting too, wild deer, maybe even buffalo, good meat for the campfire."

"Yes, we'll be able to live off the land as we go, just like an army," Luke Bouchard declared. "In a way, we'll be like pioneers, just as Grandfather was when he made the trek alone from Mobile along the winding Alabama on to Econchate.

"What sort of house will we build when we get to where we're going, Father?" Mara inquired, her sensitive face animated with mingled curiosity and eagerness.

"The weather is extremely hot, Mara, and our first concern will be to build dugouts made of adobe and logs, halfway into the ground to protect ourselves from that heat," Luke Bouchard explained. "Simata has told me a great deal about the region where we're heading, and he says there's wood enough along certain parts of the Nueces which our workers can hew and cut to size. Eventually it's my hope to have a small but comfortable *hacienda,* and of course a corral for the horses. Our eccentric but very gifted old wagonmaker has managed to get us horses enough to pull the six wagons I've commis-

195

sioned—I've inspected everything, and I couldn't have asked for better workmanship nor sturdier horses to take us on to what will be Windhaven Range."

"You will need more horses for your *remuda*," Simata spoke up, his dark eyes rolling with anticipation, "horses to help you drive your cattle in the right direction. There are many wild mustangs where we go, they can be captured and tamed and trained to round up the cattle. Eeyaah, I will teach my skill as a rider to all your blacks, Mr. Bouchard, and then they will have nothing to fear."

"I have heard that the Comanches and the Kiowas are the greatest horsemen to be found in this country, so that if you teach my workers to ride only half so well as they, Simata, I shall be more than satisfied," Luke Bouchard laughingly avowed. "But now it's time for target practice, Andy. Give us a demonstration yourself, and then you and Joe can show our women how to handle the weapons."

Djamba, Lucas, old John Dewton himself, and the other blacks from Windhaven and the Williamson plantation emerged from the house to watch. A pair of scrub pine trees stood a hundred feet away, and Andy and Joe now strode to the trees and attached home-made bullseyes.

Andy Haskins, in buckskin jacket and breeches and moccasins, nodded to his Georgian friend: "Old John's picked out a pair of each kind of firearms, and when we're finished with the shoot, they'll go back in the cases, and they've all been marked so that the captain of that packet we're going on won't know what's really inside. John's a pretty fair carpenter, and he's made the cases and boxes a mite different in size, sort of camouflage, you might say. Hand me that Spencer, Joe, I'll show the ladies first off. They ought to be lots better than me, seeing as how they've got two arms and I've just got one."

Joe Duvray brought over a loaded Spencer rifle. "I do declare, Andy, you're the biggest showoff I ever met up with. Specially when there's ladies around." Then, turning to address the absorbed women who had moved closer to the two young Southerners, he added, "Soon as Andy does his tricks, I figger I can take one of you ladies and

196

teach her while Andy's showing one of you others. That way, it'll go faster. Two of you can be learning at the same time."

"Go right ahead, Joe, that sounds like a very good idea," Luke approved.

"Now you ladies'll notice I got me a piece of leather patched to my jacket at my shoulder," Andy Haskins explained, turning slowly so that all of them could see what he meant. "That's sort of to cushion the bruise that butt is gonna give me when I pull the trigger. Tell you what, Joe, unload the Spencer, then show them real slow and easy how you load it for me. Watch close, ladies, and after you've tried your hand on the bullseyes, we're going to ask you to be mighty patient with us and learn just how it's done. Never can tell when knowing how to load your rifle real quick when you're up against it might just save your life."

Maybelle bit her lips and nervously glanced at Sybella who met her questioning gaze with a reassuring smile.

"No, Maybelle, I don't want to kill anyone any more than you do, but if some bandit or hostile Indian tried to kill you, it would be your duty to protect yourself or the children or any one of us who's in danger, just as I myself would try to protect you if you were in danger."

"I—I understand, Mother," Maybelle murmured.

Meanwhile, Joe Duvray had unloaded the Spencer and was reloading it, explaining how the rimfire cartridges were fed through a tubular magazine in the butt. "Now this is lever-operated," he went on, "so all you have to do is aim, fire as fast as you can, then cock the hammer and pull the lever to shoot again. When you've used up the one in the magazine and the seven in the chamber, it's time to put a new magazine of cartridges in—just like this." Then, turning to Luke Bouchard, he chuckled and added, "You know, Mr. Bouchard, you got a better deal than you thought from that sidewinding Yankee captain. Damned if his boys didn't bring along two Henry repeater rifles, and they're the best I've ever seen. They take a .44 caliber cartridge, rimfire of course, and they can handle sixteen shots with lever action. They've got the tubular magazine under the barrel, and I'll just bet that Henry got the idea for that design from Hunt's Volition Repeater. Best of all, you don't have to cock the hammer every time as you do with the Spencer."

"Sixteen shots, Joe? That will really come in handy if we're attacked by a large force of hostiles," Luke said.

"Well, Mr. Bouchard, they say about this model that you load the Henry on Sunday and fire all week long," the young Georgian replied. "All right, Andy, now you're all primed to go, let's see what you can do with that left-hand target."

Cuddling the butt of the Spencer against his shoulder and leveling the rifle squarely at the target, squinting along the steel sight, the one-armed Tennesseean pulled the trigger and then again and again and again until the magazine was emptied. His friend hurried up to the improvised target and whistled admiringly: "Three in the bullseye, five neat as you please between the next and the last circles. And that's without hardly even aiming. I declare, Andy, you can outshoot me with your one arm to my two!"

Next, the young Tennesseean demonstrated the carbine and finally the six-shooter, moving up to a distance of 35 feet from the target. Thrusting the revolver into the holster at his left side, looking around to make sure that he had everyone's attention, he suddenly crouched, plunged his left hand down to the butt of the revolver and emptied it. This time, Joe Duvray announced, four holes appeared in the bullseye, two about half an inch away. "Now that's what I call a lightning-fast draw. Ladies, we're not after that, we just want to show you how to aim and get away a shot as accurately as you can. Now then, I'll load them up again, and we can start our lessons."

Luke escorted Lucy to a dilapidated little shed near the end of John Dewton's back yard where, for the revolver practice, Andy Haskins and Joe Duvray had set up new targets at a 25-foot distance. Andy Haskins helped her adjust the butt of the rifle against her shoulder, level it and aim along the sight. "Now just cock the hammer and squeeze the trigger, ma'am," he counseled. "For the first time, you better not level them all off at once, or you'll have a mighty sore shoulder. Gently now, that's it."

"Oh my goodness!" Lucy gasped as the recoil of the rifle made her stumble back. "It—it kicked like a mule!"

Mara, Maybelle and then Sybella broke into compassionate laughter at the startled look on Lucy's lovely face. But, she insisted on continuing until she had demonstrated a passable ability to place several shots in the last and next-to-last circles, and to load the rifle without faltering. Meanwhile, Joe Duvray had begun to instruct Sybella Bouchard in the use of the rifle, the carbine and the revolver, trying not to use technical terms that would confuse her as to distance and wind velocity. "Now then, ma'am," he urged, let's see how you can do at the target. Take your time."

Sybella squinted along the barrel, adjusting the butt against her shoulder, cocked the hammer and then crooked her right forefinger against the lever of the Spencer. The recoil staggered her, but she hung on grimly, and when she had finished, Joe Duvray excitedly announced, "Darned if you didn't hit one bullseye and put all the others along the last two circles, ma'am! Now that's what I call darn good shooting your first time out."

"Thank you, Mr. Duvray." Sybella grimaced as she rubbed her bruised shoulder with her right hand. Inwardly, she was thinking, *If only I'd been there at Windhaven, that trooper never would have shot poor old Matthew down. Or if he had, I'd have avenged Matthew with one of these.* Aloud, she added, "I don't ever want to think of lining up that sight against a man, even if he's a bandit or an Indian after my scalp. I'll have to try to pretend it's just a target like that one in the tree."

"I understand your meaning, ma'am," Joe Duvray nodded. "What you're sayin' is that you got a lot of respect for what these guns could do, but you want to use 'em jist when you have to stay alive. That's a right sensible way to think about these things too. All right now, who's my next pupil? Miz Forsden, I'm graduatin' you right now, with honors."

It was Maybelle who followed her mother-in-law to the target on the right-hand pine tree, under Joe Duvray's able guidance, while Maxine and Mara performed creditably under Andy Haskins's instructions. Maybelle's shots with the carbine and rifle tended to be wild, but she did vastly better with the six-shooter and the target on the shed. So much so, indeed, that she showed a flash of humor for the first time in years by wryly remarking, "Maybe if I'd had one of these back at Windhaven a long time ago, I could have kept that restless husband of mine around and not let him go meandering off to New Orleans—maybe everything would have been different then."

And then it was the turn of Luke and his son Lucien Edmond and then Djamba and Lucas and, one by one, the other blacks who would accompany the Bouchards on their Windhaven venture. . . .

Luke and Lucy stood at the rail at the stern of the *William Wallace*, looking back at the receding levee as the packet majestically moved out toward the great Gulf. "It's beginning, my darling," he murmured as he drew her to him, an arm around her waist. "May God watch over us on the weary miles to our new home. It'll be a rude, primitive one at first, Lucy, but we'll all be together."

"Yes, Luke dear. You know, I've the feeling that our lives are going to be changed, especially Maybelle's. She's been so despondent, I was glad to see her perk up when we were learning how to use the guns. Wouldn't it be wonderful, Luke, if she found a nice, considerate man homesteading out where we'll be, someone who could look after her?"

"I'd like nothing better for Maybelle, my dear one. Say good-bye to New Orleans. We'll be getting our supplies from San Antonio from now on. I wonder—I wonder if I'll ever see John Brunton again. Of course we'll correspond with each other. But we'll be a very long way apart."

His gaze, fixed on the bustling crowds along the dock and the levee, was almost melancholy. He was thinking of Laure Prindeville, now Laure Brunton, wondering what sort of life she and his best friend would have together.

He did not notice, at the back of the throng of stevedores, soldiers and vendors hawking their wares, the scowling face of a man with a fastidiously waxed mustache who had just been talking to a burly black stevedore and learned where the unusually large cargo and its owners were headed.

Nor did he see the man, wearing a green frockcoat and black breeches and boots, make his way to a telegraph office just off the wharf from which the *William Wallace* had weighed anchor, and, pausing at the door, look back a last time at the departing packet, his mouth twisting in a vindictive smile.

"Can I do somepin fer you, Cap'n Soltis?" the bespectacled, gray-haired clerk respectfully asked.

"It's plain George Soltis now, Elmer. Resigned my commission. Yep, I'm a plain ordinary citizen again. But sure, you can send a message for me on to the dispatcher at the Corpus Christi station."

"Be glad to, Cap'n—heh-heh, I mean Mr. Soltis—right?"

"Right as rain, Elmer. Give me that pencil and that sheet of paper. I'll just sit me down and write it out nice and neat for you. You make sure it goes on the wire fast, there'll be a ten-dollar tip for you."

"Why, fer that money, Mr. Soltis, I'd send it ahead of President Johnson's message, effen he were to come in here right this minute 'n wanted to git his off fust, I sure 'nuff would. Take your time, Mr. Soltis."

"I've finished. Here you are, Elmer, and here's your tip and enough to cover the charges."

"Thank you, mighty nice of you, Mr. Soltis sir! Here now, lemme read it back to you jist to see if I got it right—it goes this way—

> Rutherford from G. S., get word to M., wagon train heading from Corpus Christi. Arriving *William Wallace*, just sailed. Luke Bouchard in charge, two dozen with him, believe well armed. Bouchard swindled me. Have M. get me satisfaction. Acknowledge usual way."

"You've got it perfect, Elmer. I'll be back in a couple of days for the answer. And see that you don't go blabbing about this to anybody, hear? Specially about the answer."

201

"Nobody's gonna know nuttin' 'bout this whole thing 'ceptin' you'n me, Mr. Soltis," the old telegrapher fervently promised.

George Soltis's smile was not a pleasant one as he plucked at the pointed tips of his mustache. "That's exactly the way I want it, Elmer," he said softly as he walked outside to watch the packet growing smaller in the hazy distance as it neared the mouth of the Gulf.

CHAPTER EIGHTEEN

It had been barely a year since Ferdinand Maximilian, Archduke of Austria, had formally renounced his claims of succession to the throne which his older brother Franz Josef held as Emperor, and had crossed the ocean to ascend the throne of Mexico. He and his Empress Charlotte had been assured by Napoleon III through the Convention of Miramar that France would never fail the new Mexican Empire; nevertheless, they found Mexico to be a country torn by violent strife. Even before the impractical young Archduke had been beguiled to accept this untenable throne, President Lincoln had declared that America would not tolerate any infringement of the Monroe Doctrine and that any European power who intervened in Mexican affairs would sooner or later encounter the hostility of the United States. Now that the North had emerged triumphant in the Civil War, Secretary of State Seward had refused to receive Maximilian's Consul-designate, avowing that it was not the habit of the United States "to have official or private dealings with the revolutionary agents of a country with whose legal President

(Benito Juarez) the United States is in diplomatic and friendly relations."

Against the impractical Maximillian, there stood a pure-blooded Zapotec Indian from the mountains above Oaxaca, a little lawyer dressed in a dark civilian suit, an austere man who had risen from abject poverty to become the leader of the Liberal faction in Mexico. With the help of the United States, Benito Juarez had become President of Mexico late in 1860, and one of his first decrees had been to confiscate without compensation all church property, to make cemeteries national property and marriage a civil contract so that no Mexican need pay the clergy either funeral or marriage fees. Against Maximilian's idealism, stood the unwavering integrity of Benito Juarez who was determined to govern legally and abide by the constitution, and to transform his oppressed land into a nation of small peasant-proprietors. Thus from the moment that Maximilian accepted the crown of Mexico, Benito Juarez became his sworn, implacable enemy.

It was June 26, 1865, a day after Luke Bouchard and his family and loyal workers had boarded the *William Wallace* bound first for Galveston and then Corpus Christi. It was the day on which Francois-Achille Bazaine, Marshal of France at the age of fifty-four and commander of the troops of Napoleon III whose support alone could hold the throne for Maximilian, celebrated his marriage in Mexico City to a lovely seventeen-year-old Mexican girl, Dona Josefa de la Pena, whose uncle was a former President of the Republic. And already on this very day French bankers were telling Napoleon III that Bazaine and his men must abandon this hopeless aim of conquest because there was only bankruptcy at the end of it for France.

The Zocalo, the huge public square of Mexico City, was crowded with carriages filled with attractive young women who wore their finest dresses and mantillas in honor of the wedding. Indeed, many families in Mexico City claimed some kind of relationship with the pretty young bride, and some of the women witnessing the ceremony wore hats from a new French milliner who had opened up a shop on Plateros and was able to get her wares easily

204

through customs because of her friendship with certain high-ranking French officers.

It was a gala day, with brilliant uniforms on display and a parade by the Zouaves. Archbishop Antonio Labistida had consented to perform the nuptial mass in the palace chapel, to unite the aging Marshal with his teen-aged bride, putting aside the memory of their differences of a year ago when he had threatened Bazaine with excommunication and the latter had talked of blowing in the doors of the great Cathedral with his cannon. Even though the Archbishop disapproved of Maximilian's liberal policy, the fear of an American invasion and the resurgence of Juarism compelled him into a reluctant support of this regal venture. And Maximilian himself paid tribute to Bazaine as the representative of "our great and enlightened ally," while Charlotte so far ignored her exalted status as Empress of Mexico by condescending to kiss the bride in public.

But for all the pomp of the occasion, the French soldiers felt disillusioned. Weakened by disease, exhausted by continual marches across mountains and scorching deserts, seeing little prospect of the riches and glory which the recruiting officers had promised back in France, they had already begun to wonder why they were not called back to safeguard French possessions on the Rhine against militant Prussia, rather than lying trapped in some miserable Indian village fighting for an emperor whose cause no one believed in, with allies who could quite easily desert overnight and go over to the *Juaristas*. A year ago, the native population had welcomed them as the bringers of peace, and now was either indifferent or actively hostile. For the villagers lived in terror of the bloodthirsty vengeance exacted by the soldiers of Benito Juarez once the French troops had moved on. Nor were there sufficient French soldiers to consolidate the temporary gains over all the nameless villages of the countryside.

And even the new bridegroom, the most illustrious soldier of all France, was writing home to his imperial master that the weakness of the campaign lay in the government of the Emperor Maximilian.

On the afternoon when this brilliant and joyous celebration was taking place, hundreds of miles to the north a band of thirty horsemen rode toward the little village of Miero, a dozen miles from Nuevo Laredo in the province of Nuevo Leon. At their head, on a gray gelding, brandishing a captured French rifle and with two pistols thrust through his broad leather belt, his wide sombrero tugged down over his forehead, rode Diego Macaras. He was swarthy, with a thick mustache and shaggy goatee at the tip of his doubling chin, his dark little eyes set closely to the bridge of his nose, his lips thick and sensual. He wore a green coat and matching breeches and glossy new black leather boots, and although Benito Juarez had denounced him as a traitor and *ladrón*, he continued to proclaim himself a general of the *Juaristas* and wore epaulettes on his shoulders and a handful of stolen medals on his coat.

He halted now, rose in his stirrups and lifted his right hand to order a halt. Coming up beside him, Ramon Hernandez, slim, twenty-five, his second in command, looked cautiously at his *jefe*. "Your orders, *mí jefe?*" he asked as he brought up his right hand in a formal salute.

Diego Macaras's beady eyes considered him a moment, and then in a whiskey-hoarse voice, he retorted, "You will take two men, *mí capitán*, and go to the outskirts of that wretched *pueblo*. Report back if you see any of those mutinous dogs in the streets and whether they have guns."

"*Sí, mí jefe*. But I know that village well. They have not given any shelter to the French. The troops of Bazaine have not come so far north, they do not have enough strength."

"Do you dare to argue with your general, *Capitán?*" Diego squinted at the handsome young man beside him. "I say that *pueblo* gives aid to the *gringo* dogs of the French, and we are here to punish them for it."

"I will carry out your orders, *mí jefe*." Again, Ramon Hernandez smartly saluted, wheeled his horse, but not before his leader had angrily called, "I wish to be called general, not *jefe, comprende usted?*"

Ramon Hernandez did not answer as he rode down the double column of men behind the swarthy leader, selecting two men to accompany him.

Ramon Hernandez had been born in the village of Candela, in the province of Coahuila. His father had toiled in the silver mines operated by a corrupt *federalista* under the Presidency of Miguel de Miramon, head of the Conservative Party and a staunch defender of clerical power in Mexico. Seven years ago, young Ramon had watched, powerless and weeping, as a platoon of soldiers had dragged his father out of their little adobe hut into the public square, where his wrists had been manacled above his head to a towering round wooden post set in the center of a hastily erected platform. There, at the order of the director of the mine and on the grounds of treasonable insurrection, Pedro Hernandez had been whipped to death before his son's eyes. A month later, Ramon's fifteen-year-old sister had been ordered to the *hacienda* of the obese, lecherous official ostensibly to serve as maid, but in reality to become his servile concubine. A month later, despite her Catholic piety, she had taken her own life because she could not endure the shame of her degradation.

Ramon Hernandez had vanished from Candela the day following the discovery of his sister's suicide, but three months later, as *Señor* Esteban Cordona was taking a siesta in the patio of his *hacienda*, the young *peon* had climbed the adobe wall to its top and sent his knife unerringly to bury itself into the fat official's heart. Thus at the age of eighteen, Ramon Hernandez had become a proscribed outlaw, with a price of a thousand *pesos* on his head. With the coming to power of Benito Juarez, he had joined the forces of Major Alfredo Gonzales and seen action against the civil war mercenaries paid by the clergy to fight their battles and keep possession of the rich lands and the rents and the tithes. Last year, when Gonzales had been killed by a French sniper on the road to Querétara, his troops had disbanded, fleeing in cowardly flight before French lancers. Ramon Hernandez had escaped with a flesh wound in his thigh, and friendly villagers had hidden him and nursed his wound.

Six months ago, he had heard Diego Macaras address

the inhabitants of a tiny little *pueblo* not far from the village where he had first known life, been attracted to the pompous leader who declared that he fought for the justice of Benito Juarez to free the common people against the French usurpers and to unite all Mexico in a holy war. At first, when Macaras had made quick, successful forays against small forces of French infantry and cavalry attempting to ferret out dangerous malcontents who might revolt against the rule of Maximilian, Ramon Hernandez had devoutly believed in the military cunning and the idealistic principles of his superior officer.

But then there had come one raid after another into villages where the French had never yet set foot, raids that became orgies of useless slaughter, of rape and theft, and Ramon Hernandez had begun to sicken of his pact with Diego Macaras. Indeed, this very afternoon, he had been at the point of telling the self-appointed general that he planned to ride south to join the army of Porfirio Diaz, undeniably Juarez's most gifted, fiercely loyal general.

The two men whom Ramon Hernandez had chosen from Diego Macaras's ill-assorted followers were both former *peónes*. One of them, a year younger than Ramon himself, had seen his mother slashed to death with a saber wielded by a French sergeant; his name was Roberto Nigarte. The other was a fat, bald man in his early thirties, also a former *peón*, Tomas Aguimante, who had toiled with his brother in the fields of a rich landowner in Guadalupe. The brother had been unjustly accused as a thief, whipped before all the other *peónes*, ultimately dying from the ordeal. At first, both Tomas and Roberto had enthusiastically joined this guerrilla force to wage war on the hated French as well as to avenge the tyranny of the greedy, rich landowners. But by now they had seen how too often the raids of Diego Macaras ended in the needless slaughter of old men and even children, and they had no stomach for the looting and the raping that followed.

"*¡Amigos, vamanos!*" Ramon Hernandez bade them as he wheeled his chestnut mare toward the narrow road which led into the little village. He wore a pistol strapped in a holster on the left side of his belt, and a short sword taken from a French cavalryman on his very first action under Macaras's standard. He had been made a lieutenant after that first campaign, and promoted to captain a month later; with a great show of ceremony, the swarthy leader had pinned onto the shoulders of his ragged blue coat the insignia of a French cavalry captain which had been torn from the uniform of its dead owner. Perhaps it was as well for Ramon Hernandez's peace of mind that he had not seen the announcement issued by Benito Juarez himself which, in addition to proscribing Diego Macaras as little more than a bandit and outlaw, contemptuously condemned him for issuing military promotions which had neither basis nor legality so far as the Liberal army arrayed against Maximilian was concerned.

As for the two former *peónes*, they had old Belgian rifles, single-shot, clumsy to wield as well as to load, and of dubious accuracy. They eyed each other now and flanked their young captain as all three rode warily on to this sprawling little village of adobe huts which could boast only a public square and a little fountain outside the humble church which raised its cross far above the tallest roof of those impoverished dwellings which it spiritually defended.

"*Hombre*, are you thinking what I am, Tomas?" Roberto muttered as he eyed his companion. The latter nodded, his face gloomy: "The *capitán* was right, the French have never come so far. But our illustrious general thinks otherwise. It will be an excuse to do what he likes best, *no es verdad?*"

"*Sí, hermano*. But we have little choice. The *capitán*, he is an officer, he can argue for us."

"For all the good it will do him." Tomas surreptitiously crossed himself and then drew the rifle out of the rude scabbard he had improvised out of rawhide and attached to his horse's side from the saddle.

They had reached the entrance of the village now, and the blaze of the sun was dwindling, but the air was oppressively warm. Only an old priest stood by the fountain, laboriously dipping a wooden bucket and lifting it out, then turning slowly and moving back toward the church.

"*Hola, Padre, momentito por favor!*" Ramon Hernandez called as he lifted his short sword.

The old priest set down the bucket, crossed himself and

209

waited, as the young horseman rode up to him and dismounted. "God be with you, my son. Do you bring soldiers into this poor village? You will find nothing, I am afraid, except poverty and sickness. Three of our strongest young men are down with the fever, and I go now to administer the last rites of Mother Church."

Ramon Hernandez bent his head and devoutly crossed himself. "May they be granted eternal forgiveness, *Padre*. I ask you this only, have the soldiers of the French entered this village and has anyone given them shelter or help?"

"I have seen no soldiers except yours, my son. If you will excuse me, these three poor souls cannot wait much longer to make a good confession and to have their sins absolved before they die."

"*Vaya con Dios, Padre*. I will tell the *jefe* there is no reason to come here, so you have nothing to fear." Ramon Hernandez bowed his head as he saw the old priest raise a trembling, bony hand and make the sign of the cross over him. Then, mounting his mare, he turned back to the double column which had halted, Tomas and Roberto following him at a canter.

"What have you found out, *mi capitán*?" Diego Macaras's voice was mocking and insolent.

"That there is sickness in the village, that they have never seen the French, and that the old priest from that little church goes to give the last rites to the dying," Ramon Hernandez replied.

"We shall go there anyway. I have in mind a good lesson for these little *pueblos* who let a stupid priest do their lying for them," the swarthy chief replied. Then, rising in his stirrups, he turned back to his men and bawled, "Attack, enter and attack! Kill anyone who offers the least resistance. You, *Sargento* Duerto, take five of your best marksmen, have them fix bayonets, and enter the largest of those huts. If you find gold, take it. If you find weapons hidden there, kill those who own them. *Adelante*!"

"But, *mi jefe*," Ramon Hernandez anxiously protested, "I could see for myself that no one was stirring in the village. And the old priest himself, he was weak and himself had the signs of illness upon him."

"*Señor Capitán Hernandez,* I have felt of late that you are wanting in respect to your general and to your duties. I demote you now. Tear off the epaulettes I have given you for courage—you are little more than a coward. You can redeem yourself only by joining the others and showing your valor."

"If that is all you think of me, *Señor* Macaras, then I will do better than demote myself, I will resign from your company."

As Ramon Hernandez wheeled his horse toward the rear of the double column, the swarthy leader chuckled softly, drew one of his pistols, leveled it and pulled the trigger. Ramon Hernandez uttered a stifled cry of pain and then slumped over the neck of his horse. Frightened, the chestnut mare broke into a gallop, its unconscious rider still seated, his arms dangling on each side of its neck.

"Thus with all traitors," Diego Macaras blew the smoke from the barrel of the pistol, thrust it back under his belt. "Now, *hombres,* let us teach the people of Miero the lesson of Benito Juarez. Let them learn from what General Macaras will teach them now that priests are out of fashion and as corrupt and wicked as the landowners who taxed and whipped all of you. Forward, and you Jorge," turning and grinning at a scar-faced stocky *mestizo* who held the rank of corporal and whom Diego Macaras employed to apply torture to those suspected of hoarding gold or hiding their women from him and his men, "see to it that you find me a pretty little pigeon for tonight, or I'll reduce you to a private, *comprende?*"

With hoarse shouts of anticipation, the little bandit army of Diego Macaras galloped toward the village of Miero. In the distance, the chestnut mare had halted now, turning back its head and whinnying as it perceived the inert rider still upon its back. It pawed the parched earth with one hoof, whinnied again. But the bullet which had penetrated just under the right shoulderblade of Ramon Hernandez had left him unconscious. It had emerged through his upper chest and dropped to the earth, and his blood stained the flanks of the restless mare.

CHAPTER NINETEEN

A flight of seagulls swept through the sky, dipped down over the packet *William Wallace*, then climbed upward toward the bright blue sky, uttering shrill, eerie cries. Almost since the steamboat had pulled away from the wharf at the Queen City, the gulls had followed like a kind of convoy. They had disappeared for a few hours off Matagorda, but now that the port of Galveston was in view, they returned as if to bid welcome to James and Arabella Hunter and their children Melinda and Andrew who would come to their new home.

Arabella turned to Luke, her face suddenly shadowed with concern: "Why, it's a lovely city, this Galveston! And James has told me all about the hotels and the theaters and the fine restaurants—he makes it sound just like New Orleans! But, Luke dear, he's told me into what barren country you're going to go with those wagons—I feel so selfish already, thinking that here we'll be in civilization, and you'll be in a kind of wilderness."

Luke Bouchard considered his half-sister, touched by her sudden twinge of compassion. Gently, he replied, "But, Bella dear, it's in the wilderness that a man finds his soul. We shall go where there will be few neighbors, it's true, but those whom we shall find there may be staunch companions and enduring friends. And I, for one, would rather have that than be nearer the larger towns where there still exists a prejudice against the color of a man's skin or the humbleness of his birth. What we shall forge out of this wilderness home of ours will be a new Windhaven, and it will be ours through effort and hardship, and perhaps it will be the sweetest home of all that we have ever known because it will be so dearly won. No, Bella, say a prayer for us, but don't be sorrowful and think that we'll be abandoned. Remember what Grandfather achieved after he had come as a stranger in an alien land to live with those whom many called bloodthirsty savages."

"I remember, Luke. May God be with you and your family and the good fine men who go with you to work beside you," Arabella whispered as she put her hand to his cheek and then swiftly kissed him on the lips, turning away quickly to hide the tears.

Little Andrew had come up beside her now and was demanding attention, plucking at her sleeve, "Mama, is that where we're going to live now? It looks so big! Won't you tell us what the surprise is now that Cousin Jeremy has for us? Tell me, not Melinda, I'm your good boy, Mama!"

She bent and kissed him on the forehead, and Andrew made a grimace of annoyance at this mark of affection, warily glancing at his older sister, who promptly put out her tongue at him. "But Andy, dearest," Arabella murmured, "the surprise is for both of you. It wouldn't be fair to tell you and not your sister. And I want you to promise me one thing, darling. When we get to our new home, I want you to be nicer to Melinda."

"Aw, do I have to, Mama?" His voice had the childish whine of self-pity as he again glanced spitefully at his sister. "She put out her tongue at me just then. Didn't you see it, Mama?"

"Andrew Hunter," Arabella straightened and cupped his chin in the palm of her slim hand, "if there's anything I can't stand, it's a little tattletale. And if she did, you must have had it coming. Now both of you are going to make peace with each other, or I'm going to know the reason why. Don't forget, I've got a hairbrush in my reticule, and it's for naughty boys as well as for naughty girls. Now you go over there to your father and behave yourself!"

Andrew obeyed, but not without glaring at his sister, who tossed her pretty head and turned away from him with a smile of triumph. James, who had observed all this byplay with a humorous smile, winked at Arabella and then blew her a kiss from the tips of his fingers which made her blush. In the glance which passed between them Arabella pledged a passionate reunion to the man who, from their very first meeting, had known exactly how to temper discipline with indulgence. It was James who had taught Arabella how to combine passion with domestic partnership in marriage. It was a lesson that had turned Arabella Bouchard from a flirtatious, self-seeking girl into a devoted but far from subservient wife who savored the status of near-equality to which her husband had brought her.

The *William Wallace* hove to along the dock and the stevedores began their preparations for the lowering of the gangplank and the securing of the packet to the mooring posts.

"Time to say our goodbyes, Bella," James called, and took her hand. "I can see Cousin Jeremy over there with those two fellows in white coats and trousers—do you make him out? He's the tall one with the thick sideburns, a handsome devil and a very hard worker. There'll be no loafing on this job for me, Bella, and it's a good thing. I was beginning to get a little slothful amid the fleshpots of New Orleans, I'll confess."

"Oh James," she laughed affectionately, squeezing his hand, "as if you could ever be slothful, not you! I declare, if I'd guessed how stern and businesslike you could be when you set your mind to it, I'm not so sure I would have let you cozen me into marrying you."

"I know what you're thinking," he bent to whisper in her ear, "because I heard that little business with the hairbrush. Just remember, my dear, there'll be plenty of handsome men in Galveston, and I mean to make sure you don't try flirting with them too obviously. I don't

215

mind at all if they admire you—it makes me feel all the more smug at having won you, Bella, but I'm not about to let you get smitten by anyone else. Please remember that, my dearest wife."

Arabella blushed and lowered her eyes, then gave her husband's hand another ardent squeeze. The shouts of the stevedores, the welcoming cries from the throng at the dock, and the steamboat's shrill whistle to declare itself at last in port lent a festive tone to this reunion which would be a new beginning for Arabella and her family. And as the gangplank was lowered, Arabella's eyes were again filled with tears as she bade farewell to Luke and his son Lucien Edmond, to Lucy and Maybelle, to Mara, to Celia and Prissy, and finally, sobbing uncontrollably, her arms hugging her white-haired mother Sybella, urged the latter to write as often as she could.

The blackness was fraught with waves of seething pain, and he felt vaguely like a swimmer caught up in a treacherous current who fought against its pulling him down into nothingness. He groaned softly, blinked his eyes, forcing himself out of the dark, tortured void, and above him, blurred in his slowly adjusting vision, was the anxious face of the old priest he had seen beside the fountain of Miero.

"*Hijo mio*, you have been restored to us. All praise to Him who died for our sins and to His *Madre Sanctissima!*"

Ramon Hernandez slowly turned his head, finding himself in a small drab adobe hut, lying on a straw pallet with a tattered *serape* drawn over him. He was naked save for his drawers, and he could feel the sweat along his sides and on his chest and belly. Turning his head to the left, he perceived a woman's face, round and brown-skinned, with dark eyes and full mouth. "Where am I?" his voice was weak and unsteady.

"In the village of Miero, in the hut of Magdalena Abruta, whose father was a warrior of the Tejas and whose mother one of our people," the old priest gently explained. "It was she who nursed you, my son. I prayed in the church that your life would be spared, I knew your heart was not evil."

"I—I remember, Father. And Diego Macaras and his

216

men—I told them that your village had never given aid to the French soldiers and that they should not attack it."

"Alas, my son, they did not believe you. They rode in upon us, and six of our men are dead and ten of our women and three of our children. And besides such needless murder, those men with whom you had ridden carried away three of our young girls. May God protect their innocence with His all-knowing compassion."

Ramon Hernandez closed his eyes and uttered a groan of desolate anguish. "Father," he said after a long moment, "I have sinned greatly before God. I rode with those men because I believed that their leader would defend our country against the foreign tyrants. But I had already known that the *jefe*, Diego Macaras, spoke of liberation and then looted and killed. I had sworn that I would leave him at last to join the army of Porfirio Diaz—yet I was one of those men, Father. Absolve me if there is pardon for such a sinner."

"You were not a sinner, my son, your heart was good, you came to warn us. That you could not force those men of violence to go in peace away from us was not your fault, nor was what they did your sin. *Ego te absolvo*, in the name of the Father, the Son, and the Holy Ghost." He made the sign of the cross above Ramon Hernandez's head, then gently put his palm to the young Mexican's forehead. "The fever has broken, that is good. Magdalena will bring you broth and a tortilla soon, to give you back your strength."

"When was it—how long have I been here, Father?"

"This is the morning of the third day, my son. After they had gone through our village and done what they had come to do, a few of us went out to see if they would return. It was Magdalena who found you, fallen from your horse which still stood beside you, whinnying and prodding you with its nose to waken you from what would have been eternal sleep had you not been found."

"I—I am grateful to you for life, *Señora* Abruta," Ramon Hernandez said with an effort. Already again the faces of the half-breed woman and the old priest had begun to blur.

She shook her head, smiling at him, touched his forehead again with soothing fingers. "*De nada, Señor*. Your

217

compañeros shot you down like a useless flea-bitten *sabuezo* as they did my *esposo,* Manuel."

"I am sorry, *señora.* But I was one of them, and in a way, as guilty of your husband's death as they. You should have left me to die there."

She shook her head. "*Padre* Antonio told me what you had said to him at the fountain. I knew you were not one of them in spirit, *hombre.* Now you must talk no more, but rest until I bring you food." Gently, her soft fingers touched his eyelids and Ramon Hernandez obediently closed his eyes and uttered a long sigh.

The old priest rose slowly to his feet. His brown robe was dusty and smeared with blood along the left arm. The half-breed woman, in her early thirties, went quickly to him, her eyes worried and questioning: "*Padre,* I must look at your arm again. I will brew more herbs for the wound of the sword which those *cobardes* dared to give you. *Ahimi, que sacrilegio* to break into the church itself, to steal the silver cross and the chalice—they will be damned to the fires of hell, will they not, *Padre* Antonio?"

"That is for the judgment of God to decide, my daughter. Judge not, lest ye too be judged. Yes, it was wrong of them to steal from the church, from God's own house. But He will avenge the sacrilege, Magdalena. Let us go out into my little dwelling, and you will look at my wound. But I know it is already healing, the saber cut was not deep. And then you will bring that young man food while I pray for him and for our poor village and the souls of those who perished without cause." He made the sign of the cross, turned and left the hut, the woman following him.

Ramon Hernandez had lost all track of time. The little hut diminished his world, kept him in a kind of hypnotic darkness. Later—he did not know when—the woman knelt beside him, gently slid her left arm under his shoulders, whispering, "You must eat, *hombre,* to grow strong." And, like a docile child, without argument or the strength for it, he had dutifully let her put bits of tortilla into his mouth, spoon out the nourishing hot broth. then felt the drowsiness of sleep close in upon him as she carefully lowered his head onto a blanket she had folded on the straw to serve as a pillow.

He was young and strong, and fortunate in that the treacherous bullet of Diego Macaras had made a clean exit from his body. Slowly he regained his strength, sustained by the solicitous care of the handsome half-breed woman, who nursed him like a child. *Padre* Antonio came several times during the day to visit with him and to talk of what was going on in the world, so far as news could reach this obscure village. It was said that the forces of Juarez were gathering to strike here and there at the French out of ambush and then to retreat into the countryside where it would be certain death to search for them. It was said also that the new Emperor and his Empress were estranged, and that the Pope had just issued an encyclical condemning the imperial policy of Mexico and the publication of Maximilian's decree on religious toleration. But the news which most distressed Ramon Hernandez was that Porfirio Diaz had surrendered to Marshal Bazaine after a resounding defeat at Oaxaca, which remained the chief French stronghold in the south.

"*Padre,*" he told the old priest, "even when I rode with those brigands, I had decided to join the true Juarista army. Many of my friends have told me of the skill and fairness of General Diaz, and it was my hope to make amends for having been in league with a man who was nothing more than a greedy thief and murderer by fighting for the freedom of my country under such a one as Diaz. But now, I do not know what I shall do, *Padre.*"

"He who marks even the fall of a sparrow from the sky will put into your heart what you must do, my son. You have told me why it was that you became a soldier for freedom. God will not condemn you because you misjudged the true purpose of that man who shot you down like a dog and left you to die. From what you have told me, I know that you did not have a part in the looting or the murdering of innocent people. Never fear, my son, He will lead your footsteps in the direction you must take."

Ramon Hernandez rose unsteadily to his feet, swaying with weakness, as Magdalena Abruta, with a gasp of concern, steadied him with an arm around his shoulders. "Tell me, *Padre*, when those men left Miero, did you see in what direction they traveled?"

"To the north, my son."

"So," Ramon Hernandez mused aloud, "they would have headed for Laredo. A month ago, Macaras told me that he had a good friend there who received messages from Corpus Christi by the iron wire that carries words across many miles. He boasted to me that he had a powerful friend in New Orleans who had sold him some of the best guns he had ever seen. I am sure that he and his men rode on to Laredo so that he could see whether there were more words for him on the wire. Perhaps it is thus he is shown where to attack and rob and kill. *Dios,* what a fool I was to have trusted him, but he spoke so bravely of liberating my poor country—"

"Do not distress yourself, *hijo mio,*" *Padre* Antonio gently remonstrated. "And I pray with all my heart that you are not thinking now of vengeance. Vengeance is mine, saith the Lord. Do you remember your Bible, my son, when you took instructions? Then you must know of the story of the great king of Babylon who gave a feast to praise the gods of brass and silver, of copper and of gold, and how at the height of the feasting a portion of a man's hand was seen to write upon the wall, 'Thou art weighed in the balance and found wanting, thy days are numbered.' Verily, my son, He will mete out punishment to the evildoers."

"I know, *mi padre.*" Ramon Hernandez bowed his head and crossed himself. "But I mean to go to Laredo and find the man who receives these words over the wire and tells them to that vile *cobarde.* For now I know that his ambition for gold and killing and the rape of innocent women may take him across the border to attack even the *gringos.* Perhaps, if I find this man whom Macaras called McCutcheon, I can tell the *guardia civil* of the *gringos* to watch for this man and to throw him into prison where perhaps they will put a rope round his filthy neck!"

"No, no, my son," the old priest's face was anguished "your words say one thing, but I feel that your heart says still another. You are bent on the vengeance you must not take, and besides, if this man in Laredo is a friend of the *bandido,* you may lose your life by seeking him out."

"But I shall try at least to find out for myself what kind of man this McCutcheon is and what messages he give

Macaras. Never fear, *Padre*, I shall be very careful. I have stayed here long enough, it is the seventh day now."

"No, my son, you are still too weak."

"My horse—"

"It is being cared for by Pedro Mortugar, who is our *alcalde*."

"Then tomorrow morning, *Padre*, I will get my horse and ride to Laredo. But first," Ramon Hernandez thrust a hand into the pocket of his breeches, drew out a handful of gold and silver coins, "take this *dinero* for your church and for the poor and needy of Miero. I promise you that one day I myself will replace the stolen cross and chalice."

"But you will need your money, my son, for your own journey."

"I have enough left, and what I give you now is the Judas payment Macaras gave me as his *capitán*. It is evil money, *Padre*; use it here and turn it into good. Most of it was stolen from the French soldiers against whom we fought in honor—for these last few weeks, I refused to take wages which I knew came from the looting of the poor like those in this village, *Padre*."

"Very well, my son, for the poor, and for the widows of those who were killed by those cruel men. But you are still so weak, and it is too early for you to undertake so long a journey," *Padre* Antonio anxiously replied.

Ramon Hernandez shook his head. "I'm strong enough now, thanks to you and this good woman who tended me. Once back in the saddle on Corita, I'll be strong again, never fear. Tell your good *alcalde* that I will claim my mare tomorrow and reward him for caring for her. And before I go, *Padre*, I shall come to your church to make a good confession and to ask your blessing."

"You have it already, my son. I shall be waiting for you in the confession box. And now I must go to those who mourn their dead and do my best to comfort them. Gold will buy food, but alas, it cannot buy back the lives of the dear ones. *Hasta mañana*, then, my son."

Once again he made the sign of the cross, then turned and left the hut. Ramon Hernandez cautiously tested his legs and arms, raising and lowering them, walking a few short paces within the small confines of the adobe lodging of the handsome widow. She stood watching him, her yellow cotton blouse baring her shoulders and the cleft of her generous but still firm bosom, revealing the sunbrowned satiny, strongly muscled arms; and her red skirt, falling to the middle of her sturdy calves, outlined the generous curves and thighs of a still desirable peasant woman.

He had thrown away the coat with its captain's insignia and bidden Magdalena Abruta to burn it, for it was a dishonorable uniform. His shirt was grimy and torn and his breeches dusty and ragged as well, but Magdalena Abruta stared intently at him, her face inscrutable, her dark-brown eyes unwavering.

In the troubling silence that had fallen since the priest's departure, Ramon Hernandez at last cleared his throat and awkwardly began, 'And you, *Señora* Abruta, I have little left to repay you, except a few pieces of money."

"Do not insult me, *señor*. What I did was out of kindness and pity, not for *dinero*."

"Of that I am already certain. But the food—"

"All the villagers contributed it, and I have my own little vegetable patch outside this hut, and it is enough for my needs. But there is something you can give me, and it would be far better than all the gold in the world, *Señor* Hernandez."

"And what could that be, *Señora* Abruta?" he stared uncomprehendingly at her.

"*Hombre*, my Manuel and I were married a dozen years, and he died on the anniversary of our betrothal, when *Padre* Antonio read the banns in the church, three months before he married us. We longed for *niños*, both of us, but *Nuestra Señora* did not see fit to bless us with them."

Her eyes were lowered, and her fingers twisted together in front of her as she stared stolidly at the earthen floor of the hut. Ramon Hernandez waited, uncertain, suddenly feeling himself an intruder into the poignant world of the past which Magdalena Abruta now recalled; and the anguishing knowledge that he had been one of those who had ridden in and made her a widow was a torment. He wanted to speak, but he could find no words, only to put out his hands in a gesture of compassionate apology.

"You are leaving Miero tomorrow, then, *no es verdad*?" she asked in a low voice that he could scarcely hear.

"*Sí, Señora* Abruta."

"*Es muy bueno*. If you wish, then, to pay me as you have said—"

"Forgive me, I did not mean to offend you, I should not have spoken of gold—"

"You are forgiven. But if you were to give me a *niño*, it would be the greatest gift of all. And since the people here know that I was faithful to Manuel, they will believe that *Nuestra Señora* at last took pity upon us and let me bear a child to take the place of Manuel. Would you do that, *Señor* Hernandez?"

The young Mexican colored hotly, and bit his lips and glanced nervously at the door of the hut, as if hoping that *Padre* Antonio would return and extricate him from this greatly troubling situation. Once again he floundered: "*Señora* Abruta, you know nothing about me—you know I must leave—I would not offend you—"

"I know that I am older than you, and so it is I who ask your pardon for the offense. But I shall pray to the *Madre Purissima* to let me conceive, so that when you have left Miero, it will be as if Manuel implanted life within my body before he was killed. I am not a shameless *puta*, but I ask you to consider me worthy of you for this one time alone, *hombre*. I will blow out the candle. Then you will not see if I am ill-favored or too old. Let me be your woman this night and take me as you would your own *novia*."

Ramon Hernandez caught his breath and took a step forward, a hand extended toward the handsome peasant as if to halt her. She turned toward the flickering candle, and as she did so she sent him a look of such total openness that he felt himself trembling with wonder. He tried to speak, but the sounds died in his throat. He saw her large eyes study his face an instant before the hut was plunged into darkness as, quickly stooping, she blew the candle out.

Then he heard the rustling of garments, and there could be no further doubt of what she intended of him. Yet he felt not so much desire—though, yes, there was that too—as he did a sudden overwhelming humility before the devout simplicity of her wish. He was not so experienced with women as to make the first opportunistic move toward her, even though he sensed that she was naked; rather, he had the anguished self-searching thought that he was not worthy of her, he who had come to this obscure village as an officer of a murderous bandit horde. He could not disclaim responsibility for her tragic widowhood, which had impelled her to make this supreme gift of herself—for he instinctively knew her to be chaste and loyal.

And as he stood there tortured by all these doubts and self-recriminations, he felt her arms link around him and her lips seek his to apply a kiss of the most perfect trust and acquiescence, and tears sprang into his eyes as his still outstretched hand brushed the warm satiny nakedness of her side and he heard her faint gasp which signified that her womanhood was attuned to his maleness, though they had been as strangers till this moment.

"*Hombre*," she breathed huskily as her body merged with his, exhorting him with the most elemental blandishments, "*con todo su fuerzo*, take me! Do not think of any sin, if there is such, *hombre*, it is mine—take me, now!"

He groaned aloud, stricken by the urgency that rose from deep within him; he who had not once looked upon Magdalena Abruta with lust now wakened to the subtle yet direct woman-essence of her. And of a sudden his entire world became concentrated within the narrow mud walls of this little hut; there was nothing beyond them, and what took place was timeless, primal and yet withal a sacrament shared between them.

For it was both an act of love and of pity, of deepest compassion and of poignant, almost selfless, dedication. As Ramon Hernandez lay beside Magdalena Abruta in the long dark night and heard her gentle breathing in sleep, he told himself that she had given him back not only his life, but also his manhood and his honor.

CHAPTER TWENTY

As the *William Wallace* followed the curve of the Gulf of Mexico to Corpus Christi bay, Luke Bouchard listened to the haunting cries of the gulls. They seemed to be almost a harbinger of the loneliness and primitive life which awaited him and his family and followers once they embarked on their overland journey. Nor was his first glimpse of the desolate little town any comfort. As the packet approached the muddy shallows, he saw a long line of grayish wooden shacks which dotted the desolate shore. The harbor itself seemed little more than an improvised set of loading docks, against whose round posts tiny waves lapped, and the unpainted, sunbleached wood seemed as if the water were eroding it like a slow acid. The inland part of Corpus Christi was hardly much more prepossessing: more shacks, a dusty street and a set of false-front stores, with none over a story tall.

As he turned to his left, he could make out a faint line of bluffs which rose no more than twenty feet, placed about a quarter of a mile from the docks. Undoubtedly the rest of the town must be hidden behind those bluffs, and from the looks of things already, it could scarcely be more attractive. Already the sun blazed pitilessly down from a cloudless sky, and he felt drops of sweat roll down his sides as he mopped his face with a linen kerchief.

Lucy stood beside him, contemplating the bleak landscape beyond them. "This is just a stage of our journey, isn't it, Luke dear?" she asked, giving him a brave smile and reaching for his hand.

"I'm sure it is. Simata has told me a good deal about where we're going, and I assure you it's far more scenic than this. And once we're away from the Gulf, we won't have this damp heat."

"I should think in country like this water would be very hard to find, Luke."

"From what he's told me, Mexico's rivers are all underground. And here in this part of Texas which is so close to the border, there are many hidden springs and extensions of those underground rivers. The Nueces itself runs beyond here, and it's very shallow for a good part of our trip. But if anyone can find water, Simata can. Besides, we've plenty of kegs in our wagons to keep us all going until we find our new home."

"Compared with Windhaven, it does look dismal right now, I'll confess," Lucy gave a nervous little laugh. "But I shouldn't worry, knowing that you're in charge of our little expedition. So far, my darling, you've made the right decisions, and we have always done very well."

"Don't speak so in the past tense, Lucy," he smilingly chided. He put his arm around her shoulders and drew her to him as they stood against the rail watching the stevedores begin to lower the gangplanks. "This is only the beginning. We have a new challenge before us, and there's nothing better in the world for a man at my time of life than having to forget all about the comfortable old ways and learn to cope with the new. We'll manage, Lucy. Just keep loving me, we'll manage very well, I promise."

"You don't have to ask that of me, darling," was her faint whisper. Yet all the same, as she turned to look at the nearest gangplank being swung down over the side, there was a suspicious mist in her eyes.

Mara, Maxine, Sybella and Maybelle, as well as Celia and her daughter Prissy, watched with mixed feelings as the packet came into this dreary, sun-baked port. Maybelle, uttering a long sigh, turned to Mara and murmured, "It's summer, and yet there's nothing here that's green, not like home. It's so lonely, so few people, it terrifies me."

Mara's lips curved in a mocking little smile: "Sometimes, you know, it does one's soul good to be alone, especially if the people around you aren't to your liking. Besides, we're not stopping here, we're going a long ways on, Aunt Maybelle. There'll be lots more freedom for all of us, but at the same time, we'll be closer than we've ever been before just because there aren't so many neighbors all around from the start."

"That's all very well for you to say, Mara, but you're seventeen years younger than I am, and my life's just about over."

"Now you stop talking like that, Aunt Maybelle! I declare, self-pity is just about the worst thing in the world for anybody. If you have to feel sorry for somebody, think of me, why don't you? Yes, I'm seventeen years younger than you, it's true enough, but I'm still a spinster. But you don't see me complaining."

"You shouldn't be so harsh with her, dear," Maxine Bouchard gently remonstrated with her sister-in-law. "She belongs with us, she's one of us, too, after all. And don't forget, her daughter Laurette's gone off to Chicago with her fine husband to start an exciting new life there. And maybe they'll have children soon, and then she'll have grandchildren to love her."

"I know, Maxine, I know." Mara whispered back. Aloud, she said to Maybelle, "Don't forget how you showed us all up at target practice back in New Orleans, Aunt Maybelle. We need you along with us, just in case bandits or Indians attack us. We'll all feel safer because you can shoot so well."

And Maybelle was able to force a wan smile to her lips at this good-natured teasing. But it was Sybella who, moving to her daughter-in-law, had the last and most optimistic word: "I know how Maybelle feels, girls. Why, when I married my Henry, I felt as if I were leaving one world and entering an unknown one when I had to leave my father's cabin. It's only natural to have a certain emptiness inside you when you've pulled up all your roots and you're going to transplant them in a place you've never seen before. Why, if you don't miss where you came from, it only shows you didn't love your first home and you're not yet ready for a new one. Maybelle is going to surprise us all, and that's my prediction. Now we'd better go to our cabins and be sure we've packed everything for the journey."

Meanwhile, Lucien Edmond, Djamba and his son Lucas were busy supervising the unloading of the wagons, they themselves tying ropes around the sturdy vehicles and helping the stevedores ease them down the gangplank to the heavily timbered dock. Meanwhile, the three younger blacks, Dave, Frank and Ned, took charge of the horses which Luke had purchased from the old wagon-maker, and began to hitch them to the wagons.

In addition to the dray horses, Luke had acquired durable riding horses for himself, Lucien Edmond, Simata, and Djamba and Lucas, as well as the two young Southerners, Andy Haskins and Joe Duvray. The young Kru Dave would drive the lead wagon in which Lucy and Mara would ride; Frank was to drive the next wagon carrying Maybelle and Sybella, while Ned would drive the third wagon in which Maxine would ride with little Carla and Hugo. In the fourth wagon, driven by the Ashanti Carl, who had been foreman at the old Williamson plantation, Celia and Prissy, Harry and Betty would ride together. William, the Angola from Windhaven, would drive the wagon containing the furniture and bric-a-brac saved from Windhaven, and old George, who beamed with pride when Luke smilingly informed him of his first duty as an employee of Windhaven Range, would handle the reins of the two horses which pulled the chuckwagon.

Bearded old Captain Jamie McMurtrie came down the gangplank to say farewell to his passengers, who indeed had practically commandeered his entire packet. "Mr. Bouchard," he approached Luke with a broad grin on his wrinkled face, "now that I see all of your cargo put together, I've a feeling I've helped take part in a major expedition."

"Yes, it amounts to that, Captain McMurtrie," Luke smilingly shook hands with the elderly Scotsman. "And if you feel the urge, I'm sure there'd be room for you in one of the wagons."

"Not for me, sir," Jamie McMurtrie bristled, stroking his shaggy white beard and arching his bushy eyebrows, "No, ever since I've been a lad I've been on the sea or the Gulf, and that's the way I'll die, may the Lord be willing for't! All the same, sir, you're a man that has plenty of grit in your craw, and I wish you and your dear ones all of the best. It may be I'll have word of how you fared when again the *William Wallace* drops anchor here. I hope for your sake that your journey has been worthwhile."

"That's in the hands of God, Captain McMurtrie. With a little effort on our own part, I think we'll find what we're looking for," Luke Bouchard shook hands again with the bearded captain. Then he turned to stare at the false-front shacks which marked the main street of Corpus Christi. "Houses built out of mud and wood, but they can endure the heat and stand the cold," he said to himself. "They won't be as fancy as Grandfather's red-brick chateau, but they'll keep us safe from the elements and the dangers of wild animals and those who don't take kindly to our presence." He turned back toward the north, as if summoning up for one last time the image of the chateau. "We begin again, as you did, Grandfather. Look down upon us, you and your Dimarte, approve our enterprise, grant we may all equal your courage and honor in our venture."

Then, as if impatient with himself for the emotion which came to him at the thought of his dauntless ancestor, he strode toward the lead wagon and helped Lucy clamber up into it, as Djamba handed him the reins of a roan stallion on which he would ride at the head of this procession.

Both Andy Haskins and Joe Duvray had expressed their admiration of the wagons, particularly of the metal wheels fitted to durable wooden hubs. The balance was excellent, meaning that heavy loads could be hauled with minimum difficulty, and that the wheels themselves were not likely to be dislodged when going over an obstruction. Both young Southerners advised Luke Bouchard, however, to be content with a daily trek of from fifteen to twenty miles, so that the horses would have plenty of rest and time for food and water. There would be no replacements for them, not till they reached their destination where there were many wild mustangs which could be trained to draw wagons as well as to furnish fast mounts for the riders.

Before leaving New Orleans, Luke had acquired a map of Texas as far as it had been charted at that time, and his study of it showed that the area of Carrizo Springs was roughly about two hundred miles from Corpus Christi, which meant a journey of from ten to twelve days barring unforeseen delays. Then, too, since continuous and arduous travel of this kind in open country would be tiring for the women of the party, it might be well to allow two or three days more for sufficient rest. But while fatigue was a problem, morale seemed to be improving: once the party had left the ramshackle town of Corpus Christi behind them and headed out to follow the winding Nueces River, everyone, even Maybelle, seemed to be in better spirits, in anticipation of a journey that would take them through country they had never seen before and through many miles of which had not yet been inhabited by white settlers. Thus the infallible stimulus of excitement and curiosity would help to overcome some of the weariness to be expected in so long a journey.

By nightfall, they had reached country that was mainly level for miles in every direction, with clumps of mesquite and cottonwood scrubs decorating the barren ground. Simata chose as a camping site a small knoll which rose about fifteen feet higher than the plain itself and thus gave the travelers a protective view of the surrounding landscape. He also instructed them to form a circle with the six wagons and to have some of the black workers stay on guard in shifts throughout the night.

Betty, jovial and bustling over her work as cook for the group, promptly busied herself in the chuckwagon. Soon a campfire was blazing, and the smell of biscuits, bacon and beans and strong coffee wafted through the air. It was simple fare, and yet all of them ate as ravenously as if they had been dining at Moreau's in New Orleans.

Before Simata pointed out their campsite, however, he had cautiously broken off a long dry branch from a dying cedar tree stunted by lightning, and had advanced cautiously, striking the ground and the sparse grass with the branch. "I chase away *piakwasinaboo*," he explained to Luke Bouchard who had followed him and watched with curiosity.

"That is the Comanche word for big snakes, isn't it, Simata?" he asked.

The Indian nodded. "Very big here and where we go. Snakes in water too, small ones they call coral, and the cottonmouth you have where you came from. We have this too in this land," he explained.

"I would know more of the Comanches, Simata, their customs, their beliefs. What can you tell me of them?" Luke demanded.

Simata turned, a hand to the top of his forehead, squinting into the distance, then grunted as if satisfied with what he had seen. "I thought to see the dust from many horses in the west," he explained. "It is but the wind. But in this country, a man must read all the signs and be prepared for what they foretell, or he may not live another day. Now, you have asked about the Comanches. Once, long ago, so my father told me, they and other tribes were called Snakes, and they mingled with the Shoshoni far in the northwest. Then, as they sought the buffalo, they came southward, and, finding their enemies to be the Spaniards and Mexicans, often rode over the Rio Grande to raid villages, carry away horses, cattle, even women. Their greatest warriors carry shields made from the hide of bisons, hardened and shaped so as to turn away enemy arrows, blows from lances or war clubs, even bullets. On these shields I myself saw bears' teeth, which showed that these Comanche braves were great hunters. And, too, with scalps to show that they are great warriors as well, and even the tails of horses, which is a sign that he whose shield is so decorated has won fame as a raider."

"Then, Simata," Luke said slowly, "the Comanches, had they met my grandfather, would have known him as a great hunter. For more than seventy-five years ago, when he came from across the great ocean to the land of the Creeks, to Econchaté where their *Mico*, their chief, ruled, he killed a she-bear with only his hunting knife,

231

and took its claws to wear about his neck to show the Creeks he had earned the right to live among them."

"But that was a great coup, for the she-bear is more savage than her mate when she defends her cubs," Simata wonderingly exclaimed. "My people, the Kiowas, like the Comanches, respect courage in a man, even a white-eyes. I tell you this, if we hold parlay with hunting bands I will tell them you are the descendant of a blood brother of the bear. Aiyee, they will think well of you for that, I am certain."

"But I myself have not yet counted any coup, Simata, and I must prove by my own deeds what kind of hunter and warrior I am," Luke rejoined.

Simata shook his head, touched his heart, then Luke's, and said softly, "You will count your coups, I feel it in my heart and in you. I see already you are more than worthy to bear the name of your *kaku-ai*, your grandfather."

CHAPTER TWENTY-ONE

Ramon Hernandez had said farewell to Magdalena
Abruta the next morning, had gone to the church and
made his confession to *Padre* Antonio, and then had re-
claimed his horse Corita from the gentle little white-
haired *alcalde*. In his saddlebags there was food which
Magdalena had given him for his journey to Laredo. He
wore the Belgian pistol strapped in a holster on his left
side, and he had retrieved the short sword which had
been dropped on the dusty plain when he had fallen
unconscious from his horse.

The clean wound had healed swiftly. His strong constitution and good health, coupled with his desire to bring
Diego Macaras to justice, had hastened his convalescence.
Nevertheless, he knew that it would take at least four
days to reach Laredo, allowing about twenty-five miles a
day—and even that would be an arduous test of his
slowly returning strength.

In the confession box, kneeling with bowed head as he
heard the old priest absolve him and pray for his safety
on the journey ahead, Ramon Hernandez had once again
sworn to restore the stolen cross and chalice to the little

church of Miero. This vow, too, gave him purpose for what lay ahead, and as he rode out toward the north, turning in his saddle to wave a last goodbye to the handsome peasant woman who stood on the road at the very edge of the little village, he felt also a deep and lasting tenderness for her. No matter where the road lay ahead for him, he resolved, he would find out what happened to Magdalena Abruta. And if there should be a child born from their having come together, then somehow he would make provision for both mother and child so that poverty would not blight their lives.

Midway along his journey, on nightfall of the second day, he heard from a distance the sound of horses' hooves, and swiftly led Corita deep into a thicket of mesquite, crouching beside her to remain hidden from the oncoming horsemen. Soon the sound grew louder, and there passed by him, at about a distance of a hundred yards, a dozen Comanches in full warpaint, bent on raiding some unsuspecting Mexican village where they would steal horses and carry away women to tend their campfires, tan the buffalo hides, cook the good meat and do all those many tasks demanded of a Comanche squaw—and they would do it, or they would die slowly and in unspeakable agony, he knew.

He waited for half an hour until he was certain that they had continued their ride without sending backtrackers to search the terrain, then remounted Corita and rode on. His shoulder and arm muscles ached painfully, but the new bandage which Magdelena had applied before his departure showed no signs that the wound had reopened. He fought against fatigue and the soreness of being in the saddle, and only grudgingly camped in a little cave made out of formation of chalky, white rock clusters, known in this country as *caliche*. Before dawn, he was in the saddle again.

It was late in the evening of the fourth day that he rode into Laredo and stopped at a livery stable where he found a fellow Mexican tending the exhausted horses of a stagecoach which had just ridden in under Comanche attack. *"Donde es el Señor* Ernesto McCutcheon?" he demanded.

"Yo le sabe, amigo, you will find him in the *Taberna del* Silver Star."

"*Muchas gracias, amigo.*"

"*De nada,*" the friendly stableman shrugged. "You have ridden far?"

"From Miero. And now I must see this man, McCutcheon. Will you keep Corita for me for a little while, *por favor, amigo?*"

"*Seguro,*" the wiry, middleaged Mexican smiled and nodded, taking the reins from Ramon Hernandez.

The Silver Star saloon was exactly across the street from the stable. Ramon Hernandez pushed open its doors and entered, his eyes quickly searching the men at the tables and the dance-hall girls among them.

At the bar was a fat bald man with a walrus mustache, in a dirty white apron and dirtier blue galluses which held up his black trousers. He was busy polishing glasses as Ramon Hernandez came up to the bar, and eyed the newcomer with a suspicious glint in his watery pale-blue eyes. "Whiskey, greaser?" he growled the question.

"No, *Señor*, not yet. I look for a man named Ernesto McCutcheon. If you would be kind enough to tell me where I can find him?"

"You're looking at him, greaser. What's on your mind?"

Ramon Hernandez glanced cautiously around, but no one was paying any attention to him and the bartender. To the latter's right, busily occupied in opening a bottle of tequila for a swarthy, burly Mexican in ornate poncho and sombrero, was a hunchback, with long bony nose and gleaming little eyes. With an effort, he finally got the cork out of the bottle and set it down before the Mexican, then produced a withered lime and a dish of salt for his impatient customer.

"I am Ramon, *Capitán* for Macaras," Ramon Hernandez muttered.

The fat bartender scowled, glanced from side to side, then leaned forward across the bar: "The password, before we talk."

"When we rode into Miero," the slim young Mexican answered, "it was 'A rope for Maximiliano, a bed for Carlotta, and long life for Benito.' Now, can we talk in private?"

"I guess we can." Raising his voice, the fat bartender

bawled, "Hunchy, take over for me. And be sure you charge for the salt and the lime, or I'll take it out of your wages!" Then, easing himself out of the narrow end of the bar, breathing heavily from the exertion, he gestured to Ramon Hernandez as he pulled open a rickety door that led to a windowless cubicle furnished only with a wide chair and an old mahogany secretary-desk. Easing himself into the wide chair with a grunt of satisfaction, he scowled again at the young Mexican: "Close that door, greaser. I mean, of course, *Capitán*. No offense meant. Now, what do you want of me?"

Ramon Hernandez brought his left hand up to touch his right shoulder. "I was wounded in Miero by a pig of a villager, and after the General and his men rode off, I had to force those peasant dogs at gunpoint to heal me and to give me a horse. So I have lost track of my *jefe*, and he had said that he often came to see the *Señor* Ernesto McCutcheon to get his messages which came over the wire from far away. I wish to rejoin him, you see, *Señor* McCutcheon."

The bartender reached for a scrap of paper on which was written the exact words which Captain George Soltis had had the New Orleans telegrapher send on to his colleague in Corpus Christi. Then he shoved it away and glared at Ramon Hernandez, who, however, had seen that impulsive movement and marked it. "It's funny now, the General didn't say a word about leaving his *capitán* behind in Miero. He was here three-four days ago. Now it seems to me, *Capitán*," this time he underlined the word with heavy sarcasm, "if he'd wanted you to join up with him, he'd have told me about it. I'm in partnership with him, you see. Seems to me, too, you'd know that if you still ranked in his army."

As he spoke, his left hand delved down to a narrow top drawer of the secretary-desk, but Ramon Hernandez had already seen that surreptitious movement, drawn his pistol from its holster with his left hand and fired. Ernesto McCutcheon stiffened, jerking forward, his eyes rolling upwards and a look of disbelief on his face, then slumped against the back of the chair, his head lolling to one side.

Ramon Hernandez reached across the lifeless body to pocket the crumpled scrap of paper from the top of the littered desk, holstered his smoking pistol, carefully opened the cubicle door, then nonchalantly walked toward the swinging doors of the saloon. The dwarf called Hunchy looked up from his conversation with the swarthy Mexican customer, and in a reedy voice piped, "Hey, greaser, where's Ernesto?"

"Back in his office, *hombre*." Ramon Hernandez stopped and casually shrugged. "He was showing me his gun, but mine's much better. And he says not to forget to charge the *señor* there for the salt, Hunchy. *Adios*." With this, he sauntered out of the saloon, then ran swiftly to the stable where the little Mexican was still holding the reins of his horse, mounted her and, calling back. "*Gracias, amigo*, next time I'm in Laredo I'll pay you well for helping me!" guided the fleet mare down the main street on toward the northwest. A few minutes later, angry cries announced the discovery of Ernesto Mc-Cutcheon's lifeless body, and the swarthy Mexican in the poncho and gaudily decorated sombrero hurried out, revolver in hand, to send a futile shot after the man on horseback, already dwindling in the distance.

Ramon Hernandez urged Corita on, patting her neck and talking to her as he would to a sweetheart, "That's it, *mi corazon*, faster now, faster, *linda* Corita! Soon we shall rest, you and I, and I'll give you oats and a good cool drink, but you must go now, faster than you've ever gone before—*adelante, mi querida*."

He turned the chestnut mare off the road and rode for more than a mile, till at last he was certain that there were no pursuers. Only then did he take out the scrap of paper on which was written the message about the Bouchard family. "*Por Dios*," he swore to himself, "that murdering jackal may have caught up with those poor people by now. *Caramba*! it's too late to warn them, but maybe I can pay my own debt back to this butcher who calls himself a general of Benito Juarez!"

From one of the saddlebags, he took a handful of oats and let the mare nuzzle his palm, stroking her neck. Again and again, until he was satisfied that she had been amply nourished for the time being. Then, remounting, he rode on through the dark, moonless night, his bitter thoughts eased only by the recollection of the *mestiza* who had saved his life.

By the seventh day, the six wagons of the Bouchards had come upon slightly hilly ground, and there were more thickets of mesquite, as well as isolated clumps of cedar and live oak. The blue horizon stretched on all sides of them, and the glaring sun beat down remorselessly till the ground itself seemed hard and baked. It was desolate, abandoned land, and to see no human habitation for miles around added to the loneliness. Instead, they saw from time to time sandstone and sedimentary formations, forming jagged caves and caverns on the tops of tiny, irregular hills. Sometimes a clump of wild rosebushes brightened the landscape, with the red and yellow blooms in startling contrast to the brownish, dry earth, and the chalky white rock clusters, *caliche*. As they went on, here and there, there were deep canyonlike stretches carved out by the Nueces River, where a tiny tributary had gone dry. At night by their campfires, the Bouchards and their followers could often hear the yowls of bobcats and mountain lions, and sometimes even the eerie howling of wolves.

But game indeed was plentiful, as Simata had predicted. Wild turkeys furnished a welcome substitute for the bacon and beans which had become the staple entrée of their suppers. On the fifth night, Lucas killed a wild hog which came snorting out of the mesquite thicket not far from the campsite, using one of the Spencer carbines. That night, Betty served seasoned, tasty pork and some of the sweet yams she had brought along in a bag from Windhaven.

On the seventh night, just before the wagons halted at the chosen campsite, Andy Haskins drew a revolver and fired twice at a clump of mesquite only a few feet away from the lead wagon in which Lucy and Mara rode. Dismounting, he reached up to the wagon and took down a long crooked branch from a cedar tree which he had broken off a few days earlier, and gingerly poked at the pulpy head of the rattlesnake he had just shot. Its whirring rattles had sounded harshly on the evening air as it lay coiled beside the clump. "That's a big one," he announced as he used his branch to uncoil the lifeless rep-

238

tile. "I'd say about nine feet, and look at all those rattles. It's an old one, but just as deadly as a young one. Sorry to have scared you ladies with my sudden draw, but that old rattler might have bitten one of our horses, and right now we can't spare any."

Simata turned to face the southeast, a troubled look on his face. Luke, who had dismounted and was leading his horse to tether it to the back of the lead wagon, observed the young redbone's preoccupation and called softly, "What is it, Simata? What do you see?"

"Nothing yet, But the night is very still, and I have a feeling here—" he touched his heart, then vaulted down from his saddle. "All day long, I have had the feeling that someone follows us from a distance. If that is so, and there is an enemy, he will attack at night, after we have eaten, when he thinks we sleep and are off guard."

"But I remember your telling me that your people and the Comanches seldom attack at night, since they believe that if their warriors are slain in darkness, their spirits will not find the Great Spirit in the sky."

"That is true, as I have said it. But it is not true of the white-eyes, or the Mexicano, Mr. Bouchard. It may be that he who follows us comes as a thief or a murderer, whose coup is best made when night hides him from our eyes," Simata solemnly declared.

"Then how do you advise us to prepare for an attack?"

"Have your men draw the wagons in a circle, away from the fire. If you have clothes you do not need, take branches of mesquite and stuff them, to make them look like men who sit around the fire."

"Like dummies to draw the attackers' fire—I understand, Simata," Luke eagerly agreed. "Djamba, Lucas, Andy, Joe, come here, there's work to be done," he called, running toward camp. "Have Betty hurry the evening meal and tell William, George and Harry to serve it quickly. Have Carl break out the rifles and carbines, and you, Andy and Joe, make sure they're loaded. Lucien Edmond and I will load the revolvers. I'll have Lucy take little Carla and Hugo into that grove of cedar trees and hide till we're sure all is safe. Tell the drivers of the wagons to move them into a circle, and you, Lucas, Djamba, start the campfire and then take some of the trousers and coats in the valises and stuff them to make them look like men."

At once the camp bustled with purposeful activity as the wagons were first drawn into a circle well away from the grove of cedars at the southeastern side. The meal was quickly prepared and eaten after which Djamba and his son built a large fire, then hastened to make four dummies with clothes, branches and handfuls of earth, which they placed around the fire, two seated facing to the west, one leaning against a small live oak tree with the sleeves wrapped around an old musket George had brought along as a sentimental keepsake from Windhaven.

The tall Ashanti Carl hastily passed out the weapons, which Andy and Joe inspected for priming and loading, and distributed them. Both Maxine and Maybelle energetically refused to take refuge with Lucy and Maxine's two young children in the cedar grove. Joe Duvray shook his head dubiously, "Now you ladies aren't crack shots by a darn sight yet—beggin' your pardon—so you'd best not fire till you see the rascals up close to the campfire. Lie flat inside your wagon—that old galoot back in New Orleans was smart enough to make two flaps you can unfasten and peek out to aim by, and one's about knee-high, that'll do just fine, 'n you'll keep out of most direct fire. I still don't like the idea of you ladies bein' around when bullets start flyin', though."

"I'm going to defend my children, Mr. Duvray," Maxine declared, "and nobody's going to stop me, not even you. And I'll have you know that just because I'm a woman doesn't mean I'm not smart enough to use one of these things, 'specially when my childrens' lives are in danger."

Joe Duvray scratched his head, then grinned. "You know, ma'am, I'm beginning to think whoever's gonna ride into this camp is in for a mighty big surprise. But you mind what I say, and you too, Miss Maybelle, you lie flat'n peek outa that lowest shootin' hole, and you'll do jist fine."

Sybella also insisted on helping to defend the camp, and Andy Haskins reluctantly handed her a loaded Spencer carbine. Meanwhile, Djamba and Lucas, along with Dave, Frank and Ned, unhitched the dray horses and led them to the other side of the cedar grove, tethering them securely. Luke and Lucien Edmond, as well as Simata, led the lead horses in back of the grove and, at Simata's suggestion, blindfolded them. "These horses are for fast riding, they will shy at gunfire. Cover their eyes, it will keep them from trying to break loose," the young redbone explained. At his suggestion also the dog Jubal was muzzled to prevent his barking and warning the expected attackers.

At the northwestern side of the camp was a thick clump of mesquite trees, heavy with their bean-like pods. Simata carefully explored them for snakes, and pronounced the clump ideal for ambush. Luke and his son crawled into the clump, lying flat on their bellies, with the two Henry repeating rifles, while Andy and Joe and Simata, armed with Spencer rifles, took similar positions near them. Djamba and Lucas, with their Spencers, lay under the chuckwagon. Fat jovial Betty, squealing with fright, gathered her skirts and waddled as quickly as she could toward the cedar grove to hide beside Lucy and little Carla and Hugo.

The crackling flames of the huge campfire broke the stillness which settled over this lonely place. The moon had hidden behind a cloud and there were few stars. From a distance came the mournful howl of a timber wolf, and Luke started, his eyes widening, to hear, a few moments later, the warning hoot of an owl perched atop a live oak tree not far from the clump of mesquite.

"They come," Simata suddenly hissed. "Listen, many horses, many riders!"

Cupping a hand to his mouth, Luke called, "Be ready, everyone. Let them come as close as possible before you open fire."

"Isn't it time for bed, Grandma?" little Carla suddenly piped up as she turned to Lucy, who had induced both children to lie flat on the ground, one on each side of her.

"Soon, darling, but you mustn't say a word now. Or you either, Hugo, that's a good boy. Shh now, we'll go to sleep very soon, my darlings," Lucy whispered, giving each a reassuring hug.

The sound of horses' hooves grew nearer, and then the

snorting of horses being suddenly reined in. About a quarter of a mile to the northeast, the dark shadows of about thirty men on horseback appeared. Two of them detached themselves from the main body and rode toward the Bouchard camp, then wheeled their horses and waved their rifles as a sign to follow. At once the other riders galloped en masse toward the circle of wagons, and the first two men, closest to the campfire, fired at the propped-up dummies. Djamba and Lucas took careful aim, and triggered their rifles almost simultaneously; the two Mexicans toppled from their saddles, their horses rearing, then turning round and galloping off into the distance.

"Fuego, por todos los Santos, muerte a los gringos!" the swarthy leader, in green coat and matching breeches, angrily cried as he sighted his French rifle and fired at the chuckwagon, the bullet whining past Djamba's head.

The riders broke into two columns, each circling the wagons, firing at will. From the clump of mesquite, Luke and Lucien Edmond returned the fire, and three more riderless horses broke away and galloped back whence they had come.

Sybella, opening the lower flap, crouching low, cautiously poked the barrel of her carbine out and, seeing two blue-coated young Mexicans riding toward her, pulled the trigger. One of them clapped a hand to his shoulder and dropped his rifle, swearing violently as he rode back; again she fired, and the second rider stiffened, then slid backwards, his feet caught in the stirrups as his horse dragged his lifeless body over the hard dry ground.

Andy and Joe and Simata, sighting carefully, dropped four of the bandits before the furious leader, lifting his rifle, cried out, *"Vamonos, muchachos,* the *gringo* devils have tricked us!"

Maxine Kendall, aiming out of the opened lower flap in her wagon, fired, and bald Tomas Aguimante, who had ridden with Ramon Hernandez to scout the village of Miero, coughed and slumped over the neck of his wildly neighing, rearing horse, a bullet in his lungs. As the remaining bandits wheeled their horses in panicked confusion, Djamba and Lucas felled two more with well-aimed bullets. Again the swarthy leader bellowed, *"Vamanos, muchachos*, save yourselves," and wheeled his horse back the way it had come. Sybella saw the green coat plainly in her sights, and pulled the trigger. With a howl of pain, the bandit leader clapped a hand to his left shoulder, then spurred his gray gelding on, ignoring his men who, now leaderless, took flight in all directions to escape the accurate and withering fire of their intended victims.

Luke emerged from the mesquite, anxiously calling, "Is anyone hurt?" and then hurried to the cedar grove where Lucy was doing her best to quiet the frightened, sobbing children.

Simata, Andy and Joe emerged from their hiding places and warily approached the sprawled bodies near the campfire and around the circle of wagons. Ten were dead, and Tomas Aguimante was dying. As Andy knelt down and took out a canteen to hold to his trembling lips, the former peón gasped, "Forgive me, *Señor*. It was the *jefe* who—ordered—this. I would to God—I had listened to *mí capitán* Ramon—*Nuestro Señor, perdoneme Usted*—"

His head fell back, his eyes closed. The vengeance sought by Captain George Soltis had boomeranged indeed. . . .

CHAPTER TWENTY-TWO

Frank, Dave and Ned took over the burial detail for the bodies of the eleven bandits who had fallen before the concentrated fire of the alerted Bouchards. In return, their attack had been most ineffectual: Prissy, Maybelle and William had slight flesh wounds. Betty, having recovered from her fit of hysterics, tried to make amends by brewing fresh coffee and making biscuits which she insisted on passing out to everyone.

"We'll have to be on our guard in case they try to surprise us again," Luke said to Simata, as Djamba, Lucas and Andy and Joe rounded up the horses and hitched them to the wagons as before.

The Kiowa half-breed shook his head. "They will not come back, they have lost too many men. Even if they tried, they would need more men, and that would mean they would go back across the border. By then, we shall be at the place where I guide you, and we will build strong shelters and they will not be eager to try your strength again once you are settled on the land and begin to make your home there."

"We all owe you much, Simata. If you hadn't warned us about the bandits, we could have easily been killed,"

Luke gratefully declared as he took Simata's hand and clasped it between both of his own. "It was lucky for us all that Djamba and Lucas found you in New Orleans and brought you with us as our guide and teacher."

"But you fought well, with courage and cunning, as my own people or the Comanches would fight. All I did was to warn you, so you have already proved what I said, that you yourself are a great warrior, and you will be one day blood brother to a chief. I know this in my heart. Now I go to take the weapons of the dead *bandidos*. And the ammunition too. That is always what my people did in battle, so that they would be stronger the next time their enemies came against them." With this, he respectfully inclined his head to Luke as a sign of tribute, and hurried toward the workers who were digging the graves for the dead raiders.

Luke stood watching him, strangely moved by what the young redbone had just said. Once again, there came the hoot of the owl still perched in the live oak tree, and Luke swiftly crossed himself, glancing about to make sure that no one had seen this impulsive and uncharacteristic gesture. Even though he and Lucy had been married as Catholics, there had been no church of that faith within a hundred miles or more of Windhaven; yet, like old Lucien, he had devoutly studied the Bible and known the moral leadings of his religion. Now, in this spiritually exalting moment of victory over terrible danger, he had been reminded most of all of the inexplicable symbolism of the owl whose call had heralded the danger and now announced its ending. Inside him, there welled up a surge of mystical feeling, of nostalgic grief and love and gratitude, as once again he crossed himself and whispered, for only the silence to hear, "Thank you, Grandfather, and you, Dimarte the beloved one, you have answered my prayers, truly you have safeguarded us and journeyed with us in spirit to our new Windhaven—and perhaps to yours as you look down upon us who carry on in your honored names."

Djamba and Lucas, Andy and Joe, as well as Simata, took turns standing guard all through the rest of that night, but the bandit force had been much too severely beaten to think of returning with such depleted forces. And the next morning, after a hearty breakfast, the Bouchards and their workers resumed their trek across the seemingly endless plains. During the afternoon of the ninth day, they came upon thicker mesquite and cottonwoods, and now the land began to roll gently so that from the tops of the small rises they could see for miles ahead. The bunch grass barely stirred in the sultry breeze under the parching sun, yellowed and browned in most spots, with startlingly green patches in others. "It would be poor grazing for cattle in this region, especially without water," Luke pointed out to his son Lucien Edmond. "See how many dry creekbeds running to the Nueces we can see to the south."

Simata, who was riding beside the two Bouchards, nodded. "It is because the river goes underground so often or leaves small beds which dry up after many years. But there is much water where I take you. And there is good grazing for the cattle."

"Look there, Father," Lucien Edmond pointed far to the right, where on a gentle hill rise there seemed to be a series of rectangular mounds, framed by several sturdy live oak trees.

"They are burial mounds," Simata explained. "Warriors killed in battle, or old chiefs and wise men of the tribe who have gone to the Great Spirit and wish their bones to be mingled with the earth over which they once rode."

The dust was acrid as the wagons moved onward, following the winding river, and the women had soaked their handkerchiefs in water and tied them over their noses as protection from the scorching sun and the irritating dust. As the sun began to lower, the magnificent unending panorama of orange and red and purple sky appeared before them like some fairy-like mirage to console them for the bleakness of the landscape.

Simata had found a small creek partly filled with fresh water, beside which stood three sturdy cottonwoods, and indicated that here was a perfect campsite. As the drivers drew their horses to a halt, Lucien Edmond turned in his saddle to see a rider coming toward them from the southeast.

"Father, someone's coming," he called. "Just one rider, as far as I can make out."

"Perhaps it's one of those damned *bandidos* come back to parley," Joe Duvray growled, readying his Henry and squinting lovingly down its sight.

"He's a young man, and he's been riding hard," Luke watched the rider urge his chestnut mare on toward the wagons. "His horse is wet with slaver, and look, his shoulder is bandaged."

"Then maybe it's one of those raiders we shot who got away," Joe Duvray persisted as he took careful aim with the Henry.

But the slim Mexican astride the chestnut mare raised one hand in a gesture of friendship, then drew on the reins and brought her to a halt, her sides heaving, tossing her head and whinnying. "I am not an enemy, but *un amigo*!" he called to Luke Bouchard.

Luke had given the sign for the wagons to halt, and now rode up to the stranger. "You've driven that mare of yours a long way, it appears. Were you one of the men who attacked us two nights ago?"

"No, *Señor*, I swear it. I came to warn you against the *bandido jefe* Diego Macaras. My name is Ramon Hernandez. Are you not the *Señor* Bouchard?"

"Why, indeed I am, *Señor* Hernandez. But how did you know that?" Luke wonderingly asked.

The young Mexican dug his hand into the pocket of his breeches, pulled out the scrap of paper he had taken from Ernesto McCutcheon, and handed it to Luke.

"My God," he said to his son, "that attack was planned by the man who sold us our weapons and then tried to take them back so murderously. Read it for yourself, Lucien Edmond." Then, turning back to the young Mexican, he asked, "But how did you discover this and what possessed you to ride so far and so hard to warn us?"

"Alas, *Señor* Bouchard, until a few weeks ago I rode with that *ladrón* and *cobarde*. My father had been beaten to death by a cruel *rico* and I wished to avenge his death, so I joined the forces of liberation—or so I believed. Diego Macaras had declared himself a general under Benito Juarez, and at first when he fought the French troops who were sent to support Maximiliano to be Emperor of my poor country, I followed him gladly. But I found that his way of liberation was to destroy a village and to take what money he could find from the poor *peones*. It was my wish to resign as his *capitán* and join the army of Porfirio Diaz, but he must have guessed what I thought of him, and he shot me down and left me to die at Miero."

"You're a brave man, *Señor* Hernandez. But I still don't understand how you were able to get hold of this copy of a telegraph."

Ramon Hernandez smiled grimly. "This *jefe* who is a murderer had told me that he often went to Laredo to receive messages sent over the wire from many miles to this man McCutcheon, *Señor* Bouchard. After I had recovered from my wound, I went to Laredo and obtained this paper. I had sworn to avenge myself on Diego Macaras, and it was my wish that the first step would be to warn you against him and his men."

"They struck us two nights ago, *Señor* Hernandez," Luke answered. "Thanks to our Kiowa scout, Simata, we were able to defend ourselves."

"*Gracias a Dios!*" the young Mexican exclaimed. "Have I your permission, *Señor* Bouchard, to dismount and to water poor Corita?"

"But of course. You need not ask that," Luke smilingly replied.

Ramon Hernandez drew himself up in the saddle, wincing at the twinge of pain in his shoulder. "Forgive me if I tell you of something you do not yet know because you are new upon this land, *Señor* Bouchard. It is never wise for any rider to enter a camp or to come upon strange riders and dismount without asking their permission. If he were to do it without their bidding, it would be not only ungracious of him, but also perhaps the sign that he was an enemy and sought to draw his guns the moment he reached the ground."

"I'll remember that, and I'm grateful to you for instructing me, *Señor* Hernandez. But now, by all means, rest and water your horse, and I invite you to share our evening meal."

"That is very generous of you, *Señor* Bouchard." Ramon Hernandez dismounted, stroking the mare's neck, talking softly to her, as Djamba smilingly advanced to take the reins. "*Gracias, amigo.* She has heart and courage, that little one." He turned to look up at Luke Bouchard who was in the act of dismounting. "You say that you drove them off. I pray the good God that none of you was badly hurt."

"We have said our prayers of thanksgiving already, *Señor* Hernandez," Luke softly replied. "Only a few minor wounds, no casualties. But we buried eleven of their men."

"And Diego Macaras, their leader? That is right, *Señor* Bouchard, you would not know him by sight, of course. But he wears a green coat on which are many medals—medals he stole from dead officers."

"Then I can tell you that he was wounded. My mother, Sybella Forsden, shot such a man and wounded him in the shoulder, and he rode away with what was left of his men. It appeared that they were deserting him, judging from the directions the rest of them took when they withdrew."

"*Magnifico*! Your *madre*, you say? I should like to meet her and salute her for such bravery. *Caramba*, if it is known back in my country how this thief, this *cobarde*, led his little army against *gringos* who had never before set foot in Texas and was not only driven off but himself shot by a woman, he would become the laughing stock of all Mexico!" Ramon Hernandez tilted back his head and laughed heartily, then winced again and put a hand to his bandaged shoulder.

"You do not know anything of me, *Señor* Bouchard," he went on after a moment. "But I feel a great sympathy for you and your people who come so far and have shown such courage. Before I thought to avenge my poor father's death and to help liberate my country from a foreigner, I was a good *vaquero*. As you see, I ride well, also thanks to brave Corita. If you need a horseman, *Señor* Bouchard, I would be glad to work for you. And perhaps too I can be of help if ever Diego Macaras decides to return to settle the score. He may do that, *Señor* Bouchard, with the promise of much gold and women and new weapons, and he will recruit from the poorest villages, as he did me and some of the friends I had who, like myself, believed in his lies and rode with him."

Luke Bouchard held out his hand. "It is true that I know very little about you, *Señor* Hernandez, but you are honest, you care enough for people you have never met to ride all this way to warn us, and you are welcome as one of us as a *vaquero*, if that is what you desire. Now come have some supper and rest yourself—I'll have a look at that shoulder of yours later."

CHAPTER TWENTY-THREE

Now the land before them seemed less barren, less desolate, though there were still no habitations to be seen for miles around. Here and there were small steep banks of the river which led into concealed arroyos. There was dark-knobbed prairie which gradually rose, and early this tenth morning Luke perceived four does and two bucks standing on the top of a grassy knoll far to the north. The mesquite was thicker and grew higher now, almost as tall as a man's full-grown height, and here and there were wild beds of yellow roses, drawing their nurture from some mysterious underground source of water which belied the crumbly, sun-baked earth in which they seemed to thrive. By evening, the wagons moved beside hills whose rolling swells were topped with evergreen, flanked with oak and bushy mesquite. Here and there, as if carved out by powerful rushing river water centuries ago and then left arid, were the mouths of narrow valleys, canyons in which bandits or hostile Indians might hide to ambush the unwary traveler.

A day later, they came upon a valley thriving with cedar trees, with lush green grass and gaunt cattle grazing, cattle with incredibly long horns, as much as seven and eight feet from tip to tip, bulls who glanced up at the passing wagons and shook their heads defiantly, then pawed the ground, snorting in hostility: "Those big bulls lead the herd," Simata pointed out to Luke. "And you will find many more wild herds when we come to Carrizo Springs."

"They're fearsome enough, Simata," Luke chuckled, as one of the older bulls snorted and charged toward the chuckwagon, only to wheel and lumber back to the herd of cows it was guarding like a patriarch when Dave shouted and waved his hat. "I'm sure that many a matador would have second thoughts going into the bullring against a sharp-horned bull like that!"

On the next day, the wagons passed by abandoned adobe huts, crumbling under the scorching sun, and now the hills grew steeper, flanked with the inevitable mesquite and topped at the skyline with jagged crests of bright cedar. There were other kinds of flowers now, jaunty spears of Indian paintbrush, wistful bluebonnets in isolated patches, bold butter-gold dandelions, and lacy spider lilies which bent in the faint late afternoon breeze. Now they had entered a valley which widened to about seven miles, narrowing to half that width, only to broaden again. And along the river to their left, that threading, serpentine stream of water which had been their guiding mark throughout the trek, were profusions of tall, yellowish reeds, as high as a man's head, and a broad stretch of rolling prairie dotted with pecan, elm and oak trees and even thicker mesquite. Here the soil near the tributary streams of the Nueces changed from sandy red to waxy black, and as the sun began to descend on this twelfth day of their dusty, arduous journey, the Bouchards came upon a hollowed-out valley with a high-sloping river bank to the south and jagged little hills which perched above narrow canyons to the north.

"We are here," Simata grinned with satisfaction as he dismounted. "There is water, there are trees from which you can build your shelters."

"And no one owns this land as yet, Simata?" Luke Bouchard demanded as he turned to drink in the variegated landscape, profuse with color as the setting sun's rays touched the hills and the valleys and the trees and the flowers with a master painter's brush.

"My father told me long ago," Simata replied, "that twice there were colonies here, and that Mexicans from the river towns grazed their cattle on this prairie when the Indians had not yet come to hunt the buffalo and to drive all settlers away. But he said that they did not last, and so I think this land must belong to him who can settle on and hold it." He pointed to the southwest. "About forty miles from here, if I remember from my days as a boy riding beside my father, there is a Pass of the Eagles. He told me that a Comancheria, a large village of the Comanches, was hidden there in a stronghold. I do not know if it is there now, but the Comanches always wander on the land to find the best hunting. They are many tribes, you see, Mr. Bouchard. Some are family tribes who hunt, and there are the warrior tribes who make raids across the Rio Grande and who take up their lances to drive the white-eyes from whatever land they come upon. It is those tribes which you must most fear if you remain."

"You will teach me each day more and more of the Comanche tongue, Simata, so that I can make them understand I will not spoil their hunting or be their enemy."

The young Kiowa scout dubiously shook his head. "Words are as smoke upon the wind, Mr. Bouchard. It is by the coup that my people and the Comanche understand what is in a man's heart. It is how he treats them, how he acts toward them, not what he says. You, yourself, know from where you came, that there were many white-eyes who spoke with forked tongues and drove the Cherokees, the Choctaws and the Creeks from the land which once was theirs alone. The treaties of such men were as smoke upon the wind that vanishes and leaves no trace of what has been said and agreed to."

"I know your meaning, Simata, and I will try to show the Comanches and those tribes of your people who may still hunt and live in this beautiful country that I do not make treaties but keep my word and offer friendship to all men," Luke Bouchard declared.

There was a joyous feeling now as the campfire was built and Betty began to prepare the evening meal. Here at last, after a tiring and dangerous journey over country where they had not yet seen a single settler after having left Corpus Christi, the Bouchards had come upon what Luke, still standing and surveying the picturesque landscape on every side, had determined to call Windhaven Range.

"We'll live in our wagons until our workers can build lean-tos and dugouts and shacks for us," he told his son during supper. "I've brought saws and axes and hammers and kegs of nails, and each of us will do a good day's work until we've shelter for the women first and then ourselves."

Once again Andy and Joe and Simata, and the three younger black workers formed a protective circle with the wagons, unhitching the horses and watering and feeding them. "We'll need to build a corral for the horses, with separate stalls for our own mounts," Luke observed.

"Just before we found this place, Father," Lucien Edmond said, "I saw a herd of wild mustangs over to the north. They'd make good workhorses if they could be caught and tamed."

"We'll do that too, my son. They're swift and sure-footed, and when we round up our cattle next spring and drive them to market, we'll need plenty of workhorses. There'll be time enough this fall to break some of them in and train them. But as soon as we've finished building temporary quarters for our people, you and I and Djamba will have to ride to San Antonio to deposit our drafts and open an account. Yes," Luke nostalgically looked back toward the southeast, "the Bouchard name will one day soon, I pray, be as respected in Texas as it was in Alabama when Grandfather did business in Mobile and New Orleans. It's a name to be defended with honor and dignity, and although we are new to Texas, Texas itself is to have a new beginning after this war. So it and we shall grow together in the years of peace which follow."

"How far would you say San Antonio is from here?" Lucien Edmond asked.

"By the map I brought with me, Lucien Edmond, I'd say about a hundred and twenty miles. On swift horseback, by ourselves, carrying only enough provisions in our saddlebags, we should be able to ride there in four days, and four days back. And from what Captain McMurtrie told me, we'll have to rely mainly on San Antonio for our supplies. You saw yourself how desolate Corpus Christi is—the Union blockade just about wiped it out. But trade with San Antonio flourished long before the war, especially from New Mexico. And we'll send letters from there to Fleurette and Laurette to let them know how to reach us with the news of their own new beginnings." He turned back to the blazing fire, his face exultant. "And I'll get off a long letter to my friend John Brunton, and be sure to thank him again for all he did to make this journey successful."

As he spoke the name of his close friend, Luke saw in his mind's eye the captivating face of Laure, and once again a twinge of conscience stirred in him as he saw his gentle wife seated beside the campfire with her arms around little Carla and Hugo. *How attractive Lucy still is,* he thought to himself, *for all that she's a grandmother. How many good years we've had together, how much we've shared in joy and hardship—and yet why should I concern myself over Laure who entered my life so briefly? I must drive out these thoughts, they're unfair to Lucy. It's best that I've put so much distance between myself and New Orleans, for the hard work ahead of building a* hacienda *and making this new venture of raising and marketing cattle must occupy all my energy and mind.*

He went to the fire then and squatted down beside his wife and smiled at her, and she put out her hand and he took it in his and brought it to his lips. "We're home at last, Lucy darling," he said gently, and now the image of golden-haired Laure disappeared in the dark stillness of their first night together on Windhaven Range.

By the end of the devastatingly hot month of August, this pleasant stretch of valley had taken on the semblance of a little colony. The sound of axes had rung throughout the days until sundown, as Dave, Frank and Ned, assisted by Djamba and Lucas, as well as Carl, William and Harry, and even old George himself, felled timber, dried it, sawed it into planks and nailed them into place. Luke and Lucien Edmond supervised the work, so that by the time they were ready to leave for San Antonio to open the new bank accounts for the Bouchard family, there was a spacious bunkhouse for all the blacks. In addition, they had built a number of adobe and wooden dugouts half beneath the ground for coolness, for temperatures on most of these days rose to the 100° mark and above. They had also begun work on the *hacienda* itself, which was a sprawling one-story wooden frame house with a porch shielded from the sun by a planked roof covered with tarpaulin. This would house the family, but it would not be entirely finished until the end of September, so that the wagons would continue to be used as temporary lodgings for the night. Simata, Joe and Andy at once chose the adobe-wooden dugouts which were constructed at about forty feet apart from one another at the top of a little hill: in this way, they could constantly be on the lookout for bandits or Indians. The *hacienda* itself would be at the base of the gently rolling hill, commanding a magnificent view of the wide, grassy valley beyond. And far in the distance, Luke and Lucien Edmond could already see hundreds of longhorns feeding on the abundant grass and estimate how many there might be to round up the next spring, to fatten and then drive to the nearest and most lucrative market.

The black workers also built a small corral for the riding horses, and a larger one for those which had pulled the wagons from Corpus Christi. Ramon Hernandez supervised this construction, from his own experience as a youth back in his native province. "Just before the cattle roundup, *Señor* Bouchard," he told Luke, "I will help catch some of the wild mustangs and break them in so that they can become workhorses to drive your cattle. It is not easy work, but once you have tamed them, they will work hard for you. They have great stamina and are not easily frightened, especially by stampeding herds."

Before Luke and Lucien Edmond and Djamba left for San Antonio, Luke and his son rode out to make boundary markers for the land they intended to buy. "We should count on at least two thousand yearlings, steers, cows and calves for our first drive," Luke told his son. "From all the authorities on cattle-raising that I've read and from what I remember grandfather's telling me about how it was in Normandy, you should have from two and a half to four acres per head as grazing land. So we should mark off about eight thousand acres, and since we're here first, we can pretty much choose where our boundary markers go. Then I'll draw a map and show the markers, and later go to the land office in Austin to file my claim. Land like this should be extremely cheap, and it'll be the best investment of all for our Windhaven Range."

On the first Saturday of September, Luke, Lucien Edmond and Djamba saddled their horses with ample provisions for a four-day journey and headed toward San Antonio. Each carried a Spencer rifle in a scabbard attached to his saddle, as well as a six-shooter holstered to his belt. Andy Haskins, Joe Duvray, Simata and Lucas would remain behind as the chief guards of Windhaven Range. As soon as the trio had set forth, the four defenders held target-shooting exercise for the women and the other blacks of the entourage.

San Antonio was an old city, and already the legend of the Alamo had spread around the world. For over a century white men had been living on the banks of the river after which this town was named, and the Alamo itself stood across the street from a hotel whose rickety porch was crowded with blue-coated soldiers, farmers in flat-brimmed black hats, Mexican *caballeros* with fancy *sombreros*, and even Indian fighters dressed in buckskins and stinking of rancid tallow, with patches of scalps strung to their rawhide belts. Luke and Lucien Edmond turned to look at the Alamo, a ruined mission wedged against a warehouse, glorious rubble that would not be mended or touched by any of the town's citizens but remained as a memorial to gallant men who had given their lives against unbelievable odds.

A block away was the Citizens' Bank of San Antonio. Luke, his son and Djamba entered the bank and walked to the counter just inside the door where a bespectacled little man with thick sideburns and short beard was seated. He rose at once, smiling at Luke and Lucien Edmond, the smile freezing on his tight little mouth as he saw the tall sturdy graying Mandingo standing beside them. "A good day to you gentlemen. Haven't seen you here before. My name's Pericles J. Lysander, and I'm the president of this bank. How may I be of service?"

"My son and I and Djamba Forsden would like to open accounts in your good bank, Mr. Lysander," Luke replied. "We have drafts from New Orleans which came through one of the leading Boston banks."

"No trouble at all, sir, not at all, if it's as good as you say. May I see the drafts, please?" The bank president took out a silver-rimmed pince-nez, removed his dusty spectacles and adjusted the new visual aid as he peered at the three drafts which Luke handed him. "All in good order. Let me have the privilege of welcoming you, Mr. Bouchard—and I trust this is your son? I'll personally give you receipts and indicate the amount of money—I presume you want separate accounts?"

"And for Mr. Forsden also," Luke gently reminded him.

"I see, I see," the bank president testily muttered, with a quick, irritated glance at Djamba. "You know, Mr. Bouchard sir, these are great days for Texas. Yes sir. Just a few months ago, old Andy Johnson named A. J. Hamilton as provisional governor of Texas. He was a brigadier general in the Union Army, you know, and himself raised in Austin. He didn't hold with secession, not one little bit. We'll have law and order here, and no trouble. Come along this way, gentlemen." His glance included Luke and Lucien Edmond, but not Djamba.

"I trust you intend to open Mr. Forsden's account as well," Luke Bouchard quietly insisted as he and his son and the Mandingo followed the man to a teller's window.

"I suppose. If that's the way you want it. You understand, I'm from Virginia myself, left there in the late Fifties. But my heart's still in the South, in Dixie, always will be, gentlemen. So you can understand my feelings."

"I can, but I'd prefer you not to voice them," Luke firmly interposed. "Mr. Forsden got his manumission papers nearly thirty years ago, and he's my foreman at Windhaven Range."

"Do tell! And where is that, if you please, Mr. Bouchard?"

"We've ridden up from the Nueces, near Carrizo Springs."

"I wish you all the luck in the world—and you'll need it. Why, those damned Injuns have just about massacred all the white settlers around that place for miles. So if you're after land, you can get it dirt cheap—forty or fifty cents an acre, though of course you'll have to go to Austin to stake your claim."

"We'll do that directly. The three receipts, if you please. Thank you, Mr. Lysander. I was told that this is a solid, trustworthy bank," Luke Bouchard's lips had the hint of a smile on them with this last remark.

"Solid as Texas itself, I'll have you know," the bank president fumed, glaring at Luke. "It'll stand just as long as the Alamo, and that's a fact, Mr. Bouchard. There you are, a pleasure to do business with you. I hope we'll be seeing you in San Antone right often."

"We'll come in for supplies, of course, and for mail also."

"If you've mail to send out, the stagecoach office is two blocks down from here and a block west. It'll make good connections—that is, if the drivers don't have trouble with the redskins along the run. Good day to you, gentlemen."

Luke and his son and Djamba went out into the street, and Luke stood looking at the shambles of what had been the Alamo. "Don't you mind him, Djamba," he turned to the Mandingo. "Better men than he died for the right of all men to be equal, and over there is a monument to such heroism. We'll see as little of Mr. Lysander as is possible, I promise you."

Djamba chuckled good-naturedly and shrugged. "I've a notion that man's a carpetbagger, Mr. Bouchard. Just an opportunist, and he probably had a plantation and thought he was being generous when he let his slaves sing hymns of a Sunday. I don't fret about his kind at all, not when I'm with you and Mr. Lucien Edmond and all of the family. Not when I'm with Miz Sybella most of all—'cause she was kind enough to let me use her dead husband's name. I won't ever forget that, Mr. Bouchard. I'm your man, you know that, but I'm her man too as long as there's a breath left in my body."

"I've known that for a long time, Djamba. And I think she knows it too. Now let's go get our supplies and hurry back to our ranch. With the gold I've brought along in my moneybelt, it might be a good idea to buy a wagon and a couple of good horses, with all the supplies I've listed."

CHAPTER TWENTY-FOUR

Lucien Edmond had volunteered to ride on to Austin to file claim for the land of Windhaven Range, a journey that would take him between three and four days on horseback from San Antonio. His father hesitated at first, on the grounds that so prolonged a journey for a single rider might be dangerous. But Lucien Edmond argued, "Father, you're forgetting I'm a husband with two children to look after, and if I'm going to amount to anything in this country, it's high time I started doing things for myself and by myself. That's what you've taught me to do all these years, after all."

"So I have," Luke Bouchard affectionately put an arm around his son's shoulders. "But you'll be gone at least two weeks, because the return journey to Carizzo Springs is at least two hundred miles. Be careful, travel at night and be sure your Spencer's loaded and the rest of your ammunition easily within reach. God be with you, and come home safely to us."

"With the deed to the land, Father," Lucien Edmond smilingly responded as he shook hands with Luke and Djamba, then wheeled his horse to the west and galloped down the dusty street. Luke watched him go, then turned back to Djamba as he took up the reins of the wagon he had purchased to carry back the supplies to Windhaven Range. "I'll spell you every four hours, Djamba. If you get tired of riding beside me on this bumpy buckboard, you can always take one of our mounts tied to the back of the buckboard and ride ahead and scout for me and I'll do as much for you."

"Yes, Mr. Bouchard. You know, that's a fine son you've got. I don't think you'll have to worry about him. He'll find his way back safe and sound, don't you fret now."

"Your words are heartening, Djamba. Because, you see, Windhaven Range is going to mean all the more to my son as the years go on. Right now, the thought of staring all over again excites me. I'm not old yet, not quite fifty, and by working on the soil I've kept my strength and my health as well. But the future is for Lucien Edmond, and after him little Hugo and his sister. And to tell you the truth, I'm not half so afraid of the Comanches or the bandits as I am of men like that bank president."

"Well, Mr. Bouchard," Djamba humorously retorted with a broad grin, "don't you have a saying that sticks and stones may break your bones but words will never harm you? Speaking as a fighting man, I think I'd much rather come up against a regiment of men like him than a dozen of those bandits or Comanches whom Simata's been telling me about. For certain that man couldn't ever ride a horse the way the Comanches do, and even Simata has to admit that his own Kiowas came out second when it came to buffalo-hunting and spearing one of those big animals while riding at top speed through a herd."

"I hope we'll never have to fight the Indians, Djamba. I'm hoping that I'll be able to speak their language well enough to make them understand that the land we're settling on is devoted to raising meat for the tables. And when they themselves need meat for their campfires, I'll certainly be willing to let them have it. From all I've heard about the buffalo hunters and their Sharps guns, that majestic animal will be extinct before very long, and then the Indians of the plains will have to live on beef.

And now let's head home. That word sounds good, doesn't it, Djamba?"

"Yes, Mr. Bouchard. When I first learned it in your language, I thought of my Africa and all that I left behind me. But now I think of Windhaven, and all that's happened really is that it's been moved from Alabama to Texas, isn't that so?"

Once again Luke Bouchard looked steadily at the tall Mandingo, and then he smilingly nodded. "So long as we're all together and respect and love one another, Djamba, home is wherever we are."

When Lucien Edmond rode into Austin, he saw the Union flag flying over the capitol building and the soldiers' tents dotting the green lawns in front of it. At the land office, there were only a few farmers and settlers waiting their turn, and one of them, a rawboned cowman in his mid-forties, turned to peer speculatively at the handsome young son of Luke Bouchard. "You a Johnny Reb come lately or a blue-belly?" he wanted to know.

"I believe in the Union, if that's what you're driving at, stranger," Lucien Edmond amiably returned.

"I get it. One of those secesher who grabbed hold of a pen and signed the loyalty oath and then skedaddled out where you think old Andy Johnson's bloodhounds won't find you. Didn't you see all the soldiers round here?"

"I've nothing to fear from them, sir. My name's Lucien Edmond Bouchard, I didn't catch your name."

"I didn't give it to you, that's why. Name's Hank Johnson, from bloody Kansas. I got sick and tired of all the bloody fightin' over slaves or no slaves, so when my old woman up and died on me this spring, I sold my place and rode down here to pick up some cheap Texas land. Only I don't hold with slavery."

"I thought it was over when Mr. Lincoln issued his Emancipation Proclamation, Mr. Johnson."

"That's true enough, but a lot of Johnny Rebs don't figger that way. They still have a hankerin' for what they used to enjoy before we taught them a lesson."

"My father and I and my great-grandfather before us, never had slaves and I don't believe in them either."

"Well, in that case, shake hands, Bouchard. Where's your land at?"

"Near the Mexican border, Mr. Johnson."

Hank Johnson hawked and spat on the dirty plank floor. "Well, Bouchard, all I've gotta say is you'll have those redskin varmints to tackle, and from what I hear, they're worse even than old U.S. Grant's best troops. Me, I'm buying me a piece up near San Antone. Well, it's my turn now, buy you a drink at the saloon when we've finished our business."

"It'll be my pleasure to have you as my guest, Mr. Johnson."

The lanky horseman hawked and spat again, then chuckled. "Your speechifying and manners, son, are sure mighty rare in these parts. Tell you what, you'd better brush up on handling that rifle you're carrying and that six-shooter too, because there's some folks you jist can't talk yourself out of a fight with using mighty fine words, if you get my meaning. All right, clerk, don't get so golderned impatient, you know you're glad to sell the land 'cause there ain't enough suckers around to take it all off your hands."

When Lucien Edmond's turn came, he presented the accurate survey map which his father had made, and purchased eight thousand acres for $4000 in gold. Hank Johnson, who had stepped back to watch the transaction, whistled respectfully: "Sonny, you sure were lucky no Comancheros saw you carrying that much gold."

"Comancheros?" Lucien Edmond wonderingly echoed.

Hank Johnson nodded and spat again. "White buzzards who do business with the Injuns, sell 'em anything from guns 'n ammunition to bad whiskey. Most of them are outlaws with a price on their heads. Decent white folks can't stand 'em, most times the Injuns tolerate 'em jist 'cause they can't get what they want from anyone else. There're a couple in this town, over at that saloon across the street. If you're gonna buy me that drink, we'd better go down the street a pace to wet our whistles and pass them by.

"Come on, sonny," Hank Johnson urged Lucien Edmond as they started out of the land office, "I want to make sure that three fellers I was just telling you about didn't lay eyes on me."

"Why should you be afraid of them?"

"It's a sort of long story, sonny." The rangy Kansan glanced uneasily at the saloon across the street as he took Lucien Edmond's elbow and guided him down the street to the next block west. "I met up with them 'bout a week ago when my horse went lame, and they sold me a roan mare they had in tow with a coupla other hosses. Next thing I know, I'm having a hard time explaining to a posse that I'm not a hoss thief, and I declare, I thought fer a minute they wus gonna string me up to the nearest cottonwood tree. Not much I can do about gittin' my money back, but if they see me they might be plumb riled and think I'm after their hides, and I can't draw a gun that good, not against three Comancheros I can't. Oh, Jeez, they're comin' outa the saloon, they seen me—duck, sonny—"

Lucien Edmond pulled away from Hank Johnson's grip in time to see the tall Kansan dip his right hand toward his holster just as three men emerged from the saloon across the street, one of them shouting, "Hold on there, Johnson, we got words with you!"

All three were dressed in buckskin jackets and breeches, wore beaded moccasins, and gaudily decorated *sombreros*. The one who had hailed Hank Johnson, in the middle, was short and squat, with an ugly scar running diagonally over his forehead down to his right eyebrow. The other two were tall, bearded, their faces wrinkled and bronzed from long hours on the open range and under the boiling Texas sun.

"Don't you come any closer, you hoss thieves, I'll shoot!" Hank Johnson yelled, crouching and lowering his right hand to brush the butt of his holstered six-shooter.

"Git him, Red," the scarred man called, "and that young 'un too, he's Hank's partner!"

Lucien Edmond's eyes widened at these words and he turned to Hank Johnson with an incredulous look. "Mr. Johnson, they've got it wrong—I'm not your partner—tell them that—"

But the rangy Kansan, his face warped with fear and hate, had already drawn his six-shooter, and, crouching, leveled it at the trio across the street. For a moment Lucien Edmond stood incredulous. The glare of the hot sun, the dreary ramshackle structures of sun-bleached planks and adobe on both sides of this dusty, hot street, loomed before him as a kind of nightmare, as if he had suddenly stepped into a dream in which he should have had no part. To his left, far down his side of the street, he could see two men in ponchos and sombreros, halted and whispering to each other, then point just as the boom of Hank Johnson's six-shooter made the nightmare real.

Almost in unison, the three men across the street drew their own six-shooters and opened fire. Lucien Edmond saw Hank Johnson utter a strangled gasp, saw him spin around, then sprawl full-length on the planks which served as sidewalk in front of the saloon he and Lucien Edmond had been about to enter.

"You've killed him!" he called out, his voice choked with horror, and then he recoiled as the scarred man took aim and fired directly at him. He could feel the bullet tug at his sleeve, and he cried out again, "For God's sake, don't shoot, I'm not his partner—you're making a terrible mistake—"

And now there was no time to protest as he saw the tall bearded man at the left aim at him. Tugging his Spencer out of the scabbard, he flung himself flat on the planked sidewalk and leveled the rifle at the trio. He was hardly conscious of the bruising recoil or the angry bark of the quickly snapped-off shots. Huddling himself as he lay flat to make as small a target as he could, he continued to trigger the Spencer till he saw them topple like bowling pins. The scarred man jerked backwards and then crumpled in front of the still swinging doors of the saloon. The two men flanking him stumbled forward, one toppling into the dusty street, the other clapping a hand to his throat from which an ugly red geyser spouted, then pitching forward to lie with his face pressed up against his dead companion's back.

There was an uncanny stillness along the dusty street as Lucien Edmond, pale and shivering as with ague from the aftermath of this inexplicable attack, lay waiting, clutching the rifle in both hands, not even aware that he had emptied it in the course of defending himself. At last, when he saw that his three assailants did not move, he slowly stumbled to his feet, still gripping the Spencer. "Oh, dear God in heaven," he said half-aloud, "why did they want to kill me?"

Out of the saloon into which the dead Kansan had been about to take Lucien Edmond, a heavily set, gray-haired man in his late forties, a silver star on his black vest, his frock coat open and its tails swinging as he strode forward, hailed him: "I saw it all, stranger, that was damn good shooting. A clear case of self-defense. I wouldn't be surprised if there's a bounty on all those rascals."

"A bounty?" Lucien Edmond turned, gripping the rifle in nerveless hands, still pale as death, his eyes wide and shadowed with revulsion at what he had been forced to do, still not understanding why it had had to be done.

"Sure. Know who those three you gunned down were? Red Borchard, Clem Porter, and Dick Mayberry. They've helped many a murdering Comanche shoot down innocent women and kids with rifles just like you've got there. And that Hank Johnson, he's not much better. Fact is, this morning I got a wanted poster on him from Lawrence. Seems like he held up a Wells Fargo coach and got away with twenty grand."

"He—he was in the land office buying a spread there with me," Lucien Edmond stammered.

"That figgers. I'm Sheriff Ben Wilberg. Who might you be, mister?"

"My name is Lucien Edmond Bouchard. My father and I just bought some land near the Nueces around Carizzo Springs."

"Good luck to you, Mr. Bouchard. As I was saying, those three galoots wuz in with Hank Johnson on that Wells Fargo haul. Only the way I get it, he fleeced them of all the gold and hightailed it here ahead of them to get hisself a spread and then get on to San Antone and bank the rest of his stolen cash. I guess those fellows figgered you wuz in with old Hank. Well, you can go on your way, and much obliged. Sure you don't want to get the reward for it?"

"No thanks, Sheriff Wilberg." Lucien Edmond shuddered. "I want no part of blood money. It eases my mind to have you tell me they're all criminals, though. You see, it's the first time in my life I've ever had to kill a man."

"Don't let that fret you none, Mr. Bouchard. You did a right good deed here in Austin, and I'm here to tell everybody that's a fact. Anyway, for your first time, you sure picked yourself a doozy! Well then, good luck to you. If ever you need any help here in Austin, you'll find my office down the street next to the barber shop. Glad to meet you." The sheriff held out his hand, and Lucien Edmond numbly shook it, still trembling in nervous reaction to the unexpected violence in which he had been so unwillingly a chief actor.

CHAPTER TWENTY-FIVE

They had ridden out of their stronghold not far from Eagle Pass two days ago, and ten of the warriors had gone on ahead to the east, for it was known that the long-horn cattle grazed there. These ten, the finest riders in the tribe which Sangrodo ruled, would drive off at least a hundred cattle—ten to a man, and more if they wished their names to be spoken with praise around the campfire of the Comancheria—and would drive them ultimately into Sante Fe. They would be sold there, and the money would buy guns and blankets and clothing and salt. And some of the cattle would be left back at the stronghold to be killed and eaten, doubly welcome since the meat was like that of the prized buffalo. Best of all, it would have been stolen from Texans whom Sangrodo had hated ever since the day a Texas Ranger had shot at him from ambush and instead killed his first wife Mikana.

The rest of the band, thirty in all, turned and crossed the Nueces River on their way to a small Mexican village not far from Nuevo Laredo. They had painted their faces red and most of them wore headdresses of buffalo horn. Their long lances had been painted red also, and each of the braves bore a shield of tanned buffalo hide painted in gaudy colors and decorated with a circle of feathers which fluttered whenever the shields were moved and thus helped spoil the enemy's aim. Even their mustangs shared in this adornment, for their heads and tails had been painted red, with red ribbons attached to the tails as well.

Sangrodo himself rode at the head of these thirty, and he had hand-picked them for the war party because of their bravery and because each of them had counted coup over no fewer than five enemies. The scalps of those enemies decorated the shields they carried now to prove their valor as warriors and something more: scalping an enemy prevented his gaining immortality, and perhaps also his being reborn at some future date to oppose again the path of the Comanches.

Sangrodo himself, in his mid-forties, had broken away from the Wanderers tribe and come farther south with a few young braves who, like him, wished to be free of the authority of the elders to hunt the buffalo and to loot and raid as they saw fit. He was taller than most of his warriors, his skin coppery and bronzed even darker by the sun so that at times he resembled the very Mexicans he implacably warred against. His, too, was the longest of all lances, and his shield was decorated with forty-two enemy scalps. He wore a feather war bonnet, the feathers painted red and black as was his upper body. His coarse black hair was parted in the center, and the part was painted a deep carmine, worn in braids on either side of the head, with a scalp lock falling from the top of the head. His side braids were wrapped with strips of buffalo hide, and he wore a red feather thrust through the scalp lock. His ears were pierced, and in the left ear was a ring made of white shells cast up on the bank of the Nueces, and through the right ear a ring of silver.

It had been a good summer for the tribe of Sangrodo. The buffalo had been plentiful, and the animals were fat and had shed their winter hair. Soon again, perhaps two moons from now, he would order another buffalo hunt, since by then the hides would have reached their prime. But as he lifted his lance to call a halt and turned to direct his braves across the border into Mexico, his eyes glistened with a ferocious pride to see how attentively his warriors awaited his signal. They, like himself, thought now only of the raid to be made upon Maxtime. He had raided this village a year ago, brought back horses and captive women to become squaws if they would consent and slaves if they would not, and he and his men had killed a dozen Mexicans. But the *jefe* of the village still lived, and he had killed two Comanche warriors. By the time the sun had risen and set two more times, Sangrodo promised himself, that *jefe* would pay with his own life for having slain Idalgo and Bilmane, who had been like sons to him.

Sons—his painted, harsh-featured face softened an instant as he thought of Kitante, whom he and his men called "Little Horse." The boy's mother, Amara, whom he had carried away as a girl of fifteen from just such a village as Maxtime, had died two moons ago from the wasting sickness. Perhaps he would find a new wife, for Amara had been well favored and eager on the blanket beside him and gladdened his nights, and she had loved her little son even as if she had been a true Comanche mother.

Of course, she had not been Sangrodo's only squaw. It was inevitable that many of the strongest and youngest braves should die and thus destroy the balance between male and female. With the constant warfare of recent years, there was an erosion of Comanche men out of all proportion to the natural loss by death of the women. Thus it was that only through polygamy each woman might have a husband and the birth rate be maintained to keep the Comanche nation strong.

He turned back now to stare down at the village, bathed in the light of early dawn, the shabby little adobe huts huddling in a jagged rectangle tinged with the sun's first rays which deepened with each passing moment till it seemed an invisible hand had daubed the roofs with a sinister red.

Sangrodo's face became taut, and he briskly gestured with his spear at the man nearest him, Ipiltse, He Who Rides Like Wind. Squat and short, in his mid-thirties, Ipiltse was his war lieutenant and had counted many coups on similar raids across the Rio Grande. Ipiltse rode up abreast of his chief, his swarthy face expressionless. But his eyes glowed with a ferocious pride that his chief had summoned him for what he knew would be the start of the raid.

"It is *Tzanábunit* (light)," Sangrodo muttered.

"Yes, a good *nabuniquit* (dawn)," Ipiltse laconically agreed, staring down at the adobe huts perhaps twenty-five feet below them as the Comanches waited at the brink.

"You will take your *piate* (gun) and seek out the *jefe*, Ipiltse. Let a dozen warriors ride with you into the middle—there is his hut, the largest of all. He has a *cueh* (wife); take her, see that she is not harmed."

"I hear, Sangrodo."

"*Equihtzi* (now)!" the Comanche chief shook his lance above his head.

Wheeling his mustang back to the first line of warriors behind him, Ipiltse nodded to each of them until he had counted aloud, "*Uahtematoequet* (twelve)" and then unslung the old Sharps buffalo gun from its buffalo hide sheath at the side of his mustang, primed and loaded it.

Lifting the buffalo gun like a banner above his head, he uttered an earsplitting cry and, kicking his heels hard against his mustang's flanks, rode down the ravine toward the sleeping village, followed by the first dozen warriors. Sangrodo, watching intently, pointed his lance to the far left end of the little village as a sign that the rest of his men were to strike there. As they rode down, he waited a moment till he saw Ipiltse and his dozen ride into the very center of the rectangle, as if it were a maze into whose heart the first attackers would strike, and then he too uttered his war cry, brandished his lance, and rode down into the ravine.

At the back of the little village was a wooden corral in which a dozen horses now began to move restlessly, whinnying as they saw the swarm of Comanche mustangs bearing down upon them. Two of Sangrodo's warriors dismounted, one jerking away the round wooden log which barred the gate, the other flinging open the gate and emitting a wild yell which stampeded the horses out of the corral.

The rest of the braves, notching arrows to their bowstrings, circled the village. A young Mexican, yawning and stretching, emerged from the doorway of his hut, uttered a cry of terror, *"Los Comanches, guárdese, hombres!"* and then clutched at himself and doubled over as an arrow sped into his belly. The bloodcurdling war cries of the circling riders were mingled now with the terrified screams of women and children, the hoarse shouts of men violently wakened from heavy sleep, and the boom of Ipiltse's buffalo gun as a tall, gray-haired Mexican, clad only in his drawers, rushed out of his hut, knelt and aimed his rifle at the circle of riders. He sprawled lifeless, his rifle still clutched in nerveless hands, his skull half blown away by the Sharps at close range.

An elderly Mexican in the hut nearest the *jefe*'s flung a rusty machete which knocked a young brave out of his saddle to be dragged, one leg caught in the stirrup, through the gritty dust of the village street, as his mustang bolted, whinnying shrilly in terror.

But twenty minutes later, the raid was over, at the cost to the attackers of two dead braves and a third badly knifed in the upper arm by a villager whom the wounded brave first disemboweled with his spear, then scalped. And when Sangrodo and his warriors rode back up to the brink of the ravine, they took with them three men and five women who rode at the very end of the raiding party back across the border toward the Comanche stronghold.

For the luckless captives, the journey back was harrowing, two days under the scorching sun, cramped by their bonds, haunted by the knowledge of their ultimate fate once they reached the Comancheria. At night, their horses were tethered to trees, and they were fed only a little pemmican and juniper berries, though their captors saw to it that during the day they were given water as they begged for it: they must be kept strong enough to endure what was in store for them.

At last the raiding party, riding in solemn single file with Sangrodo at their head, reached the stronghold. It was marked by a long escarpment, a clifflike ridge of grayish rock which stretched like a kind of fortifying circle within whose enclosure stood the tepees made of tanned buffalo hides, rising from twelve to fourteen feet high, upon a framework of sixteen or eighteen poles. The doors were covered by a bearskin, and there was an ingenious flap at the very peak to offer a vent for smoke. Both door and vent faced away from the prevailing wind, and these tepees were given greater stability by tying a leather rope to the poles where they crossed overhead and attaching it to a stake driven into the ground near the center of the dwelling. Within each tepee, there was a fire in the center, used both for cooking and warmth, and the ground was covered with buffalo skins to sit on and to sleep. To the west of this stronghold rose a grove of live oak trees and huge thickets of mesquite, forming an ideal camouflage against intruders. Sangrodo had brought his people here four months ago from their former Comancheria northwest of Eagle Pass. There were no white settlers here within miles, the border was easy to cross, and there were both cattle and buffalo, and much game.

As the procession neared the escarpment, squaws emerged from the tepees, their eyes shining with pride as they saw their men returning with scalps. The old women and the children gathered up pebbles and sticks and flung them at the fettered Mexican prisoners who brought up the rear of the triumphal entry into the stronghold, and two of the Mexicans bowed their heads and began to pray aloud that death might be swift. The third man, tall, with the arrogant face and look of an *hidalgo* despite his peasant clothing of rude shirt and coarse trousers, was Manuelo Arvilas, the *jefe* of Maxtime. And behind him, first of the five female captives, was his comely wife, Catayuna, twenty-six, clad only in a ragged shift through which the soft brown satin of her naked flesh was generously displayed. She rode, her head held high, a contemptuous smile on her sensuous lips, her full melon-like breasts rising and falling with an even rhythm. As the pebbles and sticks struck her back and thighs and bosom, she did not wince, but stared straight ahead—her husband rode just ahead of her.

The first stars of evening had appeared and the squaws began to prepare a communal feast of delicacies to celebrate the victorious raid. There would be curdled milk taken from the stomachs of suckling fawns and buffalo calves, boiled tripe, marrow, raw liver flavored with the contents of the gall bladder, bowls of warm blood from the freshly killed antelope, pecans, acorns, tubers, mulberries and persimmons and plums. And for the warriors, and even the old men, there would be *tiswin*, a weak beer made from herbs which the Comanches had learned to make as the Apaches did.

When the warriors were in the center of the stronghold, it was Sangrodo who first dismounted. Namine, who had been his third wife and was now in her late thirties, took the reins of his horse and led it to the largest of all the tepees, garishly decorated to proclaim Sangrodo's leadership of the tribe. One by one the squaws of the other braves came forward to take the reins of the mustangs and lead them away, till only the three Mexican men and five women remained on horseback, still bound astride their mounts, their bodies begining to droop with fatigue and lack of circulation. Yet Manuelo Arvilas and his wife continued to regard the jeering, milling throng around them with the utmost contempt, forcing themselves to sit with shoulders and backs straight, heads erect, the smiles riveted on their lips despite their weariness and secret terror.

Now in the center of the stronghold, as the flames rose high in the gathering dusk of this warm night, the old men, the children, the squaws and the unfledged braves gathered, rapt with attention, to watch Sangrodo tell in pantomime of the great victory against the Mexicans. Still in his full warpaint and the war bonnet trailing to the ground, he began to gesture. The spellbound audience could see through the movements of his hands and the flashing of his eyes the gathering of the raiding party upon the brink of the ravine. They could see his order for the first dozen braves under Ipiltse to descend to the very heart of the sleeping village. They watched with excitement as Sangrodo's expressive hands depicted the ferocious attack upon the huts of the *jefe* and the others, how Ipiltse's Sharps gun slew and disfigured the man who had dared to fire upon the Comanches—and that disfigurement was a victory, since if it were destined that he return in some future life, his skull could not be whole. They chuckled as they saw through Sangrodo's gestures the wily release of the Mexican horses, and they sucked in their breaths when Sangrodo pronounced—for the last time— the names of the two dead warriors lost in the raid. Their widows began to wail, ran to the fire and took blackened ashes and rubbed them upon their faces and throats and arms, then seized scalping knives and cut off the braids of their hair and cast them into the flames.

Never again would the names of those dead warriors be spoken in the Comancheria, nor would their widows ever again utter them. But they had died bravely, and their spirits would not grope in darkness to reach the sky. That was why the raid had waited until the first light of dawn.

And now Sangrodo acclaimed those who had been bravest in the raid, calling them before him by name, placing a hand upon each brave's shoulder and nodding his approval. Then he divided the spoils. The other ten Comanches who had been sent to drive the wild Texas longhorns toward the stronghold had returned shortly after dawn of this very day, and each of them was rewarded according to his merits.

Now, turning to face the eight captives, Sangrodo's eyes glittered with cruel anticipation. He gave a sign, and four of his braves hurried to the horses and, untying the two other Mexicans, dragged them toward an old overturned wagon which, earlier this spring, had been seized from a would-be settler making his way across the great plains toward San Antonio.

One of the Mexicans was in his fifties, gray-haired and bearded, already weeping and begging for his life. Sangrodo moved toward him and said in Spanish, "You have grown rich on Comanche scalps, Mexican dog. Now it is time to yield up your own. You will not miss one scalp after all the others you have been paid for, I think. To the wheel with him!"

The other, stocky and in his mid-thirties, spat contemptuously at Sangrodo's feet. The Comanche chief grinned humorously, and again spoke in Spanish: "You think to die swiftly by my lance, descendant of a diseased burro? You too have taken bounty from the scalps of my people and you will pay as he does."

He made a sign and moved back to watch as the braves, two holding each doomed captive, dragged him toward the wheels of the wagon and bound him head downwards. An old squaw approached with a flaming torch, and Sangrodo flung it at the rotting canvas of the wagon. There was a burst of flame, and both Mexicans began to scream in terror. Sangrodo watched impassively as the fire reached them, writhing and shrieking piteously until at last smoke engulfed them and their cries were heard no longer.

And now it was the turn of the *jefe* of Maxtime. Sangrodo stared hard at the arrogant Mexican, who had not yet uttered a single word of complaint against his impending fate, then made an abrupt downward-slashing gesture with his right hand. Two braves at once cut the thongs which bound Manuelo Arvilas's ankles under his horse's belly and lifted him down onto the ground, gripping him by the elbows, then forced him to his knees before the Comanche leader.

"We meet again, *Jefe*," he said in Arvilas' own tongue, "and this time there is a debt to be paid. Two of my bravest warriors died by your hand. Their names are not spoken, but I have not forgotten them."

"Is it a debt, then, to defend one's self and one's people against murdering savages?" the Mexican contemptuously countered.

The two warriors gripping Manuelo Arvilas angrily forced his head down till his face was buried in the sandy earth, but Sangrodo shook his head, and they righted him. "It is more than a debt," he solemnly replied, "because those of your village whom I have already killed took the scalps of my warriors and sold them as bounty. My people are the Comanches, and all others are the enemy, but worst of all are those who defile our strong men and take greedy profit from their death. Now you shall live long enough to see your woman become my squaw. Let it be done as I have said!"

The braves lifted Manuelo Arvilas to his feet, then marched him westward about fifty paces to where a large hole had already been dug into the earth. Carefully they lowered him down into it, shoving on his shoulders till at last he was buried to his neck with only his head visible. On her horse, still tied, Catayuna uttered a stifled cry of anguish, her dark-brown eyes wide and glistening with tears. And then, despite her own bitter pride, she pleaded, "Kill him quickly. He killed your men with his gun, they died fast. At least he deserves as speedy a death."

Without turning to regard her, Sangrodo answered her in Spanish, "In Maxtime there were many who took gold for my warriors' scalps. He was the chief, he could have stopped them but he did not. It shall be as I have said, woman."

Then he squatted down before his enemy, and Ipiltse handed him a scalping knife. Sangrodo held it point upwards toward the darkened sky, his eyes rolling and his lips moving silently, and once again Catayuna uttered a choking cry of abysmal torment as she saw him plunge the fingers of his left hand into her husband's thick shock of graying hair and begin the incisions that would tear his raw scalp from his head.

Manuelo Arvilas closed his eyes and ground his teeth, summoning all his powers of resistance to remain stoic. But when it was done, when his face sagged and the sockets of his eyes seemed unnaturally huge and the blood ran down his cheeks and forehead, he uttered a hoarse groan, then panted, "Do what you will with me, but spare my woman. She has done you no harm."

"If she is as brave as you, *hombre*," Sangrodo mockingly retorted, "she will replace the wife who has gone to the Great Spirit ahead of you."

He turned and dropped the raw, bloody scalp into a clay bowl which his wife Namine held out in both cupped hands toward him, and then he made another sign. Mingride, the old medicine man, hobbled forward holding a buffalo skin which had been gathered together at all four ends and bound with a rawhide thong, dropped it a few feet away from Manuelo Arvilas' head. With a mocking laugh, Sangrodo slashed the rawhide thong with the bloody knife, unfolded the buffalo hide and stepped quickly back. And then Catayuna uttered an inhuman, prolonged shriek of incredulous agony: "*Dios*, not that way, oh, quickly, I plead with you!"

Out of the buffalo hide swarmed hundreds upon hundreds of long black ants, while from behind the gory head of Manuelo Arvilas an old withered squaw knelt to smear wild honey over his face. The dirt had been packed in so that Manuelo Arvilas could not move, could only twist his head frenziedly upon his neck and roll his dilated eyes like a frightened animal.

"Now, *Jefe*," Sangrodo declared, "you shall see your woman beg to be my squaw."

"Never, never, though you kill me like him, you devil!" Catayuna cried, wrenching at her bonds. But the black mare on which she was tied was held by one of the strong young warriors who brutally jerked upon the reins till the bit drew blood from the mare's mouth, and thus controlled her, while his glittering eyes feasted on the lush half-nakedness of this captive female.

Sangrodo nodded, and four squaws set upon Catayuna, cutting the thong which fettered her slim ankles, dragging her off the mare and toward a torture frame shaped like a St. Andrew's cross some twenty feet opposite her husband's head. There they bound her wrists and ankles, spreadeagling her, tore away her tattered shift to leave her naked, the flickering play of the campfires casting weird geometric patterns on the glossy, satiny brown skin of her shuddering belly and thighs and full lush breasts.

Sangrodo approached her now, his face impassive, his eyes narrowed and appraising. Catayuna bared her teeth in a rictus of loathing and shame commingled, jerking at her bonds, but the torture frame was sturdy and the rawhide thongs had no play in them. "Woman," he said to her, "by our law, I take you as squaw if you agree before the tribe. This, or slavery. But because you are the *mujer* of him who was the enemy of my people, it will be death instead of slavery. And it will not be quick."

Catayuna stared at him for a moment, and then, summoning all her strength, hawked and spat fully into his face. A chorused gasp of anger rose from the watching squaws, and one of them picked up a stick and was about to strike her across the breasts when Sangrodo held up his hand: "Let her taste the fire, of which she is filled. Perhaps then she will choose more wisely."

"Catayuna, pray for me, *Dios*, pray for my courage!" her husband cried out as the ants approached in swarms. Circling, in single files, in columns, then black moving streams, they crawled upon his chin and cheeks and ears, and he twisted his head in vain to shake them off. Now they covered his chin and then his mouth, and he spat repeatedly, gagging and choking, but they were not deterred.

His breathing was hoarse and quick and again he cried out, *"Virgen Sanctissima*, receive me, forgive my sins!" Sangrodo, still confronting Catayuna, replied without turning his head, "Let her if she will, but I will not!"

The oldest and ugliest of the four squaws now crouched, cackling with sadistic glee before the straining naked figure on the torture frame. She held out two thin round sticks, whittled to evenness, between whose compressed ends was vised a flint arrowhead heated in the fire till it was white-hot. Slowly she extended it toward Catayuna's upper left thigh, and the naked captive stiffened, tilting her face upward to the sky, and began to pray. At that moment, the tortured shriek of Manuelo Arvilas proclaimed the beginning of his long death-agony, and Catayuna echoed it with her own raucous cry, "Murderer, coward, animal, let me join him! I would die before I would mate with a beast like you!"

Sangrodo's face darkened at the insult, and he made a gesture; the squaw pressed the white-hot arrowhead flat against Catayuna's naked thigh near the thick black *mons veneris*. She sucked in her breath, and then her head turned back and forth and she began to thrash upon the torture frame, a whining sound emerging from between her desperately compressed lips.

"May you be accursed, evil one, monster, O, *Dios*, hear my death prayer, let him know suffering such as mine!" Manuelo Arvilas hoarsely shouted.

"Once again," Sangrodo curtly directed, and the old squaw carefully moved the tongs-like sticks against Catayuna's other thigh and pressed the arrowhead home against shuddering tender flesh.

Her body jerked again and then her head slumped forward as she sagged in merciful unconsciousness. Beyond her, the sobbing cries of her husband rose now, for the torture was unspeakable, and all that could be seen of that bloody head which was not covered by the swarming black ants were his bloodshot, horribly distended eyes.

Sangrodo stared lingeringly at the unconscious naked woman, and then barked a gruff order to the squaws. Wonderingly, whispering among themselves, they cut her bonds and carried her into a tepee near his own. Then Sangrodo turned and walked toward Manuelo Arvilas, squatted down and said softly, "*Hombre*, her courage is great. Perhaps as great as yours. Curse me as you will, but I give you my word she will be a slave and not my squaw."

But there were only whimpering sobs and choking cries from the now incoherent, dying Mexican. The war-painted young warriors drank in those sounds greedily, for to them this was the proof of triumph over a hated enemy. Sangrodo turned back to his tepee, just as his wife emerged from the doorway, her face congealed in anguish. "It is your son, Sangrodo, it is Kitante. I had thought he was playing with the other boys, but just now Noriame came to me and said that she saw him ride his pony away from the stronghold soon after you returned with the warriors. Oh, Sangrodo, beat me, let me die, if I have lost the son your favorite Amara bore you." She sank down on her knees, huddled before him, crossing her arms over her breasts and wailing in her sorrow.

"The curse—it is the *jefe*'s curse," Sangrodo muttered, and glanced superstitiously up at the dark sky where only a crescent moon cast its pale glow upon the stronghold of the Comanches.

CHAPTER TWENTY-SIX

Perhaps if Namsi-kohtoo, He Who Makes a Fire Quickly, had not taunted him and called him only an *oná*, a little boy who is afraid of a *caa*, Kitante could have conquered his disappointment when he saw his warbonneted father ride back into the stronghold at the head of his warriors and the eight Mexican prisoners they had taken. But to be jeered at by the older son of Ipiltse, who, though only a year his senior, had already killed a wild boar with a spear, was simply not to be borne. So Kitante, in the hub-bub which surrounded the return of Sangrodo, had slipped away to the end of the stronghold, saddled a sturdy pinto pony, provisioned himself with a sack full of parched corn and jerky and a water bottle, and rode off toward the southeast. He had taken his bow and quiver of arrows, and he wore only breechclout and moccasins. His unruly black hair was shaped into a thick but short braid at the back of his neck, and a white headband around his forehead marked with the sign of the bear showed that he was of the tribe of Sangrodo, to whom that animal, as well as the coyote and the owl, was sacred. A few months past his tenth birthday, he was sturdy and stocky, for it was unusual among the Comanches to reach more than a height of five and a half feet; his father was the striking exception.

Kitante was not exactly certain where he was going, except that to the southeast there were no settlers and should be plenty of game. Perhaps if he shot a wolf or an antelope or even a wild boar with his flint-tipped arrows, then the braggart son of Ipiltse would no longer call him a little boy frightened by a mouse. Besides, that had been all of two years ago when a field mouse had jumped out of a sack of corn right into his face without the least warning; why, he was certain that even his own father, if such a thing had happened, would have been startled. But Namsi-kohtoo had never let him forget it, and that was why, crushed at not being allowed to go with his own father and perhaps even to count a coup over the hated Mexican enemies, Kitante had decided to demonstrate his own mettle in such a way that the stronghold would know that in his veins there flowed the blood of Sangrodo.

It was hilly country for the most part, with dry gulches and thick beds of mesquite growing in them, a sparse live oak or cedar tree here and there, and occasional clumps of wild flowers.

Aware of the danger of pursuit and even more of the disgrace in being returned to the stronghold under what would undoubtedly be the mocking gaze of his older tormentor, Kitante stubbornly urged his pinto on and on, not stopping for the evening meal until he was certain that he had covered a good twenty miles. Knowing also that the scouts of his tribe were expert in tracking, he took pains to double back several times in order to leave different directional hoofmarks and, for about a quarter of an hour, rode along the bank of a little creek which was almost dry, fording it and then crossing back over several times, again to throw any possible pursuers off the track.

By midnight, exhaustion claimed him and he tethered the pinto to the overhanging branch of a dwarfed cedar tree near a tributary of a larger creek which had already gone dry. He made a hasty meal out of a handful of corn and jerky, drank two mouthfuls of water—he had let the pinto drink at the little creek which he had forded several times—and then wrapped himself in a blanket, stretched out atop a section of fairly level shale, and promptly fell asleep.

He awoke before dawn. Starting up, he scanned the horizon in every direction. He saw no one, and that was reassuring indeed. He opened his sack of food and held out some corn to the pinto, who whinnied, and gratefully partook of the meager fare. A moment later, Kitante was back in the saddle, kicking his heels and urging the pony on. Now gradually the stunning crimson and orange of the sun tinted a cloudless sky, foretelling a searing day on what was now level ground, broken only by clumps of cacti and mesquite, with some oddly shaped formations of rock and shale which looked like old burial mounds and may well have been those of the forebearers of this nomadic tribe of Comanches centuries before.

Again several times Kitante changed directions, then dismounted and swiftly improvised coverings for the hoofs of his pinto by taking broken branches and clusters of mesquite and tying them on with rawhide thongs. Once again he continued his journey, changing directions numerous times again. The blurred and indistinct prints left by the pinto would, he hoped, confound those who were certain by now to have set out after him. He did not think his father would thrash him; perhaps his mother might—though of course she was not his real mother—but if that occurred, he would ask only that the beating be administered within the tepee and out of sight and hearing of He Who Makes a Fire Quickly. He would rather face a dozen rattlesnakes than have to endure once more that grinning, ugly face with the squat nose which had been broken once in a long run when his enemy had stumbled into a gopher hole and fallen headlong onto a rock. He grimaced with anger as the image of the older boy appeared before him, and he made the sign the Comanche makes to ward off evil and hostile spirits.

By mid-morning, the sun was merciless, creating a kind of haze which blurred and distorted the sight. Even though Kitante was used to it—he had learned to ride a pony at five, and his coppery skin had long since been darkly bronzed from daily exposure to this bright Texas sun—he stopped long enough to bathe his eyes with a few drops of water from his by now nearly depleted bottle. He also placed just over his eyelids an ingenious kind of visor made by piercing the leaves from a cedar tree with a long strip of bark.

As yet, he had come across no game, although early this morning and far to the west, he had seen what he believed to be a herd of antelope scurrying off in the distance. At noon, he halted again for food and water, letting the little pinto graze in some welcome shade. To his right, due southward in the direction of Mexico, he could make out a milling herd of longhorned cattle perhaps half a mile away. Once again he warily glanced back toward the west, but there was still no sign of pursuers, and he permitted himself a thoroughly boyish, mischievous grin at the thought that he had perhaps—if only for a short time—outwitted his own father, the feared and respected chief of the stronghold. If he could remain another day or two without capture, it would indeed be something to tell that braggart Namsi-kohtoo, yes, even if he brought back no trophies of the hunt.

By late afternoon, he found a small creek which seemed to have fresh water, and dismounted to let the pinto drink its fill. Snuffling, tossing its head, the little pony drank greedily till Kitante, shaking his head and scowling, pushed its nose away from the water. The pinto tried to nip at him, and the sturdy young Comanche boy burst into an angry tirade as he mounted once more and, kicking with his moccasin-shod heels energetically to show the pinto who was master, continued his journey, this time heading due east.

When next he stopped, it was to observe with amazement that in the distance perhaps a mile away there were buildings made of wood where, so far as he could recall, there had been nothing before except the land. These, then, would be the dwellings of the hated white-eyes who had dared to come upon Comanche land. Aiyee, but his father would welcome such news and praise him as bearer of it! Now he did not care whether he killed game or not; his father had always said that the best scouts made the craftiest warriors, and it would be as good as any *coup*, better by far than the spearing of that boar by the detestable Namsi-kohtoo. He permitted himself another grin at the thought of being praised by the elders of the council as well as by his own mighty father for the deed he was about to accomplish, and with this flare of excitement to drive away all thoughts of fatigue which had begun to cramp his almost naked young body, Kitante once again kicked his heels and urged the pinto forward at full speed.

But the pinto, too, was weary, for it had carried its young rider nearly forty miles since early evening yesterday. Besides, the terrain was uneven and suddenly the pinto, with a frightened squeal, stumbled over a small gopher hole, fought for footing, and then halted jerkily, throwing Kitante to the ground.

There was a sudden terrible whirring, rattling sound, magnified by the intense silence of this desolate area. Kitante, painfully crawling to all fours after having been flung full-length and bruising his right side, found himself staring into the beady eyes of a coiled rattlesnake sunning itself on a flat round rock only a few feet away from him. With a strangled cry of fear, the boy straightened, just as the snake struck, burying its fangs in Kitante's left calf.

The pinto was not afraid of rattlesnakes. It had killed one with its hooves nearly six months ago, which feat had decided Sangrodo to purchase it from the father of Namsi-kohtoo and give it as a present to his young son. Now seeing its young master in danger, it reared, and drove its hooves down upon the ugly oval head, stamping and stamping again while the partly uncoiled snake threshed and writhed in the convulsions of its death agony. Whinnying shrilly, it continued to stamp at the lifeless reptile until there was not a flicker of life in the mottled brown coils which ended in eight still-quivering rattles.

Kitante had stumbled back, seating himself on the ground and at once drawing his hunting knife as he began to dig around the bloody puncture left by the rattlesnake's fangs. He was trembling, and he winced at the sharp pain of the knife into his young flesh as he forced himself to keep the poison from spreading. If only he could suck the wound—

The day before, Luke Bouchard had returned from a quick journey to San Antonio to buy rope, branding irons and several new saddles, and had found a letter from Fleurette awaiting him, forwarded on by John Brunton, to whose bank she had written. In it, she announced the birth of a son, Thomas, to her husband Ben Wilson and herself. Ben was spending many hours in a Pittsburgh clinic for the poor. Though thirty-three, Fleurette joyously wrote her mother Sybella that her delivery of the child had been easy and that she expected to return to work with her beloved husband, whom she considered the most humanitarian person she had ever known. Ben had been accredited by the medical examiners as a full-fledged doctor, and was thoroughly dedicated to his work. "Perhaps, Mother," she had concluded the letter with a final section addressed directly to Sybella, "we'll bring your grandson to Texas so you can see how strong and healthy he is. Ben thinks he might be able to take a few weeks off next year once the clinic is really on its feet. God keep you and all the others, and Ben sends his best to you as well. He says he's very anxious to meet his mother-in-law so he can tell her how well you brought me up—isn't he nice, Mother dearest?"

There was a letter for Sybella from Arabella in Galveston which indicated that the once flirtatious beauty of Windhaven was making every effort to adjust to her new surroundings and her husband's new business venture. The latter, she complained, was infinitely boring: bills of lading, inspection of bales of cotton for shipment, a good deal of time spent traveling on horseback to meet with the planters and advise them. Yet withal Arabella was in good spirits, thanks to several parties which had been given in her honor by her husband's cousin's wife and also because Andrew and Melinda were keeping her busy in their never-failing rivalry, this latest phase being a heated argument over who should be entitled to outright ownership of the pony—James Hunter's surprise for his children.

Finally, there had been a letter from John Brunton, sent from New Orleans three weeks ago and addressed to Luke himself. He had read it eagerly, devouring every line, and then he had walked out of the almost-completed hacienda until there was no one within sight. He had turned his face toward the northwest, until once again he seemed to see the lofty twin towers of that red-brick chateau which had been Windhaven in the glorious twilight of old Lucien Bouchard's arduous life. And, despite his pleasure in what he and his family and workers had wrought already upon this seemingly barren stretch of Texas soil, Luke Bouchard felt a wave of nostalgic yearning seize him as he glanced down at the pages he held in his hand and read again that one paragraph which had revived the image—and with it, all the exquisite and poignant memories—of Windhaven as it had been and as he himself had taken part in its construction:

"You will recall the project you and I discussed shortly before your departure for Texas. I promised you that I would make inquiries, and they have been eminently successful, I am happy to report.

The provisional governor of Alabama is an enlightened man who has no vindictiveness towards Southerners, though perforce he must abide by the laws which a Northern-dominated Congress imposes upon him. But by the strictest terms of his tenure, he is able to sell land to freed blacks who have sufficient funds to acquire it. Thus it was that I sent as my intermediary—I should say, yours, Luke—a certain Phineas Atbury. Phineas is a man of fifty, sedate, deferential, an excellent Thespian in his own right (he has made a good many dollars playing in a minstrel show for the edification of such tourists as we now have in New Orleans), and was for some years the porter in the bank which I operated before General Butler took it over. I saw to it that he had sufficient papers of identification—I myself had manumitted him about eight years before the war—and also sufficient money to lend veracity to his story.

This was that his father had been born very close to Windhaven and, now that he himself was free and financially independent, he wished out of sentiment to return to the land where his father had first drawn breath. Accordingly, by a dispatch sent from Mobile last week, Phineas informed me that he is now the owner of Windhaven and fifty acres thereunto appertaining.

I must warn you again that even if you think of returning, it is far too soon. There are angry feelings in the North; Thaddeus Stevens stalks through the Capitol Building daily swearing that he will wreak punishment on the rascals and traitors who dared secede from our glorious Union. Yet I am convinced that within a few years this hostility will diminish, and so it will be perfectly logical for you then—if you should still contemplate such a move—to negotiate with Phineas and regain possession of your grandfather's dream which became such a magnificent reality. Do feel free to write me your thoughts, and know that I shall always be not only your financial advisor but also your lifelong friend.

John Brunton

There were two postscripts to this letter. The first was as follows:

Last week, there appeared in the *Times-Picayune* an item that may interest you. It seems that the body of a certain George Soltis, formerly a captain assigned to the Quartermaster's Division of the Union Army, was found in the river. He had been stabbed several times with a jeweled dagger, which was left in one of the wounds. The authorities suspect a young mulatto girl in whose company Captain Soltis was often seen but as yet no trace of her has been found. It appears also that court-martial charges were being prepared against him, there being some evidence that he illegally confiscated arms and ammunition from a Federal warehouse. Of course his untimely death quashes this proceeding.

The second postscript, scrawled in the former banker's boldly legible hand: "My wife Laure asks to be remembered to you and to wish you and yours success, health and much happiness in your new venture."

And why that message from Laure should have made him crumple the pages with a kind of morbid anguish, as if her quite properly conventional words had made him suddenly wish to scourge himself in penitence, he did not know. Perhaps it was a fleeting presentiment of a life that might have been if commitments had not been made long years ago and turned him upon the path on which he found himself. But because he could not lie even to himself, Luke Bouchard knew, deep within his soul, that the mere mention of Laure Prindeville who was now Mrs. John Brunton had the power to interrupt the placidity of his days upon this new Windhaven Range and to sow the seed of discontent within him. And yet there was no reason in logic or wisdom why that should be so: his life with Lucy had been joyous and serene, perhaps unexciting yet steadfastly loyal. She had fulfilled his needs for security and stability; if she was not by nature an exciting, unpredictable houri like Laure, that was no reason to tremble now like a lovesick schoolboy at the thought of the woman who had taunted him into the one unpardonable, yet unforgettable lapse from unswerving marital fidelity.

Perhaps, too, it was because of what Lucien Edmond had said to him upon the latter's return from Austin with the title to the Texas land that Luke was now so troubled. Maybe it was Lucien's news that made Luke brood about his encounter with Laure, exaggerate it out of proportion to what it really had been—an impulsive, totally uninhibited accident of carnal passion which knows no law and needs no justification. Ever since he had left New Orleans, Luke Bouchard had almost cynically told himself that if he had had the conscience of his half-brother Mark, he would by now have entirely forgotten Laure's body as well as her name. And that thought in turn led him to the sudden recollection of what his grandfather had once remarked to him, that often within a family the curious and inexplicable distribution of human genes may cause both honor and dishonor to emerge within a single family, to have such divergent contrasts between brothers that strangers would not believe the two could possibly be related by blood. Luke had long remembered the anxieties old Lucien had known in wondering if the ruthless and selfishly predatory nature of his older brother Jean might not have reappeared in Luke's own father Henry. And if that were true, Luke had already begun to reason within himself, might not those selfsame tainted genes, so long dormant, have reawakened within his own psyche and led him to the unpardonable hour with John Brunton's beautiful young wife?

Only a few nights ago, his own son had stood here beside him, brooding and taciturn, his face sobered and grave, and Luke Bouchard had suddenly felt his age just as, he thought to himself with a mordant humor, old Lucien must have felt on those mornings when he and his adolescent, hopeful young grandson walked together along the fields of Windhaven. Without a word, Lucien Edmond had handed him the deed to this unclaimed eight thousand acres of Texas land, and then stood staring in the very same direction where even at this moment his eyes were turned. Then at last, his son had said to him, "Father, for the first time in my life I've had to kill. It happened in Austin, just after I got the deed to our land."

Greatly troubled at his son's distraught mood, Luke had gently pressed him: "How did it happen, Lucien Edmond? Doubtless it was in self-defense, my son?"

And Lucien Edmond had nodded, without turning to look at him, and had said in a distant voice, "It happened so quickly there wasn't time to think. Some fellow ahead of me at the land office was telling me he'd almost been hanged as a horse thief and that some men had tried to throw the blame on him for what they'd done. And after I'd paid out the purchase price for our land, he wanted me to buy him a drink in a saloon, and as we were going there, three men came out of another saloon across the street and called him by name and opened fire on him. They killed him almost immediately before he could fire a shot, and then they started to shoot at me, thinking I was his partner. I tried to call to them, but I couldn't, and one of their bullets almost hit me. I had to use my rifle to protect myself, Father, and I killed the three of them."

Luke Bouchard had nodded, mulling over what his son had said. They had gone on for a few minutes, and then he had turned and gripped Lucien Edmond by the shoulders and said solemnly, "You had no choice, my son. You thought of Maxine and of little Carla and Hugo. You had to live for them, and it would have been stupid to have let those strangers kill you out of a case of mistaken identity. There's no law yet in this territory, Lucien Edmond. There's not likely to be for a while, I'm afraid, because even the Texas Rangers were disbanded and there's talk of preventing their re-forming. Meanwhile, many settlers are coming here, and the only law is one of self-preservation. So long as you didn't acquire a taste for killing, so long as you knew that your family was dependent upon you and acted out of natural instinct, you mustn't condemn yourself. I too had to take a man's life once, because I owed Djamba a debt when I was helping cruelly treated slaves escape through the Underground Railroad. You're younger now than I was then, Lucien Edmond; I found myself actually thinking of the moral right or wrong of the matter, and it very nearly cost Djamba his life. There are times when a man must act instinctively and pray afterwards that God was on his side and that his cause was just. I know it's poor comfort to you to say things like that, but there's nothing else I can say to you. And now let's take our walk and try to forget the horror of it. Think only that you're back with your family, that once again the Bouchards have honestly acquired land on which they can build a future and fulfill their destiny."

And now on this melancholy evening when John Brunton's letter and Laure's postscript had wakened in Luke Bouchard singularly uneasy thoughts, he remembered his conversation with his son. The future would be to Lucien Edmond, and Windhaven Range would come to term and to fruition with his own son's maturity. Windhaven Range would be Lucien Edmond's to have and to hold for his lovely young wife and their two small children. That was written in the pages of the future, but what was written for him?

And as he stood there looking back toward the northwest, he suddenly heard the distant call of a screech owl. Here in this wilderness it might well be the ruse of a hostile Comanche or Kiowa. And yet, when it was repeated a second and then a third time, it had a strangely gentle, comforting sound; and Luke Bouchard felt himself trembling as if suddenly he had walked over his own grave.

Luke Bouchard and Lucien Edmond had ridden out this afternoon to inspect Windhaven Range, and the young Kiowa scout Simata, as well as Ramon Hernandez, had accompanied them. So had Jubal, the dog which Djamba had saved from its former master's vindictiveness at the bear fight in New Orleans. Jubal had thrived under John Dewton's care, and his almost emaciated leanness and the fearful look which had accompanied it had been replaced by a sturdy body and a thoroughly contented disposition. He had, indeed, so ingratiated himself in his new surroundings with Andy Haskins and Joe Duvray that the young Southerners had already begun to test him around cattle and horses to determine whether he could be trained for eventual useful work on the range. Often both of them rode out to inspect the land, with Jubal trotting eagerly between their horses, his eyes bright and his pink tongue lolling out in what might be called as happy an expression as a dog can manage when all is well in its world, with plenty of food and kind masters to provide it.

"It would be wise, Lucien Edmond," Luke declared, "to set some of our workers placing boundary markers along our acreage. It'll be some years before we'll have fences in this part of the country, I'm thinking, but some sort of markers might discourage other cattlemen or farmers who might come upon this region and want to claim it for their own just because there aren't many settlers in the vicinity."

"That's a very good idea, Father. I'll start doing that next Monday, and George will be one of those who'll volunteer, you'll see," his son replied. "The old rascal's been dying to test his skill on a horse, in spite of his age, just so he can show off in front of Prissy."

"You can't blame a man for trying, Lucien Edmond," Luke grinned as he slowed his horse to a walk and looked slowly around in every direction. "I am so glad we have this wonderful land. I'm convinced there's plenty of water around, and maybe we can find some of it by spring. There's sure to be some sort of artesian well or hidden tributary of one of the rivers not too far from our *hacienda*. We'll need it when we think of rounding up our cattle in the spring. Simata can help us find it because he knows this land so well."

"Indeed he can, Father," Lucien Edmond agreed as he glanced over at the young redbone who was chatting with Ramon Hernandez. "You know, he's teaching me a little Comanche and Kiowa, just as he's done with you."

"That's an excellent idea too, Lucien Edmond. I'm hoping that if we both can converse with the leaders of the tribes who often cross the border into Mexico near Windhaven Range, we can work out a practical kind of

296

peace between us. I remember how grandfather used to tell me that communication of words and ideas was the one certain way of bringing about a brotherhood of man, and how his own knowledge of the Creek language let him discover what basically decent and industrious people they were. Back in New Orleans, many people I met told me that the Kiowas and Comanches were bloodthirsty redskins who should be shot on sight. Well, we've seen for ourselves that Simata, who is of Kiowa blood and the son of a former chief, is as honest and straightforward a man as one could meet anywhere."

"That's true enough, Father," Lucien Edmond's face was grave as he remembered his own sudden violent fight for survival in Austin. "But the trouble is that sometimes people shoot first and ask questions afterwards, which is a saying that I picked up from that sheriff back in Austin."

"I understand you, my son. Well, I pray God that if any Indians come upon us, we'll have the chance to tell them why we're here and assure them that we haven't come to drive away their buffalo and their cattle and that there's plenty of room for all of us to live in peace. What's Jubal barking at now?" Luke turned to stare at the rangy mongrel which had suddenly begun to bark excitedly as it ran toward a slightly sloping incline of land bordered on the north by tall clumps of mesquite and on the south by a row of little hills framed by cedar and live oak trees.

"There's someone sitting on the ground there and his pony's frightened," Lucien Edmond exclaimed.

"Why, it's an Indian boy!" Luke averred as he spurred his horse forward.

Simata and Ramon Hernandez had seen Kitante too, and they raced toward him now, the young redbone being first to dismount.

Kitante, his face contorted with pain, bending and twisting himself in a vain effort to lift his left calf to his mouth so that he could suck out the venom, saw the approaching riders. Gripping his knife, he waited as Simata came slowly toward him, then struck at the redbone, crying out, "*Wʌhkuuta, wʌhkuuta*" (I kill).

"*Tʌih, tʌih* (friend)," Simata soothingly held out his hands palms upward. Then, seeing the dead rattlesnake, he murmured understandingly, *"Kwasinaboo? Simata tʌih."*

But Kitante, his leg throbbing with pain, tears streaking his dusty cheeks, shook his head and again lunged at Simata with the knife. The young scout deftly caught the boy's wrist, twisting it till the knife dropped, then with his other hand scuffed at it to send it flying a few feet away. Now, swiftly grasping Kitante's wrists, he bent his head and himself began to suck out the venom, spitting it out in mouthfuls, murmuring in the boy's own tongue, "I am Kiowa, I am friend, let me take out all the poison and you will be well soon, I promise."

Luke and his son and Ramon had dismounted and stood watching as the boy first struggled and then, at last understanding that Simata sought to save his life, clenched his fists and closed his eyes.

"It was lucky we came upon him so quickly, Mr. Bouchard," the young redbone at last released the boy and rose to his feet. "It happened only a few minutes ago. His pony killed the snake." Then, in a kindly tone and bending to stroke Kitante's head, he asked, "Where do you come from, who are you?"

"Comanche, I, Kitante, Little Horse, son of Sangrodo, the chief," Kitante gasped, his face solemn with pride despite his obvious pain.

"I think all of the poison is gone, Mr. Bouchard. But a hot poultice will draw out what is left of the bad blood. His leg will be stiff for a day or two, but he is young and strong."

"Then we'll take him home and nurse him," Luke declared.

Simata turned back to Kitante and swiftly translated Luke's remarks into the Comanche tongue. Kitante shook his head, fearfully gasping, "No, no, I go back to the stronghold, I am son of the chief, I will not live with the white-eyes."

He tried to rise, but fell back with a groan, then glared at the four men who watched him. Then he tried to crawl on all fours to retrieve his knife, but Simata, with a tolerant laugh, picked him up as he might a baby, mounted his horse and turned it back in the direction of the *hacienda*. Infuriated, Kitante began to strike at Simata with his fists, but the Kiowa murmured something to him and the boy, with a startled look, at last grudgingly nodded and was docile.

"What did you say to him, Simata?" Luke rode his horse up beside the redbone's.

"Why, Mr. Bouchard, that I was not sure that he was the son of the chief, since he was behaving like an infant that is afraid of grown men. It is an insult, and so he will be very proud and very stubborn and also, I think, very good."

"If what he says is true, there must be an Indian village not far from here," Lucien Edmond anxiously put in.

"That, or simply a temporary camp, because the Comanches are so often on the move, from what Simata tells me," Luke replied. "In any case, what we'll do is tend his hurts and keep him with us till he's able to ride again. Then we'll take him back to his village with a side of beef for his people. It may be, Lucien Edmond, that fate has led him to us so that we could begin our work on Windhaven Range by making peace with the fiercest of Indian tribes in Texas."

CHAPTER TWENTY-SEVEN

Sangrodo, still wearing his warpaint and the long feather bonnet which signified his continued hostility against all strangers who crossed his path, chose six of his fiercest braves to accompany him on the hunt for his missing son. One of these was his war lieutenant Ipiltse, the father of Namsi-kohtoo. But as Sangrodo was making preparations for the search, bidding two braves to guard the small tepee into which Catayuna Arvilas had been carried with her wrists and ankles bound, Ipiltse scowled as a passing reflection occurred to him. Striding to his own tepee where his handsome wife Desyugata silently greeted him by bowing her head and drawing back the flap of the entry to make way for him—not without a swift smile of pride at his having been acclaimed by the entire stronghold for his part in the raid against Maxtime—he demanded, "Where is my elder son? I see there the little one Jurimano, but not Namsi-kohtoo."

"Doubtless, my husband, he is talking with the other warriors who came back from the Mexican village. You well know how he longs to ride with you and count coup, young though he is," his comely wife smilingly replied.

301

"Fetch him to me, woman, and quickly! I ride with our chief after little Kitante who has left the stronghold. It is in my mind that Namsi-kohtoo may know why this is," Ipiltse glowered.

"I obey, my husband," Desyugata hastily answered, seeing from her husband's scowling face that he was in no mood for pleasantries. Ducking low as a sign that she knew her unworthiness to be in the presence of so great a warrior, she hastened out of the tepee toward the group of Comanches who had accompanied Sangrodo on the raid. There indeed was the sturdy boy, his eyes shining with excitement as he listened to them recount the dangers they had faced in riding into the heart of the Mexican village.

Taking him by the forelock and hissing into his ear, "Come, lazy rascal, your father orders you before him," she led the reluctant boy away from the group. Namsi-kohtoo grumbled and glanced appealingly back at his mother, but he knew better than to offer too much resistance to an order from his father. When he entered the tepee, Ipiltse grasped him by the shoulders and, scowling, harshly exclaimed, "For once, my son, no boasting words and no pleas to ride with us! What I want from you is the truth with a straight tongue—I can tell from your face when you speak with a forked tongue. What have you done with Kitante?"

"But my father," Namsi-kohtoo protested, drawing himself up and facing his father as a young man might, "I have done nothing with him. It was only that I said to him that he was a little boy who would run from a mouse. That is all, I speak with a straight tongue on this, my father."

"Is is as I thought," Ipiltse grimly declared, "you have shamed the son of our chief, and this is why he has run away from our stronghold. Know this, my son, that even if it were the truth and I do not think it so, it is not wisdom to say such a shameful thing to the son of our chief. If harm should come to Kitante because of your taunting words, I could not spare you at the council if Sangrodo wished to have you beaten with switches by the women before us all."

"Oh no, my father, do not let me be punished in such a

way! I do not speak against the pain, but I am your son and you are the war lieutenant, and it is not worthy that I be punished by squaws."

Ipiltse's face remained grim, but at the corners of his mouth there was an almost imperceptible twitching; inwardly, he took pleasure in his elder son's courageous answer. Laconically, he replied aloud, "I have pledged obedience to Sangrodo. Therefore if he so orders you to be punished, I must surrender you to him, understand it, it is our law. But this is all you did, to tell Kitante he was afraid of a mouse? You did not see him after that?"

"I swear it by the Great Spirit, Oh my father!" Namsi-kohtoo earnestly answered.

"It will be as it will be, I have spoken. And now, to show that you are sorry for the insult to Kitante, you will help your mother scrape the hide of the buffalo which is to be used as a blanket for the Mexican woman our chief has made his slave," Ipiltse gruffly ordered.

"But that is woman's work, my father," Namsi-kohtoo wailed.

"And it was like a woman that you behaved when you spoke to Kitante. He has not yet had the puberty rites, and because the Great Spirit favored a boastful little boy one day to let him spear a boar, you already think yourself a full-fledged brave. That too is why you will work with your mother all the rest of this day—I have spoken and I listen to no more from you."

Namsi-kohtoo uttered a doleful groan, but took care that his father was already out of the tepee before he emitted it. Then, with a sigh of resignation, he went outside and humbly bowed his head before his mother, saying, "I will scrape the hide as my father wishes."

It was Sangrodo himself who found the first trail of the little pinto pony which Kitante had ridden out of the stronghold, and he and his braves followed it carefully. At the point where the young runaway had begun to double back, he raised his hand and halted his mustang. Turning to Ipiltse, he declared, "The boy has cunning. He is well named Little Horse. See here how he rides back and forth in several ways to trick us. But we know he will go on to the southeast. There are no white-eyes there for many miles."

303

"He is wise indeed, because he is your son," Ipiltse flattered his superior.

Sangrodo grunted, then urged his mustang on. "He wishes to be a man before he has known all the years of his boyhood. That is not bad in itself. What did you say to your son Namsi-kohtoo?"

Ipiltse's face was a study in mingled wariness and paternal pride: "It was because of his boastful words that Kitante rode away from the stronghold without telling anyone, my chief. It is your right to have him punished by the old women before all the tribe."

"No," Sangrodo shook his head, "it was not wrong for Namsi-kohtoo to make fun of my son. Has he not speared a boar? Kitante must learn that one answers idle words with silence or, better still, with deeds when he is of an age to do them. Come, here the trail changes again. He has learned much, and he has still much more to learn. We ride on."

Later they found the stretch of rock on which the little boy had slept, and the telltale sign of a few kernels of corn and mulberries verified Kitante's chosen campsite. At last Sangrodo and his six braves made their own camp for the night, but resumed their quest well before dawn. This time it was Ipiltse who saw the disguised markings left by the hooves of Kitante's pinto, when a tiny sprig of mesquite marked the pony's turning. Pointing to it, he called to Sangrodo, "Your son has all the cunning of the coyote—see here how he has tied mesquite and bits of branches to let us think that there were other horses going and coming along this trail. He is indeed worthy to be the son of our great leader Sangrodo!"

"Is he not a Comanche, Ipiltse?" Sangrodo impassively countered. "Was it not the will of the Great Spirit that we, the Comanches, ride with more cunning and swiftness than the men of any other tribe upon this earth, and is it not our creed that all other peoples, white or red or brown, are inferior to us? Aiyee, it is true that the boy shows skill, but he has not lost us as he thinks. We head to the southeast because in that isolated, unpeopled land, he would go to talk to the Great Spirit to hasten the coming of his manhood. Ho, ho, Ipiltse, I am glad that he ran from our stronghold as he did and so you need have no fear that Namsi-kohtoo will be punished. For this is a test, and because of it, my son will show his father what he has learned of the life and the ways of a Comanche."

Farther on, Ipiltse uttered a cry and pointed to the cedar tree from which Kitante had cut the long strip of bark to make himself a shield against the blinding sun. Sangrodo rode up, peered at the tree, then nodded and gestured with his spear to quicken the pursuit. Now they came toward the crest of grayish rocks on the top of the hill and, halting there a moment, Ipiltse pointed southward. Just as Kitante had earlier observed, longhorned cattle grazed peacefully. A little farther on, Sangrodo saw the hoofmarks of the pinto as it had paused to drink from the little creek, and this time the pinto's tracks were unmistakably headed toward the east.

It was nearly dusk now, and from afar there came the hoot of an owl. Sangrodo stiffened in his saddle, looking toward the direction of that sacred bird. "Ohohá speaks, Kitante near!" he muttered. "The cattle which my braves drove back to the stronghold surely came from that herd, Ipiltse. And look—there on the rock, *kwasinaboo*."

He and Ipiltse dismounted and squatted down to peer at the lifeless rattlesnake. They saw, too, the sharper, deeper marks left by the pinto's hooves when it had crushed the reptile. And as they straightened, they simultaneously uttered a gasp of surprise, for there were the great tepees of wood, well beyond them, with a tall picket fence circling the dugouts and the *hacienda* and the bunkhouse to form a sort of protective stockade.

"See, Sangrodo, the marks of other horses which come from the lodges of the white-eyes!" Ipiltse pointed to the tracks left by the horses of Luke and his son, Ramon and Simata. "They go back toward the lodges—they have taken Kitante!"

"We have not come this way in many a moon," Sangrodo angrily observed as he mounted his mustang. "The white-eyes are not content with stealing our land and driving away the buffalo, they have stolen my son as well. But their stronghold will not be easy to attack and there are only seven of us. I do not know how many are there nor whether they have the long rifles that kill from a dis-

305

tance. We shall make camp and wait to see what they do in the morning, Ipiltse."

At first Kitante felt weak and nauseous, for the long ride under the hot sun and then the sudden terror of the snakebite had taxed his strength more than he had realized. Still, remembering Simata's taunt about his being a baby, he had closed his eyes and set his teeth and lain motionless as Maxine Bouchard applied a hot poultice to the discolored marks left by the rattlesnake's fangs. Simata himself had first examined the bite, and was certain that all of the venom had been drawn out. A few hours later, Maxine returned with a bowl of nourishing broth made from herbs and some of the meat from a fat heifer which Djamba had slaughtered. Kitante was able to sit up, propped up with pillows, while Simata squatted beside him, an arm around the boy's shoulders, gently talking to him in Comanche to reassure him.

"We are friends, I am Kiowa. The Kiowas ride with the Comanches, this you know. No one will hurt you here, and these white-eyes are good people. I have come to work with them and to help them raise cattle which will bring much good beef to those who are hungry," he explained.

Kitante allowed Simata to hold the bowl to his lips and cautiously took a little sip. His eyes brightened, it was very good, there was strong meat. Soon the bowl was empty, and Kitante looked first at Simata and then at the empty bowl.

"Can you bring him more, Miz Bouchard?" the young redbone asked.

"Of course, Simata, that's a good sign that he's eating, isn't it?"

"Yes, very good. I know the poison is gone and this poultice will take away the soreness and the stiffness. He is a very strong boy. Now we must find out from where he comes. If it is true that he is the son of a chief and we can show the chief that we have saved his son's life, we shall be safer here," Simata explained. Then, turning back to Kitante, he said in Comanche, "The white-eyes, she will bring you another bowl. You say you are the son of a great chief. It may be that I know his name. Who is he and where is his stronghold?"

"I will tell you his name but not where the stronghold is. You speak my tongue well, Kiowa, but I do not yet trust you or any of the white-eyes. My father, Sangrodo, says that all who are not Comanche are enemies. You are our enemies because you come to live upon land on which we hunt. This is so."

Simata shook his head. "It is not so, Kitante. There is much land and we have not driven away the buffalo. The good broth you have just eaten comes from one of the longhorned cattle you saw when you rode toward us. They are wild and still lean, but we will let them graze till they are fat and have much meat upon their bones. Then, if the buffalo herds are small this winter, the white-eyes chief of this stronghold will see that you have much meat for your fires. I promise you this in his name, and I do not lie. My father too was a chief among the Kiowas!"

Kitante's black eyes fixed on Simata's earnest face, as Maxine entered with another bowl of broth. This time, Kitante himself reached for the bowl, put it to his lips and greedily began to gulp it down, only to stop with a grimace and gasp because it was much too hot.

"You see? Even the son of a chief can be hungry, and the white-eyes who are friends to all men will feed him well," Simata quipped.

Kitante absorbed himself now in blowing on the broth to cool it, but found time to glance curiously at his interlocutor. Finally he said in an indifferent tone of voice, "My father will come for me, you will see. He will bring many braves with bows and arrows and spears, yes, and the long rifles too. I know because I have seen these when my father's warriors rode out to raid the Mexican village. If you kill me, you will all die."

"If we had wished to kill you, would we not have left you there to die from the bite of the *kwasinaboo*?" Simata countered.

Kitante frowned, having no immediate answer, and finished his broth. When the bowl was empty, he let it drop to the planking floor and then rubbed his belly. "The white-eyes squaw cooks well. The meat was good. But do not tell her this, she is only a squaw and it is the work of a squaw to feed a warrior."

"Then I will not tell her," Simata solemnly responded, glancing up at Luke who had just entered the room and winking at him.

At the sight of the master of Windhaven Range, Kitante stiffened and sat erect, his eyes suspiciously narrowed: "Who is this white-eyes, Kiowa?" he demanded.

"His name is Luke Bouchard. His grandfather was blood brother of the bear."

Kitante started, stared hard at Luke Bouchard, then turned to Simata: "How can that be, a white-eyes, an enemy? Our tribe would not take a white-eyes as blood brother. And my father, Sangrodo, he is of the tribe of the bear, but he could not be blood brother to this, your white-eyes master."

"He is not my master. All of us are free men, even as you, Kitante. He will tell you himself in your tongue," Simata replied as he nodded to Luke who had followed the conversation with increasing interest.

"What Simata tells you is straight, brave young Comanche warrior," Luke said in Comanche. "Yes, my grandfather who lived on the land of the Creeks, who are now in the Indian Territory far to the north, was indeed their blood brother. He killed a she-bear with his knife and took her claws to make a necklace about his neck to show all men that he was a great hunter and warrior."

Kitante stared at Luke, his eyes widening. "I have never before heard of this, that a white-eyes speaks our tongue. Oh, you do not speak it well—only we Comanches have that knowledge. But for a white-eyes, it is not bad, I can understand you. Is this true, what you say of your grandfather?"

"I swear it by the bear, the owl, the coyote, and most of all, by the Great Spirit," Luke said as he touched his forehead, then his heart.

The little boy scowled, and then grudgingly replied, "What will you do with me?"

"Send you back to your father in the stronghold," was Luke Bouchard's smiling answer. "And as a sign that I mean you and your people no harm, I will send back with you a side of beef."

Once again Kitante stared with growing curiosity at the master of Windhaven Range, and then, a wily look on his face, retorted, "If you mean what you say, that you are not an enemy to the Comanche, I will show you where our stronghold is. But you must come alone with me without weapons, show there is no evil in your heart or lies on your tongue."

"I give you my word I will do as you wish, Kitante."

"That is good. Already I feel b.. c.. am not a child a weakling to lie here in a bed and be fed by a white-eyes squaw, you know."

"It was not your weakness, but the poison of the *kwasinaboo* which brought you here. And even a great chief, such as your father, can be made a weakling by its bite."

"Yes, that is true enough. But if my pinto had not stumbled and thrown me, and if the snake had not been there, you would not have captured me," Kitante insisted.

"That is true also. But then, as even your people will agree, it is the will of the Great Spirit what is to happen to us. Doubtless all of this was planned in advance, Kitante," Luke gently and persuasively proposed.

"I do not understand," Kitante shook his head. "You are a white-eyes, but you know so much about our customs and our beliefs. It is truly beyond my knowledge. Of course I am still young, but I have much wisdom from my father."

"That is well known. And perhaps your wisdom tells you that you would enjoy still another bowl of broth?"

"Well, if there is more and no one else wants it, I think I could eat it," Kitante cautiously admitted.

Young Ramon Hernandez, at Simata's suggestion, had ridden out on Corita toward a grove of live oak trees not far from the Nueces River on the morning of the very day that he and the young redbone, Luke and Lucien Edmond had come upon Sangrodo's son. He had seen a dozen gray mustangs, led by a stallion with the long legs of a race horse, a strong, barrel-like chest and a thick flowing mane, and marked the horse at once as a worthy prize. Three mares grazed nearby, and four other younger stallions not far from these, nickering softly as they tried to attract the attention of the mares. But the leader snorted and pawed the ground, lashing his tail and baring his strong yellow teeth. The younger horses feared him, so they made no move toward the mares. Just beyond, four smaller mustangs grazed, oblivious to the activities of the rest of the herd.

The young *vaquero* had already uncoiled his lariat, ready to lasso the great stallion as he watched from behind a huge clump of mesquite. There was no sound save for the droning of cicadas which mingled with the cheerful song of an itinerant brown sparrow. Cautiously Ramon Hernandez urged his mare on with the merest pressure of his knees and then, within range of the coveted mustang, drew on the reins with his left hand and murmured, "*Adelante, amiga.*" Swiftly he rode toward the leader, who, turning and whinnying, sped off with the *vaquero* in swift pursuit.

The other mustangs took flight in varied directions like a frightened covey of birds, and Ramon Hernandez raced alongside the stallion, leaning forward over his chestnut mare's neck as he awaited his chance. Then swiftly he cast out the lariat and deftly lassoed the racing mustang by the neck, drew vigorously back and planted himself in his saddle with feet dug hard into the stirrups to withstand the shock.

With an angry squeal, the gray stallion rose on its hind legs and pawed the air, turning to face its captor, once again baring its teeth in fierce defiance. Swiftly dismounting, Ramon Hernandez made the other end of the lariat fast around the base of a cedar tree. Then he waited, talking soothingly to the mustang in a soft, liquid Castilian which even as a boy he had found effective with nervous or hostile animals. Again the stallion reared, shaking its head, savagely pawing the air, then backed up and tried to break the lariat, but in vain. Its eyes rolled wildly, and as Ramon drew closer, it lashed out with its front hooves toward the young *vaquero*.

"Gently, *amigo*, gently, I will not hurt you," he murmured. From the pocket of his breeches he took out a carrot and tossed it on the ground in front of the enraged mustang, repeating his soothing words.

Then he moved back, stroking the head of his own devoted mare, who nuzzled him playfully. The gray stallion

310

watched suspiciously, its flanks heaving, and then again it tried to break free of the lariat. Ramon Hernandez stood patiently waiting, till at last he saw the stallion dip its head toward the carrot, push at it with its muzzle, and finally warily nibble at it till it had eaten all of it.

"*Bueno, amigo!* Now you see you have nothing to fear from Ramon Hernandez. Now I will ride you, *amigo*, to show you that I am gentle and respect your great strength," he called as he smilingly approached.

The *vaquero* moved trustingly forward till he was well within range of the deadly hooves, and held out another carrot.

The wild stallion darted its head toward Ramon's hand, nipping the carrot from it, crunching it, whinnying, its eyes not so wild but cautiously intent on this two-legged stranger who acted as no man had ever done before on this wild plain. Moving slowly toward the cedar tree, Ramon Hernandez kept talking to quiet the restive horse, then swiftly cut the knot at the end of the lariat and, entwining it around his right wrist, loped swiftly toward the mustang and leaped bareback astride it. "Now, *amigo*, show me how swift you are, how strong, how brave," he called as he swiftly coiled the length of the lariat and held it between both hands as a kind of bridle.

The stallion reared once again, looked back, its eyes rolling, snorting its defiance, and then its long legs thundered along the ground as it galloped, hoping to pitch its audacious rider off by the sheer headlong flight it took. But Ramon Hernandez, laughing joyously, held tightly to the lariat, crouching forward over the neck of the magnificent horse, encouraging it, applauding it, using every pacifying word he knew from the long hours he had worked with animals on his father's land.

For a quarter of an hour, the mustang raced unfalteringly away from Windhaven Range, and then suddenly halted, snorting, sweat lathering its flanks, turning its head to regard its rider. "*Gracias, amigo,* that was good for both of us! And now, let us go back to the corral and I'll give you more carrots and some hay and, if you are very good, some sugar too. *Adelante ahora!*"

The stallion bobbed its head, seeming to understand, and dutifully turned back as Ramon tugged the lariat to one side to indicate the direction to be taken. Meanwhile the young *vaquero*'s mare, knowing what was expected of it, had begun to trot back toward the wooden rails of the corral and waited there at the gate until its master rode up on Amigo—for that was the name Ramon Hernandez had given this magnificent wild horse.

At last Ramon descended, and, patting the head of the mustang, drawing gently on the lariat which still noosed Amigo's neck, urged it into one of the smaller stalls whose gate had been left open. Then he put up the gate and stepped back with a joyous laugh of triumph just as Mara Bouchard emerged from the *hacienda*, in white shirtwaist and brown skirt which descended to the middle of her booted calves. She already had complained several times to her father that now that they were out here in the wilderness of Texas, there was no reason why she should not be allowed to wear the breeches of a man, of a *vaquero*. It had been her mother Lucy who had gently reminded her, "But wilderness or not, Mara dear, the undeniable fact is that you're a woman, and the men who work for us will think it most unladylike for you to go around dressed the way they are." To which Mara had petulantly retorted, "Mother, I'm twenty-eight and a spinster already, so what does it matter if they don't think I'm a woman? If you only know how I detest wearing these long hobbled skirts and silly shirtwaists in such hot weather!"

She had walked out toward the corral and was watching Ramon put up the gate, her lovely face bleak with a sudden mood of desolation. She felt she did not belong in this strange new country, in spite of all her promises to herself that perhaps here in Texas in this new venture she might hope for a different, a freer life. That was why, piqued by the sight of the magnificent gray stallion with the lariat still noosed round its neck, she called out, "It's cruel to catch that beautiful wild horse and to put that tight rope around its neck!"

Ramon Hernandez turned, removed his sombrero and bowed slightly to the black-haired young woman. "Your pardon, *Señorita*, but there is a good reason to catch such a horse. Simata has given me the idea. He says that the

Kiowas and the Comanches are great horsemen, and if one day their braves come upon our land and are angry that we are here, it can be used as a gift to their chief to show that we wish to be at peace with him."

"But we haven't seen any Indians at all so far, and I still think it's a crime to drag that beautiful horse away and shut it up in the corral. Please let it go, for my sake, Ramon!"

Again Ramon Hernandez doffed his sombrero and inclined his head respectfully toward Mara Bouchard. "It grieves me to go against your wishes, *Señorita*," he politely answered, "but I am sure that it will not be long before Indian scouts will see our *hacienda* here and come to find out who we are and what we are doing. That is why I must keep Amigo here until Mr. Bouchard tells me otherwise."

"Oh! You—you're impossible, Ramon! But then, I might have expected a Mexican wouldn't understand what freedom means to a beautiful animal like that!" Mara Bouchard burst out and, glaring at the young *vaquero*, went back into the *hacienda*.

And so, the next morning, when Kitante admitted that although his leg was still somewhat sore but that he was still able to ride and wished to return to his father, Ramon Hernandez led the gray stallion out of the corral, saddled it with a new saddle from the equipment which Luke Bouchard had purchased in New Orleans, and tied the side of beef which Djamba had cut from the slaughtered heifer onto the saddle, after first salting it down to preserve it as long as possible under the hot sun and then wrapping and tying a blanket around it. Luke mounted his own horse, and tied a short lariat around the stallion's neck, attaching the end to the pommel of his own saddle, while Kitante on his sturdy little pinto rode ahead.

Beyond, at their camp a mile away from the *hacienda* and the bunkhouse and the corral of Windhaven Range, Sangrodo and his six braves waited, holding council among themselves.

"Look, Sangrodo," Ipiltse called, putting a hand over his eyes to shield them from the blazing sun, "there is Little Horse and behind him a white-eyes and behind that one a mustang with saddle and provisions—what can this mean?"

"Perhaps," the Comanche chief joked in a solemn voice, "that Kitante has captured the *jefe* of the white-eyes who have built those tepees of wood. If that is so, Ipiltse, my son has counted a greater coup than your Namsi-kohtoo!"

The other five warriors grunted and eyed one another, sharing Sangrodo's jest, for although they respected the valor of the war lieutenant, they were inclined to find him a braggart on many an occasion around the campfire, especially when he had drunk too much *tiswin.*

"This white-eyes carries no long rifle nor the hand gun that spits fire," Sangrodo observed as the two riders neared the clump of mesquite behind which Sangrodo and his men waited.

"That is true. And your son leads the way to the stronghold, Sangrodo," Ipiltse wonderingly agreed. To his men, he barked an order, "Surround the white-eyes chief, but do him no harm. We shall hear what Little Horse has to say about him."

Luke Bouchard saw the seven Comanches ride out of the huge thicket of mesquite, perceived Sangrodo with his long trailing war bonnet and the warpaint still upon his half-naked body, and drew his horse to a halt.

"It is my father!" Kitante eagerly cried, spurring his pinto toward the warbonneted Comanche chief as he energetically kicked his heels against the pony's belly.

Sangrodo reined in his horse and stared with mingled wonder and reproof at his son, while Ipiltse and the other five braves made a circle around Luke Bouchard and the tethered mustang stallion, eying him suspiciously, their lances and guns not yet threatening him until Sangrodo should give the sign.

"My father, the chief of the white-eyes who built these tepees saved my life," Kitante explained. "My pinto threw me and I fell before the big snake and it bit me. I could not suck out the poison, but this white-eyes has a Kiowa scout who did it. They took me to their stronghold and they fed me and now I am strong again."

"It is true what your son says, chief of the Comanches," Luke interposed in the Comanche tongue. "I wish to be your friend, and to show it, I have come without

314

weapons and I bring beef that your people may eat and think well of us on this land."

"You speak our tongue well, white-eyes." Sangrodo wheeled his horse toward Luke Bouchard and rode up beside him, staring earnestly at the handsome, alert face of the founder of Windhaven Range. "Who has taught you this?"

"It is Simata, the Kiowa who himself is son of a chief who once rode upon this land. He has come with me to help raise cattle and to teach me your ways and your beliefs as well as your speech so that you know I talk straight and am not your enemy."

"Is this true, Kitante?" Sangrodo turned to stare at his son.

The boy nodded: "He has shown me the papers he had the white-eyes chiefs write upon to sell him this land on which he will raise cattle, Oh my father. He has treated me well and he respects the Comanche. If he had not found me, you would have no son, Oh my father."

"That is true. But you should not have run away, Kitante. I have always known that it would take more than a mouse to frighten the son of Sangrodo. Ho, let us go back to the stronghold quickly then." Turning to Luke Bouchard, Sangrodo declared, "You shall visit our stronghold, and you shall see our people and we shall talk. If it is as you say, there can be peace between us. We hunt the buffalo on our land, and the soldiers of the white-eyes wish to drive us from it."

"It is not my wish, and I will not willingly use weapons against you who were first upon this land, no more than would my grandfather have done in the land far to the east where once the mighty Creeks were as you are here."

Kitante eagerly put in, "He has told me that his grandfather was a blood brother of the bear, Oh my father, that he slew a great she-bear with only a knife and took the claws to prove his coup."

Sangrodo looked back wonderingly at Luke Bouchard: "Is this the truth, white-eyes?"

"I will never speak to the great chief of the Comanches with a forked tongue. I swear it by the Great Spirit," Luke Bouchard touched his forehead and his heart.

"Ho! I, too, am blood brother to the bear, white-eyes. Who knows, it may be that there is a bond between us, even though my people are sworn to look upon all others as enemies. We will talk at the stronghold."

CHAPTER TWENTY-EIGHT

Luke Bouchard observed that the Comanche chief, his warriors and his little son did not ride directly toward their stronghold, but instead took a sweeping, circular trail to the northwest and camped at nightfall. He made no demurral, well understanding their hesitancy in allowing a white man to know the exact whereabouts of their hidden temporary village. Nevertheless, when they made their camp, they shared their provisions with him most generously, and Sangrodo gestured to him to walk away from the campfire and to talk.

"I have thought all the day long over what you have said to me," the Comanche leader declared, "and there are good signs. When we reach our stronghold, I will have Mingride read the bones of the coyote and see what they foretell between us. It is *tucan* (night) now, and what I have heard is *equebitz* (new) to my ears. You are the first white-eyes with whom I have talked thus, the first whom I have not tried to kill before he could kill me or my warriors."

"Perhaps that is a good sign, Sangrodo," Luke Bouchard staunchly replied. "And I am eager to know

317

what the bones foretell, just as my grandfather was when the *Windigo* of the Creeks prophesied his destiny on their land."

"Is is not yet your land, for all the papers on which your white-eyes chiefs may write," the tall Comanche leader contemptuously retorted, as his face grew taut with old, remembered hatred. "You are new upon this land, and we were here when there were no white-eyes, only the Mexicans who at first would trade with us and then later behaved with treachery and killed many Comanches, and Kiowas too, to collect the bounty on their scalps. That is why my men and I raided a village but a few days ago and took their women prisoners that they may become squaws and slaves of the Comanches to punish their men for what they had done."

"But are there no treaties, then, between my people and yours, Sangrodo?"

The tall, warbonneted Comanche walked slowly away, his arms impassively folded across his chest, standing looking at the crescent moon in a cloudless sky which foretold another day of scorching sun upon the arid ground of this region of the low plains. Luke waited, sensing that in Sangrodo's hostile mood he would not wish the white intruder to break in upon his thoughts, and bided his time until at last the glowering Comanche turned back to stare coldly at him and to say, "What do you, a white-eyes, know of the history of our people? Even we who have scattered into many tribes in order to survive against our enemies and to make it harder for them to find us, have forgotten all that was written by the Great Spirit hundreds upon hundreds of moons ago when all this land belonged to us who came upon it and found it good and rode like the wind under the free sky."

"I know the history of my own people, Sangrodo, and that where the white man goes, the land is taken from those who first walked upon it. It was thus in the land of the Creeks, it must be so here. But I pledge to you that I have acted with all honor; I have gone to the land office in Austin and there I have staked a claim to land which no other white-eyes has spoken for and where even the Comanches do not often go."

"That is true now; it was not so in long-gone days.

318

First we and the Kiowas knew the *conquistadores*, the Spanish settlers who traded with us even here in what you call Texas. There were the Penatekas, the honey-eaters, and the Nokoni, the wanderers, and over on the great Staked Plains to the west of here, there were the Kwahadi, the Antelope people of the Comanches. We were many miles apart, more than it would take the swiftest mustang to travel in six suns, and we went our own way and we hunted and traded and it was good. Then, when the Texicans won their independence from the Mexicans, we of the Comanche people said that there must be a boundary which would reserve our territory from all settlement by any other tribes or any other white-eyes. This the chiefs among the Texicans refused.

"Yes, your white-eyes chiefs opened their land offices, and settlers came swarming across this land. And the chiefs among you said that any citizen could be settled upon any land not occupied by a white owner and that we and the Kiowas and all others whose skins are red must keep away from those settlements no matter where they may be. Thus the herds of buffalo were scattered by these white-eyes, and we could no longer hunt. And when we tried to hunt, the white-eyes hunted us down and killed us as they would wild dogs. In return, we gave them battle. Now, here on this land which was once ours so long ago, we are like outlaws, hated and feared. And that is why we are ready to give battle so that the soldiers of the white-eyes will not think we are women and children and come to kill us in our sleep as was done with other tribes."

Sangrodo seemed to be speaking beyond Luke Bouchard, his voice angry, his eyes blazing, and the founder of Windhaven Range was silent before such furious eloquence. For he remembered as a boy his visits to Econchate with old Lucien. And he remembered also the pitiful leavetaking of those straggling Creeks, in rags, starving and derided by the greedy white land-speculators who stole away their certificates entitling them to land in the Indian Territory to the west. Yes, they too had been hunted down like wild dogs by the greedy settlers who swarmed over the rich land which once the Creeks had so patiently cultivated. And here in Texas, he knew, the pattern was the selfsame one of selfish greed, or of hypocritical treaties never meant to be kept in which nebulous boundary lines were set so that later it could be said they had been violated by the Indians.

"I cannot speak for all the white-eyes, nor for their chiefs," he at last replied when the Comanche leader turned to stare inquisitively at him. "But I can speak for myself and for my family and my workers. Let me stay upon this land which I have bought at the land office in good faith and honor, let me raise cattle and fatten them so that the meat is good and will feed many hungry families. When the tribe of Sangrodo needs such meat if the hunting is not good, you have only to ask me and I will give you cattle and seek nothing in return except your friendship and the promise of peace between us."

"You speak with dignity and with bravery. I respect these things, even in a white-eyes. I will think on what you have said, and I will see how the bones are thrown tomorrow when we reach the stronghold. But now I will tell you this because of what you have done to save the life of Kitante and because you have given me these presents of the meat and of this great wild horse which I myself shall train to guide me swiftly on my raids against the Mexicans. There are many of us, smaller and scattered tribes, and many attack first and do not listen to words, especially when they come from the mouths of your people. There are also men whose skin is the color of your own who trade with such smaller bands of wanderers, and who bring them whiskey and guns and who turn them against settlers who are white like themselves. Such men are called Comancheros. They are lower than the *kwasinaboo* and far more deadly to us, to themselves and to men like you. And there is one such chief among these smaller bands who trades with such evil men and who has already killed many white-eyes and their squaws and even their children. Beware of him. His name is Norvito. Before I left our stronghold, one of our scouts told me that Norvito and his warriors were seen many miles to the north, but it would not take long to ride down upon you if they knew you had built your tepees where they are."

"I thank Sangrodo for his advice, and I will heed it."

"Let us sleep, then, for already the owl hoots the

320

lateness of the hour and bids us close our eyes and dream," Sangrodo mystically declared. And as he did so, Luke Bouchard trembled to hear once again the soft, mournful hooting of an owl in the distance. . . .

At dawn, Sangrodo and his six warriors continued the circuitous journey back to the stronghold, and it was noon when they reached the camouflaging escarpment. As Luke Bouchard rode in behind Sangrodo and Kitante, flanked on each side by three Comanches, he observed that there were many more women than men in the stronghold. Nor was this strange to him after what Simata had told him about the history of the Comanches. From the time they had entered the written history of our nation, when they first came into contact with the Spanish people of Santa Fe in the eighteenth century, their legend had been one of continuous warfare. They had fought and defeated the Pawnees, the Osages, the Tonkawas, the Navahos, the Utes, and the Pueblo Indians in New Mexico and Arizona. They had marketed horses with the Canadian Indians, raided as deep as fifteen hundred miles into Mexico and had seen the Pacific Ocean. The Comanches had stopped the advance of Spain to the north and to the east and that of the French to the west and to the south. Now the Republic of Texas, the United States and Mexico ranked highest among their enemies—and during all these years there had been no period when the tribe in its entirety was at peace.

As Luke dismounted, he saw the braves and the squaws and the old women and children crowding around to stare at him, some with hostility, most with curiosity. He smiled and made the sign of peace, that universal gesture of the hands which all Indians recognize. Then he said in Comanche, "I am happy to see so many strong warriors and sturdy children and comely women in this *Comancheria*. It does credit to the great Sangrodo and to his worthy son Little Horse."

A pleased and startled murmur ran through the onlookers, who eyed one another and set to whispering about this white-eyes who spoke their own tongue. Sangrodo, overhearing, turned back from his tepee where he had been conferring with Namine, and, holding his arms up to the sky, declared in a guttural voice, "This man and his friends have saved the life of Little Horse, and he has done us honor by bringing us meat for our fire and this great wild horse as a gift to me who am your chief. He is welcome in our stronghold, from this day forth until the end of his days. Let it be known that he walks our way and does not mean harm to the Comanche. I will have Mingride read the bones of the coyote to tell us all what the Great Spirit plans for this new friend of our people and for us who will be touched by his coming among us."

Then, turning to Luke, he added, "You will eat with us now. I will give you a Comanche name by which you will be known here as our friend. It will be *Nimaihkana,* the one who is summoned. Thus you will be *Taiboo Nimaihkana,* the white-eyes who is summoned, and when your name is spoken at the campfire even when you are not among us, it will be as if you are here and your spirit moves with ours."

"I am honored, Sangrodo. And this name you have given me has a special meaning: you have only to send one of your scouts to summon me if I can help you and your people, and I shall come. On this I give my word in truth," Luke Bouchard smilingly averred as he touched Sangrodo's forehead with his right palm, then his own and then his heart. A murmur of approbation rose from the watching Comanches, and Ipiltse called out, "Ho, never before have I seen a *taiboo* who knew the ways of the Comanche."

"It is because I have been taught by one who is the son of a chief of the Kiowas and who knew this land as you do. I respect your ways, your people, your land. My tongue is straight as I say these words in your own language," Luke declared aloud.

"It is a good thing. For once the *kwasinaboo* has not brought death but life," Sangrodo interpolated. "Now, bring food for our friend, and let the shaman Mingride be called to read the bones."

With growing interest, Luke observed the ritual of cooking. Simata had told him that meat was often eaten raw, though it was usually roasted to some degree. At times, when the wandering branches of the many Comanche tribes were able to obtain pots and kettles, they sometimes boiled their meat and other food, but considered it the worst kind of bad luck to both broil and boil a meal on the same fire at the same time: indeed, that was, according to their superstition, as harmful as if someone's shadow happened to fall over food that was cooking. Seated cross-legged near the campfire beside the tepee of Sangrodo, he smilingly accepted a large chunk of the only partly cooked side of beef which he had brought to the stronghold, and did his best to down it so as not to give offense to his Comanche hosts. There were also grapes, currants, *lunas* of the prickly pear, pecans and acorns, as well as pemmican and marrow, and even a slice of raw buffalo liver which was regarded as a great delicacy.

And when at last the feast was over, partaken of by the six braves who had accompanied Sangrodo, with Sangrodo and Luke themselves seated side by side and intently watched by all the rest of the stronghold, the leader of the Comanches clapped his hands three times and a silence fell over the assemblage.

The old shaman, the medicine man of this tribe, emerged from his tepee, naked to the waist, his body painted with ocher to represent the symbols of the bear, the owl, the coyote and the snake, his sparse white hair pulled into a greased forelock, with necklaces of the bones of the antelope and the owl dangling from his scrawny neck. From his waist, tethered by a rawhide thong, there dangled a bag made from the intestines of an antelope.

Luke watched the shaman's approach with more than usual interest; into his mind there suddenly came the mystic foreboding which he had experienced many a time during his conversations with his grandfather, both when they visited Econchate and when they walked in the fields of Windhaven Plantation. As he turned his head to watch the onlookers, he saw squaws wearing carefully sewn and richly ornamented buckskin dresses, and moccasins garishly adorned with beads, fringes, and bits of iron and tin. The wife of Sangrodo stood nearest to him, her hair cut short, parted in the middle, (with the part daubed with color) and allowed to hang loose. Her eyes were accentuated with red and yellow lines above and below the lids, while her ears were painted red inside and each of her cheeks was daubed with a solid red-orange circle.

Under the hot sun, this symbolism seemed to take on an unearthly aspect. He began to tremble and he did not know why, except that what was about to take place seemed so momentous that he had not had time to prepare his mind to accept the meaning of it. It was unreal, an illusion, and yet the smells and the sights of this camp were so strongly vivid that he knew it was no dream, no illusion.

The shaman bowed low to Sangrodo, then lifted his arms to the sky and began an incantation evoking the Great Spirit and those lesser spirits of the demi-gods which the Comanches worshiped. At last, the old man was silent, and then he moved toward Luke Bouchard and touched Luke's forehead with the pad of his thumb, placing his fingertips atop Luke's head and pressing lightly as if to determine the shape of the skull.

This done, he untied the pouch and squatted down before both Luke and Sangrodo, with Luke at his left and the chief at his right. Opening the pouch, he held it up to the sky three times, and lowered it each time first toward Sangrodo and then toward Luke. Then with both hands he gently thrust it forward, so that the contents of the pouch tumbled upon the ground, the whitened bones of a young coyote killed during the full moon and by the shaman himself so that there would be no sacrilege.

He bent low toward the tumbled bone, both hands pressed at his cheeks, his watery eyes staring intently at their placement on the sunbaked earth. Then he said in a solemn voice, "It is good that the white-eyes has come to the *Comancheria*. He brings life though there is death ahead of him and for the most dear. Yet even in that death is new life reborn."

Luke understood the words, and was taut with attentiveness as he waited for the shaman to continue. Through his mind there passed remembrance of what old Lucien Bouchard had told him of how Tsipoulata had read the signs at Econchate which would guide and shape his future life and destiny.

"Ho, though the squaw of the white-eyes is barren, yet will he have a son, and because of this son will he return to the land which he first knew at his birth. This I see plainly, Sangrodo. You, mighty chief of the Comanches, warlord of our tribe, will owe your life to him and he will avenge, though not by his own weapons, the slaughter of innocents. It will not be many moons before all this takes place as the Great Spirit has willed it. I see no more."

He collected the bones and restored them to the pouch, retied it to his waist and, with great dignity, rose and walked back to his own tepee. In the deathlike silence, Luke Bouchard could hear his own heart pounding as he tried to interpret the mystic words of the shaman of the Comanches, as assuredly as Lucien Bouchard must have done when he sat before the *Mico* of Econchate and watched the *Windigo* evoke the spirits of the future as they meant to impinge upon his own destiny.

CHAPTER TWENTY-NINE

A month had passed since Luke Bouchard's visit to the Comanche stronghold of Sangrodo, a month well spent in strengthening the corrals and adding to the size of the original bunkhouse as well as new rooms to the sprawling *hacienda* which housed the founder of Windhaven Range and his family. It was a month of hard work and peaceful planning for the future, and because of the alliance which Luke Bouchard had won from the nomadic and powerful Comanche tribe, he and his workers could look toward each new day without fear of hostile Indian attack.

Yet Sangrodo's warning about the renegade Norvito had not been forgotten. Luke Bouchard had ordered Djamba to instruct the black workers to build a tall wooden stockade which would encircle the adobe dugouts where the two young Southerners dwelt, the bunkhouse and the *hacienda* and the main corral. In this way, if there should be an Indian attack or one by bandits, the defenders would have ample warning and time to arm themselves. Moreover, Luke urged Djamba to instruct the black workers in the expert handling of the firearms which he had purchased in New Orleans so that, when the time came for the cattle drive in the spring, he could leave enough trained marksmen behind to protect the women and children.

The end of October brought an end to the relentless heat on the high-brush plains where Windhaven Range had its site. To further the alliance between Windhaven Range and the tribe of Sangrodo, Luke Bouchard hit upon the scheme of sending a gift of five longhorn steers and heifers to the Comancheria, driven there by young Lucas. His older sister Prissy had purchased a small frame loom in New Orleans, and had begun to weave towels and small blankets for her own amusement. The day before Lucas was to drive the cattle to the stronghold, Luke Bouchard observed the woman at work on her loom and admiringly watched in silence as her nimble fingers plied the threads on the warp according to the defined pattern.

"That's beautiful work, Prissy," he observed, and Prissy sprang up, startled, apologetic: "Oh, Mr. Luke, I ought to be busy with the kitchen chores along with Mama—I just stole a few minutes away to go on with this blanket."

"Don't apologize, Prissy. As I said, it's really beautiful. Do you know what I've been thinking? Grandfather used to tell me about the wonderful crafts which the Creeks and the Cherokees practiced back in Alabama. When I visited the Comanche stronghold last month, I saw some of the women working on baskets and shaping pots and pans out of clay which they baked in the sun, then daubed with berry stains and animal oils for coloring. Do you know, I think that if you took that loom along, the squaws might want to try your way of weaving. Couldn't you make them a similar loom out of sticks and perhaps bits of metal?"

"Oh yes, Mr. Luke, it would be easy, though at first you'd have to start with little things like headbands or wristbands and such," Prissy excitedly replied.

"Well now, if you could go along with Simata, who could translate for you, you could show them what you're doing and you could ask them to tell you some of the stories of their old ways and their crafts and arts, and maybe you could even picture them in some of your weaving."

"Why, yes I could at that, Mr. Luke, that's a wonderful idea!" Prissy eagerly vouchsafed.

"So why not go along with your brother and Simata tomorrow?"

"I'll just do that, Mr. Luke. You're sure that Mama won't mind my being away and not helping her?"

"Of course not, Prissy, I'll speak to her right now."

And thus it was that on this gray, late October day, Prissy set forth on a bay mare, her hand loom carefully strapped to the sidesaddle, while Simata and Lucas rode along ahead of her, herding the five cattle which were Luke Bouchard's gift to Sangrodo and his people. The herds of buffalo which had been seen the month before had changed their pasturing ground, and Luke felt that hunting might be difficult for the braves of the man who had won the fearsome sobriquet of Red Arrow.

He had observed one other thing at the stronghold on which he had kept silent: as he had waited for the shaman to emerge to foretell the future with the sacred bones, he had seen Sangrodo's wife slip into a nearby, smaller tepee and heard voices raised in angry discussion. One of them was that of a Mexican woman, young, from what he could estimate of the tone of her voice, defiant and full of hatred. And when the squaw had emerged, he had been able to glance through the momentarily widened opening of the tepee and had seen a handsome Mexican woman wearing only a tattered shift, barelegged, her wrists bound behind her back, her hair disheveled, her eyes blazing.

He had surmised that she had been a captive taken during the raid of which Sangrodo had boasted, and Simata had told him of the laws of the Comanche regarding captured women: they either complied with their captor's will and agreed to become squaws and share in the work, or else they were made slaves, doing the lowliest menial tasks, beaten mercilessly when their work was inadequate. Yet he knew that the Comanches did not permit prostitution and that at least this handsome Mexican captive, no matter what ultimate fate she chose for herself, would at least not be coerced to carnal submission by the young warriors of the tribe. In any event, it was a harsh life, with little reward even if she should agree to be San-grodo's squaw.

And that was why, just before Prissy had set forth with her brother and Simata, he had taken her aside, described that Mexican woman in the tepee near Sangrodo's, and urged, "You speak a little Spanish, Prissy, that I know. If you have the opportunity, but without making it too obvi-ous and offending any of the guards, see if you can talk with her and learn something about her. Perhaps you can help her; perhaps you can even get her guards to let her work on your loom. It will distract her, give her some-thing to think about that is not part of the hard life she must otherwise accept."

When Lucas and Simata reached the stronghold, they learned that Sangrodo and Ipiltse were away on another raid, this time to capture horses rather than squaws and slaves. The old shaman, Mingride, had been left in charge of the Comanche village, and it was to him that Simata respectfully addressed himself, with Prissy and Lucas standing nearby to hear the translated replies.

"We bring you meat for your fires, O Mingride, as gift from him whom you know as *Taiboo Nimaihkana.*"

"That is good," the old shaman solemnly responded. "The white-eyes keeps his word even before he is sum-moned—that is very good. The bones spoke the truth, as they always do. You and your friends are welcome here."

"I thank you, oh Mingride," the young Indian respect-fully inclined his head. "These are brother and sister, workers for the white-eyes as am I. Is it permitted to speak to the Mexican captive whom Sangrodo brought back from his raid?"

"It is permitted, but do not try to help her escape. She will not be the squaw of Sangrodo; she must be the slave and serve wherever tasks are required. She is proud and angry—that is understood, she has seen her man die in an unpleasant way. But she must work to earn the meat from our fire. Soon Sangrodo will ask her again if she will become his squaw or remain a slave—it will be for her to decide."

"I had thought that the sister of this black man, who is called in our tongue Prissy, might show the Mexican woman how to make cloth upon a frame that is like magic."

The old shaman's eyes brightened as he glanced appraisingly at Prissy, who gave him back an uneasy smile. "I would see this magic of the white-eyes."

"Lucas," Simata said, "unpack Prissy's loom and let her show the shaman how she weaves."

In a few moments, Prissy seated herself on the ground with the small handloom on which a warp was already stretched, and began to move the threads in the patterned sequence that had already been started on the apparatus. Mingride watched with great interest, uttering grunts of pleasure as he observed the design brought out upon the small blanket Prissy had commenced. The motif was that of a series of arrowheads in red. Simata diplomatically explained, "It is the wish of Prissy, when this work is done, oh Mingride, to give the blanket as a gift to the mighty Sangrodo. Since he is known as Red Arrow, you see for yourself how the arrows are shaped in a row, pointed toward the sky."

"Ho! This *guaihpe* (woman) has great magic in her fingers!"

"It is a magic that can be taught, oh Mingride. And if the Mexican woman can be shown how to do this magic, perhaps it will take her mind from her sorrows over her man, and in the honor of Sangrodo to whom she belongs, she can make just such things for the tribe," Simata smilingly proposed.

"Ho, that is very good, Sangrodo will be pleased. Go then to the tepee where the woman is lodged and tell Jicinte that I permit you to have words with her. You and the two who have come with you are welcome, and we will give you food and also *tiswin*."

Simata approached the tepee with Prissy and Lucas behind him, as the Comanche guard rose to his feet, gripping his lance and readying himself. "It is permitted by the shaman," Simata said in the brave's tongue, and the latter grunted assent and walked away to take up his post a few yards distant. Simata crouched to open the flaps of the entryway, and Catayuna Arvilas uttered a stifled cry of terror and shrunk back as far as she could.

"Have no fear, we are friends," Simata assured her, this time in Spanish.

The young widow had been forcibly dressed in buckskin blouse and skirt, her feet shod in moccasins. On the brown satin skin of her calves and lower thighs, Simata could see the darkening striata of the switch, with which the older squaws had liberally beaten her when they had ordered her to work, and she had either refused or shown clumsiness.

"*Amigos!*" she repeated the word scornfully. "There is no such thing for me now. I wish only to die or to escape—and if I am killed trying, it does not matter now, *mi hombre es muerto.*"

"We know," Simata squatted down and made a sympathetic face. "But my master, who is named Luke Bouchard and who owns many acres of land to the southeast of here, has become a friend of the chief Sangrodo. We have come to talk with you, and the daughter of his foreman, whose name is Prissy, asks to be allowed to show you how she weaves upon a hand loom."

"What do I care for things like that? I have no life, they will send me from one horrid Comanche to the other," Catayuna Arvilas bitterly retorted, then bowed her head and began to weep silently.

"No, *Señora,*" Simata shook his head. "I myself am of Kiowa blood, and we are the allies of the Comanches. They do not make *putas* out of the women they capture. If you do not agree to become the squaw of Sangrodo, then you will be kept here only as a slave, to work at whatever tasks the women set you."

"Oh, that I have already learned, to my pain and suffering," the handsome Mexican widow glanced down at her striped bare legs, then bit her lips in shame. "They hate me because I am *Mexicana,* and perhaps one day I will anger them so much they will give me a quick death—not like the one they gave my poor Manuelo."

"It is best to forget such things, *Señora.* The anger of Sangrodo which took his life was not against you, nor perhaps even against him as a person, but because the Mexicans pay well for Comanche scalps and have slain many peaceful Indians out of greed."

"Do you wish to tell me, then, that I must make the

best of it and submit myself to that cruel murderer? If he had used a lance or a gun against Manuelo, perhaps I would not hate him so much as I do and always will!" she angrily flashed.

"But perhaps, *Señora,*" Simata went on in a cajoling voice, "since you know you cannot escape and you do not wish to die—you are a young, handsome woman and you can still bear many children for the man who will one day take the place of your Manuelo—would it not be wiser to think more pleasant thoughts of life and of the many ways by which you can lighten your own burdens?"

"How can that be?"

"Why, let Prissy show you how she weaves a blanket with pictures that tell a story. Perhaps, if you learn her skill, you can tell your story, of how you and your husband were taken from the village by Sangrodo, and how you fought valiantly to save him."

"Why, yes," Catayuna Arvilas wonderingly said, her eyes widening and brightening. "I would learn what this woman of yours has to show me. Yes, perhaps I can tell what hate I feel for Sangrodo in pictures made out of thread, but he will not hear those words spoken and perhaps then he will not torture me. Let her show me if she wishes."

"Now that is good," Simata grinned and got to his feet. Outside the tepee, he whispered quickly to Prissy who nodded, and then entered and seated herself beside the attractive widow. The latter smiled cautiously at Prissy, then remarked in Spanish, "I will not be a very good pupil if my hands are tied behind my back."

"Simata, tell the guard that the shaman permits her wrists to be untied," Prissy called. A few moments later, the Indian entered the tent and himself cut the rawhide thongs which bound Catayuna Arvilas' slim wrists.

"*Gracias a Dios,*" the young woman breathed a sigh of relief as she began to rub her chafed wrists to restore the circulation.

"Well, you have helped me already by coming, I would be ungrateful if I did not try my best to learn what you wish to teach me. Show this loom to me and explain how you work upon it."

And thus began the restoration of the intrepid and defiant Catayuna Arvilas, captive of the Comanches.

While Simata, Lucas and Prissy were visiting the Comanche stronghold, Luke Bouchard had ridden to San Antonio. He had bought more supplies, and found a letter waiting for him; it was from Laurette, Maybelle's only child and now twenty-eight, the very same age as Mara.

Maybelle was now a grandmother, for Laurette's letter happily announced, the first week of September, the birth of twin sons, Kenneth and Arthur Douglas, both healthy babies, fair-skinned and blond. Charles had added an enthusiastic postscript which revealed how easily he had discarded his Southern background in favor of this bustling, thriving new Midwestern metropolis:

> Laurette and I are both excited over the phenomenal growth of what they have begun to call the Windy City because of the wind from Lake Michigan. They are building, and announce it as being ready for business on Christmas Day of this year, the Union Stock Yard and Transit Company, with as many as 345 acres, at Halsted and Thirty-Ninth Streets. Here, I am told, they will receive cattle shipped in—perhaps some of your famous Texas cattle will come here on the new railroad lines. There is much business, and in the store where I work, I have already had a promotion and a raise in salary. Chicago is booming, built so rapidly there is hardly time to lay out the new sites. I feel the vigor of life here, and Laurette says she hardly misses the placid ways we knew in the South before the War. I send my warmest greetings to all of you, and, thanks to Laurette, I feel myself a kin of the Bouchard family, which has so lengthy and honorable a history. Maybe next year we can arrange to visit you in your new home, which sounds so very far away.
>
> Charles Douglas

"Our roots are being transplanted, and yet they seem strong and enduring," Luke Bouchard mused to himself. "It is Grandfather's legacy, a legacy that shows that it is not the land on which we settle, but rather the unity which holds us all together despite geographic distances, which truly perpetuates the name of Windhaven and all that it stands for."

CHAPTER THIRTY

It had rained much of this day in late November, and the branches of mesquite quivered in the gentle wind. Drops of water clung to the branches and, with the sudden faint emergence of the late afternoon sun, they had the luster of precious jewels. On the morning before, Luke and his son Lucien Edmond had, with Djamba and Lucas, built a blacksmith's forge to be ready for the spring round-up and to develop the branding irons which would allocate to Windhaven Range the steers and heifers, calves and young bulls which the riders would "brushpop." It was Ramon Hernandez who had acquainted Luke with this cattleman's expression, meaning that wild longhorns often grazed and hid in the thick mesquite bushes and belonged to anyone who could drive them out, lasso and brand them.

Luke had watched as Djamba fashioned the first branding iron to be used on this new venture, a circle in which the capital initials W R were aligned: (WR) "It'll be hard to alter that, though it looks simple enough," Luke observed as Djamba pressed the smoking iron into a piece of cedar wood to display the newly created brand. "Lucien

Edmond, in the next few months, when you ride out with Ramon and the others, watch for some of the young bull calves that can be altered into steers. Choose several that will make good leaders, docile and easily driven, whom the rest of the herd will follow. When I go into San Antonio the next time, I'll try to find out where the best and most accessible market will be for the herd we'll send from Windhaven Range. From what I've heard thus far, it appears to be Sedalia, Missouri. But I'm not yet convinced that's the place to aim for. There's still a good deal of hostility against Southerners, even in that border state, and I've no way of knowing how the townspeople would treat our riders driving along a herd of three or four thousand cattle. It may be that if my friendship with Sangrodo develops as I hope it will, he may be able to direct us to an even closer market."

"I've heard it said, Father, that some of the Comanche tribes steal cattle, trade them to the Comancheros for guns and whiskey, and then they in turn sell the herd to greedy New Mexico ranchers who don't care where beef comes from so long as they can get their hands on it."

"I've heard that too, my son. And there's one thing more. Sangrodo warned me against a renegade chief, Norvito, who he says was camped about fifty miles north of here. Simata, I think the time has come for you to ride out in that direction and see if you can find any trace of him and his band. Be very careful, take along one of the Spencer repeating rifles and all the ammunition you think you'll need."

"And one of Djamba's spears too, Mr. Bouchard," the Indian smilingly assented.

Simata had taken provisions and water, lashed one of the ironwork spears which Djamba had had made in New Orleans to the side of his saddle, and the Spencer to the other side, and armed himself also with a hunting knife. He had cajoled his bay mare, talking to her as if she were human, to explain the journey and its dangers. And, the past several weeks, he had diligently taught her to obey certain gestures of his hand and low murmured commands, a precaution against dangers which he might encounter on the trail when he rode out as scout for Windhaven Range.

He rode all afternoon and camped late at night on rocky land near a clump of scrub shin oak trees. Beyond, vaguely outlined in the dark-blue haze of twilight and approaching nightfall, was a gentle grass meadow which seemed to stretch far to the west, broken here and there by deep arroyos, where once little creeks had flourished but had dried up years ago and left canyon-like stretches of deep, dry gullies in the rich earth. "This would be a good grazing pasture for the longhorns," he said to the mare, whose ears pricked up at the sound of her master's voice. "We shall rise early at dawn and go a great ways till we are sure there are no unfriendly Comanches. But if we find Norvito, then you will have to remember quickly all that I have been teaching you these last few weeks." At this the mare whinnied and bobbed her head, and Simata chuckled, highly pleased, and gave her a handful of oats.

Just before the sun rose, Simata woke, breakfasted on a mouthful of water and a handful of dried beef jerky, then swung himself into the saddle. The bay mare instantly moved forward with her graceful, loping strides, as the Indian drew in lingering breaths of the pure, refreshing air, cooled by the heavy rain of the day before. Now he came to sparse, thin reddish-brown soil and then shallow, stony chalk. Here and there were old abandoned rock houses, and at the side of one he saw half-buried in the earth the thick feathered shafts of war arrows. The outer walls of the rock house were blackened by fire. Here, perhaps only six months or a year before, some ambitious settler had staked his claim and built a house, and now he and his family were dead. It was an eloquent sign of the conflict between the Indian and the white man, each battling for what was still primitive country, where a man survived only if he was keenly alert and had the powers of anticipation.

Suddenly he halted the mare and dismounted, squatting down and peering with a hand shading his eyes from the once again hot sun. It seemed to him that he had just caught sight of a signal fire, two clouds of smoke rising swiftly one after the other, and then half again as much rising lingeringly. "Comanche signs," he said aloud. "They are so confident that no one is around here for miles and miles in any direction that they send up smoke signals. Now, my pony, you and I must hardly even breathe as we go forward to find Norvito."

By late afternoon, Simata saw puffs of smoke ascending from a distant mesa several miles to the northwest, and reined in his mare to study them. The Kiowas themselves were famous for communication with their allies and their own tribes through the use of smoke signals, building a small fire and lowering a blanket over it in various rhythmic movements to send up smoke patterns that signified phrases or words known by all the tribes. And the Comanches had adopted this swift method of communication; as he read the signals now, he knew they were Comanche and that they summoned a meeting between a Comanche leader and his allies.

"It must mean the Comancheros," he muttered to himself as he jogged the mare forward, his eyes keenly fixed on the mesa. Halting her a little further on, he drew the Spencer repeating rifle out of a rawhide sheath he had fashioned for it as a kind of saddle holster, and inspected it to make certain that it was primed and loaded for immediate use, then replaced it. The air was cooler now, with a touch of fall, and here and there the live oak trees had changed from their rich green to a vivid yellow. He breathed in the air deeply and eagerly, and he felt alive and in the full command of his physical powers. It had been long years since he had ridden along this trail, but it came back to him now. Beyond the mesa and to the east, he remembered, was a deep *arroyo*. There men could meet in a rendezvous, and no one could see them for miles around. Yes, the smoke signals came again, and they told of that meeting place. It could only mean that Norvito and some of his warriors were about to meet the renegade whites who had no scruples about selling whiskey and guns to Indians so long as they were well paid for their risks.

But now there was no further trace of the smoke and the sky was darkening. Simata sniffed the air warily, and then leaned to murmur to his mare, "Swiftly now, *Disygata* (fleet one)! Fly over the ground so that your hooves will make no noise to warn Norvito that we come to spy on him!"

He rode for another four miles till he neared the canyon, and then swiftly dismounted, tethering the mare to a crooked sumac. Beyond the sumac rose clumps of thinning mesquite as tall as a man's head, and through this he made his way carefully, gripping the Spencer in both hands.

It was sloping ground to the top of the arroyo which he knew to be deep enough to hide even men on horseback. His father had once told him that there had been a great creek long years before, and it had eroded and shaped out a primitive canyon for about an eighth of a mile before it had dried up and left no trace of water or of its original source. He heard the faint sound of voices and flattened himself on the ground, crawling slowly forward inch by inch, until he reached the brink and peered over cautiously.

A stocky Comanche with a white headband and a single eagle feather thrust through it sat astride a huge gray mustang. He was flanked by two of his braves, who wore breechclouts and moccasins, and also white headbands, their feathers dyed blue and their chests painted with red and yellow warpaint. Norvito himself wore a shirt of buckskin, and the blue striped trousers of an infantry soldier in the Union Army, whose scalp he had taken a few months before. He also held the soldier's carbine, the muzzle lowered to the ground. His braves, shorter and wirier than he, carried lances. Facing them were two men, one with long yellowish beard and heavy sideburns, his fat face pockmarked and bathed in sweat, in a tattered cambric shirt open at the throat and black riding breeches and boots. From his holstered belt there dangled two six-shooters, one on each side, and he wore a black sombrero pulled down over one side of his forehead. His companion was a tall rangy black-haired man in his late thirties, in buckskin shirt and breeches and moccasins, such as an Indian might wear, gripping a cavalry saber in his right hand and his left hand near a leather pistol holster strapped to his hip. His face was angular, and a dirty black stubble covered his deeply cleft chin and concealed an ugly scar. He, like his yellow-bearded companion, was a Union Army deserter, and there were wanted posters picturing both men in Army forts not only in Texas but throughout the Indian territory.

"*Bueno, hombre,*" the renegade Comanche chief Norvito spoke in guttural Spanish, for he had learned this tongue from his Mexican mother and preferred it to the Comanche of his father. "You have read our signals. What news have you for Norvito? Do you bring trade goods this time?"

The yellow-bearded Comanchero shook his head and grinned crookedly. "Not this time, Norvito. Sure as my name's Ezra Baxter, it's getting harder and harder to steal guns from the soldiers. Maybe next time, soon as Charlie Arnslager here finds out when the next shipment's coming into Fort Griffin."

"But that is many miles from here, *hombre,* and too dangerous for just two men. You will tell me when it comes, my braves and I will see that it does not reach Fort Griffin," Norvito declared.

"We'll do that, sure thing. Now listen, Norvito. You've always said you had a hankering for a white squaw. Well, I'm here to tell you, Charlie and me, we been doing some scouting the last week, and about forty or so miles from here due south some new families moved in and put up a bunkhouse and a big corral and even a *hacienda*. We rode by just last week, to get the lay of the land, and me, I saw at least two squaws you wouldn't mind having in your tepee, Norvito."

"Ugh, they are young, these squaws? Norvito is still a young warrior, he takes for his *cueh* (wife) only a squaw whose *táe* (private parts) are still full of fire."

"Well now, I can't tell you exactly how they'll be on your blanket, Norvito," Ezra Baxter sniggered coarsely, as he winked at his younger companion, "but I am saying they're white squaws and young enough. Now maybe you'd like us to ride on down there and wait and see if they come out close enough to us so we can nab them and bring them back to you. How's that sound?"

Norvito nodded. "Maybe enough squaws for Nepilse and Piaisa (Young Wolf) too?" At this, the two braves flanking him exchanged a lewd grin.

"Sure, why not? But that'll cost you money, Norvito.

Mainly, we don't stay around whites much, we can operate better on our own. But because you're a good friend and customer, I'll promise to give you a fair shake."

Contemptuously, the renegade Comanche demanded, "You bring squaws, Norvito pay gold. Aiyee, do you have *pamo* (tobacco) for Norvito tonight?"

"No, I'm sorry as hell, Norvito, Charlie and I didn't have time to pick it up. Next time sure. I'll tell you what you do. You get your braves out and moving down south from here, not too close to all those buildings they just put up on their land. Looks to me like a passel of Southern folks, probably skipped out before the Northern soldiers could punish 'em for leaving the Union. Charlie and me, we'll mosey down there starting tomorrow and find ourselves a likely spot where nobody'll see us. First thing you know, some of those squaws'll come out to fetch water, and then's when we'll get 'em."

"Bueno," the renegade concurred, "I will have my warriors riding there with the next sun. We shall camp where they will not see us, these white-eyes with the *linda mujeres*. When you capture them, then we shall attack. It is a good plan. But where is your other *amigo, el barbado rojo?*"

"You mean Red-Beard Merle, Norvito?" Ezra Baxter grinned. "He's riding now with that greaser *bandido* Diego Macaras. Things got a little too hot for him in San Antone."

Norvito scowled, shook his head. "You will not use the word greaser again, *Señor* Baxter. *Mi madre* was *mexicana*, and such a word is an insult to her."

"Why, I meant no harm, Norvito, you know that," Ezra Baxter hastily amended with a servile smile. "But from what I hear, Macaras and his boys sometimes come across the border. Now wouldn't it be nice if his band and yours attacked those new settlers about the same time? Then for sure you'd have all the squaws you want."

"That, too, is not a bad idea," the renegade Comanche admitted. "You can get word to the *barbado rojo?*"

"Why sure. Told you, Charlie and me, we'll ride down that way ahead of your braves, and Charlie'll cross the border and go find Merle and tell 'em our plan. Just you hold off till we get the word back to you. They've had it easy down there so long, those damn Johnny Rebs won't be looking for anybody to bother them. You'll hit them from one side, Macaras from the other, and we'll have them like a fat nut between a nutcracker. Easy as you please. Why, hell, Norvito, you could even take over what they've built down there for your stronghold."

"I have no stronghold. My braves and I live on the land, and we move as it suits us. Also, I sent for you because there is something I hear that I do not like."

"And what's that, Norvito?" the yellow-bearded Comanchero eyed his crony, flickering his eyelids as a sign to be ready for trouble.

"I hate the gringos and I make war against them, because one of them shot my *madre* and another—a Comanchero like you, *Señor* Baxter—became the husband of my sister and then cast her aside when she was with child. I followed and killed him. And the Texicanos who come here and take away the good hunting land, I make war on them as you know. But you and your *amigos, Señor* Baxter, raid farms and *haciendas*, and you kill the men and capture the women and you leave signs as if it were my warriors who did these things. This is the act of an enemy, *Señor* Baxter. I do not need men like you to count my own *coups* or scalps. Be careful that I do not one day take yours if I find that you make war on your own people in my name!"

"Why, Norvito, there's been a misunderstanding somewhere, you know that. Hell, *hombre,* we've done business nigh on to a year now, and you've been satisfied every time. *No es verdad?*"

"With the guns and the whiskey, yes. But you do not do this as a friend, you do it because you know I will kill you if what you sell to me is not good. Do not boast of your friendship with Norvito, the wind hears it and brings it back to me, *comprende?*"

"Now, now, Norvita, no need to quarrel. Here, isn't it proof of my friendship for you that I've told you about that passel of white-eyes squaws you can have for the taking? Why, if I were out to double-deal you, Charlie and me and a couple of good boys I know I can pick up when I need them would ride off ourselves and burn that damn *hacienda* and take all the women for ourselves," Ezra Baxter blustered.

Simata, flat on the ground at the top of the *arroyo*, had listened attentively, scarcely daring to breathe lest he be heard by the three Indians or the two Comancheros. Suddenly he felt a tickling on his right hand, which clutched the butt of the Spencer. Staring at it, he saw a centipede, and grimaced as he watched the ugly insect move across his clenched fingers and then drop harmlessly to the ground. Instinctively, he shifted himself to the right and away from the poisonous insect, and the barrel of the Spencer dislodged a small piece of shale which tumbled over the top of the little cliff and clattered below.

"What the hell was that?" Ezra Baxter exclaimed. "Sounds like it came from the top of the *arroyo*. It's so damn dark I can't see anything, but let's try a couple of quick shots—that'll flush the bastard, whoever he is!"

Transferring the reins of his horse to his left hand, Ezra Baxter darted his right hand down to his holstered six-shooter, leveled it and pulled the trigger twice. Simata heard the bullets whine past his head and began cautiously to crawl backwards. As he did so, he could hear the Comanche renegade barking orders to his two braves to ride out of the *arroyo* and seek out the eavesdropper.

Simata rose and, crouching low to make as obscure a target as possible, raced toward the crooked sumac where he had tied Disygata. Just as he did so, he heard the warwhoop of the two braves who had accompanied Norvito into the *arroyo,* and saw them racing toward him on their mustangs. Quickly he dropped to one knee, cradled the butt of the Spencer against his shoulder, squinted along the sight and pulled the trigger twice. One of the Comanches toppled out of the saddle and lay sprawled face down, but the other shot had only grazed the shoulder of the second brave, who rode at him now with his lance, his teeth bared in a grimace of ferocious hate. Again Simata squeezed the trigger, and this time the Comanche stiffened, lurched to one side, dropped his spear and slid down from the racing mustang to roll over and over on the sloping ground.

Simata turned his head as he heard the sound of a horse's hooves approaching to his right, and perceived

345

Charlie Arnslager bearing down on him with upraised saber. At that moment, the Comanchero reached down toward the pistol strapped around his hip. Instantly Simata aimed the Spencer at his chest and pulled the trigger, only to have the rifle jam. Flinging it down, he lunged toward the side of his mare and unstrapped the spear Djamba had made, drew it back and, just as the Comanchero aimed the pistol at him, hurled it forward with all his strength.

There was a gurgling shriek, the pistol dropped from the Comanchero's hand as he pitched backwards to the ground with a thud. He had dropped his saber and his right hand scrabbled toward the shaft of the spear driven halfway through his chest, then his eyes glazed and his head fell to one side.

Picking up the Spencer, Simata mounted his mare and headed her at full gallop toward the south. Behind him, he heard the faint cries of Norvito and Ezra Baxter, but he did not turn to look back. Urging the bay mare on with all his skill and persuasion, he outdistanced his two pursuers as he headed back toward Windhaven Range.

CHAPTER THIRTY-ONE

The sky was still gray the next morning, and the humid air foretold more rain. At Windhaven Range the black workers busied themselves fortifying the area around the *hacienda,* bunkhouse and the adobe dugouts where Joe Duvray and Andy Haskins preferred to live because of the view they commanded of the surrounding terrain. Frank, the wiry Fulani, Dave, the Kru, and Ned, the Hausa, built a kind of picket enclosure around all the buildings which comprised Windhaven Range, including the corral. By now, too, a gate had been made in this picket barricade, about a hundred yards from the porch of the *hacienda* itself. Djamba supervised the work, and Lucas worked with the other three blacks to strengthen this fortification. One short span of fence still remained unplaced, however, near the side of the corral.

Betty had just finished preparing and serving lunch in the *hacienda,* and she and Prissy were clearing away the dishes from the dining table salvaged from the chateau in Alabama. Luke and Lucy were chatting, talking of old times, while Sybella and Maybelle were engrossed in making sure that little Carla and Hugo finished the fruit on their dessert plates.

"You know, Maybelle," Sybella smiled as she reached over to pat little Carla's head, "maybe next spring Ramon could train some ponies for the children to ride. It would be good exercise for them, teach them to be self-reliant. They're both sturdy youngsters and they haven't had a day's sickness, heaven be praised. This country is far more rugged than the one we left, Maybelle. Children will grow up more quickly here, because they'll have to."

"That's very true, Mother. Alas, about the only pleasure I have in this lonely place is taking care of those sweet children."

White-haired Sybella gave her daughter-in-law a searching, knowing look. Then she gently remonstrated, "I don't like to hear that note of self-pity in your voice, Maybelle dear. You've made a marvelous adjustment already, so don't look back."

"Sometimes I can't help it, Mother. After all, I'm forty-five and a woman's life is just about over by then. I certainly can't bear any more children, and when it comes to that, there's no man around here for miles and miles, even if I were thinking of marrying—which I'm not."

"You mustn't think that. There'll be other settlers here, and not in the too distant future either, Maybelle. And as for your being forty-five, you're still a very handsome woman. That red hair of yours still has very little gray. You watch and see, you'll find a man, a kindly, considerate man, who'll have eyes only for you. I'll be sixty-four next year, Maybelle, but I don't think my life's over yet. I'm much too excited watching my children grow stronger and wiser and take on new responsibilities."

Mara Bouchard, across from them, had been listening with a bitter smile playing on her lovely mouth. Brusquely she rose from the table: "If nobody minds, I think I'll go for a ride on Tamisin. I'd best get it in before it starts to rain again."

Luke looked up as his handsome daughter walked toward the hallway. "Don't ride too far, Mara," he lightly admonished. "Simata isn't back yet, and you know about the dangers of outlaw Indians."

"Father, there hasn't been an Indian around here in

months, and you know it," Mara irritatedly expostulated, her eyes sparkling with pique as they always did when she felt herself crossed or hampered in having her own way. "After all, didn't you tell us that you'd made a peace with that Comanche chief, Sangrodo?"

"That's very true, my dear, but he leads only one of many tribes, and there are plenty of Indians in Texas who certainly don't hold themselves bound by Sangrodo. Just be careful and don't go too far. You know how your mother worries."

"But there's no need to, Mother," Mara put her hands on her hips and stared hard at gentle Lucy. "You know that I ride perfectly well, and I know exactly where I'm going at all times. I'll be back in an hour or two. Please don't worry about me—I'm not a child any more, Mother."

Setting her lips, her head high, she walked out of the dining room. Lucy turned to her husband: "It's very hard for Mara, Luke dear, you know that. If only she could find a husband out here. I think she's beginning to resent the fact that we left Alabama, when she looks back to the neighbors and friends she had in those happy days."

"I think," Luke drily observed, "she sometimes wishes she'd been born a man. She'd be out there helping to build that stockade of ours if that were the case. I know she's restless, Lucy. She has a good many things bottled up inside her, and maybe riding will get them out of her system." He rose from the table. "I'll go out for a while and see how the stockade is coming along. It ought to be finished in another day or so. Then we'll take a nap and wait for Simata to get back. I hope he hasn't run into any trouble."

Mara Bouchard defiantly adjusted her sombrero, edging the rawhide band under her dimpled chin which she thrust out with unconscious belligerence. For the past month, she had ridden a rangy pinto mare which she herself had christened Tamisin, although Ramon Hernandez had at first politely suggested that the mare was likely to be skittish and that she would do better to choose an older roan mare which he had marked for her in the corral and which he himself had thoroughly trained.

But that advice had only irritated her, the more so as it

had followed her annoyance with him at having captured the superb wild mustang Amigo. As she emerged from the back door of the *hacienda* and made her way toward the makeshift stable which Ned and Frank had built to one side of the corral for quartering the horses, she frowned as she saw the slim, wiry young *vaquero* standing in the middle of the corral coiling his lariat and preparing to lasso another of the wild mustangs he and the two Southerners had brought in a few days earlier.

"Don't we have enough horses by now, Ramon?" she petulantly flung at him as she turned toward the stable.

"Your pardon, *Señorita* Bouchard, but we shall need a large *remuda* for the spring drive of the cattle your father intends to bring to market. It is well now in the months before the drive to gather up good strong horses and to train them so our riders will be able to move the cattle without stampedes or have too many stragglers."

"You certainly do have an answer for everything, don't you? Well, I'm going riding now. I'll take Tamisin."

"May I be permitted to ask where you're going *Señorita* Bouchard? It is not too safe to wander far from here."

"Now don't you too start treating me like a child, Ramon!" she angrily flashed. In her right hand, she grasped the rawhide quirt which Simata had fashioned for her, while at the same time cautioning her against using it except when imperative.

"I was not aware that I was treating you like a child, *Señorita* Bouchard," he said mildly, his eyes widening and a hurt look momentarily appearing in their depths. "You are assuredly a *linda mujer*, if you will pardon my saying it."

"It doesn't matter at all to me what you might or might not say about me, except to be civil, Ramon. Now, if you've no objections, I'm going to saddle Tamisin and ride her."

"*Pero, Señorita* Bouchard, I do not really think it is safe for you to ride out alone today. Simata went scouting to find the Comanche outlaw Norvito, and he is not yet returned. It may well be that some of Norvito's braves ride not far from here. And a woman without weapons would be powerless and helpless against the Comanches, who are the best riders in this country."

"That's quite enough, Ramon. I'll do what I want, whether you like it or not." She slashed the quirt at her calico skirt and turned toward the little stable.

"At least, let me ride with you," he anxiously pleaded.

Mara Bouchard whirled, her lovely face clouded with anger. "Damn you, Ramon, don't you understand English? My father hired you because he thought you did. Now you just keep away and mind your own business. I want to go for a ride by myself, I know the country around here, and besides I don't think the Indians would hurt a woman all by herself."

"*Madre de Dios, Señorita* Bouchard," Ramon exasperatedly burst out, "I do not understand why your father has not ordered you to stay at home. I know that if I were he, I'd make you do so, *para todos los Santos*!"

He had moved out of the corral now and closed the gate, stood a few feet away from her, still twisting the coils of the lariat in both hands.

"How dare you talk to me like that, you—you greaser!" In her mounting anger, Mara pitilessly flung at him the most insulting of terms to a full-blooded Mexican.

Ramon Hernandez's lips tightened and his dark-brown eyes narrowed with anger at this insult. But, controlling himself, he put up a placating hand. "At least, *Señorita* Bouchard, wait till evening when it will be cool, and do not go beyond the big *arroyo* to the southwest."

"Didn't I tell you to mind your own business, Ramon? Maybe this will convince you I mean just what I say!" Mara Bouchard exclaimed. Out of angry impulse born out of her own lonely frustrations, she drew back the rawhide quirt and slashed him across the cheek.

The young *vaquero* sucked in his breath, put a hand to his swarthy cheek, where an angry weal blazed. "*Caramba*, if you were a man—" he began. Then, mastering himself, and with a sarcastic show of humility, he doffed his sombrero and quietly resumed, "*Perdoneme, por favor, Señorita* Bouchard. I had not meant to anger the *señorita*. She is free to go where she wills, like the wind. *Vaya con Dios*!"

Mara Bouchard, her gray-green eyes bright with anger,

bit her lips as a sudden contrition mitigated her stormy mood. Yet, seeing the faintly mocking smile on the young *vaquero*'s lips, she suppressed the words of apology that surged to her throat, and stormed by him into the stable.

Leading her rangy pinto mare Tamisin out of its stall, Mara swiftly saddled the horse, then swung herself up astride, having hoisted her calico skirt and petticoat. *One of these days,* she vowed to herself, *I'll wear chaps like a man. Why shouldn't a woman be practical out here on the plains, for God's sake.* Then, pulling the brim of her sombrero down with a belligerent gesture, she rode past Ramon Hernandez, wheeled Tamisin to the long stretch of plain to the southwest, and, without a backward glance, urged her mare into a gallop.

Ramon Hernandez, still stroking his welted cheek, watched her ride off for a long moment. Then he swore under his breath and hurried to the stable. Saddling Corita and filling a leather canteen with water, he loaded his Henry rifle, packing extra bullets and powder in a pouch tied to the strings of his chaps. "*Vamonos*, Corita!" he called, and the mare followed Mara Bouchard's trail to the southwest.

After half an hour's hard riding, Mara Bouchard had begun to regret her stormy impetuosity. She had passed the low grasslands and now was entering a rocky, desolate terrain, crisscrossed by deeply eroded stream beds. As she pulled up Tamisin to a halt, looking around somewhat nervously, she suddenly stiffened when she heard the distant sound of a hoot owl. "Come on, Tamisin girl, we'll turn back now," she said aloud to the mare, who tossed its head and whinnied fretfully. Once again, there was the sound of the hoot owl, and this time it was closer.

Wheeling back, Mara kicked her booted heels against Tamisin's sides, urging it on as suddenly a bloodcurdling yell rose behind her. Glancing back, she saw three almost naked Comanche braves, in full warpaint, brandishing feathered lances and rifles. As they saw her glance back, they uttered their terrifying war whoops and urged their horses on to overtake her.

Suddenly Tamisin stumbled into a gopher hole and, with a scream of pain, pitched onto her side. Mara had just time enough to throw herself off the fallen mare, and lay sprawled as the three braves neared her, their cries gleeful now. A short squat young warrior rode up, grinning evilly, as he lifted his lance and pretended to hurl it at her, and she instinctively cringed, her mouth gaping in a strangled cry of terror, putting up one hand to fend off the deadly point of the weapon.

Suddenly there was the report of a rifle, and the Indian jerked in his saddle, dropped his lance and then slumped over the other side of the horse and lay in a fetal position on the rocky ground. Behind him, the second Comanche uttered an angry cry, lifted his rifle and fired, while Mara threw up a hand in front of her face in an ingenuously instinctive motion to ward off the bullet, though it had not been aimed at her.

Again the rifle far behind her barked, and the Comanche, with a gurgling yell, swayed, then sprawled onto the ground as his riderless mustang raced by.

Mara turned, her eyes widening incredulously to see Ramon Hernandez crouching behind a jagged boulder, hastily reloading the Henry. The third brave, the oldest, with tufted forelock, naked but for breechclout and moccasins, brandished his lance and galloped toward the boulder. "Look out, Ramon. Oh my God!" Mara cried hysterically.

The young *vaquero* leaped from behind the boulder, swinging the rifle by the barrel, and, feinting to one side, evaded the Comanche's lance thrust. Then, springing at him from the right, Ramon Hernandez swung the butt of the Henry with all his strength against the Indian's muscular back.

With a yell of pain, the brave drew his foaming mustang to a halt, leaped down and, crouching, lunged at the young *vaquero* with his long lance. Mara began to crawl toward the combatants; scooping up a handful of pebbles, she suddenly flung them into the Comanche's face just as he prepared to lunge again. As the Indian brushed his left forearm against his face, Ramon Hernandez rushed forward and clubbed him with the butt of the Henry against the side of the head. The Comanche staggered and, dropping the lance, sank down on all fours grunting in pain, shaking his head, trying to rise, but before he could, Ramon Hernandez had retrieved the fallen

353

lance and plunged it deep into the Comanche's back. Then, straightening, panting, he turned to stare at Mara, who had dragged herself to her feet. "I said, *Señorita*, there were Comanches out here, *no es verdad?*" he painfully gasped.

Tears ran down Mara Bouchard's cheeks as she stumbled toward him, and she put out a hand to touch the livid welt which her quirt had left. "Forgive me—oh my God, forgive me, Ramon, I'm the one who ought to be whipped," she groaned.

Then she sank down on her knees and holding out the quirt in both hands, offered it to him. "Whip me, punish me for what I've done—I almost had you killed because of the way I behaved—whip me hard!" she huskily murmured.

He stood over her, his face twisted and flushed from the physical exhaustion that was the aftermath to this fight against such uneven odds. Drawing in great gulps of breath, he stared at her as if seeing her for the first time, and then he turned as the pitiful squeal from the fallen pinto mare recalled him to the awareness of the moment. "It's Tamisin, she's badly hurt," he hoarsely gasped, and turned away from the kneeling young woman to stumble toward the mare. She lay on her right side, one leg doubled back under her, the other front hoof pawing at the ground, eyes rolling and glassy with pain, baring her teeth as the young *vaquero* approached. The three dead Comanches lay sprawled, stiffened in their grotesque postures, their horses having galloped off and disappeared by now. Again Tamisin squealed, tried to rise, fell back with a still more agonized, shriller cry.

"*Pobrecita,* she's broken her leg," he muttered as he squatted down to stare at the suffering mare. "I have to do this."

"Oh Ramon, must you kill her?" Mara, still kneeling, holding the quirt in her trembling hands called out, tears choking her voice.

"*Sí, linda,* and it's not safe to use the gun. If there are other Comanches nearby, they may come if they hear a shot so long after the others. Close your eyes, *querida.*"

Mara obeyed as tears ran down her cheeks, bowing her head, while Ramon Hernandez retrieved one of the feathered lances of the Comanches, moved slowly to one side, took careful aim and then thrust swiftly and mercifully into the mare's heart.

Then, his own eyes wet with tears, he moved slowly back toward the kneeling young woman. "You saved my life, *tu sabes, linda*. When you threw the stones into that one's face—he would have killed me otherwise. So we are even."

"No. I brought all this on you, I acted like a child with a tantrum, I called you—I called you a greaser, Ramon. You were so brave, you thought only of saving me, not of yourself—I deserve to be whipped like the child I am— here, use it, leave marks on me as I left on you, Ramon." Once again, opening her eyes and staring imploringly at him, she held up the quirt with both hands.

He took it from her and flung it away, shook his head. "I do not whip women, *linda*. Besides, I think I deserved it for what I was thinking about you when you came to the corral."

"You were thinking—about me, R–Ramon?" Mara quivered, not understanding, her forehead furrowed as she stared wonderingly at him.

"*Sí, querida. Te quiero mucho, Señorita* Mara! It is true that I am what you called me, a greaser, as you say. But I am all the same a man who loves a woman who has *mucho fuego*, like you, *querida!*"

He put his hands on her shoulders and Mara trembled and swayed, seeing his anxious eyes fix on her face. His fingers gripped her, and she came to her feet hardly knowing that she did, uttering a choking little sob as she flung her arms around him and offered her mouth to be kissed.

With a groan of desire he could no longer quell, Ramon Hernandez pressed her to him, his mouth fusing with hers. Mara whimpered, her own eyes closing as her lips parted to receive and to respond. She was shaken by a wild, almost agonizing yearning the like of which she had never before experienced. The thought of death, the terrors she had known when the three Comanches had surrounded her, when she had seen one pretend to spear her, when she had heard the shot of another which she had believed intended for her own heart—and the three

355

sprawled bodies of the war-painted Indians impinged upon her senses with a terrifying realism that, paradoxically, seemed to sharpen all her awareness of herself, of her womanliness, and of her virginity as well. The struggle between herself and the man whom she had despised—yet who had saved her life and avowed his passion for her—had melted the hostile reserve she had built around herself since coming to Windhaven Range. Now, heedless of the sun, of the smell of blood and death and of her own sweat of fear, Mara Bouchard quivered in awakening.

Her legs were weak beneath her, they could not hold her, and she felt him gently cradle her down onto the ground. Intuitively, inexplicably, she whispered, "Yes, yes, Ramon, oh my dearest, yes, I want you too!" as she felt his hands husk the calico skirt and the long petticoat, felt his fingers almost impatiently unfasten her camisole and part its folds to bare the heaving creamy globes of her naked virgin bosom. As she opened her eyes, she could see the pink buds of her nipples darkened and stiffened in their pale aureola, and as his fingers moved to the waistband of her drawers, again intuition arched her body willingly and longingly for his taking. The harsh, pebbly ground bit into her back and buttocks and thighs, yet the torment only seemed to whet the fiercely uncontrollable craving which rose within her, made her thighs ripple and welcomingly part to receive him.

He was covering her face with kisses now, his hands touching the swelling turrets of her naked breasts, with an urgency and yet a delicious veneration that thrilled her to the very core, for it was virile and *macho,* and yet there was a rare romantic adoration even to his swift wooing of her here near that boulder where he had fought so valiantly for her life as well as for his own.

She groaned aloud as she felt him probe her, wincing at the first twinge of unwonted maiden pain, yet even in that shrinking, she compelled herself to succor him so the debt between them would be more than paid in full. He had saved her life; her strong finely sculptured young body might well have been sprawled beside these three Indian renegades if he had not come after her and disobeyed her insolent order. Thus at first it was an overwhelming gratitude which arched her to him, and then he made himself known into her by the full force of his vigorous manhood, as his lips moved to nuzzle first one stiffened nipple and then the other, as his hands slid under her buttocks to arch her from the uncomfortable ground, as they fused into white-hot concord, Mara Bouchard understood at last the sweet fury of love born of primal hatred which is all the more tempestuous when the reason for hate is so heroically erased.

She cradled his head in her hands, kissing him as she could, abetting him, responding to him with feverish undulations, and her loins rejoiced and throbbed with the glory of first mating. She scarcely heard the broken, panting endearments which he laved upon her, but she felt everything, and sensation upon sensation raised her to intolerable rapture till at last, mouth to mouth, arms and legs entwined, they culminated in rapturous crescendo there on the field of death which had become life.

Long moments after, when he moved from her, suddenly contrite and even blushing like a schoolboy, beginning to stammer apologies for his audacity, she laughed softly and shook her head: "Stop it, Ramon. Maybe I wanted this all my life, and it took you to show me that I needed a man who wouldn't take stupid orders from a woman like me. Don't be bashful now, for God's sake—it was wonderful, wonderful for both of us—I could tell, even though it was my very first time—oh Ramon, my lover, my darling one, will you forgive me for the way I've treated you, for marking your dear face with my quirt?"

"It is a mark of love and I will wear it with pride and honor, *linda*," he knelt down, took her hand and kissed it, then kissed one creamy panting breast. "And now you'll have to ride with me on Corita, and we'd best be getting back swiftly before any other Indians take a notion to see what happened to these three. *Dios*, what an animal I was to tear your clothes like that—they're hardly fit for riding—"

"Shh, *mi corazón*," she laughed softly as she sat up and put a hand over his mouth, laughing again with pleasure as she felt his lips kiss her palm. "You weren't ashamed of my body before, why should it disturb you now?"

357

"But when you come back like that, what will they think, *querida*?"

"Help me up, darling. There now. It's not too bad, my clothes aren't really torn. Why, as to that, I'll say that I'm your girl, Ramon. That is, if you'll have me."

"Oh no, *Señorita* Mara," he shook his head, his face congealing with anguish, "not that at all! I haven't any right, and I've very little *dinero*, nothing except myself and Corita and my wages to offer you—but if you would think of it, you would do me a great honor to be my *esposa*!"

"It's such a lovely word, much sweeter than our word 'wife', Ramon. Yes, if you want me, I'll marry you. And now let's go back, so I can tell my father and mother that I'm not lonely any more on Windhaven Range."

CHAPTER THIRTY-TWO

They rode back, Mara behind Ramon, her arms clinging trustingly around him and her head cradled on his shoulder. Seated astride Corita's broad back, the black-haired young woman felt an ineffable peace and tranquility which had never been hers before. It was as if the violent antipathy which had so swiftly turned into uninhibited passion had transformed her by the sheer mysticism of the struggle between life and death. And there was a wry smile on her face as, from time to time, she tightened her arms around him and pressed a kiss against his neck or shoulder.

"I heard you tell father that you once rode with the *Juaristas*, Ramon," she murmured. "Did they have their women riding with them like camp followers? Or, in the days of Napoleon, you know, they were campfollowers who assigned themselves to any man who caught their fancy and marched beside him and saw that he was fed and had enough wine and, at night, a woman to sleep with."

Ramon Hernandez uttered a joyous laugh, then shook his head. "That is all very romantic, *querida,* but with me it wasn't at all that way. I hated what was being done to my Mexico, when the French soldiers placed that Austrian on the throne. Benito Juarez is a great man, *linda,* and one day soon he will liberate my enslaved country. But you see, the man with whom I rode was a liar and a murderer, only I did not know that until it was too late. He is the one who attacked your family on your way to settle here. And I think he will try again, for he will not soon forget that your wonderful *abuela* wounded him and drove him off like a jackal with his tail between his legs."

"You hate him, don't you, Ramon dear?"

"Sí, querida. Not for what he did to me so much as for what he did to that poor little village of Miero, killing innocent people, wounding the old priest, even stealing the altar cross from the church. I have sworn a vow that I will replace it one day—and now again that reminds me how little I have to offer you, *mi corazón."*

"Don't talk like that, Ramon. You've more to offer me than any man I've ever met, you've yourself, you're strong, brave, and you would have given your life for me back there. Besides, I'm sure that Father will give you a piece of his land and a good start so that we can have our own home together—and your children, Ramon. I want your children very much."

The young *vaquero* halted Corita, who turned her head and nickered softly as she watched her stalwart young rider turn and kiss the young woman who rode behind him. Docilely, she waited for his signal to go on, but it was long in coming.

"Pero, querida," he at last responded, "I want no gift of land, nothing I do not earn by my own labor. I am poor, but I am proud and I am a man of honor. And this is what concerns me most, because of the way I used you back there—as if you had been a *puta,* and this you are not, *mi corazón, mi linda* Mara."

"But, you silly darling, don't you know it was the way you loved me back there which made me know how much I really wanted you all this time, even when I thought I hated you? I want to be everything to you, your *puta,* yes, your *esposa,* your *mujer.* You see, Ramon, I speak a little of your language, and I will learn more so there will never be any secrets or guilt or shame between us, not ever again."

They had reached the open part of the stockade, and Ramon Hernandez dismounted and tenderly lifted her down, holding her to him and kissing her ardently on the mouth. With a moan of happiness, Mara gave him back kiss for kiss, straining herself to him till she was breathless and flushed. "I'll go tell Father and Mother, Ramon," she promised as she at last reluctantly freed herself.

"Is it wise yet, *mi corazón*? What will they thing of me, a poor *vaquero* who asks for shelter and who works as the lowliest of *peónes,* and then takes their daughter from them? Perhaps it would be best to wait till you are very sure, my darling one."

"Ramon Hernandez, you're the most obstinate, illogical man I ever met—and I love you because of it, too!" Mara Bouchard gaily laughed as she leaned forward to kiss the now fading welt on his cheek. "Besides, you can't cast me off quite so easily as that, not after I've marked you with my own brand. Now you go take Corita back into her stall and give her some extra oats for the hard work she had to do in carrying an extra rider, and I'm going to tell Father and Mother about us. No, not another word, you understand. I love you so." She doffed her sombrero, and jauntily waving it by the band, marched off into the *hacienda,* her face aglow with a serenely confident smile.

Luke and Sybella had been sharing a cup of tea, and Luke had finally revealed to his stepmother the secret he had been keeping ever since the receipt of John Brunton's last letter. "But, Luke dear," the white-haired matriarch gently declared, "is it wise to look back to the past, now that you've made this adventurous step forward and done such hard work to establish us on this new frontier?"

"I know exactly what you're thinking, Mother," Luke considered his empty teacup and uttered a faint sigh, "I confess it was a sentimental, perhaps even romantic gesture. All I know is that on the morning when we rode over to Windhaven Plantation and saw what the Yankee troops had done to it and to Matthew Forsden, my heart was sick within me. I knew then that because of the hatreds between the North and the South, that all of us would have been evicted by the new provisional government, even if the chateau had not been burned. But when we were in New Orleans, I took John into my confidence and told him how I felt about the place. He said that he would look into a possible purchase of it. Well now, as you see, he's managed to have it bought by a free black man. I told John, too, that whatever it cost to restore it, I'd be willing to pay. So now, there exists the possibility of getting it back one day, if ever it's needed. Let's suppose that Lucien Edmond doesn't find Windhaven Range as rewarding as he'd hoped. In a few years then, Mother, he and Maxine and the children could go back to Windhaven Plantation. By then the hatred between North and South would have begun to die down, and people wouldn't regard a young man like him as one of those legendary cruel slaveowners."

Sybella gave her stepson a fond smile, her eyes warm and knowing. Finally she said, "You're so much like Lucien, my dear, and I think he knew that, and I think to the very last he believed that you would be the true hope of the Bouchards. So far, the decisions you've made have been right for all of us. And I share your love for that chateau back on the Alabama River, because so much of my life was spent there, and I've so many happy memories. My life has nearly run its course, Luke, and perhaps that's why I'm all the more anxious to see what happens here on Windhaven Range and how Lucien Edmond takes charge of things from your own very capable hands—that's surely what you intend?"

"Yes, Mother. All the same, I felt I had to tell you—let's make it our secret for the time being, because there's no need to tell the others. Maybelle, for instance, would only be reminded of the unhappiness she had back there, and I don't think she'd ever want to return. But at least we'll both know that Windhaven Plantation is within our reach one day if we should ever need it. Well now, here comes Mara back from her ride." This last, as his daughter entered the living room and then stopped short, her creamy cheeks suddenly flushing with a shyness quite uncharacteristic of her.

"Oh—I—I didn't mean to intrude—" she stammered.

"And you didn't, my dear," Luke genially retorted. "Did you have an enjoyable ride?"

Mara blushed becomingly, bit her lips, then bravely

squared her shoulders and faced her father and grandmother: "More than I dreamed it ever could be. Ramon Hernandez saved my life, because I went riding in the wrong direction after he'd warned me, and three Indians captured me. Father, he—he was so brave, he killed them all, and he didn't even think about his own safety in trying to rescue me."

"Thank God for that, Mara! Where is he now—I want to thank him—" Luke began.

"No, Father, first I want to talk to you about him. I—I've fallen in love with him, and I want to marry him."

Luke stared incredulously, then chuckled and shook his head: "Only a little while ago I was telling your mother that you probably wished you'd been born a man because you were finding life so dull and unexciting here. And now you bring me this startling but certainly very joyous news."

Mara twisted her fingers together, bit her lips again, and then confronted her father with a flare of her old self-willed defiance: "It's no joking matter, Father, I assure you. I know it sounds silly because up to now you know I've never really been involved too much with any man—I won't even talk about what happened back at Windhaven Plantation—and now all of a sudden I'm telling you that I've fallen in love with a Mexican. A poor Mexican, Father, but he's got more honor and pride and dignity than a lot of rich men I met back in Alabama."

"Now, now, Mara," Luke laughingly protested, holding up his hands in mock petition for mercy, "I haven't said a word yet, and I wasn't about to bring up the facts you just volunteered. Ramon Hernandez was very honest when he told me about his background, coming to warn us as he did about the bandits with whom he'd ridden before he learned their true character. I'm certainly satisfied with him here as a worker, and he can be very valuable to the future of Windhaven Range. So far as I'm concerned, Mara, I see no possible objection to your marriage, not from my viewpoint, at any rate."

"Nor from mine either, darling," Sybella smilingly interposed as she went to hug her granddaughter by marriage as tenderly as if Mara had been her own flesh and blood.

"Oh, Father, Grandmother—I'm so happy—it's only that Ramon says he's poor and he doesn't want to be beholden to you in any way—oh, please, Father, make it possible for us to get married! I know he's the man I need, the man I want!" She was smiling through her tears now as she kissed Sybella and then flung herself into her father's arms and gave vent to the overwrought emotions which had begun with the antagonistic scene at the corral.

Luke tenderly stroked her head, murmuring words of endearment. "That's it, Mara, cry it out. They're tears of joy and they're wholesome, good tears. Don't you worry about Ramon. I'll have a little talk with him later on—I think right now would be somewhat tactless. Just tell him, when you see him again as I know you will, that I've given you both my blessing, and that I'm going to think of a way in which he can own the land he'll need to make a home for the two of you—yes, and the children you'll both want. They're the hope of the future, Mara, and if you've a strong man beside you, it doesn't matter what country he was born in. Grandfather proved that when he left Normandy to come to Econchate."

It was sundown when Simata rode back through the open part of the stockade and led his horse into the stable, then hurried into the *hacienda* to tell Luke Bouchard what he had learned.

"This is a grave matter, Simata," Luke declared when he had heard the young redbone's story. "It means we're going to have to prepare ourselves for an attack, maybe from both sides of the border. You have no idea how many braves Norvito can lead against us, I suppose?"

"No, Mr. Bouchard, there were just the two with him, the ones I had to kill. But from what this man Ezra Baxter was saying to Norvito, I'm sure he must have at least twenty or thirty in his war party. That renegade band is even more nomadic than Sangrodo's. But what was most important, Mr. Bouchard, was Baxter's telling the Comanche leader that one of his friends rides with the bandit Macaras who attacked us on our way here. He had one of his Comanchero friends with him, and that man I killed also. But it is my fear that this man Baxter may himself ride on across the border and bring the bandits back to strike at us at the same time that Norvito plans to attack."

"You are probably quite right, Simata. I'm very grateful to you for what you've learned, and I'm only sorry that I had to send you into danger."

"It might have been still more dangerous, Mr. Bouchard, if *Disygata* had not been able to outrun the horses of Norvito and Baxter. The rifle I took with me jammed after I had fired it three times at Norvito's two braves. Here it is. I do not understand. It is supposed to fire all the shots in the tube."

Luke Bouchard frowned as he examined the Spencer rifle which the young redbone handed him, and began to take it apart. "I see the trouble, Simata," he pronounced. "The ejection mechanism was worn down so that it didn't clear the spent cartridges. That's why it jammed on you. It appears that the man from whom we obtained these weapons was not altogether honest—but fortunately, from the news I have had from New Orleans, we shan't ever have to worry about Captain George Soltis again. Give this rifle to Djamba, and see if he can't tool the ejection mechanism back into shape."

"I will, and thank you, Mr. Bouchard. What do you plan to do to prepare against the attack?"

"You've told me that the Comanches won't attack at night."

"That is true, but they would attack as dawn breaks, or just before sundown. They will ride in and encircle our compound, and perhaps they will use fire arrows to keep the defenders busy so that they can climb the stockade."

"I'll have Lucas and Frank see to putting picket poles into the space we haven't finished yet near the corral. They'd better work on it this evening so that we'll be ready by tomorrow. And perhaps, Simata, some of our blacks and you and Joe and Andy could ride out, well armed, to scout the territory, to see if Norvito's braves are heading toward us and also if there's any suspicious activity south of us."

"Yes, Mr. Bouchard, that's a good idea too. I'd better

ask Djamba to inspect all our carbines and rifles just to make sure they'll work when they're needed."

"Thank you, Simata. I'll tell the women to be particularly careful and to keep inside our stockade for the next few days."

CHAPTER THIRTY-THREE

Early the next morning, Luke Bouchard, Ramon Hernandez, Djamba and Lucas, as well as Dave, Frank, and Ned, rode out to survey the terrain around Windhaven Range. There was no sign either north or south of any intruders, and early that afternoon, Simata himself rode out on his mare to look for tracks which the others might have missed. But when he returned at sundown, he reported that there was as yet no sign of the renegade Comanches led by Norvito, nor had he seen any smoke signals from the north which would indicate that the Comanches were preparing an attack.

The stockade had been completed by now, and here and there on all sides were chinks of space between the tall posts from which the defenders of Windhaven Range could fire. As Luke himself pointed out to his son, it was better to have the problem of defense than of attack, since here, secure within their little fortress, they could see the attackers coming and repel them with heavy losses before any breach in the stockade could be made.

The next day was as peaceful as the preceding one, and this time Joe and Andy rode out for a quick inspection

367

tour, only to report that there was absolutely no sign of any riders coming toward Windhaven Range from any direction.

At about four o'clock that afternoon, Maxine Bouchard, who had been playing with little Carla and Hugo, smiled indulgently when they both declared that they were thirsty. "All right, darlings, I'll go fetch a bucket of water from that little creek, and I'll also pick some of the pretty roses near the bank for you, Carla."

"Oh yes, Mommy, I like roses," the little girl solemnly declared, while Hugo sniffed disdainfully and then interposed, "Maybe Mama can pick some berries for me, can you, Mama?"

"Why, of course, I can, Hugo dear. Now you stay here and don't tease your sister, and I'll be back in a jiffy, I promise," Maxine assured them.

The young woman wore a ruffled shirtwaist and blue cotton skirt. Since the sun was still hot even at this late hour, she wound a bandanna around her forehead, went to the kitchen and took one of the larger wooden buckets. Betty at once protested, "Now, Miz Bouchard m'am, no need for you to go fetch water, ah kin do it mahself."

"Never you mind, Betty," Maxine laughed, "I can get it myself. Have you seen my husband lately?"

"Mr. Lucien Edmond, he just saddled hisself a hoss, he go ridin' wid dat Injun—de nice one, ah means."

"You mean Simata, Betty," Maxine smiled. "Well then, I'll be back before he misses me, won't I? See if you can't make the children a little pudding or something special tonight. I think they're a little fretful from all this hot weather we've been having. My goodness, I thought with the coming of fall, we'd have much cooler weather, but I suppose we're much too close to the Mexican border for that."

Maxine left the kitchen and circled the *hacienda,* opening the gate, then closing it behind her. Humming a wordless tune, her hazel eyes wide with pleasure at the sight of the spacious land that stretched beyond to the farthest horizon, the tall clumps of mesquite, the patches of unexpectedly beautiful wild red and yellow roses, she walked confidently toward the little creek about a quarter of a mile from the *hacienda.*

On the way, she carefully broke off a full-blooming yellow rose for Carla, deftly breaking off the stem and avoiding the thorns, then thrust the shortened stem into the pocket of her skirt. There would be wild blackberries down by the creek, and both Carla and Hugo would enjoy them. Perhaps she could use her bandanna to carry them in one hand and the bucket in the other. She smiled to herself, thinking how important it was to keep one's promise to a child, no matter how young. That was what her own father had told her back in Baltimore when she had been a little girl.

She walked carefully, her eyes searching the ground ahead of her, remembering the danger of rattlesnakes and the far deadlier little coral snake which sometimes lurked near stagnant pools of water as well as along the banks of creeks and rivers.

There was a well-beaten pathway to the creek, for Simata had found the creek when they had first decided on this site for the building of the *hacienda* and the bunkhouse and the corral and the dugouts, and proclaimed it fresh water from an underground source. He had promised also that in the spring he would dig for what he was certain would be hidden wells of pure fresh water.

Here at this point where the beaten pathway reached the lowest bank of the little creek, it was easy to squat down and to dip the bucket into the clear cool water. She could see how magically it seemed to come from that hidden source underground, bubbling up from the bottom. She lowered the bucket slowly, glancing about to make sure there were none of the snakes which Simata had warned about, and then suddenly she uttered a startled gasp, for the shadow of a man standing at her right fell between her and the water. As she glanced up, she saw a man with a long, yellowish beard and thick sideburns, his plump cheeks pockmarked, his blue eyes squinting at her. Before she could utter a cry, he had swiftly knocked the bucket from her hand back into the creek, and clamped his palm over her mouth while his other hand drew one of the two six-shooters which dangled from his holstered belt. "One yell, sister, and I'll kill you, savvy? Now, you just do as I say, maybe you'll live a while, hear me? Nod your head!"

369

Paralyzed with terror, Maxine Bouchard managed to nod, her frantic eyes fixed on his ugly features, seeing as if in an irrelevant awareness the black sombrero pulled down over one side of his forehead.

"That's showin' sense, honey. Now, jist you git down on all fours and start crawlin' round this side of the creek and over to that tall clump of mesquite, you hear me?" He prodded her shoulder with the muzzle of his six-shooter, and Maxine Bouchard nodded again, fighting the wave of hysteria that threatened to overpower her, as she sank to all fours and meekly began to crawl in the direction he had indicated.

Glancing furtively around, the fat man crouched low and followed along beside her. "That's fine, honey, keep movin', fast as you can. There now, that's good. Now we'll jist go behind this nice tall mesquite so nobody'll see us, and I'll fix you up nice and comfy for a little horse-back ride."

"My God—who are you—where are you going to take me?" Maxine Bouchard managed to stammer in a trembling voice.

"Why, honey, to a redskin who'll pay plenty for a piece like you."

"Oh God—no—aah!" At her sudden outcry, the bearded man had savagely backhanded her across the cheek, making her sprawl on the ground where she lay sobbing.

"I told you not to make any sound, honey. Hate to mark up a nice piece like you, but maybe it'll teach you a lesson. Now git behind that mesquite like I said and do it fast before I really hurt you!" he growled.

Maxine Bouchard obeyed, and as she looked up, she saw a saddled gray mustang, tethered to the top branch of the tallest mesquite. Before she could say another word, her assailant tore off her bandanna and used it to gag her, then ripped off his cambric shirt, tore it into several strips and promptly bound her wrists behind her back. Even as she struggled, he muttered in a low menacing voice, "Don't fight me too long, honey, I get mad and then I'll really hurt you. Won't do you any good anyway. You're worth a lot to me, not only for the gold I'll get from Norvito when I bring you in, but because he'll see I'm his real friend after all. Now, I'll help you up on that horse, right in front of me, so I can manage you all the time and don't forget it. Up you go, spread those legs, that's it. You ride a horse real nice, honey," he added with a snigger as he forced her to mount.

Her eyes rolling, nearly fainting with terror, Maxine Bouchard stared desperately at the distant *hacienda* as her abductor swiftly mounted behind her, seized the reins in his right hand, clamped his left arm round her middle and urged the mustang on till he was lost from view in a copse of live oaks and cedar trees.

When Lucien Edmond and Simata returned a quarter of an hour later, and Betty had tearfully told them that Maxine had not yet returned from the creek, they rode back there, and Simata quickly found the tracks of the mustang. He scowled as he held up a strip of the ripped cambric shirt to Lucien Edmond: "I have seen this shirt before, Mr. Bouchard. It was worn by the Comanchero who calls himself Ezra Baxter and is an ally of Norvito. It means he has taken your wife to Norvito and that the braves of that hostile chief have camped not far from here."

"Can we go after them, Simata?"

"We should need all the people here to do that, Mr. Bouchard. I have a better plan. I will ride now to Sangrodo's stronghold; he is an enemy of Norvito, he and his braves will help us. Take the Southern boys Andy and Joe with you, see if you can follow the tracks of Baxter's horse and learn in what direction he went. It is my thought that Norvito, after leaving the *arroyo* where I saw him meet this Comanchero, rode southeast with his warriors and must be camped somewhere on the low plains, waiting to attack Windhaven Range."

Lucien Edmond ground his teeth in powerless rage. "I didn't want to kill those three men in Austin, Simata, God knows I didn't. Yet, God forgive me now, I'll kill any man who mistreats Maxine."

The Indian sympathetically nodded, touched Lucien Edmond's shoulder in a gesture of understanding. "You would not love her otherwise, Mr. Bouchard. It will soon be dark, you'd best start looking for the tracks, and I go now to Sangrodo's stronghold."

"Do you actually think he'll help us find my wife, Simata?" Lucien Edmond anxiously demanded.

"Yes, Mr. Bouchard. He has sworn a pact of friendship with your father, and to him Norvito is a man who kills and tortures without reason. It is true that Sangrodo himself is cruel, but only against those Mexicans who kill his people for the money paid them for scalps. It is only justice that Sangrodo seeks, although the white man cannot always understand such things. But now I must go, for it may be that Sangrodo and his warriors have left the stronghold to raid across the border or else to hunt the antelope and the buffalo." Raising his hand in salute, he wheeled his mare toward the west and galloped off, as Lucien Edmond stared despondently at the pieces of torn cambric shirt which marked the abductor's attack on his beautiful wife.

Ezra Baxter chuckled to himself with anticipation as he galloped eastward, following the Nueces River for about ten miles and then crossing it at a shallow ford near the Mexican border. Here, in a dry gully, he prepared to camp for a few hours, comfortably certain that any pursuers would not believe he would halt his journey quite so soon or that he would cross the river toward Mexico. The darkness and the natural camouflage of the site he had chosen aided him. Moreover, he had eaten nothing since breakfast and it would be well also to see to his captive's physical needs.

Maxine Bouchard winced as he dragged her down from the mustang and set her on her feet, her hair disheveled, her shirtwaist ripped at one shoulder to expose the creamy curve of shoulder and upper arm. He drew his six-shooter and prodded her belly as he muttered, "I reckon you'd like to go off into the bushes by now, honey, and maybe rest your bottom a spell before we get back to traveling, eh? Now I'm going to take this gag off, and you be real careful about opening your yap, because if I have to, I'll kill you, and that's a promise. Now, are you going to be good?"

She faintly nodded, staring at his ugly face, and sadistic

grin as he reached out to unknot her bandanna. "There now, just remember there's no good yelling your fool head off. I covered my tracks pretty good crossing the river a little while back, and they're not going to think of looking for me this far south. Want some food first, or do you have to go tend to yourself, honey?"

Maxine shuddered with revulsion at the sly lechery in his words and grin. "I want no favors from you. But I warn you, my husband and his men will track you down no matter where you go, and you certainly can't think of selling me to a Comanche. You're a white man—"

"Sure, sure, honey," he mockingly interrupted. "Everybody wants to tell poor Ezra Baxter what to do all the time. Well, I had a captain over me during the war and he was a miserable bastard, riding me all the time. Sloppy uniform, he used to keep saying, put me on report, got me doing latrine clean-up work—you know what that's like, I guess. Well, honey, I settled his hash before I left the army, and I killed a couple of other men who thought I ought to do what they said. So don't you be going and telling me that you're white like me. Anyhow, I owe Norvito a big favor, 'cause he's a little unhappy about some of the raids my boys and I've been pulling. So when I bring you in, he'll make me a kind of blood brother, and he's a powerful friend to have when you want to keep your scalp. Now, like I said, do you want to eat first or go into the bushes over there?"

Maxine Bouchard turned scarlet and lowered her eyes as she nodded, not wanting to give him the satisfaction of a reply.

"Guess you'll need your hands then, won't you, honey?" he sniggered. "All right. I'll untie them for now. But I'll watch you, and I'm a damn good shot. Just don't try running off. Most likely, you'd stumble onto a rattler or a coral, or maybe a *javelina* might run you down and gore you. Wouldn't want you to get marked up any before I turn you over to my redskin blood brother now, would I? There you are. Don't take too long, either. I'll come after you if you do."

His obscene laughter followed her as she made her way toward a clump of bushes on the other side of the dry gully, and she closed her eyes to try to drive away the tears that stung them, tears of powerless indignation and hatred. For an instant there, when he had lowered his six-shooter and taken his knife to cut the improvised bonds on her wrists, she had been almost tempted to lunge for the gun and turn it against him. But her wrists were numb from lack of circulation, for he had tied them cruelly tight; and she knew that he would not hesitate to kill her, just as he had threatened. Mercifully, the thick bushes concealed her, but even as she was tidying herself and rising, she heard him coarsely call out, "That's time enough for whatever you have to do, honey. Now come back here on the double or I'll come in there after you!"

"I—I'm coming now," she called, once again a wave of furious hatred and shame seizing her.

"Now that's a good girl. Your hubby trained you pretty nice, I'll say that for him. Only Norvito's more a man than the one you got, he'll keep you busy so you won't miss your man too much," he guffawed. "Want some jerky?" He took a piece of dried, smoked beef out of the pocket of his black riding breeches and proffered it to her.

Maxine Bouchard shook her head. "I told you I don't want anything from you."

"Well now, that's being real huffy now, honey. Anyhow, you're sort of beholden to old Ezra, aren't you? Wasn't I nice letting you attend to yourself just now? That ought to be worth a kiss at least. That's all I want now, I'm saving you for Norvito," he sniggered as he moved toward her, the six-shooter leveled at her heart.

Maxine Bouchard closed her eyes and stiffened as his left arm clamped around her waist and pulled her up against him. The unwashed smell of his half-naked body, the moist thick lips which forced themselves on hers made her gorge rise, but she submitted without a whimper, her arms and fists tight against her sides.

"Well, that was better than nothing anyhow," he mockingly declared as he at last released her. "Say, what's that ring you've got on? Your wedding ring, maybe?"

"No. It belonged to the mother of my husband's great-grandfather," Maxine tersely explained. "Are we going to stay here for the night or go on riding?"

"We'll ride soon as I've had a chaw or two of this jerky. I'll bet you're just dying—hey, I see you tore off

374

part of the sleeve of your shirtwaist, honey. And I'll bet you left it tied to one of those bushes, sort of a signal. You're smart, real smart, but it's not gonna do you any good, so just forget it. And you don't have to start peeling yourself down to leave more markers either—Norvito'll do that for you, haw haw!" he guffawed again, pleased with his obscene wit.

Then, keeping the six-shooter in his right hand, he proceeded to chew on a few mouthfuls of the jerky in his left, eying Maxine with unmistakable lechery. Once again she could not help turning scarlet under his humiliating gaze, but she stood courageously, arms at her sides, head erect and shoulders straight, trying her best to ignore his presence.

"There now, that'll have to do for a spell. Norvito'll have some real good chow for us when we get there, honey." He pocketed the rest of the jerky and then gestured with the six-shooter. "Put your wrists behind your back. I'm gonna tie you up again real tight, and gag you, too."

"I—I won't scream—please, it's very uncomfortable—" Even as she spoke, Maxine hated herself for asking even this indulgence from this ruthless Comanchero.

"Don't tell me what to do, woman, like I just told you!" he suddenly snarled, his eyes narrowed and glinting with fury. "Nobody pushes Ezra Baxter too far. No, not even that dirty redskin Norvito. Now do what I told you to, and fast!"

There was no help for it. Maxine Bouchard put her wrists behind her back, while Baxter gagged her again with her own bandanna and then used the same strips from his discarded cambric shirt to bind her wrists and her elbows together as well, adding extra knots to make the fetters cruelly tight. She winced, but remained silent.

He lifted her up in his strong, pudgy arms, placed her on the mustang, then mounted up behind her. Once again, his left arm fitted around her waist like a vise, his right holding the reins, he urged the mustang on back across the river and toward the east.

It was nearly noon when he reached the abandoned adobe huts which Luke and Lucien Edmond Bouchard had observed on their first trek toward what would be

Windhaven Range. Ezra Baxter had broadly skirted toward the west the valley which had led away from those adobe huts, in his desire to puzzle the pursuers, and now sharply turned the mustang southward and rode till he reached the jagged crests of little hills topped by cedar. Then, dismounting, leaving Maxine bound and gagged astride the rangy gray horse, he cupped his palms to his mouth and uttered twice the hoot of a screech owl. From one of the abandoned huts, there came an answering, low call, and the Comanchero chuckled triumphantly: "Yep, honey, your new man's here and waiting, with about twenty of his braves, I'd say. So just a little friendly piece of advice before I take you to him—you'd better be real nice to Norvito, or he'll throw you to the others. These renegade redskins don't exactly honor females the way some of the Comanche tribes do. Now with Quanah Parker or maybe even Sangrodo, you might be a slave, but you wouldn't have to share the blanket unless you took a fancy to some strong buck. It's not like that with this tribe, so think it over."

He lifted her down now, wrenched away the gag, and Maxine attempted a final plea: "For God's sake, I'm a decent woman—I've got two little children—for their sake, if not for mine, don't sell me to an Indian!"

"You'll forget all about your kids, honey, once Norvito makes you his squaw. He's got enough juice in his *cojones* to give you a whole passel of brand-new brats to make you forget the ones you left behind. It'll be a real excitin' life for you, honey, and if you cuddle up to him real nice on the blanket, he'll deck you out with jewels and feathers like some fancy gal in a New Orleans cathouse." Once again he bared his yellowish teeth in an obscene grin, and Maxine Bouchard shuddered and dug her fingernails into her palms, realizing the utter uselessness of any decent appeal to the Comanchero.

Then, gripping her by an elbow, he forced her down the slope toward the row of adobe huts, and her eyes widened as she saw the renegade Comanche chief come out of the first hut and stride toward them.

He was clad in his usual buckskin shirt and blue striped Army trousers and moccasins, white headband around his high-planed forehead with the single eagle feather thrust through it at the right. His scowling face was hideous to Maxine, seeing the strong angular jaws and deeply cleft chin, the squat, seemingly broken nose and the thin cruel lips, his cheeks bedaubed with red and yellow and black paint in the symbols of his tribe and hostility to all strangers. Two of his braves emerged from the hut next to his, one with a lance, the other with a carbine, watching intently as their chief, gripping his carbine by the barrel in his right hand, confronted the Comanchero and his abducted prey.

"You keep your word, *Señor* Baxter. That is good. Ho, this white-eyes is *muy linda*. She will be my squaw now—you have told her this?" Norvito spoke in Spanish.

"Of course, aren't we blood brothers now? I told you Ezra Baxter's word could be relied on, Norvito. Now what about the gold you promised me?"

"One thing more I must ask first. Have you sent word to the red-bearded one who rides with the *bandido* Marcaras to join our forces in the attack against the *hacienda* from which this squaw was taken?"

Ezra Baxter chuckled and shook his head in amusement. "Norvito, I swear you're getting more forgetful every day. Hell, man, don't you remember I told you to let me have one of your braves and I'd tell him where to find Merle Kinnick? He's bound to have reached him by now since we had our meeting out there in the canyon."

"*Sí, es verdad,*" Norvito grudgingly admitted with a scowl at the Comanchero to rebuke him for this tactless remark before the white female captive. "*Bueno.* I will have Surbide bring you the gold as I promised. There are other squaws at the *hacienda,* did you see them?"

"I told you before, there were a couple there the first time I scouted the place. I rode round it and across the border and waited yesterday afternoon on the chance one of them might come down to the creek for water. Sure enough, this one did. Now don't be greedy, Norvito, this little spitfire'll give you all you can handle till you and your braves can raid her ranch. Now where's the gold?"

"Who talks of being greedy now?" Norvito growled as he made a sign to the brave with the lance, who nodded, disappeared into the hut, and then loped back with a rawhide pouch which, at Norvito's sign, he handed to Ezra Baxter.

The Comanchero opened it, thrust his hand into it and drew out golden coins, clinked them together in his palm, then dropped them back into the pouch and retied it, thrusting it into the pocket of his breeches. "Always a pleasure to do business with you, Norvito. Now if you don't mind, I think I'll ride south and see if I can pick up old Merle's trail myself. Might not be too healthy in these parts. For sure this little hellcat's man is going to be coming for her."

"We are Comanches, and one Comanche is worth at least thirty of the white-eyes," the renegade leader contemptuously declared. "If you wish to save yourself, go then. There is no reason for you to stay, you have been paid for the white-eyes squaw who is now mine."

"Well, seeing as how you feel that way, Norvito, I'll mosey along. I'm going to try to get to Merle and see if I can't bring him and Macaras's band back to raise a little hell over at that *hacienda* where I found this tasty filly for you."

"Let it be so. But Norvito does not need to wait for help when he raids the white-eyes," the Comanche renegade boasted. "My warriors have counted many coups, have taken many scalps. By the time you bring back the *bandidos,* there may be nothing left of that *hacienda* and the white-eyes who have built it on land they stole from the Comanche!"

Then, his dark eyes glistening with lustful anticipation, he gripped Maxine's bound wrists with his left hand and, the fingers of his right hand twisting her disheveled hair, forced her ahead of him back toward the adobe hut.

Ezra Baxter snickered, adjusted his sombrero and called out, "Remember what I told you, honey. Forget your man and your brats, you'll wind up being queen of the redskins round these parts!" Then, with a brutal laugh, he mounted his mustang and, without looking back, rode toward the Mexican border.

CHAPTER THIRTY-FOUR

Lucien Edmond Bouchard, accompanied by Andy Haskins and Joe Duvray, had followed the tracks of Ezra Baxter's mustang eastward, and Joe had discovered the place where the Comanchero had crossed the river at its shallowest point and made his temporary camp. Night had fallen, and the half-moon was obscured behind masses of ominously dark clouds.

"Likely to be a windstorm, might even be rain," Andy Haskins warily glanced up at the sky as he dismounted. "Let's see if we can find where that blasted Comanchero went back across the river." Squatting down, he took a tinder box from the pocket of his buckskin jacket, tore off some dry mesquite leaves and soon had them burning. Breaking off a branch, he held it to the little fire till it ignited, and then, leading his horse with the reins in his left hand, crouched low to the ground as he held the improvised torch ahead of him. "Here it is, and see how deep the hoof prints are, Mr. Lucien Edmond," he called. "That means your missus rode on the same horse with that devil. They headed east, and like as not that's where that redskin's hideout is."

"I'm going on, Andy. If you and Joe want to come along, that's fine, but this is my fight."

"Look, Mr. Lucien Edmond," Joe protested, "we know just how you feel, but it'd be suicide to go on in single-handed against a Comanche war party. Hell, he must have at least twenty or thirty braves with him, and all you'd do is get yourself killed."

"Maybe so," Lucien Edmond replied, "but at least I can try to settle accounts with the man who carried her off. My guess is once he's delivered her, he won't stay around long. He might even be heading back this way."

"That's fair reasoning, Mr. Lucien Edmond," Andy drawled, scratching his neck and eying his young crony, "but you'd better take us with you. That'll mean three carbines instead of one, and we brought along plenty of ammunition. Why, with that firepower, we could just about wipe out Norvito's band if we found ourselves a good place to ambush them."

"Simita has ridden to Sangrodo's stronghold to bring help. How long do you figure it'll take before our Comanche friends can pick up our trail and join us?"

"He can't possibly get to that stronghold before tomorrow noon, Mr. Lucien Edmond," Joe Duvray volunteered. "And if Norvito's braves stay put where they are, my guess is it'll take two days of hard riding after that. Simata'll find the trail, don't you worry about that, and old Sangrodo's a pretty smart chief, he'll figure out where Norvito's holing up."

"Then I'm going after that Comanchero. I'll make him pay for what he did to Maxine, as God's my judge." With that, Lucien Edmond Bouchard spurred his chestnut gelding to the east. Andy Haskins and Joe Duvray exchanged another pitying look, then rode on after him.

Norvito, cruelly twisting Maxine Bouchard's hair, forced her to stoop in order to enter the old abandoned adobe hut and, laughing brutally, shoved her forward so that she sprawled on the floor and lay panting.

"*Mujer*, you are my squaw now," he said in halting, guttural English.

"Never! You can kill me, torture me, but I won't give in!" she hysterically cried.

"Ho, ho, we will see. It is well known the white-eyes are cowards. If you do not obey me, I give you to my braves. They will know how to tame you," he chuckled as he squatted down and examined her tightly bound wrists and elbows. "What is this?" His dark eyes saw the antique ruby ring which Laurette de Bouchard had given her younger son Lucien seventy-six years ago and which Luke had in turn given to Maxine as an omen of good fortune for the new life they were to have on Windhaven Range.

"You shan't take that, my husband gave it to me! You've no right!" Maxine shrilly defied him as she rolled over with an effort and tried to sit up to face him.

With a braying laugh, the renegade Comanche leader put his hands to her torn shirtwaist and viciously tore at it, then tore off the cotton camisole beneath, baring her to the waist. He sucked in his breath as her magnificent, pear-shaped creamy breasts appeared, swelling voluminously in her distraught emotion. *"Lindas tetas, mujer!"* he grunted, "they will give suck to Norvito's papoose. You will be my squaw, I have spoken. But that ring, once I take it from you, it proves you have no other man but Norvito."

Savoringly, catching sight of a little mole at the base of the cleft between Maxine Bouchard's superb naked breasts, he poked a forefinger at it, and Lucien Edmond's wife, with a cry of revulsion, jerked back, then spat into his face. "Animal, don't touch me!" she exclaimed in a voice that trembled with near-hysteria.

Raging at this affront, he cuffed her cheek so viciously that she fell back against the wall of the little adobe hut. Gritting her teeth, she suppressed an outcry at that bruising blow, which left an angry, discolored mark on her sun-tanned satiny cheek. Then, with a snarl, he seized her by the hair drawing at last a shrill cry of pain from the helpless captive as he pulled her forward onto the ground before him. Squatting down over the middle of her back, he seized the ruby ring and wrested it from her finger, despite her efforts to bend her finger and prevent the theft.

With a laugh, Norvito began to place the Bouchard heirloom on his own left hand, but it would fit only the

381

little finger. Moving backwards, he again plunged his right hand into his victim's tumbled hair and lifted up her contorted face, showed her his left hand. "See who wears your man's ring now, white-eyes squaw!" he cackled. Then he attacked the fastenings of her skirt and tore it off, and then her drawers, leaving Maxine naked except for shoes and stockings. With a shriek of disconsolate, helpless shame, she again summoned her only resource and spat into his face.

"I will teach you not to insult Norvito, chief of the Comanches!" he snarled, livid with rage. Once again, he grasped her thick tresses, twisting them mercilessly, he backhanded her with his left hand across first one cheek and then the other, but Maxine Bouchard stoically endured the painful blows, summoning a contemptuous sneer to her exquisite face.

He chuckled then, capriciously pleased with her defiant spirit. "Ho, it is good the white-eyes *mujer* does not obey her man's will the first time. It is plain she is no *puta,* but a *mujer muy fuerte.* Ho, that is very good. She will give Norvito a warrior son. And so first my braves and I will destroy your white-eyes stronghold, woman, and when you have seen your man and your friends dead under our lances and guns and tomahawks, then you will know whose squaw you truly are. But first, a lesson in manners, so you will know the next time Norvito comes to you with the scalps of your white-eyes friends that a squaw does not spit at a great chief!"

So saying, the renegade Comanche began to slap her with the flat of his hand, attacking her breasts and belly and the insides of her thighs. Groaning, Maxine Bouchard feverishly rolled over onto her belly to escape the atrociously painful slaps to her tenderest parts, and with great glee, Norvito amused himself by slapping her buttocks and thighs as he cackled, "So I have heard the white-eyes punish their young when they do not obey! It is very good, ho, for you are a naughty child even though your *tetas* and your *táe* (private parts) are truly those of a fine squaw! There, *mujer, ne tza osupanact* (I know) you wish your hands were free so that you could try to kill me, *no es verdad*? But you will not kill me, white-eyes *mujer* with the big fine *tetas,* you will be my *cueh* (wife) when I have come back from the raid on your people, and then your *táe* will know the power of my *guea* (penis)!" As he spoke, he rained stinging slaps all over Maxine's legs and buttocks, as she lay grinding her teeth with stoic endurance, preferring this humiliating chastisement to the torture of her breasts and loins. Nonetheless, tears streaked her flushed cheeks, and when he had finished, her body throbbed with the hot pain of his sadistic reprisal.

"Now it is finished—for this time. You will stay here, one of my braves will bring you food and drink. He will not touch you, woman, but if when I return from the raid on your stronghold, you are not then ready to be my squaw, all of my warriors shall enjoy your white-eyes flesh, this I promise you!"

He took a rawhide thong and lashed it painfully tight round her ankles, then, with a last derisive bark of laughter, left the adobe hut. Maxine Bouchard burst into uncontrollable tears, and her lips moved as she faintly murmured, "Lucien Edmond, I won't ever give in to him, I'd die before that, my beloved husband!"

Lucien Edmond and the two young Southerners had ridden at breakneck speed all through the night, stopping only now and again to let their horses rest and water while Andy Haskins again used his tinder box to make a torch and to look for signs that the Comanchero was continuing in an eastward direction with Maxine. Simata had told Lucien Edmond as well as Joe and Andy what he had overheard when he had hidden at the top of the *arroyo* to spy on Norvito and Ezra Baxter, and it was because of this that Maxine's distraught young husband was convinced that the Comanchero had kidnapped her for the sole purpose of taking her to Norvito's stronghold.

And so it was that a little more than an hour after Ezra Baxter had delivered Maxine to Norvito at the desolate rendezvous of the abandoned adobe huts that Lucien Edmond, Joe Duvray and Andy Haskins, exhausted and dripping with sweat, reined up their horses a few hundred yards west of the jagged crest of little hills which topped the row of huts. The threatened storm had passed over, though the skies were still dark and gusts of wind tugged at the branches of the cedar trees.

"Look, Mr. Bouchard," Andy Haskins whispered as he pointed to a little gully which dipped below the cedar-decorated hill, "we've found the Injun hideout for sure! They've got about twenty mustangs tied up down there, and just one redskin guarding them. My God, sir, if we can drive their horses away, they'll be pinned down in those adobe huts until Sangrodo and his braves can deal with them. And Joe and I can stay here with our carbines and snipe at them if they try to come out of those huts, that'll keep 'em honest till our reinforcements arrive."

"It sounds like an excellent plan. Look," Lucien Edmond had dismounted and led his chestnut gelding back down toward the bottom of the gully so as to be out of sight from the huts, "did you see that just now? Way over in that last hut, I saw two Comanches crawling out for a looksee and then back in again. My God, Maxine must be in there, in one of those huts—but which one?"

"We'll just wait and find out, Mr. Bouchard," Joe Duvray whispered. "We don't dare risk any wild shooting, bullets'll go through that mud and they could kill her just as easy as not."

"Joe, I'll take care of the redskin, then you help me stampede those mustangs, and maybe Mr. Bouchard can look for that Comanchero's tracks. Chances are pretty good he hightailed it out of here once he brought Mr. Bouchard's wife to that damned murdering redskin," Andy Haskins vehemently declared.

Putting a finger to his lips, the young one-armed Southerner flattened himself on his belly, drew out his knife, and crawled along the top of the gulley till he was within range of the Comanche, wearing only breechclout and moccasins, who stood with his back to Andy. Carefully, drawing back the knife, he flung it with all his strength: the unsuspecting Indian stiffened, then reached back with a shaking hand as if to tug out the imbedded blade, then toppled forward without a sound. One of the mustangs, startled by the sprawling body so close to it, whinnied shrilly and backed away. Joe Duvray, who was holding Andy's horse's reins in one hand and those of his in the other, was hard put to suppress a whoop of triumph as he hissed, "Nice throwin', Andy—now let's lose their hosses for them fast!"

Tethering their own mounts to the branches of the cedar trees, the two young Southerners slid down into the gully and quickly unfastened the reins of the Comanche mustangs. Then they began to whoop and yell, slapping their sombreros against their thighs, and with snorts and squeals, the nearly wild mustangs poured out of the gully and headed, some to the east, some to the south.

An angry yell came from the hut from which Norvito's two braves had momentarily emerged, and one of them crawled out carrying an old Sharps buffalo gun, aimed it at the hill and pulled the trigger. Andy and Joe had flung themselves down as soon as they saw the Comanche aim his gun, while Lucien Edmond coolly aimed his carbine, stood his ground and pulled the trigger. The war-painted Comanche uttered a shriek, dropped his buffalo gun and sprawled lifeless on the ground, arms spread out in a cross.

"Damned good shooting, Mr. Bouchard," Andy Haskins whispered. "You go look for that Comanchero, me 'n' Joe'll stand them off. You saw the track of the horse he was riding back there a ways, think you can recognize it again? Remember, this time they won't be as deep. He'll be riding alone as fast as he can make it!"

"I'll find him. I'll look to the south, he might have gone over the border toward Mexico, it would be the logical thing to do," Lucien Edmond panted as he mounted his chestnut gelding. "Don't take any unnecessary chances. Ride back to the *hacienda* as soon as you can, they won't get far without their horses."

"If you don't mind, Mr. Bouchard, sir," Joe Duvray respectfully said, "we'd just as soon stay here and keep those red devils from getting away till Sangrodo can catch up with them. There's berries and acorns and roots around here, we won't want for food, and I saw some water off in that little creek just southeast of here. Never mind us, you go after that traitor—hell, a man who'd sell guns and whiskey to the Indians and then steal a white man's wife and turn her over to them doesn't deserve to live, in my book!"

"Nor mine either," Lucien Edmond muttered as he

waved his hand in salute and rode slowly out of the gully toward the south, looking for signs of Ezra Baxter's mustang.

The yellow-bearded Comanchero had jogged off at a leisurely canter to the south, certain that by now any pursuers had either lost his trail or been dissuaded from engaging in a direct attack against Norvito's murderous war party. As he patted the pouch of gold which he had stuffed into the pocket of his breeches with his left hand, he grinned as a new plan occurred to him. He had paid his debt to the renegade Comanche by having abducted Maxine Bouchard; he had been paid as agreed, but it did not bind him to joining the attack against Windhaven to which Macaras and his men would be summoned by Norvito's courier. For that matter, if he could intercept the bandit's men, he might even be able to persuade Macaras to go on raiding the little Mexican border towns where there would be no danger of heavy losses. Those damned Mexicans wouldn't be armed, and they had plenty of damn good-looking women for the taking. Besides, he hadn't liked the way Norvito had mentioned about his maybe losing his scalp: that Comanche outlaw was just devil enough to use his help and then maybe arrange to put him to the torture in some of those filthy ways Comanches had of killing their enemies. No, it would be much smarter to steer clear of Norvito from now on in. He'd been hankering for a spell in Mexico, now here was his chance. And if Norvito and his men rode against that *hacienda* and got slaughtered—and from what he'd already figured, the people there had plenty of weapons and ammunition—then he'd never have to worry again.

In great humor at his own cunning, Ezra Baxter stopped by a little creek to water his mustang and dismounted, still naked to the waist. The air was humid and oppressive. The mustang, whinnying at the prospect of water, moved down to the lowest part of the creek and dipped its muzzle into the muddied water, then uttered a shrill squeal of indescribable agony and reared into the air, pawing with its front hooves.

"Jesus, what the hell was that? Diablo, what's got into you, boy?" the Comanchero called, moving down toward the end of the creek. He stopped short as he saw a little reddish-brown snake wriggle back into the muddy water and disappear. "Oh Christ, a coral snake—my horse—"

Diablo's sides heaved, its eyes rolled to the whites, foam flecked its gaping mouth, and then the mustang collapsed and fell heavily, its head submerged beneath the water.

"My horse," he repeated incredulously, a look of terror warping his pockmarked face. He took a step toward the inert mustang, clenching his fists, as if willing it to regain its feet, to prove that this was only a hideous mirage born out of his headlong flight and the brain-clouding fever of the relentless sun. But it lay quite still; not even its visible side heaved. He was alone, condemned to go on foot. If there were pursuers, they could easily track him down, and there was nowhere to hide. Whirling, he stared hard at the north, blinking his bloodshot eyes to clear them. No, thank God, there was still no one in sight—but he would have to keep going to put as much distance as he could behind him. His chest heaved as he fought for breath in the humid, choking air. Glistening with sweat as he was and naked to the waist, he attracted swarms of chiggers and little black flies, and he swore violently, as he slapped at them with his sombrero, panting, his corpulent body unused to such exertion.

He knew himself to be only a few miles from the Mexican border. Once across it, there were little villages where he would find shelter and a fresh horse. He would lie low for a few months, perhaps even ride with the *bandido* Macaras until word came to him of the extermination of this mad-dog renegade. Then it would be safe to go back and collect the hoard of gold he had deposited in the San Antonio bank under the name of Ezra Conlon, which had been his dead mother's name. And then back across the border into Mexico, where with all that gold a man could live like a king, with many handsome *putas* to serve his every need, where he could build himself a *hacienda* as grand as the homes of the silver-mine owners.

Then he swore angrily, remembering that he had forgotten to take his canteen of water from his dead mustang. He still had food, however, as he remembered the piece of jerky he had offered Maxine Bouchard last night. He dipped his hand into his pocket, took it out and

387

bit off a chunk, chewing it slowly, while he looked around warily, panting with exertion. Here the ground was uneven, and there were many cacti and thick clumps of mesquite and wild flowers growing between the stretches of rock which dotted the gentle slopes of small hills off to the southwest. Glancing upwards, he swore again to see the black outline of a *zopilote,* the wattled buzzard which was the desert's scavenger. In a sudden impulse, he drew one of his six-shooters from its holster, aimed and fired. The buzzard plummeted downwards, falling into a dry gully off to his right. Again he bared his yellowish teeth in a triumphant grin: "You won't feed on me," he chuckled. Then again his face twisted with anger at his own stupidity: the sound of that shot might well attract a pursuer, even though he was sure he had sufficiently covered his trail last night to be safe enough.

The flies, the chiggers and the mosquitos now seemed to attack relentlessly, and as he stumbled southward, he repeatedly slapped at himself with his sombrero, cursing volubly. From time to time, he patted the pocket in which Norvito's pouch of gold was tucked away, and his dry cracked lips curved into a greedy smile as he kept doggedly on.

There was sure to be water, there were many little creeks, and if he had read the dark clouds correctly, there must have been rain far to the south last night, so there would be pools of water here and there, even in the driest gullies and arroyos.

Now the sun emerged from behind a cloud, beating down pitilessly on the half-naked bearded wanderer. At last Ezra Baxter seated himself cross-legged near the protective shade of a clump of mesquite, fanning himself with his sombrero, again and again reassuring himself that the pouch of gold was still in his pocket.

Lucien Edmond Bouchard, after much searching, had found the unmistakable set of hoofprints which the big mustang Diablo had left when the Comanchero had ridden over the jagged little hills and disappeared toward the south. Intent upon them, he went slowly, stopped to take a swig from his canteen, as well as to check the priming of the carbine. Half an hour later, he came upon the bloated, blackened body of Ezra Baxter's dead mustang, and his lips tightened with a grim satisfaction as he headed his horse due south, his narrowed eyes following the marks of the Comanchero's boots. He clucked encouragement to the gelding as he gripped the butt of his carbine more tightly, leaning forward in his saddle and squinting to see if he could catch sight of his now horseless enemy.

Ezra Baxter froze as a sudden sibilant noise and then a whirring of rattles broke the stillness of this desolate landscape. Licking his dry lips, his eyes wide and glazed with exhaustion, he drew out the six-shooter holstered on his right hip and stared in the direction of that terrifying sound. A dozen feet away, to his left, a rattlesnake lay coiled, its forked tongue flickering out of his ugly, blunt oval mouth. With an oath of fear and revulsion, Ezra Baxter aimed and fired, and the rattlesnake jerked and threshed, its rattles whirring, till at last the life ebbed out of it. Scrambling to his feet, the Comanchero began to run again, glancing back over his shoulder, mumbling to himself.

God, but he was thirsty! He'd give almost half this pouch for a good long swig of cold well water, the kind he used to have as a boy back in Ohio. Even back there, the other boys had picked on him after he'd had the smallpox because of the marks on his face, and he'd had to thrash a few of them to teach them that you didn't fool with Ezra Baxter. And then there'd been that simpering blonde Alice, that farmer's bound girl who'd let him tumble her in the hay because she was fool enough to think he'd marry her. Then when she'd told him she was carrying his child and started giving orders about the kind of house she wanted, he'd had to throttle her. As if he'd give his folks' house to a stupid little bitch like her—so he'd had to join the Army because the sheriff was beginning to get a little suspicious when Alice hadn't been found and everybody knew that he'd been sparking her. All down through his life, people had had it in for him, and all because he'd had smallpox. *Damn it to hell, it just wasn't right the way a decent man was treated these days—what was that?* He whirled, thinking he heard the sound of a horse's hooves, but there was nothing, only the hazy, wavering blur of the mesquite and the cacti and the uneven reddish ground along the way he had come, distorted by the ferocious sun.

There was a creek ahead of him; by God, he could have all the water he wanted, even roll over and over in it and drive those damned insects away! Whimpering with relief, Ezra Baxter stumbled on a piece of shale and went down on all fours. Then he crawled doggedly toward the little creek, lined with live oak trees. There'd be shade there, he could drink his fill and then rest. Nobody would wander onto this desert, he was just imagining things. Norvito and his braves would have found anybody who'd been coming after him; they'd have killed him by now for sure.

Lucien Edmond Bouchard stopped again and squinted. Far ahead of him, perhaps half a mile, he could see the tiny outline of a man, stumbling along. He urged his chestnut gelding on, kicking his heels against its belly, and the gelding whinnied, bobbed its head and began to canter.

Ezra Baxter reached the edge of the little creek, bent his head and sucked in the water. It wasn't very cold, but at least it was clear. When he had drunk his fill, he buried his head and shoulders in it, sighing with pleasure at the relief it gave his insect- and sun-tortured skin. He drew himself back, shaking his head, then bent down again to drink more. God, it was better than the finest beer or champagne even if it wasn't cold!

As he knelt, he heard the distinct sound of a horse's hooves, and stumbled to his feet, turning around. He could see a black-haired, slim man on a chestnut gelding, and with an oath he pulled out his right-hand six-shooter, leveled it and fired. But the range was still too distant and the bullet whined harmlessly and dropped far ahead of Lucien Edmond Bouchard.

Enraged, he fired again and again, till the six-shooter was empty, and then, cursing, flung it down and shot his right hand to the left-hand holster to clear his remaining weapon.

As he did so, Lucien Edmond sighted along the carbine and pulled the trigger. With a bellow of pain, Ezra Baxter dropped the remaining six-shooter, and stared incredulously at his bleeding, broken hand. Then he bawled, "All right, all right, you got me, don't shoot, I give up!"

Maxine's husband approached, holding the chestnut gelding to an ambling walk, his carbine readied in his right hand. The yellow-bearded Comanchero stood, his booted feet in the water of the little creek, his hands upraised and blood streaming down his right arm. "You got me," he querulously insisted, "you can see I'm plumb out of weapons, don't shoot again, my Gawd, you broke my hand!"

"You're Ezra Baxter, the Comanchero. You're the one who kidnapped my wife, aren't you?"

"Sure, sure, Mister, but I took her to Norvito, I didn't hurt her none, you gotta believe that! He gave me lots of gold—he swore he'd kill me if I didn't—I had to—gimme a chance, fer Gawd's sake!" the Comanchero whined.

He took a step forward, holding out his left hand in a begging gesture, and Lucien Edmond Bouchard aimed a quick snapshot of the carbine which came perilously close to Baxter's right booted leg. With a howl of fear, Ezra Baxter backed up into the water, not seeing that he was close to a live oak tree which rose above his head. Along a crooked branch which angled down toward him, there seemed to be a mottled, yellowish-brown vine, wound round the dry branch. Ezra Baxter did not see it, his feverishly bloodshot eyes fixed on Lucien Edmond Bouchard's stern, unrelenting face. He raised his left hand a little higher, whined, "Gimme a break, Mister, you don't know what those Comanches are like—hell, he'd have scalped me alive and fed me to the ants if I hadn't done it—he won't hurt her none—here, you can have back the gold he gave me—now that's fair enough, just lemme be, lemme get across the border, you won't ever see me again!"

Slowly he lowered his hand, took out the pouch which Norvito had given him, held it aloft for his armed adversary to see, and then tilted back his arm in the gesture of throwing it. At that moment, the slithering vine came to life, and the fangs of a cottonmouth buried themselves in the hairy back of Ezra Baxter's upraised left hand.

He uttered a gurgling shriek, lowered his left hand to see the cottonmouth still wriggling and dangling from it, its fangs imbedded in his flesh. Then, making hideous, mewling sounds and staring pitifully up at Lucien Edmond Bouchard, who sat impassively astride his horse, he tried to dislodge the snake with his bleeding right hand. The pouch dropped into the water of the little creek, and at last the cottonmouth followed it, disappearing in the stagnant, muddied water.

"My Gawd, Mister, gimme a chance—there's still time—gimme a knife to cut the flesh away, I can still suck the poison out. Please—look—take the gold, see, I've got plenty more stashed away. Jesus, look, my hand's turning black—aw please, I don't wanna die like this," he babbled, taking a stumbling step toward his silent pursuer.

At last Lucien Edmond spoke in a cold, hollow voice: "No, that's true, I don't want the snake to cheat me of my revenge for what you did to Maxine."

As he spoke, he brought up the carbine and squeezed off a single shot. Ezra Baxter jerked back. He took a faltering half-step forward, then pitched backwards, his eyes rolling to the whites. The water of the creek splashed about his beard, which floated on it; there was a faint cry, and then all was still.

Joe Duvray and Andy Haskins, lying on their bellies on one of the jagged little hills which looked down on the row of adobe huts, their carbines trained to pick off any Comanche who ventured outside, exchanged a confident look. "Now their horses are gone, we can hold them off until Sangrodo and his boys get here, that's for sure, Joe," the young one-armed Southerner said.

"Hey, look there, Andy. Looks like a flag of truce out of that first hut!"

Norvito had taken Maxine Bouchard's torn-off shirtwaist and thrust his feathered lance through it, then, cautiously crawling forward on all fours out of the hut, lifted the lance as high as he could to signal for a parlay.

"It's a white flag—you think that redskin devil is up to some fancy trick, Joe?" Andy Haskins anxiously demanded.

"Won't hurt to see what he's got on his mind, Andy. The way it stands now, his braves can't move out of their huts, or we'll pick them off like shooting geese in a gallery," Joe Duvray gleefully chortled. Raising his voice, he called, "All right, speak your piece and make it fast!"

"I am Norvito, chief of these Comanches!" the renegade Indian called in a deep sonorous voice. "In my hut there is the white-eyes squaw the man Ezra Baxter has sold to me. If you do not ride away with your guns, I kill her!"

"He's bluffing!" Andy Haskins hoarsely whispered.

Joe Duvray shook his head, whispered back, "I don't think so." Again he called out: "Let's see if you've really got her, Norvito. Get her out where we can see her, then we'll think about what you've said."

"Norvito do," the renegade mockingly called back. Crawling back into the hut, he dragged the bound, naked young woman out of the hut, bowing his head down against her panting naked breasts to make certain that the two young Southerners would risk the danger of killing her if they shot at him. "You see white-eyes squaw? Norvito does not lie!"

"That redskin son of a bitch!" Andy Haskins swore under his breath. "What I wouldn't give for a snap shot at him—but I can't take the chance from this angle. We're licked, boy!"

"Guess we are," Joe Duvray muttered, then called down: "All right, Norvito, you win for now. But you haven't got any horses, and it'll take you a long time to find them. Sangrodo and his braves will be hunting you down, just remember. If you hurt Mrs. Bouchard, you won't live to boast about it, that's a promise."

"You go now!" Norvito called, "Or I take lance and kill white-eyes squaw now!"

With a frustrated groan, Andy Haskins straightened, made his way to his horse, Joe Duvray following behind him. "We'll ride back to the *hacienda*, Joe," the one-armed Southerner told his friend. "We'll try to head off Sangrodo and his boys so we can steer them direct to where we saw this tricky redskin! We'll have to tell 'em about Mrs. Bouchard, and Norvito will keep her close to him no matter what happens, you can count on that. She's the best hostage he's got. Let's go now!"

With a last glance backward down at the row of adobe

huts, the two young men rode back at full speed toward Windhaven Range.

By this time, Simata had reached Sangrodo's stronghold and swiftly told him what had taken place. Summoning Ipiltse to him, the tall Comanche leader gave orders that forty of the strongest, youngest braves join him against the outlaw Norvito, and with Simata leading the way, the Comanche band thundered eastward at a gallop, their pintos and gray mustangs raising a cloud of dust as they rode with breakneck speed.

Lucien Edmond Bouchard had wheeled his chestnut gelding back northward, and ridden back to where his wife was kept prisoner. When he reached the irregular row of little hills with their fringe of cedar trees, he uttered a cry of anger and disappointment. There was no sign of life; indeed, as soon as Joe Duvray and Andy Haskins had left their vantage posts, Norvito had untied Maxine Bouchard's ankles and had dragged her out of the hut and summoned all his braves to make for the higher plains to the northwest. There were caves there and burial mounds, and they could put up a good fight and lie in ambush for their pursuers, he had declared.

Lucien Edmond Bouchard rode after them, taking care not to come too close, but keeping the last straggling brave in view about half a mile away. Again and again, he looked back toward the west, praying that Sangrodo and his men would be seen. All too well he remembered how the young Southerners had told him it would be at least two days, even with the swiftest riding, before the Comanche allies could come to his wife's rescue.

He kept following at a distance until nightfall, and then made his camp in a thicket of cedar trees and mesquite, about five miles from the higher plains and the abandoned Indian burial mounds. There was a kind of reddish-brown escarpment above those mounds, and here and there there were black openings, old caves which centuries ago the Lipan Apaches and the Kiowas and the Comanches themselves had used when they went on a buffalo hunt or a raid against a Mexican village. He took a swig from his canteen, ruefully noting that it was almost empty, and seeing a patch of wild berries nearby, made a frugal supper. Then, seating himself tailor-fashion, his carbine readied in his lap, he waited through the long night, hearing the sighing of the wind, the chirping of the insects, and twittering of nightbirds, his mind tortured by the thoughts of what cruelties the renegade Comanche and his men might inflict on his helpless young wife.

When dawn broke, he rode the chestnut gelding a little closer to the mounds and the obscure cave openings, but he saw no sign of life. All through the day he waited, and at last was rewarded, about twilight, by seeing a stocky almost naked figure crawl out of one of the caves, squat down and cup his hand over his eyes to stare out over the rolling landscape. There was no sign of human life anywhere except that one, but Lucien Edmond Bouchard's heart leaped with joy: now he knew that Norvito's men and his captive wife were hiding there, confident that they could fight off the most heavily armed pursuers, since in battle the odds would favor the defenders who where higher-placed and looked down upon a comparatively flat terrain across which Sangrodo and his men would have to move.

Once again he dozed through the night, and he was awakened suddenly by the sound of horses' hooves, then fired his carbine into the air.

"Friend, friend," he called out in the Comanche tongue.

The tall war-painted, bonneted Sangrodo rode up to him on the strong gray mustang, lowered his feathered lance. "Simata has told us that Norvito has your wife. We followed their tracks from the adobe huts."

"They are still there, Sangrodo. But my wife is there with Norvito, he will surely kill her if you attack."

"We will ride around those caves, and my warriors will crawl down into them. We will take them by surprise. We will go with our horses to the east as if we were riding past and did not know where they are hiding," Sangrodo explained, and Lucien Edmond Bouchard nodded eagerly: "It's a good plan, it might work. But leave Norvito to me."

"If the Great Spirit so wills it, you shall save your wife and slay him," Sangrodo proclaimed. Then, lifting his lance, he gave the signal for his warriors to ride swiftly eastward, and Lucien Edmond Bouchard mounted his own horse and rode with them, skirting Norvito's hiding place by several miles before doubling back and coming to the top of the ridge. There, half a mile from that escarpment, the friendly Comanches tethered their horses, and crouching low, moved forward silently, armed with knives, tomahawks, and lances.

As they lay in wait at the top of the escarpment, Lucien Edmond Bouchard pointed down as he suddenly saw the Comanche guard emerge from the cave, and Sangrodo nodded. Lifting his spear, he flung it downwards with unerring aim, and the breech-clouted Indian sank down on his knees, then fell slowly forward in death. Now, one by one, Sangrodo's warriors let themselves down over the top of the escarpment, dropping to the narrow dirt path in front of the caves, brandishing their weapons and entering. Screeches and yowls of agony ensued, as Lucien Edmond Bouchard, waiting his chance, leaped down toward the very first cave, then crouched outside the opening, his heart thudding wildly, his carbine readied. "Come out, Norvito, or are you a coward who can fight only squaws?" he cried out in Comanche.

There was a guttural snarl, and Norvito came out of the darkness, lunging at Lucien Edmond Bouchard with his lance. Behind him, there was an hysterical cry, "Look out, darling, oh my God, be careful, Lucien Edmond!" from Maxine.

Norvito had missed with his ferocious lunge, but now, seeing Lucien Edmond to his right, swung the lance like a flail and before Maxine's husband could fire off a shot, had knocked the carbine from the young black-haired man's hands. Desperately, Lucien Edmond Bouchard seized the lance and began to wrestle with Norvito for it. The two men stood locked together, their eyes glaring at each other, and then, exerting all his strength, Lucien Edmond Bouchard thrust the lance downwards and brought up his right knee into Norvito's belly. Taken by surprise, the renegade Comanche uttered a strangled grunt of pain, and Lucien Edmond drove his fist with all his strength into Norvito's mouth, feeling the Comanche's teeth break beneath the savage blow. Then, as Norvito fell back, Lucien Edmond Bouchard flung himself down upon the chief, his hands gripping Norvito's throat and tightening like a vise as the Comanche threshed and kicked and twisted, frenziedly trying to break that fatal stranglehold.

Lucien Edmond Bouchard felt his senses waning, exhaustion seeped through every fiber of his being, but he hung doggedly on, his thumbs thrusting down into the jugular, until at last Norvito's body slumped and lay inert. Staggering to his feet, his chest heaving, he could see in the obscure darkness the creamy naked body of his bound wife. He groped towards her, and as he gathered her into his arms, he began to weep with joy.

CHAPTER THIRTY-FIVE

It was the last month of the year of 1865, and all the seceded Southern states except Texas had fulfilled President Andrew Johnson's requirements, elected Federal representatives and senators, and were ready for recognition. In Texas, the remaining loyal Confederates still held out against returning to the Union, their pride sustaining them in their defiance of the Federal government. Yet even in this Reconstruction, there were ominous signs which showed that the bitter hatred between North and South would not be washed away by mere statutes: Mississippi had just passed a vagrant act which was to begin the "Black Codes" of the new South and lead, a year later, to the organization of the vile Ku Klux Klan at Pulaski, Tennessee. In the northern section of Texas itself, the former Confederate residents still maintained their contempt for blacks, and the knowledge that these blacks were now free and equal to whites rankled in their minds, poisoned their thinking, and made impossible any peaceful reconstruction of this vast new state.

Yet it could hardly be otherwise, since on December 14, the House of Representatives had appointed members of the Joint Committee on Reconstruction, with the notorious Thaddeus Stevens of Pennsylvania as chairman. Four days later, Secretary of State Seward formally proclaimed in effect the Thirteenth Amendment of the Constitution, which abolished slavery in the United States and had been ratified by twenty-seven States of the re-established Union.

When Sangrodo and his braves had returned from their rescue of Maxine Bouchard, Luke invited them to a feast in the bunkhouse, and Frank, Ned and Dave killed two young longhorned bulls, while Betty, though plainly terrified by the half-naked and war-painted visitors, outdid herself in cooking an exceptional dinner and even helping serve it. As she later confessed to Celia, "Ah wuz so scaired dey wuz gonna scalp me, ah jist had to make sure dey got plenty to eat so dey wouldn't git mad at me!"

And there was welcome rain for several days in a row through the month of December, when Luke Bouchard, his family and workers celebrated their first Christmas on Windhaven Range. As he sat at the dining table which had been salvaged from the chateau, Luke could see the happiness on the faces of his son Lucien Edmond and his wife, whose nearly tragic ordeal had brought them closer together than ever. It was a sight that strengthened his heart in the future of his only son, and perhaps even then subconsciously he thought to himself that Lucien Edmond had once and for all proved his manhood, his endurance, his ability to meet adversity and overcome it in what was as much a wilderness as ever had been the forests of Econchate where Grandfather Lucien Bouchard had begun his strange, yet wonderfully rewarding new life.

There were other signs that this Windhaven venture was taking roots and forming itself into an enduring enterprise. The handsome quadroon Prissy had become a frequent visitor at the stronghold of Sangrodo, often riding there with either Simata or her brother Lucas, and sometimes both of them, to visit Catayuna Arvilas and continue the lessons in weaving on the hand loom which had been specially constructed for the use of the widow. Indeed, when Sangrodo and his braves had stopped at Windhaven Range before returning to the stronghold, Prissy had boldly unfolded a blanket which Catayuna herself had woven and laid it on the table before the tall Comanche chief. She had learned a few words of Comanche, which Simata and even some of the squaws in the stronghold had taught her, and she had said to him, "The woman who is your slave hates you, but respects you as a great warrior. See, how in this blanket she has shown you and your braves circling the little town from which you took her?"

Sangrodo had grunted and stared at the blanket, its colors red, blue and brown, showing the rows of adobe huts, and the horses with their crouched riders circling them. "Here," Prissy had continued, pointing to a rider who dwarfed the others in proportionate size, "is you, the leader of the Comanches."

"Ho, that is very good. She sees that I am tall and strong, then. But you have spoken with her many times, and I have not asked you what she has said about me. She still hates me then, for what I did to her man?"

Prissy had shaken her head. "Perhaps if you had given him a kinder death, she would not remember his agony so much. She understands better now, for truly she did not know that her husband and those other men you took from the village were given money for the scalps of your warriors. It saddens her, for she had always thought her husband a good man who would not wish to grow rich by the murder of peaceful men, even if they were Comanches."

Sangrodo had scowled and reflected on this for a long moment, then nodded, his face softening as he finally declared, "I respect her too. She has great courage, she would make a squaw worthy of a chief. It may be that the Great Spirit will change her hate to love, and I will give orders that she be treated no longer as a slave but as a free woman."

"Thank you, Sangrodo. She will respect you for that," Prissy had smilingly avowed.

And Prissy, Luke observed with secret satisfaction, seemed to have more reason than ever to smile these days. Just a few days before Christmas, when she had ridden back with her brother Lucas, Luke Bouchard had been in the corral and come out to greet her and her brother and to ask the news from the Comanche stronghold. As

401

Prissy dismounted, she lowered her eyes and visibly blushed, as she groped for words. It was Lucas who chuckled and explained, "It seems Prissy's found herself a man, Mr. Bouchard. It's Jicinte, the brave who guards that Mexican widow's tepee. He speaks a few words of Spanish, and lately, every time Prissy's been going in there with the woman to help her with her weaving, he's shown a lot of interest and asked Prissy a lot of questions. Why, just before we mounted up to come back here, he asked Prissy if she would consider being his squaw, and he promised that he would pay you many fine horses and a strong bow and quiver of arrows that will never miss their mark."

"I'd say he'd better make that offer to Djamba, since Djamba's Prissy's father," Luke came over to take the reins of Prissy's mare and to stare with pleased interest at the attractive quadroon. "How do you feel about it, Prissy?"

"Well, I never did think I'd end up marrying a redskin, Mr. Bouchard," Prissy finally managed, unable to suppress a giggle, her blushes further deepening, "but he's mighty respectful and he seems to take a real fancy to me. I was thinking something else—"

"Yes, Prissy?" Luke prompted.

"Well," Prissy frowned as she concentrated on the way to express her thoughts, "seeing that you and Sangrodo have a sort of peace agreement worked out between our people and his, maybe it wouldn't be such a bad idea. I mean, one of us marrying one of them, wouldn't that help make the peace treaty more binding?"

"I'm sure it would, Prissy, but you know all of us want only your happiness. If you really like Jicinte, you'll have to remember that he may want you to go live with him in the stronghold, and maybe you'll not see Djamba and Lucas and your mother Celia as often as you'd like, or the rest of us for that matter. And, too, Sangrodo has been telling me that the buffalo are moving northwest, and he may not always stay in that stronghold. The Comanches are wandering tribes, and I'm afraid that with this Reconstruction going on, one of these days Texas is going to be much more under military control than it ever was even during the war. That would mean the soldiers might try to exterminate the Comanches if they can't make sensible treaties with them."

"Well, I didn't say yes yet, Mr. Bouchard," Prissy bridled prettily, scuffing at the ground with the heel of her boot and giving her brother a vexed look as if to reprimand him for telling tales out of school, "only so far it's the first real offer of marriage I've ever had."

"You'll break old George's heart if you up and marry a Comanche, Prissy, I suppose you know that," Luke Bouchard couldn't help teasing.

"That man!" Prissy eloquently rolled her eyes and looked heavenward, "Why, he's old enough to be my grandfather."

"Not quite, my dear." Luke chuckled, shook his head. "But if you do decide, just let George down gently. He's been mighty useful to us here on Windhaven Range, and I think you're one of the prime reasons for all his youthful activity."

A new year began now, a year at last which was to know none of the bloodshed of the Civil War. And with it came a kind of post-war depression, with a rapid decline in prices for foodstuffs and other commodities needed by settlers. Luke Bouchard had ridden into San Antonio to bring back supplies, and was pleasantly surprised at the lower prices he had had to pay for flour, coffee, beans, salt and other provender. A letter awaited him from Charles Douglas and Laurette, whose twin sons were thriving, and Charles himself had just had a handsome raise in salary for his work in promoting greater sales in the store where he was now full-fledged manager. A letter came also from Ben Wilson and Fleurette, announcing that little Thomas was cranky over cutting a new tooth but otherwise robust and healthy as his parents. Ben was taking his medical examination and would be permitted to call himself "Dr. Ben Wilson," and perhaps even be assigned to Pittsburgh's largest hospital as a member of the staff. Once again Fleurette had added a postscript in which she sincerely hoped that perhaps this next summer they might manage a trip to Texas.

And finally, there was another letter from John Brunton, mentioning that he had been in touch with Phineas Atbury and was arranging to advance him funds for the restoration of the old chateau. John had intimated to Atbury that it was entirely possible that, within the next few years, an offer might be made to the freed black to purchase the chateau back from him at a handsome profit; at the same time Atbury was to keep John Brunton constantly informed of the prevailing mood of the provisional government toward any such transfer of property.

This time Laure had not added a postscript, but her husband had: "My beautiful wife should soon be presenting me—the doctor says by early March—with our first child. Needless to say, the prospect fills me with great joy, and it certainly makes me feel younger than ever before. I hope that you and your family and workers have overcome the initial difficulties of Windhaven Range, and I shall be eager to hear from you how your first cattle drive prospers."

On a rainy late Monday morning of the second week of January, Luke and Lucien Edmond had saddled up and gone out with Ramon Hernandez to appraise the wild herds of longhorned cattle. "We'd best be thinking of rounding them up, branding them, and driving them by the end of March," Luke said. "Do you agree, Ramon?"

"*Sí, Señor* Bouchard," the young *vaquero* nodded. "Lucas and Dave and Frank and myself, we have already gelded a few of the young calves and the youngest bulls, so we can fatten them and also train leaders among the steers for the drive. And I, myself, have taken Jubal out a few times and let him run alongside some of the cows to see how well he can do directing them. He is taking to it, I think he will be very useful."

"That's good news, Ramon," Luke rejoined. "I wish I knew exactly what market to aim for. The last I heard, some of the Texas cattlemen were having very bad luck getting their steers to the market in Sedalia. I'd like to know a little more about what other possibilities there are before we make definite plans. Lucien Edmond," he turned to his son, "how many cattle would you estimate we've seen the last few days?"

"I'd say about thirty-five hundred, Father."

"That's about my tally, too. Charles Douglas has written that the new Stockyards in Chicago will be ready to accept many large herds. There'll be good prices, and since this cattle has cost us nothing and is ours for the taking, most of the sale will be clear profit for us. All the more reason I'd like to make our very first drive a successful one."

"It's a pity we don't have more settlers around here who've had some experience with the various markets and could advise us, Father," Lucien Edmond soberly reflected.

"*Señor* Bouchard," Ramon suddenly called, rising in his saddle and turning toward the southeast to point, "speaking of settlers, there seems to be a wagon coming just beyond our boundary."

Luke Bouchard turned to look in the direction that the young *vaquero* was pointing, and frowned. "We'd best go meet them and see where they're headed for, Ramon. Have your carbines ready just in case there's any trouble."

The three horsemen spurred their mounts into a gallop to head toward the heavy "prairie schooner" with its dingy white canvas covering propped inside by rigid poles, much like the legendary "covered wagon" with which so many ambitious pioneers had crossed the great plains and headed westward.

As they drew up close to it, Luke could see a middle-aged, plump, pleasant-faced man holding the reins of four visibly exhausted dray horses, with a young girl in a faded pink bonnet and homespun dress seated at his left and a freckle-faced, wiry boy no more than twelve with wide-brimmed soft black hat, a torn shirt and tattered cotton breeches, seated at his right.

"Ho, there," Luke Bouchard called, raising his right hand in a friendly gesture, "where are you bound for, sir?"

"Whoa, whoa there, consarn you critters!" the man dragged on the reins and slowly brought the wagon to a lumbering halt. "Name's Henry Belcher. I'm from Sedalia, and this is my boy Tim and my girl Connie."

"Sedalia—you've indeed come a long way!" Luke Bouchard exclaimed.

"I had me a farm back in Sedalia, but when I came back from the war, 'twasn't much good. Then my wife

Millie died with river fever, and I got sick of the whole thing, so I figured I'd come out here and look for some nice land I could farm on, something to give the kids as a grubstake when I'm gone."

"You're welcome to share our noon meal, and your youngsters look as if they could stand a little rest," Luke Bouchard said kindly. "I'm Luke Bouchard, this is my son Lucien Edmond, and Ramon Hernandez, one of my top hands."

"If that don't beat all tarnation!" Henry Belcher slapped his thigh and shook his head. "Fact is, Mr. Bouchard, I was given your name by the cap'n on the boat that brought us as far as Corpus Christi. Let's see now, what was it—Devries, that's what. Told me I most likely would find you around these parts. Spoke highly of you too, sir. Now you're sure we won't be any trouble, barging in on you like this?"

"Of course not, and we'd welcome visitors. In fact, you'll be the first we've had since we came out here last summer," Luke countered as, dismounting, he moved over to the prairie schooner to help the shy, blonde girl down from her father's side, while the boy leaped down by himself and looked around almost defiantly.

"What I'm after," Henry Belcher explained as he walked back with Luke and Lucien Edmond to the *hacienda*, while Ramon Hernandez took the reins of the latters' horses and led them back to the stable, "is a small parcel of land I can farm, without too much trouble. I'm nigh on to forty, and I don't mind telling you, Mr. Bouchard, it wasn't only the war aged me a spell, it was coming back to Sedalia and seeing what's going on there. My heart just wasn't in it after Millie died, what with all the bushwhackers and the fight over slavery and such. Myself, I joined up early, and that was when Millie had her older sister and husband to look after her and my kids here."

"I take it you were on the Confederate side, Mr. Belcher?" Luke Bouchard hazarded as he opened the door of the *hacienda* and graciously ushered Henry Belcher and his two children in.

"Yessir, and proud of it. Only one thing keeps sticking in my mind, sort of like a ghost, you might say. You saw

406

that gun I had on the seat right beside me, next to my boy?"

"I didn't get too good a look at it, Mr. Belcher, but it looks like a beautifully handcrafted weapon."

Henry Belcher sighed. "It's a Whitworth, Mr. Bouchard, with a thirty-three-inch barrel and side-mounted telescopic sights. I was lucky enough to get one because I got sharpshooter's marks during my training. You know that Missouri stayed on the Federal side, but when Governor Jackson tried to secede with the rest of the South, I knew where my duty lay. Mind you, I only had me about two niggers, and I worked with them in the fields and they was almost kin to me, but I just couldn't see the Feds telling me I had to turn 'em loose just on their say-so. It riled me. Well, sir, they issued me one of these Whitworths, good enough to hit a target over a mile, and you had to allow for nearly twelve feet at that distance."

"That's really shooting!" Luke Bouchard admiringly declared.

"Yessir." Again Henry Belcher sighed. "Well, they sent me along with old Jube Early when they attacked Washington in '64. A couple of the boys and me, we were hiding in farmhouses a couple of hundred yards from the Union trenches, and danged if I suddenly didn't see through my sights a tall, ugly-looking feller in a black top hat standing on a parapet behind the lines. I just couldn't believe what I saw, Mr. Bouchard. That's why I couldn't pull the trigger—later, they told me it was for sure Mr. Lincoln. I don't know, I keep thinking all this time, what if I'd pulled the trigger, would the war have been over any sooner, would the South have won?"

"Only God could know that, Mr. Belcher," Luke Bouchard said softly.

"Yes sir, that's what I believe. But that's my secret, and it's one I'm going to have to live with the rest of my life. I never had any hatred for the feller, I didn't call him Abe the Ape like a lot of my friends did. Only thing was, we thought this war was a matter of principle, that no government could tell a feller what to do and how to run his life. So there you have it. I didn't mean to talk you to death, Mr. Bouchard."

"And you didn't. I'm anxious to have your views, Mr. Belcher, and especially on what you think of Sedalia. You see, my son and I are getting ready for our first cattle drive, and a lot of people have said that Sedalia is the best available market."

"Don't you ever believe that, Mr. Bouchard!" Henry Belcher emphatically shook his head. "No sir. Mainly, there's the bushwhackers, and they've already taken plenty of herds of cattle from honest folks, beaten them, killed them or left them for dead or worse. And besides, a lot of the folks in Sedalia are starting to talk about the fever Texas cattle bring in from the ticks on them. Why, just before I left to go on down to New Orleans and then get me this little wagon and some supplies, there was a herd of about two thousand cattle, I'd say, and the citizens formed a sort of posse and met the owner and his drivers outside the town. They were all armed and they told him he'd better take his damned cattle back the way he'd come or he wouldn't live to see what was going to happen to them. I never did hear tell what finally became of him, but he for sure didn't sell them in Sedalia."

"I see," Luke Bouchard gravely responded. "I'm very grateful to you for this news. I'm going to have to think of a different plan, then, to sell the cattle we have in such abundance on Windhaven Range. Now you and your young ones make yourselves comfortable here at the table, Mr. Belcher. I'll have our cook Betty get you up a good lunch, and some nice fresh water to start with."

"That'd be real nice, I'm awful thirsty," the thin little girl spoke up, with a fleeting, wan smile as she nervously glanced at her father. He turned to look at her, and his homely face brightened as he reached out to stroke her curls. "This one takes after my Millie, you see, Mr. Bouchard," he clumsily explained, and blinked his eyes, reached into his pocket and produced a red bandanna with which he violently blew his nose as if disclaiming the touch of emotion he had just shown.

Luke had gone into the kitchen to tell Betty to set places for the three guests, and Lucien Edmond now rose as Maxine entered, followed by Sybella, who was tending Carla and Hugo, and Maybelle. Henry Belcher looked

408

round, and hastily rose, bending to whisper sharply to his son to imitate him.

"I'd like to introduce our family, Mr. Belcher. This is my wife Maxine," Lucien Edmond smilingly gestured toward the young woman, "my grandmother, Mrs. Sybella Forsden, our two children Carla and Hugo, and Maybelle Bouchard."

"A pleasure to know you all. Like I was telling Mr. Bouchard here, my Connie and Tim and me—I'm Henry Belcher—took off from Sedalia and came just about the same way you did, from New Orleans on with old Cap'n Devries to Corpus Christi, then came across country with our wagon looking for some land we could settle on to farm."

He looked admiringly at Maybelle, who flushed under his intense scrutiny and then impulsively went to the little girl and hugged her: "I declare, that's the prettiest dress, honey!"

"I did most of the sewing on it myself, m'am," Connie Belcher volunteered, "didn't I, Papa?"

"That she did, Miss Maybelle. Her mother learned her real good. She can cook a little too, and she helped out a lot when we were coming out this way," her father declared.

"I'm ten, and my brother Timmy's twelve," Connie felt it necessary to explain.

"Why, I think that's wonderful!" Maybelle beamed, as she moved away to take her place at the long table. "Here's Luke with some water for you folks, I'll bet you're thirsty more than hungry. My oh my, but this Texas can be hot even in January."

"We don't exactly have blizzards down in Sedalia too often, m'am," Henry Belcher chuckled as he nodded his grateful thanks and accepted a glass from Luke Bouchard's hand. "Mind your manners now, Tim, don't gulp it all down at once, you'll get a bellyache—begging your pardon, ladies."

"No need to," Sybella gently smiled. "We don't stand on ceremony here. You say you're from Missouri, Mr. Belcher. And you were in the war?"

"Not on the Federal side, Mrs. Forsden." Henry Belcher took a sip from the glass, then set it down as he

409

turned to face Sybella. "I was telling Mr. Bouchard I just couldn't see the sense of taking orders on how my life was to be run for me. I crossed over into Arkansas and volunteered in May of '61. Came through the war without a scratch—God was good to me, but he took my Millie in return when I got back home, more's the pity. That's why I just picked up and made up my mind to start out somewhere where I could forget all about the war. I talked to a few people in New Orleans, and they said that the part of Texas near the Mexican border was likely to have all the freedom a man could want, so here I am with my kids for better or for worse."

"I think, Mr. Belcher, that there's about a hundred acres of good land just south of my own boundary. Of course, I went over to the land office in Austin and staked out my claim, but so far as I know, that hundred acres belongs to the first man who claims on it. It's good rich soil, near plenty of water—as a matter of fact, I've a feeling we're going to find some artesian wells around here next spring or summer. But what water you'd take for your farming wouldn't interfere with the cattle I'll be rounding up in spring," Luke Bouchard pleasantly stated.

"That sounds just fine, Mr. Bouchard. You're sure you won't mind having a dirt farmer for a neighbor?"

"I'd welcome it. And I've some blacks who'd be happy to lend you a hand putting up a little wooden house for the three of you."

"I declare, that's more than I bargained for. But then, don't you see, I'd be in your debt right off and I'm not hankering to do that. I've got a small grubstake, Mr. Bouchard, I'm not a rich man, but I can afford to pay for my necessities."

"But you're only one man, and your two children can't cut wood and put it together. I've some extra workers who won't be too busy the next few weeks, and they'd welcome a chance to keep in practice. If you feel obliged to pay me, I'd welcome some fresh vegetables and fruit for our table come next summer or fall, and we'll call it a good bargain."

"I declare, this is the first good piece of luck I've had since the war started, Mr. Bouchard. And just look at that plate of chicken your cook is carrying in—Tim, Connie, now mind you watch yourselves, leave some of the food for these good folks."

"Dey's more where dat came from, suh," Betty proudly said as she set the platter of fried chicken down in the center of the table. "Dey's mashed potatoes 'n gravy, 'n cornpone too, 'n ah got some fresh blueberry pies."

"It sounds like heaven," Henry Belcher sighed happily. He glanced around at Maybelle, who flushed and lowered her eyes. As she fumbled for her napkin, she rebuked herself for acting just like a silly school girl.

CHAPTER THIRTY-SIX

During the next month, while Luke Bouchard invited Henry Belcher and his young son and daughter to make their home in the *hacienda,* Frank, Dave and Ned busied themselves building a frame house for the widower just beyond the southernmost boundary of Luke Bouchard's land and nearest to the supply of water. In addition, at Luke's suggestion, they marked off with round posts every hundred yards the hundred acres for which Henry Belcher would file his claim in Austin. There was little likelihood that any other settler would speak for that land, isolated as it was from other whites and so close to the Mexican border which was considered still perilous for newcomers because of Comanche and bandit raids.

During this time, it was evident that Maybelle Bouchard and Henry Belcher had developed a growing affection for each other, and Maybelle particularly warmed to the children, Connie and Tim. Quickly understanding that the boy desperately wished to be more grown up than he was, so that he could stand beside his father in the beginning of their new life together, Maybelle soon broke down Tim's outward hostility by talking to him exactly as if he were an adult, and by suggesting diversions for him and his sister in such a way that they seemed to be his own ideas. And when the new house was ready, the last week of February, Maybelle herself insisted on cooking the first dinner in it for the Belchers.

It was a momentous week indeed in the nation's history. Having warned Napoleon III that the United States did not welcome the French in Mexico, Secretary of State Seward finally demanded that Napoleon III set a time limit for the entire French evacuation of Mexico—thus foretelling the ultimate doom of the idealistic Maximilian. When this news reached the *Juaristas,* they celebrated by making guerrilla raids against French troops, inflicting heavy losses. At about the same time, President Andrew Johnson vetoed the bill to extend the life of the Freedmen's Bureau, which was to widen the breech between himself and Congress. A few days later, speaking from the steps of the White House, he violently denounced the Joint Committee on Reconstruction, thereby losing considerable partisan support for his administration and preparing the way for the first impeachment of a President in United States.

In the wake of Secretary Seward's declaration, the expertly led armies of the *Juaristas* began to unify their efforts against the French. They understood that once the formidably armed French troops were evacuated, there would be no longer any support for the usurper Maximilian, and then at last the dream of a Republic of Mexico could be realized. By this time also, the marauding and murderous tactics of Diego Macaras had been observed by many *Juaristas,* who in turn reported the activities of the bandit and his raiders to General Porfirio Diaz, the ablest of Juarez's generals who held the southern stronghold of Oaxaca, within striking distance of Mexico City.

A punitive expedition of some two hundred men had been organized against Macaras, and he had escaped an ambush not far from Miero, which he had raided again, this time with little profit to himself or to his by now grumbling men. Accordingly, disgruntled and angered by the threat of near-mutiny in his ranks, the wily *bandido* made his way to Nuevo Laredo, and remained there for many weeks, drinking and carousing, content to spend the gold he had already gained from previous successful raids and to promise great future exploits to his dissatisfied followers.

It was in Nuevo Laredo that Ikanito, Norvito's chosen courier, found Macaras, after spending several fruitless weeks in tracking him down from the locale where Ezra Baxter had told Norvito that the bandit and Baxter's own crony Merle Kinnick might be found. Tethering his mustang to the wooden rail outside a cheap saloon, where bawdy shouts broke the silence of a late December night, the Comanche warrior, dressed in buckskin jacket and breeches and moccasins, his greased black hair stiffened into two long braids, cautiously entered the saloon. The Mexican bartender uttered a cry of terror and at once ducked under the counter, but Diego Macaras rose, swaying unsteadily from too much tequila, held up his hand and bawled out in Spanish, *"Amigo, adelante!"*

"My friend Ezra must have got old Norvito to send this redskin down here with some sort of message for us," Merle Kinnick grinned crookedly as he got to his feet and put his hand to his heart and then his head, in the Comanche sign of friendship. Then he beckoned to Ikanito, adding in Spanish, "Keep that gun lower down to the floor, we are friends here, all friends."

Merle Kinnick was well over six feet tall, with a long red beard—which indeed had given him the nickname by which Norvito had called him in that meeting in the *arroyo* between himself and his two aides and Ezra Baxter and his other Comanchero crony. He had just turned forty, had been born in Baltimore, joined the Union Army at the outset of the Civil War to escape being imprisoned for debt as well as suspicion of the murder of a Baltimore faro dealer who he claimed had cheated him.

He had hated women most of his life because his parents, who had been Bible teachers, had appeared to show far more affection to his older sister than to him. Before he had left his home in Maryland at the age of eighteen, he had lured his sister into taking a walk with him. Once in the woods, he had bound and gagged her, ripped off her clothes and brutally raped her, then taken a clasp knife and cut his initials into each of her meager breasts. Later, when he chose the livelihood of a professional gambler, going from town to town as long as his welcome lasted, he made a practice of beating up prostitutes to force them to depraved acts.

Because he was an excellent shot and because his recruiting sergeant sensed the instinct of a killer in the man, Merle Kinnick managed to escape court-martial on several occasions during the first year of the war and, indeed, won a sharpshooter's medal at Manassas and another medal at Antietam. At Antietam, he single-handedly killed a dozen Confederates with his bayonet, despite being wounded twice himself, and he was thus able to pave the way for his company's taking a small enemy ridge.

But with his bloodlust was mixed a greed for power and money which hand-to-hand fighting could not earn him: shortly after Antietam, he deserted and, donning the uniform of a dead Confederate officer, made his way to a small Virginia town where he broke into the plantation home of a recent war widow and her two teen-aged daughters. At knifepoint, he forced the mother to give him a fresh horse and what money she had in the house, then bound her daughters while he raped her, and then the daughters in turn. After that act of depredation, Merle Kinnick, miraculously fortunate in evading detection or questioning in his stolen Confederate uniform, finally made his way to New Orleans, won a large stake at faro from a Creole gambler, and was able to buy his way on a paddleboat to Galveston. There, hearing of the exploits of the notorious Comanchero Ezra Baxter, he decided that here was exactly the sort of companion who could bring him adventure, gold and women, and a few months later met up with the yellow-bearded Comanchero in a little town not far from San Antonio.

For the past six months, Kinnick had been riding with Diego Macaras, except for an attack of dysentery that had forced him to miss the raid on Miero where Ramon Hernandez had been so treacherously shot down and left for dead. Now he was restored to good health, and Macaras was counting on him to turn future forays into profitable successes and at the same time escape the vengeance of Porfirio Diaz, who had declared Macaras a traitor and sworn that he would be hanged without trial upon capture.

Now, in the saloon in Nuevo Laredo, Kinnick and Macaras watched the renegade Ikanito approach their table. Two girls who were with them, seeing the scowling face of the buckskin-clad brave, uttered squeals of fright and tried to rise, but Merle Kinnick guffawed and, seizing each girl by a shoulder, commanded, "Sit still, *queridas*! He won't hurt you unless I tell him to, *comprende*?"

Fearfully, they obeyed, exchanging a look of dismay but not daring to brave the wrath of the red-bearded Comanchero. The latter chuckled, satisfied with the effect he had produced, and turned to the brave: "What is the message from Norvito, *mi compañero*?"

Then, turning his head, he bawled to the bartender, "Jorge, *por favor*, a bottle of tequila *pronto aqui*!"

The bartender produced a bottle of tequila, a fresh lime and a cup of salt, and made his way to the table, his eyes as fearful as the girls'. He set the bottle, the cup and the lime on the edge of the table and backed away, only to be recalled by Merle Kinnick: "For Chrissake, you stupid greaser, bring a glass! Just because he's a Comanche doesn't mean you can't be polite, savvy?"

"*Sí, Señor* Merle, forgive me," the bartender babbled and hurried back to the counter for a glass which he wiped with his dirty apron and then gingerly set down beside the bottle.

"Make yourself at home and have a drink—*qual es su nombre, amigo*?"

"Ikanito, *Señor*."

"Here, I'll show you how to drink this rotgut stuff, Ikanito," the red-bearded Comanchero genially lifted the bottle, put it to his teeth and pulled out the cork, then poured a generous swig into the dusty glass. Next, drawing his clasp knife, he sliced the lime into three sections, took one, doused some of the salt onto the back of his left hand, rubbed the lime on it, then picked up the glass, took a sip, then sucked at the lime. "Like this, Ikanito, *comprende*?"

"*Sí, Señor*. It like whiskey?"

"It's got a more powerful kick, but you can't really

taste it. That's why they use the lime and the salt. Go ahead, see for yourself."

Diego Macaras, pulling his girl onto his lap, hand roving under her skirt, was whispering obscenities into her ear and making her giggle. He watched with amusement as the Comanche imitated Merle Kinnick, gulped half the contents of the glass down, made a wry face, then sprinkled salt on the back of his hand and rubbed a section of the lime and sucked at it. He made a face, threw the lime down onto the floor and shook his head: "No like. Whiskey good, no like salt and what I suck."

"Well, no accounting for tastes, as the farmer said when he kissed the cow," the red-bearded Comanchero chuckled, as he leaned toward his girl, who was not more than nineteen, plumper than her cousin whom the bandit leader was fondling so brazenly, and pinched her nipple through the thin stuff of her dress. She uttered a cry of pain and slapped his hand away, at which he drew back his right hand and slapped her viciously across the cheek, so harshly that she was nearly pitched from her chair onto the floor.

"Don't you ever lay a hand on me again, you Mexican slut," he snarled, his blue eyes narrowed and glistening with sadistic fury. "I owe you a little something for that, Rosa, and you'll get it when our palaver with the redskin is done, don't you forget it." Then, turning back to the brave, who had just poured himself another drink from the bottle, he demanded, "Let's get down to business, Ikanito. What's the word from Norvito?"

"He meet with your friend, the one with the yellow beard."

"Ezra Baxter, by God! Sure he did. So what did old Ezra have to say to me?"

"It is many weeks since Norvito and your friend sent me with the message, Señor. I have been tracking you through the villages here. But now that I have found you, I am to tell you that there is a new white-eyes hacienda, not far from the place that is known as the Springs of the Reeds. There are many squaws there, young squaws like these two here at the table," he gestured with this thumb at the two shrinking Mexican girls, "and your friend says that you and the jefe with whom you ride can attack from the south while my chief and his men attack from the north."

"Now that's not a bad idea, Diego," Merle Kinnick leaned across the table and eyed the bandit leader. "Once we get out of Mexico, you won't have to worry about your neck being stretched by one of Benito's generals."

With a solemn, owlish dignity, already half drunk, Diego Macaras shoved the pretty young Mexican girl from his lap and staggered to his feet, hammered his fists on the table: "No one will dare hang Diego Macaras, for I am a true *Juarista*, I am one of the saviors of my country. Do not say such things to me, *Señor* Redbeard!"

"Calm down, Diego, calm down, of course they won't hang you if you get out of the country. Now if we go along the Texas border and bide our time, we can pull off a couple of raids and get plenty of gold and prettier bitches than these here," Merle Kinnick told him, contemptuously regarding his own cowering, frightened companion.

At this point, Diego Macaras scowlingly rose to his feet and called to the bartender: "Out of here, *hombre*! What we have to discuss is important business, and we want no spies or traitors to hear our words. Go out and take a *siesta*!"

The bartender gulped and nodded and scrambled out of the tavern. With a braying laugh, the bandit turned to the two young Mexican girls: "You too, *muchachas*. This is men's business, the time for *putas* like you will be when we have finished with it, *sabe*?"

The red-bearded Comanchero reached across the table to grasp young Rosa's wrist, just as she began to rise. "Only be sure you're in your room when I come looking for you later, you slut. You've punishment coming, and you'd best not try running away, because I'd only find you and then it would be worse, wouldn't it?"

"*Sí*, S—Señor M—Merle," she pathetically quavered. He grinned savagely, released her wrist and nodded curtly, and she and her cousin hurried out of the squalid tavern.

"Now then," the bandit leader resumed as he reached for the bottle and poured himself a liberal portion, which he downed at almost a single gulp, "it so happens I have unfinished business with those *gringos*. From what your friend the *Señor* Baxter has sent our Comanche friend to tell us, I have a feeling in my bones it is those accursed *Yanquis* whom we attacked on their way from Corpus Christi to Carrizo Springs—that is the place of the reeds, *es verdad*. Do you know, *Señor* Merle, that they were well armed and that an old woman shot me? I, Diego Macaras, the best general Benito Juarez ever had and who does not appreciate him, may that little Indian lawyer roast in the deepest fires of hell! I have thought all this time of my revenge, and now the *Señor* Baxter wishes me to join the attack against those *gringos*. You see, I knew about them at first through a *Yanqui* friend of mine in New Orleans who sold me at times guns and ammunition for the great cause of liberating my homeland."

"Come off it, Diego," the red-bearded Comanchero sneered, "you don't have to talk patriotism to me. I know what you are and what you're after. I'm after the same thing, so cut out the fancy oratory and let's get down to cases. If they're well armed as you say they are, you'll need plenty of men to attack them and you'll have to take them by surprise."

"Not if Norvito attacks at the same time with all his band. Now what we must do is have this Ikanito go back and tell Norvito that we will attack when he gives the word. Let him set such and such a time. Let me see now—it is about a hundred miles from here to Carrizo Springs. *Bueno,* that will take three days of good riding. Now then, Ikanito, how many warriors can your chief bring to fight against the *gringos*?"

As he spoke, he shoved the bottle across the table, and the buckskin-clad Comanche who had been staring wistfully at it all this while, seized it in one hand, tilted it and downed a long swig, his Adam's apple convulsively working. He set it down with a thud on the stained and badly scarred table, patted his belly, "Ho, good firewater, burns Ikanito's belly good." Then, recovering, he added, "When I left to search for you, Norvito had riding with him perhaps thirty-five warriors."

"Well," Diego Macaras pursed his lips and frowned, "I can count on about eighteen of my men to go along with me. I've had a few mutinous dogs leave my little army the last few weeks, because not enough gold has come in to suit them. But that's over fifty men. That should certainly be enough, if we attack from both sides at the same time, to kill all those accursed *gringos.*"

"Except the women, Diego, you're forgetting them," Merle Kinnick interposed with a humorless grin.

"*Sí, sí,* that is understood, *amigo.* Meanwhile, I think we are safe here in Nuevo Laredo for a time. That bastard Diaz who has said that I am a guerrilla and not a *Juarista,* he is too busy with the French to look for me so close to the border. So my men and I will stay here, and there are a few little villages off to the west from which we can take what we need. There are always churches where one finds silver and gold which can be melted down and sold for *dinero.* So that is what we will do." He pointed to the Comanche and gloweringly concluded: "Go back to Norvito then, tell him that we are ready when he is. Tell him it will take three long days to reach the *gringos,* but he must give us plenty of time once he sends you back with the signal to us."

"I understand it. I go back to Norvito now. I will find you here again?"

"Most likely. If not, Carlos, that fat fool who brought you the bottle of tequila, he will know where I am."

"I go then." The Comanche looked down at the almost empty bottle, seized it, drained it, tossed it to the floor and silently and swiftly left the tavern.

It was two weeks before Ikanito returned, having had to track his chief's movements from the rendezvous with Ezra Baxter, and following the trail of the Comanches' horses to the abandoned adobe huts and then again beyond to the burial mounds and caves where he found the bodies of Norvito and his renegade followers, hardly recognizable after the sun, the vultures and the wild animals had had their way with them. And when he observed the hideously grimacing face of his dead chief and saw the black marks of strangulation which Lucien Edmond Bouchard's fingers had left on Norvito's throat, he cried out in horror. In his savage credo, the soul and breath were one: if Norvito had died by strangulation, his soul could not make its escape from the body and was forever imprisoned within the lifeless corpse. As he backed out of the cave, his eyes bulging and his mouth agape, he seized Norvito's spear and, lifting his knee, broke the wooden haft across it and flung it down to the plain below, then ran like one possessed back to his mustang, mounted it and rode back toward Nuevo Laredo.

CHAPTER THIRTY-SEVEN

It was mid-January before Norvito's courier was able to find Diego Macaras and his Comanchero ally Merle Kinnick, since the two marauders had left Nuevo Laredo with a band whose numbers had thinned to fifteen, the others having become disgruntled with the paltry earnings their-self-styled general had gleaned for his men since the raid on Miero.

A rumor that a contingent of *Juarista* troops was on the hunt for him, under an intrepid young Mexican captain who owed his promotion to Porfirio Diaz himself, had reached the ears of the bandit chief two days after the Comanche courier had brought Norvito's message to the tavern in Nuevo Laredo. Diego Macaras, fearing that he might be captured and hanged out of hand, had rallied his remaining loyal followers with promises of much gold and women to be had by attacking the somewhat more prosperous village of Qualixo, some twenty-eight miles northwest of Nuevo Laredo and not far from Piedras Negras on the banks of the Rio Grande. Moreover, as Macaras assured his men, Qualixo lay only some forty miles over the border south of Carrizo Springs, which would be their richest strike of all when Norvito and his braves joined forces to attack Windhaven Range.

As hostages, the bandit leader and his Comanchero ally took with them the young cousins Conchita and Rosa, mounting both of them on a single horse with their wrists tied behind their backs, a rope binding their waists together and circling the belly of their mare, and their ankles equally pinioned. Both girls had been cruelly marked by Merle Kinnick's quirt; the night after Ikanito had come to the tavern, the red-bearded Comanchero had vented his sadistic lust on the two girls by having Diego Macaras tie both of them by the thumbs with a cord that was drawn up to a peg in the ceiling, forcing them to sway on tiptoe, naked and facing each other; he then plied the rawhide whip over their writhing naked bodies till, at his depraved order, they tearfully performed a lesbian act as Diego Macaras watched. Then he and his Mexican crony, pitilessly ignoring the agonized girls' pleas for mercy, sodomized them together savoring their shrieks of pain and babbled, hysterical plaints to be spared more torture.

However, Merle Kinnick's plan to keep these girls captives was not entirely motivated by his twisted lust: he foresaw that they could be useful in the forthcoming attack on Windhaven Range, and Diego Macaras had heartily agreed with him once the red-bearded Comanchero had proposed his idea. "Let's face it, Diego," Merle Kinnick had almost tauntingly avowed, "you don't have the manpower you used to, and you're not likely to pick up any more volunteers, not when practically all of Mexico knows there's a price on your head and even that big Mexican general himself is after you. Now suppose we were to make Conchita and Rosa go by themselves to your *gringo* friends and ask to be taken in. You and your men could wait in ambush just on the other side of the Nueces River, and while they're busy being good Samaritans to these little bitches, they'll be distracted enough so that they won't be ready for us. Then all we'll need is Norvito coming in with his braves from the north, and we'll have them between a pair of pincers and we can squeeze the lives out of all of them, except the women, of course."

"*Amigo*, you are a man after my own heart." Diego Macaras had guffawed, clapping Merle Kinnick on the back. "And then, of course, we must not forget that while the *muchachas* are with us, they will provide much amusement for us and our men, in case we do not find all the women at Qualixo that I have promised, *no es verdad*?" he had bawdily winked.

And so the little army, sworn to pillage, rape and murder under the guise of *Juarista* retaliation against those who had given comfort to the French, rode toward the town of Qualixo. It numbered perhaps three hundred inhabitants, with a wealthy *alcalde* whose handsome wife and two teen-aged daughters were undoubtedly the most attractive ladies of Qualixo; an old church whose one priceless possession was a huge silver crucifix which had been blessed by the Archbishop of Mexico himself; a tavern, offices which a doctor and an aspiring young lawyer shared, and a little general store. Its commerce was mainly farming, though at times many of its men went to work in a small silver mine some sixty miles south. Diego Macaras had long since noted the location and wealth of that mine, but he had never had the force to attack it. What was more to the point, however, was that he knew the inhabitants of Qualixo to be poorly armed and that many of them had died in a raid two years ago carried out by the Comanche chief Sangrodo.

At nightfall, he and his men rode onto the slope of a wooded hill which looked down upon the sleeping little town, and he turned to Merle Kinnick and chuckled, "It will be easy, *Señor* Red Beard. Do you see there, off near the church, that little wooden house? It belongs to the *alcalde* and his family. *Dios*, but how proud he is of that. And I am told that this woman and daughters are tasty morsels. We shall take them prisoners, so that poor little Conchita and Rosa will have time to rest from their duties with our brave *compañeros*, do you not agree?"

"Sure, Diego," the red-bearded Comanchero grinned as he reached for his Henry rifle in its saddle sheath. "Women are always handy to have around when we're not busy. But what about gold?"

"*Amigo*, you talk my own language. How strange it is that your good friend the *Señor* Baxter does not join

425

us—what an army we would have then! But as to gold in Qualixo, there is a precious silver crucifix in the church. And doubtless the good *alcalde* has in his fine house a hiding place for the gold he has taken in taxes which he has not given our worthy *Presidente* Benito Juarez. Oh, there will be other objects of value for our saddlebags, I am certain, *amigo*. But first let us take this village, kill as many men as we can, and then we can see to the division of the spoils."

"Just a minute, Diego. What sort of fire power are we going to run into? I like to know the odds, even when they're in my favor," Merle Kinnick scowled at the bandit leader, who wore as always his green coat and matching breeches and shining black boots, with the epaulets on his shoulders and his stolen medals on his chest.

"You are a most suspicious *hombre, Señor* Merle," Diego Macaras chuckled and shook his head. "Have I not told you that they lost many men and most of their weapons when Sangrodo swooped down on this dreary little place? I marvel that the wise Comanche chief did not capture the *alcalde*'s females at the time. But since he was thoughtful enough not to do so, he has left them for us. To answer your question, *amigo,* there are perhaps three or four old Belgian single-shot guns in the entire town, a few machetes, perhaps a pistol or two, and the knives which the *mujeres* use for cutting meat—that is all. And here are we with our guns and pistols and plenty of ammunition, and we take them by surprise before perhaps they can even fire a shot. Does that satisfy you, *mí compañero*?"

"I'll tell you when it's over, Diego. I'm ready when you are."

The swarthy Mexican nodded, then raised his hand and swept it down in the direction of the village below. "Quietly now, *mí soldados*, kill swiftly, spare no one except the *mujeres*."

They rode down into the sleeping village, and Merle Kinnick went to the little church, dismounting, carbine in hand and flinging open the door. There an astonished gray-haired priest, kneeling at the altar, turned and uttered a cry of horror: "What sacrilege do you do, my son?"

426

For answer, Merle Kinnick shot him through the forehead, and from the pews where half a dozen women knelt in prayer, there came shrieks of horror and disbelief.

With a dry chuckle, the red-bearded Comanchero made his way down the aisle, callously shoving the sprawled body of the dead priest aside with his booted foot to seize the magnificent silver crucifix from the top of the altar. He tucked it under his left arm and then, whirled to stare at the peasant women who stared at him as if he were indeed the very devil.

"Now you just stay here, *muchachas*," he told them in their own tongue, "and you won't get hurt. Stick your faces outside this church till we've finished, and it'll be a different story, *sabe*?" Then he strode out of the church to join the other marauders.

There was little resistance; of the hundred and thirty men of Qualixo, fifty were away at the silver mines, hoping to return within a week or ten days to bring back belated Christmas gifts for their wives and children. The old women and the children, as well as the wives, could do little except hide when they heard the gunfire, and pray that their loved ones would be spared. Several of the peons who did manage to reach their machetes and their ancient guns were cut down as they emerged from their huts before they could even use their weapons. In twenty minutes, a dozen of Diego Macaras' band had lined up all the male survivors in the village square, while the bandit leader himself, Merle Kinnick and the other two guerrillas forced their way into the *alcalde*'s house and made him, his buxom thirty-eight-year-old wife Catarina, and their daughters, Isobel and Dolores, thirteen and fifteen respectively, quaking prisoners.

The mayor, fat, bald, nearly fifty, clad in only his nightshirt, stammered hoarsely, "Spare us, *Señores,* we are loyal Mexicans, we have never aided the French, I swear this on the cross itself!"

Then, as he heard the sudden cracks of carbine and rifle shots and the distant sounds of screams and groans from the village square, he crossed himself and panted, "In the name of God, what is that, *Señores*?"

"All of your men are being executed, *amigo*," Diego Macaras genially told him as his beady eyes laved the

427

shrinking woman whose unbound black hair floated nearly down to her waist against the glossy white silk of her shift. "It is a precaution, *Señor Alcalde,* because we wish to stay a time in your fat little village, fat with much *dinero,* I am sure."

"But it isn't true, *Señor,*" the mayor groaned, wringing his hands and biting his lips as the ominous gunfire continued, "the men of Qualixo who are at the silver mines, surely you do not believe they bring home what they toil for? There is nothing here, all of us are poor—"

"Except you, *Señor Alcalde,*" Diego Macaras made an ironic bow toward the terrified man. "Perhaps a little persuasion will loosen your tongue to tell us where you have hidden your treasures. But we will start with your wife, since I am sure that you must be very brave to be the *alcalde* of Qualixo. Jose, Pedro, tear off the shift of that handsome *señora* and use it to bind her wrists to the bed. Then take your belts and whip her a little until her husband is ready to talk."

"Oh no, don't hurt Mama, please don't hurt Mama," Dolores cried as she ran forward and hugged the sobbing woman toward whom the two grinning bandits now purposefully advanced.

"Don't interfere, *muchachita,* or we shall be forced to spank you and your sister a little too," Diego Macaras sniggered, then made a sign. Merle Kinnick stepped forward, tossing the crucifix to the floor as he seized each young girl by the wrist and dragged them both off to one side.

Suddenly the fat mayor, stricken by the sight of his terrified wife's anguish as the two bandits neared her, lunged at one of them and tried to tug his pistol out of his holster. Diego Macaras calmly unholstered his own pistol and shot him through the back of the neck. "How very brave and how very stupid. Now then, *Señora,* I fear it will be up to you to tell us where your husband's gold is hidden, or when we finish with you, we shall start on the little *muchachitas,*" he declared.

"I swear there's nothing, oh my God, my poor Alfredo—you've killed him—you monsters—help me, oh God in heaven, help me—stop—let me go—"

Jose and Pedro had seized her, ripped the silken shift

from her body, revealing the opulence of her glossy brown flesh, and while Jose held her wrists in one hand and twisted the fingers of his other into her tumbled long black hair, Pedro tore the shift into strips to be used as pinions for her wrists which they bound to the uprights at the foot of the bed. Then, unbuckling their leather belts, they began to slash her from neck to heels, while she shrieked and implored mercy, and her two weeping daughters, cruelly restrained by Merle Kinnick, poignantly begged the bandit to spare her, to whip them instead.

But at last Catarina Concilardo, half-fainting under the burning kisses of the leather belt, could bear no more: "Enough, enough, *por el amor de Dios*," she shrieked, twisting her contorted fear-ravaged face back to her two torturers. "There is some money in the little chest at the foot of the chapel altar. Take it all, and be merciful, spare my poor little girls, they've done no harm to anyone!"

"Jose, Pedro, go find the chest and bring it here," Diego Macaras commanded. "And you, *linda,* if I find you've been lying to me, my men will take the skin off your big *tetas* with a real thrashing, after which you will watch your pretty *muchachas* obliged to service their *cojones*!"

The two bandits, winking at each other and eying the two pretty teen-aged girls who cowered beside the red-bearded Comanchero, flung down their belts and strode off to the little room in which, like so many pious Mexicans, the mayor kept a chapel with altar, crucifix, and an oil painting of the Virgin Mary. They found the chest as described and carried it back, and set it down before their leader who impatiently nodded to them to open it.

Inside the chest was a magnificent silver bowl encrusted with turquoise, the work of a gifted young villager who hoped one day to set himself up in Mexico City as a silversmith and whose generous English employer at the mine, having observed this talent, had allowed him to take enough silver ore to fashion this reliquary. There was also a purse containing several gold and silver coins.

"Well now, Catarina," Diego Macaras approached the almost fainting woman and tilted up her chin with his pudgy hand, grinning evilly at her. "You didn't lie after all. So you've saved yourself a really good thrashing, but now, as you can plainly see, my soldiers need a little reward for all their hard work. Or would you prefer to have your daughters satisfy their honest needs?"

"In the name of merciful heaven, no, take me, take me, but spare the girls, I beg of you," the woman pleaded.

He nodded, and Jose and Pedro swiftly untied Catarina Concilardo's wrists, dragged her to the bed and flung her down on her back. While Jose knelt behind her and pulled her wrists out behind her head, calling obscene encouragements to his crony, Pedro flung himself upon her and brutally possessed her. Then he, Jose, replaced him while Isobel and Dolores, closing their eyes, averted their tearstained faces.

Merle Kinnick smiled cynically at their prayers, and when the two bandits had vented their lust on the nearly unconscious naked captive, ordered, "Now then, *amigos,* take that carrion outside and dig a grave for it. Your general and I are going to take over the mayor's house, so everything must be neat and orderly."

And after the two bandits had trundled out the lifeless body of the *alcalde,* Merle Kinnick turned to Diego Macaras and proposed, "It will be a safe hideout for us, Diego. When the other men come back from the silver mines, we'll dispose of them as we've done with the others. Meanwhile, take your pick of these two little bitches. They'll amuse us while we're here, since by now Rosa and Conchita no longer amuse us as they did. Why not let the men have them? These girls are younger, they'll make better hostages and we can teach them how to go beg for sanctuary at the *hacienda* of the *gringos.*"

"*Muy bueno,*" Diego Macaras approved, his eyes glistening as he approached the two cowering teen-agers. "I will take this little one here," he reached for Isobel's shoulder and she uttered a shriek and tried to escape. "Not so fast, my little pigeon, do not fly away from Diego!" he guffawed as he teased her. Then, lifting her over his shoulder with a triumphant laugh, he carried her out of the bedroom into her own room across the hall and there, on the bed which the two young girls shared, savagely took her virginity. Merle Kinnick, meanwhile dragged Dolores over toward the bed where her naked, near-swooning mother lay. Then, gloatingly, he stripped

430

her, pinching and slapping her until she hysterically agreed to submit without resistance, and violated her with gusto as his eyes drank in the opulent nudity of the mother sprawled beside them.

All this while, weeping bitterly in apprehension of their ultimate fate, the young Mexican cousins Rosa and Conchita had remained tethered on their burro, bound and gagged so that they could not call out a warning to the unsuspecting villagers, and it was only at midnight when, sated with his lustful carousing, Diego Macaras remembered them and sent Jose and Pedro to free them from the burro and force them to the sexual service of any of his followers who desired them.

It was therefore in Qualixo that Ikanito at last found Diego Macaras and Merle Kinnick, who with their men had taken over the entire village and by now had looted it of every possible valuable, even to the paltriest trinket. There had been more executions, these of some of the old women and the wives who had openly rebelled against the bestiality of their captors. Each of Macaras' men had been assigned two of the comeliest women of the village as his personal attendants, to cook for him and wash his clothes, and of course to submit at all times to his slightest erotic whim. It was a reign of terror, and those women who managed to steal over to the little church at night and to pray implored a just God to wreak His vengeance on their brutal captors.

The Comanche found Macaras lounging in bed, clad only in his boots and his bemedaled green coat, being served tequila by Catarina Concilardo, who was obliged to go naked except for her shoes and a shawl in his presence. Merle Kinnick, across the hallway, was again amusing himself with Isobel and Dolores, forcing both naked young girls to lie on each side of him and ply him with caresses, threatening her who did not please him the most with a sound whipping. Through his sadistic tutelage, both teen-aged sisters had become the most accomplished *putas*.

"*Hola, amigo,*" Diego Macaras drained his glass and handed it back to the cringing naked widow, "it's taken you a long time to find me. Well then, what's the news? When do we attack the *gringos*?"

Ikanito shook his head, his face shrunken and tortured with the knowledge he had so terrifyingly acquired: "Our chief is dead, and all his braves with him."

"Diablo!" the half-naked Mexican guerrilla abruptly sat up, his swarthy face twisted in an angry scowl. "All of them? Who did it, Ikanito?"

"I do not know, *Señor*. It could not have been the *soldados,* so I think it may have been the *gringos* you and Norvito planned to attack." Ikanito shook his head, "He who killed our chief put his hands to Norvito's throat, and never will the spirit of our chief reach the sky. Whoever he is, he has great magic power to do such a deed. Now I have no tribe, I am a wanderer."

"Then join my men, Ikanito. You see how I live, and all my men have a *linda mujer* to wait on them as this *puta* waits on me now." With a wide sweep of his arm, he gestured toward the shuddering naked Catarina, overcome with the deepest, most helpless shame. "Did you see the *hacienda* of the *gringos* before you came back to find me, Ikanito?"

"Yes, *Señor*. I could not come too close, I did not wish them to see me, but there are as many men as you have in your band. And they are armed with the long guns that kill from a distance."

Diego Macaras scowled again, then made an angry gesture toward Catarina: "Bring more tequila, stupid bitch, enough for my friend Ikanito here. Hurry, or I will have you whipped in front of the church for all your friends to see!"

Dully nodding, her eyes lusterless, bloodshot from countless tears, the handsome widow stumbled out of the room.

"If you wish, Ikanito, you may have her. I am tired of her already. But I think I have a plan, and the men we have will be enough to kill all those *gringos* and take their women and their gold. That bitch you just saw, whose name is Catarina, has two young daughters. We will have them go to the *hacienda* and say that they have escaped from an attack by the Comanches on their parents' wagon train, that all are dead except them. While the *gringos* are

432

busy comforting them and perhaps sending some of their *pistoleros* out to look for these *Indios,* we shall fall upon them."

Ikanito considered this a moment, then nodded. "It is a good plan."

"Yes, but we must wait some little time. There will be men returning to Qualixo from the silver mines very soon and we shall kill them. Then we shall remain in this village until it is nearly time for the *gringos* to think of rounding up their cattle and driving them to market. They will be so busy thinking about such things that when the girls run to them for help, they will suspect nothing. Also, it will give my men time to grow strong, yes, and hungry for more gold too."

"You make good plan, *Señor.*"

"You stay with me, Ikanito, and you'll become a chief of a new tribe, I promise it to you. *Bueno*, here comes your woman with the tequila. Catarina, stupid bitch, on your knees and serve my good friend Ikanito his tequila. You will have him as your master now, I have given you to him."

The trembling naked widow almost dropped the glass of tequila which she had brought in on a little glazed clay tray. She sank down to her knees, holding up the tray with its brimming glass to the buckskin-clad Comanche, while looking back toward the bed and poignantly imploring, "I beg of you, *mí general,* do not do this! I am afraid of *los Indios.* I will try harder to please you, I swear it, only out of pity, not the Comanche!"

"You see, Ikanito?" Diego Macaras grinned. "She finds you ugly, *hombre*. For that, I would beat her well!"

"I shall do that. A Comanche does not let his squaw insult him," Ikanito stared coldly down at the naked woman kneeling before him, picked up the glass and drained it. "Come, woman. It will not be the first time I have had a Mexican woman, *Señor*. I know how to tame them." Stooping toward her, the fingers of his left hand twisting into her hair, he yanked cruelly at it, and with a sobbing cry, Catarina Concilardo was forced to follow him out of the room as Diego Macaras leaned back and burst into obscene laughter.

CHAPTER THIRTY-EIGHT

By mid-February, Luke Bouchard had decided that his first cattle roundup and drive would be aimed at the market of Santa Fe. Henry Belcher's report on the bushwhackers and the hostility of the citizens of Sedalia had decided him to abandon that originally intended drive. Yet the journey to Santa Fe, well over six hundred miles, would be through barren country, much of it controlled by the warlike Apaches, and from what Ramon Hernandez had told him, Luke was aware that the average distance covered during a day in a cattle drive was not much more than between twelve to fifteen miles. At that rate, it would take at least two months to reach Santa Fe, not allowing for stampedes, attacks by bushwhackers or rustlers or the Apaches themselves.

Accordingly, he had sent Simata to Sangrodo's stronghold to submit a proposal that might solve the friendly Comanche chief's own problems of having meat enough for his people, since the herds of buffalo had already moved to the west. What he proposed was that Sangrodo provide him with an escort of Comanche warriors whose presence alone would be enough to deter the Apaches, since they were allies under their own existing peace treaty. In return for this, he promised Sangrodo two hundred cattle of prime stock, mainly yearlings and a good number of heifers and calves. In addition, he agreed to set aside a sum of money after the cattle had been sold in Santa Fe which would be used to purchase weapons, blankets, salt or whatever else Sangrodo's people required for their comfort.

To his great delight, Simata returned to tell him that Sangrodo had agreed and would send twenty warriors, well armed and on the fastest horses, to accompany the Bouchard cattle drive which was now planned for the first or second week in March. As a further precaution, aware of the ever-present danger of attack by bandits and renegades, Luke Bouchard dispatched Ramon Hernandez to Nuevo Laredo for the purpose of hiring eight or ten *vaqueros*, to whom he promised wages of thirty dollars a month and board, with the promise of a bonus to be paid out of the receipts of the cattle sale in Santa Fe. Andy Haskins and Joe Duvray, as well as Lucas and Djamba, had made an estimated count of the longhorns already branded: there would be over three thousand, and these *vaqueros* could be put to work at once rounding them up over the many miles they had strayed away from the grazing area near Windhaven Range and running the wildest cattle until they were tired enough to be amenable to moving in an orderly herd.

This first drive, then, could not possibly realize the profits Luke Bouchard had hoped for when he had first thought of raising cattle and driving them to a convenient market: if there were a way to get a good-sized herd to the Chicago Stockyards, he might have been able to count on as much as $50 or $60 for each longhorn, with an average weight of 80 pounds, since that was the prevailing price in Chicago. But as yet there were no railroads strategically placed to receive cattle at the end of a long drive—or at least not without such dangers along the way, as in the case of Sedalia, that would threaten to wipe out the tempting profit at the end of the projected drive. But still and all, from what Simata had been able to glean from his discussion with Sangrodo, it appeared to Luke that he could expect to realize from six to ten dollars per animal if in prime condition. And with a herd that would number over three thousand, it was assuredly a tidier profit than even old Lucien had made in his first years selling cotton down the river to Mobile. Best of all, the cattle themselves had cost not a penny; they were the property of anyone who could rope and brand them and herd them to market. Yes, even deducting the wages of the new *vaqueros* and the cost of Sangrodo's escort, Luke foresaw a profit that would begin Windhaven Range on what he hoped would be a cycle of growing prosperity that would insure the well-being of the Bouchards in Texas for long years to come.

By the time Ramon Hernandez arrived at Nuevo Laredo, the news had already arrived of Diego Macaras's massacre of the men of Qualixo. Thus it was that when Ramon Hernandez entered the tavern presided over by the fat bartender Carlos Asunciata, he stood at the bar and ordered a tequila as he listened carefully to the men gossiping on each side of him. And from this it was that he learned the whereabouts of the man whom he had once mistakenly considered as one of the saviors of his homeland. When the time was right, he drawled, "I was once an officer in the *jefe's* army, *Señores*. But he did not pay well enough, and so he and I parted company. Now I am here to hire *vaqueros* who will work for honest *gringos*, just across the border. The pay is good, they are decent men, not rogues like my former *jefe* who pretends to free our enslaved country while he loots and kills."

The bartender glanced nervously around to make sure that none of the bandit leader's men were there to hear what he was about to confide: "Listen *amigo*," he whispered, "that man is a *demonio*." He made the sign of the cross, "It is said that the French troops must one day leave our country, and when that happens, our *Presidente* will soon rid us of murderers like that one. But I have heard just now that he and his men left Qualixo, perhaps hearing that a troop of true *Juaristas* was too close for comfort. *Madre de Dios*, he is a butcher, that one! Why, the night he was here and that *Indio* came to see him, I feared for my own life, I tell you the truth, *Señor!*"

437

"An Indian?" Ramon interestedly pursued. "Another tequila, *por favor*." He drew out money and tossed it onto the counter of the bar.

Carlos Asunciata pocketed it, nodded eagerly, bent to procure the bottle and filled Ramon's glass to the brim. "*Sí, amigo,* and I have seen men of his tribe before. He was a Comanche, I swear it on my mother's hope for paradise."

"You did not hear what he said to this *jefe* whose orders I once took, then, *hombre*?"

Carlos Asunciata shook his head, wiped his sweating face with his dirty apron, warily glanced around again before replying. "Oh no, *Señor,* he and his friend, the red-bearded one, a *gringo,* ordered me out and the girls too. They said they had business that was not for our ears. From what I have just heard, *Señor,* he and his men left Qualixo to go along the border of the Rio Grande. It is said that they plan to cross over and to attack a rich *gringo hacienda.*"

"My thanks, *amigo,*" Ramon Hernandez smilingly nodded. Then, laying down more money, he ordered a bottle of tequila, and beckoned to several of the younger men whom he saw lounging against the wall nearby and whom he recognized from their apparel as being *vaqueros.* Within an hour, he had engaged eight men to ride back with him to Windhaven Range. But even more important, he felt certain that at last Diego Macaras intended to take his revenge for the defeat he had suffered at the hands of the Bouchards when they had been on their way from Corpus Christi to Carrizo Springs. And as he and his new companions rode off toward the Rio Grande late that night, he murmured a prayer that a just God would give him the chance to pay Diego Macaras back for that bullet of dismissal which had been meant to kill him.

Satisfied that he could glean nothing more from Qualixo, and once again apprehensive over reprisal by the real *Juaristas,* Diego Macaras and his followers, with Merle Kinnick and Ikanito accompanying them, rode westward near the Rio Grande, their saddle bags loaded with

438

plunder and the weapons which they had seized from the murdered men of the little village. Behind them, hands bound behind their backs, the reins of their burros tethered to the pommels, were the last riders in that procession: Conchita and Rosa, and the disconsolate daughters of Catarina Concilardo beside them. Their tears mourned not only their own atrocious fate, but also their courageous mother: a few hours before the bandits had prepared to leave Qualixo, Catarina had tried to sneak out of the house, had actually mounted one of the bandits' mustangs and had just begun to ride down the street in a desperate attempt to find the nearest *Juarista* soldiers, when Diego Macaras appeared in the doorway, and sent a bullet into her head. When Dolores and Isobel, seeing their mother dead, had shrieked in anguish and tried to run to her, Merle Kinnick had dragged them back. "Don't try running, *muchachas*. Otherwise, you'll wind up just like your poor *mamacita*. Too bad, she was a tasty morsel. But then, we'll have to make do with you, won't we, *queridas*?"

Some seventeen miles from Qualixo, they came upon a tiny hamlet, known as Morsucion, a stone's throw from the Rio Grande. There were at most thirty adobe huts, a small church made of the same sun-hardened yellowish clay, and a small public square whose only feature was a well with a trough for horses. Diego Macaras held up his hand and turned back to bawl to his men, "We shall make our headquarters here till it's time to attack the *hacienda* of the *gringos*. I know this little village, and there are only *peónes* and a few *mestizos*. Perhaps among them, since they have *Indio* blood in their veins, we may recruit a few more men to strengthen our forces." Merle Kinnick gave him a cynical look, and the bandit leader scowled angrily as he raised his voice: "Ride in there, *hombres,* with your weapons ready. Leave the *muchachas* on their burros till we have taken the town—they won't try to run away, they miss you too much already." Obscene sniggers down the line of horsemen greeted this licentious sally.

Flourishing his sombrero, Macaras gestured toward the little village and raced forward, the others following him

439

at a gallop till they reached the public square. He and Merle Kinnick dismounted, guns at the ready, while the frightened villagers emerged from their adobe huts. As he had said, these were mostly *peónes* and a few men whose mothers had been Mexican and fathers Indian. In all, there were perhaps sixty inhabitants, including old women and children. It was a village that had never before been raided, even by the Comanches, for it was impoverished. There were a few vegetable gardens on the outside of the little town, but most of the *peónes* either worked in the silver mines or for wealthy landowners at starvation wages. And for exactly that reason, Diego Macaras had chosen it to give him and his men ample concealment until it was time to attack Windhaven Range.

There was practically no resistance. One of the younger men, brandishing a machete, denounced the bandit leader, who laughingly unholstered one of his pistols and shot him through the heart. Then, addressing the terrified inhabitants, he proclaimed that he took possession of the village in the name of Benito Juarez, and that he and his troops would be quartered here to make certain that no aid would be given to the hated French oppressors. Anyone who sought to leave the village without his permission would be summarily shot. Then, seeing that his words had had their expected effect, Diego Macaras ingratiatingly continued, "I offer those of you who are brave and true patriots at heart the chance to fight for your beloved country and to have much gold, good food and drink, and beautiful women for the taking. Before we ride out of here, my *coronel*, the *Señor* Kinnick," here he gestured toward the red-bearded Comanchero, who gave him a mocking wink and nod to acknowledge the military title just conferred upon him, "will talk to those of you whose valor and courage will lead you from your dusty little hovels to glory for Mexico!"

The stooped, crippled old priest now emerged from the little church, and Diego Macaras turned to contemplate him. Merle Kinnick had drawn one of his pistols but Diego Macaras shook his head warningly: it would not do to antagonize these humble people if he wished to enjoy a peaceful rest before summoning all his strength against the hated *gringos*. "*Padre,* we are come in the name of Benito Juarez and we stay here with you a little time. Here is for your poor," and with a grandiose gesture he flung a handful of silver into the dust of the square at the priest's feet.

The old man, nearly blind and deaf, began to bless this generous benefactor, as he groped for the coins. "Aid the good father, *mi coronel,*" Diego Macaras smilingly turned to his red-bearded aide. With a grimace of distaste, Merle Kinnick dismounted, squatted down, collected the coins and put them into the priest's trembling, outstretched hands. "Pray for us, *Padre,*" he said softly.

A few minutes later, the bandit leader was quartered in the home of the elderly *alcalde,* a childless widower, while Merle Kinnick moved into the little rectory beside the church. The other men and Ikanito were equally accepted by the other villagers, except for the buxom, still young wife of the man whom Diego Macaras had shot down. But the renegade Comanche moved beside her and whispered, "If you do not take me, *Señora,* the *jefe* will give you to all of his soldiers like a *puta.* I will console you for the loss of your *hombre,* you will see." Grinning evilly, he gripped the woman's wrists and forced her to lead him to her hut.

After all these arrangements had been made, Diego Macaras rode back to fetch the two burros with the four helpless female captives he continued to hold as valuable hostages, and led the burros to the stable at the end of the village, where he locked them up for the night. "If you are good girls, *muchachas,*" he taunted them, "*mi coronel* will bring you something to eat and drink. Perhaps he will also amuse himself a little, but that is the price you must pay in this desolate country for your lives. We are an army, *mis bonitas,* and nothing that travels with an army can be wasted if we are to win our battles. *Adios* for now!"

Ramon Hernandez and his eight newly hired *vaqueros* reached Windhaven Range several days before Henry Belcher and Tim and Connie moved into the house which Luke Bouchard's workers had built for the Sedalia widower. It was a mild evening when he rode into the corral, and invited the *vaqueros* to meet their new employer in the *hacienda*.

"I'm glad to have you back, Ramon. In another ten days, we should be starting our roundup and begin for the drive to Santa Fe," Luke Bouchard enthusiastically declared. "A fine group of horsemen. I can see that from the way they're dressed and the way they look."

Indeed, all eight were muscular, their faces bronzed from the sun. Most of them wore knives in scabbards, attached to belts decorated with silver, and all of them wore chaparreras made of the skins of Angora goats which had long and naturally curly, silky hair. They carried coiled *reatas*, lariats which could hold a huge longhorn in check and topple it to the ground so that it could be branded. Some of these *reatas* were eighty feet long, made of eight strands for heavy work and about three-quarters of an inch in diameter. The men all wore sombreros, some of them black and decorated around the brims with silver, others white with deeply creased crowns. The jingling of their spurred boots made a pleasant sound as they walked into the broad living room of the *hacienda* at Luke Bouchard's invitation, where Betty, goggling again at their strange garb, served them coffee and some of the spiced cakes she had just finished baking for the evening meal.

"Each one of these men, *Señor* Bouchard," Ramon Hernandez explained, "has his own six-shooter, and three of the men have old Belgian rifles, single-shot but very efficient at long range. Let me introduce to you: Paco Alvarez, Jose Martinez, Jorge Feliz, Felipe Rodriguez and his brother Manuel, Pablo Toldanos, Luis Garcia and Sebastiano Galvez."

"*Bienvenidos, Señores!*" Luke Bouchard smilingly greeted them and went to each to offer his hand. "You will be paid exactly as Ramon told you, and when we have sold our cattle in Santa Fe each of you, according to the work he does, will receive a bonus. Those of you who have the rifles, I should like to stay here at the *hacienda* to guard it."

"I am one of those, *Señor* Bouchard," young Pablo Toldanos spoke up, a slim black-haired young man of twenty-four, with a short pointed beard. "I know also who it is that may attack you, for Ramon Hernandez has told us about this *bandido*. My cousin was killed in the town of Miero, which this *cobarde* raided in the name of Benito Juarez—I hope that I may have him in my sights, and that I do not miss when I pull the trigger."

"Then you'll stay on guard here, Pablo," Luke Bouchard decided. "And who are the others who have rifles?"

"I, *Señor*," and "I, too, *Señor*," came from Jose Martinez and Sebastiano Galvez as they stepped forward. "They're tied to our saddles, *Señor*," Sebastiano Galvez volunteered, oldest of the eight men hired. "I can hit a *zopilote* at a hundred yards, *Señor*, without even aiming. If this liar and murderer comes closer than that, he will be as dead, *seguro*."

"And I sincerely hope that you will have your chance, Sebastiano," Luke chuckled and shook hands again all around. "And now, we'll find you places in the bunkhouse where you can store your gear, so rest up a bit after your long journey, and then tonight my cook will have a very good dinner for all of you."

On the evening of March 1, Maybelle Bouchard had just finished serving supper to Henry Belcher, Tim and Connie.

Lucas had lassoed a wild hog and slaughtered it that very morning, and Maybelle had cooked ham slices with currants and a little sugar to sweeten the gamy flavor of the meat. She had served fluffy biscuits, liberally smeared with wild honey. The meal had made the middle-aged widower nostalgic. Accepting a second cup of coffee, he declared with a long sigh, "I swear, Miss Maybelle m'am, I can't remember when I've ever had better vittles—leastways not since I lost my Millie."

"Me too, Pa," Tim chimed in.

Flustered and pleased, she couldn't help blushing. "Oh now, Mr. Belcher, you're just saying that to be nice. It was just an ordinary supper, nothing special."

"No it wasn't, Miss Maybelle," Now don't you go downgrading yourself. I've noticed you've been doing a lot of that ever since I met up with you. Land sakes, you're a fine upstanding woman, and I—" Suddenly fearing that he had gone too far in voicing his thoughts, he pretended to cough over a mislodged mouthful, put his napkin to his mouth and finally took a long swig of milk. "Guess I must have got something in my windpipe. But I was saying, that's the best cooking I've set a knife and fork to in longer than I care to remember. Now, Tim and Connie, you go help Miss Maybelle with the dishes—"

"Oh, no, I wouldn't hear of it! Really, Mr. Belcher, there aren't very many and it keeps me in good practice."

"You know, Miss Maybelle," Henry Belcher ventured as he saw his children hurrying out to the little kitchen in anticipation of the chore, "it's a mite too soon to talk about things like this, but I've been feeling this for some time now and I just wonder—say, what was that?"

There was a sound of booted footsteps, and then a red-bearded tall man in buckskin jacket and breeches strode into the room, a six-shooter in his right hand. "Now nobody move or fuss or do anything rash, maybe you won't get hurt," he drawled.

"Who—who are you?" Maybelle Bouchard quavered, putting a hand to her mouth as her eyes widened in fear.

"Never you mind who I am, sister, you just go on nice and easy. Now then, you, Mister, you're not one of those Bouchards, are you?"

"No sir, I'm not, I'm Henry Belcher and I'm from Sedalia, not that it's any of your business," the widower tartly spoke up, far from being cowed by the gun leveled at him.

"A Missourian, eh? Seems to me like you're trying to get that saying about you folks proved mighty quick, that you're from Missouri and you want to be shown. Well, Mister, just you make one yell, and I'll pull this trigger and you'll be one sure as hell dead Missourian, savvy?"

"I reckon that's plain enough to understand, Mister," Henry Belcher gave him back, undaunted.

"All right." The red-bearded man glanced at the table. "I could use some vittles myself. Got anything strong to drink?"

"Just milk," Maybelle acidly retorted, dropping her

444

apron and staring angrily at the intruder. What piqued her most was that she sensed that Henry Belcher had just been on the verge of a momentous avowal, and the interruption, for all its dangers, galled her more than the sight of the gun and the nasty look of the man holding it on the widower.

"Well, it'll have to do. Bring me whatever you've got, plenty of it, and fast, sister. Those your kids?" he gestured with the muzzle of the gun as Tim and Connie came back from the kitchen, halted, Connie uttering a stifled little cry of fright at the sight of the stranger.

"They're mine, Mister, and I'd appreciate it if you wouldn't point that six-shooter at them. You can see how young they are, they're not likely to do you any harm," Henry Belcher indignantly stated.

"All right, don't talk so high and mighty, and don't think that just because you haven't got a gun, I wouldn't shoot you down if I'd a mind to," the red-bearded intruder growled. "You kids, go over in the corner and sit down on the floor and not a peep out of you, hear?"

'Why—yes, s–sir," Tim quavered, "but please don't you hurt Miss Maybelle or Pa."

"If he minds his business the way I hope you're gonna, kid, I won't have to. Now take your sister over there and sit down and keep quiet, quick now!" Again he made a menacing gesture with the gun.

"Come on, Connie, don't cry, you'll be fine," Tim reassured his sister as he took her by the hand and led her over into the corner, then drew her down to sit beside him on the floor. Both children looked on with growing anxiety as the intruder pulled out a chair and seated himself astride it, keeping his six-shooter leveled across the table at Henry Belcher's heart.

Maybelle was trembling, but she fought the sick nausea of fear and forced herself to carve a liberal slice of the ham and ladle out the currant and sugary syrup, brought the plate out and set it down before the gunman, then went back to the kitchen and piled four biscuits on a plate, poured out a glass of milk and set these down beside him also. Then she retreated to the end of the table, gripping the top of a heavy wooden chair for support as she watched him take out a clasp knife, cut the ham into pieces which he stabbed with the tip of the gleaming, sharp blade and wolfed down.

"Not bad chow, sister. Now, you say you aren't related to the Bouchards?"

"I told you that once," Henry Belcher doggedly replied. "I'm just a farmer here, and Mr. Bouchard helped me claim a hundred acres near his holdings, that's all. Miss Maybelle just came over to help cook supper for the kids and me. I lost my wife back in Missouri."

"Well now, I guess maybe I interrupted some sparking, then," the red-bearded intruder chuckled nastily.

Henry Belcher's face flushed. "Mister, I'm not aiming to do anything foolish, but I'd be much obliged if you wouldn't make any comments about the lady like that. It's none of nobody's business anyhow."

"You're real touchy. Where there's smoke there's fire, they say. Well, tell you what I'm gonna do. I've got a few boys along here and we're gonna pay the Bouchards a little visit. I'm staying here to make sure that none of you goes running off to tell them they've got callers, understand me?" Merle Kinnick cocked his six-shooter and the dry click added a grim punctuation to his words.

"Oh my God!" Maybelle Bouchard murmured faintly to herself, closed her eyes, swaying against the chair.

"Like I said, you might all get out of this alive if you just stay here and keep shut. Let's have some more milk, sister. Sure you haven't got any whiskey or tequila in the place?"

"I told you once no. Milk will just have to do you," Maybelle disgustedly flung at him as, drawing a deep breath, she walked over to him, took up the empty glass and walked slowly back to the kitchen.

As she reached for the pitcher of milk, her eyes fell on the sharp short-handled knife with which she had cut the ham. At that moment, Connie began to whimper, and Merle Kinnick whirled in his chair and snarled, "Stop that squalling, you little bitch, or I'll stop it for good, you hear me?"

"She's frightened, Mister, no need to talk to her like that," Henry Belcher indignantly put in.

"You shut your trap too, if you know what's good for you. All right, kid, make your little sister stop that blubbering, or I'll give it to you both, I mean it," the red-bearded Comanchero directed.

Maybelle swiftly grasped the knife by the handle and slid it up her left sleeve, which was of puffed cambric. Then, clutching the pitcher with both hands to steady herself, she filled the glass, and walked slowly back with it toward the Comanchero.

Connie was doing her best to hold back her tears, but the sight of the intruder's ugly face and the angry tone of his words had been too much for her, and she began to cry in earnest now.

With an oath, Merle Kinnick shoved back his chair and was about to rise when Maybelle, drawing the knife out of her left sleeve, plunged it into his back, using both hands and driving downward with all her might. He stiffened, his right hand went up, his trigger finger reflexively tightened, and there was an explosion as the bullet buried itself harmlessly at the top of the wall beyond. Then the gun dropped from his hand, as he reached behind him, slowly turning his face, trying to understand what had happened to him. "You—you—b-bitch—I'll get you—oh Jesus—oh Gawd—"

He stumbled backwards, and Maybelle put her hand to her mouth to stifle a cry of terror, as he grasped hold of the back of the chair and tried to straighten himself. Then he crumpled to the floor, pulling the chair over with him, jerked fitfully and lay still.

"Oh my God," Henry Belcher whispered in awe as he got to his feet. "Oh, Miss Maybelle, do you know what you've done? You've saved our lives, that's what—my God, I'd never have thought you could have done it, that man was a killer, a killer for sure—oh Miss Maybelle honey, don't cry like that, it's all over now, it's all over!"

For Maybelle was weeping bitterly in his arms as he comforted her, and Tim and Connie had sprung to their feet and run to their father, hugging him and Maybelle in their near-hysterical release from tension.

"Do you know who he was, Miss Maybelle honey?"

Henry Belcher at last demanded when Maybelle's tears had subsided somewhat.

"Oh no, Henry, but you remember he said they were going to pay a visit to the Bouchards—maybe he was one of those bandits that attacked us when we came from Corpus Christi—that must be what it is—I remember now how we all left the wagons around the campfire so they'd think we were still in them, and we were ready for them and drove them off—maybe that's why they're back now, to pay us back for the damage we did then—"

"Then we've got to warn them!" Henry Belcher valiantly cried. "I'll get my old Whitworth and I'll fire a shot to warn them. It's dark now, and we don't know how many men they've got along there with them, and if I was to go out now and try to get to the *hacienda,* like as not they'd shoot me down. Now you just stay there—kids, don't look at that awful man. You go to your rooms now, that's good children. Oh God, Miss Maybelle, when I think what he could have done to them—yes, and to you—"

There were tears in his eyes as he took her by the shoulders and stared at her until at last she lifted her face, her lips trembling, her eyes appealingly staring into his. "He said we were sparking, Miss Maybelle—well maybe, I guess we were at that—leastways, I was in a mind to try. And now, the way you've shown how you could take over and save Tim and Connie, I'd be much obliged, real obliged, Miss Maybelle, honey, if you'd consider making it a permanent job for life. Think you could? I know I ain't much to look at, and I'm never gonna be rich, but my kids like you a lot—"

"Oh Henry, stop talking, you silly darling, and just hold me and kiss me, oh Henry darling!" Maybelle sobbed happily as she hugged him and put her mouth to his and eagerly gave him back kiss for kiss.

CHAPTER THIRTY-NINE

Djamba had turned Jubal loose to patrol the stockade as the first shadows of this early March evening fell. Strong and sleek, the once stray dog of New Orleans strutted with pride around the pickets which enclosed the *hacienda,* the corral, the bunkhouse and the adobe dugouts where the two young Southerners still kept their bachelor quarters and guard post.

Inside the *hacienda,* Betty had busied herself preparing supper for the Bouchards, while Celia and Prissy stood ready to carry platters of food to the bunkhouse for the free blacks and the new Mexican *vaqueros* whom Ramon Hernandez had engaged in the name of Luke Bouchard. It had been an exhausting day for Luke and his son Lucien Edmond, and the new *vaqueros* had already earned their month's wages by riding down stray steers, young bulls and heifers, lassoing them, while Djamba and Lucas quickly branded them with the capital letters WR.

There was already a warm spirit of camaraderie between the Mexican horsemen and the freed blacks. Some of the blacks indeed, like Ned and Frank, had learned a little Spanish from their occasional visits to Mobile with the produce crops which Luke Bouchard had had ferried down the Alabama River. For words they lacked, they compensated with gestures and hearty bursts of laughter. The spirit of a brotherhood had already come to the bunkhouse of Windhaven Range. It was one which old Lucien Bouchard himself would have welcomed.

Lucien himself had learned the lesson of brotherhood from the Creeks. His grandson Luke believed that after the grueling, hateful war which had robbed the nation of so many strong, adventuring young men, the hope of the future could only lie in a sharing of all adversity and triumph, a free expression of patient tolerance. Luke saw no difference in a man because of the color of his skin or religion or ethics, and looked back with gratitude to his friendship with John Brunton, whose advice had been to choose this isolated part of Texas where he would not be forced into onerous contact with former Southerners who still believed themselves racially superior to the black.

It was a new world, still primitive and yet with the portents of a great future in which a man could achieve his full potential through strength and courage. It was not yet an Eden, and perhaps would never be: yet already Luke Bouchard could justly feel that what he had wrought out of this abandoned wilderness would be a fitting heritage for Lucien Edmond, Maxine and their children Carla and Hugo. Just in itself, that was nearly reward enough for the harrowing difficulties which he had encountered since he set out on this venture—which now seemed to last an eternity.

At this moment, from the southeast, two shadowy figures began to jog toward the gate of the picket fence which faced the sprawling *hacienda*. Farther beyond, just across the border of the river which was shallow and narrow at this point, hidden by a thick copse of live oak trees and tall, irregular clumps of blooming mesquite, twenty-two horsemen waited in the shadows. Diego Macaras had been able to recruit six *mestizos* from the little village of Mursucion. Impoverished all their lives, and with an inborn hatred of the *gringo,* they were easily won to the promise of plunder and riches and *gringo* women for the taking. Ikanito, seated on a rangy sorrel and carrying a lance in one hand and a Belgian rifle in the other, turned to the bandit chief and muttered, "By now, the *Señor* Red Beard has captured that other house of the *gringos*. I had not seen that one when I rode by this place, *mí general*."

Diego Macaras beamed at the Comanche's use of his self-bestowed title. "*Es nada, amigo,*" he assured the Comanche. "It is a little house, *muy poco*, and I am sure that the *Señor coronel* has already killed all of those in there—unless there are some pretty girls he has tied up to keep for our loyal soldiers after the battle is won. What have you done with Conchita and Rosa?"

Ikanito shrugged. "They made too much noise, *mí general*. I cut their throats a few miles back and left them for the buzzards." Besides the daughters of that woman of the *alcade*, they are younger and have more life.

"It is a matter of no importance. Two mouths less to feed, and as you say, Isobel and Dolores are *muy linda,*" Diego Macaras smirkingly agreed. "Now we shall wait," as he turned back to beckon to his two lieutenants to come up closer to him, "till we hear the *muchachas* call out for help against the wicked *Indios*. *Comprende*? Then Ikanito and I will ride to the gate, which the girls—if they do not wish to be whipped to death, as I have already told them—will have had the sense to leave open for us—and the rest of you will circle and keep firing whenever you see a target. Where you can, you will climb over those accursed fences and get into the *hacienda*. Do not kill the women. There is one there with whom I have a score to settle." He scowled as he touched his shoulder, remembering the wound which Sybella had inflicted. Just as Ramon Hernandez had foretold, news of his defeat at the hands of the members of the Bouchard wagon train had already filtered across the border, and there were still some taverns where men laughed softly as they talked of "La Vieja," and "El General."

"Agreed, *mí jefe*," Carlos Muñez, who of all his followers had put in the longest time of service and proved himself to be the most ruthlessly faithful, assented. "Are we to use fire?"

"If we do not break down the fence and kill all the *gringos* at first, *sí*, and I will signal for it, *mí capitán*."

451

The lean, wiry Mexican, a man of thirty-five, with several missing teeth and a purplish scar running from his right earlobe to the jawline, grinned and touched his sombrero to acknowledge this field promotion from lieutenant. "We will kill them all, the accursed *gringos*. We will not have to use fire, I am sure, *mi jefe*. There go the *muchachas*!"

"Yes, and let us hope they do what they were told, or they will wish they had never been born," Diego Macaras sullenly muttered.

Earlier that day, Jubal had discovered a little round mound of earth dug up not far from the porch of the hacienda. Now that he was safeguarding the entire fenced-in area, and the people whom he loved best were safely inside, he decided to investigate this phenomenon. Wagging his tail and sniffing noisily, he pawed at the upturned earth, and for an instant uncovered a tiny mole which at once lowered itself back to subterranean safety. Angered at its escape, Jubal barked, and began to use both front paws as he scrabbled to dig down to the mole's hiding place. It was at this moment that Isobel and Dolores approached the gate and began to cry out, "Help us—oh please, in there, help us—our family's been killed by Indians, please let us in!"

Thirteen-year-old Isobel, her long black hair descending almost to her hips, wore a dirty, yellow dress which Merle Kinnick had appropriated from one of the women in the village, while her older sister Dolores, somewhat shorter and more buxom and with fluffy dark-brown hair that fell just below her shoulder blades, was clad in a tattered calico dress which had similarly been taken from its rightful owner. Both girls were barefooted, their faces smudged with dirt to add authenticity to their story.

Luke Bouchard was at that moment conferring with Lucien Edmond, Djamba and Lucas in the living room of the *hacienda* on the forthcoming cattle drive and the placement of the newly hired *vaquero* escorts. Sybella and Maxine were chatting in a corner, while Lucy was trying to comfort little Carla, who had just discovered that her favorite rag doll was missing. "Don't you remember when you had it last, darling?" Luke's grayhaired wife solicitously asked.

"It was outside, near where all the horses are, Grandma," Carla sniffled, her lower lip trembling pathetically. "I want my rag doll right now, Grandma!"

"All right, dear, I'll go outside and help you look for it. First, let me get a lighted candle so I can see out in the dark. Come along now." Taking Carla by the hand, Lucy fetched a candle and led the sobbing little girl out into the back yard. The bunkhouse was perhaps a hundred feet away to the southwest, and lights glimmered there already from the shuttered windows.

The gate in the center of the fence directly in front of the *hacienda* was closed at night by placing two horizontal wooden planks across it on the inside. The height of the fence made it impossible for the girls to reach over and draw away both planks, and Isobel, having already attempted to reach her arms up and over the top of the fence, grasped the uprights and began to shake them, crying out again, "*Por favor*, help us! Doesn't anyone hear us in there? The Indians killed our folks and they might be coming after us too—oh please, won't someone let us in?"

Hearing the younger girl's shrill cry, Luke Bouchard had excused himself from his conversation, gone to the door and reached for the loaded Spencer repeating rifle. Carefully he unbolted the front door of the *hacienda* and peered out into the growing darkness. "Who's there?" he called out. Jubal, forgetting his quest for the elusive mole and attracted by the cries of the two young girls, had raced toward the gate and was barking furiously, turning his head back to his master and then springing at the gate in a vehement effort to make Luke Bouchard open it.

"Oh please, Mister," Dolores now cried, feverishly glancing to the south where the hidden riders waited in ambush, remembering what dire punishment she and her sister had been promised if they bungled their assigned task, "Help us, *por el amor de Dios! Los Indios*—they killed our *madre* and *padre*, we ran away to escape them, oh help us, we don't want to die!"

Luke Bouchard came out onto the porch, looking warily around. Then cautiously he advanced step by step toward

453

the gate. Jubal continued his impatient barking, running back to Luke, whining, then back to the gate against which he sprang again and again.

"Quiet now, boy!" Luke shushed him, pointing his forefinger in an abrupt downward-descending gesture. Jubal stopped obediently, wagging his tail, crouching, a faint grumble in his throat showing that every canine instinct made him want to disobey his master's order. And in that moment, Luke Bouchard heard the snuffling of the horses in the clump of live oak trees. A moment later, there was the sound of a shot from the little Belcher house, as Henry Belcher bawled out, "It's the bandits, Mr. Bouchard, don't open the gate, it's a trick!"

Diego Macaras swore viciously, and then, lifting his sombrero, swept it down in the signal to attack. "*Muerte a los gringos, todos!*" he angrily cried out as he urged his horse forward, while his lieutenant signaled to half the riders to circle the stockade from the other side.

In building this protective fence, Djamba had arranged that at every eighth upright post, there was to be a small rectangular space at about the level of a man's shoulders, so that if Windhaven Range were attacked, the defenders could aim their weapons and have good visibility. Luke now ran, crouching like an Indian, toward the open space a few feet to his right of the gate and quickly peered out into the darkness. He saw the stocky form of Diego Macaras followed by six other men, quickly aimed and triggered the Spencer. At the first bark of the rifle, the rider just behind the bandit chief twisted in his saddle and then fell sideways to the ground. Diego Macaras leveled one of his pistols and fired, the bullet whining past Luke Bouchard's head.

Hearing the shots, Lucien Edmond had seized a carbine and hurried out to join his father. In the bunkhouse, meanwhile, Ramon Hernandez, the blacks and the *vaqueros* ran out with their weapons, stationing themselves at strategic points behind the tall wooden fence, using those defensive open rectangles for the placement of their pistols, rifles and carbines, and began to open fire at the circling riders, who returned the fusillade with sporadic shots.

454

Lucy Bouchard was still in the yard with Carla when the shooting began. "Grandma, there it is, there's my dolly!" little Carla cried as she saw the large, floppy rag doll on the ground near the well.

There was the thud of a bullet hitting the rim of the well and the whine of a ricochet as the little girl ran toward her doll. With a cry of fright, Lucy rushed forward and picked Carla up, turning to go back to the kitchen, when one of the half-breeds whom Diego Macaras had recruited in Morsucion aimed his old Belgian single-shot rifle and fired into the space of one of the rectangles between the upright fence posts. A moment later, Ramon Hernandez's carbine turned his face into a gory mask and he was felled from his saddle as if by an invisible hand as his horse raced off, wildly neighing.

Lucy Bouchard had stumbled, then regained her footing, her face twisted with pain. On the back of her blue dress, a red stain was spreading.

"Grandma, Grandma, you're holding me so tight you hurt—Grandma, what's the matter?" Carla petulantly complained. "My dolly—please get my dolly—"

"No, darling, we—we have to go back to the house, we have to—I have to get you there—please be good, Carla honey—" Lucy chokingly gasped. A sudden swell of hot pain from the wound made her close her eyes and totter for a moment, and then, with a tremendous effort, she stumbled toward the kitchen door, clutching the little girl tightly in her arms, her eyes glazed, as Betty, with a cry of fright, opened the door and rushed out: "Oh, Miz Lucy, you hurt—gimme dat gal, ah got her now, Miz Lucy. Carla, you go back with your folks, you mind Betty now! Oh my Gawd, Miz Lucy, you's hurt bad—my Gawd—"

"I—I'll be all right—just let me sit down at the table here, B–Betty," Lucy faintly gasped as the fat black cook held onto her, tears running down her cheeks, solicitously aiding her to reach the chair. "Don't tell Luke—don't tell Mr. Bouchard—I–I'll be—" she seated herself, and then her head fell forward onto the table as Betty, flinging her apron over her head, raised her hands and burst into frantic lamentations.

From his position at the side of the gate, Luke Bouchard called out, "Girls, lie down flat on the ground, keep out of the way!" as he waited for the circling riders. On the other side, at the bunkhouse, the raiders had drawn first blood: Paco Alvarez was instantly killed by a pistol shot, and Jorge Feliz dropped his pistol and sank down on his knees, clutching his right shoulder which had been broken by a rifle shot from another of Macaras' riders. The renegade Comanche Ikanito had ridden behind the stockade and, guiding his mustang up against a post, had agilely caught hold of it and leaped over, his scalping knife in his right hand, his pistol in his left. Crouching low, he ran toward the side of the bunkhouse, but Ramon Hernandez, wheeling, saw the vague outline in the shadows, knelt down and pumped three shots from his carbine at the scarcely visible target. Ikanito uttered a wild yowl of agony, sank down to his hands and knees and painfully began to crawl toward the young *vaquero*. Tightening his finger on the trigger of his pistol, he fired it, but the ball whistled past Ramon and thudded against one of the fenceposts. The momentary flare from the Comanche's gun provided Ramon with a perfect target: one quick shot of the carbine and Ikanito sprawled with a bullet through his brain.

Pablo Toldanos, Sebastiano Galvez and Jose Martinez stood against the fence, their rifles extended through the open rectangles, returning the bandits' fire unflinchingly. Despite a slight bullet crease at the right side of his head, Pablo returned the riders' shot with deadly accuracy, and another bandit toppled from his horse, his foot caught in the stirrups, as his mustang dragged his lifeless body away from the stockade. Two more bandits fell to the accurate aim of Sebastiano and Jose.

Infuriated at the loss of his men, Diego Macaras began to curse them in the most voluble and obscene Spanish, branding them as cowards and women, threatening to shoot them down if they did not breach the stockade. Two of his men dismounted, leaning from their saddles to grasp the tops of the posts and to hoist themselves over as Ikanito had done. Djamba, who had run out of the kitchen and briefly noticed the slumped body of Lucy

Bouchard at the table, carried one of the ironwork spears he had made in New Orleans. Running forward and drawing back his right arm, he flung the spear at one of the bandits, who uttered a shriek and doubled over, his hands scrabbling at the wooden shaft whose deadly sharp point was buried in his belly. The other bandit, scrambling to his feet, aimed a pistol at Djamba, but the powerful Mandingo dropped his left hand to the holster of his six-shooter, squeezed off a shot, and the bandit uttered a gurgling shriek as he fell with a bullet in the throat, kicked convulsively, rolled over and lay still.

Thus far, Diego Macaras had escaped unscathed, though one bullet had tugged his sombrero out of his hand and another had plucked at the shoulder of his coat. His face livid with rage, he wheeled his gray gelding away from the murderous fire from the stockade, and called out at the top of his voice, "Ernesto, Humberto, *fuego,* burn the *gringos* out, *pronto*!"

But his last two men, convinced that the battle was lost and fearing for their own lives, had ridden off across the Nueces River on to the safety of Mexico, and the self-styled general of Benito Juarez was alone. He had no more ammunition left for his pistols, and with a cry of agonized rage, he flung them at the indomitable fence, then reached for his French rifle in its scabbard, aimed it and fired into the yard. Ramon Hernandez had hurried to his companions, squinting through one of the rectangles as he seized a carbine from one of the blacks, aimed it at the bandit leader and pulled the trigger.

Diego Macaras' gray gelding squealed shrilly, staggered, and the swarthy bandit chief, with a shriek of fury, leaped off the dying horse before it fell onto its side, clutching his rifle, brandishing it back at the defenders of Windhaven Range, and then began to run as fast as he could away from the disastrous carnage which spelled the end of his hopes for gold and helpless women.

"Leave him to me, Ned," Ramon Hernandez muttered to the Hausa whose carbine he had taken. "I have a score to settle with *mi jefe.*" He threw down the carbine, took hold of the horizontal plank near the top of the fence, and nimbly hoisted himself upwards, then swung himself over to the ground. Catlike, regaining his footing, he began to run toward the fleeing bandit chief.

His breath wheezing, Diego Macaras reached a cedar tree, knelt down, and feverishly began to reload the single-shot weapon.

The sound of his raspy, exhausted breathing reached Ramon's ears as he hurried forward in the darkness, crouching to make as small a target as possible if there should be any bandits left to fire at him. As he approached the cedar tree, a look of exultation came on his handsome face to see the green coat with medals and the stocky man hastily forcing a cartridge into the breech.

"Bienvenido, mí jefe," he mockingly called out. "We meet again. It has been a long time since Miero, *no es verdad?"*

"Por todos los Santos!" Diego Macaras gasped, crossing himself. "Ramon Hernandez—but I killed you—"

"No, *mí jefe*. The old priest and the woman whose husband you killed cared for me. And now it is between us, is it not, *mí jefe*? No, your fingers are all thumbs, you do not even put the bullet in right—let me show you—" Like a cat, he sprang forward and wrested the rifle out of Diego Macaras' sweating hands.

"Mercy—don't kill me—I only meant to wound you, a lesson in discipline, that was all—no, I am rich, Ramon, much richer than you think—there were spoils I took in Qualixo, and I have other things, jewels and much gold hidden in an *arroyo* near Nuevo Laredo—I'll take you to all of it, you shall have all of it, but let me go!"

Ramon flung the rifle with all his strength as far away from him as he could. "I would not waste a bullet on you, *mí general*," he contemptuously responded. "And it is the last time you will be called general by anyone on earth, for surely the next one to call you that which you never were will be *El Diablo!"*

He bent down and seized Diego Macaras by the neck, dragged the whimpering bandit leader to his feet, then drove his fist as hard as he could into the pit of Diego Macaras' belly. The bandit leader screamed and doubled over, sprawling forward on his knees, his arms clutching Ramon Hernandez' boots babbling, *"Por piedad,* for the sake of old times, *mí capitán*! *Misericordia*, I do not want to die, have mercy on me!"

"As much as you showed me, *mí jefe*. The same mercy you and your murderers showed the priest at Miero, the husband of that poor woman who made me well again. Their vengeance is what I execute upon you, Diego Macaras. Stand up, you sniveling offspring of a diseased burro—and you talked of how you would save our beloved Mexico—my sin was that I listened and I believed, Diego Macaras. But I know you now for what you are, the spawn of hell itself—rejoin the others in the eternal fires!"

Once again the young Mexican caught hold of the slobbering bandit, lifted him to his feet and then drove his fist as hard as he could against Diego Macaras' nose, breaking it. A plaintive shriek arose as the outlaw fell backwards, his fingers trying to stanch the flow of blood, whining, "You have broken it—mercy, mercy, Ramon, I swear I did not mean to kill you—have pity, I am helpless!"

"Not till you are dead, murderer, bandit, blasphemer, liar!" Ramon Hernandez knelt down, thrust his wiry hands against Diego Macaras' fat neck, and began to throttle him. Kicking and threshing, his bloodied hands convulsively trying to tug Ramon's away, Diego Macaras fought for life. Slowly, his eyes narrowed and his lips set, the young *vaquero* tightened his hold till at last the bandit's face blackened and his eyes bulged, unseeing.

Ramon Hernandez straightened, turned his back and walked slowly back to where the gray gelding lay. He opened the saddlebags, and caught his breath as he saw the silver cross and the chalice from the little church of Miero, and the great silver crucifix of Qualixo. He crossed himself reverently as he kissed each of them, then said to himself, "I can keep my vow." Raising his eyes to the velvety black sky whose moon had hidden behind a heavy cloud, he murmured, *"Gracias, El Señor Dios,* for helping me to keep it."

CHAPTER FORTY

"Ah tried, Mistah Luke sir, ah tried mah best to tell her t'warn't no good goin' out dere," Betty sobbed. "But she jist insisted she had to find l'il Carla's rag doll, no matter wut! And now she dead." The fat cook pulled her apron up over her eyes and burst into uncontrollable sobs.

Luke Bouchard, his face drawn and pale, stood in the kitchen staring at the table on which Lucy's head was slumped in death. Behind him, hushed and grave, stood Sybella and Mara, Maxine and Lucien Edmond. Carla and Hugo had been quickly put to bed against their peevish remonstrations.

Gently Luke reached down to touch Lucy's hair in a reverent caress, then murmured, "May God rest her sweet soul."

"Amen to dat, Mistah Luke!" Betty's sobs grew louder as she turned her back to them and, bending down over the kitchen counter, gave full vent to her anguished grief.

Mara put her hands to her face and brushed away the tears which coursed down her cheeks, while Lucien Edmond came forward to put his arm protectively around her shoulders and to whisper what words of consolation

461

he could find. Maxine had begun to sob. "It was so needless, so useless," she turned to Sybella, her lips trembling, "I don't know why Carla had to take it into her head to have that silly doll at that particular moment—I feel responsible—I should have taken the children to bed right after supper and it wouldn't have happened—"

"There now, dear," Sybella drew Maxine to her, "You mustn't think or say that. Remember, she died saving Carla's life. So it wasn't needless or useless. We can't always see or understand God's ways and reasons, and He had set Lucy's time for now. You must always remember that she thought of others in her last moments, and that's the greatest love of all and God knows it, Maxine, dear."

Again a hushed silence fell upon them, broken only by Betty's pitiful sobbing as Mara and Maxine valiantly strove to suppress their tears. Luke Bouchard straightened and turned to face them. "I think she loved best here that little grove of cedar trees near the river," he said in an unsteady voice. "And she loved the birds that perched in the branches. That's where she shall rest."

Djamba entered the kitchen and halted, uttered a stifled groan as he saw Lucy's head bowed on the table, and then his eyes sought Sybella's. Still with her arms around Maxine, Sybella gave him back an unflinching look and then imperceptibly nodded, sensing what he sensed, that this tragic moment recalled to them both the death of Matthew Forsden, a grief which both had shared so intensely on that first day of decision which was to begin Windhaven Venture. And each sensed, too, the parallel between that first brooding tragedy and this, each born of violence and hatred that was alien to the Bouchards themselves and those who worked for and loved them and shared their courageous lives.

"I want to help, Mr. Luke," he said gently, and Luke Bouchard nodded. "Thank you, Djamba," he said softly as he reached down and very gently lifted Lucy's body in his arms and strode out of the *hacienda*.

The others followed at a respectful distance, and now the moon had come out from behind the cloud, and the night was bright and cool as if the darkness and evil fury which had threatened the Bouchards had been dispelled.

Luke walked slowly, stopped to kiss Lucy's forehead, then her eyes, and moved on toward the little grove of cedar trees, Djamba behind him with a broad spade.

As they neared the river, the sound of the water splashing was restful and gentle, and Luke nodded to a little knoll at the right of the trees and Djamba, without a word, began to dig a grave.

As he laid her body down gently, he turned to Djamba and said, "She has the locket that I gave her in New Orleans, the locket with (WR) on it. She lived long enough to see us free and on the threshold of our new lives, Djamba. She was my sweetheart and companion and her spirit will be with me always, as Dimarte's was with my grandfather so long ago."

"Yes, Mr. Luke. She was kind and thoughtful, always. She never said a mean word about anyone, she didn't. God rest her soul in peace forever."

Luke knelt down and crossed himself, and Djamba slowly began to fill the grave. And when it was done, Luke Bouchard remained on his knees with his hands over his eyes and at last the tears came as Djamba silently went back to the *hacienda* and the others, understanding Luke's need to be alone and to commune, followed.

The moon's rays luminously bathed the little knoll where Lucy rested, touched his haggard face lightly so that the tears glistened. He prayed silently, hands clasped and head bowed, and then he shuddered as he remembered the locket which had been buried with her and which, in New Orleans, she had welcomed as a gift of fealty and love, as the symbol of the beginning of their new life together. How short a span of time there had been for them after that memento! And yet almost a full lifetime of hardship and danger and violence and staunch loyalty had taken place after the giving of that gift. But now, with a terrible clarity, Luke Bouchard remembered that that memento had been an impulsive gift—an impulse to conceal his one lapse from the fidelity he had sworn with his marriage vows. That stolen hour with Laure, that unreasoning and uninhibited surrender to carnal passion against which he had been powerless, in spite of all his moral precepts and high-flown code of ethics, had motivated that gift. He flagellated himself now at Lucy's grave by thinking, it had been a kind of Judas gift, and now how deeply and sorrowfully he wished he might have bought it before he had met that golden-haired, tantalizing young woman who had goaded him beyond what he had believed was impregnable endurance.

He wept again in his shameful realization, and then he said in a hoarse voice, "Forgive me, my darling. I did not calculate it or seek it, and I had no defense or excuse. Know that I loved you and that, like Dimarte to her Lucien, your spirit will be with me to the end of my days, no matter where they take me or how they deal with me."

As he slowly rose, there was the sudden hooting of an owl from one of the trees near the grave, and with a gasp he looked up to see the owl take flight, a dark shadow against the filtering moonrays.

He crossed himself, and then he turned slowly back toward the *hacienda*. As he did, he saw the young *vaquero* hesitantly approaching, sombrero clutched between both hands, nervously twisting the brim.

"I ask your pardon, *Señor* Bouchard," Ramon Hernandez apologetically murmured. "I did not mean to intrude upon your grief."

"You didn't, Ramon. I have said my prayers. She's at peace now. Tell me," Luke straightened, his face again calm and impassive, "how are the men?"

"Four wounded and one dead, *Señor* Bouchard. As against that, sixteen of the bandits will not see the sun tomorrow morning; the others rode away when they saw there was no hope for them. And their leader—I myself have seen to it that he will never attack Windhaven Range or any harmless and innocent little village again."

"Then it was Diego Macaras, of whom you warned me."

"*Sí, Señor* Bouchard."

"God sent you to us, Ramon. I believe that. You came to warn us, and though you were too late, you forearmed us for the future. You have more than earned the right to marry Mara, and she's lucky in her choice of a good man like you."

"I did only my duty, *Señor* Bouchard." Ramon Her-

464

nandez bowed his head, twisting his sombrero back and forth, embarrassed by the older man's words.

"In my grandfather's country, Ramon, it was customary for the parents of the bride to give a dowry. I intend to go to Austin after the cattle drive is over, and there I shall deed over two hundred acres of this land in your name. You can have your own *hacienda,* and thus Mara will still be close to her family while she begins her new life as your wife."

"You are too generous, *Señor* Bouchard."

"No, Ramon. I have come to love you as I do Mara. Besides, it is an investment in the future. She is a Bouchard, you are a Mexican. The mingling of your blood on a new land which is at the beginning of its future in a nation now unified should bring a rich harvest. Your children, yours and Mara's, will be citizens and workers of the future, building toward the strength that is inherent in this land. You have both faced danger together, you have overcome it. She has learned most of all from you to overcome prejudice. That is why you both are more fortunate than most young couples who bind themselves together. God grant you and Mara many long happy years, fruitful ones." Luke Bouchard put out his hand and Ramon grasped it, and there were tears in his eyes now as well.

After a moment, Ramon falteringly spoke, "I ask a favor, *Señor* Bouchard—a little time to carry out a vow I made before I came here."

"I'd say you've more than earned some time for yourself."

"*Gracias, Señor* Bouchard. I told you that this bandit *jefe* shot me and left me for dead in the village of Miero. He stole the altar cross and chalice from the church, and I found them in his saddlebags, together with a great silver crucifix which was taken from some other village. I told the priest of Miero that one day I would return these things stolen from the house of God, and that is what I wish to do now, with your permission."

"You have it. Take all the time you need, Ramon. We'll start the cattle drive next week, and since we have the good *vaqueros* you so ably engaged for me, as well as

Sangrodo's braves to escort us, it's not necessary that you go with the herd to Santa Fe."

"*Gracias* again, *Señor* Bouchard. I'll leave in the morning, after I've said goodbye to Mara."

As the sun was setting on the third day of Ramon Hernandez' journey from Windhaven Range, he rode Corita into the little town of Miero, dismounted in the public square, unfastened his saddlebag and took out the silver cross and bowl which had been stolen by Diego Macaras. Kissing each, he walked into the church and as he reached the last row of pews, genuflected and bowed his head. As he rose, he saw *Padre* Antonio kneeling before the altar. In the first pew at the very front, a woman sat, her head bowed, her hands clasped in prayer. He moved slowly down the aisle, and waited until the old priest had risen after prayers, then moved forward.

"My son, my son!" the old priest exclaimed, his voice trembling with joy. "You have returned to Miero."

"Yes, *Padre,* I have kept my vow. I bring you back the blessed treasures of God, and I ask you to pray for me." He handed the chalice and the crucifix to the priest, knelt down and clasped his hands.

"It is a miracle, my son. God will not forget your goodness of heart nor your honoring Him." *Padre* Antonio made the sign of the cross over the kneeling young *vaquero,* "May Mary the Mother and Jesus the Son and God the Father watch over you and yours and bless them from this day forward." Then, his face radiant, he went back to the altar and placed the crucifix and the bowl upon them, knelt down and prayed aloud in his gratitude.

Slowly Ramon Hernandez turned his head to look at the woman in the first row. She too had turned to look at him, and he recognized Magdalena Abruta. He uttered a stifled gasp, staring at her, his face suddenly taut with remembrance.

At last the old priest rose and came down toward them. "How perfectly God works His wonders, beyond the knowledge of us poor mortals," he said jubilantly. "Just now, before you came, my son, *Señora* Abruta came to tell me that she wishes to be wed in this little church to a fine man of our village. She is with child, and Mary the Mother has blessed her among women, for it is late in the years of the women of our people to conceive, you know, my son."

"Yes, *Padre*," Ramon Hernandez murmured, his eyes never leaving the handsome, eloquent face of the woman who had tended his wound.

"Tomorrow, *Señora* Abruta, I will pronounce the banns. You will bring Tomas Burcano with you, that he may share the blessing. But now you two have much to talk about. Go and be blessed, both of you, and you, my son, if you will come back to see an old man for a few moments, I will be very grateful."

"Of course, *Padre* Antonio." Ramon Hernandez bowed his head to the old priest and then followed Magdalena Abruta up the aisle and out of the church.

She turned to him, put a hand on his arm. "You are well, *Señor*?"

"I am well, Magdalena. *Gracias*. And you—you are going to be married?"

Her face was radiant, her eyes serene, as she nodded. "Tomas is a good man, much older than I, but he has cared for me for years. He will be the father of my child."

"Magdalena—I—" Ramon Hernandez began.

Gently she put a hand to his mouth to silence him. "I know. It is your child. Dear old *Padre* Antonio knows that as I do, Ramon. He knew it when I made my confession to him after you had left Miero. He is kindly, and he forgave me the sin, and he told me that God and the Holy Mother would not punish the child because of what I had asked you to do."

"But I feel guilt, Magdalena. And worst of all, I went to live with the *gringos* whom I tried to warn against that *ladrón* who killed your *hombre* and wounded *Padre* Antonio and stole the treasures of God's house. And I—I fell in love with a *gringa,* the daughter of the man for whom I work."

"And her father, he does not mind that you are Mexican?"

"No, Magdalena. God touched his heart long ago with tolerance and kindness for all men."

"Then you are blessed again, Ramon Hernandez. I wish you a long life and much happiness and many children with your *esposa*."

He could not see her face for the tears that suddenly blinded him, as he went down on his knees, took her hand and brought it to his lips, kissing it fervently.

"Oh no, you must not kneel to me, I am only a poor peasant woman, Ramon Hernandez. Besides," there was a soft laugh now to her voice, but one of joy and not mockery, "what will poor Tomas and the villagers think if they should see you do this here in the public square?"

"Forgive me, Magdalena. I owe my life to you. And yet I cannot leave Miero with the thought that you bear my child and I, I have done nothing for you—"

"Never say that again. I asked you to give me a child because my man was killed, and you did. And you had heart enough to come back, to bring back the stolen crucifix and the chalice to *Padre* Antonio and to think of me. I am not a woman who needs money from a man to be remembered by him, never that!" She drew herself up proudly, her dark eyes flashing.

"Again I ask your pardon, I have offended you without meaning to," he stammered. "But this village is so poor—I have my wages—would you not let me give you a gift that you might buy toys or what the little one would need?"

"No, Ramon Hernandez. Tomorrow *Padre* Antonio will say the banns in the church for Tomas and me. And my child will be christened in that church as the child of Tomas Burcano and his wife Magdalena."

"I do not know what to say or what to do, Magdalena."

"I have no hold upon you, nor you upon me, but I will always remember you, Ramon Hernandez. *Vaya con Dios.*" She turned away, and then turned back again to add in a very soft voice, "But if it is a son, I will ask my husband if I may name him Ramon after a dear friend who once gave me life and hope."

He watched her walk back into the adobe hut where he

had lain in feverish agony and from which he had emerged to go on the mission which had changed his life so wondrously and perilously. He watched a long moment and then, rubbing his sleeve over his eyes and snorting with impatience at himself, he walked back into the little church.

CHAPTER FORTY-ONE

It was the fifteenth day of March, a bright, cheery day, an augury of good fortune for the first cattle drive of Windhaven Range. Ramon Hernandez had returned a few days before, serene and comforted after his final confession to old *Padre* Antonio. He had found the other stolen cross in the saddlebags of Diego Macaras' horse, and had taken that with him as well to Miero in the hope that the little priest might know from which church it had been stolen. And so *Padre* Antonio had indeed, recognizing it at once as the blessed cross from the village of Qualixo. Ramon had left it there, with a few silver pieces for the poor, and the new, much younger priest, who had replaced the one the Comanchero had shot down in cold blood at the altar, had been bewildered by this apparent miracle. But the young *vaquero*, disclaiming effusive thanks and prayers, had said only, *"Gracias, Padre.* It was part of a vow I made, and I have kept it. I wish only your blessing for a safe journey back to *mi corazón,* to my new life. *Adios!"*

The Mexican *vaqueros* had worked assiduously, not only out of pride in their profession as men who knew how to work cattle, but also in memory of their companion who had fallen in the battle to save Windhaven Range. The Indian scout Simata, and Dave, Ned and Frank, along with Djamba and Lucas, and Lucien Edmond himself, had ridden beside them day after day, completing the branding and the tallying of the herd that would be driven to Santa Fe.

True to his word, Sangrodo arrived with twenty of his warriors, on the day before the drive was to begin. Luke Bouchard went out to meet him, and he saw that the Comanche chief's face was grave.

"I will not hold you to your pledge, Sangrodo, if it will deprive your stronghold of warriors you need for the hunt," he declared.

Sangrodo shook his head. "My brother, my stronghold numbers seventy warriors, more than twice as many women and children, to say nothing of the old men and the old women who sit around the fires and tell stories of Coyote and his cunning. And those warriors who remain in my stronghold are fierce hunters and have counted many scalps in the days of war. Now, thanks to you, we are at peace, but there are others who would destroy us. This is what I fear."

"Who would destroy you, Sangrodo?"

"A day's journey from our stronghold, there is a fort where soldiers live. It is on the east bank of the Leona, near the land where long ago my grandfather and his braves fought against a captain of the Mexicans who drove them to the rocky divide along the Llano River. I have been told his name by my father who had it from his father: Juan de Ugalde. And since then, they have called the canyon the *Cañon de Ugalde*, and now it is called Uvalde."

"And you say there is a soldier's fort there, Sangrodo?"

"That is true. Until now, there were men who wore the gray uniforms of your white-eyes brothers of the South, but your war is over and they long ago abandoned it. Now there are soldiers dressed in blue."

"Northerners, yes. But they are there because the North won the war of the white-eyes, Sangrodo, and they keep the peace. In a way, they are like the Rangers who once kept law and order in all of this vast country."

472

Again Sangrodo shook his head. "These soldiers in blue are not like the Rangers, this I know already. Their leader is a young man who does not think that the Comanche, the Kiowa, and the Apache should be allowed to live on the land which was always theirs. He has said so, a trader of goods who has been to the fort and who has come to our stronghold to bargain with us has told me this. And, if this captain sees as enemies we Comanches who are at peace with you because you are our blood brother, he may wish to strike all of us down, yes, even our old men and women, and our children. And that will be war between us and the white-eyes. You see me now—I do not wear the warpaint."

"I see that you come as my friend, Sangrodo."

"And what I feared would happen has happened already," the Comanche chief went on, his face solemn and drawn. "The killing of white-eyes men and women and even children, who came here as you did to settle upon the land, which was done by Norvito, this trader has said to me, has been marked against my people and me. It is true that Norvito was one of the Comanche tribes, but not mine; he was an outlaw and he hated all men. Yet because of his deeds what I fear is that this white-eyes captain with his soldiers will seek us out and try to drive us from our stronghold and from even the western land which my grandfather and his people once dwelt upon."

"Then," Luke Bouchard abruptly decided, "I shall not go on the cattle drive with my son, Sangrodo. My blacks and some of the *vaqueros* will stay here, and I will see that this new captain does not make war against you. I shall ride to your camp, to make certain it is secure, then meet with the soldiers."

"That is good. Truly you are my blood brother, *Taiboo Nimaihkana*." Sangrodo lifted his lance in salute. "Simata says that the bandits and the white-eyes who was the friend of that traitor who joined the followers of the mad dog Norvito attacked your stronghold."

"Yes, Sangrodo, but the Great Spirit smiled upon us and helped us defeat them. They will trouble us no more."

"That is good." Sangrodo stared compassionately at

Luke Bouchard, then softly added, "Simata has told me also that your squaw has been called to the sky. I sorrow with you, my brother."

"You are kind to say it, Sangrodo. She died trying to protect the little girl who is the daughter of my son's wife."

"The Great Spirit smiles upon her and already calls her the beloved woman, then."

At these words, Luke Bouchard trembled: well he remembered what his grandfather had told him of Dimarte and how the Creeks had called her by that gentle, revering name. He said at last, "She was indeed beloved, my blood brother."

"And Simata says also that two young squaws were taken in the battle. Perhaps the words of Mingride, when he threw the bones for you at our stronghold, will thus come true if you choose one of them as your new squaw."

"Oh no," Luke Bouchard shook his head, "they are very young girls, Sangrodo. The chief of the bandits killed their mother and took them with his men to use in deceiving us. They came to the gate and cried out that the Indians had killed their father and mother and that they wished us to help them, so that when we opened the gate, the bandits could fire upon us."

"It was a great sin to use them so, my blood brother."

"Yes, Sangrodo, but the sin was not theirs, and we are caring for them till they are strong again. Then one of my *vaqueros* will take them back to their village and perhaps the priest of the village will find them a new home where they can begin to forget the evil that was done to them."

"Ho, that is good. I respect you, *Taiboo Nimaihkana*."

"Then it is decided, Sangrodo. I shall stay here. I shall have ten good men who can ride with me to the fort and talk to this officer who seeks to drive you from your stronghold. I will tell him that you are at peace and that you do not threaten either his men or men like myself who settle on land and offer to share with you the bounty of it," Luke Bouchard spoke in the Comanche tongue.

Again Sangrodo lifted his lance in salute. "Then, my blood brother, I go back to the stronghold with a lighter heart. My men go with your cattle, as I pledged. My other braves and I will go on a hunt for the buffalo, but we will not go too close to the soldiers' fort. And one thing more I would tell you—you will pass near the land where Jutsi, chief of the Mescalero Apaches, dwells. It would be well for you to make him a present of cattle, so that he and his people will have meat and will look upon you with friendship."

"That's an excellent idea, Sangrodo. We have just made our tally of the herd we shall drive to Santa Fe, and I will tell my son Lucien Edmond to keep a hundred cattle for the chief of the Mescalero Apaches."

"For such a gift, he may even send some of his warriors to escort you back," Sangrodo jested, his strong face breaking into a broad grin. "You will cross the Pecos River on your way to Santa Fe. Before you reach there, there is the fort which you white-eyes call Sumner. The soldiers there will want your beef, and it may be that you can sell many hundreds to them."

"I will tell Lucien Edmond this, and again, all my thanks, my blood brother."

Sangrodo nodded, and then with a sly grin, added, "Jicinte is one of the warriors who will ride with your herd, *Taiboo Nimaihkana*. He has told me that he wishes to take a squaw, the woman of color who has taught Catayuna how to tell stories on the blankets that she makes for the village of Sangrodo."

"You mean Prissy," Luke Bouchard chuckled delightedly. "I've a hunch that when I tell her, she'll want to go along with Betty in the chuckwagon. Well then, my good friend, once more I give thanks to the Great Spirit that you are my friend, that you have helped me. I will have Lucien Edmond, as he drives the herd toward Santa Fe, take twenty-five of the cattle and send them into your stronghold so that you too will have meat for your cooking fires."

"Your gift is generous, my blood brother, and is welcome. Already the buffalo go to the west faster than even our ponies can track them down, and it may be, as Mingride says, that we must find a new stronghold before another winter comes upon us. I go back to the stronghold now, and may you walk tall in the sun always, *Tai-*

boo Nimaihkana." Once again the Comanche chief lifted his lance in salute, wheeled his mustang, shouting a command to his escort of twenty braves, and galloped toward the west.

Captain George Munson unbuttoned his sweaty coat, uttered a weary sigh, and stared dully at the rough draft of a map of Texas which he had found in one of the drawers of the desk that the Confederates left behind last September when they had at last realized the hopelessness of the Southern cause. His handsome face was sour with disappointment and boredom, and he for one was heartily sorry that the war was over.

Just twenty-nine years old, with curly shoulder-length hair, a neat Van Dyke beard, and a trim mustache of which he was inordinately proud, George Munson cursed the bad luck which had got him transferred to this miserable hellhole of a Fort Inge. True enough, it was a cavalry troop, but it comprised only a hundred men of whom only about seventy could be really considered fit for active patrol. The rest were the usual contingent of clerks, elderly quartermaster and drill instructor personnel, a consumptive doctor who had the rank of first lieutenant and whose connections in Washington and his own fierce pride had kept him in the service and got him transferred here from the East in the faint hope that the climate might cure him, and a few stablehands including a blacksmith who Captain Munson was sure wouldn't know how to fire a rifle if they were issued one.

Out of fretful pique, Munson crumpled the map in his hands and flung it to the floor. Already in March, the weather was intolerably hot, a far cry from his native New York state. It was his firm belief that there was no more desolate, damnable, useless post in the entire Union command than Fort Inge. And simply because he had made the blunder of courting a young lady who he thought preferred him to a fussy dandy of a major, he now found himself here instead of Washington or Baltimore or even New York. There would be no quadrilles or officers' parties here. And Betty Miles herself, the treacherous little bitch, had actually dared to complain to the major about

476

his "importunities." How was he to know that Major Ashby Donovan was a distant cousin of a brigadier general who could reach out and scribble his signature on a War Department order that would banish him to this God-forsaken, Indian-ridden, pestilential spot?

He had started the war as a lowly corporal in a platoon, shown some expertise with horses and got himself transferred to a cavalry unit. He'd even ridden with Phil Sheridan against J.E.B. Stuart in the attack against Richmond in which Stuart himself had been mortally wounded and his vaunted cavalry defeated. That had won him a first lieutenancy on the battlefield. All he'd sustained had been a slight saber cut in his left shoulder, and a bullet nick that had creased his right calf, after four years of bloody fighting. After Lee's surrender, he'd gone back home on furlough, and that's where he'd met Betty Miles and believed she was really fond enough of him to marry him. And then the world had collapsed when he'd been summoned before her major and two other high-ranking officers on the charge of—of all things!—attempted carnal misconduct unbecoming an officer.

Now, of course, looking back, he could see that it had been a filthy bluff for that gutless major to have called his friends in and threatened him with a court-martial on such a trumped-up charge. But he'd been so stunned to find out that Betty had played him false, that he'd acted like a whipped cur with its tail between its legs: he told the major that he'd accept duty elsewhere, that he'd made a mistake, that he certainly had never meant to force his attentions on Betty. Still, the upshot had been that he'd got a captaincy as a sop to his running up the white flag and then, just to make sure that he would never bother Betty or her major again, assignment out here. At least if it had been Fort Griffin, he could have tolerated it a little more. There was more action around there to the west, a better caliber of men to command, and plenty of dirty redskins to teach a lesson to. Captain George Munson had his own very definite ideas about Indians, and they were even more vitriolic than old Andrew Jackson's; his grandfather had been scalped by a Delaware brave and his mother had told him many stories as a boy of the savagery and bestiality of the Indians.

He glanced again at the formal order which had come through by courier from San Antonio just a week ago. He was to maintain the fort, rehabilitate it after the Confederate tenure, to keep his men alert, well drilled and to make certain that their horses were well cared for. There was nothing in that order which could lead to a promotion, not here. Not unless he protected the settlers against those damned Indians, and God knows there were plenty of them here in Texas: Comanches, Kiowa and Apaches, and other tribes whose names he was just beginning to learn and to hate as much as he hated the name of Delaware. And what settlers there were in this lonely southwestern part of Texas were likely to be nothing else than damned Johnny Rebs, still thinking they'd won the war, hiding out here where nobody could find them, certain to hate him and his men even if he saved them from the Indians. It was banishment pure and simple to be here, and there was absolutely nothing he could do about it. Even Major General Phil Sheridan, who had personally recommended him for that medal and battlefield promotion, couldn't get him out of this; not when he'd thrown himself like a sniveling coward on the mercy of those two officers and that son-of-a-bitch major simply because he'd seen right off the reel that if they'd wanted to, they could have got him drummed out of the Army and blacklisted for the rest of his life on those trumped-up charges.

At least there was enough to eat here at Fort Inge, thanks to plenty of wild game and fresh water. But so far, in the month and a half that he'd been here since receiving his field orders from the War Department in Washington, he'd had the sort of duty you could expect at a military school. No excitement, and of course not a woman in sight for God knows how many hundreds of miles. Damn Betty Miles to hell and gone.

Gloomily he reached down for the crumpled map he had discarded, smoothed it out on the desk and stared wearily at it again. If he could read the Confederate major's scrawl, it appeared that there was some kind of Indian village about forty miles southeast of here. Of course, everybody knew that Indians were always on the move, especially after they'd wiped out a wagon train or a little farm village of helpless settlers. Still and all, it wouldn't do any harm to check out that map. It would give the men something to do, help whip them in line. A surlier, more listless lot he'd never seen in all his days during the war. And if they came upon one of those murdering bands of Comanches and wiped them out, the news would get back to Washington as fast as he could telegraph it, maybe even reach Phil Sheridan himself, and get him a major's oak leaf and a new command in some civilized part of this country.

Just as Luke Bouchard had predicted, Prissy, seeing that Jicinte was one of the braves who would escort the herd of longhorns on to Santa Fe, insisted that she go with Betty to help preside over the chuckwagon. And when Jicinte, his homely face beaming with pleasure—for just as he had taught her many Comanche words, so she in turn had taught him English—heard her declare to her mother Celia that she wouldn't take no for an answer, he dismounted and hesitantly approached the mulatto woman.

With great humor, Celia eyed her daughter and then the Comanche brave, and said to Prissy, "Are you sure now, girl? If you are, you're going to have to tell this redskin that I want you to come back an honest woman. There'll be a priest in Santa Fe, and I suppose you'll probably have to marry him Comanche style when you get back, but you're going to promise me that you'll have a proper marriage at the end of the drive."

"Oh yes, Mother, oh thank you, Mother!" Prissy happily exclaimed, and then, greatly to Jicinte's embarrassment and the snickering of his mounted tribesmen, went up to him and hugged him.

"Well, I guess that about decides it. Pack what gear you'll need, because the herd's ready to move. And one thing more," Celia warningly shook her forefinger at her smiling daughter, "there'll be no blanket sharing till after you two come out of the church in Santa Fe, just understand that, girl."

Then it was Prissy's turn to blush and hang her head, while the *vaqueros* chuckled and called out compliments to the attractive quadroon. Luke, mounted on his horse, said to Lucien Edmond, "I'll ride with you as far as Sangrodo's stronghold and deliver the twenty-five cattle I promised him, then you'll be on your own, my son."

"I can handle it, Father. The *vaqueros* and Andy and Joe have been running a small part of the herd for a few days just in practice, and they tell me that if I don't have any problems with stampedes or really bad weather, I ought to be able to average fifteen miles a day. Let's see now, that would mean about forty days to reach Santa Fe, give or take a few."

"Perhaps it would be as well to enter the money in a new account in the bank at Santa Fe, Lucien Edmond," Luke Bouchard counseled. "That's just in case there isn't any railroad to the northwest by the time next year's drive rolls around. From what I've been told, Santa Fe is a thriving market and a very old one."

"Yes, Father. Well, any time you're ready. See, even Jubal is going with us!"

Indeed, Jubal was already barking impatiently, running back and forth, eager to signal his readiness to herd the stragglers back into line as he had been so well taught.

"You've got plenty of food for the extra men, Lucien Edmond?"

"Yes, Father. Plenty of flour, beans, molasses, bacon, coffee, salt, and kegs of water just in case we run into a dry spell. But Sangrodo told me that we'll find plenty of water for the cattle all along the trail, except for one or two bad places, and there's grazing land to the west, so we ought to put quite a few pounds on those bony steers before they get to Santa Fe."

"Fine. And you've got plenty of extra horses for your *remuda*?"

"Ramon advised me to take along at least five horses for each of the *vaqueros*. And of course I've added a few extra for Sangrodo's braves. I've made Felipe Rodriguez and his brother Manuel the point riders, to go up front ahead of this big herd and lead them in the right direction.

We've got a couple of tame steers that the rest of the herd seems likely to follow."

"Good, good! You're taking six of the *vaqueros* and the twenty braves, so you'll have plenty of swing riders. And what's your final tally, Lucien Edmond?"

"Pablo Toldanos just gave it to me, Father. It's thirty-three hundred forty exactly."

"Less the twenty-five for Sangrodo and the hundred for the Mescalero Apaches, of course. But I'd say that before you reach Santa Fe you'll probably have a few additions. That reminds me—are you adding at least one extra wagon for the new calves that are likely to be dropped before you finish the trail, Lucien Edmond?"

"Two extra wagons, Father."

"Then everything's in order." Luke swung back in his saddle to wave to Sybella, Mara, Maxine and Carla and Hugo, who stood on the porch of the *hacienda*. Ramon Hernandez, sombrero in hand, stood beside Corita and glanced adoringly at the lovely black-haired young woman who was soon to be his bride. At peace with the world, his last misgivings removed by his conversation with old *Padre* Antonio, he was impatiently counting the days when Mara would become *Señora* Ramon Hernandez.

Lucien Edmond waved his sombrero and galloped along the restless herd far ahead to where the two *vaqueros* rode the points. It was the signal to begin, and Luke Bouchard, riding slowly alongside the last Comanche who acted as swing rider at the tail end of the huge herd, smiled exultantly to see with what enthusiasm and determination his son had assumed the role of foreman and drover. One of the *vaqueros,* turning toward a huge clump of mesquite, shouted and slapped his sombrero against his chaps, and a heifer, mooing discontentedly, wheeled out of the mesquite and docilely trotted back into the orderly herd. Clouds of dust rose from the cattle's hooves far along the trail, but this was a new trail, the very first taken from Windhaven Range, and for Luke Bouchard it was immensely satisfying.

The *vaqueros* were picturesque, with their bright red bandannas above their collarless shirts, sitting straight in their saddles, heavy and broad of horn, each with double cinches, their stirrups covered with metal discs. The *reatas* at each saddle-horn were thin, of closely braided hide, pliable and tough as steel. All of them had their own newly purchased rifles or carbines strapped alongside their saddles, with holstered six-shooters at their belts. And several of the Comanche braves whom Sangrodo had sent as escorts for the herd had old Sharps rifles which had once been used by Confederate soldiers.

At the end of the second day, Luke Bouchard and one of the *vaqueros* diverted twenty-five long-horned cows and steers into the stronghold of Sangrodo, and the *vaquero*, saying his farewell, saluted the founder of Windhaven Range as he rode back to join the others.

A few of the oldest braves had remained in the stronghold at Sangrodo's order to take charge of the cattle and to drive them into a hastily constructed corral. Luke dismounted and approached the tepee of Catayuna Arvilas who, having heard the sounds of the cattle as they entered their new enclosure, came out to meet him. She wore buckskin jacket and skirt, her feet thrust into beaded moccasins, her hair slicked back and twisted into a long braid, Comanche style. The sun had bronzed her magnificent dusky skin, and he would have taken her for a Comanche squaw had he not known who she was.

"The men of the village have gone on the buffalo hunt, *Señor* Bouchard," she told him. "Sangrodo says it will be a week, maybe two. The buffalo have gone to the west. But he is glad that you have brought this meat for the people."

"And you, Catayuna, how goes it with you?" he solicitously asked.

"*Bueno, Señor* Bouchard. I accustom myself to my new life. I have no other choice, but at least I am not a slave any longer." She looked down at her moccasin-shod feet, then regarded him intently with those great lustrous eyes. "It is you I have to thank for that, *Señor* Bouchard. How kind it was of you to send Prissy here to show me how to weave. I remember my grandmother did it, but as a little girl I had no time for such things. My mother planned a wonderful life for me, I would wed a rich man and have many servants so that I need not concern myself with the

482

affairs of the household except to rule over it. And now—" She shrugged, scanning the tepees of the stronghold, seeing the old women and children at their tasks, playing, talking, and she sighed, "My mother was right, for I married Arvilas, and I had servants, but I was a barren wife to him, though I prayed the Holy Virgin to give me a child."

"But your life is only beginning, Catayuna. Sangrodo respects you, and the blankets and the other things you have woven which tell the story of this village will be handed down long after you, and others who follow you will tell the story of the proud woman who gave up one life to begin another."

"Perhaps that is true, Señor Bouchard. It is strange—I can no longer hate him. I have prayed many times at night when all the others have gone to sleep to understand why this is. I loved Arvilas, I suppose because I had never known any other man and because I was betrothed to him since I was fourteen. I think now how little I knew of him and of the others in my village, and perhaps I begin to understand why it was that I was captured. The old hatreds, the old vengeances, they are like things in a story book until they happen to you. And then you are helpless and you do not know why they have touched you and made you a part of them."

"I think that is God's doing, Catayuna. I myself do not know what will happen to my life now that my wife is dead."

Her lips formed a soft, compassionate curve, as she slowly nodded. "Sangrodo told me. I will pray for her, Señor Bouchard. She did not suffer?"

"No, Catayuna. We had many years together, good happy years, and I wish only that she might have lived to see how well our son takes hold on this new land in his new life."

"She will know in heaven, Señor Bouchard, of that you may be sure."

"I believe that, Catayuna. But I came also to warn you and the others. Sangrodo has told me of the Union soldiers in Fort Inge, and how their commander has no love for Indians. As soon as I go back, I shall bring my *pis-*

toleros and ride to them and tell them that there is no better friend and ally than Sangrodo, chief of the Comanches of this stronghold."

"That will be a good thing, *Señor* Bouchard. I know how my people feared the Comanches, and yours must fear them also when they come here for the first time. But I do not think that soldiers will make war on old men and women and children."

"I pray God they will not, Catayuna, and I shall do everything in my power to make sure it does not happen. *Adios*, and may good things happen to you."

"*Vaya con Dios, Señor* Bouchard," she gravely told him, respectfully inclining her head, and then went back into the tepee.

CHAPTER FORTY-TWO

Luke Bouchard rode back to Windhaven Range as soon as he had delivered the twenty-five Texas longhorns to Sangrodo's stronghold, and, hardly stopping for rest or food, reached the *hacienda* by mid-morning of the next day. He had the brooding presentiment that the presence of Union soldiers at Fort Inge threatened the peaceful alliance, which he had been able to effect with this tribe of Comanches. Indeed, they had stayed longer at their stronghold than most tribes would have done, and the reason had been mainly because of his having shared his cattle with them, as well as other provisions from time to time.

Yet in a sense the Union troops menaced his own peace of mind for the security and well-being of his family: Texas had not yet been declared by President Johnson as entitled to representation in the Congress, since it had not yet complied with Presidential requirements in electing Federal representatives and senators and shaping its state constitution to fit the Northern demands for acceptable Reconstruction. That being so, the troops at Fort Inge, particularly if they were under the command of an inimical officer, might well regard the Bouchards as only another contingent of displaced secessionists.

And that was why, as soon as he reached home, he summoned a council of the defenders of Windhaven Range.

"I'm going to ask for volunteers to go with me to Sangrodo's stronghold and to see if we can head off the new commander at Fort Inge," he declared. "Sangrodo has taken the rest of his braves on a buffalo hunt, and there is no one left to defend his stronghold. The new commander has no love for Indians of any tribe, and I fear that he and his soldiers may ride in on that village and find it undefended and so attack it."

"I think you are right, Mr. Bouchard," Simata gravely agreed. "I know well how many white-eyes fear the red man, because he is first upon the land and tries to keep it because it was his from the beginning. My father told me many times how the white-eyes would make treaties and promise peace, only to break their word. It is a bad thing. I will ride with you."

"I too, *Señor* Bouchard," Jose Martinez spoke up, scowling and twisting his ornate mustache, a characteristic gesture when he was excited.

"My old pappy used to tell me how they ran the Injuns out of the South," one-armed Andy Haskins spoke up. "There were the Creeks and the Chickasaws, the Cherokees and the Seminoles. Seems like to me they minded their own business pretty well until the settlers tried to push them around."

"That's true, Andy," Luke Bouchard assented. "In my grandfather's day, it was true because President Jackson had no love for any of the Indian tribes. And as Simata says, treaties were made with them, they were promised land in the west, they were given certificates which dishonest traders and speculators stole from them in exchange for trinkets or a bottle of whiskey, and they were herded like so many cattle on the long march to what was to be called Indian Territory. I can foresee that when the railroads start to build across the plains and create new markets to which cattle can be driven to reach the big new Stock Yards in Chicago and other markets in the East, they'll be moved again to even less desirable land."

"But this Texas is so big, Mr. Bouchard," Lucas earnestly argued. "Don't you think it's possible for the government to work out some sort of peace treaty between the Indians who were here first and the people who are moving in?"

"Treaties are pieces of paper, Lucas, worth only the honesty and the integrity of the people who make them. So long as there are men who are greedy for land at any price, so long as they are in power and make those treaties, the Indians will be cheated. It won't be long before Texas is admitted back into the Union, and when that happens, there'll be plenty of settlers from the North wanting the good fertile land here. And that will mean that the Comanches and the Kiowas and the Apaches and the Navahos and all the other tribes here in the southwest will have to move or fight—and I'm afraid they'll fight to defend what they sincerely believe belongs to them, just as you or I would to keep this land of ours which we believe we bought fairly and in the doing of it deprived no one. That was why I was eager to meet Sangrodo and to see that he and his people had food when their hunting was not successful so that they would understand that we did not come to steal their birthright from them."

"Ah wants to go 'long with you, Mistah Bouchard suh," old George spoke up. He had learned of Prissy's decision to marry Jicinte and he was plainly heartbroken, his face long and morose, his voice saddened and self-pitying.

"It's a bit too strenuous for you, George, but if you can still ride a horse forty or fifty miles and not hold us up, I've no objection at all. You'd better pick yourself a gentle horse and saddle it up and come along with us, and don't forget to bring a six-shooter," Luke Bouchard smilingly directed. "We still have a dozen Spencer repeating rifles and the five carbines, and a half-dozen six shooters. So all of you are coming, is that it?" For all the men in the bunkhouse had nodded. "Well, that makes a round dozen with myself as the baker's dozen, then. William's busy in the *hacienda,* and I am sure he can take care of things. We're not likely to be under any attack for a while, anyhow, not with the bandits driven off and Norvito's band permanently put out of circulation. Let's mount up, then."

Half an hour later, Luke Bouchard led the way towards Sangrodo's stronghold, followed by Ramon Hernandez, Djamba, Lucas, Simata, Andy Haskins and Joe Duvray, Dave, Frank, Ned, Carl, Jose and white-haired George, for whom Simata had picked the gentlest of the mares.

It was time, Captain George Munson decided, to find out a good deal more about the terrain which his fort was supposed to guard. The weeks of inactivity had worn his nerves to the breaking point. The war was over, there were no Southerners left to fight, but there were Indians whose very presence menaced the safety of those farmers and ranchers who would be sure to come from the North. He was weary already of sending weekly reports to Washington of how his lackluster days were spent in rehabilitating a fort which the Confederates had occupied for so long. And his restless men were every bit as miserable as he in this barren, unpromising pinpoint on the map.

Besides, a little hard riding and some alert surveillance would do these malingerers a world of good. He had just about come to the conclusion that out of sheer malice aforethought, the War Department had assigned him an outfit most of whom had had disciplinary problems and very narrowly escaped genuinely deserved court-martial. There was Corporal Hosmer Turlow, a sullen blond lout in his early thirties who had twice lost his sergeant's stripes for insubordination, and who had a hair-trigger temper. He had already spent four days in the military barracks for having broken the jaw of Private Abe Denton, who had twitted him about his reputation as a lover. Unfortunately, the joke had been in the very worst of taste so far as Corporal Hosmer Turlow was concerned; he had been discharged from his Pennsylvania regiment and gone back home to Philadelphia only to find that his fiancée, who had written him ardent letters declaring her eternal fidelity all through the war, was pregnant by her elderly civilian paramour. After beating up the civilian, he had re-enlisted and got sergeant's stripes at once, only to lose them in a drunken brawl in an off-limits tavern with three corporals from a rival regiment.

There was Second Lieutenant Evan Brodie, a tall, black-haired man of twenty-eight, who had been a captain at the outset of the war and broken down to a mere private after Bull Run because of a misinterpretation of a dispatch from his commanding officer to fortify a certain position. He had distinguished himself in subsequent battles enough to win a promotion to a first lieutenancy, gone back home after the war to discover that his older brother had gambled away the farm and the money of which he was to have had a rightful half. His re-enlistment had been celebrated by a classic week of drunkenness, which had dropped him down a military notch and promptly got him sent out to Fort Inge. He was probably the best officer under Captain Munson's command so far as knowing the intricate details of military procedure, but he was taciturn and morose and went for weeks without speaking to his fellow officers or the enlisted men.

And then there was his ranking officer, First Lieutenant Leopold Turner, a bespectacled, dapper young man of twenty-six who had managed to keep safely out of combat all through the war by being assigned to the Quartermaster Corps by a doting uncle who happened to be a major general on Grant's staff. He had arrived at Fort Inge with a trunkful of books, and spent his nights assiduously reading them. Self-consciously aware of his lack of military aggressiveness, First Lieutenant Turner hoped to assimilate enough strategy and tactics from his reading to reflect glory on his uncle. Every Friday afternoon, Captain George Munson staged target practice for the officers as well as the enlisted men, and First Lieutenant Turner was undeniably the worst shot in the outfit.

The only man in whom Captain George Munson felt much confidence was his top sergeant, Fred Wilton, forty, stocky, his sun-browned face made even more melancholy by a huge walrus mustache. Fred Wilton was a Kansan, and he had been a private in the army of General Zachary "Old Rough and Ready" Taylor on that memorable day of January 13, 1846 when President James Polk had given orders to advance the American forces from the

Nueces River to the Rio Grande. He had gone back to Emporia and married his school sweetheart, seen her and his two boys die of milk fever, and re-enlisted in time to see action through all four years of the war between the North and the South. Fred Wilton had never been given to heroics, had never won any medals, but his superior officers had thought well enough of him during his soldiering to give him a master sergeant's stripes, and now, with the cessation of hostilities, learning of his familiarity with Texas from his record in the Mexican War, had assigned him to Fort Inge. If only for the accuracy of his paperwork, Fred Wilton's status as the top ranking non-commissioned soldier was the one bright spot on an otherwise dismal roster so far as Captain George Munson was concerned.

And that was why, this March morning, brooding over his fate, Captain George Munson left his office and stood before the desk of Corporal David Sedgewick, a pimply-faced, lean, conscientious, twenty-five-year-old recruit from Massachusetts who was his personal orderly.

"Go find Sergeant Wilton, Corporal," he barked. The swift scrambling of his orderly from the desk and the frantically hasty salute lifted Captain George Munson's flagging spirits; by God, he was going to see some action today or know the reason why.

"You sent for me, Captain?" Fred Wilton stiffened to attention and saluted smartly. His superior's face brightened with a satisfied smile: a response like this reminded him of the glory days back during the Wilderness campaign, and the hell-bent-for-leather chasing down of old Jeb Stuart's will-o'-the-wisp cavalry.

"Yes, Sergeant, I did. I want you to assemble as many fit men as can ride thirty or forty miles, get them out there with their horses, saddled up, provisions issued for at least two days, and ready to patrol," he ordered.

"Right away, Captain. Would the Captain care to tell me where the men will be headed for, sir?"

"I've taken a look at the Confederates' map, Sergeant, and there's something about a Comanche band roving around these parts. I want to find out if they're still around because they're likely to cause trouble. Murdering devils, all of them."

"Yes, sir," Sergeant Fred Wilton stolidly assented. "You'll be wanting the men to carry side arms as well as rifles and sabers, then?"

"Naturally. On the double, Sergeant!"

Once again Captain George Munson was gratified to see the smart salute, to see the sergeant wheel, click his boots together and, a few moments later, blow his whistle and bawl, "All right, you lazy goldbrickers, you're going to start earning your pay. On the double, boots and saddles!"

Captain George Munson rose, turned to stare with satisfaction at his own reflection in a dusty mirror at one end of his office. Then, going to the closet, he took out his pistol holster and saber belt, and then strode outside, where one of the stablehands sullenly stood by holding the reins of the roan mare which Captain Munson had named "Betty" out of spiteful pique.

Mounting the mare, he moved to the head of the line, turned back to Sergeant Wilton and demanded, "Ready on muster, Sergeant?"

"That's right, sir. Thirty-two men, not counting the officers, sir."

"Very good, Sergeant. Lieutenant Turner, give the orders to move out!"

The gates of the fort were opened and Captain George Munson led his contingent forward, heading southeast and in the direction of Sangrodo's stronghold. It was a full day's journey, and the sun was already beating down on the uniformed soldiers with their full packs of provisions and arms. There was glowering and muttering in the ranks, but Captain George Munson paid no heed to that. Everybody knew that soldiers grumbled; when they didn't, he'd been told, then was the time to worry. By God, he'd wake them up and show them some action if he had to go looking for it, he told himself.

At nightfall, the cavalry troup bivouacked, on a rolling little hill crested with cedar, live oak and some cypress trees. It had been a hot, hard ride, with no sight of hostiles in any direction. Nor were the men happy over the order that there were to be no fires, no coffee, no smoking. They had to make do with hard tack and jerky, and some of the salted meat was already beginning to turn rank. Indeed, at the mess hall the past week, some of the men had been profanely outspoken about the quality of provender being served them, declaring that even in a Federal prison they would eat better than at Fort Inge. Nor were their tempers mollified when, just before making camp, Sergeant Wilton had drawn his six-shooter and killed a rattlesnake coiled and sunning itself on the jagged flat rock at the base of the little hill.

Captain George Munson found it difficult to sleep, and paced back and forth, clasping his hands behind his back and scowling, unconsciously imitating the behavior of General Phil Sheridan just before the decision to attack Richmond. The night was still, only the occasional fretful call of a nightbird or the lonely wail of a distant coyote breaking the silence and the undertone of the troopers' whispered remarks. He had seen to it that they did not raise their voices above a whisper; a sudden tingling excitement had taken possession of him, just as it had before he had ridden into action behind his adored general. Perhaps tomorrow would bring the chance he'd hoped and prayed for, a daring attack on hostiles that would make the territory safe for settlers, prove once and for all that it was an injustice to maroon a courageous and imaginative cavalry leader like himself out here in a wilderness.

Once again the sun was hot at the very break of morning, as they saddled up and continued their journey. A little before noon, Lorimanta, the wizened Kiowa Apache scout whom Captain George Munson had inherited from his Confederate predecessor, rode back at a gallop toward the troop and pointed in the direction of the distant stronghold which he had just spied.

"Comanche, many tepees, maybe hundred, maybe more live there," he grunted in his guttural English.

"We'll take them by surprise," Captain George Munson tugged at the point of his beard, his eyes sparkling with animation. "Sergeant Wilton, have the men make sure

492

their weapons are loaded and ready, and draw sabers as we reach that village Lorimanta has just reported."

"Sir?"

The questioning note in Sergeant Wilton's voice made the blond officer turn in his saddle with a vexed scowl: "Anything wrong, Sergeant?"

"I mean, sir, not questioning orders, but are we going to fight them? We don't even know if they're hostile or peaceable, do we, sir?"

Captain George Munson glared at the stolid non-commissioned officer: "All Indians in this part of the country are presumed to be hostile, Sergeant. Maybe you haven't heard of the raids of the chief called Norvito, wiping out little farms and ranches, carrying off women, killing children. Well, I have. That's why I'm in command. Do what I told you to!"

"It might be wise, Captain," Second Lieutenant Evan Brodie mildly spoke up as he drew his horse abreast his superior's, "to have Lorimanta go close enough to the Indian village to see how many braves are there. They might just be off on a hunt, and they'd have only the old ones and the women and kids left behind."

"When I want your advice, Lieutenant Brodie, I'll ask for it. Troop, forward ho!" Drawing his saber, Captain George Munson brandished it aloft and then galloped forward. With a sigh, the second lieutenant shrugged, then gave the signal for the enlisted men to follow with sabers drawn.

As they neared the northern side of the escarpment, Lorimanta halted his horse and gesticulated excitedly. "Men come, white-eyes, not Indian," he called out.

"What the devil!" Captain George Munson angrily exclaimed. "You say they're white men?"

"Yes, white-eyes with long guns, they come toward us now," the scout gestured again. With an oath, the blond captain unbuckled the case of field glasses strapped around his neck, adjusted them and swore again: "Damnation, there's a dozen or thirteen of them, and you're right, they've got rifles and carbines! Might be a band of Johnny Rebs, planning to start the war all over again! Get your side arms ready, and watch for my signal."

Luke Bouchard rode forward now, holding up his hand in a sign of peace, and approached the fuming commander of Fort Inge. "My name's Luke Bouchard, Captain," he said without any preamble. "I'd hoped to head you off before you got to Sangrodo's stronghold."

"Who the devil are you? The name means nothing to me. A secessionist, I'll be bound," was the surly answer.

"Not entirely, Captain. All I did in the war was to furnish food, and I've bought my land near Carrizo Springs and I'm raising cattle. Sangrodo's at peace with the whites, and he and his men are off on a buffalo hunt. There's no one in the village except the elderly and the women and children. The way your troop has its weapons at the ready, I was afraid you might be contemplating some rash action."

"Rash action?" Captain George Munson's voice rose shrilly in his thwarted fury. "You call Comanches peaceful? Mister, I'm commander at Fort Inge, and my orders are to keep this territory safe against murdering Indians. You're dealing with the United States Army, mister, and I'll thank you to mind your own business."

"These people are my business. They helped me rescue my son's wife from a renegade band of Comanches, Norvito's."

"I've heard of him, but this Sangrodo can't be much better."

"That's where you're wrong, Captain. Norvito and his men are dead. And there were a few Comanchero friends of his who did a little killing and looting themselves and left signs so that people would think it was all done by the Comanches. I can personally vouch for Sangrodo. He's sent twenty of his men to escort my herd to Santa Fe and to Fort Sumner to furnish good beef to soldiers like you. For that matter, if your men need meat, I'll be glad to let them have cattle at a fair price."

"That's not the question at the moment, Mr. Bouchard," Captain George Munson's temper was noticeably fraying at the edges. "I don't know you from Adam, and I'm not taking a Southerner's word that any Comanches are peaceful. If we find any braves with weapons in

494

that village, we'll take steps to make them permanently peaceful, if you get my meaning."

Luke Bouchard cocked his Spencer rifle, sitting quietly in his saddle and placing the gun across his lap with the barrel aimed at the blond officer. "Understand me, Captain," he said calmly, "I'm not one to defy the Federal government. I'm as loyal to the United States as you are. No one more than I deplored the needless bloodshed of the four years our country's just been through. But I tell you that if you massacre the innocents in that village, I'll personally shoot you down out of hand. Because that's what it would be, massacre pure and simple. There's not a brave left there with any weapon, and old men and women and children aren't any menace to you and your soldiers or to us settlers."

"Are you threatening me, Mr. Bouchard?"

"If it comes to that, yes. If you'll look around, you'll see that my men have carbines and rifles and six-shooters, plenty of ammunition, and they're all expert marksmen. Don't provoke a fight needlessly. Go back to your fort and try to make peace, instead of wanting to kill those who would never raise a weapon against you in the first place. I've made a treaty with Sangrodo and his men, and I've kept it and he's kept his word all these months. I'd trust him sooner than I would a soldier with a gun in his hand and murder in his heart."

Captain George Munson looked back at his troop, gnawing his underlip, his eyes narrowed and bright with fury. A glance back at Luke Bouchard and his riders told him that despite having nearly three times as many men, he was woefully outnumbered when it came to fire power.

"Very well," he grudgingly conceded, his voice trembling with anger, "all right, Mr. Bouchard. You win for now. I guess I'll have to take your word that this Sangrodo and his braves aren't in the village. But I'm going to keep a watch for them, and if they come by the fort and they look as if they're on the warpath, you'd best stay out of it. They'll be hostiles, and the Army deals with hostiles in just one way."

"If they attack you, that's a different story. Then it'll be out of my hands and in the hands of God. And now, Captain, I'd feel a lot easier and so would my men, if you'd order your troop back to Fort Inge," Luke Bouchard gravely declared.

Captain George Munson stared at the tall graying founder of Windhaven Range. Then, cursing under his breath, he wheeled his roan mare round, again flourished his saber, and gave the order for his men to follow.

CHAPTER FORTY-THREE

His lips tightened, his face red with the intolerable shame of having been discountenanced in front of his own men, Captain George Munson rode stiffly back toward Fort Inge. His mind raged within him. His first command, and he had backed down to a damned Johnny Reb! What colossal nerve that aristocratic bastard had had, sitting there so calmly and actually threatening to shoot him, Captain George Munson, down, and he an officer in the victorious Northern Army which had taught those traitorous secessionists a good lesson.

But those rifles and carbines were the latest issue, he'd seen at a glance, and most of his men had only single-shot rifles and the clumsy six-shooters. It would have been sheer insanity to have risked a shoot-out; half of his men would have been killed before any of them could have got off any retaliatory fire at all. And the smug self-assurance, the galling conceit of that damned Johnny Reb, that dirty Indian-lover, actually daring to tell him to go back to the fort and mind his own business, as if he were preaching a sermon on a Sunday to a schoolboy!

As he sheathed his saber, he could hear the faint murmuring behind him. He could imagine what the troopers were saying to one another, that their commanding officer didn't have any guts, that he'd backed down at the first show of a fight. It was already hell enough to be abandoned out here, his chances for promotion just about nonexistent, and now it was going to be infinitely worse. Every time he came out to lead the troop on maneuvers, there'd be knowing looks, whispered innuendos, disrespectful snickers—he could imagine what they'd say in the mess hall tonight. And if an officer like Brodie took it into his head to write some of his friends back in Washington about what had happened this morning, he might even find himself summoned before an honest-to-God court-martial, stripped of his rank and pay, his life over before he was even thirty.

He halted his mare, looked back around. The tiny figures of Luke Bouchard and his riders had all but disappeared on the horizon. By God, he'd send a courier to Austin and find out if that Luke Bouchard was lying about buying land and settling down here like an honest citizen. Honest be damned, talking about a Comanche chief as if he were an equal, calling him peaceful—it made a man want to upchuck!

As he was about to turn to signal the troop forward, First Lieutenant Leopold Turner rode up and gave him a slow salute, his homely face quizzical. "What is it, Turner?" he growled.

"Begging your pardon, Captain, are we just going to ride back to the fort and do nothing?"

"Damn it, Turner, are you questioning my command? I outrank you, don't forget it. Would you have wanted me to tell the men to fire, when those bastards had their Spencers cocked and ready to mow us down? Sabers and six-shooters and single-shot rifles aren't much good when a bunch of fools with those repeaters have the drop on us, you know," his voice dripped with vicious sarcasm.

"But they're out of sight now, Captain, what's to stop us going back and doing what you came out to do?" his first lieutenant persisted.

The blond captain stared intently at his ranking second; he was well aware of Turner's background and influence, enviously aware of it, for that matter. And what if Turner took it into his head to write his uncle a letter about what he'd just seen and heard? "I take it you feel the way I do, then, Turner," he shrewdly hazarded.

"Yes sir. We came out here to drive off the Comanches, didn't we? Let's give those Rebs time enough to get back where they belong, and then go have ourselves a look-see. If it's true what he said about their men going off hunting, we won't have to worry about being attacked, will we, sir?"

"That's right, Turner." Captain George Munson permitted himself a crafty smile. By God, he'd show that damned Johnny Reb! And he'd let the men think he'd planned it this way all along, to pretend to buckle in to that Bouchard fellow, and then go on in and do what he'd come out to do in the first place. That way, the troop would have to admit they had a commanding officer with some gumption.

"All right, Turner. For your information, I didn't want to risk any of the men's lives in a fight with settlers. They're white the way we are, and the war is over. If I'd fired on them, now that the peace was signed at Appomattox, it would be a critical incident and could lead to the outbreak of hostilities again, you see that, don't you?"

"Oh, yes sir!" Turner's face was glowing with enthusiasm.

"Then tell the men my plan. We're to rest here a bit till we're sure those Johnny Rebs are well out of the way, and then we'll skirt that Comanche village to the south and go in and destroy it."

"You mean, burn the wigwams or whatever it is they live in?"

"I mean, destroy it, Turner. That's clear enough, isn't it? Tell the men we'll go back southeast in about ten minutes."

"Very good, Captain!" First Lieutenant Leopold Turner gave him the smartest salute he'd had since he walked into the office at Fort Inge to take over his new command, and rode back to Sergeant Fred Wilton. He saw the walrus-mustached non-commissioned officer squint at him, shake his head, then turn to talk to Turner, saw Tur-

499

ner talking back with an earnestness and authority that he'd never shown before. Good! If that veteran of the Mexican War could be convinced that he'd figured this out all along, the rest of the men would follow him hell-bent for glory.

Catayuna Arvilas looked up from her loom and smiled at Namine, the plump, good-natured wife of Sangrodo who at first had been her chief tormentress and was now her understanding friend. "You like it, Namine?" she held up a section of the blanket she was weaving.

"Ho, it is very good. It is he, riding with his braves, driving his enemies before him," Namine agreed. "You are happier now?"

The handsome Mexican widow nodded. "I am no longer a slave, therefore I am happy," she said in laconic words which she had painstakingly learned. At first, learning the harsh Comanche tongue, for which there was no help in her native language, no root or source to grope for, was extremely difficult. She had learned the language in order to distract herself, early in her captivity. But now it was with keen interest that she had mastered the Comanche tongue, for it brought her back into the world of the living, let her understand the feelings of the women around her and know what their lives were and how they adapted to the arduous toil extracted from them.

"It is more than that," Namine murmured. "I know. I have been his squaw for fifteen years now, and though I am barren, he treats me often like a friend, sharing his thoughts with me, learning mine. I tell you, woman, what he feels for you now is neither hatred nor possession. What you have done here with your fingers and that strange thing on which they work has given him much pride. Even Mingride, the old shaman, says that your coming was foretold and that there will be life out of the death which marked your coming here."

"But perhaps he will give me to one of the warriors," Catayuna persisted.

Namine shook her head, a wry smile curving the corners of her mouth, then quickly vanishing. "He will not do that. No other warrior would dare ask for you now.

You are set apart from the others because of what you have done to tell his deeds and his courage by these pictures made of threads. And this peace which he has made with the white-eyes whom we call *Taiboo Nimaihkana,* that is something I have never known before of Sangrodo. In a way, you have brought this about, and for this too he honors you."

As Namine's eyes lingered on Catayuna's expressive, lovely face, the Mexican widow lowered her eyes and felt herself blushing violently, much to her perturbation. It was strange now that when Sangrodo entered her tepee, she felt not the slightest hatred, and it seemed that even the death of her husband had been blotted out of her mind and that this Comanche had become the very center of her life. And yet exactly because she did not know what he intended for her, there were times when she found herself alternating between an almost impatient anguish to know his will and a gnawing fear that what he wished would be to cast her to one of his braves as a prize for having counted a great coup in battle or on the hunt.

Namine shook her head, and now her smile was gently evident: "I can read your thoughts. Sangrodo will not give you to any warrior. You know our custom, that men take several wives, often sisters, and sometimes there is jealousy between them. If it should be that he would wish you to become his squaw, I should not be your enemy but your friend. And Kitante has told me that you are kind to him, that you talk to him as if already he were full grown and a warrior."

Catayuna Arvilas fought against the growing confusion within her at these benevolent words. "He is a fine strong boy with a good mind. He is resourceful. And in a way, Namine, it was he who brought about the peace between the white-eyes and Sangrodo in running away to prove that he was already a man."

"Yes, that is true." Namine suddenly started, her eyes widening with alarm. "But look! White-eyes come, on horseback, in blue coats—I am afraid!"

Captain George Munson reined in his mare and held up his hand to halt the troopers as they approached the entry to the Comancheria. "Pistols and sabers ready! Marksmen, have your rifles ready at command!" he called.

The Kiowa Apache scout Lorimanta rode up beside him, squinting at the tepees in their rows on either side. "Sangrodo hunts. There are no braves here, just as the white-eyes stranger said," he muttered.

"So much the better," the blond officer irritably declared. "Who's that old man, coming out, shaking his rattles?" For Mingride had emerged from his tepee, shaking the bag of bones in his left hand, and the rattles of a snake in the other, his face solemn with anger.

"That medicine man," Lorimanta asserted. "he make sign, go in peace. Comanches not at war with white-eyes soldiers."

"Oh, does he now?" Captain George Munson sneered. Unholstering his pistol, he fired into the air. "Let's just see if any Comanches are skulking around waiting to ambush us. Be ready, men!"

Once again Mingride shook the bag and the rattles, then gestured toward the entry of the Comancheria, swept his arms wide, lifted his face to the bright cloudless sky.

At this moment, Namsi-kohtoo emerged from his father's tepee, and, seeing the assembled cavalry troop, uttered a cry of anger. Seizing his bow and drawing an arrow from the quiver strapped to his back, he notched it and sent it flying toward Captain George Munson. It fell fifty feet too short, but Corporal Hosmer Turlow, with an oath, dragged his rifle out of its scabbard, quickly leveled it and pulled the trigger. There was a cry of surprise and pain as the boy, still clutching his bow, tottered, took a step backwards, then bowed his head and sprawled on the ground before the tepee. His left hand moved fitfully back toward the quiver of arrows, and then halted forever.

"Attack!" the blond officer cried, and galloped his horse forward toward the old shaman. Mingride stood fearlessly as the roan mare thundered down on him, lifting the bag and the rattles toward the sky as, with a vicious oath, the commander of Fort Inge cleft his skull with a savage downswipe of the saber.

Catayuna Arvilas uttered a shriek of horror, turned to

502

Namine and panted, "Get a horse, ride to Sangrodo in the west, bring back the warriors—they will kill us all, they are evil!"

As Namine scurried toward the side of the tepee, one of the privates in the troop squinted along the sights of his Sharps and pulled the trigger. Sangrodo's squaw pitched forward without a sound and lay still. Crouching on her knees, Catayuna Arvilas stared at the advancing troop, then cried in Spanish, *"Son amigos, todos! Amigos!"*

"That's no Comanche woman, that's a Mexican," Second Lieutenant Evan Brodie rode up to his superior officer, pointing toward Catayuna. "She says they're all friends here. For God's sake, Captain, you're not going to slaughter women and children, are you?"

"I'm going to exterminate a Comanche stronghold, that's exactly what I'm going to do, Lieutenant," Captain George Munson coldly retorted as he loaded his pistol. "If you don't feel like killing Indians, you can just gallop yourself out of here and put yourself on report, you understand me?" Then, raising his voice and turning in his saddle, he brandished his saber and shouted, "Circle the tepees and open fire at will!"

Kitante, who had been in his father's tepee, now ran out, uttered a cry of horror to see his friend and rival Namsi-kohtoo stretched on the ground near him, and ran back into the tepee to find his bow and arrows. Catayuna followed him, sobbing distractedly, and as he emerged, she flung her arms around him and shook her head, saying in Comanche, "No, Little Horse, no, they'll kill you like Namsi-kohtoo! You can't fight them, they've guns, your arrows will never reach them! I beg of you, in your father's name, hide—"

A rifle shot interrupted her as Corporal Hosmer Turlow, grinning like a fiend, leveled and pulled the trigger. She felt a fiery blow at her left shoulder, and with all her remaining strength, clutched Kitante as she fell on top of him, panting, "Don't move, Little Horse, pretend to be dead as I will. Oh my God, they've gone mad!"

"No, no, let me up, let me kill them—they've hurt you, Catayuna—please—get up, get up!" the boy pleaded. But

503

Catayuna Arvilas, though she could feel the blood trickling down her left arm and staining the side of her buckskin jacket, forced herself to cling to him, panting, "Oh Holy Virgin, give me strength, let me keep him under me so they won't kill Sangrodo's son—help me, Blessed Mother—*ayudeme Dios!*"

Kitante could hear the staccato reports of pistols and rifles, the shrill cries and screams of the women and old men who, emerging from their tepees, were shot down without mercy. A bloodlust had taken possession of the troopers, and Corporal Hosmer Turlow, having exhausted the ammunition for his rifle, rode down an old crippled man and skewered him in the back with his saber, wrenched it clean and laughed exultantly as he galloped on toward another fleeing victim.

Sergeant Fred Wilton shook his head and crossed himself as he reined his horse beside that of Second Lieutenant Brodie: "My God, sir, they've gone stark raving crazy—it's cold-blooded murder, that's all it is—there isn't a full-bodied man among those poor damned Injuns!"

"You and I know that, Sergeant," the officer gasped, his face pale and twisted with the sick nausea of what he saw, "but in Captain Munson's report, it's going to sound as if they wiped out a whole battalion of Comanches on the warpath! By God, can't anybody stop them?"

"I can try, sir, if you'll order me to do it," the walrus-mustached sergeant offered.

At the lieutenant's nod, he raised his pistol and fired it into the air, bawling out, "Cease fire, cease fire, reassemble to retreat!"

But the troopers had broken out of the column and each rode helter-skelter on his own individual path, racing after a stumbling old woman, a frightened young girl, a shrieking boy, and sabers dripped with blood and the crack of pistols and rifles resounded until at last there was only a gruesome silence. At last Captain George Munson, his eyes blazing, a feverish grin on his lips, waved his saber and cried out, "Cease fire, reassemble, back to Fort Inge! Maybe we'll come across Sangrodo's braves, and we'll give them just as good a fight as this one, men! I'm

504

proud of you, damn it, proud for the first time since I took command! Now reassemble on the double!"

Sergeant Wilton blew his whistle, and slowly, silently returned, as the troopers wheeled their horses and docilely came back to form the column. At their head, the blond officer rode, his shoulders straight, his head erect, the same grin on his lips. *General Phil Sheridan would hear of this, and maybe there'd finally be some strings pulled to get him back where he belonged in civilization!*

Catayuna raised her head, her body throbbing with the agonizing pain of her wound. Her left arm hung uselessly at her side as she at last released the sobbing boy whom she had covered with her body to shield him during the massacre. Wincing, but trying to smile, she put out her right hand and stroked his cheek. "Little Horse, tell me where your father has gone to hunt, please, you must!" she whispered hoarsely.

He sat up, his eyes wide and his mouth agape as he beheld the sprawled, bloodied bodies of those with whom he had lived all his life. Namsi-kohtoo lay only a few feet away from him, that lifeless hand still reaching for another arrow. He ground his teeth, trying hard not to cry, for a warrior must never do that, especially in front of a squaw.

"Tell me, please, Little Horse! I have to go to him, I have to bring him and the men back so they will punish these evil white-eyes," Catayuna urged him in his own tongue.

"To the west, beyond the big creek where the Valley of the Winds begins."

"How far is it from here, Little Horse?"

"A day and more by horseback for a warrior—you cannot go, you are hurt, you are bleeding, Catayuna!"

"No, Little Horse, you stay here, go see if there are any still alive and if you can help them. I will go to Sangrodo."

Slowly she rose to her feet, setting her teeth against the sudden spasm of hot pain from her wound, and then she sank back down on her knees. "First, Little Horse, help me put medicine bark on the wound and tie a bandage around it to stop the blood," she urged as she fumblingly began to undo the jacket.

Kitante understood. He hurried to the tepee of the dead shaman, came back with a dark-brown bark which he knew Mingride used to press upon the wounds of his father's warriors. The bullet had gone clean through, leaving a small puckered hole to the right of her armpit. With his knife, the boy had cut strips from the shaman's blanket, and now as he put the bark upon the bleeding wound and Catayuna thrust her forefinger against it to hold it in place, he swiftly wound the strips of the improvised tourniquet as tightly as he could.

"Good! Now go help those you can, Little Horse. I will get to your father, he will avenge those who died so needlessly at the hands of the soldiers!"

Catayuna totteringly got to her feet, and moved behind Sangrodo's tepee toward the little corral where the Comanche chief kept his own string of horses. Kitante saddled one of the gentler mares, led it out, then helped the handsome Mexican widow to mount. Catayuna swayed in the saddle, her eyes closed, beads of sweat trickling down her cheeks as she fumbled for the reins.

"See if there's anyone left alive, Little Horse," she hoarsely gasped. "Then ride to the *hacienda* of the man who saved you from *kwasinaboo*," she insisted.

Kitante held onto the bridle and urged the mare out of the little corral, then closed the gate. "I will ride to him, he is the friend of my father. But I still think I should be the one to bring Sangrodo back, Catayuna. It hurts you, you sway in the saddle—"

"I must go to him. He will want to hear it from me, who was once his enemy and am now his willing captive," she answered. Then, kicking her moccasin-shod heels against the sides of the mare, she headed toward the west, while Kitante, scratching his head, looked after her, his sturdy young face set in a puzzled scowl. "Who could understand what a squaw says, anyhow?" he grumbled, half-aloud. Then, almost sulkily, he leaped astride a gentle gray pinto, headed it toward Windhaven Range. In his haste to bring help, he had forgotten Catayuna Arvilas's insistence that he first try to help the survivors. Yet it did not matter: Captain George Munson's troopers had left no survivors in the stronghold.

CHAPTER FORTY-FOUR

It had been a bad week for the buffalo hunt. Ipiltse had sighted a herd of buffalo about five miles northwest of the rugged country to which Sangrodo had taken his warriors, and he and fifteen braves had pursued them. But the herd had been sparse and it had scattered, and when Ipiltse and his men finally rode upon their prey, they found only a few old bulls and several young cows. They killed these, cut away as much meat as they could take from the cows, and took only the intestines and hearts of the bulls. They bound the dripping slabs of raw meat to hastily contrived triangles made of solid wooden branches fixed securely with rawhide thongs, and tied them to the tails of their mustangs.

Sangrodo had taken his other warriors to the northeast, and found only a few wild turkeys and several stray antelopes. Already the game was moving far to the west, the Comanche chief gloomily declared. "We shall move from our stronghold within a moon," he told Ipilste when the latter returned with the relatively meager supply of buffalo meat. "To take so many warriors and to come back with so little for our campfires is a bad sign."

509

"Ne tza osupanact, it is indeed a bad sign," Ipiltse sorrowfully agreed. "Do we move to the west, then?"

"I have seen the buffalo go each year farther and farther towards where *Taabe* (the sun) sets," the Comanche chief broodingly replied. "But the other tribes who hunt on the Great Staked Plains will not be glad for our coming there, and there will be war."

"But our warriors are the bravest and the strongest, we shall defeat all others, for are we not Comanches?" Ipiltse loyally avowed, his eyes shining at the thought of battle. Truly it was more rewarding in the life of a warrior to do battle with a foe than to hunt even the lumbering buffalo. And the old bulls, one of which he himself had killed, had been starved and full of ticks, and their eyes had been red, and that too was not a good sign.

"That is so," Sangrodo conceded, "but we do not have enough *natzahcuinó* (six-shooters) like the white-eyes, and even better would be the long guns that speak with fire and thunder and strike down from a great distance which *natzahcuinó* do not do."

"Yes, that is true also," Ipiltse unhappily assented. "Shall we break camp and return to the stronghold, then, after this night?"

"I have a bad feeling that we should go back, yes. I do not know why it is, even with the good friend who is our *Taiboo Nimaihkana* to guard against our enemies while we are away, but I do not like this place."

"Nor do I, oh Sangrodo," his war lieutenant quickly agreed. Springing to his feet from beside the little fire, he stalked off in the direction of the creek to the south, and then suddenly he shouted, "Someone comes!"

Sangrodo rose, and hurried toward where Ipiltse stood. "Yes, someone rides to us. I cannot yet tell if it is a friend or an enemy. Tell Tikora to have his *piaet* (gun) ready if I give the signal. And let Dontiri ready his *pacendé* (arrows) in case Tikora misses when the rider comes *icmitz* (very near)!"

Ipiltse cupped his hands over his mouth and called softly to two of the nearby braves. One of them seized his old Sharps buffalo gun, the other fitted a long feathered

510

arrow to his longbow and took aim, glancing back at Sangrodo for a sign.

The sorrel pinto, bearing an almost unconscious Catayuna Arvilas came into view just as the moon passed from behind a cloud to light her face, the bloodsoaked buckskin jacket, her useless, dangling left arm, her right hand still desperately clutching the reins of the exhausted pony.

"Catayuna!" Sangrodo cried, gesturing to his two armed braves as he hastened toward the animal, reached up and gently lifted Catayuna down. She drew in great gulps of breath, shuddering violently as she forced herself to speak in a faint, trembling voice, "The stronghold—the soldiers—they rode in, they killed all they could find—your wife Namine—"

"What of the others, woman?" Ipiltse fiercely demanded.

"Your son—your wife—they too are dead—Kitante lives—when the soldiers shot me—I flung myself over him and warned him to lie still and pretend to be dead so they would not kill him too—he rode to your friend, the *Taiboo Nimaihkana*—" Catayuna gasped.

Sangrodo, his face stricken, cried out in a harsh voice, "We ride! Let four warriors bring back the meat we have taken at their own time, the rest with all speed follow me!"

"To the stronghold?" Ipiltse demanded.

"No. The soldiers will be waiting for us to come back there. We go to my friend, we ask his council. How can it be that his men could not make the soldiers know we are at peace with the white-eyes?"

"Because there can never be peace with the white-eyes, oh Sangrodo," the war lieutenant angrily countered. "We are Comanches, we are the enemies of all, and all others who are not Comanches are our enemies. It is the ancient law and you have broken it by your alliance with this white-eyes.

"You are wrong, Ipiltse. We will go there first, you will hear what he has to say before we judge him. Catayuna—she is hurt—the soldiers have shot her—oh Great Spirit, save me this squaw's life, for she is truly of

511

the blood of Comanche—do you not see, Ipiltse, the blood of her wound, yet how she rode all this way to find us? She shall not be a slave or a captive, she shall be my squaw. I shall honor her for what she has done. Bring *tiswin,* have the warriors mount their horses, we go to the *hacienda* of our friend!"

Cradling her sagging body in his arms, Sangrodo gently laid Catayuna down on a little grassy knoll and with almost reverent fingers unfastened her jacket. "Ho!" he grunted, "the wound is bound and the medicine bark of Mingride helps it heal. She is weak, small wonder, she has ridden fifty miles to warn us. Truly she is worthy to be *cueh* of the chief of all the Comanches, even a Quanah Parker, so says Sangrodo of the Wanderers!"

"The *tiswin,*" Ipiltse knelt with a crude leather bottle, and Sangrodo took it, gently putting his left arm under her neck and lifting her head as he put the mouth of the bottle to her lips. "Drink, beloved woman! It will give you strength, it will bring you back to the land of the living! We need your strong brave spirit, beloved woman—hear me, hear my words and drink all you can!"

Wanly Catayuna Arvilas' eyelids fluttered open and she stared into the drawn, solemn face of the man whom she had first hated with the most intense passion. "Do not waste time on me—hurry back, avenge yourself, Sangrodo! They came upon us without word or warning, they killed Mingride because he made the holy signs to the Great Spirit that we were at peace with them—they fired the long rifle at Namine—oh, Ipiltse, your wife and son were slaughtered too by the blue-coated soldiers—"

Ipiltse uttered a cry and hammered his fists upon the ground, then rose and drew his claspknife, seized his scalplock and severed it with a single slash of the sharp blade. "By the Great Spirit who hears me, I swear I shall not grow it back until the blood of all the white-eyes soldiers spills upon the ground. I, Ipiltse, war lieutenant of the Wanderers, swear this that all men may hear and know my vow!" he cried in an agonized voice.

"Drink, beloved woman," Sangrodo softly urged Catayuna. "You shall ride with me, I will hold you so it does not hurt. Do you think you can make the journey?"

"With you, yes, Sangrodo—it was you I thought of, you and Kitante when the soldiers came," Catayuna Arvilas whispered, and then she drank from the bottle like an obedient little child while he smiled down at her, his face soft with joy, despite the sorrow and the hate.

And soon, with Catayuna seated in front of him, Sangrodo led the way back to Windhaven Range.

It was nearly midnight of the next day when Sangrodo and his braves reached Windhaven Range and the Comanche chief, gently lifting Catayuna Arvilas down, carried her in his arms toward the gate and called out in a loud voice, "*Taiboo Nimaihkana,* I, Sangrodo, call you!"

The door to the *hacienda* opened, and Luke Bouchard appeared, a quill pen in his hand. He had been composing a letter to John Brunton, telling him of Lucy's death and of the abduction and rescue of Lucien Edmond's wife. In the other hand, he held a carbine, and hearing Sangrodo call out again and recognizing the chief's voice, he hurried to the gate and opened it.

"This beloved woman, oh *Taiboo Nimaihkana,* was shot by the soldiers of Fort Inge, yet rode far to warn me of their treachery."

"I know," Luke Bouchard bowed his head. "Your son Kitante came to tell us, he is here, he is safe, Sangrodo. The soldiers were mad dogs, but I swear to you by the Great Spirit that my men and I rode out to intercept them, to tell them that you were my ally, to tell them how you had saved my son's wife from Norvito's men, how we were blood brothers. My men and I took with us the guns that speak often, so that we would be well-armed to convince them. I told them that only the old men and women and the children were left in your stronghold while you were hunting, and that you sent twenty of your best braves on the drive to Santa Fe."

"And did they heed you, oh *Taiboo Nimaihkana?*"

"I swear by the Great Spirit that I thought they did. I told them to go back to their fort and not to wage war on innocent people. My men and I watched as they rode back to Fort Inge and then we rode back here. I swear to

513

you on my honor and our friendship that it is as I have told you."

"I believe you, my brother. And would you have shot the soldiers if they had defied you and fired upon you?"

"Sangrodo, you must surely know that we have had four years of terrible war which put brother against brother, the North against the South. You know also that I am from the South, though I did not carry arms against my country. These men who wear the blue uniforms are of the North, and they have won the war, and they look upon me as a rebel from the South—so it was their leader told me. And if I had fired upon them, my countrymen would have regarded it as treason. Yet I swear to you that if they had tried to go on into your village, intending what they came back to do by so cowardly and treacherous a trick, I would not have hesitated to try to defend your people—I am sorry that my men and I could not have been there, could not have understood the crafty mind of that commander of Fort Inge and prevented this shameful massacre, Sangrodo."

"Yes, I believe you, *Taiboo Nimaihkana*. Here, will you not take the beloved woman and have your own women tend her wound? I wish her to live, for all of us respect her, she has shown the strong blood of the Comanche in her bravery. She has ridden, suffering though she was, all those miles to come to me, caring nothing for her own life, and now that my squaw is dead, I will ask her if she will take her place. I beg you this favor, my blood brother."

The elderly Angola, William, had come out of the *hacienda* and Luke Bouchard turned to him. "Help me carry the *Señora* Arvilas into the house, William, and ask Mrs. Forsden if she and Maxine can look after her."

Sangrodo watched as Luke Bouchard and the black gently took Catayuna from him and carried her into the house. A few moments later, Luke returned, leading Kitante by the hand.

The Comanche boy ran to his father, who embraced him, not ashamed to show his emotion. Then, staring intently at Luke Bouchard, Sangrodo said, "I do not ask you to bear arms against your own people, for as you have told me, you would be condemned and driven from this land where you live in peace. But I am a Comanche, and when an enemy comes like a hissing serpent into my house when I am gone from it and strikes down those who are dear to me, I will crush it. I will seek it out no matter how long it will take."

"I will lend you my guns and ammunition, Sangrodo. What that officer did is in my mind a crime before God and all his angels. It is a sin before your Great Spirit too, and perhaps I can help you without myself taking part because it is your vengeance. Let me call Simata." He turned to William who had come out again solicitously to inquire if he might be of further assistance, and whispered to him. The Angola nodded and hurried toward the bunkhouse. A few moments later, Simata joined Luke Bouchard on the porch of the *hacienda*.

"Kitante has told me what the soldiers have done, Sangrodo. My heart is as heavy as yours, because the Kiowa is brother to the Comanche. When the white-eyes who fear us and do not try to understand us or to share the land with us do evil things, it is all of us who suffer, no matter from what tribe we come."

"That is so, Simata," Sangrodo slowly nodded.

"This man whom you call *Taiboo Nimaihkana* cannot ride out and take vengeance upon the soldiers, because he is not a soldier himself. This you know. But I, Simata, whose father was a chief here in this land, I will fight with you because such men have killed my people just as they have now killed yours."

"We cannot ride against the fort."

"No, Sangrodo. They will shut themselves up and they have guns. But you know that the man for whom I am a scout has guns that shoot faster and farther, and he will lend them to me to give your warriors. Now we must think of a plan to bring the soldiers out of the fort to ride after us, Sangrodo."

"Yes, that is the best way."

"Do you not remember the place that is called the *Cañon de Ugalde* where once the Mexicans fought your forefathers?"

"I know it well."

"Give me fifteen of your braves and let me lead them past the fort. The soldiers will think we ride to join the rest of your band. Let the rest of your men hide among the rocks at the top of the canyon, and we will draw the soldiers into it and then you will have your vengeance, Sangrodo."

"Ho, it is a good plan. I will give you my horse, my lance and my war bonnet so the soldiers will think that you are the chief, and they will follow."

"That is very good, Sangrodo," Simata smiled as he extended his hand to the Comanche chief, who took it and gravely nodded to seal their pact.

"Captain Munson, sir, Captain Munson!" Corporal Sedgewick, who had hastily knocked at the commanding officer's door and then burst into the office, excitedly exclaimed.

"What the devil are you doing, Corporal? Don't you bother to salute any more?"

"Oh yes sir, excuse me, sir," the Massachusetts recruit turned red with embarrassment as he stiffened to attention and saluted. "Sergeant Wilton's here to see you, Captain. Says he just saw a bunch of Comanches ride by the fort heading towards the Llano River."

The blond officer sprang to his feet, his eyes glistening. "The tricky redskin bastards," he gloated. "This time we've got them where we want them. Tell Sergeant Wilton to have the bugler summon the entire troop—I want every man unless he's in sick bay, and I want him out there on the double, and see that extra ammunition's issued."

"Right away, sir, I'll tell the sergeant," the excited corporal stammered as he whirled around and hurried out of the office. Captain George Munson, this time, did not admonish his orderly for failing to salute; now he could envisage the perfect end to his unjust disgrace and banishment to Fort Inge. Even with single-shot rifles and six-shooters and sabers, his full troop would be more than a match for those Comanche devils: they might have a few rusty buffalo guns, but mostly bows and arrows and lances. He'd mow every last one of them down, and then

516

he'd send a telegraph to General Phil Sheridan. The newspapers would get hold of it, he'd be summoned to Washington and maybe personally decorated by President Johnson for bravery beyond the call of duty. Then wouldn't Betty Miles wish she hadn't been such a deceitful little bitch!

Outside, he heard the bugler's call to assembly, the voice of Sergeant Fred Wilton bawling orders to Corporal Jack Hayes, who was in charge of the storeroom where ammunition and extra sidearms were kept. He grinned at himself in the dusty little mirror, put back a hand to fluff out his blond curls, and stiffened to attention. "Your picture is going to be in all the papers, you watch and see, George Munson," he said aloud. "*Major* George Munson. Hell, maybe even Colonel!"

Then, buckling on his saber, drawing his pistols out of the holsters and priming and loading them, he strode out to mount his horse and to lead his troop toward the hilly terrain in whose direction Sergeant Fred Wilton had seen the Comanches head.

"Forward ho!" he shouted, nodding to the bugler to sound the call that would set his cavalrymen into full gallop toward the enemy objective. By God, this was more like it, and as the blood coursed through his veins, he felt as he had when he'd ridden against that wily Confederate fox, J.E.B. Stuart.

Second Lieutenant Evan Brodie drew abreast of him, saluted and called out, "It may be a trap, Captain! We'll be heading for that canyon about three miles from here. I wouldn't put it past them to be hiding on top of the rocks waiting for us to go through. Maybe we ought to send scouts out."

"To hell with scouts, Brodie!" the blond commander of Fort Inge vehemently exclaimed, "Just make sure your men have their weapons ready and use them at the first sign of those Comanche devils! I don't want a one left alive, you understand me? Now get back to your place in the column!"

Grudgingly, the taciturn lieutenant gave him a slow salute, wheeled his horse and held it as half the column

517

went by, then rode alongside the men at the right, his forehead creased in an anxious frown.

But Sergeant Fred Wilton had an afterthought that was bothering him, and so he turned his horse back and waited for his superior officer to catch up. As the latter drew alongside him, the sergeant saluted and exclaimed, "Sorry to bother you again, sir, but when we hit that Indian village, I didn't see you firing any shots."

Second Lieutenant Evan Brodie gave him a steely look. "Come to think of it, Sergeant, I didn't see you in the action either. Let's say no more about it."

"That's what I thought, sir," the non-commissioned officer saluted and resumed his place alongside the galloping column.

A mile ahead of them loomed the canyon, narrow and winding, its rocky crags framing the tortuous enclosure at a height of about twenty-five feet. Captain George Munson held up his hand to slacken the pace of the hard-riding cavalry behind him, then fumbled for his field glasses, focused them and uttered an ecstatic cry: "There they are, they're just entering the canyon to join the rest of those murdering bastards at the end of it! After them, men!" as, replacing the field glasses in their case, he brandished his saber and spurred his snorting mare to its utmost gallop.

Behind him, Sergeant Fred Wilton was calling orders to his men to have their weapons at the ready, to check the loading and ammunition, to fire at effective targets and not to panic. Second Lieutenant Evan Brodie, saber in his right hand, the reins in his left, glanced moodily upward at the grayish rock which topped the narrow entry to the *Cañon de Ugalde*.

Simata and the decoying warriors of Sangrodo's band had halted their horses to allow the soldiers to come within full sight of them, and Simata nodded to his companions and pointed back toward the galloping troop. "They come now, let us ride to the end of the canyon as we had planned," he told them. "When it ends, there is a sharp turn to the right and a narrow pathway which leads up to the rocks where your chief awaits them. As soon as we have ridden up out of the canyon, the warriors will push down the heavy boulders and block their exit, and then they will be at your mercy."

"After them, men!" Captain George Munson hoarsely shouted, looping the reins of his mare over the pommel of the saddle and drawing the pistol from its holster at his left side as he continued to flourish his saber toward the retreating group of Comanches led by Simata. "Riflemen, shoot down those red dogs!"

Corporal Hosmer Turlow drew his rifle out of the scabbard sheath, aimed it and pulled the trigger. The bullet richocheted off one of the rocks at the side of the canyon a dozen yards from Simata's head, and at the same moment there was the whistling hiss of an arrow and the ghastly *thuckk* as it buried itself in the corporal's throat. With a screech, he tumbled off his galloping horse, his right booted leg caught in the stirrup as his lifeless body was dragged over the rocky ground.

On each side of the canyon at the top of the crags, Sangrodo's braves had concealed themselves, and now poured down a withering fire of arrows, whose vicious hiss was interspersed with the crackle of carbine and rifle fire. Before Captain George Munson could call out the order to dismount and take cover, a dozen soldiers lay dead or mortally wounded along the winding trail.

"My God, it's an ambush, just as I knew it would be!" Second Lieutenant Evan Brodie cried to Sergeant Fred Wilton as he leaped off his horse, and ran, crouching low, toward the almost perpendicular wall of the canyon to take what shelter he could in a clump of mesquite. But the sergeant was kneeling down and taking aim with both pistols at the craggy rocks from around which the painted faces of Sangrodo's braves appeared like grim wraiths. Both pistols barked at the same time, and one of the Comanches flung up his carbine with a wild scream and catapulted down to fall like a squashed bug beside one of the dead troopers. His companion, seizing the fallen carbine, aimed swiftly and levered the trigger. Four shots rang out and Sergeant Fred Wilton clutched at his chest, blood spurting from his mouth and nostrils, then slowly bent forward on his knees with his forehead pressed against the dust.

The rest of the troopers had taken what cover they could against the walls of the canyon, using their rifles or six-shooters to fire desperately and usually inaccurately at the faces which peered down at them from the top of the rocks, only to vanish and reappear at a farther distance. First Lieutenant Leopold Turner, sobbing hysterically, the crotch of his uniform trousers wet with the urine of fear, aimed his pistol in a trembling hand and pulled the trigger. But the firing pin was loose and the gun exploded in his hand as, with a shriek of despair, he tried to rise and wave his arms as a signal that he would surrender. Ipiltse, squinting down the sights of one of the Spencer repeating rifles, grinned savagely as he squeezed the trigger, and the young officer plunged back against the wall of the canyon as if an invisible hand had flung him there.

Only six troopers were left alive now, besides their commanding officer and Second Lieutenant Evan Brodie, who, crouching down in the mesquite, calmly reloaded his pistol and took careful aim, waiting for one of the Comanches to peer out from between the jagged rocks. He pulled the trigger, and there was a yell of pain as one of the Comanche braves staggered back with a bullet in his shoulder. "Kill them, kill them, don't waste your fire, kill the bastards!" Captain George Munson screamed, brandishing his saber and, seeing Ipiltse leap agilely onto one of the rocks, aimed his pistol and pulled the trigger. The bullet whined harmlessly past the Comanche war lieutenant who uttered a jeering laugh, then took aim with his carbine and fired three times, the bullets raising clouds of dust near Captain George Munson's neatly polished boots. With a cry of fright, the blond commanding officer of Fort Inge ran toward the clump of mesquite where his second lieutenant was crouching, flung himself down on his belly and panted, "Brodie, what can we do? My God, all our men are dead, those murdering bastards tricked us—"

"As I knew they would, Captain. We're paying for that heroic action the other day, you know," the tall black-haired junior officer looked contemptuously at him.

"What are we going to do, Brodie? My God, tell me,

you've had experience under fire, more than I have even, what are we going to do?"

"All we can do, Captain, is die like men," Brodie muttered. Seeing Ipiltse leap back onto another rock now, he aimed his pistol and fired again, the bullet glancing off the rock a few feet from where the war lieutenant stood. Ipiltse laughed grimly, aimed his carbine and fired three more times. Second Lieutenant Evan Brodie rose to his feet, his pistol dropping from a nerveless hand, his eyes staring, and then fell headlong to sprawl on the dust of the canyon road.

"Brodie, my God—I'm the only one left—help me, someone—oh dear God, don't let me die!" Captain George Munson screamed, for suddenly a terrifying silence had engulfed the canyon. His tear-blurred eyes saw only motionless men in blue uniforms around him, and he could hear in the frightening silence the whinnying and snorting of their horses who had raced to the end of the canyon. Since the boulders had not been dropped because of the success of the Comanche ambush, the terrified animals galloped on and out of this labyrinth of death.

Ipiltse still stood on the rocks, mockingly calling down, "Where is the chief of these brave men, where does he hide?"

"I'll show you, you murdering bastard you, I'll show you!" Captain George Munson screamed as he hastily reloaded his six-shooter, aimed and fired till the gun was empty. Fumbling with his other hand for ammunition, he uttered a cry of horror to discover that there was none left. With a sobbing cry, he flung the useless pistol out into the winding road, and then knelt down, hunching himself, making himself as small as he could, wringing his hands and weeping.

Ipiltse laughed triumphantly, and disappeared behind one of the huge gray rocks. Now that the horses had fled to safety, leaving their riders behind for the already circling buzzards, the silence became overwhelming and the scorching sun blazed down relentlessly.

And then there was the sound of a horse's hooves, coming slowly from the eastern opening of the canyon, and Sangrodo, in war bonnet and paint, carrying the feathered lance, slowly approached on his powerful gray mustang. "I challenge the chief of the white-eyes soldiers to fight me," he mockingly called, and from behind the towering rocks there came the laughter of his warriors.

Captain George Munson was sobbing like a child as he slowly rose from the sheltering clump of mesquite, clutching his saber, tottering step by step out into the road. "I surrender, I surrender," he screamed, "look, I'm throwing my saber away—I surrender—don't kill me, please don't kill me—I surrender!" He flung the saber toward the opposite wall of the canyon and held out his arms to the approaching chief of the Comanches.

Sangrodo dismounted, holding his lance in both hands, his lips curved in a thin, merciless smile. "But I, Sangrodo, do not take prisoners except the *Mexicanos* whom I save for slow torture. Here I am, brave chief of Fort Inge. I am not a woman or a child or an old man, so come kill me, you who have killed so many others of my people who could not fight you."

"But I can't fight you—I've no weapon—don't you see? I ask for mercy—I had my orders—you've massacred white settlers, I had to kill your people, don't you understand?" Captain George Munson sobbed as he kept both arms high in the air, his face uncontrollably twitching and wet with tears.

"I too have my orders, brave white chief," Sangrodo scornfully countered as he moved forward till the sharp point of the lance brushed the belly of the cringing, weeping blond officer. "It is the order of the souls of those whom you killed without mercy when we were at peace, they order me to send you into the darkness, never to join them. For then you would return one day as enemy of the Comanches, and that is not to be." His strong wiry hands shoved the wooden handle of the lance a little forward, till Captain George Munson could feel the first bite of its deadly tip against his flesh. With a shriek of terror, he clasped the iron end, trying to force it away from his body, but Sangrodo implacably moved forward, step by step, till at last his quarry stood pinned with his back against the wall of the canyon, spittle running down his chin, sobbing hysterically, his words inarticulate and choked by his sobs of fear.

"I pity the brave men that followed such a cowardly dog to their death," Sangrodo said, his English words slow and guttural as if he chose each with deliberate care. "I send you now to darkness. Darkness forever for your spirit. Your men who died like men shall not be touched, so their spirits will find the sky. *Adios,* brave white-eyes chief of Fort Inge!" As he spoke the last words, his powerful hands shoved the lance forward, impaling the blond officer through the belly. Then he jerked out the bloodied lance and stepped back, as Captain George Munson, screaming like a woman in labor, clutched the gory wound and tried to stanch the flow of blood, staring down at it as if he could not believe his eyes, staggered, then fell onto his side, holding out one bloodied hand toward the grim-faced Comanche chief who watched him with piercing, unwavering gaze.

Sangrodo took the lance between his strong hands, lifted his knee and brought the wooden haft down with full force, breaking it, then flung it into the road. Then he drew his scalp knife, knelt down beside the sobbing, moaning, dying captain, and calmly and slowly cut away Captain George Munson's scalp, turned to hold it aloft. From behind the rocks his braves appeared, brandishing their weapons, shouting his name as their victorious leader, "Sangrodo! Sangrodo, he who leads us against our enemies!" And then, leaving the dying man to writhe and scream for what little time was left him, the chief of the Comanches mounted his mustang, signaled to his men to follow him, and rode out of the *Cañon de Ugalde.*

CHAPTER FORTY-FIVE

When Betty, two days later, saw all of Sangrodo's warriors in their full warpaint and with their weapons arriving at Windhaven, she wrung her hands and uttered fearful lamentations.

"Don't take on so, Betty," Luke Bouchard chuckled, patting her shoulder. "They're our friends, don't you recognize them? You fed them once, you know—maybe not so many, but they're from the same tribe."

"Mebbe so, Mistah Bouchard," Betty tried to control herself, dabbing at her eyes and her nose with her calico apron, "but come nighttime, dey looks awful mean! Does ah hab to feed all ob dem redskin critters now, widout no warnin' or nuttin'?"

"I don't think so, Betty. I'll go out and talk with them, and don't you fret." He went out of the *hacienda,* opened the gate and walked forward to where Sangrodo sat astride his mustang. It was two days after the battle in the canyon, and Simata, dismounting and tethering the reins to one of the pegs in the stockade fence, smilingly approached his tall gray-haired employer. "Sangrodo has come to return the guns we lent him, Mr. Bouchard, and to claim his woman."

"The beloved woman," Sangrodo smilingly interrupted as he lifted his hand in the sign of peace toward Luke Bouchard. "We have come from the stronghold where we put to rest those who were slain by the white-eyes soldiers." His face was solemn as he added, "None lived, and so my braves are like you, *Taiboo Nimaihkana*—each man has lost his squaw—and worse still, his children."

"My sorrow is great for Sangrodo and his men," Luke Bouchard replied.

"I have come to say farewell, my blood brother."

"You will seek a new stronghold, Sangrodo?"

"Not here on this land. There will be other white-eyes soldiers who will hear of what was done in the *Cañon de Ugalde*, and they will ride out to kill the Comanches for their battle against the soldiers of Fort Inge."

"And those soldiers—" Luke stared into the unflinching face of the tall warbonneted chief.

"Their spirits have gone to the great sky, all but one—their evil chief will wander in darkness throughout all time. I myself took his scalp—it dangles from my belt so that never again will he come back to earth to kill the old men, the women and the children of the Wanderers or of any other tribe."

"If soldiers come to me and ask me what I know of this thing, Sangrodo, I will say the truth, that your people were massacred without pity and that your battle was against armed soldiers who might have killed you and your warriors, but that your skill brought victory to the Comanches."

"You and I well know that your words, though spoken straight and with a good heart, will not turn the soldiers who will come on the path of Sangrodo. We go across the Rio Grande." Sangrodo smiled humorlessly. "In the past, we have taken squaws and slaves from the villages to the south of the great river. Now my men, who have no squaws or slaves, or children to follow them as warriors, perhaps will take new squaws and we shall live as we can, as the Great Spirit wills."

"There are still at least a hundred of the long-horned

526

cattle near my *hacienda,* Sangrodo. Take what you need for your campfires as you travel to your new stronghold."

"With your permission, then, my warriors will drive off twenty only. It will be meat enough till we find a new home."

"And for you, take my rifle, the best of the lot I bought in New Orleans when I came here to defend my land and my family." Luke Bouchard handed the mounted chief of the Comanches his Spencer repeating rifle.

"Ho, it is a fine gift, and I will long remember the giver, *Taiboo Nimaihkana.* I have a gift for you in return, a relic of our ancient people, handed down by my father's father, who in turn had it from his father's father. Ipiltse!"

"I come, my chief," the war lieutenant exclaimed as he rode his mustang up toward the gate, dismounted and came forward toward Luke Bouchard. In his hands he held a rawhide thong which formed a kind of necklace in whose center was a jagged, raw turquoise. At Sangrodo's nod, Ipiltse put the thong around Luke Bouchard's neck and saluted him by inclining his head and spreading out his arms, palms downward toward the earth.

"It is a priceless gift, Sangrodo. It is too much—"

"It is the spirit of our people," the Comanche chief replied, "and the shaman whom we mourn once said that if it should depart from the tepees of our tribe, it could be given only to one who has that spirit in his heart and who is our blood brother. That is you, *Taiboo Nimaihkana.*"

"I am honored, Sangrodo. But if you give me this talisman, will you not deprive your tribe of its strong spirit, its good fortune?" Luke Bouchard spoke in Sangrodo's own tongue, so that there could be no misunderstanding of his words.

"No, my brother. The spirit lives, because you gave life back to my son Kitante, who one day will be the chief when my spirit has gone to the sky. Before the soldiers came upon our peaceful stronghold, our shaman foretold a strange thing—of this I had not yet told you. He had thrown the bones as he had done for you when you visited us for the first time, my brother, and he said that we who are the Wanderers would know the sorrow of death

527

and the joy of rebirth in a new hunting ground. And he said that he who had come among us to show us that there are white-eyes who do not fear or hate us—that is you, oh my brother—would mourn a death and take joy in the birth of new life in a land he had once known long ago."

Luke bowed his head, unable to speak. Behind him, the door to the *hacienda* opened and Kitante, with a cry of joy, ran forward toward his father. In the doorway, Catayuna Arvilas stood, wearing a homespun dress which Sybella had given her. Her eyes shone with pride and love as she watched the little boy clamber up to sit in front of his father astride the great gray mustang.

"The beloved woman," Sangrodo said gently, "honored of our tribe, you are free. Go where you will, and go with the respect and honor of all my warriors and of my own self."

"Then, if you will take me with you, I go with you, Sangrodo," Catayuna Arvilas replied as she came down the steps of the porch and walked slowly out toward the Comanche chief.

"You are certain? You are free now, remember that. Your life is yours, as it was before I took you from your village."

She shook her head, held up her hand to him and he grasped it, and she said softly, "I did not know it, but even then I was not free. But now that you tell me I am, I have made my choice. If you will have me, I will be your woman. And I pray your Great Spirit that I will give you a son who is as strong and brave as Kitante."

Sangrodo's face glowed with joy as he beckoned to Ipiltse: "Bring a horse for the beloved woman. She rides with us, Ipiltse."

"I obey, Sangrodo."

Sangrodo watched as Catayuna Arvilas, hiking up her skirt, eagerly and nimbly mounted the horse the war lieutenant had brought up for her, nodded as she took the reins and smiled with approval as she wheeled the horse to move alongside his.

"I do not know if we shall see each other again, *Taiboo Nimaihkana*," he said to Luke Bouchard. "But when you look upon the spirit of our tribe, when you touch it, when you feel it upon you, then will you know that Sangrodo, your blood brother, sends good thoughts to you that you may walk straight without fear in the sun, that your family will honor you and follow in your footsteps of honesty and friendship to all men even if they are not like you, my brother."

"Go with God, Sangrodo, you and Catayuna and Kitante and your warriors. I too will send my thoughts to all of you, and I will wear this talisman to keep those thoughts forever."

Sangrodo nodded, then held up his hand, and rode forward while his warriors respectfully drew back their horses to make a pathway for him to take his rightful place at the head of their band. And with him rode Catayuna Arvilas, who looked back once toward Luke Bouchard and raised her hand and then turned back, quickening her horse that she might keep up with the chief of the Comanches.

Luke Bouchard stood watching as the soft darkness enveloped the land, the trees, the clumps of mesquite, and watched until only the shadowy outlines of the riders could be seen. Across the river they rode slowly, and on the other side, having taken the shallowest ford, Sangrodo turned and lifted his hand in farewell. Straining his eyes to see, Luke Bouchard raised his in salute. And then they merged into the darkness and there was nothing except the sound of the nightbirds and the soft splashing of the tributary of the river.

It was the twentieth of May, 1866, and Texas, last of the Confederate states to do so, had completed Reconstruction in conformity with the plan of President Andrew Johnson. The Fourteenth Amendment to the Constitution had been passed by Congress and sent to the states for ratification, but it was to be rejected by twelve of the thirty-seven states including all Confederate states except Tennessee the following year and would be defeated for the time being. Luke Bouchard had gone first to Austin to keep his promise to Ramon Hernandez by transferring two hundred acres of Windhaven Range into the young

529

vaquero's legal ownership and had put the deed into his saddlebag as a present to Ramon and his daughter Mara. He rode then to San Antonio to pick up supplies and letters.

There were three letters, one from Fleurette, a second from Arabella in Galveston, and a third from New Orleans which bore the familiar seal of John Brunton, but was addressed in a woman's hand. Quelling his impatience to read the last one, Luke Bouchard walked into the bank and transacted what business he had, and when it was finished, walked over to a counter near the door and opened the letter from New Orleans. He caught his breath as he recognized the handwriting, for it was Laure's:

Dearest Luke:

On March 19th, I gave birth to a healthy son, weighing, as the doctor told me, nearly eight pounds, with fair hair and blue eyes. John was already sick with the yellow fever which was to take him from me exactly six days later. I sent word to the hospital by one of my girls at the house, telling him of my son's birth and asking if I might name him Lucien in honor of your grandfather, whose memory he always cherished. He sent back word that he himself could not have chosen a worthier, more honorable name.

We had so little time together, it seems, and yet I think in that short time I was able to make John happy. How strange that he was always talking of you and wondering how your venture in that huge and dangerous and uncharted Texas would turn out. Of course you already know from him that Windhaven Plantation was purchased by his black factor so that the chateau of your grandfather and fifty acres of land adjoining it can one day be yours if you so wish. As for me, I shall not want for money, thanks to John's generosity. My own life will be devoted to bringing up little Lucien and hoping that one day he may be worthy of your grandfather's name and perhaps even do great deeds as your grandfather did. As for the house, I have told the girls that the need for it is ended and that they would do well toward fitting themselves for honorable marriage. They are lovely and generally good of nature, and with all the newcomers pouring into New Orleans, I do not think they will want for understanding, devoted husbands.

You have not written to John in so long that I am a little concerned about you and Lucy and the others. You know how I wish you well, and how I shall never forget you. It would be asking too much, I know, and it's presumptuous of me to say it—but if you should ever come to New Orleans again, do please call upon me. Perhaps you will be a godfather to little Lucien. Since I have no family, only him, I hope you will understand and forgive this selfish wish of mine.

Laure Brunton

He lifted the letter and he could smell the musky perfume that she had always worn. Very slowly he folded it and put it back into the envelope, and then forced himself to read the other two letters. They were cheerful, Fleurette's happily avowing Ben Wilson's absorption and dedication to his flourishing medical career, Arabella's chatty and gossipy, with news of her children who were demanding more and more of her time and attention.

With a sigh, he walked outside and got into the buckboard in which he had placed his supplies, and started back toward Windhaven Range. Once out of San Antonio and on the familiar road back, he stopped the horses and took out Laure's letter and read it again. And as he reached the last words, he lifted his face to the sky and wonderingly repeated the words of old Mingride of the stronghold: "Though the squaw of the white-eyes is barren, yet will he have a son, and to this son will he return and to the land which he first knew at birth."

"He spoke the truth," he said aloud, "like the old *Windigo* who foretold my grandfather's destiny, he spoke the truth. My wife is dead, and I feel certain Laure's son is mine, not John's. And Grandfather's chateau is waiting for us both." Then, his face alight with a strange joy, a joy that brought tears, Luke Bouchard urged the horses on along the trail to Windhaven Range.

He stood, dressed in buckskin as once Lucien Bouchard

had dressed at the village of Econchate, in the living room of the *hacienda,* with his son Lucien Edmond, his daughter Mara who stood beside the joyous *vaquero,* white-haired Sybella, Maxine and Maybelle, who was now Mrs. Henry Belcher, and his eyes rested fondly on each as if inscribing their features on his memory for all time to come.

"I have something to tell all of you," he began, struggling through his emotion to find the proper words. "Mother knows part of this already—that when I was in New Orleans, I urged our good friend John Brunton to see if he could buy back Grandfather's chateau on the Alabama River. And some months ago he wrote me that a freed black man, his factor, had been able to buy the chateau and fifty acres around it. At the time, I thought to myself that perhaps if we found this new venture in Texas too arduous, too full of dangers for the future well-being of all the Bouchards, we could return there where we were once happy and lived in peace with our neighbors and tilled the earth and brought forth food for the hungry. But now that Lucien Edmond has come back, has sold all the cattle at a fine profit which will enable all of you to thrive and to have the material things needed to make this range into one of the richest in all Texas, I can see that my son has already carved out his destiny and is content with it. Isn't that so, Lucien Edmond?"

Maxine walked over to her handsome husband, put her arm around him, and both smilingly nodded.

"But, Father," Lucien Edmond began, "it sounds as if you were saying farewell to us."

"There you have it, Lucien Edmond. Yes, it's true. And this is the other part which even Mother doesn't know—in New Orleans, I'm not ashamed to say it, I met the young woman who was to marry John Brunton. She helped me find the man who sold us the weapons of which we made such good use defending ourselves against the bandits when we came across this country, the weapons which avenged Sangrodo's people for the shameful massacre at his stronghold, the weapons which my son and Sangrodo's friendly warriors used to restore his beautiful, courageous wife to him. Well, John Brunton is dead of yellow fever and his wife Laure delivered a son in March—my son."

"Father!" Lucien Edmond gasped, looking wonderingly at Maxine.

Luke Bouchard stood unflinchingly, his shoulders erect, his face serene. "Yes. You know how I loved your mother, Lucien Edmond, and I was faithful to her except for one mortal hour when, I shall not seek any reason to justify myself, I broke the vow I had sworn to your mother on our wedding day. And thus the son is mine, and because she is alone, with no relatives and few friends to stand beside her now that she is widowed and with a child, I propose to go back to New Orleans, to marry her, and perhaps if it is possible within the next few years, to restore Windhaven Plantation to what it once was in the days of Grandfather."

Sybella impulsively came forward and put her hand on Luke Bouchard's shoulder. This is so good and honorable—and so like you, Luke. You mustn't judge yourself harshly, nor would Lucy judge you. Yes, I think I knew all along that your heart was still back at Econchate. Perhaps in a way mine is too, but I shall stay here and watch your son's children grow, and watch over Maybelle and her new family. But my thoughts will be with you always, my son Luke, my dearest son Luke."

He embraced her, and now his unashamed tears flowed freely as he kissed her. Then, his arm around her shoulders, as he turned her to face the others, he said in a voice that strove to be steady, "Don't think that this farewell of mine means that we shall never see one another again. For this is the great legacy of the Bouchards, that even if we are many miles apart, all of us are bound together by love and understanding, by compassion and the need for sharing our innermost thoughts and feelings. As our country restores itself after this tragic war which brought us here, I foresee swifter communication between all the peoples of this rich young land. We shall see one another again, I'm sure of that."

Then, with almost banter in his voice, he added, "Now, Lucien Edmond, don't forget our talks about interbreeding various types of cattle so you'll get stronger, sturdier animals for the market and you won't have to worry about Texas fever."

"I shan't, Father."

"And you, Ramon and Mara, be happy with each other, and if you should have a son, if you should think kindly enough of me to name it after me, you'd make me very happy."

Mara blushed becomingly as she squeezed the young *vaquero*'s hand and nodded, "We're to be married two weeks from now in San Antonio, Father. And I promise to do just what you want—unless of course it's a girl." Then, abashed, she blushed furiously and hid her face against Ramon Hernandez's chest as he hugged and kissed her and whispered endearments.

"I shall leave at once for New Orleans," Luke Bouchard declared. "I'll ride back along the way we came from Corpus Christi, and take the steamboat back. And as I ride, remembering how we came across that uncharted trail to find Windhaven Range, I'll pray for all of you and for your long life and good fortune. Remember most of all, your legacy is in yourselves, the good and the compassion and the love and the willingness to work hard for what you seek—and to seek far beyond material possessions and mere comforts. It is a legacy which the land itself gives us, and that was Grandfather's secret and he learned it in the fields of Yves-sur-lac. God keep you all and bless you."

He kissed Sybella again, came forward to shake his son's hand, to kiss Mara, Maybelle and Maxine. Carla and Hugo looked wonderingly at him, not having understood all that he had said but sensing that he was saying goodbye to them. He lifted each in his arms in turn, and kissed little Carla, took Hugo' hand and shook it gravely.

Then, feeling his eyes blind with tears, he turned abruptly, opened the door of the *hacienda* and went out the open gate, beyond which Simata stood, holding the reins of his horse.

"Look after them, Simata."

"I will, Mr. Bouchard. Go with God."

"Amen to that, Simata. And thank you for all you have done. My son will talk to you soon about a piece of good land he wishes to give you in return for your loyalty and courage."

He took the reins and with his right hand touched the huge turquoise which hung upon his neck. Then he turned to look at the porch and lifted his hand in farewell to all the people he had loved.

Djamba, the powerful Mandingo, hurried out of the bunkhouse and called to him, "Mister Luke, Mister Luke, wait—I just heard Simata saying you were leaving—"

Luke turned in his saddle and smiled down at the man who had shown such self-effacing loyalty to Windhaven Plantation, who had saved his own life and who, he had always known, loved and revered Sybella. "Yes, Djamba, for New Orleans, and then one day back to where you first came to live with us and help us grow and find our strength in love."

Djamba shook his head, blinked his eyes, cleared his throat, then held out his hand which Luke reached down to take and clasp warmly. "I'd like it mighty fine if you'd take me with you, Mister Luke."

"It's good of you to say that, Djamba. But you and I both know," he lowered his voice so that only the Mandingo could hear, "that your heart is here now with Mother—and with Celia, Prissy and your fine son Lucas. My son Lucien Edmond will need you and Lucas much more, Djamba, though selfishly I'd be proud to have you back with me at Windhaven Plantation."

"Thank you for saying that, Mister Luke. I'll pray for you every day of your life, and so will my wife and Prissy and Lucas—for all you did for us."

"God bless you, Djamba. Look after Mother all you can."

"You know I will, Mister Luke. She's the finest woman I ever knew in all my life." The Mandingo blinked his eyes again, then stepped back as Luke Bouchard waved a last time to the others on the porch.

The sky was majestic, with the purple and red and orange of the setting sun. Luke Bouchard rode slowly, looking back again and again at the *hacienda* until finally he could see it no more. And then, touching the turquoise at his heart, he rode on swiftly toward the south.

The exciting Windhaven Saga will continue for several more volumes as Marie de Jourlet recounts the lusty adventures of the Bouchard family, which parallel the tempestuous story of the American nation being created. With historical authenticity and rich, true-to-life detail, Marie de Jourlet has brought a bright, new storytelling talent to the bestseller lists. It may be interesting to note that she has developed this series under the direction of Lyle Kenyon Engel, the man responsible for producing the phenomenally successful American Bicentennial Series by John Jakes.